Boniface Box Set

the first three Boniface novels in one volume:

The Murder of Henry VIII
Pollute the Poor
Tattoo Your Name on My Heart

Simon Cann

Coombe
Hill
Publishing

Published by Coombe Hill Publishing
33 Melrose Gardens
New Malden
Surrey KT3 3HQ
United Kingdom
coombehillpublishing.com

Cover design by Ishtiaq Ahmad (behance.net/ishtiaq-ahmad).

ISBN: 978-1-910398-06-7 (paperback)
ISBN: 978-1-910398-07-4 (ePub)

18 March 2017

The Murder
of Henry VIII

one

"Asshole," Boniface mouthed, snapping his phone shut with a flick of his wrist. Had Trudgett taken lessons in how to be annoying, or did he spend all day planning how to exasperate?

Boniface straightened, turning into the room. So this was what hand-printed wallpaper looked like up close. Burgundy highlighted with a deep red pattern—a texture of repeating geometric shapes—overlaid with gold leaf.

Lots of gold.

Gold applied without restraint.

Gold applied without any consideration for taste.

Gold applied without any consideration for cost.

Enough gold to fund the debt of all developing nations, leaving sufficient change to embarrass the zillionaires in Silicon Valley.

To Boniface it looked like the wallpaper he saw in Indian restaurants, but this came at an eye-watering price tag—apparently into seven figures for this reception area alone. All that for something displaying the subtlety of a vulgar property developer or the restraint of an oil-rich sheik.

The three pairs of eyes that had been on him since he arrived were still locked on him, emotionless but judging. Three men: one behind the desk, two in front. All standing. Each with the confidence of a man who had, and was prepared again, to defend himself physically. Each with the posture of a man conditioned to the discipline of the military. Each, in addition to his manifest physical presence, with a sense of menace seeping through his pores.

Veronica had told him about Kuznetsov's ex-Spetsnaz bodyguards. Russian Special Forces who learned their trade under a regime that needed its soldiers to have near-superhuman powers, requiring them to succeed at any cost. And what weapon was issued to these human death machines? A shovel, apparently.

Whatever powers they had, whatever training they had received, they hadn't been taught how to make a guest feel at ease. Boniface was avoiding eye contact but could still feel his skin blistering where the fixed gazes burned into him as he self-consciously moved to one of the sofas, relaxing into its delicate embrace as he released his weight.

The furniture mirrored the wallpaper—well-stuffed chairs, covered in thick fabric repeating the pattern of the wallpaper. On the table in front of him—gold-framed, with a glass top—three newspapers had been arranged with architectural precision. In a room that was clearly intended as a defiant statement of opulence, the newspapers would usually have seemed somewhat incongruous, but these were a selection of newspapers owned by Kuznetsov and were left as a statement, not for information.

Without picking up a paper, Boniface scanned the headlines. The theme was similar—the continuing call for a referendum. Unsurprising, given that the man he was about to meet for the first time, Ivan Kuznetsov, was widely rumored to want to be the first British president, despite many unconvincing public denials, and it was his newspapers that conceived, launched, and supported the Referendum for Democracy campaign.

Boniface knew the argument he was going to hear when he got to meet the Russian: "The UK is a disgrace. You talk about being a democracy, but the head of state is only the head of state by an accident of birth. You have more influence over which singer gets chosen to keep singing on a Saturday night television show than you've got over who governs you. And this is the twenty-first century—why are you still voting on scraps of paper?"

The contradiction being that, as far as Boniface could tell, Kuznetsov had no interest in democracy.

Democracy was just a useful slogan to make a grab for more power and influence, and if that failed, then hopefully someone would be installed whom Kuznetsov could buy.

But it was still hard for Boniface to see a firm link between the task he had been hired to achieve—to handle the public relations for the launch of a book recounting, on the most flimsy evidence, the murder of perhaps England's most famous monarch—and an attempt to start the process to replace the hereditary monarch with an elected president.

The tallest of the three men flicked his eyes to Boniface, dismissively wrinkled his nose, and gave a nearly imperceptible nod of his shaved head to the other man standing in front of the desk; then closed his eyes as if to confirm his affirmation. The other man, whose face was lined with a scar, turned silently, walked to the elevator, punched the lower button, and departed.

As the sound of the descending elevator faded, the man with the shaved head turned to the man behind the desk—a swarthy man, with hair just long enough to start to curl—who started to turn as if to come out from behind the bombastically ornate desk. The opulence of this piece of furniture desk wasn't lost on Boniface, as he noted the massive pieces of mahogany, inlaid with rosewood and ebony, and with a corporate logo detailed in flamed maple.

The man with the shaved head looked at the swarthy man. Keeping his arm by his side, he lifted his hand as if telling a dog to stay, then walked to the elevators and jabbed the higher button. His boots, displaying a shine that only comes with many, many layers of polish applied with rigorous discipline, scraped through the thick burgundy pile with gold corporate crests.

The gold elevator doors opened, and the man with the shaved head glared at Boniface while gesturing into the waiting elevator. Boniface jumped up, hastily pulling together a few papers he had slipped out of his briefcase, and scurried over.

After a few seconds, the doors opened and Boniface stepped out of the elevator into the Observatory on the seventy-first floor of Kuznetsov's London re-creation of the Chrysler Building, the building Londoners called the Silver Spike. The elevator doors—on this floor, exotic hardwoods with delicate fretwork—closed on his escort, leaving Boniface alone.

Where he had sat in an enclosed lobby on the lower level, this whole floor was open. There were no internal walls apart from the elevator block running through the central core, which had become more prominent as the building tapered toward its eponymous spike. The dull electric light from ornate gold lamps on the lower floor had been replaced by muted daylight straining through the triangular windows arranged in a sunburst arc on each wall, giving an effect of a child's picture of the sun.

Boniface paused to take in the room. Apart from the large flat-screen television with a 24-hour news channel silently recounting the latest developments, one disproportionately sized chair, and a stand-up desk, the interior looked like a color re-creation of the black-and-white photos he had seen of the original building in New York.

Unlike the reception area, with its oppressive darkness and overly rich decor, this was a refined and perfect re-creation of the art deco interior, complete with starscape murals suggesting that the height of the skyscraper put the room into space, and with lights hanging like planets, in case you missed the allusion.

A slight shift in the shadows around the room alerted Boniface to the silent arrival of Ivan Kuznetsov. "Mister Boniface."

two

Montbretia had been quite clear in her instructions: "Wear the dark blue suit, the one we bought when I last stayed with you. No, don't wear pants. Sure, they're functional, but this is television: You get shown from the neck up—you're not going horseback riding."

She didn't stop there. "Wear a skirt because men will look at you differently. If you get interviewed by a man"—and 99 times out of 100, for a political piece Ellen was interviewed by a man—"then the interviewer will be a preening alpha-male type, or at least a wannabe alpha-male. He will want to stand in front of the camera and grab all the attention, so by definition he'll want to call the shots. And if he's that type, then he'll be kinder to you if you're wearing a skirt. Sexist, absolutely. But do you want to come across well on television, or do you want people to watch a narcissistic Neanderthal bullying you?"

The logic was sound, and Ellen couldn't argue with her sister. "So can I wear my cream suit?" she asked and was promptly told no.

"Wear the blue one. Very sober, very businesslike, and the skirt is such a good cut. It fits you perfectly. Wear your glasses, too. It gives you that whole repressed-sexuality vibe that the English men go gaga over."

And she continued without pausing. "Jewelry. One item and one item only. And something that doesn't make a noise; the microphone will pick up any rattling or jingling."

"So a brooch, then. Blouse?"

"Yeah, that would be good, sis. Not sure you're ready yet to get your whammers out on national TV, are you? Wait until you're a bit more famous, and then make some real money."

And she continued without a pause. "Make sure the blouse is one color. Avoid polka dots, stripes, and patterns—they all interfere with the cameras. Make sure it's cotton. Not silk. Silk looks like cheap polyester on TV. And wear heels."

"For the alpha-male interviewer?"

"No, because you're short."

"Not that short."

"But you're not tall. If you're standing next to someone who's taller, then the camera will only see the top of your head. Or if the others are giants, you'll just be a gap between two people." A day spent in any heel too high would hurt, so the agreed compromise was kitten heels. And as Ellen walked from Westminster tube, her feet agreed it was a sensible compromise.

She looked up and checked the time; according to Big Ben, she had five minutes to spare. Crossing the six lanes of traffic, she followed the railings around the Houses of Parliament and then crossed to College Green, which, as usual, was filled with several production crews. This was what passed for normal for Ellen these days—looking to figure out which TV crew she should be talking to.

Two years ago the book was published. The logic was simple. The logic was straightforward. The logic was perfect. It was a path trodden by many academics before her: Publish a book, sell a few copies—they talked about a print run of 2,000, so expectations weren't that high—cement your reputation as an expert within your field, and live out a quiet life in academia, but with your reputation assured because you've published a book, so you must be an expert. And that was what Ellen did, confirming her position as the leading authority on the English constitution, an ironic distinction given that she was an American citizen.

But then one of the newspapers had started agitating and had launched its Referendum for Democracy campaign.

The basic thrust of the argument was reasonable, and some of the ideas suggested were quite forward-thinking. In the twenty-first century, in a country that called itself a democracy, it wasn't that outrageous to expect the head of state to be elected by the people, was it? Other than to encourage tourists, there was no benefit in having a hereditary monarch.

As the campaign caught the media's attention, Ellen had been dragged from her cozy academic life and thrust in front of a television camera whenever producers felt they needed an expert to prove that their program was serious. So thanks to the newspaper owned by the Russian who had built the thing they call the Silver Spike because no one could pronounce its Russian name, this American had become what in common parlance was known as a media personality.

And boy, did she loathe it. The title and the role. The English constitution still fascinated her, but the media frenzy was a joyless experience—answering the same facile questions from overly aggressive, insecure, cardboard-cutout journalists who might look good on camera but who had absolutely zero skills when it came to intellectual rigor and recognizing, then dealing with, fallacious arguments.

If there was an upside, at least the book was selling well—more so since the publisher, Richard Sherborne, as overly familiar as he was overweight, had become involved and demanded a substantial reprint while making sure that his PR people got behind the book. As a result, Ellen was scheduled for even more interviews.

She looked at her interviewer and cringed with a sense of what was coming. Did this interviewer care that she was a historian, not a political animal grasping for power? Ellen studied the past, noting each historical event and its implications for the current state of society. She was an expert on the historical basis of the English constitution—she wasn't a politician who was happy to answer any question, however ignorant of the facts they might be.

Ellen's phone rang, reminding her to ask Montbretia how to change the ringtone. She had understood how to use her last phone, but this new one? This was real space-age technology, but it was the one that Montbretia thought was best, and it did let her do a lot of things without needing to turn on her computer. As well as calling, she could email, check her calendar and to-do lists, blog, tweet, buzz, squawk, and do all of those other social-networking things Sherborne's PR people told her she should do to help promote the book. And not only did the phone let her leave her laptop at home, it also pinpointed her precise geographic location, and some clever gizmo then highlighted her current position on her website to show everyone that she was a real person who didn't spend all day in some ancient university.

At least that's what the PR people had told her.

"So what did Boniface say?" she asked, catching an angry glance from the producer. "Well, I'm not surprised. It's never going to sound good if you tell people you've just come from the police station... Look, I've got to go. I'll try and make it, but I've got another two interviews after this. I'll call you when I'm finished."

Calls from Nigel never helped when she was trying to focus, especially when Nigel was so excited. But what was his big secret and why did he want to tell her face-to-face? He was still buzzing after "helping the police," but the call was more than his usual combination of insecurity and desire to please, made worse by the arrogance that came from him feeling that he had finally been recognized for his expertise.

She checked her hair and added a few dabs of powder—a superstitious gesture to appease gods who would otherwise make her face look overly shiny in front of the camera—as the producer started counting down for the live broadcast.

three

Turgenev stood in the doorway to his office off the reception area and stared at the PR man who had just met with Kuznetsov. The Russian sized him up. Five eleven, one-hundred-and-sixty pounds, short hair—not military short, but long enough to suggest he bothered about styling, although the gray flecks suggested that at least he didn't dye it—blue pinstriped suit, a shirt and tie that the Englishman doubtless thought made him look superior to a former soldier, and shoes that only shone that way because they were new.

He snorted. The Englishman wouldn't make it past the first punch.

The man changed elevators, exiting the only elevator that could access the Observatory and Kuznetsov's private floors, exchanging it for one that would drop him to street level. The Russian made, and held, eye contact with Boniface, who seemed to wither in his gaze.

The doors closed on the PR man, and the Russian took the vacated elevator and ascended to the Observatory, stepping out to find Kuznetsov watching television and shaking his head in disagreement. He watched his boss, waiting for his cue to interrupt.

On the television, the short woman with blond, slightly curly hair; thick-framed glasses; and a blue jacket appeared to be an academic—Professor Armstrong, he thought the interviewer said. For some reason, the woman conducting the interview seemed to have taken against this academic and was singling her out for a metaphorical beating, while ignoring the male politicians flanking her victim.

Kuznetsov started talking at the television, his voice a rising crescendo that soon became a shout.

Turgenev maintained his silent vigil. The blond academic's comments were annoying Kuznetsov, but Turgenev wasn't sure what was particularly annoying him—was it what she said, or was it that she was too close to Sherborne? When Sherborne came up in conversation, Kuznetsov would usually start shouting, and this woman seemed to have something to do with Sherborne.

Turgenev watched the television, trying to listen to the conversation and ignore his boss's rants. "If I could correct you," said the blond woman, stopping the interviewer. Turgenev could feel the temperature plummet and cold wind blow out of the television. Silently, war had been declared. Even he knew that if you made an interviewer look stupid on live TV, they'd bring out the big guns.

And the interviewer did. "Look. It's a straightforward question for the country's leading expert. Could we have a straightforward answer, please?" And if the big guns didn't work, then the interviewer would cheerfully tear the professor to pieces with her bare hands.

The academic retorted, "It's not a straightforward answer. You're trying to bring many different and unrelated issues, and you want a simple answer. This isn't a binary issue...it's not yes or no. It's more a question of yes or no to a whole range of sub-issues."

The interviewer had seen weakness in her victim's response and went for the kill, but the academic fought back. Turgenev checked Kuznetsov. His face remained impassive, but the back of his neck was turning pink, then red, finally darkening to a raging purple, like a cartoon thermometer set to explode.

Turgenev continued watching. He still didn't understand what she was talking about, but he could see how the small blond professor was getting increasingly combative in her response, having seemingly decided to elaborate sufficiently in her answers to highlight the extent to which the questions she was being asked were matters that she thought any fool should understand. And like the balance on a set of scales, as her authority rose, Turgenev could see Kuznetsov's spirits seem to fall.

Kuznetsov spat out a few words, looking like a man both disgusted and disappointed. A man who could not be consoled. Turgenev went to speak but stopped himself, instead returning to the elevator.

four

"The man is a menace."

"And good afternoon to you, Boniface." Veronica's head remained down as she lifted her eyes to look up from her desk. "I'm busy. Can we do this later?"

The room was as Boniface remembered—the walls, painted a delicate shade of yellow, almost bordering on gold under a white ceiling, with lights hanging from the beams encasing the building's steel skeleton. Veronica sat in her corner office behind her understated but functional cherry-wood desk, positioned as if to brace the corner of the building. Her chair—leather, and the model of comfort—was backed into the outside corner.

Square windows to her left and right provided a view over the London's West End. For the second time that day, Boniface gazed at Big Ben. When he was with Kuznetsov in the Observatory, the clock tower beside the Houses of Parliament was more than 600 feet below them. Now, somewhere around 200 feet below Kuznetsov's Observatory, the change in perspective made the face of that most iconic landmark more readily visible, like a carriage clock on a low table.

Backed against one outside wall and obliquely facing the desk sat an armchair. Again leather. Again designed for comfort, but chosen so that whoever sat there was not placed at a psychological disadvantage. On the near side of the room was a meeting table, again made from cherry wood and surrounded by six leather-upholstered chairs, three on either side. Against the far wall, growing in large terracotta pots standing on the dark green carpet, three Acers—Japanese Maples—each about four feet high, were just coming into leaf. Mounted on the wall, squeezed in the corner diagonally opposite her desk and just inside the doorway, a television was showing 24-hour news on one of the Murdoch channels.

Boniface ignored his former wife's preoccupation. "He's a complete menace. This isn't a kid who likes to pull legs off spiders. This is a man who has grown up and wants to pull limbs off human beings. This is someone intent on the power play." He dropped his briefcase on the floor and slumped into the leather armchair across from Veronica's desk. "Call me Vanya, he says. Vanya. Russian for Johnny."

Veronica sighed as Boniface continued.

"Vanya. And then he says, 'When I am at home, people call me by my full name, Ivan Konstantinovich Kuznetsov, as a mark of respect, but my friends call me Vanya, so you should call me Vanya, too.' And apparently I'm Sasha. That's the diminutive of Alexander, you know. I tried to tell him that only my mother calls me Alexander, but that only seemed to set him off on another course—no, in Russia she would call me Alexander when she was scolding me. Then there's what's-his-name? The shaven-headed one with the big boots."

"Turgenev," said Veronica, making some notes on the document in front of her.

"Turgenev. Right bloody charmer he is. Head of Security? Yeah...thug-in-chief, more like. Stares at you through those eyes with no life, making it quite clear that if he wants you dead, then you're dead. And then there are his mates who all dress the same. I know you said Kuznetsov has security, but you didn't tell me he has a private army."

Veronica deliberately put down her pen and looked directly at Boniface. "New suit?"

"Yup."

"But still the same tailor?" She nodded as if confirming her approval. "Well, you're looking good for it. Just don't go and put on weight—or grow any taller."

Boniface leaned forward. "Kuznetsov does know this is an unwinnable war, doesn't he? He does know he's not going to get a referendum—and if he does get a referendum, he'll never win?" He tried to keep the exasperation out of his voice. "Am I meant to take him seriously when he says that he thinks *The Murder of Henry VIII* will, and I quote, *help to inflame the national consciousness*?"

Veronica reached to her right and pulled out two cut-glass tumblers from her desk. "Sure I can't tempt you back to the dark side?" Boniface slowly shook his head. "Or rather, are you sure I can't tempt you back into the light? You seem to have chosen to hide in the shadows since you stopped. But I guess that's where your demons live."

"Can we not have that argument again? Please." Boniface kept his voice calm.

Veronica's face softened as she filled the bottom of her tumbler and placed the bottle on her desk without replacing the cap.

"It's all about disappointment, Boniface. Don't disappoint the man." She took a sip. "And I mean don't disappoint him, ever. Don't think that because you've done exactly what he asked you to do—and more—he will be happy, because he won't be. For him, disappointment is measured in the moment. If something goes wrong and he thinks you're the one who disappointed him, then life is shit. Well, on a good day your life is shit; on a bad day..." she trailed off.

"So you've got me a job, and all I can do is disappoint this menace with his own private army of dead-eyed psychopaths." Boniface's throat tightened, his voice straining.

Veronica took another sip. "Look, we both do things for money. We're two of a kind. You're unemployable, so you had to set up your own agency, and I'm working for the only person I can work for—there are no other options for me. The only way forward is to persuade the big man to carve out a new role for me overseeing several papers, and then I might be able to move up a few more floors."

She pointed to the ceiling as she walked around to the front of her desk and sat, her hands folded on her lap, holding her tumbler. "I got you the job because you need the money. You do still need money?"

Boniface looked down. "Lots." He blushed. "And fast. How quickly will they pay once I send my invoice?"

"What's gone wrong now?" she asked.

He sighed deeply, resigned to admitting his folly. "I borrowed money."

A look of disappointment spread across Veronica's face.

Boniface winced. "I wasn't that stupid, but I needed money to get the office, and I'm not a good risk for the banks given my...shall we say...history."

"What did you do?" Her voice was disapproving but resigned to acceptance.

"I borrowed what I thought was family money." Boniface felt the self-criticism twist his gut. "But my kindly lender was happy to take risks and liked to gamble, and one evening, finding himself rather short, he used my loan as a stake. Lost. And the winner sold the debt on to a gentlemen who has decided it's time to call in the loan."

Veronica raised her eyebrows. "When?"

"Today."

"No. I mean when do they want their money back?"

"Today." Boniface was more emphatic. "And to make sure I really understood the message, they put holes in my office wall, and now I need a new receptionist." He exhaled loudly. "But let's not dwell on that."

"Focus on the job, Boniface, and you'll get paid."

"But..."

Veronica stopped Boniface with a look that he knew she had honed over many years. He sat in silence as she took another sip before continuing. "All you have to do is avoid failure." She waited, watching, as if calibrating his understanding. "And as long as you avoid failure, everything will be fine. As you've said, how hard can it be to babysit a professor? You hardly need danger money, unless you count the danger of getting bored to death."

"Or annoyed beyond reason." Boniface recalled his conversation with the professor as he waited to meet Kuznetsov. "He's very annoying. You will visit me in jail if I can't resist the compulsion to ring his scrawny little neck?"

Veronica frowned, slowly tilting her head from side to side as if weighing up the request. "Look, Boniface, Kuznetsov is fighting this battle on many fronts—you just have to make sure that your front isn't the place where the enemy breaks through. The rest of us are out in the trenches too, each with our separate campaign. I'm trying to undermine the royals, and others are making the arguments for representative democracy."

Boniface laughed. "Like he cares about democracy."

Veronica looked hurt, narrowing her eyes at the unnecessary barb. "All you have to do is make sure the message gets out that Henry VIII was murdered and so all the so-called descendants are impostors and crooks, or whatever it is Kuznetsov wants to call them. Hold the party line and make sure that nothing goes wrong. Make sure you can't be identified as being the reason he couldn't get a referendum."

He looked down, staring at the carpet, and didn't notice the man walking in. "Oh. I'm sorry." Boniface looked toward the voice. He didn't know the man, but he recognized the type on sight—longtime journalist, probably quite good in his day, but drank too much and couldn't hack it, so now he had been given a courtesy title—deputy something that sounds important—to make him feel good, and he would stay in the office and remain employed until he ceased to be useful.

Since he wasn't out on the streets, he had become fatter, and the cheap suit—the same suit he wore every day with a jacket that lived on the back of his seat so it looked like he was in the office even when he was in the pub—was now so tight that his gut flopped over the top of his belt, which was open as far as possible. It was impossible for his shirt to circumnavigate his stomach, so it was always at least partially untucked. "I'm sorry. I didn't realize you were...er... Give me a call when you're, you know..." He turned and rolled away.

"What are you up to?" asked Boniface as the unhealthy specimen departed.

Veronica raised the side of her lip in a dismissive sneer and casually waived her hand as she stood.

"Your man had a picture of Oscar—Sherborne's kid, Oscar—on the top of the file he was holding." Boniface's ex-wife shrugged. "You can't go after him again, not after you accused him of being the father of that child and then had to print the retraction."

"You know that wasn't me, Boniface. I was on holiday when that broke."

"I know. And don't get me wrong, Oscar is a noxious little spoiled brat, and I spent years trying to bury Sherborne—you know—and you know that I still want to get him, and my new friend Vanya would reward me well if I could stab Sherborne in the back for him. And I'd take that job—Sherborne was the one that took me from broken-down alcoholic, to unemployed alcoholic, to unemployable."

"Unemployable and divorced. I know, Boniface." There was a slight coloration in her cheeks. "You will remember we were married at the time."

"I know. I'm sorry." He paused. "But for all he did to hurt me...to hurt us... I never tried to get at Sherborne by attacking his kid, or at least, the guy we think—but have never been able to prove—is his kid."

Veronica sat down behind her desk and stared at Boniface, seemingly willing him silent, before she carried on in a soft, measured voice. "We're going after Oscar von Habsburg, not because of any rumor about his daddy, but because after tonight we will have proof of his criminal business deals. We've known his partner is dirty for a while, but we also know that Oscar doesn't have the wit to stay alive in the drug trade. After tonight we should be able to prove that his club is taking a cut from the dealers it lets trade on its premises. Not only is this a great scoop, but it helps Kuznetsov." Boniface frowned quizzically. "We don't know for sure who his daddy is, but we know who mummy is."

Boniface's mouth dropped open as he tried to speak. "Heidi. Princess Heidemarie."

"And if we can find a way to embarrass the royal family through proof that the junior royals are...well, let's be frank, criminals, then I get a gold star from Kuznetsov. I'll get another gold star when you succeed, because I brought you in for the job, and I need all the gold stars I can get at the moment."

"Well, no one's giving me a gold star," said Boniface, rising from his seat. "However, they will send thugs with shaved heads and big boots if I don't get to Hampton Court to hold Nigel's hand at the launch. And then maybe Kuznetsov's guys could help me with the small matter of the outstanding loan?"

Veronica smiled. "I'm here all evening. As you've figured, I'm not going home until the snare has tightened around Oliver and the first edition has been put to bed, so call me if you want a chat. If I'm not around, it probably means I'm upstairs having something to eat with the big man. I'm in favor while I'm earning gold stars."

"Upstairs? The Cloud Club? Very impressive. Playing with the big boys."

"Indeed. Floor sixty-six." Veronica emptied her glass as Boniface left.

five

Turgenev was already walking to his office as the gold elevator doors opened. The boss was angry, and he should be the man to fix it for him. Kuznetsov's words had been clear and unambiguous, and had not required any discussion or elaboration, or even a response from Turgenev: "Professor Armstrong must cease to be an irritant to me."

This was an easy job and one where he could show what he could achieve and how he could be trusted. He paused. Should he check with the boss?

No.

It was time to move up, and an opportunity like this didn't present itself very often.

This was the smart strategy. Sure, he could ask for more responsibility, more pay, his own share, funding for a business, but why should he? And why should he force Ivan Konstantinovich Kuznetsov to consider such a request? Kuznetsov had already given him a position of responsibility, and he was trusted; to ask for more would be disrespectful. But if—through his own initiative and actions—he demonstrated that he could be more useful, then that took the risk out of the boss's decision.

Turgenev put on a pair of latex gloves; opened his safe; flicked through a stack of Russian passports, dropping one on his desk before he replaced the pile; and took out a pistol. He checked the magazine, firmly pressing it back into the gun, which he placed on his desk before closing and locking the safe.

With two clicks of a mouse, he had a travel website open. With a few key taps he had the flight to Moscow Sheremetyevo selected. He input the details of the traveler and his passport reference, clicked through to the payment page, lifted the receiver on his phone, and dialed a familiar number.

"Yuri. Mikhail. I need a clean credit card number...no, not much, two-hundred-and-thirty-three...pounds sterling... No, it must be clean and not traced back to us...a flight, to be taken tomorrow morning; after that I don't care if they find that the card was stolen." Turgenev input the card details and clicked the pay button. "Perfect. Thank you, Yuri. Payment authorized." He hung up and printed out the receipt and boarding pass, adding them to the pile with the passport and the gun.

He unlocked his bottom desk drawer, took out a set of car keys and a phone, then rummaged in the top drawer of his desk and pulled out a list of names and phone numbers. Halfway down the list he found the number he wanted; marking his place on the list with his left hand, Turgenev programmed the number into the phone with his right.

Turning back to his computer, he called up another website, entered the phone number, then clicked the mouse and waited. About fifteen seconds later, the phone beeped. He opened the SMS message, followed the instructions to acknowledge it, and turned back to his computer, clicking the maps link on the open webpage. A map of central London loaded with St Giles' Circus in the middle. An arrow appeared, moving toward the center of the map, coming to rest on the Silver Spike.

He placed the phone on his pile of unrelated objects, which was now beginning to look like a child's memory game.

One of the advantages of working for a man who owned a number of newspapers was intelligence—or as the newspaper staff preferred to call it, the Oracle. The papers kept huge databases about anyone who had ever blipped on the public's radar for whatever reason. Scoutmasters who liked little boys, sportsmen who liked white powder, and little old ladies who liked to grow flowers in their garden—they were all there with their details logged and cross-referenced with any and every other piece of information that the paper could get hold of, whether that be voter registrations, credit scores, or anything that came at a price. It all went into the database, and then all anyone had to do was click a button, and the data was there. And not simply there—it had been verified from multiple sources, making it as accurate as any information was likely to be.

In the case of someone like Professor Armstrong, it wasn't hard to pinpoint the individual Turgenev was looking for. First, there was the name. Check. The profession. Check. Recent media interest. Check. Publications. Check. Which all pointed to one person at one address. Turgenev looked back to his screen, opened Google Maps, and put in the address. Almost perfect, go west, drop south over Kew Bridge, into Richmond, and you were virtually at the front door. The route out was equally straightforward. Keep going on the main road into Kingston, turn right, go over the river, and then it was a pretty straight route to Heathrow.

GPS systems could be unreliable in the field. They broke; they gave the wrong route; they gave directions in English, which didn't help if your man barely spoke the language; they could be hacked and tracked; and most significantly, they left a history. They left a trail of breadcrumbs that could be traced, and if you were stopped, it was really hard to get rid of a whole GPS unit with the route stored deep in the memory. Paper was far more reliable, and if anything went wrong, the evidence could be destroyed. A single page could be burned or eaten—quickly and completely.

Turgenev went to his shelves and picked the top copy from his pile of London street atlases. It was an old and tattered edition, barely holding itself together. He checked the location in the index and opened to page 183, comparing the map to the image on the screen. He took a pen and marked "Professor Armstrong," putting an X to mark her house and writing the address on the page, then snapped the book shut and watched as a few loose pages fluttered to the floor. He picked them up, looked them over, and dropped them in the trash.

He grabbed a large envelope and delicately filled it with the gun, the atlas, the boarding pass, the phone, the car keys, and the passport, and then folded the top twice to close it before throwing his gloves into the trash on top of the discarded map pages. Then, with a click of his mouse, he switched off his computer.

six

Boniface was caught between the stone balustrade and the angry rush-hour traffic, threading his way through the directionless tourists meandering in the opposite direction over Hampton Court Bridge toward Hampton Court train station.

The sun-baked path was still radiating heat, and even after the early evening breeze skimming off the river had washed away some of the closeness, Boniface could still feel his shirt sticking to his back under his jacket.

Walking down from the bridge, he turned through the pillars of the outer gate—a lion on one side of the entrance and a unicorn guarding the other—to face Hampton Court Palace as he started on the path from the outer perimeter of the grounds to the main gate. He crunched down the broad stone track before spinning and returning to seek out the guard, who was bound to be in the hut by the outer gate.

He found him. A tall man in his seventies with good posture. Probably former military—in other words, a man who understood logistics and who could be reasoned with, but who wouldn't mess around. Boniface introduced himself and chatted for a few moments. The war stories started. Definitely an ex-soldier.

When it was polite to move on, Boniface asked his question. "We've got some cabs arriving to pick up our guests from the event tonight; they should be ready to leave around eight-thirty. Can you send them straight through to wait outside the Great Hall?"

"I'm sorry, sir. We don't allow vehicles through the main gate." Boniface waited to see whether a compromise was offered. "But what I can do for you is get them to line up on this side of the main gate. That space to the right, overlooking the river..." He pointed to the main gate to the Palace at the other end of the entrance drive. "If we do that, your guests only have to walk across the courtyard from the Great Hall, rather than come all the way out here."

Boniface stuck out his hand. "Deal." The guard shook it, and Boniface recommenced the long walk to the main gate with the comfort that a cab would carry him back when he left.

As he reached the Palace and passed under the arch of the main gate, he checked the time on his phone—less than 30 minutes to make sure everything was in order—and looked up to see Nigel. How could he do it? How could someone so intelligent be so stupid? How could someone who dedicated his whole life to understanding and interpreting nuances miss the obvious? How could someone who had written extensively about how the outer appearance is a metaphor for the inner manifestation of power be so unaware of his own appearance?

Boniface remembered the conversation with Nigel, virtually word for word. "So you're going to get a new suit for the book launch."

"Of course."

"And you understand what this suit needs to do for you."

"I do."

"You understand that you need something classic. It shouldn't be on the cutting edge of fashion."

"Do you see me as male-model material, Boniface?"

"Equally, it shouldn't give off that dusty-professor-who-only-wears-tweed-that-he-acquired-through-inheritance type vibe."

"Believe me, I've met those professors, and I'm not like that."

"And it shouldn't be what you wear on a day-to-day basis."

"Like this jacket," Nigel had said, indicating the dull sand-colored corduroy jacket with patches on the elbows that he was wearing at the time. "It will be nothing like this."

"Great. But you do understand this is quite a tough balancing act. Modern, but not too modern, and certainly not fashion-victim modern. Showing personality, you don't want to be bland, but not showing too much personality. Serious, in no way frivolous or open to ridicule. It's all about getting the balance right."

"I understand."

Now this. Nigel had called him when he got his new suit. "I did exactly what you told me," he proudly confirmed, and Boniface had relaxed.

Mistake.

He should have checked the suit. He should have made sure someone was there when Nigel went shopping. No, that wouldn't have worked; he should have sent Nigel to his own tailor—that would have been the only way to keep control of this situation.

And who still sold suits like this? In the twenty-first century? Who still made corduroy? Surely these suits were banned by some sort of United Nations convention at the same time that landmines or biological warfare agents were banned. And what color was that? It certainly wasn't one that appeared in nature. It wasn't blue, it wasn't gray, and it wasn't slate, but there were elements of all. Equally, there were hints of green and brown in there, maybe even some red, but no single identifiable color, and no color you could name to suggest the tone. Perhaps it looked good in a nightclub or under the lighting that technicians had in those crime-scene programs?

But this was all irrelevant. There was a book to be launched; the guests had been invited and were on their way. And the first task was to deal with the grinning idiot in that repellent suit, and to stop him from talking about whatever stupid things he'd been up to today with the police.

The police.

That last conversation with Nigel—"I've been helping the police with their inquiries"—came flooding back to Boniface.

"Nigel. Good to see you." Like all good PR men, he could lie on cue. Heck, he didn't even realize he was doing it and didn't feel guilt or remorse. Boniface looked him in the eye; it was time to be reassuring and to calm Nigel's over-excitement, which was radiating like nuclear waste.

So what was the best strategy here? Probably best to lance the boil, let all the puss spill out, and then get some disinfectant and put a sterile dressing over the wound. "So tell me about your adventures with the police."

Nigel excitedly began recounting his day, and at the point where Boniface felt that the only two options were physical violence toward Nigel or returning to his life as an alcoholic, he stopped him. "Quite an adventure. Now look, for tonight—*just for tonight*—it's probably best that you don't mention this tale. There are going to be a lot of journalists—drunk journalists, drunk and lazy journalists—around here tonight. You mention that you were at the police station today, and the next thing you know...well, you can guess."

"But you haven't heard the best part," whined Nigel. "I have now seen the evidence..."

Boniface cut him short. "Whatever you have seen, we can't reprint the book within the next ten minutes, can we?" This was progress; Nigel no longer emitted unrelenting excitement. "We need to remember what we're here to do. And we're here to do one thing: to sell your book."

Nigel perked up; the subject had moved back to him. Boniface pushed forward before Nigel could start talking. "There's only one thing we need to think about for tonight, and that's your chat about your book."

"Yes."

"Now, please tell me you've got something prepared as we discussed."

"Yes."

"You've practiced it, and remembered it, so it feels like it's a natural conversation. This isn't a lecture; you're only saying a few words. Casually, off the cuff; only you and I need to know you've prepared."

"Yes, yes."

"And these informal and casual comments have no jokes."

"Well...you can't not have jokes."

"You can. Cut them." Nigel's rising enthusiasm seemed undaunted. "And you're sure that you won't speak for longer than three minutes."

"Yes."

"And you confirmed this by saying your speech out loud, including pauses for you to breathe and breaks to acknowledge audience feedback?"

"Yes."

Which probably meant no, but in reality Boniface knew that Nigel would most likely dry up after about 90 seconds. However, everyone who turned up to one of these events understood the rules. You got free food and free drink in an interesting venue, and you got to meet some other interesting guests and do a bit of networking. The price was that you had to listen to some tedious author meander through the story behind his book, then laugh and clap at the appropriate place. The PR would keep it short and jump in, as Boniface would do with Nigel if—or should that be *when*—it looked like Nigel was losing the audience's charity.

"Now clearly, the chat is your big piece, and I'll introduce you. But before that, you need to circulate. You want to meet everybody, and that means you need to keep moving. Don't spend any more than three minutes with any one person. For tonight, everything's limited to three minutes."

Nigel smiled. Good. He had got away with justifying the three-minute rule when all he wanted to say was: Don't spend more than three minutes with anyone, because you're a tedious dullard and everyone will want to wring your scrawny neck. But perhaps he could soften the blow: "You need to do enough to convince them that you're an expert. Move in, radiate gravitas"—he could see that Nigel liked that idea—"and then move on before you get into any in-depth questioning."

"But isn't this about the in-depth questioning?" Nigel seemed worried.

It was time to have the serious talk. "No. We don't do in-depth. Remember, drunk, lazy journalists looking for an easy story. They can only understand one thing. They think they're smart and they think they can multitask." Boniface shook his head firmly. "They can't."

Nigel seemed to be understanding the concept. "Give them one message and only one message. Don't confuse them by telling them what you know. Tell them what they need to know to write their story, and then your book will sell millions and you can buy another new suit...or perhaps a car. Do it right, and by the end of the week you can buy yourself a Ferrari."

"But I've got a car," Nigel was whining again. "A 2CV." Boniface knew what was coming. A history lecture from a historian about the worst car ever made. A car designed for French peasants and taken to their hearts by vegetarians. Great for French peasants, awful for London, where any crash would guarantee immediate death as the whole contraption dissolved into dust and a few rusty component parts. A few smart ads in the 1980s, but production had long since ended.

Boniface jumped at the only option he knew. "Then you can get another. Perhaps get a whole fleet. Get them restored. Pay for a garage to store them all."

He waited for Nigel to mentally process the image of a fleet of French vegi-mobiles and continued. "So you're happy? You know what we're doing?"

"Certainly." Nigel had given him this unwavering confirmation before, and what had happened next?

That suit.

"Then we've got radio tomorrow and the TV interviews the day after, and I'll be with you through all of these. But tonight is all about you."

Nigel beamed. "Now, where are we set up?" asked Boniface, looking for any excuse to get away from that awful suit, wondering where he could emigrate to in order to hide from his new friend Vanya, who was sure to be very disappointed very soon.

seven

The elevator reached street level and Turgenev stepped into the central concourse walled with flamed Moroccan marble. The triangular floor plan funneled people left, right, and forward, giving an immediate impetus to move.

He gripped the envelope containing the tools of the mission and headed out of the central entrance, as he always did casting a glance back to his left, the Porsche showroom, and behind him on his right, the Ferrari showroom. The Rolls-Royce showroom at the back of the building was of less interest, but perhaps he might acquire a taste once he had his own chauffeur?

The Silver Spike stood on its own island—which for some reason he didn't understand they called St Giles' Circus—and traffic found its way around, but with typical English town-planning priorities there was no clear path through this untidy conjunction of island and roads. A mishmash of bad compromises that black-cab drivers alone seemed able to divine how to navigate.

He checked the traffic and moved forward, finding gaps created by the panic of tired taxi drivers afraid to hit a pedestrian and lose an evening's income explaining the accident to the police. Reaching the far side, he walked up Tottenham Court Road through the mass of people, some heading somewhere, some heading nowhere, all moving slowly in the fading heat of the early summer afternoon. He passed the theatre, which was still showing a musical based on the songs from a famous 1970s rock band, and took the first right into the quiet of a side street.

Great Russell Street had a different character with a mixture of cheap construction crammed against decaying Georgian terraces, office fronts, and a few business hotels where the architecture had been sympathetically restored to follow the Georgian origins. Nestled about halfway down on the right was Sodom and Gomorrah, where the two doormen ushered him inside.

As Turgenev was subsumed into the belly of the club, he lost contact with daylight and any other outward signs that might suggest the time of day, or even that there was any world outside the sealed bubble.

The only sign of time passing was the women around him, who he could see visibly age as he watched. Years of extreme sun and tanning beds, frequent and cheap cosmetic surgery, cheap food eaten infrequently and at odd hours, diets to keep a figure, nicotine as a food substitute, alcohol, alcohol as a food substitute, party drugs, drug addictions, harsh chemical treatments in the name of beauty from skincare and hair products had aged these women. They were like the result of some bizarre Nazi research experiment where through inhuman treatment, twenty years of research data could be generated within three years of what passed for a normal routine.

Some of the younger ones had yet to develop the rhino-hide skin, but it was only a matter of days before regular moisturizing could no longer mask the accelerated passing of time.

While they fought the aging battle, they had already lost another battle: They were here. Some would be paying off family debt at home, others would have come for promises of bright lights and modeling careers. All would have been lied to. All would have been given enough drugs to become addicted. Most would have been beaten, and all would eventually work to start paying what was owed—and once the debt was satisfied, most then stayed in the only place where they could find some sort of security, with the twisted form of camaraderie that is shared between victims of a natural disaster or a terrorist outrage.

Turgenev knew better than to look into their eyes; the eyes would always sparkle back. But that was a conditioned response. When you looked closely, you could see that the sparkle was a cover, and usually the result of eye drops to combat the effect of air conditioning. Underneath there was nothing. Not life, not death; nothing. He had seen this before when he was a soldier. Even the new kids who got shipped in had the look of a broken and defeated conscript army. They had gone beyond the hurt, the loss, the bereavement, the fear, the terror, the anger, and they had reached nothing. Whatever had connected their soul to their body had snapped, and their body just moved around.

Turgenev had once dreamed of owning a club like this, and Kuznetsov would probably set him up in business if he asked for his help.

But not now.

Now he could see the cliché: pretty girls, fast cars, and people spending other people's money. Now he could see it would be like commanding another army of conscripts again. Instead, he wanted freedom. He wanted to break free from the ties of loyalty that, in truth, were ties of fear, and Professor Armstrong had given him a way to take that first step to establish his independence.

The pounding beat of 1980s hair metal was oppressive but useful, and while a Whitesnake power ballad played over the sound system, explaining unsubtle horizontal ambitions, no microphone would be able to hear his conversation.

He looked around the room; the men either wore business suits or boots, jeans, and leather jackets. Sitting in the far corner was the man with the scar across his face. Turgenev held his gaze, breaking when the man acknowledged the unspoken order.

"Get a room; I'm going to give you a private dance." The man with the scar turned and led Turgenev toward the back of the club. Two men with tuxedos and bowties stood guard over a narrow passage, not moving as the man with the scar approached. With a backward tilt of his head he indicated the higher power, stepping out of the line of sight of the guardians so they could see Turgenev.

"Room three," said the gatekeeper, stiffening as Turgenev passed.

As the two men walked into the burgundy-painted room, Turgenev shut the door behind him and looked up at the security camera on the wall above the door. "Put your jacket over that." The man with the scar complied, and in an exaggerated gesture, like an unctuous waiter, Turgenev offered a seat on the leather banquette spanning the back wall of the small room.

Closing the door had muffled the sound, making it slightly less bright but still as loud. Turgenev sat close to the man with the scar so he could be heard without needing to shout. "You're going home tomorrow morning, but I've got a job for you first. A job that must be completed tonight."

He unwrapped the two folds at the top of the envelope, pushed the sides so the mouth opened, and offered the aperture to the other man, who removed each object in turn, placing it on the only other piece of furniture in the room—a small table, still sticky with spilled drinks and whatever other fluids had been spilled by the previous occupants of the room. "Put the gun in your jacket. We don't want anyone getting a surprise, do we?"

When the man with the scar had sat down again, Turgenev continued. "Page one-eight-three in the atlas." The man with the scar opened the map book, put a finger to the name and address written on the page, and returned his concentration to the shaven-headed man. "Professor Armstrong must cease to be an irritant to someone who is very important to both of us. Professor Armstrong must cease to be an irritant permanently, and tonight."

The man with the scar nodded his affirmation.

"Listen. This is what you will do." The man with the scar focused on Turgenev. "Take the car: It's a little red Toyota, completely anonymous, no one will notice you. Drive to Richmond."

The man with the scar nodded, glancing back to the map and running his finger over the page.

"When the professor returns, complete the task. You're a good shot, but this is a residential area, so get next to the professor before you pull the trigger. You need to be fast, accurate, and achieve the outcome with the minimum of fuss. Shoot once, then leave. Drive slowly; you've got plenty of time before the flight. You're on the first flight that's available, but it doesn't leave until nine-thirty tomorrow morning, so you've got the whole night."

Turgenev cocked his head toward the map, holding his finger away from the page while pointing. "Drive out this way and then get something to eat. You can stop around here; there's bound to be somewhere suitable. I want you to stay close in case there are any other loose ends that need to be tied up. You've got the phone; I'll call you if I need."

The man with the scar gave a confident nod.

"When you've found somewhere to eat, then call the number that has been programmed into the phone. And you know the drill if you get caught: Eat the SIM card so that no one finds the number. The number is for some friends of ours. They don't know what's going to happen, but it's important that they are the first to find out about the professor's accident. They will then report the professor's sad demise."

Turgenev persisted. "When you've had something to eat, drive into Kingston. You see, it's a straight road. Go under the railway bridge and turn right." The man with the scar followed the directions on the map. "When you get to the bridge over the Thames, stop and drop the gun. Then it's an easy route to the airport."

The man with the scar on his face looked at the map, flipping pages as he followed the road to Heathrow.

"Leave the car on a street. Somewhere away from the airport. Somewhere away from CCTV. A quiet residential street, something like that. Then walk to the airport, but don't get there too early. Flights start landing from six in the morning, so after that time it should be much easier to blend in. Leave the phone under the driver's seat. We'll track it, get the car, and make sure everything is cleaned up."

The man with the scar nodded. "One other thing," said Turgenev. "They're very suspicious about people without luggage, so make sure you take a full bag. If there's anything you can't fit in or don't want to carry, leave it, and I'll get Sergey to send it."

Turgenev stood, and the man with the scar scrambled to his feet. "Thank you, my friend. Your dedication is appreciated and will be rewarded." The two men embraced. "Who is your favorite?" He tipped his head backward in the direction of the noise.

"Kristalle," said the man with the scar. "But her real name's Olga."

"Well, she is going to give you a very special going-away present. My treat to you my friend. Here's..." Turgenev took the cash out of his back pocket and started to count it. "Two hundred and fifty pounds. I will pay, but you can look like a hero to her when you give her a tip. And here's another fifty for your dinner tonight," he said, giving the man with the scar his last bill.

eight

The Great Hall, Hampton Court. Location of the first documented performance of Shakespeare's *Macbeth*, and tonight, the location of the launch of Professor Nigel Trudgett's new book, *The Murder of Henry VIII*.

Henry would be weeping with the decline.

Nigel had explained the theory several times, and each time Boniface cared less. There was no grave for Wolsey—Cardinal Wolsey, the King's chief administrator and trusted confidant—so any stories about Wolsey's death were simply rumors to explain away his disappearance. He disappeared so that he could metamorphose into the King. Not being within the line of succession, he couldn't become King by inheritance, so he had to take the role through a bit of sixteenth-century identity theft, which also involved a swift murder. As Nigel was forever saying: "Have you ever seen a picture of a slim Wolsey? But you've seen a picture of a slim Henry and a fat Wolsey? Okay, now join the dots."

Boniface looked up. He had been here as a kid, and looking at the ceiling he still found it stunning today. Even though he vaguely knew the building—and he had read the guidebooks and checked out Wikipedia's references to the *sumptuously decorated hammer-beam roof* when he prepared the invitations—as he stood right underneath it, breathlessly looking up, he marveled at how impressive it was, and how impressive it must have been for the thousands of people who ate under this roof when Henry reigned.

He stood, fixated on how the crossbeams appeared to have had their middle section cut out. Each end of the protruding beam was then supported by curved braces meeting the wall below, and the arched ceiling was balanced on top of these supported beams. The detailing was exquisite; Boniface could find no other word. It was like a doll's house but more intricate and bigger, much bigger—as in probably the biggest of its kind when it was built—and it had survived for more than 500 years.

Around the walls hung tapestries. Nigel had told Boniface that these showed the story of Adam and that they had been restored for a huge cost. Tens of millions spent on restoring something that, while it was hugely impressive, had been rendered pointless by central heating, Swedish furniture stores, and cheap labor in Vietnam.

His contemplation of the treasures of the Palace was disturbed by the caterer. Bloody prima donna. She stood in a room like this—self-obsessed and yet lacking the self-awareness to see her own lack of talent—and thought what she created was art. You put her next to true beauty and grace, and she just couldn't see it. At the planning meeting Boniface had lost interest. He'd said finger food; the managing editor had suggested finger food with a Tudor twist.

Boniface didn't even know what that meant. Swan vol-au-vents perhaps? Mini sparrow pies? Spit-roast stag, washed down with a flagon of the finest mead? Figuring the catering shouldn't affect how the book was reviewed in the papers, he left the catering arrangements to the managing editor, who had apparently delegated the task to her secretary—an arrangement Boniface was now regretting.

He turned away, trying to concentrate.

Time for a final run-through of the mental checklist. Most things seemed covered; there were stacks of books, and someone had even taken them out of the boxes and laid them on the table. A table...fabulous. A small raised stage, so everyone could see Nigel.

And where was he? People were starting to arrive.

It was stunning how someone so non-descript could be so completely defined by a single clothing choice. Nigel was five-foot-three and slightly built, made even slighter by his hunched shoulders. His hair, usually greasy, was only lank today, and like the rest of him, his clean-shaven face had no distinguishing features, but for Boniface, finding Nigel was as easy as finding an emergency beacon tied to the end of his own nose. "They like the suit," Nigel said, beaming like a six-year-old who has been told he looks exactly like Superman when he wears his underwear on the outside.

"Huh?" This wasn't the line Boniface was expecting.

"I was standing behind those people there"—Boniface looked at a cluster who had seemed particularly keen to get to the wine—"and the blond one"—the overly-peroxided one, thought Boniface—"said 'Love the suit.' And she must mean it because she didn't even realize I was there."

Boniface didn't know where to begin in the explanation of the concept of sarcasm, so he moved on. "Well, it just goes to show, doesn't it, Nigel? But remember, it's like a party dress—now that everyone's seen the suit, they shouldn't see it again, so you will wear something different for the TV stuff, won't you?"

Before Nigel could do much more damage on a one-on-one basis, it was time for him to address the gathering. This was the PR equivalent of crop spraying with highly toxic insecticide: necessary, but there might be casualties, although of course all appropriate precautions would be taken.

Boniface led Nigel to the stage and watched as the bravado, bolstered by the apparent positive perception about his new suit, crumpled, like the suit without Nigel's insubstantial frame to hold it.

Boniface surveyed the unintelligible hum of human interaction echoing around the room, waiting as a polite hush settled over the gathering, leaving whispers, a few clinking glasses, and the sound of a caterer performing her art. After a few gentle jokes, Boniface introduced Nigel and stepped away to allow the audience to focus.

Surprisingly, Nigel seemed to have prepared quite well and engaged the audience much more successfully than Boniface had expected. He touched on most of the points he seemed to mention every time he opened his mouth...Henry VIII was murdered...by Wolsey...with the lead pipe in the conservatory, perhaps...no, apparently there was now evidence of a plot with Anne Boleyn...

Boniface guessed he must have misheard. Nigel had told him the Wolsey/Anne Boleyn story several times, but it was always a theory; there was never definitive evidence. No matter, Nigel was on a roll, so Boniface didn't need to pay too much attention, and he casually moved next to the pile of books. This was the first time he had held a copy; until now he had only seen pictures of the cover.

He picked up a copy from the nearest pile, felt the weight, and flicked through a few pages. He was surprised: Somehow, it looked much more impressive than he was expecting. He turned to the back cover.

Henry VIII came to the English throne on 22 April 1509 at the age of 17, following the death of his father, King Henry VII.

The new King was a fit, good-looking, clean-shaven man with a passion for sport. He was a world-class tennis player, a skilled archer, and an accomplished horseman who would take on all-comers during a joust. He also enjoyed fishing and hunting.

He was well educated and spoke several languages, as well as being a devout Catholic and a scholar of the Bible. His (Roman Catholic) Christian belief was shared with his devoted (Roman Catholic) wife, Catherine of Aragon.

While he keenly embraced the pomp and ceremony of the monarchy, the affairs of State did not interest the young King, except when it came to war. He was well regarded as a soldier and led his troops in battle, in particular against the French.

When he first became King, due to his age his aunt, Lady Margaret Beaufort, acted as regent and performed the duties of the monarch. When Henry reached the age of 18 and the full power of the monarchy was vested in him, he still had little interest in the day-to-day business of the state. Instead, he left the administration of the country to his advisers, in particular the most trusted among their number, Cardinal Wolsey.

So why is it, in the twenty-first century, 500 years after this young man came to the throne, that Henry VIII has a reputation for having six wives, for being morbidly obese, for being little more than a tyrannical dictator who was ready to put his enemies (and some of his wives) to death, and for breaking with the Roman Catholic Church, which led to the founding of the Church of England?

Or is the man in our history books not Henry VIII?

A bit long and a bit wordy, but an interesting question. If Boniface hadn't met Nigel and didn't know what a twat he was, then sure, he might be interested in the book. Until he read it, of course... If it was written anything like Nigel usually talked, then he wouldn't get past the first page without wanting to throw the book across the room in anger and frustration.

Boniface glanced up and calibrated the responses. The mood had shifted. Nigel paused and Boniface took two steps forward, catching the eyes of two or three people in the small gathering. The audience understood the cue and started clapping. "Congratulations, Nigel. Great speech. They loved it."

"But I..." Boniface hustled Nigel back into the crowd, leaving the academic to move like a hunter finishing off the lame animals who didn't run swiftly enough.

nine

"Thank you so much. You were great in there." Ellen tried to focus on the producer but found herself distracted watching the other woman who was tightly gripping a cup of coffee but sloshing the liquid as she scratched the back of her other hand. "I am so, so sorry that we kept you waiting for so long. I hope you can forgive us."

"It's not a problem; I'm pleased to have been able to help, and if it sells more books..." Ellen felt sheepish, cringing at how commercially she was thinking.

"Well, it's your website you've got to thank. When I looked at the map and saw how close you were, I figured it was worth giving you a call."

"It's my sister that takes all the credit there," said Ellen lightly. "I don't understand all these gizmos, but she seemed to think it was easy: She took me to the shops and told me which phone to buy, did something on the website, and well...now you know where I am."

"Anyway, it was a pleasure to meet you." The producer seemed unable to focus on Ellen and was twitchily looking around the corridor.

"No, the pleasure's all mine. It was a joy to be interviewed by someone with a grasp of the subject. And if you need me again, well..." She looked down, her cheeks beginning to redden. "You've got my number and you know how to find where I am."

"Thank you. I'm sure we'll want to call you again," said the producer. "Let me show you the way out."

Ellen walked out of the studio and onto Millbank, following the River Thames upstream; checked her watch; silently cursed; and pulled out her phone. "Nigel, hi... Yes, I've just left my last interview. I'm at least forty-five minutes away."

Ellen was surprised that Nigel didn't seem disappointed. Not even vaguely annoyed. Instead, he seemed preoccupied. He was hyped up, but even by his usual standards of over-excitedness, there was something much more important preoccupying him. He was desperate to talk but didn't want to talk on the phone.

She checked her watch again. "It'll be quicker for me to go straight home; I should be there in under thirty minutes. Why don't you finish up there, then come 'round and you can tell me all about your evening and whatever it is that's exciting you."

She held the phone away from her ear as Nigel's babbling excitement seemed to ratchet up another gear.

"I can't be too late... Mmm, that's right. I've got to be up at some ridiculously early time to meet Montbretia at Heathrow... No, still don't know what we're going to do, but we'll figure something out. Call me when you get close."

She held the phone in front of her and started typing a text message. "Hi Monty, Nigel really excited. Perhaps he's found a pot of gold!?! I'll let you know. Maybe he'll let us spend it :-) So looking forward to seeing you tomorrow. Love E."

She hit the send key.

ten

By the third loop of the Richmond one-way system, the man with the scar on his face had figured out how it worked. It had been easy to reach Richmond, but he seemed to spend longer driving around the town than he had getting there.

The car was where Turgenev had said it would be. The route he had set out was simple, and once he got out of that bloody loop thing in the middle of Richmond, the route up the hill was straightforward. As he reached the top, the villas on his left side looked like they had been constructed as part of a BBC period drama, but he guessed these must be the real thing that had inspired the TV set designers. To the right the hill fell away, and at the bottom meadows ran down to a river that curved along the side of the lush grass. It was like a picture postcard of what England was supposed to look like, but he had only driven a few miles from the heart of London. From there it was a short drive to Ham Common, where Turgenev had marked Professor Armstrong's house.

The north and south sides of Ham Common were bisected by a main road—the exit route specified by Turgenev, which led first to dinner and second to Kingston, where he was to go over the river and dispose of the gun.

The professor's house was easy to locate on the north side of the common. It was on a road that ran parallel to the loop road, separated by a strip of land about sixty feet wide with grass and a few trees. The building was a small semidetached cottage in a row where there were houses on only one side of the road, facing out across the common.

Having completed his reconnaissance and double-checked his exit routes, the man with the scar found a place to park his car outside a church on the common's perimeter road, about 100 yards away from the professor's house. There was a certain irony in parking next to a church when he had come for such an ungodly act, but it was secluded, with the surrounding trees and bushes offering some cover, and with no streetlights to highlight his presence.

He waited for a man with a white terrier to pass, then took out the gun Turgenev had given him at Sodom and Gomorrah. By force of habit, he removed the magazine, confirmed again that it was loaded, and returned the pistol to his jacket pocket. He checked the phone—not that he was expecting any calls, but it was another habit to make sure that he had a signal and enough power.

Having checked his tools, he was ready to get in position before the light faded. Looking to make sure the man with the white dog had gone, he got out of the car and stretched, surprised at how relaxed he felt. Turgenev was right; Kristalle had helped him to clear his mind. He could now focus.

Across from Professor Armstrong's house, the common was wooded with dense, prickly undergrowth. The man with the scar found an old tree stump in the minor suburban jungle and sat, waiting under the protection of the natural camouflage, ready to be at the front door as soon as the professor returned.

eleven

Boniface and Nigel followed the last few stragglers from the Great Hall into the cobbled courtyard between the third gate—which was apparently called Anne Boleyn's Gate—and the Palace main gate, which Nigel made sure everyone knew was actually called the Great Gatehouse, not to be confused with the gate on the outer boundary, which was a modern construct.

"So why is it called Anne Boleyn's Gate? I thought it was called the Clock Tower." Boniface regretted his question immediately but remained stunned by the majesty of this third gate's architecture. In the dark, the two octagonal towers on either side of the gate were less prominent, but three floors above the archway was the exquisitely decorated astrological clock, now floodlit and now commanding everyone to stop and pay attention to its beauty. Kuznetsov could learn something about using gold for effect if he paid a quick visit here.

Before Boniface had the chance to slap himself for his stupidity, Nigel's phone rang. He watched as Nigel seemed to go through the whole range of emotions: excitement, enthusiasm, disappointment, hope, and back to puppy-dog enthusiasm building to unrestrained excitement.

As they walked through the Great Gatehouse archway, Boniface saw the line of cabs confirming that his chat with the ex-soldier on the outer gate had been worthwhile. He said his goodbyes and thanks to the last few departures and stood between the last cab and his corduroy-clad tormentor with his fingers crossed. "You live quite close, don't you, Nigel?"

The professor ended his call and looked down at his phone. "Yes. Thames Ditton Island." A flash passed across Boniface's face, his raised eyebrows acknowledging his approval and his slight surprise that Nigel would live somewhere so unique. "It's just over a mile or so if you walk, less if you want to swim."

"I know it," said Boniface. "Well, I know *of* it. It's on the bend behind the pub. I've seen it many times, but I've never been onto the island."

Nigel beamed. "But I'm not going home right now."

"So where are you going, Nigel?"

"Ham Common. My friend Ellen…"

"Oh, that's fine. I'm going to Kingston. Jump in. I'll get out at the bottom of Kingston Hill, and you can take it round to Ham."

Nigel grinned again like an inane child and continued on his line that Boniface had interrupted. "My friend Ellen. I've mentioned her before, and you've probably seen her on TV: She's the English constitutional expert. I want to tell her what I found out today when I was at the police station."

Boniface opened the cab door and Nigel scampered in, continuing to fiddle with his phone as he had been since his call ended. "Kingston, please," said Boniface to the cabbie. "Foot of Kingston Hill for me, and then could you take his nibs on to Ham Common?" The cabbie raised his eyebrows wearily.

"So is she your girlfriend?"

"Who? No." Nigel seemed to be encouraging his phone to perform an important task.

"But you'd like her to be?" Boniface didn't know why he asked these questions. It was probably some knee-jerk reaction from his journalist days, as hard to give up as the drink.

Nigel shifted awkwardly in his seat but managed to revert to his earlier subject. "As I was trying to tell you earlier, Boniface, the police called me because they had this guy who had found himself stuck in a hole."

"But you're an expert on history, Nigel. In particular Tudor history—you've written a book about Henry VIII. Why did the police need your expertise on people stuck in holes? Have you been keeping your talents with a pickaxe hidden from me?"

The cab jerked away, heading for the outer gate. "Tudor history is my thing, so when the police found an intruder stuck in a hole in Hampton Court, and with 'old bits of paper,' as the sergeant called them..."

"Old bits of paper?"

"What I call priceless documents, Boniface. They prove I was right, and that there is an heir to Henry VIII. This means the book is out of date, which is great news: The book's out of date because we've now got evidence, real documentary proof, of the aftermath of the murder. We just need to find some more of these documents to complete the story. This guy in the hole had some of them when he was picked up, and he wasn't telling us where he found them."

All Boniface could hear were Kuznetsov's words bouncing around his head. The point of tonight was to prove that the Royal Family had stolen the English crown, not to prove that there had been another heir to the throne.

He tried to calculate how many millions Kuznetsov had spent on his campaign to undermine the monarchy and to position himself as the obvious choice for first president, and figure how Nigel—who was still fiddling with his phone—had managed to subvert the whole campaign with his bumbling enthusiasm.

"You haven't told anyone about this, have you?"

"No. You told me not to when we spoke earlier."

"You're sure."

"Sure. I mean, obviously the police know."

And so it started. He had told the police the implication of the finding but was disappointed with their apparent complete disinterest—if they even understood the point he was making. The guy who got stuck in the hole had overheard this conversation and had said to Nigel that he could get more of these documents. Nigel had left Ellen some messages but didn't think he had given her details. "And I was about to mention it tonight, but then I remembered what you told me about reprinting the book."

So in short, lots of people knew—even if they didn't understand *what* they knew—and there was no way to get these worms back into the can. The only hope was that people hadn't been listening to Nigel and that what they had heard, they had forgotten.

The cab reached the end of Hampton Court Road, spun three-quarters around the roundabout, and headed over the River Thames into the Kingston one-way system. Boniface cursed under his breath. The driver. That was another person who had heard. Nigel looked up. "These photos are taking far too long to upload."

The comment begged to be ignored, so Boniface did, not that he even understood what Nigel was trying to tell him. Instead, he leaned closer to the academic and whispered, "Look. I can't explain here, but we need to talk tomorrow."

"Could you speak up a bit?" asked Nigel, drawing attention to Boniface's attempt not to alert the driver.

Boniface stared at Nigel, waiting for him to make and keep eye contact. Nigel flicked his gaze around the cab, finally finding Boniface's stare and locking onto it. A single shake of the head conveyed the response and the gravity of the matter Boniface was about to mention. He leaned in to Nigel. "Do not, I repeat, *do not* under any circumstances talk to anyone. Anyone. Not your mother, not your cat, and definitely not your friend Professor Ellen. Do not talk about your visit to the police station and what you found out. And," he lowered his voice further, "don't talk about a line of succession and this proof that could still be in Hampton Court."

Nigel's face took on a solemnity, like a seven-year-old trying to join the grown-up world.

"Not anyone," said Boniface, letting his voice reach a normal level, "including..." he lifted his eyes to indicate the cabbie and held up a single finger. "We will discuss this tomorrow, when everything will become clear."

"Okay..." said Nigel hesitantly.

"Okay," said Boniface, closing the subject.

The cab had found its way through the one-way system and was reaching the foot of Kingston Hill. "Drop me on the corner," Boniface called to the cabbie.

The cab pulled up, and Boniface let himself out. "Until tomorrow," he said to Nigel, lowering his head so he could look up for added emphasis. "You go and have a good evening talking about history. She's sitting there waiting for you, is she?"

"Should be," said Nigel, indicating to Boniface to come closer. As Boniface leaned in, Nigel whispered, "And tomorrow I'll tell you about the descendant of Henry. His direct heir...the true heir to the throne... He's living in London."

Boniface leaped back to see Nigel grinning. Subtly, he raised a finger to cover his lips; then pushed the door shut with a clunk.

He checked the meter and took a few bills out of his wallet without looking at the amount. "Thanks, mate. If you could now take my dear friend to Ham Common." The cabbie winked conspiratorially as he took the cash.

Boniface let the cab pass, feeling incapable of moving his feet and having difficulty putting his thoughts in order. How was he going to keep a lid on Nigel's discovery for long enough to keep Kuznetsov happy?

Standing by the side of the road wasn't helping. Curry might.

twelve

The man with the scar across his face identified the professor as the cab pulled up.

Why did all professors look the same? They were all uniquely different, but somehow they all looked the same. They always had lank, unkempt hair and slightly too-open eyes, and their sense of dress was always at least two decades out of date, even to the untrained eye. Even to the eye of a soldier who didn't understand fashion. And they all always dressed in weird colors. This one was dressed in a color that almost occurred in nature, but not quite. And in a weird material that looked like bits of string stitched together. It was almost what the man had heard called "peasant chic" but it still screamed "professor". He watched as the professor with the strange-colored suit made a big show of using his phone, like the taxi driver would care...

And as the taxi started to pull away, the man stood up and swiftly moved toward his prey.

■ ■ ■ ■ ■

"Hi Ellen, guess who? This call has gone through to voicemail, so you're probably on the phone. Anyway, I'm outside your house now, so if you're in, you can open the door. And if you're not in, then I'll try Hilda next door and see if she'll let me in. I've got lots to tell you. Ellen, you're not going to believe it; I've finally got the proof, and it was murder."

"Professor Armstrong?"

Nigel picked up on the thick Russian accent immediately. Or did the accent originate from farther south, from some other part of the Russian Federation? That didn't matter for now; all that mattered was giving the right answer, and that answer was obvious: Yes, this is her house, but no, I am not her.

Nigel trawled his brain for the right words. Da is yes. Dacha is a house... But can a dacha be a main home? Or is a dacha only a second home, sort of like a summer cottage? This was Ellen's home, after all, and not a summer residence. This house was a cottage, so perhaps it could be regarded as a dacha, or did the fact that it was the main home rule out that option? There was a lot Nigel needed to find out from his Russian and Eastern European colleagues when he was next at the university, or perhaps this fellow might tell him.

"Professor Armstrong?" repeated the man in front of Nigel, looking at him with an intimidating intensity. It had been a very pleasant evening, and now a big Russian—or at least someone who appeared to Nigel to be Russian—wearing boots, jeans, and a leather jacket, and with a large scar starting at his nose and crossing his cheek, was demanding to know whether he was Ellen. Clearly there was some misunderstanding.

The man stared at Nigel, his eyes insisting on an immediate answer, and Nigel hesitantly started to answer as best he could while he tried to find the right words to give him the answer in Russian: "Da..."

■ ■ ■ ■ ■

The man with a scar pulled out the pistol and placed one shot between the professor's eyes. With a single flowing movement, the gun had been removed, discharged, and replaced in his pocket. There was no need to check that the professor was dead or to put another bullet into his body. That one bullet, placed accurately, was sufficient.

His task now was to leave rapidly and without drawing any attention to himself. He moved swiftly and noiselessly through the trees, looking to confirm he hadn't been seen before he drove away, taking the road away from the professor's home and the lifeless body, following the perimeter of the common as it circled back to the main road.

At the junction he turned left and followed the route toward Kingston. As he crossed the end of the professor's road, he saw the man with the white terrier kneeling next to the fallen body. The man seemed torn between trying to help the professor and keeping his dog away from the body.

He continued to follow the main road, pulling off to park in front of a parade of shops, where he picked up the phone, selected the number that Turgenev had programmed for him, and notified the man who answered that Professor Armstrong had been shot dead outside his home on the edge of Richmond.

Grabbing the map book on the passenger seat, he flicked to page 183, ran his finger—again—over his route for departure, and, having fixed the image of the route in his mind, tore the page from the book. Dropping the book back on the seat, he opened his car door and set fire to the page with a plastic lighter he pulled from his pocket, twisting the burning paper to make sure every detail was caught by the flame, dropping the last unburned corner when every other detail had been obliterated.

His task complete, he looked up at the Chinese restaurant on the other side of the street.

thirteen

As every kid who has ever visited Hampton Court Palace knows, each resident changed something.

Cardinal Wolsey when he acquired the location from the monks, Henry VIII when he acquired the Palace Wolsey had constructed, each of Henry's wives, and every resident since has changed it. Some added bits. Some removed bits. Some replaced bits. Some changes were structural, others decorative. Some changes were gorgeous, others were hideous. But everyone changed something.

The end result is a complete hodgepodge.

There are odd angles and illogical layouts. Corridors end unexpectedly. Room sizes and dimensions don't make sense. Where there are new rooms next to old rooms there are gaps and crevices. Sometimes these are filled but sometimes not, and sometimes these are quite interesting spaces...if you're the kind of person who likes to find his way around.

And that was what Peter Winckley had been doing. It started more than a day ago, shortly before closing time at the Palace.

Pete had bought himself a ticket and started to look around. The public lavatories were not the most salubrious location in the Palace, but they were a useful place to hide if you were looking to get yourself *accidentally* locked in. Having succeeded, Pete only had to wait a few hours for the cleaning crew to pass through, and then he was free to roam. His only concern was to ensure that he didn't bump into the security staff, but those old soldiers were so noisy that he could hear them coming from a mile off. Whoever made those big clompy boots, he owed them.

There was a gap that Pete had wanted to look at for a while. He'd seen it next to a new wall—new as in several hundred years old, but newer than the older Tudor walls—which seemed to cut off one of the very old parts. This created a gap.

The gap was tight, but Pete was skinny and accustomed to a tight squeeze—literally and metaphorically. He had pushed into the gap and followed a right and then a left right-angle turn before a wall, built to the height of about five feet, cut the passage. But there was still a gap above the bisecting wall that he could scramble over.

As Pete had dropped over the wall, there had been a delicate ripping sound—like gossamer threads being pulled apart. He had switched on his light to find he was not the first living being to have had the idea of taking a look around. With each stab of light into the darkness of the room, it had become apparent that industrious spiders had spent several hundred years working on a very special project. Where some residents choose to paint their rooms and others choose wallpaper, the spiders had focused on soft furnishings and had attempted to cover every surface and all the space between with webs.

He had turned to look around the room and felt a clump of webs stick to the right side of his head. Reflexively, he had shaken his head and raised his hand to remove the mess—his ponytail had flicked more webs, and by the time his hand had reached his face, he had been wearing a cobweb glove.

They say dust only gets so deep. Pete had wondered whether there was a limit to the number of spider webs that could fit into one room as he had pulled his hands inside his sleeves and chopped through the blankets in front of him, and then kicked at the webs holding his legs.

Against the long wall on the other side of the room appeared to be some bookcases, and Pete had guessed the lumps were cabinets. Holding his light in his mouth, he had ducked his head and pushed forward to the nearest piece of furniture, a long table.

He had tried to move the gossamer blankets; each time he had picked up a web, he needed to flap his hand to try to drop the clump he had just grabbed, but he failed as it stuck to him. In frustration, he had pushed the morass to reveal the top of the table and what looked like some old pieces of paper.

It was no good; he was getting nowhere. He would have to come back, but with a stick or a saw or something else to cut through the mess. Five minutes on Google, and he would find the answer for dealing with spider webs, but for the moment he had done enough—he had maneuvered himself into one of the very old parts of the building, and he had found *something*. It still wasn't clear what the room was; it certainly didn't show up on any of the histories that he had read or in any of the floor plans he had seen. He had guessed it was an old storage room that had been split and permanently sealed when a new room was built, and on first glance there didn't seem to be anything of value that he could sell easily.

He had turned back to the wall he had climbed over to enter and then stopped himself, remembering the documents on the table. Cautiously, he had picked them up and returned to his exit.

Getting out, it had been harder to scrabble over the wall. Where it was five feet high on the outside, on the inside the drop was deeper, probably by another two feet or so, plus he had the documents and the spider webs still sticking to him.

He had balanced on top of the bisecting wall for some time, listening to boots trample up and down the passageway outside. It had seemed like there was a convention of security guards outside his crevice. When he finally was convinced they had left, he had dropped into the gap. On the second right-angle, he had wedged his foot in a place that, given what followed, could've been regarded as a bad place to put his foot.

Having put his foot in a less than ideal place to negotiate the corner, Pete had twisted his leg and fell sideways, wedging his body in the gap, which he had found narrowed toward the bottom, and had trapped his right arm underneath him. While his body had fit along the bottom of the gap, his head had stuck out into the passage, far enough to see that although he had thought there were no guards, he had been wrong.

After their convention the guards had dispersed, but they had left one of their number who had decided to sit down on a bench in the passage. He had been contentedly having a quiet nap when he was rudely interrupted by Pete's fall.

In a slight state of shock, having woken too quickly, the guard had overreacted. The control room, hearing his radio call, had picked up on the panic in his voice, and rather than simply calling for additional guards to assist, they had also called for the police. It must have been a slow night at the station, because the police had arrived before most of the guards.

As soon as the police had arrived, they had taken charge. This was unfortunate for Pete; if he had been dealing with the old men, he might have been able to talk his way out of trouble—or at least offer some plausible explanation as a delaying tactic while he pondered his next move. But this option hadn't been available to him.

Instead, the first policeman had taken the papers he had discovered, which he was still holding in his free left hand, as evidence. Doubtless, one or more of the guards would be admonished for letting these valuable new finds leave the Palace by the same Palace authorities that had hired old soldiers drawing their pensions as guards, knowing that they were cheap labor.

After making a cursory check to ensure that, as far as they could tell given the circumstances, neither his back nor his neck were broken, the remaining police had then dragged Pete from his resting place, taking special care to ensure that it was as inconvenient and humiliating for him as possible.

He had been bundled into the back of a police car and taken to the station, where, of course, he had become the butt of every joke. What sort of thief gets stuck in a hole?

The police didn't have much evidence. It's hard to suggest that someone is guilty of breaking and entering when there's no broken window or busted lock to prove that your suspect broke in, and the entry is to a public place. But still, his questioner had persisted.

And then the King of Corduroy had turned up.

Pete had watched the man in that horrible suit, the kind of suit that wasn't even fashionable in the 1970s. And what color was that anyway? The man in the suit, Pete had soon learned, was Professor Nigel Trudgett, a leading expert on the Tudor period. An expert who was sufficiently well regarded that he had published a book. A committed expert who lived and breathed his subject: He had even boasted that he lived on Thames Ditton Island and could see Hampton Court Palace from his back window.

The professor had become very interested, very quickly. This wasn't simple interest; this was a man driven, like a cocaine addict searching for his next fix. This was something big. The professor had become quite insistent that he should be allowed to try to find out where the documents came from, and then *bang*. He had mentioned it: valuable. These documents had value, and that value would be significant to someone like Richard Sherborne.

In the end, probably to shut him up, the police had allowed Professor Trudgett to sit in on the interview. "There's more," Pete had said to the professor. That was all that was necessary to get his attention in a brief moment when the police were distracted. "I'll show you." The deal had been sealed with the professor, and the academic had gone silent and remained silent.

Later, as Pete was going through the discharge formalities, signing pieces of paper for the return of his possessions—unfortunately, with the exception of the papers he found at Hampton Court Palace—the station started buzzing about the shooting. It began with a call about a shooting and, within minutes, news came in about Professor Trudgett's murder.

Pete was sad to hear about his death. He had liked the man. Well, perhaps *like* was too strong a word. He was impressed by the man's enthusiasm for his subject, and he respected his breadth of knowledge. The way he had been able to take new information—kindly supplied by Pete's hard work—and put it into context, linking it with other historical information, was impressive.

It was even more striking that the prof had been uninterested by the financial value, even though he seemed to know who would want to pay money for this 500-year-old information. He had been quite dismissive about that aspect and didn't want to soil his hands. Instead, there was something else in the papers that interested him more.

But now he was dead.

■ ■ ■ ■ ■

Pete walked out of the station, removed the elastic band holding his ponytail in place, shook his hair free and tugged out some more spider webs that were still stuck, then pulled his phone out of his pocket and called directory enquiries.

On the third attempt, he got lucky.

"Richard Sherborne, please." The voice at the other end was pompous. He sounded like a Richard Sherborne, so Pete continued. "This is one of those 'you don't know me but…' phone calls." It was rare that he got to use such a clichéd line. "I've got some documents that I believe could be very significant for you." It took some time to interest Sherborne. "Definitely authentic. Verified by Professor Nigel Trudgett; I'm sure you know him."

Once interested, Sherborne seemed quite willing to pay money for the documents. "Of course, as you will understand, the documents are in a secure facility. I'll need a few hours to get hold of them, and I'll bring one or two samples to our first meeting so that you can appraise what's on offer."

Sherborne seemed quite open to this approach.

Pete hung up and went to find the next bus headed toward Thames Ditton. It couldn't be that hard to find Professor Trudgett's house on the Island. Once there, he was bound to find something he could sell to Sherborne—and maybe the professor had a suit that he could borrow for the meeting.

Hopefully his suits weren't all corduroy.

fourteen

As Ellen's cab pulled up, her phone beeped—a missed call and voicemail from Nigel. Ignoring the phone until she got inside, she continued to look through her purse for some cash and found a bill that she pushed through the glass to the driver.

"D'you wanna receipt, love?"

"Yes, please," said Ellen.

"There you are, my darling," said the cabbie, passing the receipt and Ellen's change. "Not sure what's going on over there." Ellen looked to where the cabbie was indicating: the path to her house. Several people were standing around, all looking flustered. Each seemed to be looking outward for the answer, as if they were expecting a knight to ride up on his trusty white steed.

It took Ellen a moment or two to realize that they were standing around someone, someone who seemed to be lying on her front path. She looked again at the faces; this wasn't just concern she was seeing.

This was shock.

This was panic.

As the sound of the cab's engine faded, she stood frozen, becoming increasingly aware of several sets of sirens, each with a different tone and character. Hilda Longthorne, her neighbor, came toward her.

Hilda was in her seventies, but despite being in apparently good health, she looked older: Dry, wrinkled skin; colorless gray hair; and an old brown floral dress with a faded green cardigan all displayed her age but hid her warm heart. Ellen looked into the old woman's eyes and could see a desperation to look sympathetic, but an inability to hide her horror. "Your friend," said Hilda, her old skin crinkling as she trembled. "It's your friend."

Ellen threw a look of panic. "Nigel?"

"Yes, dear. He's been shot." The siren from the paramedic's car drowned out Ellen's scream.

In the evening gloom, the flashing blue lights on the paramedic's green-yellow car gave the street the stop/go effect of a 1920s monochrome movie, slowing down time. Ellen watched as the paramedic walked over to where Nigel lay, getting closer with each flick of the lights, and knelt beside him.

As an ambulance arrived and shut off its siren, the sound of another emergency vehicle could still be heard in the distance, but nearing. "That'll be the police," said Hilda. "Now come on, dear, he's being looked after by the best people for the job. You need a cup of tea, or maybe something stronger."

Hilda took Ellen's arm and pulled her toward the shared path to their houses. "Look away, and I'll guide you through," said Hilda, but it was too late. Ellen had already seen Nigel, who had fallen onto his back with his head pointing toward her front window.

He looked as he always did, apart from the new suit and the round hole in his forehead where a small trail of blood oozed. Ellen looked up at the front of her house, a few feet away from where Nigel must have been standing when he fell, and noticed the splattering, as if someone had thrown a cup full of dark, sticky liquid mixed with shredded raw meat.

"Is he…?"

"I don't know," said Hilda, ushering her past Nigel and the paramedics, and through the older woman's front door.

"He is, isn't he?" said Ellen, starting to cry uncontrollably.

fifteen

"What and why?"

Veronica Rutherford leaned back in her chair, twisting her fingers in the end of her hair as she contemplated the woman standing in her office door.

What lipstick was left was badly applied; the rest had been rubbed off, hopefully only on a coffee cup. The lipstick that still clung on clashed with her fuchsia jacket, which exaggerated her peroxide-scorched hair. Burst capillaries—hieroglyphics that, when decoded, told a story of too much alcohol, too little sleep, followed by too much caffeine, all in the name of career, and some misunderstanding between career and self-worth—strained like gauze holding back the last remnants of youth, before the floodgates of age opened. And with age and experience came competence, so Veronica listened.

"Our bitter and twisted little man who Sherborne never appreciated, but who we are being kind to, called. Something is going on. Something has caught Sherborne's interest in a big way." She pursed her lips. "But we don't know what. All we know is that he's called in the big guns—outside muscle to keep him safe."

Veronica let go of her hair and slumped. "So what—precisely—has happened?"

"Difficult." The fuchsia jacket pondered. "As far as we can tell, Sherborne received a phone call from someone who he has apparently never met. He got excited by the call and is expecting the caller to get in touch with him later today."

"So...they're going to meet? What does this mean?" Veronica sat up, shoulders lifted, palms up. "Some sort of trade? Blackmail?"

"That was my least implausible conclusion." The fuchsia jacket sounded noncommittal. "Sherborne has called in the cavalry, which is how we got the tip. And he wants brawn, not brain, which tells us something, although I'm not quite sure what."

"So where is Sherborne at the moment?" Veronica knotted her eyebrows. "Where does he want the reinforcements? Home or the office?"

"Home. In Richmond."

"At home, protected by the redoubtable Ada. I'm surprised he feels the need for anyone other than Ada to defend him. Perhaps he's getting sentimental in his old age."

The fuchsia jacket's concentration remained fixed on her boss. "Shall we send someone to sit on him for a few hours? Perhaps see if we can recognize the source before he gets to Sherborne?"

"Let's do that. Send Whittaker if he's not still sulking." The fuchsia jacket frowned but seemed unwilling to ask for an explanation. "We're chasing a lead on Oscar—and before you say it, I doubt it's connected to this, but I guess we'll find out. Anyway, we've got a sting to catch Oscar, and Whitters doesn't look the part, so we sent someone else, and young Whitters..." She pushed her nose, putting a kink in it.

"Out of joint, big time." The fuchsia jacket smirked conspiratorially. "I see. I'll be gentle. I'll tell him that you handpicked him for this mission."

Veronica smiled broadly. "Thank you." The smile dropped. "Just make sure he gets that this is all about subtlety. I don't want Sherborne to know we're there. I don't want him to think that anyone's on to him. If he starts thinking that way, he's going to get paranoid, and if he gets paranoid, then he's going to start looking for spies. 'Traitors, dear Vron. Traitors, the damned blighters.'" She dropped the Sherborne mimicry. "And if he starts looking for spies...well, there's always a chance that he might suspect our bitter and twisted little friend. Even if he can't prove anything, we risk losing our source, so tell Whittaker not to be noticed. By anyone."

Veronica loosened the crick in her neck with a gentle twist of her head, then shook her hair free in an involuntary reflex. Her dark auburn mane convulsed and gently settled itself. "Sherborne may seem like a buffoon, and he is in so many ways, but he's not stupid. Remember, we don't know what security he had before the reinforcements, and much more importantly, we don't know who else might already be chasing this. The last thing we need is a branch meeting of the National Union of Journalists outside his front door."

"Aye aye, Cap'n," said the fuchsia jacket, saluting as she turned to leave.

Veronica sighed, reaching into her desk to pull out her whisky, and filled her tumbler, which was still sitting on her desk from when she had seen Boniface. She turned to her screen to skim the next day's layouts while taking the occasional sip.

There was a soft tap on her door, and she spun. The fuchsia jacket's tanned hide was looking pale. "I was passing the duty office on my way out..." She hesitated, a slight tremble audible as she continued. "Professor Ellen Armstrong was murdered tonight. She was shot dead outside her house in Richmond."

The room was silent. Veronica took a deep breath, held it, and then slowly exhaled while closing her eyes. "Is it confirmed?"

"The call came direct, and apparently the caller was certain about the identity. We haven't got a second source yet, but I've got calls out."

Veronica paused, moving her lower jaw from side to side. "Has anyone else got it yet?" A single shake of the head. "Then we'll run it. Check and double-check with whatever sources you can find, but unless Oscar makes his mistake soon, that's the lead story. Let's get it out to the TV stations; maybe we can get the lead on *Newsnight*. But try and get more information and a second verification before the presses roll."

"On it."

sixteen

Boniface stared at the wall on the other side of the restaurant.

He didn't want to be with people. He didn't want conversation—he had spent too much time with Nigel, too much time in a room with too much alcohol, and too much time had been wasted with half-drunk people he thought he had escaped from. Then, to put the cherry on the top, Nigel had blurted out that he had found the heir to Henry VIII living in London.

He wanted quiet. And if he couldn't have quiet—which was difficult to achieve in a restaurant that was open to the public—then he wanted to be left alone.

He couldn't stop fixating on the implications of what Nigel had said: If there was a living heir whose ancestry could be proved, then Kuznetsov's plan to undermine the monarchy on the grounds that they were frauds would be irrelevant, and his ambitions for a republic—with him as the president, becoming the de facto first tsar—were in tatters.

The last three, four, five, or however many years of Kuznetsov's pursuit of his ambition would all come apart as a direct result of the job that Boniface had been given. Sure, if there ever was a referendum, it would be virtually unwinnable, but now any failure to achieve a referendum would be directly attributed to Boniface rather than the fact that it was a stupid idea in the first place—and, as Veronica had so succinctly suggested, that would be a bad thing.

Boniface had been assigned one mission, and it was a simple one. But he had failed.

Someone was bound to have listened to Nigel. One of the cops would have taken him seriously and called the papers. The cabbie almost certainly heard. Nigel was bound to have told someone at the book launch. And then there was the guy who got stuck in the hole at Hampton Court, who had actually found the documents. He wasn't going to sit back, was he?

There were two questions that needed to be answered: How was the story going to get out and how angry would Kuznetsov be? Never-work-again-in-this-town type of angry, or send-around-one-of-the-guys-with-big-boots-and-a-worn-leather-jacket angry? Probably the guy with the scar across his face; he looked like he could be good with his hands, and if not him, then Turgenev, who would kill him just with his looks.

Boniface's stare remained fixed; he didn't even notice the annoying background sitar music. His empty plate sat in front of him, with the greasy yellow stains on the over-starched tablecloth proving that he was both messy at serving and messy at eating. But he didn't notice; he kept staring at the dark-red flocked wallpaper, which seemed far less tasteless than the wall coverings in Kuznetsov's reception.

"Mister Alexander, you're being very quiet tonight." The proprietor stood by attentively.

Boniface pulled himself out of his trance-like state. "I'm sorry, Shankar. Lots to think about, I'm afraid." He looked sheepish, still half-dazed with Nigel's revelation, when his phone rang. "Yes, that's me, and it's Boniface, please, no mister." His smile for Shankar turned into his fake reassuring business smile, and then dropped to reveal his un-faked worried look. "The police? How can I help you?"

Shankar shared Boniface's look of worry. "Yes, I know Professor Trudgett. I was with him until about an hour ago." Shankar's look of worry relaxed. "Dead?" Shankar took the form of a cartoon character, with his eyes out on stalks.

Boniface felt winded. The life force was being sucked out of him. He was supposed to be the expert on handling situations, and now he didn't know what to do. He was already dazed, thinking about how widely Nigel had spread his revelation, but now he sat and listened to the policeman, repeating back odd phrases like a three-year-old trying to say big words. "Shot...dead...his phone...I.C.E...in case of emergency, oh... my number...really, oh...no, I don't know why...oh...no, I don't know why anyone would want to shoot...did he...I mean...pain, suffer...doc says instant...oh...Ellen Armstrong...yes, his friend...no, never met her...shocked...she would be...they were at Cambridge, I think, together...doubt they were more, but I don't know...his publisher is my client..."

Boniface continued talking with the police, or rather listening and mumbling odd phrases. As he ended his call, he said "gotta go" to no one in particular and dropped a few bills on the table before heading into the cool night air.

seventeen

Ellen felt like she had been wailing forever.

In reality, she had been sitting, gently sobbing, in Hilda Longthorne's sitting room for less than an hour while Hilda kept vigil, silently offering support.

The room was typical of old-woman chic. Two old armchairs with an unpleasant floral design sat on the edge of a heavily worn carpet betraying its 1960s vintage and exposing old floorboards where the fabric rectangle didn't extend to the walls. The wallpaper was of a similar age, reaching up to a ceiling that had once been white and now wasn't, but did have numerous fine cobwebs thoughtfully hiding the cracks in the plaster. The television seemed nearly as old but was functional. The picture was on, but the volume had been cut when Hilda went to investigate the loud noise outside.

The police had asked to talk with Ellen, but Hilda had refused. She had politely offered tea to the officers, the paramedics, and the doctor who had arrived to confirm that Nigel was indeed dead, but no one had accepted her offer. Hilda had offered alcohol to Ellen, but Ellen was happy with a cup of tea as she sat motionless, apart from her tears, staring at her phone, looking at the message notification.

Eventually she pushed the button to retrieve her voicemail, heard it ring, and heard the computerized voice giving her the menu options. Too much. She couldn't go through with it and hung up, continuing to stare at the phone. She tried again but only got as far as the ringing before she hung up. On the third attempt, the voicemail system spoke to her: "Message one was received at nine-oh-five pm today from zero-seven…" It was Nigel's number. Ellen hung up without listening.

On the fourth attempt, she heard his voice: "Hi Ellen, guess who?" Ellen smiled at his goofiness and felt a new torrent of tears flow down her cheeks. She missed most of the message, only hearing the last line: "Ellen, you're not going to believe it; I've finally got the proof, and it was murder."

Murder, and then he gets murdered.

The police called again; a gentle tap on the front door was enough. Hilda sent them away again and returned. "Bob…"—she saw Ellen's confusion—"the man with the white dog. He saw a man parked up near the church earlier in the evening when he took the dog out for a walk. He thinks he saw the same man sitting and watching from the other side of the common for about an hour or so. It was as if he was waiting for Nigel to turn up."

"But he can't have been. I only invited Nigel 'round when I finished that last interview—I was meant to be at Hampton Court, not here, so he can't have been waiting for Nigel. Bob must be wrong."

"I don't know, dear. He's a very nosey man and tends to notice things. You may not want to pass the time of day with him, but he can tell you every car that has parked up the street, the time they arrived, and the time they left."

A silence fell over the room as the two contemplated the new information. The television flickered as the previews for the next day's programs flashed, and then the titles for *Newsnight* started running. In her stunned state, Ellen stared at the flickering screen. It was the very stern presenter tonight—the one with a reputation for tearing politicians limb from limb. On any other day, if he had been doing a political interview, it would be worth watching. But Ellen wasn't in a mood for blood sports tonight, not with the amount of blood that had been splattered over the front of her house.

Ellen's picture came up on the screen, and she snapped out of her daze. It was like she had been given a year to mourn, all the sleep she needed, and a refreshing bath. "Turn it up," she said to Hilda, suddenly regretting that she was commanding, not asking. "Why am I on television? I didn't talk to them today; why am I being featured?"

The presenter was in the middle of the sentence by the time Hilda found the remote control "... the sad news about the murder of Professor Ellen Armstrong, who initial reports say was shot dead at her south London home tonight. The professor has recently made several appearances on this program..."

Ellen stood, clenching her fists, every muscle in her body tightening. "Why do they think I'm dead when Nigel's dead, Hilda? Something must be wrong."

Hilda's face remained serene. "It's probably a silly mistake, dear, don't..."

"Don't what?" Ellen snapped, and then regretted the target of her anger, slapping her hand over her mouth. "I'm sorry." She hugged her neighbor. "I'm sorry." She released Hilda and looked her straight in the eyes. "Someone has told the media that I'm dead. You're not going to tell me that this is all a coincidence, are you? There's a man waiting outside my house, Nigel finds something, Nigel gets shot, and then they say I'm dead." Ellen found she was gripping the sleeves of Hilda's dress. "I'm sorry... It's..."

Hilda's voice was soft; her tone practical, matter-of-fact. "What can I do?"

Ellen released Hilda's sleeves and stood back. "I don't know, but I can't stay here—not if the killer knows where I live." Hilda listened intently as her neighbor continued. "I don't know why Nigel was shot, but I do know it's not good to know someone who's just been killed, especially if they tell you they've got a secret. People tend to think you might know the secret too, and want you dead or want to force you to reveal it. But as I don't know what he found out, I'm going to go to his house before anyone else gets there and have a look 'round."

"Go out the back. I'll hold off the police." Ellen frowned quizzically. "I have my ways, dear. I've learned a thing or two," said Hilda, picking a bottle of sweet sherry from her shelves, and snapping the seal as she twisted the lid before pouring herself a small measure. "Awful stuff. Why do people think that you'll like it because you're over sixty?"

She took a sip, pulling an exaggerated face, swilled the liquid around her mouth, gargled, and looked around as if she had lost something. Spotting a small African violet sitting on the windowsill, she picked it up. "Pah. Horrible stuff," she said, spitting the sherry onto the violet.

A mischievous grin came over her face as she put her fingertips into her glass and then dripped sherry onto her wrists, which she rubbed together and then rubbed on the side of her neck. "Dotty old bird... I can keep them talking for hours. They'll think I'm drunk..." she put her thumb into the middle of the V neckline of her dress, giving it a noticeable tug down "...and desperately lonely. That's the scariest thing for a young policeman."

She winked at Ellen, who was seeing a resourceful side of her neighbor she had never seen before.

"Go out the back. Hop over the fence." Hilda cocked her head and looked Ellen up and down. "That's not the best skirt for fence climbing, and those aren't the best shoes, but you're young, you'll manage. Bert's got the garden at the end. He'll be in bed by now, so he won't notice you going through. His gate is never locked, but he gets upset if it's not closed, so do shut it after you go through. Turn right, and you'll reach the main road. I'll keep them busy when they next knock, and when they get insistent, I'll tell them you're asleep upstairs. It should be hours before I have to tell them that you must have slipped out while I was getting some more sherry. And while they think you're here, so will the man with the gun if he comes back."

"Thanks, Hilda. I owe you."

eighteen

The old leather creaked as he leaned to replace the receiver. The leather creaked again, and the whole chair groaned as Richard Sherborne moved his bulk back to sit squarely.

Ada had arrived at her sister's, where she would spend the night.

In safety.

He had fought quite a battle with her. She was unquestioningly loyal and only agreed to stay at her sister's when he agreed to bring in two guards for the night. And now she was safe, so he didn't need to worry about her.

But safe from what? He wasn't quite sure—this was probably a setup. The question was who was doing the setting? The obvious answer was Kuznetsov, but it didn't have his usual fingerprints: a call from a phone where the number wasn't withheld, a call to him personally at a time and place where he wouldn't usually be, the sums of money didn't seem huge—but that could be a double bluff—a proposition that hadn't been rehearsed, papers verified by one of Kuznetsov's authors... Sherborne sighed; Kuznetsov would never be that obvious. There was a ring of truth somewhere in the dirt, and if the documentation was authentic, then it would be worth paying money. But all his intuition said it was fake.

And in case it was something else, then Ada was safely stowed with her sister, and the cavalry were here.

Sherborne pushed his chair back from his leather-topped desk and stood. With his expanding waistline, standing was becoming less of a straightforward task. It wasn't that he weighed more than he once had; after all, the tweed jacket he was wearing was at least 25 years old—Ada had done a splendid job with arm patches and stitching up the burst seams over the years—and his brown trousers were probably 20 years old. But they were both tight. The trousers, naturally, around the waist, although as his gut pushed them downward the constriction became less of an issue, but it did mean he needed to think about asking Ada to take up the legs. The jacket hadn't been buttoned up since 1980-something, and now it was getting tighter under the arms and across the back. This was a new and, to be frank, rather unpleasant experience.

Having managed to lift his bulk and balance on top of increasingly tired legs, Sherborne paused to catch his breath. He looked up and exhaled, then looked down. It was a familiar sight: an old checked, brushed-cotton shirt and a tie covering a large gut, but no feet in sight. He steadied himself on the chair with his right hand and leaned over. Yes. His feet were still there, brown brogues as expected—old, but spit-and-polished to perfection by Ada. That was a relief and something that should be celebrated with a drink while he contemplated.

The drinks cabinet was on the left-hand side of the study. Sherborne placed a crystal tumbler on the dark wood; dropped in a few ice cubes; put in a good measure of gin; topped it up a bit further, and a bit further again; added a slug of tonic; and threw in a lime slice.

He took a sip and distracted himself by looking at the spines of his first editions, arranged conveniently just below eye level. He could see the contents of the first two shelves, but below that he needed his glasses or a chair to sit on, as bending wasn't a practical proposition. From the filled dark mahogany bookcases covering the left wall, he turned to the window looking across his architecturally ordered garden in the direction of the Thames. In the gloom he could see shadows, but no signs of any of Kuznetsov's men ghosting across the manicured lawns.

Walking around his desk, he dropped into his Chesterfield sofa with its back to the right wall, which was also covered in mahogany bookcases, like the others, filled to overflowing. On some shelves, books were stacked on top of books, and on others there were two rows, one behind the other.

Sherborne flopped his arm over the scrolled back of the sofa and stared up at the ceiling while he slowly sipped. Then he turned and placed his drink on a mahogany end table, exchanging his tumbler for the TV remote control.

He sat back and recalled his words during the strange conversation earlier that evening. "An offer I can't refuse? And yet somehow, I feel compelled to say no." That was enough to convince the individual to explain what he was about.

He checked his watch and clicked on the television, switching to *Newsnight*. He was shocked by the headline: Ellen Armstrong, his favorite historian, had been murdered. Shot outside her house less than two miles away.

He made a mental note to pay his respects in the morning. He didn't know whether the professor had any family in this country, what with her being American, but he would offer his condolences and any practical help—in particular by making sure royalties on her book were paid to the beneficiary in her will—where he could.

nineteen

Hilda had been right. It wasn't easy getting over the fence, but it was possible. Ellen would've preferred to have gone home and changed, perhaps slipped out of her skirt and put on some sensible shoes. Home wasn't that far—it was next door to Hilda, across a shared path with facing front doors—but that would have meant seeing Nigel, the remains of Nigel still over her house, the police, probably the press by now, and all of those other well-intentioned but ultimately annoying neighbors.

And she might have seen the man with the gun. And he, her.

So she had gone out the back way, climbed over the fence, skinned her knees but kept her suit clean, passed through Bert's garden, closed the gate as instructed by Hilda, and walked to the line of shops at the end of the road. There she had been fortunate and seen a cabbie who had said he had just come out of the Chinese restaurant. You couldn't usually find a cab for hire at that time, but tonight she had been lucky, and so she had been able to get to Thames Ditton in less than ten minutes.

Ellen asked the cabbie—a strange-looking man, who was balding but kept what hair he did have collar-length at the back—to drop her at the roundabout in the middle of the High Street, and from there she headed toward the river.

She walked up Thames Ditton High Street, a road she had always found cute in a Ye Olde English type of way. Given its history, Ellen always expected this to be a more substantial road. According to Nigel, when Henry first took ownership of Hampton Court Palace, the island—Thames Ditton Island—didn't exist. Instead, it was part of the bank on which the Palace stood. Supplies for the Palace would be brought up the High Street, and at low tide there was a ford to cross the river. If the tide was in and you wanted to get across, then you had to pay a ferryman.

To travel to the Palace, the King would be rowed up from Westminster. But Henry was dissatisfied with the lack of grandeur on arrival, particularly when he was receiving guests at this country Palace. So he had ordered the river be dug straight. The land that was cut off when the river was cut straight became a separate island. Ellen remembered how excited Nigel had always been, living somewhere created by Henry.

She reached the sharp bend at the junction between the High Street and Summer Road, and crossed, following what had been the route of the road into the ford, but which now led into two parking lots: the one on the left attached to a pub and the other a more informal space that doubled as a slipway into the river.

She stepped onto the footbridge, and at the security gate halfway over the river she punched in Nigel's code 1-5-0-9-4-7 and smiled: always the Henry VIII obsessive. Each resident on the island had their own security code for the gate—Nigel had been so pleased that he had been able to set his code to reflect Henry's period as King, 1509 to 1547. Or rather, the historically recognized period during which Henry was King. In reality, Nigel believed that Henry had probably been murdered sometime around 1530, so maybe he should have changed his entry code. Ellen wiped away a tear. It was too late to tease Nigel about that now.

As she hit the last digit, the lock clicked and Ellen pulled the gate, then strolled the short distance to Nigel's house.

Nigel had given her his door key several years ago. She wasn't quite sure why, and she had never reciprocated. She wasn't even sure whether the key would fit; she had never tried it, as she had never been on Thames Ditton Island without Nigel.

The key fit—of course, Nigel would have checked several times to make sure—and the lock turned smoothly and silently. Ellen removed the key and pushed the door open, remaining on the step.

There was an unpleasant stillness to the house. Perhaps it was always this way when Nigel wasn't there, or perhaps it was her thinking too hard. She reached inside to switch on the light, then waited as her eyes grew accustomed to the electric glare. When her pupils had stopped reacting, she craned her neck to look into the house before gingerly taking a step over the threshold and quietly shutting the door behind her.

twenty

What was this English obsession with sending the traffic in one direction? He had once heard them called one-way systems, and now tonight, the man with the scar on his face had found two, and both had confused him. Say what you like about the Soviet days, but central planning had some real benefits for its citizens.

When he arrived in the Chinese restaurant there was one other customer, a balding man with longer hair at the back of his head who was reading a newspaper while he ate his meal. This emptiness didn't give the anonymity that he had hoped for, but he was hungry and Turgenev had told him to stay near, so he stayed. The balding man soon finished his meal and was gone before the man with the scar's first course had been delivered.

When the meal arrived, he finished it swiftly, all the time reflexively checking the phone, then left, leaving a fifty pound note on the table. Following the map in his mind, he drove in the direction of Kingston, reaching an intersection immediately before the railway line where the road fanned into three lanes. He took the right-hand lane, ready to turn right as he went under the railway bridge.

As he came up from under the railway line, he was surprised to see that the three lanes all flowed to the left. To his right, in the direction he wanted to go, was a large pedestrianized area, with another road heading in the direction of the bridge on the far side. Driving over pedestrians was not the sort of low-key exit he had been instructed to make.

He followed the three crowded lanes as they went left, finding himself blocked, confused, and intimidated in his small car as he tried to figure out how to get back on track. The three lanes then curved right, and he found himself in the left lane, approaching a junction, where he was again surprised, this time to find his lane filtered left. For a country that prides itself on its freedom, the UK didn't seem to give its motorists much freedom of choice, and he was now going away from the river, although this road did at least go in both directions.

He spun the car and headed back to the last junction, taking the road that would have been the first right turn. This was a two-way road but narrower than the other roads he had followed since he had turned left. He followed it until it came to an abrupt end.

Cursing under his breath, the man got out of the car. In front of him were some red phone boxes, about ten in total, but apart from the last one they had fallen over like a series of toppling dominoes. On the other side of the phone boxes were some railings preventing him from driving through to the road that he guessed was the road he should be on.

The man with the scar across his cheek took out the map book and flicked through, looking for his location, then swore again—the pages were missing. He threw the atlas across the street, its remaining pages coming unglued and scattering, before getting back into the car, feeling the gun in his pocket niggling him that it should have been at the bottom of the river by now.

Nagging him that he had already made too many fuckups and needed to sort out his fuckups.

Immediately.

And ideally before Turgenev found out.

twenty-one

Ellen stood with her back to the front door, which she had shut as she stepped in, looking around a large, open plan room.

On her left, toward the front, was an L-shaped kitchen area following the outer wall. Nigel was never much of a cook, but at least there weren't any dishes left or any evidence of rotting food. The room was bisected by two high-backed armchairs facing French doors that looked out from the other side of the house and over the river, the chair backs facing the kitchen area. In front of the chairs was a low coffee table, positioned so that you could reach it while sitting but still walk around the other side and open the French doors to access the small back lawn separating the house from the river.

To her right there was a small bathroom. Ellen looked in quickly and decided there probably wouldn't be any clues in there. In the back-right corner was Nigel's bedroom. So, where to start? Kitchen or bedroom?

Ellen took the coward's option and started to open the kitchen drawers underneath the counter.

There was nothing of interest. Knives, forks, assorted cutlery, a can opener, a wooden spatula, and some other cooking implements that were old but didn't show signs of heavy use. In one drawer, there were some candles and matches together with some string—brown string on the left and white string on the right—a bottle opener and some folded supermarket bags. In another, opened bills, a few rubber bands, two screwdrivers, a selection of rusty screws, a pair of pliers, an adjustable wrench, and several sets of keys—car keys and the keys for the back door, Ellen guessed.

Moving past a washing machine, she opened the first cabinet. Nothing seemed out of place. Cleaning supplies—bleach, dish washing liquid, laundry detergent and softener—were as expected in the cabinet under the sink. The sink was placed squarely under the front window so Nigel could look out at his neighbors on the other side of the island as he did his dishes.

The corner cabinet had a stack of plates showing a faded blue floral decoration and a collection of assorted mugs. She pulled a mug out: "Tudor Historians do it..." Enough. Too tedious. She put it back without finishing the pun, closing the cabinet door.

Turning the corner, the final cabinet had a stack of old, worn pots and pans, and a burned frying pan on the top shelf with plastic food containers jumbled on the bottom. Ellen closed the door and stood up. On the counter a kettle with coffee, tea bags, and a jar with sugar stood ready to offer refreshment, and above that a cabinet hung on the wall. Ellen opened the cabinet: food. Nothing special, a few cans and some packets. Nothing suggesting Nigel had hidden the greatest secret of his life there.

Next to the end cabinet was an electric cooker, old but clean. Ellen opened the top oven and looked at the grill pan that had been pushed in and then opened the bottom oven, which was empty. The kitchen ended with a fridge freezer. She pulled the top door. Again, it was clean and largely empty, only having some milk, butter, cheese, ham, and a bottle of lemon juice. She closed the top door and opened the freezer door, pulling out each drawer in turn. Frozen peas, frozen bread, what she guessed was chili but could be Bolognese.

Nothing dating from the Tudor era.

She closed the freezer and turned to face the room. What had seemed like a burning sun when she first switched it on now revealed itself to be a dull, glowing low-energy bulb with a dirty shade.

The room was beige; there was no other way to describe it, in terms of both color and character. The walls were flat and featureless, without pictures, ornamentation, or any form of decoration or personalization. The carpet was old, and the two chairs reminded her of Hilda's chairs, both reflecting a certain age of furniture and the solitude of the owner. But whereas Hilda was happy to live alone, Nigel's solitary life had been less of an option and more of a consequence of Darwinian natural de-selection.

Ellen slowly and carefully surveyed the room. From her recollection of previous visits, nothing was out of place. Well, there wasn't much there that could be out of place, and nothing new had been added. Certainly no pile of papers with a nice sign saying, "In case of my death, this is the important stuff that you should read first."

She felt a shudder. She was intruding, digging through a dead man's house less than two hours after he had been shot on her doorstep. Shot for a reason she didn't understand. Shot after having found something that he thought was very important, but that he wanted to tell her about in person. Shot by a man she wouldn't recognize.

Over the ten years since she had first met Nigel, she had never had a conversation with him that touched on anything of a sexual nature. A few times she had wondered if he was trying to make an advance, but he had always seemed to feel even more uncomfortable raising the topic than she had been rejecting his inept, naïve overtures, so she had steered the conversation in a different direction, and the subject had not been raised for many years.

But Ellen had always wondered.

It was impossible to believe that he was completely asexual. It was easy to suppose that he couldn't sustain a relationship, and she understood how few friends he had, especially female friends, of whom she was the one and only true friend. But just because he didn't have a girlfriend, that didn't mean he wasn't interested. Perhaps he used prostitutes? Perhaps he kept a crate full of porn? Perhaps he kept that porn collection in his room? Perhaps he was into kids and that was the simple and straightforward reason he was murdered?

Ellen had been into Nigel's bedroom once, when she first visited the house—as an observer, not a guest, and had remained standing and fully clothed with no bodily contact. As she stepped in, the room was as she remembered, with closets along the wall shared with the bathroom. On the back wall was a window, and the other two walls were filled with shelves loaded with books. Somehow a bed had been fitted into a space between the shelves on the far wall, and an old desk had been slotted into a gap on the near wall behind the door.

On the desk was a moderately new computer. Ellen looked for the power button and pressed it. The computer buzzed and beeped, whirring to life, and while it clawed its way to consciousness and performed whatever checks and tests computers feel they have to perform in the five minutes before they are happy to interact with human beings, Ellen turned her attention to the wall of closets.

The obelisks that had probably arrived flat-packed many years ago now stood like wonky soldiers guarding her dead friend's secrets. Ellen wasn't sure where Nigel had bought the furniture, or how it had been constructed and installed. By the way it stood she suspected that Nigel had been the architect and the builder for this project. If that was the case, then he had probably made the right career choice, choosing history over construction.

She pulled the first door. It squeaked in the early part of its travel, the squeak mutating into more of a grinding sound from the midpoint in its arc. Ellen pushed the door and reopened it. It made the same noise on closing and on reopening. She thought back to the kitchen—there hadn't been any oil, not even cooking oil that she could put on the hinges.

From the top to the bottom were filing boxes, each about twelve inches high, four inches wide, and, by the look, deep enough to hold a full-sized sheet of paper in a folder. Ellen read the end notes on each box: Research Papers 1998 Box 1, Research Papers 1998 Box 2, Research Papers 1998 Box 3. There was nothing from this century and no hints as to what could be in each box beyond research papers.

She closed the door and opened the next closet, finding herself taken aback to see clothes. On the top rail there were some jackets: his sand-colored corduroy jacket with the arm patches, his blue corduroy jacket with the arm patches, his brown jacket...with the arm patches, and a selection of dull-colored pants hanging from the rail with a few belts hooked over the hangers.

On the rail below was Nigel's shirt collection, a mess of indistinct colors and old fabrics. Ellen would have thought she was in a secondhand shop if she hadn't been so acutely aware that she was standing in her dead friend's bedroom, trying to understand why he was dead, and hoping for any clues as to why the TV news had said she was dead.

She opened the next closet and felt her heart sink: If Nigel had any secrets, this was where they were buried. If there was going to be any porn, any fetish gear, any toys or signs of sexual deviance, or something that was so sexually repellent that she had managed to mentally block out its possibility, this closet was it.

The top half had shelves of sweaters. Nigel didn't wear sweaters very often, but he had a wide collection, in a range of textures and in varying primary colors. She flicked through the accumulation, pushing her hands into the gaps between each garment, looking for anything hidden between or behind.

There was nothing.

She took a deep breath, steeling herself before looking at the lower half of the closet, then opened the top drawer.

She exhaled deeply, with relief, realizing that she had been holding her breath. Socks. She quickly rifled through the socks, again looking for anything that had been hidden.

She held her breath again and opened the next drawer. Yuck. Underwear. Woman-repelling underwear at that. This was the epicenter of possible hiding places. Ellen gingerly moved the first item, getting bolder and moving more earnestly through the contents of the drawer. Finding nothing, she closed it.

If there were no horrors in the first two drawers, then logically, anything that Nigel didn't want to be found would be in the bottom drawer. Ellen sat on the floor and pulled the last one, finding that it opened far more easily than expected. She looked down: empty.

She let out another sigh of relief and stood, kicking the drawer shut and closing the closet door.

The computer beeped and whirred, drawing attention to the desktop image: Hampton Court Palace. Nigel was a man obsessed and possessed.

She fired up his word processor and opened his most recent documents.

The first was a shopping list.

The second was his to-do list. Nothing about any big secret there.

The third was his draft speech that, as far as she knew, he gave tonight at the launch of *The Murder of Henry VIII*. She had spoken to Nigel about it—Boniface had given him strict instructions to make sure he kept it to three minutes, including pauses. Sure enough, Nigel had even put the pauses for breath, and in a few places he had marked "hold for laughter." So he did pay attention occasionally... Ellen scanned the note; there was nothing new.

The fourth and last document was Nigel's conspiracy theory explaining why Henry had been murdered. This looked like the points she had heard him expound many times, but she still skimmed the points:

- Wolsey was Henry's lord chancellor, chief executive, and general go-to guy

Urrggh. It was loathsome when Nigel tried to use Americanisms to sound cool. Somehow it didn't work for the Brits.

- Wolsey was resentful of the King. His extravagance. His irresponsibility. And most of all, his taking Hampton Court Palace.

- In 1530, Henry VIII and Wolsey argued. Wolsey had failed to secure Henry's divorce from Catherine of Aragon. [question: was this failure intentional in order to bolster Wolsey's standing with the Pope—the only source of power that could balance Henry?]

Always good to see questions. He was the leading expert on Henry and Wolsey, but he was humble enough to know that he couldn't second-guess Wolsey's true intentions.

- Wolsey was stripped of his position within government and sent to be Archbishop of York.

- Wolsey was charged with treason and summoned to return from York. On the return journey he "died" and was "buried" in Leicester. However, there is no marked grave.

- In reality, this was a fiction, created by Wolsey to cover his next move plotted with Anne Boleyn.

There was nothing new here. It was Nigel's standard argument and the basic outline of his book. She scrolled down a few more lines, continuing to read. "Alright, that's interesting."

She continued nodding and talking to herself as she finished the last few bullet points, then closed the word processor and opened his internet browser, clicking the history button.

His viewing over the last few days was what she expected: Boniface's website, articles by Boniface, articles about Boniface, links to Nigel's book on Amazon and a few other large bookstores, publicity about his book. In short, lots to do with his book, and thankfully no porn.

Then something caught her eye. She had missed today's entries. She clicked, and a long list unfolded. These must have been the articles Nigel looked at after he left the police station and before he went to his book launch at Hampton Court.

She looked at each in turn. It didn't take long for a theme come out: Sherborne, Sherborne's relationship with Princess Heidemarie, Princess Heidemarie's suspected illegitimate child, speculation about the father, and so it continued.

Ellen froze. She could hear someone trying the front door lock.

twenty-two

Mikhail Turgenev sat in his office reading the news ticker on the silent television screen. Breaking news: Professor Ellen Armstrong had been shot dead outside her home.

He was now another step closer to independence.

The phone rang. His private line. The number ID was a cell phone, but he couldn't recognize the number. Hearing the voice at the other end he relaxed, leaning back and throwing his feet onto his desk. "You have done well tonight. It is all over the news." He beamed like a proud parent. "So why are you calling, my friend?"

The humor fell from his face as he dropped his feet to the floor and sat upright. "Shot him? *Him?*"

There would be a time to be incredulous. There would be a time to be angry. This was not that time. For the moment, there were practical issues to be addressed, such as the lack of death of Professor Armstrong—at least the lack of death of the professor at the hands of the man he had sent to kill her—and ensuring that Kuznetsov did not learn about whatever had already gone wrong that evening.

"You say you shot a man. Professor Armstrong is a woman." He waited for the realization to hit, and for the excuses. "I don't care if he said 'da.' Da! An Englishman trying to speak Russian, and you shot him for that."

He cursed and started punching buttons on his keyboard, then clicked violently with the mouse. "This is all wrong. Where are you?" He picked up his keyboard, blew into it, turned it over, banged it on his desk, placed it the right way up, and started typing, his fingers hammering the keys.

"Surbiton? How the...?" He looked at his screen. "The map is right. I couldn't believe you would be that stupid and that far wrong." He zoomed out of the map and looked at the escape route he had planned. "So what went wrong? Go straight, at the railway, turn right, go over the bridge, drop the gun. Easy."

He pointed to the map on the screen. "Look. There. There. There. There," and then threw himself back in his chair in frustration, looking at the map.

"So where..." The caller had been expecting the question. "Burned it." The next excuse took him by surprise. "Pages missing?" He looked into his trashcan. The latex gloves were on top, underneath were the loose pages he had dropped in earlier in the afternoon. He picked them up and looked at them, raising his eyebrows. "So you're in Surbiton, you say?"

Turgenev threw the loose pages back into the trash and returned to his computer, opening the newspaper's database. He looked at the summary and clicked a link, which opened a web page. As the page loaded, a broad grin spread across his face. "I love it when other people tell you where they are," he muttered under his breath.

"We're on to a new plan. Are you listening?" Turgenev looked intently at the map on his screen and explained the directions. He waited while the man with the scar repeated the instructions back to him. "You're going into a place called Thames Ditton. I'll spell it for you, it's T-H-A-M-E-S D-I-T-T-O-N. Go up Saint Leonard's Road, and when you reach a roundabout, turn right. Follow that road for a short distance, and the road will kick to the left. This is where you want to be; you should be able to get down to the river at that bend. More to the point, you should be able to see Thames Ditton Island, and on Thames Ditton Island you will find…?"

Turgenev waited for the reply. "Yes, that's correct. Professor Ellen Armstrong, who is a girl, not a boy."

He flipped the map on his screen from street view to the satellite view. "There's a bridge going over the river, and that bridge starts where the road kinks. As far as I can see, Professor Armstrong is in the middle of the island. The best way to find her is to call her—listen for the ring of her phone; then you'll know where she is."

He dictated the phone number, listening to the man with the scar as he repeated the number. "Get there and check out the place. It's an island—all you have to do is make sure she doesn't leave."

twenty-three

After his call with Richard Sherborne, Peter Winckley, or Pete the Winkle to his mates—a nickname reinforced by his slight stature and his squirming personality— was mentally counting out the cash he was about to be paid.

It was a shame that the police had kept the documents he had liberated, documents that had not been seen in 500 years. But it was only a problem of timing: The documents wouldn't be listed anywhere in the Hampton Court archives, so when the police couldn't prove they were stolen, he could claim ownership.

But more to the point, he knew where they had come from and was slim enough to get back there again. The documents had been there for 500 years, and it didn't seem like anyone else had been in a hurry to get in there—and if someone *did* want to get there, they would need to be smaller than him to fit through the gap. Added to which, he had told everyone he was hiding in the gap, not that the gap led somewhere, so there was little chance of anyone nosing around. And he could be confident that they wouldn't fill the gap, because that would affect the fabric of the building, and the Palace was a protected historic monument, so it would take years of planning even to block the small cavity with a plank of wood.

Having the professor authenticate the documents was a huge bonus. It was a shame that he was now dead; he had seemed genuinely interested in the find and had, albeit inadvertently, alerted Pete to the value of the papers as well as confirmed their historical significance.

But as one door closes, another one opens. If the prof was dead, then that was an opportunity for Pete. The prof wouldn't mind him having a quick look around his house—he had obviously been proud of it; otherwise, why would he have kept talking about it? And in a police station? A place where you know you're going to find criminals.

Pete stepped off the bus and shook his hair loose. Within five minutes he reached the High Street and followed it to the two parking lots next to the bridge crossing the river to Thames Ditton Island. Two wooden steps led up onto the steep curve of the bridge, and in the middle he reached the gate with barbed wire and spikes protruding in an arc around its outside.

The keypad to the right of the gate gave Pete a moment of nostalgia. He remembered when people actually thought these things were secure; now these old models were as much use as having a "please do not steal" sign on a car with the keys in the ignition.

He guessed that each resident would have their own code. But there would be a separate override code for the engineers, so his only question was four digits or six. He guessed six and punched 9-9-9-9-9-9. There was a buzz, and the lock clicked open. Pete pulled the gate and walked through, listening to the squeal followed by the solid clunk, with a vibration echo that he felt through his feet as the gate slammed behind him.

He took the two steps off the end of the bridge and onto the island. To the right was a small fenced area with a few trash and recycling bins together with a junction box fed from some cables that appeared to be suspended under the bridge. To his left was a central path through the island, gently illuminated by the light seeping out of the homes on each side.

Some of the newer buildings were sturdier brick buildings; others were wood-framed beach huts on stilts, which looked as if they would bend in the wind. None had a big sign over the top saying, "Hey Pete, this is the professor's home." None even seemed to give a subtle hint.

He walked down the central path looking to his left and right, hoping for anything that might tell him which house belonged to the professor.

About 50 yards up, he saw it: a mock-Tudor beach hut with brick pillars to the left and right of the front door. On the left pillar stood a lion, and on the right pillar a unicorn: a miniature re-creation of the outer gate at Hampton Court. Maybe it wasn't a big sign hanging in the sky, but it was enough of a sign for Pete.

The prof had clearly been here since he left the police station—he had left a light on, which he would only have done in the evening.

Pete knelt as if to tie his shoelaces and worked a straightened paperclip out of the hem of his jeans. Having taken a quick look around, he stood and went straight to the front door. For the second time in 90 seconds, he found it hard to believe how little people cared about security in the twenty-first century. First there was the security code at the gate, and now there was a pin-tumbler lock on the door. Clearly the prof had too much confidence in the security gate and the river acting as a moat.

He bent the paperclip back on itself and jiggled it into the lock, feeling each pin in the tumbler. He turned it slowly, felt some resistance, jiggled a bit more, tried again, still felt some resistance, and pulled out the clip. Holding it gently between the thumb and middle finger of each hand, he made a few delicate bends and then returned the clip to the lock. He jiggled, turned, jiggled, turned, and mouthed a silent "yay" as the lock yielded to his most delicate request and opened.

The door banged behind him, and he stepped into the room. Before he could look around, he heard a noise from the second door on the right, and a short blond woman dressed in a blue suit and kitten heels appeared.

Not expected.

Not part of the plan.

He held out his hand. "Hi. I'm Pete. Is the professor here?"

He gauged the blond woman's reaction. His brazen approach was working so far; she wasn't screaming. His guess was she was stunned, but there seemed to be some upset, maybe some anger there too, and there was a serious amount of apprehension, which wasn't unreasonable for a woman who, until a moment ago, appeared to have been on her own.

Slowly she held out her hand. "Ellen. Professor Ellen Armstrong." Pete took her hand, careful to grip it firmly enough that it wouldn't feel like he had a limp handshake, but not so tightly that it would hurt. The woman continued, "I'm sorry. I don't recall Nigel mentioning your name. Are you a student of his?"

"No. No. I'm not a student." Pete gave his best reassuring look. "I've only met the prof recently. I'm what you might call an archaeological specialist. I deal with the practicalities of buildings rather than the intellectual study of them. I like to use a hands-on approach instead of looking at blueprints. We were working on some previously undiscovered documents in Hampton Court, and he suggested I stop by this evening."

"Oh," said Ellen, looking both reassured and slightly shocked. "Then you had better sit down. And perhaps you'd like a cup of tea?"

twenty-four

The swarm around Surbiton station soon thinned as the man with the scar on his face drove down the hill, following the instructions from Turgenev.

Within five minutes he reached the sharp left-hand bend in Thames Ditton and looked ahead: two parking areas; the one on the left seemed to be attached to the pub. The other, on the right, seemed to have no particular allegiance and no lighting.

Quietly slipping into the irregular parking lot on the right, he brought the small red car to rest between a beat-up Land Rover and a convertible. As he got out, he noticed that the lot seemed to double as a slipway into the river.

He turned to look at the pub. It was an English style he recognized: brickwork painted white with black woodwork around the windows and doors. The S-shaped ends of tie-rods—steel rods inserted into the building to hold together the bowing walls—suggested that the two-story building was old. The sagging of the bay windows on the upper floor suggested very old. He looked at the roof: a nasty mixture of clay tiles and slates. Old, probably very old, but people had messed with it over the years and had repaired it cheaply; instead of a quaint pub, the building was a brightly lit white lump that vibrated with the noise inside.

From the parking lot behind the pub, an arched bridge reached to the island in the river. He looked up and down—this was probably the island that Turgenev meant. There were two other islands downstream, but those both seemed small, not linked by a bridge, and he couldn't see any houses on either, whereas there were houses around the outside of this largest island.

The first task, before he did anything else, was to reconnoiter the area. Instinctively, he felt for the gun in his pocket as he walked back to the road and looked left and right. An unimpressive stretch of asphalt, the most noticeable features being its narrowness and the sharp bend on the corner where he was standing. He waited for a minute or two to check the traffic. One car passed—there probably wouldn't be much congestion when he left.

Cautiously, he walked into the next parking lot, noticing the two steps up to the steep slope of the bridge as he went around the back of the pub. Like the parking lot next to it, this one ended at the river. Unlike its neighbor, this didn't act as a slipway; instead, there was a wooden landing stage running along the edge of the river, with a ragtag collection of boats moored next to it. Some stacked two deep, others three deep.

He followed the landing stage as it went behind the pub, running up the river and parallel to the island. Before he went over the bridge, he wanted to cast a soldier's eye over his target to assess its access points, its escape routes, and its terrain, although to be frank it looked like a fairly flat lump of land.

He counted twenty-three houses on the closest side of the island, which suggested there might be around fifty properties in total. Each building was a single story with a piece of grass leading down to a continuous landing stage circling the island, with one or two boats for each property.

The island was longer than he expected. He estimated around 200 yards; he couldn't be sure of the width until he saw the island from the other side, and he wasn't about to steal a boat to check his precision.

The pub landing stage ended before the end of the island. He looked farther up the bank of the river. There were small boats moored at the ends of private houses. He contemplated crossing the ends of the backyards but decided against it. All he needed to do was to trip a security light, and someone might call the police. And if the police were sniffing around, then he couldn't get to the professor.

Turning back along the landing stage, he followed the passageway that passed to the other side of the pub. If it was in better condition and if there was more space to turn in from the narrow road at the front, then you could probably get a car down there. He didn't have time to put his car there, but for the man with a scar, it was another useful possible exit route.

At the road he turned right, walking away from the parking lots. He followed the asphalt for a few minutes, and when he was satisfied that there were no other access routes to the river, he crossed and headed back toward the pub.

As he came up on the inside of the bend, he saw a figure ahead of him. The man turned his head to check the road before crossing, then walked into the pub parking lot, heading in the direction of the bridge.

The other man hadn't made eye contact, but his face was familiar. The man with the scar had seen him recently. He had seen him this afternoon in the Silver Spike. He was the man who'd had a meeting with the big boss in the Observatory.

twenty–five

The man on the phone seemed calmer. Turgenev wasn't sure whether it was fear or anger at himself.

He'd find out soon enough. "I'm going to get on my bike and come down and help you. Together we can make sure that all the loose ends are tied up, and then I'll give you your own motorcycle escort to Heathrow." He kept smiling while he lowered the phone into its cradle. His face fell as he released the handset.

Turgenev lifted down his black leather jacket that hung on the back of his office door and slipped it on.

How could he get simple instructions so wrong? All he had to do was find Professor Armstrong, walk up to her, confirm her identity, shoot her, and leave. What was so difficult about that?

Instead, he had shot someone—someone whose identity was a mystery to both of them—and had then become lost on his way to the airport. He was meant to be a soldier, but what sort of a soldier can't find his way around a traffic diversion?

Turgenev looked at his computer. Professor Armstrong still seemed to be on Thames Ditton Island, where she had been while he talked to the man with the scar, and the man with the scar seemed to be on the bank near the island. Hopefully that meant he was checking out the area as he said he would.

Turgenev pulled out his phone and tapped the screen to open a map—with a few button presses he had two red dots: Professor Armstrong and her hunter. With a few more presses he had a map showing his route. It estimated a travel time at forty-six minutes. He laughed to himself. Forty-six minutes if you keep to the speed limit translated into 20 minutes on a bike, and with the way he rode, maybe 10 if he was lucky.

He went to retrieve a gun, but turned before reaching the safe and sat down again, pondering whether a plausible excuse could be found for carrying a gun in a country where firearms were largely illegal. It wasn't a problem for him, but it would be embarrassing for Kuznetsov if his staff were found with illegal weapons, and there was already a gun that should be at the bottom of the river by now.

Finding no reason, he stood, picked up his helmet, and headed for the elevator. "I'll be back soon. Probably in about an hour," he said to the swarthy man behind the desk without waiting for a response.

In the bowels of the building, he walked past the parked cars to his bike. The machine was perfect. A Russian Ural Wolf. Pure Russian engineering, and this model had a heritage dating back to Stalin's time, having been built in a former state-run factory 1,300 miles east of Moscow in the Ural Mountains. Turgenev knew this firsthand; he had visited the factory to specify his custom modifications and later to pick up the machine before he rode it back to Moscow.

The factory had told him that his was the only completely black model they had ever built. Every piece of paint was black; every bit of chrome was replaced with a hard-wearing black powder-coating. Every nut, bolt, and screw was black. The only pieces that weren't completely black were the mirrors, which were tinted, and the lights, which had been darkened.

It was a black Wolf, ridden by a black wolf.

Turgenev threw his leg over, clipped the phone with the map onto the handlebars, and then kicked the bike into life, feeling the solid rumble and hearing the throaty purr as it idled, roaring on the twist of his wrist. He slipped on his helmet and followed the underground parking to the exit ramp. Through the barrier, he turned onto St Giles's Circus, pointed the bike toward southwest London, and opened the throttle.

twenty-six

Boniface was still trying to get the smell of vomit and cheap Z-list-celebrity-endorsed perfume out of his nostrils. He hadn't enjoyed waiting in line for a cab, but after walking around for fifteen minutes it seemed the only place to get one was outside one of the nightclubs in Kingston, so reluctantly he joined the queue with the lightweight partygoers who couldn't hold their drink and were already going home.

He had contemplated going home, going to the office...going anywhere, but Boniface knew that it was only a matter of time before the police would search Nigel's home. Since his house wasn't the immediate crime scene, the cops wouldn't be able to access the property without a warrant or permission from the owner, and as the owner was dead, Boniface had a few hours, if he was lucky.

The journey had been swift, and the cabbie dropped him by the roundabout halfway up the High Street. As he walked to the end of the road, he found that he could begin to breathe through his nose again. By the time he got to the pub by the river, he was pleased for the refreshing breeze coming off the water. He crossed the road, went through the parking lot, up the two steps, and onto the curved bridge leading to the island.

When he reached the gate at the apex of the bridge, a well-padded middle-aged woman was coming out. "Let me hold that for you," said Boniface, opening the gate she was struggling to push.

Stepping off the bridge, he followed the central path, unsure which house was Nigel's. About fifty yards up, he saw a mock-Tudor beach hut with brick pillars to the left and right of the front door. On the left pillar stood a lion, and on the right pillar a unicorn. Boniface tried not to sneer.

He had spent the evening with an historian. If history teaches us anything, it teaches us that people forget, mislay, misplace, and lose their keys. So any smart historian without many friends would hide a key somewhere near his house.

Walking up the path, Boniface looked at the two figures, each standing on top of a four-foot brick pillar. He looked to the left, then to the right, and back to the left. Deciding on the lion, he grabbed it with both hands and lifted, resting its weight on the edge of the plinth on the top of the pillar. In the gunk accumulated under the lion was a key; he picked it up and returned the lion to its place.

After wiping it with his fingers, then surreptitiously wiping his fingers on the plinth under the lion, the key slid into the lock and turned effortlessly. As Boniface stepped in, he noticed the light was on, which wasn't surprising, and that the kettle was boiling, which, while it was welcome, was not expected.

Two chairs in the middle of the room pointed away from the door—and from the chairs two faces swung around to look at him. In the left chair sat a scrawny man of around fifty with long hair; a small blond woman wearing a blue jacket was on the right. She stood up. "Mister Boniface." She corrected herself "Sorry, just Boniface. You're in time for tea."

"Ellen?" Boniface wasn't sure whether this was Professor Armstrong—he had never met her—but she certainly looked like the woman who regularly appeared on

TV. However, it was surprising that she was there, if she was Ellen. When he had spoken to the police, they had told him that she was in her neighbor's house and was too upset to talk.

The woman looked as if she had been crying, but the prime emotion she now seemed to be displaying was relief. Could it be that she was relieved he was here? It was almost as if she felt intimidated by the man who was sitting in the other chair.

And who was this guy, anyway?

"Yes, I'm Ellen. I'm so pleased to meet you. Nigel was always talking about you... he was in awe of you." Boniface blushed. "'Boniface,' he loved to say, 'my PR guru.' When you were first hired, he spent hours checking you out on the internet. He thought the stories of your exploits while you were a journalist made you cool. And then the time with the government sealed your reputation in his eyes."

"You make it sound like I was James Bond. I was once the press officer for the Minister of the Environment. I was hardly out there shooting baddies with a laser hidden in my pen."

Ellen's voice was soft. "But you impressed Nigel. He always liked the cliché that you don't know where the edge is until you go over it. You went over the edge, and he figured that made you a rock star among PR guys." Her smile was almost apologetic. "He also liked the stuff you wrote and thought you were working hard to make his book a success, as well as having some really smart insights."

Boniface's face cracked, and he let out a gentle laugh at the memory of Nigel. He could picture the professor's enthusiasm and how he would have loved the notion of this idealized figure working with him. It was a shame that the reality was far more mundane, and finding the edge, as Nigel put it, had, with Richard Sherborne's help, destroyed the tattered remnants of Boniface's career, pushing him to the edge of bankruptcy and necessitating a few loans that he now needed to repay as a matter of urgency, rather than making him some sort of rock star.

But it's always fun to know how other people think of you. Boniface thought of himself as an alcoholic who hadn't had a drink for a while. Someone who was doing the only thing he could, having closed down every other avenue and alienated most of polite society during his apparent rock-star years. Strange how a moody photo on a website and a well-crafted bit of copy could change people's perceptions.

"I'm not sure how to respond to that," said Boniface, "but it's a pleasure to meet you, and I'm sorry for your loss. Nigel thought a lot of you, and I'm sure you'll miss him."

The electric kettle clicked off as Ellen turned away, seemingly hiding her tears. "Tea for everyone?" she asked, her voice unsteady, as if she was holding back the sobs.

"You've clearly been in England long enough to realize that we live on the stuff," said Boniface. "And I'd love a cup, please."

"Me too," said the long-haired man, rising from his chair.

"I'm sorry, I don't think we've met," said Boniface, offering his hand. "As you can tell, I'm Boniface. I am—or rather, I *was*—Nigel's PR adviser for the launch of his book." He reached into his top jacket pocket, pulled out one of the few remaining cards he hadn't passed out earlier in the evening, and handed it to the stranger.

The other man inspected the card. "Pete. Peter Winckley. As I was telling Professor Armstrong, I'm what you might call an archaeological specialist. I deal with the practicalities of buildings rather than the intellectual study of them. I like to use a hands-on approach instead of looking at blueprints. Nigel and I were working on some previously undiscovered documents in Hampton Court, and he suggested I stop by this evening. Obviously that was before..."

Boniface gave his best interested-to-hear-what-you've-got-to-say smile. "Really," he said reassuringly. "So you were working with him recently?"

"I was." The man stood straighter, as if trying to raise his status. The look of a scrawny, unkempt man with long, unwashed hair, grubby jeans that seemed to have cobwebs on them, and a fraying sweater over a dirty T-shirt didn't quite fit with Boniface's preconceived notions of one of Nigel's colleagues.

"There's your tea," said Ellen indicating the two cups on the counter. "The sugar's there if you want." She tilted her head toward the sugar as she picked up her cup and returned to her chair.

"Thank you," said Boniface, turning back to Pete. "So you were the specialist he was dealing with this week?" It was Boniface's best earnest and impressed look.

"Yes," said Pete, apparently pleased to be acknowledged.

"You're the guy who got stuck in a hole?" Pete's blush answered in full. "So is there any good reason we shouldn't call the police now?" asked Boniface quietly.

The grubby man turned to the counter, put two large spoonfuls of sugar in his tea, and took a sip. "Good tea." He walked between the two chairs, placed his cup on the table, and then returned to stand by the fridge.

"Let me make an observation," said Pete in a rough but unsettlingly high-pitched voice. "I think it's interesting that I am someone who has opened the lock with a paperclip; someone who you have just figured out was arrested today; someone who has done time inside, as Professor Nigel found out; and yet you're both talking to me." Boniface caught Ellen's eye. "You see...most people's immediate reaction would be to call the police, not to engage in conversation. And the phone is there." He pointed to the phone on the kitchen counter. "So that leads me to wonder..."

The intruder let the end of his sentence trail into an uncomfortable silence, which settled over the room as he stood smirking. Ellen looked up from her seat. "Well...I..."

Boniface caught her glance and softly shook his head. "I'm looking after my client." The other man frowned. "Whitefoot Thorpe Publishing, Nigel's publishers, is my client. I'm here for them, in case there's anything I should know."

The intruder acknowledged this and stepped to the table to take a sip of his tea before sitting in the chair he had been occupying when Boniface had entered. Boniface looked to Ellen, shrugging and giving an I-don't-know-what-the-heck-I-should-say look.

"And Professor Armstrong is here as Nigel's friend." Ellen nodded, sniffing.

Boniface felt more confident. "And for you, it's lucky to have us both here, as we can help you with whatever you've found. Remember, in this room, you've got a PR guru, as Nigel apparently liked to call me, and one of the leading experts on the English constitution, and quite a historian herself." Boniface gestured toward Ellen, who bowed her head, apparently uncomfortably self-conscious about the compliment.

Boniface put a teaspoon of sugar into the last cup, stirred it, and took a sip. "Good tea. Thank you." He walked behind Ellen's chair to the other side of the coffee table, placed the cup on a coaster, and stood up straight again, facing the other two.

The small man looked at Boniface. "Now please don't misunderstand me. I'm not ungrateful for your offer, but I've found something that has been hidden for the last five hundred years, and without me, it will probably remain hidden for the next five hundred years. And this is good stuff...Nigel was very excited about the few samples I took with me. He was very keen to take photos but was a bit annoyed that he only had the camera on his phone. I think he wanted to take the documents to be professionally photographed."

"He would," said Ellen. "He's got someone who will do that sort of thing, making sure the documents aren't touched, exposed to harsh lights, or any processes that could damage them. We can put you in touch with that photographer if you want."

A slight sneer crossed the man's face. "These are kind offers, but I don't think you quite understand. I've already got enough interest; I've got a buyer who wants the documents, and I'm sure this buyer will be interested in everything else I can bring to him."

Ellen slumped back in her chair and looked up at Boniface, who took the cue and proceeded. "Look, can I summarize the situation?" The thief took another sip of his tea, returning his cup to the low table. "You have found some documents of value. I presume Nigel saw them and agreed there is value."

The longhaired man nodded.

"So you have some documents, and you have a buyer."

The man nodded.

"Out of interest, who is the buyer?"

"Nice try, Mister Boniface, but no."

"Please, just Boniface, no mister." He gave a reassuring tilt of his head. "Seriously, who? There's a good chance that one or both of us knows him."

"Or her," said the intruder.

"No, this is a him," said Boniface. "And as we are likely to know *him*," he stressed the gender and continued when the smaller man nodded his surrender, "then we can help you with the historical context and veracity of the documents, and also with the negotiation. Think about it—do you *really* know what those documents are worth?"

He softened his voice and pointed at Ellen. "She does. And while I'm sure that you're going to tell me that only you know where the documents were found in Hampton Court, there's a good chance that at some point the location will be found, especially when you have a leading historian," he gestured toward Ellen again, "on the case. Now that we know there's something to look for, other historians can go looking. And when—not if, *when*—we find those other documents and whatever else is there, the scarcity value of what you have will fall quite considerably. So get us on board, and we'll get you a deal at the earliest opportunity."

The intruder subtly bowed his head as Boniface pushed on. "And without wishing to sound too pissy about it, there's also the fundamental issue that you came here for a reason. If you had everything you needed, then you would be off selling whatever it is you've got and taking the cash to buy your yacht. But instead, you've broken into the home of a dead professor."

"Sure. I hear you," said the scruffy man. "But remember, at the moment I'm holding the cards, and you don't know what I know." His face cracked a thin smirk. "And without wishing to get too pissy about it, you don't know much at the moment."

twenty-seven

The man with the scar on his face retreated farther into the shadows on the inside of the bend as he watched the man he had seen at the Silver Spike disappear, heading into the parking lot and toward the bridge to the island.

Swiftly and noiselessly, he crossed back to the slipway and crouched behind the wall separating the two parking lots, looking up at the bridge as the other man neared the gate halfway across. There was a creak as the gate moved, and then a squeal as the gate opened more quickly. "Let me hold that for you." It was the man speaking. He stood back, and a fat woman waddled out. There was another squeal and the gate slammed shut, leaving the earth under his feet shuddering.

The man with the scar watched as the fat woman came down from the bridge. With each step she got closer and the ground shook more. Gracelessly, she took the two steps down from the bridge and caught sight of where he was standing. "Oh yuck. Don't piss there! Go in the pub if you really can't hold it in."

"Sorry," he said and turned, crossing behind her as she walked through the sloping lot to a small silver car. The car's suspension groaned as she got in, and he was certain it was leaning dangerously to her side as she drove out, leaving a gap next to one of those old French peasant cars.

He scanned the parking lots as he mounted the bridge and walked up to the gate. He tried it. It was locked, and the keypad to the right suggested it wouldn't be easy to get open quietly. It would be far simpler to climb around when all he had to deal with were a few spikes and a bit of barbed wire. Nothing difficult—it wasn't as if there were guns shooting at him.

The spikes were each about two feet long and arranged as an arch over the gate, which then continued to the level of the bridge floor. He turned to the shadows on the right, away from the glare of the pub on his left, and eased himself over the handrail, letting his feet down until they reached the lip of the bridge floor.

Silently, he moved up to the spikes and, holding the handrail in his right hand, crossed his left hand to grab the outer fitting, which held the spikes in position. A firm tug told him it was solid. He crossed his left foot onto one of the lower spikes, which jutted out horizontally; and with his left foot secure, he released his right hand and swung around the spikes, grabbing the rail on the other side. In one continuous and silent movement, he was over the handrail and back on the bridge, walking as if he had stepped through the gate.

As he took the two steps off the end of the bridge and onto the island, there was a small area to his right with a few trash and recycling bins that had been fenced off, and a neat junction box fed by some cables suspended under the bridge.

Turning away from the fenced area, he looked toward the central path with the single-story buildings to the left and right. Each dwelling was different in its own way, but none had any distinguishing features. He walked to the far end of the path, acting like a lost visitor, and returned to the fenced area at the end.

The junction box gave him an idea. If the fat woman he had seen earlier was any indication of the residents, then it should be easy to get them to move off. Hopefully the professor had other reasons for being here and would stay, and it couldn't be coincidental that the man in a suit was here, could it?

After looking around the bins for a moment or two, he found a length of rusted pipe and levered the padlock off the junction box to reveal a tangle of wires. He turned back to the trash and looked until he found a discarded plastic container. It was three steps down to the river to fill it. He returned and emptied the water over the electrical tangle.

There was a crackle followed by a low-frequency *pffft*, and the island went dark.

He moved in behind the bins and waited. A few residents came out of their front doors and looked around, and then, at a house about fifty yards up on the right, the man he had seen in the office took a few steps out and looked around.

Now all he had to do was wait.

Slowly, starting with one or two people, but increasing in number, the residents began to leave their homes. They all seemed to mutter and complain; the only clear word he could make out as they passed was "pub."

He counted 82 people leaving and then waited. There had been five minutes of complete stillness when he stepped out. Without the glow from the houses, the central path was much darker. There were three houses with a flicker of light—at a guess, one was kerosene and two were candlelit. His target, where he had seen the man who had been in the office come out, was the second candlelit house.

Slowly he moved into position to look through the window, staying far enough away that he could reach cover if anyone looked out. In the flickering candlelight, he could see two people standing. At the far end of the room was the man he had seen. He was talking quite intently to the other person, whose back was to him. Long hair: This must be Professor Armstrong.

He moved closer, taking out his gun and phone. He dialed the number that Turgenev had dictated to him: the professor's number. It took about ten seconds until he faintly heard a phone start to ring in the house in front of him, signaling that he should pull the trigger.

He didn't need much light to see the side of a head explode, and when he saw splatter like that, he knew his job was done. He ended the call before the phone was answered and slipped back into the shadows, ready to leave the island.

In the distance he could hear the distinctive throatiness of the Ural Wolf. Even this far away the sound was reassuring, like picking out your hometown accent in a foreign bar. Turgenev was close, and now he had something positive to report.

Now he had corrected his earlier failure: The professor was dead.

twenty-eight

Boniface had several images flashing in his consciousness and was trying to arrange their sequence in chronological order.

He had been talking to the guy with long hair, and he thought he was close to convincing him that he and Ellen could help. But then a phone had rung, there had been a noise outside, the front window had broken, something semi-liquid but perhaps containing solid particles had splattered across the wall, and the long-haired man had fallen down, hitting the chair as he fell.

Then Ellen shrieked.

A short shriek, but now she was still.

He looked at Ellen sitting in her high-backed chair, illuminated in the gloom by two flickering candles. She had drawn her legs up and was sitting in the fetal position, staring at the splatter of what he guessed was brain, blood, and bone across the wall, with her lower jaw trembling. "He's been shot." Her voice a whisper. "That wall looks like the front of my house where..." Her voice trailed to silence, but her mouth kept moving.

Boniface remained paralyzed. As his website announced, one of the services he offered was crisis management. This seemed like something of a crisis, and for the second time that evening he felt unable to think, to function, or to move. He was aware that he was breathing. From the pounding in his ears he was conscious that blood was pumping through his body, but apart from that he wasn't sure what time it was, what day it was, or what he was doing there.

"Boniface." It was Ellen, now standing near to the French doors but with her stare still fixed on the wall. "He's been shot. We need to get out of here."

"Huh?" Boniface moved toward the front door, his gaze still draw to the spatter on the wall, visible in the candlelight.

"Where are you going?"

"To have a look..."

"Not that way. Man with gun..."

The last comment shocked Boniface, and he turned to stare at Ellen. He held her glance for several seconds and then broke, snapping out of the gaze and coming out of his trance. "What the fuck just happened?"

"A bullet came through the window and hit him." She was fixated again on the splatter across the wall, her voice small and trembling, her face cracking as tears started to flow. "Is he dead?"

Boniface craned his neck to look, unsure about stepping closer. "If he's not dead, he should be. He would want to be."

"So what are we going to do? You're meant to be the expert in this situation." Ellen's voice was started to crack.

"You don't happen to know where Nigel's car is, do you?"

"The parking lot on the other side of the bridge."

"And the keys?"

"Third drawer, I think," said Ellen, pointing to the drawers under the kitchen counter. "You'll also find some other keys in there. One set must fit this door." She softly tossed her head toward the French doors behind her.

Boniface walked to the drawers. "So who were they after? You, me, him...what was his name?"

"Pete, I think he said, but I'm not sure."

Boniface retrieved a handful of keys and walked over to Ellen. "Can you drive?"

"Yes."

"Good. Here's the key." Boniface passed an old key with a battered Citroën logo on a keychain with Nigel's work identification attached. "Now, which key opens this?" He gestured to the doors and held several bunches of keys in his hands.

Ellen looked at the keys, sizing each one, as if visually imagining whether it would fit the lock. "This one." She picked a brass key on a ring with several others, placed it on the lock, and twisted. "Can we get out of here now?" She pushed, and the door swung open.

"One thing," said Boniface returning to the open drawer and dropping in the remaining keys. Ellen looked at him quizzically. He picked up the phone and dialed three digits, waiting for it to be answered. "Police. Murder." He laid the receiver on the counter and walked toward the door, raising his eyebrows to point Ellen outside.

The stillness of the night was broken by the throbbing sound of a motorcycle approaching from a distance. "Here come the filth hounds of Hades," said Boniface. "They're close. Probably going to the pub."

The stretch of grass between Nigel's house and the river was damp in the evening dew. As they got to the end of the lawn, they looked down to the wooden landing stage surrounding the edge of the island. Boniface jumped down and looked back at Ellen. "Neither of us is really dressed for this, are we?" He held out a hand for Ellen to steady herself as she cautiously stepped down, using a heel to stop her slip.

The motorcycle cut out, leaving the sound of boats clinking with the constant movement of the flowing river.

Boniface looked up and down the slim wooden platform, flanked along its length by boats. There were small cruisers, boats that would normally be powered by outboard motors, a rowboat, and lying on the stage were several nasty plastic kayaks. About twenty yards up, Boniface spotted what he was looking for. "That's the one for us." He led Ellen to a battered plastic boat, largely rectangular but with rounded corners.

Ellen stared at Boniface. He ignored the question implicit in her incredulous stare and looked around as if searching for something he had misplaced, then raised his eyes, purposefully strode out, and returned holding a single paddle with a hand grip at the end.

"We need to get out of here, Boniface," said Ellen, her voice finding an urgency that hadn't been present moment ago.

"On the other side of that house there's a man with a gun, so our options are kind of limited: It's a case of swim or get in a boat. That's a nice suit, and those are great shoes you've got there, but you're not dressed for swimming, and I'm a physical coward. This"—he held up the paddle—"seems the best thing to use to try to steer this boat."

Ellen shrugged with little commitment, continuing to stare at the small vessel.

Boniface knelt by the side of the boat, holding it with one hand and offering his other to Ellen. "This boat seems to be the easiest to get into and out of." Ellen took his hand and cautiously lowered a foot into the boat. "Most of the other boats are narrower, so they would probably wobble, and they have a point at the front."

Boniface released his hand as the professor sat in the bow of the boat, the front edge straight, stretching the full width of the vessel. "Now, notice the floor of the boat," said Boniface. "I'm sure there's a nautical term for the floor, but you know what I'm talking about. See how it rises to meet the top rim of the boat? I figure that when we reach the bank, we need to run aground and we can get out. If there was a point, well, we might need to jump."

"It sounds like a good plan." The academic spoke slowly.

"I knew you'd see it that way. Hold this." Boniface passed the handle of the paddle to Ellen and proceeded to untie the boat, throwing the two ropes into the vessel. The professor gave a slight look of horror as the boat moved freely without Boniface having hold. Her face relaxed when he sat on the landing stage, dangling his legs into the craft. "Hold tight," he said and moved into the stern of the boat, rocking it from side to side as he shifted his weight.

As the boat found its new equilibrium, Boniface asked, "Have you even been in a boat like this?" Ellen shook her head, her blond curls flicking with each twist. "May I make a suggestion then?"

She inclined her head slightly.

"The river seems to be moving quite quickly."

Ellen looked at the river. "You're right. That's fast. Are you sure…?"

Boniface cut off her question. "Nigel's car is by the bridge?" Ellen nodded. "All we have to do is drift downstream"—Boniface made it sound like a romantic afternoon on the Thames—"but instead of paddling, we'll hold on to the moored boats as we go. Once we can see around the end of the island, then as long as there's no one there with a gun, we'll try and use that paddle thing to get across to the car."

Ellen made an unconvincing sound of acknowledgement, gripping the landing stage more tightly.

"And if that fails, we'll duck down and keep drifting until we run aground somewhere." Boniface grinned.

Ellen's eyes darted around. "Couldn't we…no…perhaps…?"

"What, go the other way? Go upstream?" Ellen opened her eyes widely, questioning without articulating. "Too much fuss, too much noise, too hard to paddle against the current. This way we can stay pretty silent, and all we need to do is wait until whoever is around the corner has gone. Now that there's no light from the island, we should be able to stay in shadow, as long as we stay out of any light streaming from the pub."

Ellen shrugged. Boniface kept his gaze fixed on her. She shrugged again. "Okay. Let's do it."

"Then put the paddle down," said Boniface. "We don't need it yet. For the moment, let's get past these boats here. Hang on to them, and we'll do the hand-to-hand thing to move along the edge of the island."

Ellen laid down the paddle. "So how do we do this?"

"Push your end out… I'll keep hold of the landing stage but will move us along. When you can reach that boat, there," Boniface pointed to the small cruiser immediately downstream of them, "grab the rope around the outside, then I'll let go, and we should be one step closer to getting out of here."

"Or one step closer to drowning."

"Or one step closer to drowning," Boniface muttered cheerily.

They moved past the small cruiser and a nearly duplicate boat next to it, past a rowboat at the end of Nigel's property, and past several other craft. It took a while to get the rhythm and longer to build up the confidence in the direction that the boat was drifting. When they were sure that the general trend of the current was toward the bank, they became less concerned about drifting and focused their efforts on moving toward the end of the island.

Ellen broke the silence. "You were going to do a deal with him, weren't you?"

"Who?"

"Mister Longhair...the architectural specialist."

"No. I didn't come here to do a deal with a thief."

"So why are you here, Boniface?"

"Because..." He sighed. "It was something Nigel said."

"It sounded like you were going to do a deal."

"Of course it did. He was obviously after something, and by talking to him we found out that he's got a buyer." Boniface felt the impatience in his tone. "But I wasn't going to do a deal."

"So if you weren't going to do a deal, why did it sound like you were ready to?"

"Because he had a point. We don't know anything." He stared directly at Ellen. "I didn't want to do a deal; I just wanted to know what he knew and how he got stuck in the hole. Nigel didn't explain that to me." Ellen looked confused. "It's a whole long stuck-in-a-hole-at-Hampton-Court story; he got stuck, then arrested, the police called Nigel... Anyway, I figured if he thought that we could do something to get him some cash quickly, then we could get the information out of him, and we might get a step closer to figuring out who killed Nigel and why he was killed." He paused. "You don't happen to know why Nigel was killed, do you?"

Boniface watched as Ellen processed his logic. "But you do know something, don't you, Ellen?" She tilted her head slightly. "If there wasn't something to find out, you wouldn't have come here, would you?"

"Hold on. You haven't finished yet, Boniface. If you weren't going to do a deal, then why are you here?"

"What's this?" said Boniface. "I'll show you my motivation if you'll..." Ellen pushed out her bottom lip. "I told you, it was something Nigel said this evening. I came here to see what Nigel had left around. There was a loose end."

Ellen looked at him quizzically. "Loose end?"

"Given what has transpired, it's probably nothing," said Boniface, turning away to hide his blush. "You understand it's bad for business when a client gets killed. I take it personally." He watched, waiting as Ellen blinked her acknowledgment. "Now, I think it's time for some reciprocity."

"No, not yet. What did Nigel tell you?"

Boniface raised his eyebrows. "Not much. I stopped him talking at the book launch about whatever it was he found. It's not good to tell people why the book you're launching is out of date before it's in the shops."

Ellen smiled softly. "That's Nigel."

"Then, in the cab on the way to Kingston, he seemed to spend the whole time dicking about with his phone. I wasn't listening to what he said, something about it being too slow."

"So what was he doing with the phone?"

"I don't know. Something with photos? Perhaps the photos he took of the papers Mister Longhair stole?" Boniface exhaled. "I don't know, I'm guessing. Longhair said Nigel took pictures with his phone, right?"

They were approaching the end of the island, and the boats were thinning. "See that mooring post." Boniface pointed at a post past the end of the island, maybe twenty or thirty yards away. "If we drift, we should be able to grab that post. In fact, if we drift from here, we'll probably hit it. When we reach it, we can tie up." Boniface scrambled for the rope lying in the bottom of the boat, which had one end tied to the stern of the plastic craft. "Once we're stationary, we can sit and wait for a few minutes to make sure there are no nasty men with guns before we do our bit of paddling."

"You reckon we'll reach the post and won't drift past." Ellen let go of the boat they were passing and turned to face Boniface.

"I do." Boniface pushed away, letting their craft drift toward the mooring post. "And when we're tied up, you can tell me what you found."

twenty-nine

Fourteen minutes door-to-door.

Mikhail Turgenev rolled his Ural Wolf into the parking lot, pulling into a space beside an old Citroën 2CV, and killed the engine. He took off his helmet, yanked the phone off the cradle on his handlebars, and zoomed in, straining at the screen. It was too small; all he could see were two overlapping dots, suggesting Ellen Armstrong and the man with the scar on his face were both on the island.

All he had to do was find the man with the scar, tie up the loose ends, and get back to the office before anyone noticed things had gone wrong. And when the problem caused by the other man became apparent, neither of them would be implicated.

The Russian jumped off his bike and looked around. There was a brightly lit white pub and, to its right, the bridge connecting the island. The island seemed to be in darkness. He had expected that there would be more signs of life; otherwise, what was Professor Armstrong doing there?

The parking area didn't seem very well organized. It was an irregular shape on a piece of sloping, twisting land, and each car seemed to have parked without a thought for other drivers. The slope seemed strange; he was surprised that the ground hadn't been leveled. His eyes followed the slope, reaching the river, and it made sense. It wasn't a parking lot; it was a slipway where cars happened to be left.

His eyes followed the slope into the river, and he watched the swift current, becoming aware of the clink of the boats moored along the bank and around the island, mixed with the gentle hum from the pub. His musing was interrupted by someone coming out of the pub. He looked. Big mistake. With the background light spilling out of the pub, he lost some of his night vision.

It was disorienting. He thought he heard a phone ring out on the river; by instinct he would have placed it around the end of the island, but when he looked he couldn't see anyone there—not that he could see so well having looked toward the light. By the pub door there was a man on his phone, but the ring didn't seem to have come from where he was standing. Even with bouncing echoes, something still didn't seem right. Turgenev looked out again onto the river. It was as if he could hear whispers. But however hard he looked, he couldn't see anything; it was too dark, and his night sight was still shot to pieces.

Someone was coming over the bridge; he couldn't make out anything beyond a shape. Whoever it was seemed to be looking in his direction. He casually took some cover behind the wall separating the two parking lots and maintained his surveillance.

The shape reached a gate in the middle of the bridge. There was an electronic clunk and a squeal as the gate opened, followed by a squeal as the gate closed and a solid slam with vibrations he could feel through his feet. He watched the shape maintain its progress; he was still looking at him when the shape raised his hand in acknowledgement.

Turgenev stepped into the open. The man with the scar took the two steps down from the bridge and rounded the corner into the second parking lot. The men embraced, slapping each other on the back.

"It is good to see you, my friend," said Turgenev. "Have you found the woman?"

"Mikhail Igorovich Turgenev," said the man with the scar. "I have done more than that. I have fixed the error I made. The woman is now dead. I shot her; I saw her head explode."

Turgenev felt an overwhelming wave of relief. "That is good, very good. Tell me what happened."

The man with the scar explained how he had checked out the area, made his way over the bridge, knocked out the junction box, and then located the house. "In the candlelight I could see the woman with the long hair through the window; I called the phone number you gave me so I was sure I had the right house, and when I heard the phone, I pulled the trigger. Her head exploded. There is no doubt that she is dead."

Turgenev felt his head involuntarily rock forward and back, keeping sync with his slowing breathing. "This woman had long hair."

"Yes. Long, dark, straight hair."

Turgenev recalled the image of Professor Armstrong he had seen on the television in Kuznetsov's office. You could argue about whether her hair was short or shoulder length. What was beyond doubt was that it was blond with curl. Not long, dark, and straight.

"You have done well, my friend. Very well."

He flinched, bending his knees to reduce his size, slightly hunching, and looked to the left, pointing with his eyes. The man with the scar picked up on the danger sign and turned to look in the direction indicated by Turgenev. As he did, Turgenev exploded, his bent knees straightening to increase the force of the single blow from the outside of his right hand, which landed on the other man's windpipe.

The man with the scar on his face fell to the ground.

Turgenev went through his pockets, removing the gun, the phone, his passport, and the car keys before dragging the body along the slipway into the river, stepping into the water to hold the man's head under. When no more air bubbles came from the man's nose and mouth and Turgenev could feel no pulse, he rolled the inert lump in the water until it was face down, and then pushed it into the current.

Somewhere in the distance he could hear sirens.

thirty

The boat drifted, aiming squarely at the mooring. Boniface leaned over Ellen to wrap the rope around the post, then tangled the end in a vain attempt to make a knot that would hold. He tugged the rope, felt the tension, and guided the boat away from the post before sitting to wait for the drift to pull the line tight.

They jerked to a stop and the line stretched, holding the boat stationary in the current. There was quiet, apart from the distant sounds of the moored boats banging and clinking, and the rushing sound of water passing the flat, square stern of their boat. Across the river the white pub glowed like a beacon, and a gentle burble of noise echoed.

Ellen and Boniface sat looking toward the bank, neither breaking the hypnotic stillness.

"So," said Boniface, his voice gentle. "Tell."

The still was shattered by Boniface's phone. By the second ring he had muted the noise, leaving the sound to echo around them and diffuse into the rumble of someone coming out of the pub, talking loudly on his phone.

Ellen pointed to the bank.

Boniface frowned.

Ellen pointed again, but with more emphasis. Boniface re-scanned the bank and saw a solitary figure in the lower of the two parking lots. From a distance he looked to be wearing a black jacket, but all cats are gray in the dark, right?

Boniface looked back to Ellen with wide eyes. A look passed between them, and they returned their gaze to the lone man. Without breaking his attention, Boniface whispered, "So what did you find?"

"Quite a lot, but not enough." Ellen lowered her voice, taking out some of the harshness in her tone. "I went through his closets."

"And?"

"And nothing. I thought it would be stacked with porn, but it wasn't. I was looking through his computer when Mister Longhair came in, then you arrived, and the power went out."

"So what did you find?" Boniface had not been a patient child, and he hadn't grown up to be a patient adult. "What did you look at on his computer?"

"I looked at his word processor documents and had just finished checking his internet history when I was interrupted."

"Wrong order. Always start with the email, then the calendar."

"Thanks. Next time you get there first and do the digging." Boniface could hear the edge of annoyance in Ellen's voice.

"Sorry," he mouthed. "So what did you find?"

"A lot of it was standard Nigel conspiracy stuff. You know, Henry didn't break with Rome, Wolsey did. Wolsey never failed at anything, so the failure to achieve a divorce for Henry must have been for a reason, perhaps so he wouldn't have to deal with people in the church who would recognize him after he took power."

"Really?" said Boniface.

"Perhaps. Maybe part of it was Wolsey's anger at his mistreatment by Henry. If someone took Hampton Court away from you, wouldn't you be pissed? Perhaps he wanted all the power for himself. Maybe he felt that Henry didn't fight hard enough for him to become Pope, which would have effectively made him King of the Vatican, so he became King of England in the old-fashioned, violent way."

"But this isn't new." Boniface wanted to scream, but while floating in a small boat when someone with a gun may be after you is neither the time nor the place.

"No, it's not new. But Nigel's view was that Wolsey was Lord High Master of the Paperclip: He kept every document, every bit of paper, anything written down. It was a good job there wasn't toilet tissue in Tudor times, because he would have filed that, too."

Boniface grimaced.

"Nigel's logic was that there must be a piece of paper somehow confirming that Wolsey murdered Henry. Nigel was convinced that when he found the proof that Wolsey had murdered Henry, he would also find how he achieved the cover-up."

"Was Wolsey that much of a paper-pusher, or is this just a wacky theory of Nigel's that seemed interesting to him but had little validity?" Boniface struggled to keep his voice quiet. "I mean, I thought this was just an interesting idea and that he got the book deal because it supported the notion that the monarchy was a busted flush in the sixteenth century and therefore had even less of a place in the twenty-first century."

"No, no. Nigel was serious about this. Even to the point of chasing down any facts that could undermine his theory—like look at Wolsey's death. Conventionally, Wolsey is believed to be buried in Leicester Abbey. To Nigel's way of thinking, that lack of certainty is one possibility why Wolsey could have died in 1530 when the accepted history suggests he did."

A breeze came across the river, and Ellen pulled her jacket tighter, crossing her arms across her chest. "Nigel was always of the opinion that Wolsey would have ensured that there was a grave, even a very simple grave, to give definitive evidence of his own—albeit faked—death. In other words, if he had murdered the King so that he could replace him, then he would have done everything necessary to prove and authenticate his own death. But that lack of grave was one angle Nigel could never resolve."

Ellen fell silent and pointed to a figure on the bridge. Boniface looked and returned his view to Ellen. Ellen shrugged at Boniface, who exaggerated a shrug in return. "Not a clue," whispered Boniface. "Our shooter?" Ellen's head moved slowly, bobbing like a twig on the river before she pointed to the man on the bridge followed by a man on the bank. Boniface pushed out his bottom lip, exhaling.

The man reached the middle of the bridge, opened the gate, and let it slam behind him. As he continued, he made a small gesture with his hand. Coming off the bridge, he spun into the lower parking lot, embracing the man who had been in the shadows.

There was a low rumble of sound as they talked. Boniface strained but could not hear what they said.

His concentration was broken when they both appeared to be startled and looked toward the pub. Boniface could see nothing in the direction they were looking. Another swift move, the sound of flesh hitting flesh, and one of the men was on the ground with the other over him. Then the man still standing dragged the other man into the river and squatted, holding his head under water.

"Shit!" spat Boniface under his breath, looking at the shaved head of the man in black who was holding the other man underwater. "We're fucked. It's Turgenev."

When she spoke, there was grit in Ellen's voice. "What? At a time like this you're making up names that sound scary to amuse me. Is this your idea of a joke?"

"No. We're in deep shit. That's Kuznetsov's head of security." With the words *head of security*, Boniface made quote marks with his fingers. "I don't know if he's after you or me, but he's not here to take the night air."

"So?"

Boniface sighed. "It's probably not a coincidence that he's near where there's been a shooting, and my guess is that if he finds us, we're both dead. And it won't be a nice death: He's got his own special version of the Kama Sutra with his own special ways to fuck you. He'll fuck us any and every way he can, and then kill us."

They sat in silence, watching Turgenev turn the man over and push him along the river. The body started to move with the current, sinking below the surface. Turgenev stood, fixated on the spot where the body had disappeared, before turning and heading onto the bridge. He stopped at the gate, the light from the pub bouncing off his shiny head.

He tried the gate, and a frustrated rattle drifted over the Thames as the lock refused to open. He looked over the left side of the gate, and his head followed the outline of the spikes up, over the arch, and down onto the right side before he eased himself over the handrail and clumsily clambered around the spikes, giving a low grunt as he caught his leg.

"That's a man on a mission. That's a man on a mission who's in a hurry. We need to move. We need to be gone, now." Boniface pulled on the rope tying the boat to the mooring post and started picking at the tangle, swearing under his breath. "Are you any good with knots?"

"That's what you're calling it now, a knot?" Ellen's tone was flat. "Why don't you untie the other end? The nice, easy, dry knot that someone else tied to the boat. It's not as if we're going to need that rope once we get to the car."

Boniface reached for the other end of the rope, fiddled with it, and cast off the line, leaving the boat to start floating with the current. "And for that, you get the privilege of being first to paddle," said Ellen, handing Boniface the oar.

Somewhere in the distance a siren was wailing. Ellen looked at Boniface. "Paddle faster."

thirty–one

As he took the two steps down from the bridge, Turgenev felt a twinge in his calf where he had caught his leg on a spike as he negotiated his way around the gate.

It might be unrelated—there didn't seem to be anyone around who might have called the police—but the sirens were unlikely to be coincidental. Whatever the case, he needed to find out what had happened and get out.

Quickly.

The first challenge was to find the house. To the left, along the spine of the island, was a pathway with houses on either side. Most houses were dark, but there were lights from three of them. One seemed to be lit by a kerosene or gas lantern; the other two seemed to be candlelit. The man with the scar on his face had said he shot a longhaired woman in a house with candlelight, giving Turgenev a choice of two.

Silently he moved along the path, sharpening his senses to notice any change around him.

The front window of the second candlelit house was spider-webbed with a hole in the middle. From his place in the shadows, Turgenev became aware of the sirens being drowned out by the sound of a car trying to start. Or at least he presumed it was a car. If it hadn't been nighttime in suburban south London, he would have assumed it was a lawnmower or an agricultural vehicle starting.

He paused for a moment, watching for any sign of movement in the house, then walked up the path. There were two pillars; each seemed to have a separate animal on top. Perhaps it would be clearer with some light, but in the gloom they just looked ridiculous.

The car, or agricultural machinery, or whatever it was that was trying to start, took a break, and the sound of the sirens became clearer. After a cursory glance through the cracked window, Turgenev pushed the front door. It didn't move. Turning his back to the house, he waited; as the car tried to start again, he back-kicked the door, which swung open, slamming into the side wall.

On the third attempt, the engine caught and the car chugged into life. Whatever it was, it had less power than his bike, and that revving wasn't going to impress anyone.

The sound of over-revving and grinding of gears was joined by a third sound of squealing brakes and skidding. It sounded like someone had left the pub and was now trying to move a car around the parking lot. He turned, stepped into the room, and wasn't sure where to look first: at the body or at the spatter on the wall. Instinctively, he went to close the door behind him, but it wouldn't shut properly with a broken jamb.

There were two doors to the right. In the first he could see a bathroom, and he guessed the second would be a bedroom. The rest of the house seemed to be made up of the open plan room where he was standing.

At the front was a kitchen area with a burning candle standing on the counter next to the stove. The room was divided by two high-backed chairs with their backs to the kitchen area. Behind the left-hand chair—which had a blood smear down the back—and in front of the fridge was the body. Up close it didn't look very female, and even by candlelight the long hair clearly needed a wash and some serious hair-care products. The ladies of Sodom and Gomorrah could've offered him some advice.

In front of the chairs was a low table with some cups and two lit candles giving enough light to illuminate the blood, bone, brain, skin, and hair splattered across the left wall. Turgenev cursed under his breath: How could someone who could kill so perfectly fuck up so completely in identifying his target?

Twice?

He knelt to look at the body, moving the hair away from the face. Definitely not female. Probably around 50. Not a clue who he was or what he was doing here. Turgenev quickly patted the man's pockets, pulling out the contents where he felt a bulge. A phone, some change, a few tissues, and nothing more.

From his kneeling position he looked around. At his eye level, hanging in the lock of the French doors, was a set of keys. He walked around the table and tried the door, which opened onto a small area of grass. Quietly he jumped from the grass onto the landing stage to look up and down the wooden jetty skirting the island. Lots of boats, but whoever had gone out through the back door wasn't there now.

He walked back into the house. The different perspective made him reconsider the table. Something was wrong. Three cups. He reached over and felt them individually. They were all still warm, and by the look of them contained tea. How English.

Three cups? Three people. The guy with long hair and two other people, and the two other people—two witnesses, the professor, probably, and someone else—had most likely gone out the back as he came in the front.

He pulled out his phone and called up the map. The two dots had separated. One was where he was standing, which was to be expected as the phone he had taken from the man with the scar was now in his pocket. The other, Professor Armstrong's, was now on the riverbank, on the road running parallel to the river, going away from the High Street. The dot wasn't moving quickly, but it was moving.

Was that the car he'd heard?

Turgenev ran out the front door. The sirens had stopped, to be replaced by the oblique reflection of blue flashing lights. At a guess, they were in the parking lot by the bridge.

He went back inside and hefted the front door closed, applying his boot to make sure it would at least look locked from the outside, then slipped on the security chain and turned to blow the candle on the counter before walking around to the coffee table and extinguishing the last two candles. He took the keys out of the French door, locked it behind him, and walked down to the landing stage.

thirty-two

On the fifth attempt Ellen managed to get Nigel's 2CV started and jerked it round in the parking lot, pulling to the top of the slope. "Which way?"

Boniface sat uncomfortably in the passenger seat. "Flashing blue lights and nasty sirens in that direction; let's go right."

The car kangaroo-hopped onto the road, finally finding some equilibrium, but with the engine straining. "Where's second gear?"

"I dunno. Where was first?" Boniface fiddled under his seat, looking for some way to adjust the medieval form of torture he was strapped into. "Find first gear, then move the knob in the opposite direction."

"I don't know if I'm in first; I pulled the lever and the car moved. I don't do stick shifts, and as for clutches..." Two police cars drifted behind them, their sirens silenced but the blue lights on each roof still flashing as they entered the parking lot. "And why am I driving, Boniface, instead of you? You know where we're going."

"I can't drive."

"Can't or won't?"

"Can't. Rather a hangover from that rock-star behavior. Her Majesty's justices felt it would be best if I didn't take to the wheel for a while."

"Oh." Ellen stepped on the clutch, slid the gearshift, and released the pedal. The high-pitched squealing was almost drowned out by the graunching sound of the gears, neither of which could distract from the violent shaking as the car came to a halt with the engine dead. "I told you I don't do stick shifts."

Boniface understood when blame was being ascribed. The silence seemed to agree that Ellen might have a point, so Boniface changed the subject. "You still haven't told me what you found on Nigel's computer."

Ellen narrowed her eyes and turned her head to face Boniface. "Aren't there more pressing matters? We just saw someone get shot. There's a homicidal maniac about fifty feet away over there." She pointed through the buildings separating the road from the river, in the direction of the island. "There's a dead body in a room that has both of our fingerprints all over it, and we've run away from the scene where the police have just arrived. And to make matters worse, I can't drive this horrible car, and we're sitting in the middle of the road looking really conspicuous." Her eyes filled with tears. "That's before we talk about my friend who was killed tonight."

Boniface pondered. Go for glib. Go for sympathetic. Go for practical. Go for angry. Go for indignation. In the end, he decided to leave the car seat alone and go for silence. A car came up behind them and angrily flashed its lights, the driver gesticulating as he passed the badly parked 2CV.

Ellen bowed her head to wipe her tears with her sleeve. "I'm sorry, Boniface." She lifted her head to look up at him.

"It's alright," he mouthed silently. Ellen smiled cautiously, like a child looking for reassurance. "Really, I get it. Well, I get some of it... I was only there for the second shooting...and the first drowning." He watched tentatively, trying to judge the reaction. "This French peasant-wagon can have a real emotional effect on people, can't it?"

Ellen laughed guiltily. "He loved this car, you know."

"Unfortunately, I do," said Boniface. "Nigel told me all about it this evening. Now, shall we get moving? I feel you're right that we're probably a bit too close to danger."

"Where are we going?" sniffed Ellen.

"Hampton Court," said Boniface confidently.

"Why there?"

"Got any better ideas?"

"No."

"Me neither. And as it's the only idea we've got, we'll start there."

"Let me try and figure out where the gears are." Ellen jiggled the gearshift up and down. The only sounds: the lever squeaking through its hole in the dashboard and the movement of machinery in the engine block, with an occasional low squeak as she pressed the foot pedal. "It's not going to be perfect. Nothing with a clutch is going to be anything near good for me, but I'll try." She inhaled, seemingly finding new resolve. "Hampton Court?"

"Hampton Court, please, Driver, and you can tell me what you saw on the computer as we drive." Ellen turned to scowl at Boniface, who was giving his cheesiest grin. "Before you forget, of course."

"Let's get the car started first," said Ellen. She stomped on the clutch and turned the key. Slowly and painfully, the engine spluttered to life, the car's body rising by two or three inches as the suspension filled. "That always freaks the hell out of me."

"But that's how the peasants could drive across fields," said Boniface, glancing over his shoulder at the blue flashing lights reflecting off the windows of the buildings along the street.

Ellen dropped the gearshift into place with minimal grinding and lifted the clutch. The car jerked, finding how to combine forward movement with some smoothness. "Ready?" said Ellen.

"Huh?"

"Second gear." She hit the clutch, slid the lever out of gear and jiggled it, all the time the car slowing. "There," she said, pushing the gearshift forward. The car jerked again as she lifted the clutch and strained to accelerate. "This really is a pile of shit, Boniface."

"Don't judge it yet. We haven't done corners, and by the way, you want to take the next left."

"Left?" said Ellen. "Don't we want to go straight and then turn right?"

"We do," said Boniface, "but you can't turn right at the end, so we'll follow the back-doubles and come out farther up the road."

"Whatever you say," said Ellen, easing the car into the left-hand bend, her hands tightening on the wheel while Boniface looked for something to grip.

"It feels like we're at about forty-five degrees."

"More," said Ellen, straightening the wheel. The car slowly returned to the vertical, bouncing from left to right and up and down until it stabilized. "And you bring us the route with road humps," she said hitting the first bump.

The car stayed perfectly level, its suspension effortlessly absorbing the traffic-calming measure.

Ellen and Boniface looked at each other in open-eyed amazement. "So this horrible little peasant car, which is impossible to control and has all the power of a sewing machine, the aerodynamics of a sewing machine, the road-holding of a sewing machine, the grace and comfort of a sewing machine, is actually the best vehicle ever when going over humps," muttered Boniface. "I'm stunned. Put the pedal to the metal, and let's go."

"My foot's flat," said Ellen. "This is the top speed, unless I change gear again."

"Well, don't go wild," said Boniface. "There's a junction coming up, and I guess it's not going to be graceful."

"So what's the strategy when we get to Hampton Court?"

"First..."

Ellen smirked, not meeting Boniface's gaze. "Well, for all the buildup, there's not much to tell. As I said, the documents were all as you would expect. There was Nigel's speech for tonight."

"He really did write it down and memorize it?" Ellen made a noise that might have been acknowledgement. "I'm impressed."

She pulled the car through the right bend. "Is it meant to lean like this?"

"Probably not." Boniface grimaced.

"So how was his little chat?"

"It was quite good, actually. I shouldn't say I was surprised, but I was. Anyway, please continue—your search of Nigel's computer."

"There was his standard conspiracy-theory piece, you know—it was Anne Boleyn and family aided by Wolsey, and once Wolsey had power, he started to wipe out anyone who could possibly blackmail him, in particular, Anne. She was probably his first significant victim, but he decided to leave the kids, at least initially."

"Kids? Plural? As in more than one child?" Ellen nodded as Boniface continued. "But wasn't there only one child when Henry was done in?"

"Nope," said Ellen with a small grin pushing her cheeks. "Not at this point."

"I thought Elizabeth came later," said Boniface, hearing the bewilderment in his voice. "I thought she was fruit of the unpleasant union between Anne and Wolsey, after he started playing Kings and Queens."

"In Nigel's view, Elizabeth's father could be either man, although it probably was Wolsey. But you're still missing Henry's second child: his son."

"Now I'm confused," whined Boniface. "I thought that Edward came later, when Henry—or Wolsey acting as Henry; it all gets very confusing—married Jane Seymour."

"He's child number four," said Ellen. "You're missing child number two: Henry FitzRoy."

Boniface looked ahead at the road. "At the roundabout, you want to turn right..."

"Gotcha." Ellen's view remained fixed on the road.

"Forgive my ignorance, but who was Henry FitzRoy?"

"Short version?"

"Mmm."

"He was Henry's illegitimate son by his teenage mistress, Elizabeth Blount, who became Lady Clinton in later life. An interesting name for an adulterer, don't you think?"

Boniface sighed sardonically. "So the short version."

"Henry FitzRoy was born around 1519 or 1520, when Henry's marriage to Catherine was on the rocks because she couldn't produce a son, let alone any other child.

So FitzRoy was born after Mary, but before Anne came on the scene. And you get bonus points if you can guess who FitzRoy's godfather was."

"What do I win?"

"A smooth journey round the roundabout." Ellen threw the car into the roundabout, the wheels barely maintaining grip with the surface as it leaned precariously through the three-quarter circuit.

"I choose death; it's less scary," said Boniface, feeling the car rocking from side to side as it righted itself while it pulled off the roundabout.

"Go on, guess," said Ellen.

"I don't know. Keep going straight here; you know where you are."

"Stop changing the subject and guess."

"Thomas Cranmer."

"Have you been paying attention? Wolsey. Wolsey was the godfather to Henry's illegitimate first-born male child. Henry's first-born male child who was considered as a potential heir but who died at the age of seventeen, sometime around 1536, in other words..."

"Not that long after Wolsey would have become King," said Boniface triumphantly. "And if he had become King, and had become King by murder, then it's not unreasonable to assume that FitzRoy was ultimately murdered so that there were no male heirs if the death of Henry became public knowledge, or perhaps FitzRoy was putting the squeeze on Wolsey."

"Precisely."

"See, I did pay attention to Nigel," said Boniface, pondering the significance. "But none of this is new information, is it? None of this relates to what he might have seen at the police station." Ellen shook her head as Boniface returned to his questioning. "So what else did you see? You mentioned websites."

"He was a big fan of yours, Boniface. He spent a lot of time looking at your website and Googling articles by you and about you." Boniface groaned as Ellen smirked. "He was smitten with you."

"But there must have been more," said Boniface.

"Obviously there was a lot of stuff about the book. He had Googled pretty much every online retailer, and read every review..."

"I feel there's a *just one thing* in here," said Boniface, desperate to tease out any last detail.

"There is. Do you know my publisher, Richard Sherborne? He owns..."

"Know him?" Boniface felt his throat go dry as he tried to keep the incredulity at the question out of his voice. "Do I know dear old Dickie S? He's the reason I'm virtually unemployable. He's the reason I've had to set up my own business instead of getting a proper job."

"I'm sorry, I didn't realize," said Ellen, flinching. "Then I'm not sure whether it's good news or bad news, but from this afternoon's browser history, Nigel seemed to be looking at a bunch of websites that talk about Sherborne, his relationship with Princess Heidemarie, Princess Heidemarie's son, and speculation about the father of the child. You get the idea."

Boniface laughed out loud. "Nigel's last internet search...and he was looking for gossip about Sherborne... Shit... He could have asked me. I've got a lifetime of dirt on that unctuous little—sorry unctuous *big*—corpulent creep. I would have told him." Boniface sneered. "I would have given him archives and research to last until doomsday."

"Well, you were one step ahead of Nigel without knowing it, and now I've told you everything. So it's my turn for a question, and all I want to know is, what's our plan?"

Boniface smirked. "Don't get dead." Ellen flashed a look of disappointment. "Seriously. Stay alive."

"Nigel thought you were a strategic genius, and all you can come up with is don't get killed?"

"Yup." Boniface was resolute. "But the key issue is how we don't get killed. How we stay alive."

"You have a ready audience here, Boniface. Tell me, how do we stay alive?"

He relaxed into his seat, which hadn't become any more comfortable with time. "Well, the strategy is easy. The implementation may be tougher; but the strategy is easy. First, we find out who wants us dead: We need to know who they are so that we know who to run away from."

"But isn't that easy?" Ellen asked impatiently. "It's that man with the shaved head. The one who was in the parking lot and who climbed over the bridge."

"Perhaps," said Boniface. "But we don't know who gave him his orders. If there's someone else pulling strings, we need to find them; otherwise, they'll send someone else with a gun, and because we won't know what they look like we won't know to run away from them. If it's Kuznetsov sending people, we've got a problem—he's got a whole army of ex-Spetsnaz guys."

Ellen remained focused on the stretch of comparatively straight asphalt ahead. "Don't we need to know why they want us dead?"

"That's tomorrow's problem," said Boniface. "For today, let's focus on the *who* issue and the second part of the strategy: We make sure we're more valuable alive than dead."

"That's it?"

"It's simple. If someone believes they've got more to gain by keeping us alive, then they won't kill us."

"That's the big strategy?"

"Yup. And until we find something better, we need to find something so that whoever finds us thinks they will lose something by killing us."

"Someone? Something? You think this is going to work? Or perhaps we should try something a bit more vague?"

Boniface grinned. "I'm open to ideas if you want to suggest anything better." He looked at Ellen, who remained silent with her eyes on the road ahead.

thirty-three

Turgenev stood on the landing stage that ran around the perimeter of Thames Ditton Island, looking at the blue flashing light reflecting off the downstream river.

He felt in his pocket for the gun he had taken from the man with the scar on his face. Pulling it free and weighing it in his hand, he contemplated his options and then tossed it. The gun hit the river, disappearing, the disturbance immediately lost in the fast-flowing current. He looked at the keys from Nigel's back door, raised his eyebrows, and dropped them in the river, too. The phone he had retrieved ended in the river as he started to walk up the landing stage.

The boats bobbed and clinked; there wasn't one that he would want to choose. The rowboats looked old and heavy. The small cruisers, assuming he could start one of them, would be slow and noisy, and the small boats without their outboards were pointless.

Two yellow kayaks lying on the landing stage looked old but were probably the best option. On the fourth house he passed, he saw what he was looking for: a double-ended paddle resting against the back wall. He took the paddle and returned to the kayaks, lowering the larger onto the water.

The Russian sat on the landing stage with his feet bracing the kayak against the current and pulled out his phone to look at the single dot marking Professor Armstrong's location. According to the map she was on the road that ran parallel to the river, roughly level with the top end of the island.

And was stationary.

He looked downstream at the flashes of blue that pulsed regularly on the water. An occasional voice could be heard, probably shouts from the police. Somewhere he heard a car start and gears grind.

There were two choices: Go and get his bike so he would be mobile, or try to move upstream and get onto the bank, where he could find the professor while she was still close.

He moved into the kayak. When he was satisfied that the craft would hold him, he checked his phone again: The professor's dot had moved—not far, but it had moved. That was enough to make the decision: He needed to be mobile; he needed the Wolf. He slipped the phone into his pocket, grabbed the paddle, and pushed off from the landing stage, letting the flow of the river take him downstream.

He took a stroke or two, feeling how the kayak maneuvered, and then took a few backstrokes to slow himself as he drifted. Past the end of the island there was a mooring post; Turgenev held his paddle in the river, guiding and slowing the craft, and as he reached the post he stopped the boat with his arm, holding onto a piece of rope tangled around the post while he looked back at his bike.

The river was moving faster than he had expected, and the sound of water rushing past the boat was distracting, drowning out the fragments of conversation from the police standing in the parking lot.

In the flashing blue lights he could see six officers and two cars, one parked in each of the two lots. The one in the lower lot had reversed into a space next to his bike, and two officers were admiring the machine.

Scratch plan A, on to plan B.

He pulled out the phone and called up the map. Professor Armstrong had moved. By the look of the map, she had gone up the road and turned left.

With the phone securely returned to his pocket, he let go of the rope. The kayak drifted while he held the paddle in the river to pivot 180 degrees, and then he began paddling, careful not to draw attention as he began to move against the flow of the Thames.

Having pulled past the end of the island and out of sight of the police, he paddled harder, applying additional power each time the blade cut into the water. Slowly, he felt himself gain additional momentum, and the boat moved upstream.

About a quarter of a mile up from the island, he saw what looked to be some sort of boating club with a large landing stage on the side of the river where the professor had passed. Grabbing the stage with one hand, he retrieved the phone with his other. The map showed a road running perpendicular to the river, about half a mile up from where he was. Professor Armstrong's dot was slowly moving along the road from left to right.

The Russian looked ahead: On her current course, the professor would pass over the bridge crossing the river. After that, the road split. One road continued away from him, running parallel to the river. The other went along the edge of the area marked as Hampton Court Palace Golf Club.

The kayak wasn't going to be fast enough. He checked his side of the river: There was a railway line and another river joining the Thames—both inconvenient hazards to cross, both made the decision easier. He returned the phone to his pocket, pushed off, and paddled furiously for the other bank.

It took a few moments to find somewhere to get out, and as he scrambled up the bank, the kayak began to drift. Professor Armstrong's red dot was still moving, as he started jogging in the direction she was heading.

thirty-four

"So why is Nigel dead?"

"Dunno."

"Why is Mister Longhair dead?" Ellen seemed to be keeping the car moving as fast as it would go, passing Hampton Court train station and heading toward the bridge over the River Thames.

"Dunno... Lack of attention to personal grooming?"

Ellen smirked. "You don't know much, do you, Boniface?"

"Nope. But I do know this roundabout isn't going to be pleasant."

Boniface looked at the view of the main entrance to Hampton Court Palace for the second time that day while Ellen drove over Hampton Court Bridge. As the car descended from the apex of the bridge, she let it coast, losing speed before the 360-degree spin around the roundabout.

"I feel seasick," said Boniface as the car righted itself and Ellen turned into the outside gate. He tilted his head toward the lion and the unicorn on top of the pillars. "Look, they've stolen Nigel's idea."

Ellen jerked the car to an undignified stop as the guard came out of his hut behind the gate. Boniface recognized a familiar face and scrabbled around, looking for the door handle. "Leave it with me," he said to Ellen, who seemed to be feeling for the window crank.

Boniface found the handle and stepped out; walking around the front of the car, he offered his hand to the guard. "Good to see you again. I had hoped to see you someday, but I wasn't expecting it to be quite this soon."

"Mister Boniface." The guard seemed pleased to be remembered. "It's a pleasure to see you, too."

Boniface saw Ellen give up her search for the window crank and look at the side window, scanning the horizontal split halfway up the pane. Her raised eyebrows seemed to say "aha" as she saw a catch at the bottom of the glass. Her hands went to the catch, and the lower pane flipped up from the hinge in the middle of the window.

She twisted her head to look out the opening. "Y'all know I've got to be at the airport at sunup, and I need ma phone."

Boniface was momentarily stunned to hear a Southern accent that hadn't been apparent while he was in the car, but he took the cue. "Yes. My friend left her phone in the Great Hall. Could we dash back and pick it up. As she says, she's flying out first thing in the morning, so we can't come back tomorrow." Boniface grimaced his apologies, holding out his hands in a what-are-you-going-to-do gesture.

The guard looked at his watch. "We're running a bit late tonight, what with your bash and some of the cleaning crew being sick, but if you hurry." He turned to Ellen. "You know where you left it?"

"Sure do, sir."

"Be quick. The guys will probably be around at about half past eleven, so you need to find it before then." He turned to Boniface. "And you remember where to park?"

"I do. Thank you for your help." Boniface shook his hand again and jumped into the car.

As the car jerked, crunching gravel, Boniface turned to Ellen. "How long have you been channeling Scarlett O'Hara? I was in the car, sitting next to a woman from Richmond, Virginia—didn't Nigel say that's where you're from?—but now living in Richmond, London, and when I get out, the next thing I know there's some southern belle telling lies."

"I told the truth," said Ellen huffily. "I have got to be at the airport first thing tomorrow, but to pick up my sister. You lied when you constructed the notion that I was flying out. And as for Scarlett O'Hara, there's something deep in the English psyche that makes men go weak when they hear a Southern accent. I don't understand it either, but it always works. And we need to get in here, don't we?"

"We do." Boniface looked up at the building, looking as Cardinal Wolsey would have seen it, but with the addition of electric floodlighting pinpointing the Palace against a blanket of darkness. "It's magnificent, isn't it?"

"Stunning," said Ellen, twisting the steering wheel to keep some sort of control as the car wobbled up the grand drive. "If I don't crash this thing and kill us both, I should bring Montbretia here."

"Who?"

"Montbretia. My sister. Remember...we've just had that conversation—she arrives tomorrow, and I have to pick her up at the airport. I'll take her around the Maze and show her the rest of the Palace." She sighed lightly, her tone softening. "I wish we had Nigel here to give her the detail, but it'll be fun."

"Who will win the race to the center of the Maze?" Boniface regretted a question that didn't move the conversation away from Nigel.

"She will. She always wins anything competitive. But she's made me get this clever phone with GPS and all that sort of stuff. I don't understand it; it's all to do with my website. But anyway, maybe I can use the GPS in the Maze?"

"He wants us to park up over there." Boniface pointed to the right of the Great Gatehouse, managing to move the subject away from Nigel. Ellen slowed the car, following a large loop to bring it pointing in the direction from which they had come as she jerked them to a stop. Boniface pulled a quizzical face and asked gently, "Why?"

"If you can figure where reverse gear is, then we can go backwards. Until then, we go forwards," said Ellen definitively. "I've done my bit of thinking, so tell me, oh great strategist, we're still alive and we've got past the gate. What's the plan now?"

They stepped out of the car and gazed up at the Great Gatehouse, which commanded their attention. Boniface started talking softly, almost absent-mindedly. "Now...? Now we go in. Look. See what we can see. Perhaps accidentally, very accidentally, get lost and see if we can figure where Mister Longhair found his papers. But whatever happens, get out quickly and get away from here before a tall, shaven-headed Russian figures that we're here."

Ellen remained entranced by the architecture.

"Let's start moving," said Boniface, indicating the bridge that led across the dry moat, the path then passing under the Great Gatehouse arch.

They walked through the gate, entering the courtyard with Anne Boleyn's Gate at the far end. "If I marry my Prince and then become a Queen, my King will definitely have to build me something like that," said Ellen wistfully, looking at the golden astrological clock illuminated like a sun over the courtyard, her kitten heels clip-clopping as they walked.

Reaching the far corner of the courtyard, Boniface indicated the door. "The Great Hall?" she asked.

Ellen led them through the entrance, immediately turning right, following the passage to the Great Hall. The main lighting had been extinguished, leaving the hammer-beam roof in darkness, its dulled timbers visible but the detailing of the master craftsmen lost in the gloom. Muted safety lights let off a gentle glow, enough to see the room but not enough to be a fire risk.

Boniface let out an expletive as he surveyed the mess of the room. "Useless people." Ellen paused, seemingly waiting for elaboration. "Look." Boniface pointed around the hall without identifying any particular object. "The caterer hasn't finished clearing up." He walked over to a tray of half-eaten food and looked down a row of several tables covered with the detritus of finger food. "In fact, hasn't started clearing up. Swan vol-au-vent? Probably with added salmonella by now, along with the other bacteria from people prodding and poking them."

Ellen looked at the tray of food and made a face. "Yuck. People ate that?"

"Not me," said Boniface, turning to look at the rest of the room. "Now that's just stupid. You get a stack of books printed, and then you leave them laying around after the event."

"It's a mess, but isn't that good for us?" Ellen turned to Boniface. "Doesn't that mean that whatever was here won't have been disturbed?" Ellen watched as Boniface looked back at her. "That's good, right? We can forgive the laziness and be thankful?"

Boniface nodded. At first, a small nod of the head, but then increasing the swing of his skull. "Well, get looking then," he said. "I've got a call to make."

thirty-five

Boniface moved to the side of the Great Hall, pulled out his phone, flicked his wrist to open it, then hit a speed-dial button. "Hey, it's your favorite ex-husband...only ex-husband, so I must be your favorite... How're you doing? Have you nailed Oscar yet? Got your big scoop to make Mister Kuznetsov proud?"

He watched as Ellen started to work her way around the room, systematically checking each and every object. She looked under tables; on, under, and behind chairs; under the detritus left on tables and on the floor; and she delicately peeked behind the tapestries hanging on the walls without touching them. Each time she satisfied herself that there was nothing to be found or that what she had found was of no interest, she moved on: a one-woman grid search applying cold, hard logic and pure persistence to a problem.

Boniface huddled around the phone, holding it tighter. "Look, I've got a problem. There are three dead bodies, and I think Turgenev is chasing me. What have you and Kuznetsov got me into?"

He listened, more attuned to how the response was delivered than the words that were being spoken. "I'm not sure you're taking this with the same seriousness that I am. Nigel is dead...he was shot. I watched some complete stranger get shot as he stood next to me, and then I saw Turgenev drown a man and float his body down the river."

He turned to look at Ellen continuing her progress around the room, then turned back, keen to shield her from the conversation. "Yes. Yes... Nigel was shot outside Professor Armstrong's house." He listened, understanding that the journalist instincts would be kicking in at the other end of the line.

"Apparently I was the emergency contact number programmed into his phone, so they called me first... Definitely outside Professor Armstrong's house... Well, there you are; there's your scoop. Now you know whose body that is. So when you ask Mister Kuznetsov why Mister Turgenev is following me, perhaps you could tell him about Nigel and say sorry, I didn't mean to get him killed."

He waited, walking in small circles, looking at his feet. He knew the game. A journalist had new information, and Veronica was more than a simple journalist; she was responsible for a whole newspaper, so she needed to get someone working on the story first. And it was to his advantage to let her clear her mind. That way, he could rely on her giving one-hundred percent focus to him.

Veronica came back on the line and Boniface listened. "No. Not dead... Very much alive... Why did you think she was...? I'm looking at her now, and she's very alive. Who was the source?" He looked up at Ellen, making sure she was occupied and not aware that she was the subject of conversation.

"My location? Let's just say London. You're not the only one to hold back information." A broad smile broke out across his face. "Right. You go find out why there are gentlemen with guns running around, and I'll go and see what the not-dead professor has found. Speak soon." With the well-practiced smoothness of a gunslinger, he flicked his wrist and returned his phone to his pocket in a single movement.

"Talking about me behind my back?" asked Ellen, her stern face giving way to a guilty grin.

He lifted the sides of his mouth weakly, wondering when she had started listening, becoming aware that the look of joy and expectation was not fading from her face and that she was standing with her hands behind her back. "What have you found?"

"*Ta-dah.*" Ellen held out a battered leather satchel briefcase. Boniface raised his eyebrows in a so-what motion. "Nigel's briefcase."

The cynicism dropped from Boniface's countenance, to be replaced by enthusiasm and his own version of childlike wonder. "Where was it?"

"The books at the end…" Ellen tilted her head in the direction of the table on the small stage at the end of the Great Hall, piled with hardback copies of *The Murder of Henry VIII*. "Under there."

"No," said Boniface. Ellen nodded as Boniface's astonished face morphed into a large grin. "I'm guessing we've got all that's worth finding here, so let's get moving." Ellen turned toward their exit. "But do you fancy accidentally taking the wrong turn on the way out? Perhaps we might see where Mister Longhair decided to get stuck in a hole. It may not tell us where the other documents are, but at least it's a start."

"Lead on," said Ellen, indicating the door.

"I was rather hoping you would lead," said Boniface. "After all, you are the historian."

"But…"

"But nothing." Boniface was resolute. Ellen moved toward the door, signaling her assent. "And while we walk, you can tell me what's in the briefcase."

Ellen gave a maybe-yes, maybe-no side-to-side tilt of her head, then returned to her excited grin as they turned out of the door, walking in the opposite direction from which they had arrived. "Okay, and then you can tell me what you said about me." Boniface opened his mouth to speak and found that words didn't come out.

"Shut your mouth, Boniface, and start walking. I don't know where we're going, and I'm making no guarantees that we'll find anything, but I've got a few ideas. How long have we got?"

"Dunno. Not long, I guess."

"Alright then." Ellen started to stride out, Boniface trailing behind. "Some pieces of paper."

Boniface stared blankly at Ellen, trying to keep up with the pace but unsure where the conversation had gone.

"The briefcase. You wanted to know what's in the case, and the answer is, some pieces of paper. His speech, I think. A few handwritten notes, something that looks like a hand-drawn family tree… A few printed pages, some handwritten pages, and that's it. All of the paper is new, as in there are no historic documents. But it was too dark in there to really read it. I even tried snapping a few pages with the camera on my phone—trying to see whether the flash illuminated it enough—but it was no use, so can we go somewhere with enough light to see past the end of my nose."

Somewhere in the dark there was a shout and the sound of running boots. "You asked how long we had?" Ellen looked back at Boniface, waiting for him to answer his own question. "Well, I think our time's up."

thirty-six

Nigel's 2CV sped along the main drive as fast as its 602cc, 28-horsepower engine would let it move when loaded with two adults. It was going somewhat faster than jogging pace, but the zero-to-sixty time was more of an aspiration than something that was ever going to be achieved and measured scientifically.

"What was going on there?" asked Ellen, her foot flat and her eyes fixed ahead, hands twisting the steering wheel, continuously nudging the car in a straight line as it spat out the gravel along the drive.

"I don't know." Boniface looked behind him, searching for any clue. "There's a time to be brave, a time to stand up and be counted. And there's a time to run like hell." He smiled softly. "Call me a coward, but I'm a live coward, and I vote that we run."

The guard stepped out of his hut to face the approaching car. "Better say goodnight," said Boniface as Ellen started bringing the car to a jerky stop, skidding the last few feet on the loose gravel.

Boniface flipped up his window and twisted his head to face the guard, who was peering through the rear door at the back seat of the car before bending to look directly through Boniface's window. "Did your friend find you?" he asked.

"Friend?" Boniface couldn't keep the questioning tone out of his voice.

"Yes, the young lady's friend. He said he had your phone, and as I knew it's urgent with you flying out tomorrow, I sent him straight through."

"What did this man look like?" asked Boniface.

The guard frowned and took a step back. "Tall." He held out a hand to indicate his height. "Black leather jacket. Shaved head. Had an accent, Russian perhaps? Said he had run after you. He was sweating a bit but didn't seem out of breath—he looked fit, muscular. From his posture, I would say he's a soldier, or he's been a soldier."

Boniface was glad for the darkness hiding the pallor of his skin. "He's no friend of ours." His tone was flat and commanding. "Call the police. Now. Get ambulances; you have a serious emergency on your hands." The guard stood frozen. "Now," said Boniface, waving in the direction of the hut as the man started to move, suddenly galvanized by Boniface's instructions.

"What now?" asked Ellen.

"Go left." The car started to move away with its customary lack of decorum, the engine complaining as it got onto the main road before Hampton Court Bridge. "Your phone?"

"My phone?" said Ellen.

"This clever stuff your sister set up?"

"Yes."

"Did she do anything to tag your location? You know, so your photos, tweets, posts, and whatever have some sort of location?"

"Of course," said Ellen. "This is the twenty-first...oh shit. I get it... Shit. Shit. Shit." She hit the brake. "Shit. Shit. Shit." The car pulled to a stop on the brow of the bridge, and she reached into her pocket, handing Boniface the phone. "Take it. Throw it in the river."

Boniface opened the door and got out of the car, then immediately got back in. "I've got a better idea. Drive."

Ellen eased the car forward. "Where to?"

"Over the bridge, then pull in to the station on the other side." Boniface pointed. "See up there?"

Ellen pulled into the station, and Boniface got out of the car. "Go and park up the other end; turn off the lights and kill the engine so you can't be seen. Then wait—I'll only be a minute." As Ellen moved off, he slammed the door and ran through the ticket office and along the concourse toward the platforms. "I'm sorry, sir. After the train has the signal to leave, we cannot let anyone board." The over-officious guard stood to protect the entrance to the platform.

Boniface kept running, dodging the man. "My wife's phone," he shouted, waving Ellen's phone at him. He passed the first two carriages and jumped into an open door on the third, surreptitiously slipped the phone onto the luggage rack above the seats as the doors started to beep, then turned, pushing his way through the sliding doors as they closed on him.

He walked back up the platform. Seeing the guard at the gate, he held his hands in an I-surrender pose. "I'm sorry. The wife scares me more than you do." The guard gave a knowing nod as Boniface walked past and back along the concourse.

He reached the exit from the ticket office and stood back from the door, looking across the drop-off area. Nothing seemed out of place as he edged forward, looking in the direction they had driven from. A few cars passed. A night bus. No man in black with a shaved head.

He turned left and jogged down the parking lot, looking for Ellen, and found the car backed into a concealed gap. "So you found reverse gear?"

"It's me they're after." As Boniface got into the car he could see the tears streaming down Ellen's face, her arms wrapped tightly clutching her stomach. "It's me, isn't it? It was my phone they tracked, and having that briefcase just makes me an even bigger target. Get rid of it. Now."

"I don't know," said Boniface, trying to work out the best lie to tell his driver. "But if you're right, we need to move. We need to get off the route your phone passed."

He waited, watching the academic shrivel, pushing herself back into her seat.

"Please." He kept his tone soft.

"You go." Her voice was strained. "It's me they're after, not you."

He leaned over, reaching to twist the key in the ignition. The engine turned over, then died, and the dull lights briefly illuminated the parking lot. "Well that didn't help," muttered Boniface. "If they didn't know where we were before, they will now." He sighed and stared at Ellen, who wouldn't meet his gaze. "Please. One-hundred yards up the road." He continued to stare at her, watching her eyes flick around the car but still not meet his. "Please."

thirty-seven

How did Henry VIII get anything done? He must have spent his whole time trying to find his way around the Palace. Or perhaps he had some flunky whose only job was to guide him around the buildings. He had somebody to do everything else for him—as every Russian schoolchild knew, he even had someone whose job it was to wipe his bum. And that person had the most prized job in court. Now that really was Western decadence...

He hadn't found Professor Armstrong, but he knew she had a man with her. It was kind of the guard to tell him. It was kind of the guard to be gullible enough to let him past just by waving a phone. But what was that he said? Something about needing it because she was leaving tomorrow? He hadn't been paying attention; he was running again by then.

If he had paid attention, he might have heard where the professor and her escort had gone. Instead, he tried to find his own way through the labyrinthine layout of Hampton Court and ran into the two guards. The first one tried to play the hero and ran at him, so he hit him. A younger man could have taken the blow, but this was an older man, and he fell on contact.

The other guard shouted, and that brought two more guards. They all had the look of old soldiers: upright posture, gleaming uniforms, slavish observance to detail, and fatally, a belief in immediate action. It's one thing to take action when you're a seventeen-year-old conscript being shot at from all sides. It's another when you're over seventy—in fact, probably closer to eighty—and the last time you saw active service was in Korea.

Of the final three, the first had come at him, his head bowed as he tried to over-power with his shoulder. In a single move, Turgenev had twisted his neck, feeling it crack as he dropped the lifeless body at his feet. The next two thought they had safety in numbers. They were wrong. They were even more wrong to think that the flashlights they carried were any sort of weapon.

It took two blows.

The first he hit squarely in the middle of his face with a flat hand. He felt the nose crumble and the old cheekbones crack. The Russian wasn't sure if the man had survived, but he stopped fighting after that one contact.

Turgenev then turned, stumbling over the body of the man with the broken neck, and, as he righted himself, he powered the butt of his hand up into the jaw of the last man. His neck snapped backwards. If that didn't kill him, then he would be in a wheelchair to the end of his sorrowful days.

The silence in the middle of the courtyard as he stood surrounded by four bodies was broken by a car starting. It sounded like the car he had heard while he was on the island, but this time it started on the first attempt and moved off immediately, with no crunching of gears.

Turgenev ran through an arch under what looked like a golden sundial suspended between two imposing octagonal pillars, entering another larger courtyard that he sprinted across, passing through another arch that took him outside the Palace building at the end of the drive from which he had entered. At the opposite end of the drive, he saw the taillights of a car pulling out, turning left onto the main road and passing onto the bridge.

He looked at the map on his phone: Professor Armstrong's red dot was moving over the bridge. He put the phone back and started to sprint up the gravel path to the main gate.

As he approached the gate, the guard who had let him in came out. "Hey you. Yes, you—I want to talk with you."

The Russian slowed to a walking pace and looked behind him. There was no one else; the guard was definitely addressing him. Turgenev smiled broadly, moving directly to comply with the instruction. "Certainly. How can I help you?" The guard stood firm, waiting for the man with the shaved head to reach him.

As he reached the hut, Turgenev gave a submissive bow of his head, gesturing inside the hut. "Please...how can I help you?"

The guard relaxed, turning toward the hut. "If you would just..."

Like the others, this guard needed one blow. This time, the side of his hand slammed into the old man's neck was sufficient. Turgenev grabbed the old man under his arms and dragged the inert body into the hut, looking for the darkest corner in the gloomy chamber to drop the corpse.

He flicked the light switch, extinguishing the glow as he exited the hut, closing the door behind him. As the door clicked, Turgenev became aware of sirens for the second time in less than an hour.

He jogged through the outer gate, turning left and heading over the bridge.

thirty-eight

The Citroën steadfastly refused to contemplate any speed in excess of 23 miles per hour, less as the car turned the gentle bend and headed into a light oncoming breeze.

"You were talking about me, Boniface." Ellen's voice was quiet but barbed. She hadn't asked a question, but the statement demanded a response. Seemingly, her fear—having concluded that she was the target of the Russian who was chasing them—had mutated into hostility toward Boniface.

He reflected on what his former wife had told him: Ellen's attitude during an interview that afternoon had upset Kuznetsov. It might be true, but it was a detail that Boniface was struggling to fit into the context of the last few hours, and in any event, Veronica was certain that Kuznetsov would not sanction the killing of an academic on a London street.

Blurting that she had annoyed someone she had probably never met was also likely to infuriate Ellen, and given her fragility, he didn't want to divert her from her present focus of driving them as far away as possible—and as quickly as possible—from the pursuer.

"It didn't start that way, but you came up in conversation." Boniface tried, and failed not to look sheepish.

"Elaborate," said Ellen, her tone calmer, more measured, but still expecting an answer.

Boniface softened, trying to sound reassuring. "I didn't know about the news reports saying you had been shot until I had that phone call. That's how you came up." He paused. "I'm sorry. It must have been awful for you."

"It's worse for Nigel," said Ellen, almost apologetic.

"But it's not pleasant." He gauged the minute reactions—a twitching ear, a tightened grip, a darkening of the skin—trying to collate the individual elements into an understanding about how his driver was feeling. "I didn't know about the story because the police called me and told me about Nigel. Apparently I was his emergency number."

Boniface watched as Ellen's bottom jaw tightened. Sensing he had been wrong to bring to her attention that she wasn't Nigel's first choice in case of an emergency, he elaborated. "Your apparent death was reported by the papers tonight. You know that, of course. But I don't know whether you know that the paper that broke the story is owned by Ivan Kuznetsov, as in the man who owns Whitefoot Thorpe Publishing, publisher of *The Murder of Henry VIII*."

Ellen nodded as Boniface kept talking. "The paper that made that first report is edited by Veronica Rutherford. Have you heard of her?"

"No. Well, I guess I've heard the name, but I couldn't pick her out in a lineup." Boniface couldn't read anything in Ellen's face as she kept her gaze on the road ahead.

"Sure. There's no reason you would know her, but I do." He waited a beat. "She's my former wife, and she is who I was talking to. About you."

"Oh."

"And while we're getting things into the open, it was my ex-wife who made the decision to publish the story about your death. She also works for Kuznetsov, and yes, that's the same Kuznetsov who employs the man with the shaved head who we saw drown the guy and then climb over the bridge to the island." Boniface watched Ellen nodding slowly. When he was sure she had taken in each separate fact, he continued. "My ex-wife also did me a favor by recommending me for the PR job representing Nigel's book. In other words, she's the hub from which most of the spokes radiate."

"Question, please," said Ellen.

"You want to know how they got the story?" Ellen stared at Boniface, her eyes wordlessly asking Boniface to explain. "They got a tip. Someone called in with very specific details."

Boniface watched as Ellen tried to form a question, her lips quivering as she seemed to try to make a "wh" shape.

"Whatever you want to ask next, I don't know the answer. I'm as mystified as you are as to why someone would report you as being murdered."

Ellen's mouth kept moving until she formed a question. "But why did they run the story if all they had was a tip from a phone call? Don't they try to verify these things?"

"They do." Boniface weighed how to explain the story Veronica had told him. "There was a lot of interest because you've been in the limelight recently with the campaign for the referendum."

"Really?"

"Yup. You are now officially a D-list celeb."

"You say that once more, Boniface, and I'll crash this heap of junk, killing us both."

Boniface smiled, noting his driver's attempt at humor but feeling she might not be entirely unserious. "Alright, I believe you. Back to the explanation: When the journalists started looking into your death, there was confusion. They asked the police, the police said there was a male body, the press said 'No, we're after the dead female,' the police said, 'There is no dead female,' and it all descended into chaos. No one cared who the dead man was, no one could find you, and anyone official either didn't know or denied everything. You get the idea, complete chaos."

"They could have called—I did have a phone. Then."

Boniface gave a resigned nod. "I'm sorry about your phone. Let me buy you a new one."

"I'm sorry, I didn't mean..." Ellen's voice trailed off as she flushed slightly.

"You're right, they could have called you—they could have called me, and I would have told them about Nigel. But they didn't and they had a deadline. They knew something had happened. They knew someone was dead. They printed your name. It was a mistake."

"Oops, sorry. We made a mistake." Ellen turned to face her passenger, her tone souring.

Boniface met her watery gaze and flicked his eyes forward, noting how the skin on her fingers was turning white as she returned her eyes to the road. When he recommenced, his voice was soft but resigned. "It happens."

Ellen let out a sigh of exasperation, slowly shaking her head. "This isn't helping, Boniface. This isn't getting us any further."

"But if..."

"No, Boniface. No." Ellen hit the brakes and fought with the steering wheel as the car slowed. A front wheel bumped over the curb at the side of the road, and eventually it came to a halt with the engine stalled, the weak headlights throwing their muted beam into the gutter.

She turned toward Boniface, tears streaming down her cheeks, banging her arms on the steering wheel as she shouted. "This isn't helping! I saw my friend's dead body tonight. I saw his brains splattered over my house. I might not look it, but I'm very upset about it, and if I had my way, I would be at home sobbing on my bed. But then someone said I had been murdered and that there was a man with a gun outside my house, so I got a bit windy and I ran. And then someone got shot in front of me, and that man was drowned, and the guy with the shaved head was chasing me at Hampton Court, so I'm really not having a good evening, and to be quite honest, suddenly finding that you're on their side makes me pretty scared."

The car vibrated with the aftershock of Ellen's outburst. Boniface sat and watched as she turned away, burying her head in her hands. Gradually the sobs became less frequent, and she started to wipe her eyes. Boniface wriggled uncomfortably to get his hand into his pocket and pulled out a handkerchief, offering it to Ellen. "It's clean."

She took it with a mumbled "thank you" and started to mop her eyes and wipe her dribbling nose. Boniface remained motionless in his uncomfortable seat, watching. "I'm sorry... I'm a mess... I'm not used to this sort of thing."

He waited. Ellen looked up, giving an embarrassed grimace. He tried to look reassuring. "This is tough..." He struggled, trying to sift through the usual platitudes and clichés that came to mind. "You've managed to avoid two bullets tonight; I think we should try to make sure there isn't a third."

"You mean they're..." Boniface could hear the rising panic in Ellen's voice.

"I mean, I don't know." Boniface kept his voice calm, trying to be reassuring. Hoping if he faked being in control of his emotions, it would come true.

"You don't know why they said I was dead. You don't know why the shaven-headed guy is chasing me. You don't know what Nigel found. You don't know what we're going to do next. Really, Boniface, you don't know much!"

The two sat, staring at each other, tears running down Ellen's face.

Boniface felt the edge of his mouth twitch and tried to suppress a smirk.

"I'm serious, Boniface."

"So am I," he replied, now making far less effort to hide his inability to stifle his grin as Ellen started to smile through her tears.

"I'm deadly..." He stopped himself. "I'm very serious." He exhaled. "But here's the thing—do you want to hang around and get answers? We're less than two miles from Hampton Court—do you want to go back and find Turgenev to ask him why he seems to be chasing you?"

Ellen raised her shoulders, giving an almost imperceptible shrug.

"There have already been two bullets near to you—they may have been meant for you. I don't know. They may have been meant for me. I don't know. But what I do know is that a moving target is much harder to hit, and that a target that is hidden from the shooter is almost impossible to hit. So I suggest we keep running and follow what few leads we've got until we find something we can bargain with."

He tried to reassure. "Remember, we need to be worth more alive than dead, so let's get somewhere where we can have a proper look inside Nigel's briefcase."

Ellen's jaw fell open. "You didn't tell your wife about Nigel's briefcase?"

Boniface kept his voice soft. "I didn't know about the briefcase, so Ronnie certainly doesn't know about it. Ronnie doesn't know about our trip to Hampton Court. Ronnie doesn't know about Mister Longhair and what Mister Longhair might have found." He exhaled. "To be frank, Ronnie doesn't know much, apart from the fact that she needs to print a groveling apology to you."

"I still think we should get rid of the briefcase," muttered Ellen.

thirty-nine

By the time he had passed the brow of Hampton Court Bridge, Turgenev's head was gleaming like a disco ball. Out of sight of the main entrance to the Hampton Court grounds, he looked over the river as he pulled out his phone, then zoomed in on the map.

He watched the red dot as it moved away from him, keeping parallel to the road. "The road's there...not there," he said to the phone. The red dot moved in a straight line, keeping parallel with the map of the road. He watched the dot as it passed the point on the map where the road bent to the right, but still the dot carried on in a straight line.

He shook his head, catching sight of the building on the other side of the bridge. "Shit. A train." He slipped the phone back in his pocket as he started running, increasing his pace as he freed his hand.

He came off the bridge, sprinted the short distance to the station, passed through the ticket office, and turned right, crossing the concourse toward the gate. A man in uniform was pulling a latticed security grille across the entrance to the platforms. Turgenev slowed as the guard looked up. "I'm sorry, sir, you've just missed it." He threw his head in the direction of the train lines, and somewhere in the distance the red taillights twinkled."

"When's the next one?" asked Turgenev.

"Five fifty-four tomorrow morning, sir," replied the guard. "Someone else will be here for that."

"Thanks," said Turgenev, turning to walk away. He took a few steps and spun his head without breaking his step. "Where does that train go...the next stop?"

"Thames Ditton."

"And after that?"

"Surbiton." The second mention of Surbiton in one night. First the man with the scar on his face got lost and ended up there, and now the train carrying Professor Armstrong was heading there.

"Okay. Thank you. Is there a phone around here?" said Turgenev, picking up his pace.

"Big red box. Through the hall, turn right, and turn right again." Having closed the gate, the guard was now offering directions with his hands.

Turgenev held up a hand to acknowledge his thanks as he turned into the ticket office, then right out of the entrance, and right again at the end of the building. He pulled the heavy phone-booth door and stepped in. The door closed slowly as he picked up the receiver and punched three buttons. "Police."

forty

The 2CV chugged with a bad temper along the tree-lined main road heading away from wherever Turgenev might be. Boniface broke the contemplation. "Waterloo."

Ellen kept her foot pressed hard to the floor. "Eighteen-fifteen. Napoleon surrendered. You English are rather proud of it. Still."

"No. Waterloo train station. Middle of London. South of the River Thames."

"I'm sorry, Boniface. You've lost me. I mean, yes, I know Waterloo station—who doesn't—but why are you telling me? Do you want me to drive there?"

Boniface chuckled. "No. That's where your phone has gone. I figured that if Turgenev is following your phone, we should at least try to send him in the wrong direction. And as the train keeps moving, he'll keep chasing it."

"That's priceless."

"And there's a chance you'll get your phone back. Call lost property tomorrow—someone's bound to have handed it in. Or better still, call your phone and see who answers."

Ellen kept her eyes on the road ahead. "So if we're not going to Waterloo, where are we going? Or do you want me to keep driving until we run out of gas?"

Boniface ignored the question. "Nigel's phone..."

"His second most prized possession, after this fine piece of automotive history," said Ellen, seemingly adding as much sarcastic sincerity as she could muster.

"It's the key to this, isn't it?"

"How so?"

Boniface sat back in the seat, winced, and twisted. "You didn't seem overly enthusiastic about the contents of the briefcase, but his phone has the photos he took in the police station. The documents or whatever they are that Mister Longhair recovered."

"Yes."

"And that phone is in the possession of the police." Boniface chewed his bottom lip. "So do you think...maybe we should...I don't know...what do you think?"

"What do I think about what?"

"Should we try to get it back?"

The contemplation was filled with the sound of the straining engine and Ellen crunching into third gear. "Why would we?"

Boniface tried to keep the exasperation out of his voice. "Won't the photos answer all our questions? Or at least all of our questions for which there is an answer."

"You're missing my point. Why would we try to get the phone when we're bound to fail and there's a faster way to get the pictures?"

Boniface turned his head as if his neck were spring-loaded. "What?"

"You said Nigel was messing with his phone."

"Mmm."

"Nigel uploaded everything."

"Uploaded? Uploaded where?" asked Boniface. "Nigel said something about the photos taking too long to upload, but I didn't understand what he meant by that, so I ignored him."

It was Ellen's turn to fail to stifle a sigh of exasperation. "He will have uploaded the photos to an online storage service."

"But how can you sound so certain about that?"

"Because Nigel kept all his files online." Boniface frowned and Ellen continued. "Nigel wanted his computer files to be accessible wherever he was."

"Couldn't he just use one of those thumb-drive things you plug into your computer like the rest of us?"

Ellen shook her head. "Not Nigel. He didn't trust those things—he thought they were always faulty—plus he didn't want to have to remember to copy specific files. He wanted everything available everywhere, and with online storage all he had to do was remember his password."

"Look, I've got a Stone Age phone, but you're saying he will have done this with pictures on his phone?"

"If the pictures mattered, then yes. That way he could share the photos, and they would be safe if the camera got lost... You know, like if someone put it on a train or something strange like that."

Boniface ignored the quip. "So how do we get at the pictures?"

"If I had my phone, I could tell you which service Nigel uses, but since it's on its way to Waterloo, then get me to a computer and I'll check my email to tell you. It was something like online-file-store-dot-net, but I can't be sure. Then all we need is his password, and we're in." Ellen gave a self-satisfied look.

"Go. Go fast. Well, go as relatively fast as we can go."

"I am. Look at my foot, it's flat." Boniface craned his neck to look, gave a brief nod, and slipped back into his seat, listening to Ellen. "So where's the nearest computer? We can't go round to Nigel's, and mine is probably not the best place to go to at the moment. Have you got a computer somewhere?"

Boniface pondered for a moment. "The office is too far. The closest I can think of is Surbiton."

"Surbiton?"

"Mmm. There's an internet café opposite the station. As far as I know it's open twenty-four seven. It'll probably be filled with students, but at least we can sit down, and we might also be able to look at Nigel's briefcase in something approaching a reasonable light."

forty-one

Turgenev opened the door of the red phone booth and stepped out with a schoolboy grin across his face. He pulled out his phone and called up the map for the route back to the parking lot by Thames Ditton Island: Head west, take the first road on the left—Summer Road—and follow it. It would only take a few minutes if he jogged.

As he got close to the island, he crossed to the path on the inside of the bend. About fifty yards away he stopped running, choosing instead to walk, but walk and make a lot of noise: He scuffed his feet, whistled loudly, and kicked stones and tin cans—anything that would alert people to his presence.

The two police cars were still in the lots and had been joined by other official-looking cars and a white van. The gate in the middle of the bridge had been propped open, and from the other side of the road, Turgenev could see a young police constable, no more than twenty-two or twenty-three years old, still very pink-cheeked and soft-skinned, standing guard a few feet from the bridge steps.

The Russian crossed the road, walking toward his bike. He stopped once he was sure the young officer was watching him, and looked around. "What's happened?"

"I'm afraid there's been an incident, sir," said the officer, with the gravitas of a young man trying desperately to bring all of his people-handling training into practice.

"An incident?" said Turgenev, raising his eyebrows. "It must be very serious with all of this." He loosely pointed to the official vehicles. The officer followed his direction, nodding as if acknowledging that he had heard the comment. Turgenev mirrored the young policeman, exaggerating the nod, and keeping up the momentum asked, "A murder?"

"I'm sorry, sir; I can only say that there has been an incident. As I'm sure you can understand, we can't prejudge the situation until we know more details."

"How shocking," said Turgenev, as if he hadn't heard the officer's reply. "You don't usually get crime like that around here."

"You don't, sir."

"Well, I'll pick up my bike and get out of your way." He moved toward the Wolf.

"Is that yours?" Turgenev had heard the question many times before. He nodded, waiting for the follow-up question. "What sort of bike is it?"

"A Ural Wolf," he said, lifting his helmet off the mirror. "I would offer you a ride, but"—he shrugged—"you don't have a helmet." The officer gave an envious look as Turgenev threw his leg over the beast. "Perhaps next time."

He didn't hear the reply under his helmet as he kicked the bike to life.

forty-two

The 2CV made a fuss about the slight incline in the road leading toward Surbiton station. "Park it around the corner," said Boniface, pointing to the road on the left. The car complained a bit more as it turned and vigorously expressed its displeasure as Ellen parked it.

The two got out, Boniface with Nigel's briefcase, Ellen with the key attached Nigel's work pass; both stretched as they released themselves from the unnatural position required to stay seated. "I wouldn't bother locking it," said Boniface under his breath. "We're going to be quick, and no self-respecting thief would be caught dead in one of those things."

As they reached the junction across from the station, one train was motionless and virtually deserted. Small clumps of people spilled from the station onto the streets, and on the platforms station staff wearing Day-Glo jackets were officiously bossing passengers. Some staff had managed to find megaphones and were using them with the relish of an army guard commanding concentration-camp arrivals, with the last few former passengers being heckled to disembark and evacuate the station.

"Any clue?" asked Ellen.

"Nope," said Boniface, twisting his head to exaggerate that he was listening to something in the distance. "Sirens. Again. I don't know about you, but I'm starting to twitch when I hear those things. Let's get in and out; I don't think we want to be hanging around here."

Ellen wrinkled her nose.

They pushed through the few people on the street who were starting to congregate and turned into the internet café, which seemed to have become the first point of refuge for the train evacuees. There was one spare computer terminal in the middle of a row of four. Boniface pointed. "Go."

With two steps Ellen was at the terminal and seated, the mouse in her hand. "Right. What am I looking for?" she asked as Boniface reached her, having pushed his way through the mass of late-night students and misplaced passengers, combined to form a morass of indecision.

"This online storage thing you mentioned? I don't know—you sounded like you knew what you were talking about."

"Sorry, mate." A student with dilated pupils knocked into Boniface and made his best effort to construct a sentence. "I...you know...it's crowded."

"It's okay," said Boniface, taking stock of the rising flood of humanity drowning the small room. He had no clue what the walls or the floor looked like. All he could see were people trapped under a suspended square lattice ceiling holding dirty tiles and the occasional banks of neon lights flicking and buzzing like some form of highly stylized torture imagined in a Hollywood movie.

Ellen tapped away at the terminal in front of her as Boniface lifted the briefcase, flipping the flap open and peering inside. Another drunken student, wearing a tie-dyed T-shirt with a peace sign, walked into him, spilling his can of lager. He looked at Boniface, Boniface stared at him, and the student turned, puking on three other students behind him.

For the second time that evening, Boniface's nostrils were filled with the smell of vomit. He snapped the case shut; whatever was in there would have to wait until he could find somewhere less crowded. He turned and bent over Ellen. "Any luck?"

"Nope. I can't get the pictures; I tried all the obvious passwords, but they don't work."

"Is there anything more you can do here?" Ellen shook her head. "Then let's get away from this stench." She stood and turned to the door. Boniface shook his head and pointed toward the back of the café, leaning to whisper in her ear, "Sirens, police. Maybe I'm being paranoid, but I'm sure there's a back exit."

The overwhelmed cashier stepped out from behind his counter with a mop and bucket, struggling to reach the location of the latest puke eruption. Checking that Ellen was behind him, Boniface pushed through the crowd and headed behind the counter, turning right through a doorway.

"It might smell of rotting food," said Boniface, wrinkling his nose and looking at the overflowing bins, "but it smells better than the puke and unwashed students in there." He closed what turned out to be the fire-exit door, cutting off their main source of light and muffling the sound of the internet café. "So did you find anything?"

"I found who he's with—it is online-file-store-dot-net—but, apart from that..." She sighed. "Nothing."

"Pity," said Boniface as he started making out shapes in what seemed, with his limited night vision, to be an alley behind the storefronts.

Ellen shivered in the breeze coming down the alley and pulled her jacket tighter. "So what do we do now?"

"I need to make a call." Ellen looked sternly at him. "I might be talking about you, but you can listen."

He took her softening look as agreement as he put his phone to his ear. "News?" His face remained impassive as he listened. "Okay. That's good... No, I haven't heard anything about the dear fellow—why would I? I was rather hoping you were going to tell me he died from a coronary after tonight's sting. Or is that me dreaming? Moving on: computer hackers. You must have a tame one somewhere."

Boniface registered a slight squeak—which might have been shock—from Ellen. "A bit of hacking into one of those online storage thingies... Must be good...deniable for both of us would be sensible...but primarily good and quick. Do you think you could get one of your contacts' contacts to find one?" He paused, waiting for the indecision at the other end of the phone to pass. "Great. I'll get back to you with the details in a couple of minutes. There's somewhere I need to be first." With a flick of his wrist, his phone was shut and re-pocketed.

"Hacking? Isn't that a bit extreme and—I don't know—against the law?" Ellen seemed concerned.

"Murder is against the law, but that didn't seem to slow any bullets tonight." Boniface was quite matter-of-fact. "In any case, we won't be doing the hacking, and you're focusing on the unimportant details." Ellen went to ask the next question, but Boniface kept talking. "Nigel's office?"

"Mmm."

"Do you know where it is?"

"Of course."

Boniface raised his eyebrows. "And would the university extend the courtesy of access to a visiting professor at this time of night?" He listened, unable to see her features clearly, but imagining her collecting every reason not to try, and carried on. "Before you say no... First, his office will be quiet, which..." he threw his head back toward the café, recalling the vomit that had started to flow across the floor, "will be a significant improvement, and second, isn't that the sort of place where he might have noted his password?"

"But isn't..." began Ellen.

"I take it his office is on the campus just up the road. That's less than a mile, so even our grumpy little car should be able to make it in under six hours."

Ellen gave a resigned nod. "So what else did your ex-wife have to say?"

"Two things. Let's start going back to the car." Boniface pointed somewhere in the general direction of where he guessed they had left the car as they started along the back alley. "First off, Kuznetsov definitely does not know what Turgenev is up to. Veronica said he seemed quite shocked. And he was sorry to hear about Nigel."

"So we're safe?" Ellen stopped walking and spun to look at Boniface, her face like a child on Christmas morning.

"Not quite." He kept walking, leaving Ellen to scramble to keep up in the poorly lit passage. "If Kuznetsov didn't order Turgenev to kill you, then we can't be certain about Turgenev's motives. So we can't be certain that you are the target. I might be the target, or it might be coincidence that he's following us." Ellen looked up, the hope draining from her eyes. "And the bigger problem is they can't find Turgenev, so they don't know where he is or what he's up to."

"And you didn't tell her that he's roaming around south London, drowning people for sport, because you don't want her to know where we are?"

"Yup. And I don't know about you, so just for the moment, I'd rather sit in a quiet little office that neither of us has a connection to and look through the papers in this briefcase, safe in the knowledge that Mister Turgenev will not be dropping by for a chat."

"So what else did she have to say?"

Boniface looked up; they were approaching the end of the alley. "Ronnie's other point is far less interesting. She was asking—being as I am with you, and given my history with your publisher, the delightful Mister Sherborne—whether I had heard anything about him."

"What? She wanted you to try to get information about Sherborne out of me?"

"No. Apparently he blipped on the radar tonight. Another tip. You'll understand they are a bit cautious of tips at the moment. She was wondering if I had heard anything, and because you have been at my side since we last spoke, you know that I haven't."

They reached the end of the narrow alley and joined the road where they had left the car. Several police cars seemed to have been abandoned in haste in front of the railway station, their engines off, doors open, and blue lights still flashing. An area around the front of the station was being cordoned off with crime-scene tape, and the police were trying to encourage the displaced passengers and rubberneckers to disperse.

"Maybe they're not after us, but it doesn't look like the place we want to be."

forty-three

It felt good to be back on the Wolf.

Turgenev had ridden slowly down Thames Ditton High Street while he knew the fresh-faced policeman would still be watching him, but he let rip as he turned out of sight. When he got to the main road, he held back the speed and kept his revs low. Everything to minimize his visibility as he followed, in reverse, the directions he had given the man with the scar on his face.

Motoring up the slight incline toward Surbiton station, he was pleased to see a lot of activity. It was amazing what you could do with one phone call.

About fifty yards short of the station, he parked and walked up the slope, passing an internet café, which seemed to be the only place still open besides the burger stand from which the owner had been evicted by the police. Glancing through the window, the internet café looked like an unpleasant mass of drunk and stoned students crammed into a very small room.

There were two police cars outside the station. From the angle at which they were parked and from the way the doors had been left open, he guessed they had arrived in a hurry. It wasn't clear where the police were, but one of their number—another fresh-faced young idealist—was busy fixing crime-scene tape around the outside of the station forecourt area in an attempt to create some sort of cordon.

Turgenev gave a wry grin as he saw the officer struggling to attach the tape, looking forlornly for the next sturdy object he could wrap his ribbon around while the guy from the burger stand berated him. Like that thin strip of plastic film would stop a bomb blast...

Not that there would be a bomb, but the police didn't know that. As far as they knew, the train from Hampton Court station had a bomb on board.

As far as Turgenev knew—and he did know more than the police; after all, he had called in the bomb threat—there was no bomb on board. However, it did seem a simple way to stop the train and get all of the passengers onto the street, where it would be easy to pick out Professor Armstrong and the man who was with her.

He walked around the perimeter, mimicking the behavior of the other rubberneckers, pretending he felt safer at a distance, but looking for somewhere from where he could watch for two specific people and not be obviously seen, either by any CCTV or by the two as they exited the station.

The main road from Surbiton to Kingston ran perpendicular to the station; it was the natural path for anyone to follow if they were looking for alternate means of public transport. Turgenev walked down the street, ducking into the shadow of a shop doorway to look back at the station.

The police and railway staff seemed to have cleared the station but were taking their time with the only train that was still standing at the platform. There seemed to be some confusion: Turgenev guessed they were trying to figure whether they were there to evacuate, to find the bomb, or to look for witnesses.

The red dot on his phone was stationary; he was almost close enough to be able to reach Professor Armstrong and snap her neck with the flick of his wrist. In a few minutes she would be evacuated from the train, and he would see her walking out of the station. All he had to do was to get her on her own, and then he could be back on his bike and back at the Silver Spike.

When he saw Professor Armstrong during her interview that so enraged Mister Kuznetsov, she had been wearing a blue jacket. There was a good chance she hadn't changed, but he couldn't be sure. He wasn't sure about her height—on the television she had been shorter than the other two interviewees, and she had also appeared to be shorter than the aggressive woman conducting the interview. All he could really be sure about was that she had shoulder-length curly blond hair and that he could track her phone.

He looked back at the map on his phone. The red dot wasn't moving, but there didn't seem to be any passengers still on the train. From where he was standing, it appeared the police were going through the train looking for any last stragglers and trying to locate anything that looked like it could be a bomb. He looked harder at the platform on the other side of the chain-link fence that separated the line from the drop-off area at the front of the station. The police seemed to be drawing a blank, which wasn't surprising.

The last few people who had come off the train were dispersing. Professor Armstrong had yet to appear. She definitely hadn't come out, which meant she was either hiding somewhere or she had stepped off at the last stop and left her phone behind. Turgenev stepped from the shadow of the doorway, cursing silently. If she had disembarked at the previous station, there was no way to know where she was.

He checked the dot again. Definitely stationary.

Most of the passengers had dispersed. Some were standing around making calls; others were walking with a purpose, heading for some other form of transport. The younger people seemed to have gravitated to the internet café.

There were even fewer people around the station as Turgenev started walking back toward his bike. As he looked to cross the road where he had been standing, he caught sight of two figures leaving a side alley: a taller man and a shorter blond woman. A shorter blond woman with curly blond hair, wearing a blue suit.

A broad grin spread across his face as he subtly changed direction, moving back into the shadow to watch them walking down the street.

They reached a battered car and got in: she in the driver's seat, he in the passenger's, both ignoring the comments from a group of students standing near the car. As the man opened the door, he looked behind him toward the station.

Turgenev felt a jolt of recognition and a spark of elation as he realized who he was looking at.

Now that he knew where Professor Armstrong was, he could complete his task. Not only that, he could also tell Mister Kuznetsov that the man he had met this afternoon was working with the professor. Working with Sherborne's woman. Sherborne had managed to get someone close to Mister Kuznetsov, but he, Mikhail Igorovich Turgenev, had used his initiative and had found the infiltrator.

If this didn't prove his value to Mister Kuznetsov, then nothing would.

The professor started up the car—Turgenev laughed out loud. That was the ridiculous sound he had heard from the island. They were making it so easy to follow them; he just had to use his ears.

He started jogging back to his bike.

forty-four

"Drunk but harmless," muttered Boniface under his breath as he and Ellen approached the car, where a group of students had gathered to laugh at the museum piece.

"D'you want a push, mate?" one asked, his friends laughing out loud as Boniface and Ellen got in.

"I can walk faster than that drives," offered another, frowning and looking around when his comment didn't generate the expected mirth from his comrades.

Ellen started the car on the first attempt. "Now please, little car, I know I've thought unpleasant things about you, but please, just this once, please move off without any drama." She slid the car into gear, there was a mechanical clunk as the gear reached home, and then the vehicle moved off slowly and without incident.

"I'm impressed," said Boniface, graciously waving at the students as the car chugged past.

"Now impress me, Boniface. Tell me what we're doing. Tell me what the plan is."

He picked up on the tension in Ellen's voice. "You're worried about this computer hacking thing," he said as another police car sped toward Surbiton station, its blue flashing light announcing its urgency.

"I can't say it's been one of my ambitions. So are you going to explain what we're doing?"

"There's not much to explain," said Boniface. "First we're going to Nigel's office to see if we can get into this online file storage thing while we don't have the pressure of people puking over us, and while we're there, we're going to have a look around. That's not too outrageous, is it?"

"I'm confused," said Ellen. "If we can access the photos from the university, then why do we need the hacker?"

"I hope we won't need a hacker, and anyway, it's a bloody dangerous strategy to get a stranger to open up files for you. I've asked Ronnie to find one in case we need it. That way we won't have a delay once we've exhausted our options." Boniface watched Ellen as she reasoned the proposition internally.

"This is where we need Montbretia to help us. She understands these things much better than I do. If we can wait until tomorrow morning, then she'd be ready to have a go." Ellen paused. "Tomorrow morning."

"Tomorrow morning?"

"Montbretia arrives—you remember, we had this conversation. I've got to pick her up at the airport. Now, apart from the fact that I haven't booked a cab..."

"Who needs a cab when you've got a car?" asked Boniface, holding his arms open and looking around the car.

"Yeah right. Even if I leave now, I won't make it in time, and not without doing serious and permanent damage to my skeleton. No, the problem is that she's going to call me as soon as she lands, and my phone is... I don't know, Boniface. Where is my phone at this precise moment?"

Boniface smiled. "It should be just outside Waterloo, being pursued by a shaven-headed man who likes to drown people."

"So that leaves the challenge as to how my sister and I communicate."

"Not a problem," said Boniface. "Tell her to call mine."

"Could I?" said Ellen. "Really?"

"Sure. Do you want to send her a text now to tell her to call this number?"

"Really?"

"I might not be the most technologically advanced, but I can just about manage to send one hundred and forty characters typed awkwardly on a phone keypad." Boniface pulled out his phone and flipped it open. "My price is that you explain why you got the conventional—very pleasant, but conventional—name and she got the wacky one."

"We both got…interesting names, but I use my middle name. And no, I'm not going to tell you."

"Is it a flower?"

"Our mother was a hippie. That's all I'm saying," said Ellen, blushing.

"So why didn't Montbretia change her name?" The urge to keep digging was starting to kick in.

"Because her middle name is Sylvia—which I never really liked—and after our mother died, I wouldn't let her change her name. Also, it shortens well to Monty, so it's not as bad as…"

"As?"

"Nice try, mister. Can we get on with the SMS? We can talk about weird names later, if that's alright with you, Alexander?"

"Touché. What's her number?" Slowly he input each figure, repeating as he went. "What do you want me to say?"

"Hi sis, really looking forward to seeing you, got lots to tell you…"

"One hundred and forty characters, not words."

"Sorry. Okay then, hi sis, lost my phone, call me on this number, love E. How's that?"

Boniface manipulated the tiny keypad, squinting at the screen. "Eighty-seven characters to spare. I've sent it."

"But I…"

"We can send another if you want," offered Boniface.

Ellen shook her head. "Later. Let's do what we need to do here first."

"So where's your sister coming in from?"

"Turkey. Istanbul."

"Very nice. Does she live there?"

"No, she's been doing some traveling. She did the whole mature day job for a few years, but she didn't enjoy it and so figured she would go wild for a while, before knuckling down and accepting that she had to be sensible and admit she was an adult."

"Like becoming a university professor and getting shot at?" Ellen remained impassive as Boniface continued. "Does she have a big plan, or is she going where her heart tells her until the money runs out?"

"Mostly the latter, but some of the former. She writes everything she does in this blog. It's a real hoot—some of the things she does are pretty risky. As you've probably guessed, I'm the quiet one, I'm the one who reads books; she's the more out-there sister."

"How out there?"

"Well, two days ago she was swimming across the Bosporus at midnight. That's nearly a mile: Europe to Asia. I mean, do it, but not at midnight in the freezing water with jellyfish, passing tankers, and I don't know what else floating in the water."

"So she hasn't inspired you to dash back to the Thames for a post-midnight dip when we're done?" Boniface let the question hang as they approached the front gate of the university.

"How do we play this?" asked Ellen. "There's a guard. He's going to ask some awkward questions, isn't he?"

"Act casual...act relaxed..." He sighed. "Nigel must have told everyone about his book—that was rather in his nature."

Ellen had a look of slight disappointment.

"And he's probably told everyone about one or both of us?"

More disappointed nodding.

"The one person who can't run away is a security guard. He probably had to listen about both of us: you the brilliant professor, always on television, me the maverick whatever I am. And he probably knows that Nigel's book launch was tonight. So the guard will know us, we've got Nigel's car and his pass on the key ring, and all we need to do is tell him that Nigel rather overdid things and we're here to collect some papers he needs for tomorrow morning. Look—we've even got his briefcase. What could be better proof?"

Ellen nodded in resignation as she turned into the university entrance.

"But don't embellish. Stick with the simple story. Don't go Scarlett O'Hara on me again."

forty-five

As he crossed in front of the station, Turgenev became increasingly aware of what he wasn't seeing.

The two police cars were still there, along with a third that had joined them—their unsynchronized lights continuing to bend and break—and the tape to cordon off the station forecourt was still in place, but for all this activity, there were few people.

The young, fresh-faced policeman who had diligently stretched the tape around the perimeter was not in sight, and the last two police officers who had turned up were on the platform, looking anxious and self-important, and badgering the train station staff.

The train was still in the station, with one officer seeming to want to have a final look for the bomb.

Turgenev paused, muttering under his breath: "Very clever, Professor Armstrong. You almost had me fooled." He smirked. "Perhaps you will thank me if I return your phone."

The route to the train meant going up the stairs that crossed the line, then down onto the platform that stood between the train lines—far too much chance of being stopped, especially when all he had to do was get over the chain-link fence topped with three rows of barbed wire.

He sprinted across the forecourt to the chain-link fence. Placing one hand between the barbs and the other on a concrete fence post, he levered himself over, landing on the stones beside the tracks. He jogged around the back of the train, then jumped onto the platform before ducking into the last door of the end car.

He pulled out his phone, smiled as he hit the call button, and started to walk up the central corridor of the train. As he walked through the connecting doors joining the next car, the call passed to voicemail. He hung up and redialed, continuing to walk up the central passage.

As he opened the door to the third car, there was a single ring. He stabbed his phone with his finger to redial. The parcel shelf by the door started ringing as the lone policeman checking the inside of the train came into the car. "Hey! There's a bomb. Get off the train."

Turgenev ran, grabbing the phone as he passed, sidestepped out the door, and accelerated up the stairs, not stopping until he reached his bike.

As he passed the place where the 2CV had been parked, a group of drunken students were milling around. At the sound of his Ural Wolf, all turned, some pointed, most mimicked *Easy Rider* poses.

A five-way junction marked the end of the straight road. The road he had followed behind him, a perpendicular main road going left and right, and two roads in front, splitting in a V-shape.

A junction, but no French car.

He killed the engine and slipped off his helmet. The acrid smell of a car burning oil filled his nose. The sound of the French car had lost none of its distinctiveness: It was on one of the roads in front of him. He leaned over, careful not to drop the bike, and looked down the left fork. No cars moving. The right fork curved away, obscuring anything around the bend.

He replaced his helmet, kicked the bike into life, and followed the curve of the right fork. As the road started to straighten, a junction at the end came into sight. A junction where an old, noisy French car was clumsily turning. He dropped the power, keeping his distance, and followed.

The car tracked the road through a right dog-leg and started to pass in front of a long three-story building. The building was, by English standards, comparatively new, probably late 1960s or early 1970s, and had then been built to a low budget and without any concern for aesthetics.

Reaching the end of the building, the car turned right into an entrance. Turgenev pulled up short and killed his engine. The car went across the front parking lot, pulling up to a barrier protecting a gap between two buildings. A short, scrawny man, seemingly prematurely aged by his unhealthiness, came out from the small hut next to the barrier and was met by the man he had seen in the Silver Spike, who got out of the car. After some discussion, the guard seemed to recognize the occupants and become far more relaxed with them, shaking hands before he walked back to raise the barrier, allowing the car to pass.

Turgenev kicked the bike back to life and moved. Drawing level with the barrier, he saw a gap between the buildings wide enough for cars to be parked on both sides. Professor Armstrong and the man Turgenev had now decided to call *the traitor* were getting out of their car and heading into the gloom next to the building on the right. He strained to see, but couldn't tell whether they had gone through a door or if they had followed some other passage behind the building.

He waited for a moment or two, then started to follow the perimeter. About fifty yards down, a minor road wound around the back of the site, passing buildings displaying a nasty mix of cheap construction and poor planning, coupled with no clear sense of space.

At the very back there was a large parking lot with no barrier and no guard. Turgenev carried on past the lot, following the perimeter road until it connected back to the main road, where he turned back on himself and headed to the rear lot.

He parked, pulling the Wolf into the darkest shadows, obscuring it from the road, and looked for any obvious road to drive through from the front of the site to the rear, but found none. Each new building seemed to have blocked off everything except a few narrow rat-runs for pedestrians. There was only one exit route for the French car.

He walked around the inner perimeter of the site, his eyes scanning like a bird of prey, and jumped over the low wall when he reached the front. Across the road, opposite the entrance, a brick-built Victorian hall with circular stone steps and a circular awning held up by four pillars provided an ideal place to sit and watch the sole exit.

He took stock. The guard had retreated to his hut. The car that Professor Armstrong and the traitor had arrived in was where he had seen it parked. The building to the right of the road behind the barrier was still in complete darkness. The building to the left was lit, and Turgenev could hear the thump of music being played. No one entered, no one left.

With his position staked out, he slipped out the phone he had retrieved from the train and started flicking through. It didn't make much sense, but it was interesting.

There was a text message with someone called Monty. The sentence "Perhaps he's found a pot of gold!?!" caught his eye. That alone bought Professor Armstrong five minutes longer to live while he extracted the details from her.

The photos were also interesting. Interesting in their dullness. No one took dull photos—what looked like photos of pieces of paper—if the photos didn't matter. He checked the timestamps: They were shot less than an hour ago.

It was going to be an interesting chat with the professor.

There was a sound from the hut. Turgenev jerked his head up to see the guard out of the hut and looking agitated. He had a phone in his hand, which he was clumsily dialing.

The shaven-headed Russian watched as the guard lifted the phone to his ear and started talking. The guard looked up, down, left, right, and several times at the 2CV. He pointed, gestured with his head, stood still, started to move again, nodded vigorously, and then put the phone in his pocket, remaining outside the hut like a small child desperate for the lavatory, nervously trying to control himself and stay strong.

After twitching for a while, he raised the barrier as if expecting someone to arrive, and stood in the middle of the road, waiting.

forty-six

Ellen led Boniface from the corridor into the office.

The very small office.

Against the wall separating the room from the corridor were three four-drawer filing cabinets, each a different color and showing a different manufacturer's logo, and all showing signs of wear with dents, scratches, rust, and paint patches. All had the customary two holes drilled above the lock to gain access when someone had lost their keys.

A small desk—at least Boniface guessed it was a desk under the stacks of papers and files—faced the door with its edge against the wall. One pile of papers was acting as a telephone stand for a gray phone with a knotted cord, and toward the wall sat an old computer, complete with 12-inch cathode-ray-tube monitor and circa-1983 clicky keyboard. A gap of about two feet was left to act as a passage between the desk and the filing cabinets, guiding the occupant to the chair behind the desk, which looked to have about as much comfort as one of Nigel's car seats.

"So how do we get from the secretary's office into Nigel's?" asked Boniface.

"Very funny."

"You're kidding." Boniface opened his eyes wide and let his jaw drop for emphasis. "This is it. This? This is Nigel's office. I was doing the press for a bloke who wasn't even worthy of a window? No wonder he was a bit nutty. I'd go like that if I had to spend all day in here."

Ellen followed the well-worn trail on the carpet and sat behind the desk, turning on the computer. "Clear off the top of the filing cabinets and lay the papers out there." She pointed with a sweeping motion to the tops of the three cabinets, which were covered with dying plants, dust, and more unspecified piles of papers, books, and files.

Boniface picked up the first flowerpot, finding it to be much lighter than he expected. "Nigel didn't have green fingers, did he?" Ellen drew her mouth tight and shook her head. He picked up the other plant, which was equally light, and placed the two in the corridor outside Nigel's office door; then proceeded to move the papers, stacking them in the free corner, finishing his edifice by lining the books along the wall.

He opened the case and rested it on one of the piles on the desk, removing the contents. The paper was new, but for Boniface it could have been historic archives. Careful to ensure no damage and that none of the papers had stuck together, he laid them out over the top of the cabinets, taking time to place each page and then reorder their positions until he was sure each page had been laid near to other pages with similar information.

"What am I looking for?" He turned to Ellen, who was transfixed in front of the computer screen, her head balanced on her hand, propped up by an arm resting on her knee.

"I don't know," said Ellen, her lower jaw remaining stationary on her hand, with the top of her head moving up and down as her mouth opened. "I guess that what he wrote in those notes was a combination of old information he was trying to link with the new material, so it would be good to know where one starts and the other finishes."

She sat up and started typing as Boniface tried to make sense of the contents of Nigel's briefcase. "No...not that...try something else..." Ellen had started to grumble, each grumble being followed by a burst of clicking.

The concentration was broken by Boniface's phone ringing. "It's for you," he said, opening the phone and passing it to Ellen.

"H...h...hello...? This is Ellen." Boniface returned to his papers, reading and reordering without finding any sense. "Monty!" In the short time he had known Ellen, he hadn't heard her so enthusiastic or excited. "No, I'm fine. It's been a bit of a long day. Shouldn't you be asleep? You haven't been watching the UK TV news? Good. No. Bit of a strange story...nothing to worry about... I'll explain it tomorrow, but if you see anything about me, ignore it... Yeah, big mistaken-identity thing."

Boniface looked over, catching Ellen's eye, and whispered, "Ask her about those storage things... Can she get in?"

Ellen mouthed "yes," and Boniface turned back to his conundrum, allowing Ellen to chat without being watched or overheard.

"I'll pick you up at Heathrow tomorrow morning. Yes, I'll be with Boniface." Boniface heard his name and spun to see Ellen staring straight at him, finishing her call. "Montbretia's looking forward to meeting you." She held out her hand to return the phone.

Boniface took it, his face registering confusion.

"She's heard the whole Nigel hero-worship take on you." Ellen grinned mischievously. "She wants to know if you're really that good."

"You seem to tell your sister a lot."

"We're close. We talk. It's not unusual, Boniface."

He pondered, carefully choosing his words. "No, but...now don't misinterpret this...and I know you've had a really bad night, but you seemed different talking with her. Your voice had some real enthusiasm, some real warmth." Ellen's eyebrows moved closer. "It's not a bad thing...quite the contrary. It's...I dunno...nice."

"We're close. We talk a lot. Well, talk, email, send text messages, whatever. We communicate a lot." Her face fell slightly, looking more serious. "We're sort of all each other has got."

The room was silent. Boniface waited, watching as Ellen connected with something deep in her subconscious.

"We've always been...it sounds pretentious, but I guess you would call it connected. Always. When mom died, we were the only ones who understood each other. But when dad died two years ago..."

"Jeez, I didn't know, I'm sorry."

"It's alright, we're... She's my sister." She sat straighter. "Anyway, apparently everyone uses these online storage things these days—thumb drives, hard drives, they're all for old fogies." She grimaced, slightly chagrined. "Tells me, doesn't it?"

"And me too," said Boniface, feeling mildly scolded and embarrassed by Nigel from the grave. "Once she finished telling you off, was she able to help?"

"I tried what she suggested, and it didn't work." She forced a weak smile. "Monty said that maybe we could get the password reset."

"Why don't we do that?" Boniface heard the enthusiasm in his voice.

"Because then they'd send a new password to Nigel's email address."

"What's the problem with...?" Boniface paused as the realization clicked. "And we don't have the password for Nigel's email."

"True." Ellen stood and walked to the cabinets, casting her eye over the papers. "So what have we got?"

"Not a clue. You're the historian," said Boniface. "As far as I can tell, there seem to be two family trees. One is the Henry and/or Wolsey tree, setting out the offspring attributed to Henry. Even if, after a certain point, Wolsey may have been Henry. It sort of seems to fit with what we know, as in he's looking at four children, including FitzRoy, the illegitimate one."

Boniface laid a finger on one of the papers and waited for Ellen's gaze to reach his finger.

"And while I'm in a pointing mood, this name," Boniface slapped his finger on another piece of paper, "seems to be coming up a lot tonight." Boniface moved his finger around as Ellen followed the references. "But I don't get the link. Or rather, I see the link; there's some guy called John Stephens who seems to have been alive, but young, during the reign of Henry and/or Wolsey, and this John Stephens has some descendants who are quite familiar to us." He stepped back, allowing Ellen to move closer to the cabinets. "You can see Nigel's drawn out the family tree."

She raised her eyebrows.

"So let me throw out a bit of idle speculation." Ellen frowned and looked toward Boniface. "Mister Longhair, may he rest in peace, implied that he had a buyer for his information."

"He did," said Ellen.

"Given the name that's on these pieces of paper, it would seem reasonable that he was a potential buyer, would it not? He has all the necessary qualifications to be a buyer: delusions of grandeur and stacks of cash."

"Perhaps." Ellen turned back to the papers, following the family trees with her finger.

"Have a look and tell me; I've got some hacking to get fixed. And maybe after that, we need to pay a visit?"

Boniface stepped back to carry on his conversation while resting against the doorframe. "Guess who?" He had connected before he heard the ringing tone. "I'm somewhere in London, but given that your boss's henchman has been chasing us around, you'll understand my caution while talking to you on your work-provided phone."

Boniface waited for the hurt feelings to subside before he continued. "I've got details of the online storage thing for you. Have you got someone lined up for us? All I need is for him to send me the password, and I'll take it from there."

He watched as Ellen studied the paper arrayed over the tops of the cabinets.

"So can he do it as soon as?" Boniface waited, listening. "Sure, I understand. Give me a call when he's on the case." Ellen swapped two sheet of paper. "By the way, any word on Mister Turgenev?" Ellen looked up, as if she had received a mild electrical shock. "No, we haven't seen him or heard from him for a while, but I'd rather not bump into him for a day or two... Okay... Thanks."

Boniface flipped his phone shut. "Have you found anything?"

"Nothing." She sounded disappointed. "I think we need to make the visit as you suggest."

"You've been there before. Will there be a computer there?"

Ellen grimaced. "Technically, I think it's called a computer, but what I saw last time was rather steam-powered."

"But it will connect to the internet?"

"I suppose." Ellen did not radiate confidence.

"And I'm presuming you can talk us past the front door. As you know, my relationship isn't exactly warm."

"There's little choice. I'll do what I can do." A door squeaked at the end of the corridor. "What was that?"

"The noise?"

"Mmm."

"We're not expecting visitors, are we?"

forty-seven

Turgenev became aware of a flickering light some way off accompanied by engines straining and wheels squealing: the sound of cars being driven at high speed.

He stopped looking through the professor's emails on her phone, slipping the device he had spent most of the evening chasing back into his pocket as the flickering soon turned into flashing blue lights, and the sound of speed turned into two silver BMW 5 Series with police markings turning through the main university entrance and heading toward the sick-looking guard, anxiously waiting by his raised barrier.

The guard bent down to talk to the passenger in the first car, pointing in the direction that Professor Armstrong and Boniface had gone. Slowly he returned to vertical, indicating their car, and then pointed to a few other points of interest, getting into his stride as a fellow member of the extended law-enforcement community. Finally, he stood back as the two cars accelerated through the gate.

Four officers got out, had a brief conversation, and then disappeared into the same dark hole where the occupants of the French car had gone.

The guard watched the police. As they disappeared, he closed the barrier and returned to his hut, walking with a swagger that hadn't been present a few minutes ago—in fact, probably had never been present in his life.

Turgenev waited for thirty seconds and then started walking toward the barrier. He feigned interest as he walked up to the security guard, who had boldly strutted out of his hut to greet the approaching stranger. "Busy night?"

"It is." The guard had the look of a man still feeling the pump of adrenalin and wanting someone to listen to his tale.

"What's going on?" asked Turgenev, looking around as he approached the guard, becoming aware of the pounding beat from the building behind the hut.

"You'll never believe who's just gone into the offices over there..." Turgenev raised his eyebrows. "She's the one on the news who murdered that..." said the guard, tucking in his stained shirt as the Russian stopped in front of him. Turgenev's right hand flashed forward, slamming the butt of his palm into the guard's solar plexus.

The guard crumpled like a pile of dirty laundry in front of Turgenev, who then crouched next to the body lying at his feet. Taking the guard's head, he twisted sharply, releasing as he felt a sharp crack. He looked around and fixed on a row of dumpsters at the far end of the parking lot. With a single movement he picked up the guard's corpse and carried it over his shoulder, as if it were no heavier than a backpack.

The Russian opened the lid to the first dumpster. Full. The second. Full. The third. Half full. The fourth. Empty. Perfect. He eased the body into the dumpster, closed the lid, and walked back to the guard's hut, placing his hand on the door handle.

There was a noise, shuffling of feet, voices, and laughter. "I am so wasted." Two guys, looking like students, stumbled out from the building behind the hut. "It's too loud in there, but I still need some..."

"Alcohol?" offered the other, turning to see Turgenev by the guard's hut. "Hey man…where's…?" He tapped his finger as if tapping an invisible horizontal bar, looking for Turgenev to supply the answers.

Turgenev raised his eyebrows. "He's gone to…"

"Have a piss," continued the first student. "That guy's never here. We're going to get some more alcohol, so you"—he pointed to Turgenev—"you are in charge until he gets back. And I want a full written report on my desk by the time I return." The two burst into laughter and started moving toward the outer gate.

The Russian waited until he was sure that their goldfish-like brains had forgotten him, then tried the handle.

The door opened, releasing the stale smell of cheap coffee, even cheaper cigarettes, and poor choices in personal hygiene. Turgenev wrinkled his nose in an attempt to block his nostrils as he let the foul air rush out, each individual molecule desperate to be gone from the fug. "There'll be no widow weeping beside your grave," he said as he stepped into the hut.

A small television showing 24-hour news flashed up Professor Armstrong's picture, followed by a live report from outside a small floodlit house surrounded by crime-scene tape. Next to the television sat a few chipped and dirty coffee cups, an overflowing ashtray, a small pile of newspapers, a few official-looking forms, and a battered clipboard listing people and vehicles who had come and gone. Collectively, the debris managed to hide the desk on which the clutter stood, which in turn obscured the filled trashcan sitting on a cheap piece of linoleum worn through in places, with tracks remembering the route into and out of the box, the position of the feet of the occupant as he sat watching TV, and the route of the casters on the chair as it moved in its tiny orbit. "Would it have hurt you to tidy up?" Turgenev asked under his breath. "After all, you're not that far from the dumpsters."

He turned off the television, flicked the switch to stop the buzzing strip light, and stepped out of the cabin. Sucking in clean air, he closed the door behind him and lifted the barrier.

forty-eight

Eric Whittaker quietly closed the car door as he tried to relax into the thinly padded seat after another fruitless attempt to find out what was happening with Richard Sherborne at Trumpeters' House.

He was still pissed about being excluded from whatever was going on tonight—someone said they had a sting set up to catch Oscar von Habsburg—but instead, he had been told to sit outside the fat man's house. The woman in the fuchsia jacket told him he had been chosen by the editor, Veronica Rutherford, but he could smell bull when he heard it.

He had lost count of how many loops he had made, but still he diligently recorded his notes from each reconnaissance. This last loop had been the outer circuit, the route he followed for every two inner loops that he completed. He preferred the outer loop: It was more scenic, and he could also complete it much more incon- spicuously. It took him down Old Palace Lane where he had parked, and when the road ended at the River Thames, he would turn left along a broad stone path past a classical three-floor sandstone-block mini-mansion.

After a high wall, an iron fence separated Trumpeters' House and its long orna- mental garden from the path. Beyond Trumpeters' House, there was another high wall shielding something that he couldn't see in the darkness but that he suspected was an apartment block, and finally there was a short row of three houses at the end of the path. He would then turn left from the river into Friars Lane—a wriggling back street with a mix of old terraced houses, a parking lot, a converted church, and some newly constructed houses built with old bricks—which led him back onto Richmond Green.

Around the edge of the Green were imposing three-story Georgian townhouses, brick-built with white plaster details, sash windows, imposing wooden front doors, and iron railings to the street. After the townhouses came another high wall; on this one, every brick looked about five hundred years old. This wall curved sharply to the left, going through ninety degrees before meeting the building behind it at an arched gateway over the road: The Wardrobe, a strange name for a road, but he couldn't change that.

The inner loop was riskier, and so the need for a disguise—to be changed for each loop—was greater. He looked to the pile of clothes thrown across the back seat: a gray, shapeless jacket, old combat pants, a nylon rainproof jacket, a flat cap, a fedora, and several different-colored baseball caps lay on the top of the heap. Each chosen, alone or in combination, to give him a different look when he stepped out from the shadows and onto the broad footpath that ran perpendicular to the road as he began his inner loop.

The wall on the left of the path offered him fresh shadow cover as he passed some newer—1970s, Eric guessed—houses. The next houses were set back from the path. These looked like a row of almshouses but were probably converted to executive homes by a smart developer whose mantra was location, location, location.

After this, the path ended abruptly, tossing him into Old Palace Yard: a teardrop of grass encircled by buildings.

In the corner was Trumpeters' House—Sherborne's home, and the place he was watching. Like the townhouses around Richmond Green, this was brick-built, with white plaster detailing in the central core and sash windows to the outer flanks. But this house was detached and much wider than the other houses.

Joining the other end of Old Palace Yard was The Wardrobe. Trumpeters' House was impressive, but the buildings along The Wardrobe were spectacular. A simple row of brick-built structures that looked to date from the Tudor period.

From Old Palace Yard he would walk the few steps to the Gatehouse arch and out of The Wardrobe onto Richmond Green to follow the same path as his outer loop. When the road around the perimeter of Richmond Green turned right to follow the outer edge, Eric took the left fork and followed the road as it snaked around into Old Palace Lane, straightening shortly before he reached his car.

It was during one of his inner loops, as he was leaving The Wardrobe, that he had to jump out of the way as the first car sped past, driving up to the gates of Trumpeters' House. A second car arrived not long after, and within a few minutes they had both left.

He couldn't tell how many people had arrived—four, he thought—with three leaving. As was expected of him, he had recorded their details and called them in. By now the owners of the cars would have been traced and every detail held about them on the oracle would have been sent to Veronica Rutherford.

He hadn't seen the next two cars arrive. If he had, he would have hung back and not stepped out from the passage and into the Old Palace Yard as he followed the inner loop. Once he was there he couldn't stop walking, but he had been able to hear the voice of the first man shouting to the second, who was getting into his car before driving away. The man who shouted was young and, from his accent, a Londoner. Eric didn't see what he looked like, but the other man who drove away was probably in his twenties, at least six feet tall, and well built. Eric had carried on with his circuit, calling in the plates and what he had seen before starting another swift circuit, where he had found the yard deserted.

That was an hour ago, and now he was bored and tired.

forty–nine

Turgenev stood, listening to the voices two floors above him. How had he missed finding the business card on the dead body? That was a mistake, but it was interesting to find that the dead man seemed to be a business associate of the traitor, Boniface. This was turning into an interesting story to tell Mister Kuznetsov.

The deeper voice continued. "Mister Boniface. With all your persuasive words, you seem to be forgetting that we have evidence of you having been at a murder scene. As well as finding your business card on the victim, you were identified crossing the bridge onto Thames Ditton Island shortly before the emergency call was made."

When the shaven-headed Russian had followed the route that Boniface, Professor Armstrong, and the four police had taken, he had found that instead of there simply being a dark abyss, around the corner and slightly set back from view there was an entrance. The foyer and stairs covered all three floors, and unlike the brick structure of the rest of the building, this was shielded from the weather by wired safety glass held in a flaking dark-stained wood frame.

The double doors on the ground floor led into a small lobby with vinyl floor tiles and white or beige—he couldn't tell in the gloom—painted plaster walls. Going away from him, the vinyl tiles led down an undistinguished corridor.

To the right, the staircase led to the next floors. The tiles followed the staircase on its slow progress, and the brown wooden handrail mirrored the dull wood in the window frames.

Turgenev stepped into the shadow of the corridor as the sound of Boniface and his escorts arrived at the top of the stairs, the incessant chattering from Boniface digging like a knife into his concentration.

The party began to descend. "What do health and safety say about this?" asked Boniface. "Surely we must be breaking all sorts of regulations? A man with his hands cuffed. I could have a dreadful accident and sue."

"Don't worry, sir. We'll catch you." The second voice was mirthless and insincere, characteristics that were probably finely honed over years of dealing with overly talkative criminals. Turgenev could imagine the look passing between the police at that moment—a wish, a hope, an aspiration, just once to be able to push and administer swift, unequivocal justice.

Without any hurry, the party came to the foot of the stairs. Boniface in the lead, his hands behind his back, two officers behind him—one to either side, going through the monotonous procedure of taking another fool into custody. Being required to hear, but not listen to, Boniface's continuous jabbering, which seem to be lulling the two into a trance.

As they came off the last step, turning toward the brown wood-framed door with its unpleasant wired safety glass, Turgenev silently stepped forward, sliding an arm around the neck of the closest officer and dropping him to the floor before crushing his windpipe under his boot.

Before the second officer could break out of his Boniface-induced coma, he was overpowered, Turgenev dropping his body next to the lifeless corpse of his recently deceased colleague.

"Thank God you're here, Mister Turgenev. You need to help us... I know Mister Kuznetsov's best interests would be well served if you could sort things out. Professor Armstrong is upstairs; she's been arrested too, and she's got the briefcase..."

Turgenev stared at Boniface, held up a single finger, and hissed "Shut up." Boniface went to talk. Turgenev shook his head in a small but decisive move. "Shut up, completely. I want silence." Boniface's body tensed and the bright cockiness in his eyes dulled. Turgenev jabbed his finger at him, like a shepherd telling his dog to stay. "And don't move." Boniface nodded once to affirm, the rest of his body motionless.

The two police radios crackled, breaking the still demanded by Turgenev. He reached down and pulled the first, then the second handset from their attaching wires, silencing them individually, and then searched the officers' pockets. Returning to his customary erect position, he looked at Boniface, murmured "not a move," and then dragged the first body into the shadow of the corridor, returning to remove the second.

He returned, looking through a set of keys, and pushed Boniface toward the door. "Move."

Boniface led as Turgenev directed him to the back of the closest police car. "In," said Turgenev, opening the trunk. Boniface went to speak as Turgenev pushed him, folding his head and legs into the cramped space before he closed the trunk.

As Turgenev reached the top of the stairs, he found the remaining two officers escorting Professor Armstrong, her hands also handcuffed behind her back.

Turgenev stared straight into Professor Armstrong's eyes and watched her quiver. "Good. You've got her," he looked to the first officer. "Did you retrieve the briefcase she stole?" The officer stared blankly. "The briefcase! The briefcase!"

Professor Armstrong relaxed as the two officers looked at each other in confusion. "I'm sorry, sir, we didn't see a case."

"Then come with me," said Turgenev. The officers exchanged a glance. "You come," he pointed to the first. "You stay," he pointed to the second. "She's only a woman. She's in handcuffs—she's not going to do anything."

The first officer started moving back along the narrow corridor, speeding up as Turgenev got closer. They rounded into an office, and Turgenev saw a brown satchel-like briefcase lying on top of a pile of papers on the small desk facing the door. While the policeman still had his back to him, the Russian reached, putting one hand over the officer's mouth and the other over the back of his head; with a single jerk, he twisted.

As the body hit the floor, Turgenev went through his familiar routine: disabled the radio, frisked the body, found another set of car keys, then picked up the briefcase, looked inside it, dropped it, and left the room.

Reaching the other officer, Turgenev smiled broadly. "Your friend is coming. He said he's just checking..." He unleashed a single blow, striking the officer on the side of the head with the base of his hand.

The officer's neck twisted, giving an unnatural deep cracking sound as the rest of his body convulsed, compensating for the force needed to keep the head attached to the top of the neck. As his body moved, the officer stumbled, falling against the top of the banister, continuing to follow the inertia of his head. Turgenev gave a firm push to the officer's shoulder, and the momentum took the body over the rail, landing with a cluster of dull, soggy, impacts.

Turgenev turned to Professor Armstrong, who had tears starting to form in her eyes, and pointed toward the stairs. "I'm not going to have any trouble with you, am I?" She shook her head, taking her first steps.

As they reached the bottom of the stairs, Professor Armstrong delicately walked around the edge of the indistinct lump dressed in dark blue. Turgenev performed his customary procedure, then stood back, muttering to himself, "Why bother?"

He shoved her through the double doors and toward the car, opening the back door. "In."

Professor Armstrong gingerly put one foot inside the car, leaning to support herself while trying to reach with her hands still cuffed behind her back. "Faster," said Turgenev, pushing her as she fell in a heap in the rear foot well, before slamming the door with a kick.

He pulled out his phone and opened the map, waiting a few seconds for the data to download, then zoomed out until he saw the river. He moved the map, following the River Thames downstream, searching for a place to float two more bodies once he found out what they had to tell him. He flipped to the satellite view. It was perfect: a small, quiet access road, a discreet parking place by the river, no overlooking houses. What more could he ask for?

fifty

The road had changed.

There had been a very twisty-and-turny section—they had turned right out of the university, so Boniface guessed that was the Kingston one-way system—which then led to a fairly straight but lumpy road. At some point the car had turned off that road and had travelled more slowly on a road with a smoother, undulating surface.

The undulation gave way to an uneven road with potholes, which then seemed to be replaced by stony ground, with the car kicking up rocks under his head. After several twists, the car skidded to a halt, relieving Boniface's handcuffed body of the shakes and jolts of traveling.

Unaccustomed to the silence but becoming aware of the ringing in his ears, he listened and felt the movement of the vehicle. The driver got out, opened the rear door, and said something. Boniface couldn't make out what he said, but he guessed the passenger in the back was being invited to take some night air.

The car leaned. The passenger was probably being encouraged very strongly to stand up and come outside. As the car righted itself, he listened to the sound of footsteps on the stones. One set was sturdy, strong, and sure-footed. The other set of footsteps was lighter and uncertain, each step either a hesitant stumble or a move to correct a stumble.

After about ten steps, the sound of footsteps ended. This was probably where the stones ended, guessed Boniface. His conjecture was confirmed when he heard one set of feet—the heavy, sure-footed set—return.

The trunk lid opened, and Boniface took a few moments to allow his eyes to adjust to the light, even though it was only the ambient light from a few stars and a new moon. He became aware of Turgenev's presence as the Russian's arm came toward him, first pulling his feet over the lip, and then reaching back to lever the rest of his body out of the trunk. Flipping over the lip of the trunk, Boniface stumbled and fell, confirming for himself that the car was parked on some large and roughly cut stones.

"Get up," said Turgenev, slamming the trunk and pulling Boniface by his handcuffs, already in motion away from the car. Like a wild animal that is born as the herd migrates, Boniface had to walk or perish. By the third step he had found his balance.

After a few more steps, the stones ended, giving way to a grass verge, the junction demarcated by a row of vertical wooden fence posts, occasionally interspersed by large rocks. Boniface looked ahead: The man was obsessive; they were by the river again, and he remembered what he had seen the last time Turgenev was beside a river.

Boniface was jerked to the right and saw Ellen, kneeling, perhaps five feet away from the river, her hands also cuffed behind her back. Turgenev pushed Boniface next to her. "Kneel."

"Not really dressed for this, are you?" Boniface saw her eyes fill with a mixture of joy, hope, and then fear as she winced, watching Turgenev slap Boniface.

"Shut the fuck up, Mister Boniface. And if you can't be quiet, you can watch your girlfriend swim, and if she doesn't swim very well, then you can go in and help her."

"This isn't a good place to dump bodies," offered Boniface, forcing an air of joviality into his voice but watching Ellen's face register growing terror. Turgenev swung around, and Boniface flinched. "I'd prefer it if you don't hit me. But I am serious; look at the river." Turgenev raised his head and looked. "The river's tidal here, and you can see the tide is coming in; so if you dump us, we won't float away."

Turgenev's face registered a strange combination of anger and relief as the other man looked back to the silver BMW, pointing at it with his eyes. "But you have already decided to get rid of that, haven't you?"

The Russian cocked his head, an implied question without losing face by asking.

"By now they're going to have noticed a missing car…" said Boniface, as if to imply it was obvious, "and they'll be out looking. They'll be able to track it."

"Of course," said Turgenev, looking marginally surprised to be agreeing with Boniface.

"If you put it in the river, then that'll focus them on the car—they won't know which direction you went."

Boniface caught a change, as if Turgenev had recognized that he was trying to take control, and he continued less forcefully. "We'll stay here. You go and deal with the car." Turgenev looked to the car, then back to his two prisoners and back to the car. "Come on, we can't go anywhere. Look at her heels. She's not going to do any running in those, is she?"

Turgenev reluctantly started walking backward toward the car, keeping his body facing the two. He pulled the door open, looking puzzled.

Like a ventriloquist, Ellen murmured, "Why do you want him to dump the car?"

"Not a clue," said Boniface, his mouth equally fixed. "We need to slow down whatever happens next. I haven't really been in this sort of situation before."

"Silence!" There was no ambiguity in Turgenev's instruction, but he was now on the move, looking for something. He picked up one of the rocks around the edge of the parking area, walked back to the car, and sat in the driver's seat with the door open, the rock on his lap, and one leg trailing out of the door.

He started the engine and eased the car back from the wooden pickets around the lot; slipped the car into drive; stood up, keeping one foot on the brake with the other on firm ground; and dropped the rock onto the gas. As the engine picked up revs, he jumped back, releasing the brake to let the car leap forward, snapping the wooden barrier like a row of lollipop sticks.

The police BMW bounced over the grass verge between the parking lot and the river, losing momentum on the uneven ground but moving to the bank, which fell away to the river. As the front wheels passed the precipice, the car fell onto its belly, being pushed by the rear wheels, which increasingly lost their grip, starting to spin in the soft grass as the car slowed to a stop.

Progressively the wheels dug deeper, inching the car forward until eventually the silver vehicle started to tilt on the fulcrum of the edge of the bank. The nose dropped as the rear lifted, raising the wheels from the mud, which then splattered behind as the engine raced.

The car continued to overbalance and started to slide. As the front wheels reached the river, the underbelly slid and the rear drive wheels, spinning rapidly, made contact with the fulcrum, propelling the front of the car into the river and covering the engine and the driver's door. As the River Thames consumed the machinery, the engine started to splutter, the sound muffled by the water. Slowly, starved of oxygen and fed water, the engine moved from spluttering to occasional coughs and then, having taken its last gasp, fell into silence, its rear wheels shuddering to a halt.

Turgenev was back behind Ellen and Boniface, who were transfixed by the drowning car. "What sort of police force doesn't carry guns? It would be much easier and, to be honest, less painful in the long term for both of you, if I had a gun."

"We don't have a police force," corrected Boniface. "We have a police service. You are disparaging the Metropolitan Police Service. The Metropolitan Police Service whose car you have just dropped into the River Thames."

Turgenev lazily slapped him with the back of his hand. "Shut. Up."

Boniface instinctively moved to soothe the pain but found himself pulling on his handcuffs. Slowly he turned his head to face Turgenev. He couldn't make eye contact with the other man, but still he proceeded. "Look... We need to talk..."

Turgenev swung and Boniface flinched, relaxing when the blow didn't land. "We get it. For whatever reason you're not having a good day at the office." Some of the anger seemed to fall from Turgenev's scowl. "We don't care. Really. That's not something that worries us. It's just that we've found something that's kind of interesting, and we were working on it at the university, and we thought—thought—that what we found might be interesting to you."

Turgenev shook his head, menacingly revealing his teeth.

"I know this seems desperate. And believe me it is. Listen for a moment, please." Boniface tried to keep the tension he felt in his throat from reaching his voice, but only partially succeeded. "This whole thing started because of Mister Kuznetsov. Your boss..." Given that Veronica had told him that the Russian didn't seem to be responding to calls from Kuznetsov, Boniface wasn't sure whether to go with boss or former boss, but stuck with the positive.

Turgenev remained impassive.

"What we have found out in the last few hours will be important to your boss. If you can give him this information, then you'll be his hero." Boniface looked closely at Turgenev, noticing an involuntary flinch of excitement he had been hoping to elicit. "If we're dead, then that information dies with us."

He stopped and watched Turgenev, who seemed to be ready to listen but not willing to talk. "All I'm suggesting is that you listen to what we've got to say. Nothing more. Then decide."

"So talk," said Turgenev.

"Not here. How long until the police turn up? Five minutes? Perhaps ten? We need to be somewhere else. Anywhere else." He looked around. "Where are we, anyway?"

"Ham House," said Ellen.

"That's your neck of the woods, isn't it? Don't you live up the road? Can't we go round and have a cup of tea to talk things over?"

"Sure. It's about a mile or so back that way." She tossed her head behind her. "Why don't we all go? I'm sure we could have a very interesting conversation with the police who are bound to still be hanging around."

"Okay. Point taken," said Boniface. "I suggest we go down-river."

"Why?" Turgenev suddenly sounded cautious.

"Because that's where we've come from," said Boniface, pointing with his nose.

Turgenev jutted his chin, apparently accepting the simple logic. "To make sure we're clear, Mister Boniface, we walk in silence. If you feel the need to open your mouth for any reason—any reason—then you will find your mouth open in the river, with my foot on your throat. Clear?"

Boniface nodded, the last of the color in his face draining as Turgenev yanked him to his feet.

fifty-one

The path running parallel to the river was well worn, the embedded stones polished smooth by years of passing feet. To each side was a soft grass verge, onto which Boniface had fallen twice and Ellen once. At no point had Turgenev shown any sympathy, only frustration at the slow progress and apparent dumb insolence.

After about ten minutes of stumbling, Turgenev stopped the route march.

"Kneel."

Ellen and Boniface both complied, the dampness soaking into their knees as they sunk into the moist ground. "Decide now. Which one of you wants to be drowned first?" The anger in his voice was apparent, but the tone softened, becoming more sinister. "I like water. It's very cleansing. It removes so many forensic details. And we're far enough downstream that you won't float up to the car before the tide turns."

"But you haven't heard what we've got to say," said Boniface. "There was no point in letting us stay alive back there," he threw his head in the direction of the drowned car, "only to bring us here to kill us after we've scraped our knees a few times." Turgenev remained impassive. "But if you need to make a decision, then she goes first."

Ellen shook herself loose from her hypnotic trance. "What? You..."

Boniface laughed. "Kill her, and you lose everything. She is the most important person in your world at the moment."

"So I kill you?" asked Turgenev, his voice flat.

Boniface shook his head, softly tutting. "No. That would be an even worse strategy."

"So I kill Monty? Is that the answer?"

Ellen screamed, "No! Leave Montbretia alone. She's got nothing to do with this. She knows nothing. Leave her alone, and I'll give you whatever you want."

Turgenev stared at her, a big grin spreading across his face, as he reached into his pocket and pulled out a phone. "I believe this is yours."

"My..."

He turned to Boniface. "Your idea, I presume, the phone on the train. She's clever, but I'm guessing you're the cunning one."

"If I was that cunning, I wouldn't be in handcuffs, would I?"

"Enough." The Russian's tone was icy.

"One ques..."

Turgenev glared. "I ask the questions. You answer. That is the only time I need to hear from either of you."

Boniface blurted. "Why does Vanya think you're missing?"

"What?" All emotion had dropped from the Russian's voice.

Boniface talked hesitantly. "Vanya doesn't know where you are—you haven't been returning his calls. It's alright; I told him you were with me and the professor, so you don't need to worry about calling." Boniface relaxed, watching Turgenev's face, partially hidden by the darkness but clear enough to see that the certainty and the absolute resolve, so ever-present, had temporarily deserted him. "But you probably need to worry about keeping us alive, since he thinks that's what you've been doing."

"See, I said you were cunning. I didn't realize that you're a cunning liar."

"No lie." Boniface was almost casual. "I've told my friend Vanya where you've been tonight. I told him you came to Thames Ditton Island, then to Hampton Court, and then to Surbiton. You're not going to deny this, are you?" Boniface saw Turgenev stiffen. "So why did you send that other guy to shoot our friend here, Professor Armstrong?"

Boniface watched the twitches on Turgenev's face, a slight tightening around the eyes and mouth, a wrinkling on the bridge of his nose, perhaps the slightest frown, darting eyes that were just visible in the darkness, each showing as a small flash of light.

"So it was Professor Armstrong that you were after?"

"Why?" Boniface could hear the confused desperation in Ellen's voice, and watched as she asked herself questions, trying to understand the parameters of the enormity of being a murder target, while unprepared to react to such a situation, having spent a life spent in academia.

"It's okay," he whispered to her. He raised his eyebrows and smirked at Turgenev. "I'll explain." Softly he bit his lower lip, a mischievous smile slowing starting to break out. "Were you there when she annoyed Vanya? Did you see him watch that interview and decide to show him how you could sort his problems? A bit of pro-activity in the workplace...but it didn't quite work out like you had hoped, did it?"

There was an unblinking refusal by the Russian to acknowledge. Ellen looked confused and muttered, "I've never met this Vanya. How could I have annoyed him?"

Boniface ignored the professor. "So that's it. You tried to play the big boy, but you don't know who got shot, do you?" He watched as Turgenev tried to keep an impassive face. "Boy, are you in the shit."

Boniface hung his head, trying to keep the glee out of his voice as he continued. "So the shooting outside Professor Armstrong's house. The shooter was your guy. Then you figured the wrong person had been shot, and you tracked her to Thames Ditton Island. I'm presuming it was the same guy who then took the shot through the window?"

He looked back at Turgenev and read the confirmation in his face. "And for the second time, you don't know who was shot. Do you?" He smirked. "Honesty is the best policy. Insanity is the best defense. But for you...I'd leg it. Do a runner, and make sure Mister Kuznetsov can never, ever, track you down."

Boniface looked at Turgenev; he wasn't sure whether he could see rage, confusion, or both, but he took a moment or two to collect his thoughts before he continued. "Your man shot Professor Trudgett. You know, the respected historian and Kuznetsov's golden boy who was going to prove the monarchy are usurping frauds, thereby triggering a nationwide demand for a referendum about replacing the monarchy with a president."

Boniface calibrated the tightening of the muscles in the other man's face. "So aren't you glad we're here to show you a way out of this mess you've created for yourself?"

Turgenev stiffened. "You're talking bollocks, Boniface. Do you think I care about you? I would shoot you here if I had a gun, but I don't so I'll break your neck." He placed one hand on each of Boniface's ears. "All I have to do is twist."

Boniface felt the heat in the hands burning against his ears, heavy exhaled breaths from the other man's nose on the top of his head.

The Russian twisted—his movement a blur of speed—but released the pressure enough so that his hands slipped with rough skin burning against Boniface's cheek and ripped at his ear.

Boniface reflexively sucked in air, and Turgenev returned his hands to their menacing position. "I'll tell Kuznetsov that I found you were working with the professor here. Sherborne's very own historian." He sneered at Ellen. "When I tell him that I have found and fixed his problem before he even knew about it, I'll be his hero."

Boniface felt his heart thumping and his breathing become shallower. He concentrated, trying to regain some calm. Turgenev remained impassive, his hands still in position to twist. "You misunderstand; Vanya already knows he's got a problem with you." He felt the grip on his head tighten. "Maybe you don't get it, which isn't that surprising since you seem much keener on snapping my neck than on listening to a route out."

Turgenev relaxed his grip slightly. "I don't listen because you talk too much. Your talking is giving me a headache."

"I'll be quick," said Boniface. "But could you let go of my head? What you're doing really isn't comfortable."

Turgenev stood up and walked in front of Boniface, facing him, and gave a small shrug, holding out his hands, his wrists exposed while he craned his head forward.

"Be quick and say less. Don't talk faster so that you can say more."

Boniface looked up at Turgenev's scowl and proceeded. "Trudgett was on to something and was about to tell Professor Armstrong when your man splattered his brains over her house. This was inconvenient, so the two of us..." he tilted his head toward Ellen, "the two of us went looking for details. Long story short, there was a loose end, and that loose end seems to be very significant. We were working on it at the university when the police came in...and then you...found us."

"So tell me about this loose end."

"Well, it's loose. We haven't been able to..." Boniface flinched, searching for the word, "tie it up yet."

Turgenev grabbed Boniface's hair, pulling him toward the river. Boniface fell forward, twisting and landing on his arm, which dug into the mud. "No, listen. This is the important point. This is how you get out of here alive."

He hadn't wanted to sound desperate, but he had failed. Turgenev released his hair, letting his head fall to the ground, then rested his boot on Boniface's windpipe. "Get. To. The. Point."

Boniface tried to speak, but found the weight on his throat too intense to create more than a faint hiss. He strained: "If you could release a bit of pressure, please." Turgenev relented, removing his boot, stamping it down in front of Boniface's nose.

"I know I'm not in much of a position to argue, but could we stop the histrionics?"

Turgenev frowned, then his boot connected with Boniface's stomach. "Next time, something will rupture."

"And if you kill either of us, you die." Boniface twisted in pain, gasping for breath. "But if we stay alive..." He waited for Turgenev's attention. "If we stay alive, well, that could be to your advantage. Wouldn't you like some information that Mister Kuznetsov would pay money for?" Turgenev focused on Boniface, his eyes boring into his skull. "Think what you could do. Trade it for cash. Trade it for your life. Trade it for both."

"A desperate gamble on your part, Mister Boniface." The Russian looked ready to strike again.

"Ask yourself one thing." Boniface heard the hint of confidence in his voice. "If Professor Armstrong and I weren't on to something, then why didn't we go to the police? Even a prison cell would be preferable to—and safer than—this."

"So what is this information?"

"If we knew that, do you think I'd be lying here? Don't you think I would've told you that before you tried to twist my head of?"

Turgenev went to kick him again but stopped before making contact, instead turning to watch the river. Boniface released the tension in his neck and laid his head on the wet grass, following Turgenev's movements with his eyes.

The Russian turned back to stare at Boniface. "So you're saying I shouldn't kill you because there's something important."

"Right," said Boniface.

"But you don't know what it is, and the person that did..." the Russian let his dull eyes fix on Boniface, "is dead." His eyes remained on the man lying in front of him. "This is not a compelling proposition, Mister Boniface. I don't see what I lose by your death."

"Again, you're contemplating decisions based on incomplete information." The Russian's face twitched, as it did with each implicit criticism by Boniface. "I don't know what there is—I'm not a historian—but I know there are documents. And I know what these documents show."

"You mean the documents photographed on this phone?" He pulled out Ellen's phone again and tapped the screen. "*Hi Monty, Nigel really excited. Perhaps he's found a pot of gold.* That's what you wrote and then you photographed some pieces of paper." He jabbed his head toward Ellen, who was still silently kneeling a few feet behind Boniface and starting to shiver.

"The documents in those photographs were written five hours ago," said Boniface. "I'm talking about documents created five hundred years ago."

The Russian went quiet. He looked down at the phone and then at Ellen. "So everything on this phone is worthless?"

"Not to me." Ellen's voice was pleading.

"Oops." The Russian lazily flicked his wrist. The phone spun in an arc, hitting the surface of the river about five feet from the bank before it disappeared. "Oh, I'm sorry about that. How clumsy of me." He turned to Boniface. "My patience is wearing thin. You're about to go and make a call on that phone if you don't convince me."

Boniface turned his head back to face Turgenev, rolling his nose through the mud. "There are two threads here—could you hold off with your boot until I've finished?"

The Russian said nothing as Boniface continued. "You saw the dead body on Thames Ditton Island—the guy with the long hair..."

Turgenev's face remained blank, his eyes holding Boniface motionless with their stare.

"He found the documents. He knew where there were more." Boniface watched the unchanging emotion of the other man. "He was talking to us about what he had found when a bullet... Well, you saw the mess."

"Shhhhit." Turgenev spat under his breath, turning away from his two captives.

"So, you understand, the two people who knew the most are now dead." Boniface kept his face blank. "But before he died, Professor Trudgett photographed some of the documents our long-haired friend found and uploaded them to an online storage service."

Something changed on the Russian's face.

"We've tried to access this storage thing but we can't, so we've got a hacker on the job, and we're waiting for him to call back. When he does, we need to be in front of a computer to access the documents."

"How is this hacker going to contact you?"

"He'll phone," offered Boniface.

"And your phone is where?"

"My jacket pocket." Boniface gestured downward with his head toward an internal jacket pocket. The Russian slipped his hand under the other man's jacket, then stepped back, examining his new acquisition.

"And this leads us to the second aspect." Boniface inhaled deeply. "In all our digging tonight, one name kept coming up, and we need to ask that person some questions about his connection."

"The name?"

Boniface tried to guess the likely reaction as he exhaled slowly. Then he braced himself. "Sherborne."

"Now you're fucking with me."

Boniface shut his eyes, bracing against the next kick. When it didn't come, he opened one eye and looked up to see Turgenev smirking at him. "I admire what you're trying to do, but do you think it's not obvious to me that you have been working for Sherborne all along? With that detail, I can explain everything."

"It would appear than you may again be laboring under a false apprehension, and in the interests of me not talking too much, can we just say there is some history, or if you would prefer, unrestrained animosity, between us. So when I say we need to see Sherborne, I'm not kidding." He grinned enthusiastically. "But if you don't like what Sherborne has got to say, then I'm quite happy if you want to kill him. His computer will still work even if he's dead."

"And how do we get to Sherborne?" Turgenev's voice was flat.

Boniface threw his head backward toward Ellen. "He's her publisher; she's been to his house." Turgenev grinned; Boniface corrected him. "She has been to receptions at his house. She couldn't tell you how his bedroom ceiling has been decorated."

Turgenev stopped sneering and looked at Ellen. "And where is this house?"

"About a mile in that direction." Ellen pointed downriver with her head.

"We're going to need a car," muttered Turgenev. "Can you get a car?" He looked back and forth between Boniface and Ellen, both shaking their heads, before grabbing Boniface's handcuffs and yanking him to his feet. He looked to Ellen. "Where's the nearest road?"

fifty-two

Walking on the path had been unpleasant in kitten heels and a fitted skirt, but it was manageable. Leaving the path had taken the experience to a new level of disagreeability.

Rather than follow the established track, Turgenev had taken them diagonally across the meadow at the bottom of Richmond Hill. Ellen lost count of how many times she had slipped or fallen, but now she had ripped her skirt as well as having mud everywhere. Everywhere. And it didn't taste good. Her shoe had become stuck in the mud, twice, and now her feet were encased with gritty mud, which was then wrapped tightly in her shoe. She had cut her knee and grazed her face, and worst of all, she had cow shit in her hair.

Did she say worst of all? No, worst of all—apart from being with a homicidal maniac and a man who seemed to get overly talkative under stress, which led to him trying to cut any sort of deal to stay alive—apart from that, the worst thing was the cow shit.

As they reached the far side of the meadow, there was a steep tree-lined slope, mostly mud, although a few ground plants tightly held onto the embankment between the tree roots, which lay in wait to trip the unwary.

"You." Turgenev directed Boniface to come closer to where he was standing. Boniface took the two steps toward him as Turgenev rummaged in his pockets. "Turn around." Boniface complied. The Russian grabbed the Englishman's handcuffs, lifting them and causing Boniface to bend forward. He tried the small key, which Ellen guessed he had removed from the dead policeman less than an hour earlier, and unlocked the cuffs.

Before Boniface could react, Turgenev jerked him backward, putting his back against a tree, and relocked the cuffs on the other wrist. He turned to Ellen. "It's up to you now. By your actions, you decide whether he lives or dies. And by the way, if he does die, he'll die here. He won't have a calm and relaxing death in the river. It will be slow and it will hurt. And once he's dead, then I'll have a lot a free time to go and find Monty—or what is it you called her, Montbretia?"

Ellen froze, staring straight at Turgenev, defiant but resigned, and with a mud streak across her face, covering a graze.

"Are you paying attention? This is quite simple. You do what I say, or he dies and then Montbretia dies." Ellen bobbed her head once. "Come here. Turn around." Turgenev removed Ellen's handcuffs, slipping them in his pocket. "Up that slope."

Ellen shot him a look of disbelief and was met with an unyielding stare.

"Now."

He shoved her, and she fell forward, beginning the slow ascent up the sharp slope, keeping at least three limbs in contact at all times and using her heels as climbing spikes. She reached the plateau with two shoes and only one kitten heel, puffing through the last few steps, slowly righting herself to find Turgenev waiting.

"We need a car, and you're going to get it." From the plateau, the ground leveled toward a small stone wall. On the other side a car sped past.

"But I don't have a car, and we left the last one at the university when you...when we came with you."

Turgenev looked at her with a mixture of disappointment and frustration. "The road." He pointed to the road the car had passed along. "Stop a car. Make the driver get out and bring them over here."

Ellen stared back.

"And make it convincing. You know what happens to your boyfriend and Montbretia if you mess about."

Ellen looked for any hint of humanity. Any softer side she could appeal to. Any rational logic she could deploy. She found none, just a single finger pointing toward the road.

Across the wall, on the other side there were some bushes and then the road. A few awkward steps—trying and failing to ignore the uneven heels and grit inside her shoes—and she reached the wall, where she sat, lifted her feet, and twisted, adding another rip to her skirt and another bruise on her leg. She then added a further rip as she pushed her way through the bushes to the side of the road.

A small, rusty, Korean-manufactured car headed away from Richmond. She watched it pass and then moved to the side of the road. A pair of headlights came up the hill and turned onto the road heading toward Richmond. Ellen took two steps forward and stood in the middle of the road. There was no need to fake the tears or the rest of her casualty look: The torn clothing, mud spattered everywhere, cuts, grazes, and bruises were authentic.

The headlights hit her squarely as she waved her arms and started to shout, "Stop! Stop! Please stop!"

The driver pulled up and jumped out of the dark blue sedan, leaving the engine running and his door open. A tall, slim man in his early thirties, dressed casually in jeans and a sweater, with wire-rimmed glasses. "What's up?"

"Please, you must help," said Ellen, tears running down her face and mud holding her hair in place. She grabbed his sleeve, bunching the wool in her hand, and pulled him toward the wall. As they passed through the bushes at the side of the road, there was a bright smacking sound—flesh on flesh, and Ellen felt the wool pulled out of her hand as the man fell to the ground.

"Congratulations," said Turgenev stepping out of the shadow. "This way." He pointed back to the car.

Reaching the vehicle, he opened the passenger door. "Please have a seat." Ellen got in and sat compliantly. "Your hands." Ellen looked confused and delicately offered her hands. Turgenev grabbed both arms, clamping them together with one hand, returning the handcuffs to her wrists with the connecting chain hooked over the passenger grab-handle.

And then Turgenev was gone. She saw him briefly look at the body of the man who owned the car, and then she looked away, focusing on the road.

She became aware that Turgenev had returned when the trunk opened: Someone was being stuffed into it. Whoever it was, they were being very compliant but seemed to be trying to engage the killer in conversation.

Turgenev shut the trunk before coming to sit in the driver's seat, closing the door behind him. He pulled out his phone and called up a map. "Show me. Where is Sherborne's house?"

Ellen looked to her hands, shackled around the grab rail, and back to Turgenev. "Could you... The cuffs are really digging into my wrists."

"No. Tell me. We are here." He pointed a dirty finger at the screen. "Where next?"

"To the town center. When you reach the junction with the bridge on the left, going over the river..." Turgenev scrolled the map with his finger, "then you keep going straight. The road goes downhill from there. At the bottom of the hill...look you can see...the road turns right, there's a big shop...well, at that point you want to take the left turn so you sort of go straight. Now pull the map a bit further."

Turgenev complied.

"That road leads onto Richmond Green. Halfway down on the left-hand side, there's a road that turns off."

Turgenev moved the map and zoomed in.

"That road is called The Wardrobe." Turgenev grunted as Ellen gave directions, each location appearing on his map. "As you follow The Wardrobe, you go under a gatehouse—it's a big brick arch. When you come out, Sherborne's house is in front of you."

"Here?" Turgenev pointed a dirty finger that seemed to cover most of Richmond.

"Move your finger back so I can see where you're pointing," said Ellen. Turgenev obeyed. "Yes. That's it."

"But that's impossible to approach without being seen."

"We agreed to take you there. You can't hold us responsible for the architecture. Anyway, I'm sure Boniface can help us get in. Where is he?" Turgenev pointed toward the back of the car with his thumb as he started to rev the engine.

fifty-three

"Here."

Turgenev took the left turn and followed the small side road lined with boutiques, restaurants, and bookstores, all closed. "This leads to the Green?" Professor Armstrong pointed with her eyes as Turgenev pulled to the side, looking at the map on his phone.

He grunted, took another look at the map, and slipped his phone back into his pocket. He edged the car forward, rolling it out of the feeder road at the bottom corner of Richmond Green. On reaching the perimeter road, he turned left. "Not here," said Professor Armstrong. "You turn farther down."

Turgenev checked the road sign: Friars Lane. He followed it, slowly, and as the map had told him, before the road turned to the left there was a public parking lot. He relaxed: lots of shadows.

He backed the car into the darkest corner of the empty lot and then jumped out, opened the professor's door, and leaned in to remove her cuffs. "Get out." As she stood, he bear-hugged her, returning the cuffs with her hands locked behind her back. "This way." He pushed her door shut and led her to the back of the car, flipping the trunk.

"Can I get out now?" Boniface was motionless apart from his head.

"Company for you." He turned to the professor. "Sit." He patted the sill of the trunk. She complied, and he put one hand behind her head while sweeping her feet with his other arm. There was a gentle rip of her skirt as he slid her into the trunk facing Boniface, who grunted as Turgenev pushed the professor fully into the trunk before slamming the lid and returning to the driver's seat.

Retracing his route along Friars Lane, he drove back and rejoined the perimeter road around the Green, slowing as he passed The Wardrobe. As Professor Armstrong had said, there was a brick gateway set back from the road, and although it was dark, he could make out that there were buildings on the other side. There was a slight movement—it might have been a figure coming from the other end of The Wardrobe; he couldn't be sure.

He continued following the perimeter road as it turned right at the corner of the Green, and then parked. As he turned to look back at the entrance to The Wardrobe, he saw a figure walking out from under the gate, wearing an incongruous mixture of a tweed jacket with a blue baseball cap.

The Russian kept the figure in view as it reached the perimeter road and turned left, following the road—behind his stolen car with the two passengers in the trunk—and taking the other fork in the road. According to the map on his phone, the road the man with the tweed jacket and blue baseball cap was following led to the river.

He sat and waited, looking at the road behind him in his mirrors. After about fifteen minutes another figure came out from The Wardrobe. This new figure had a similar height and build to the person who had passed earlier and seemed to have the same gait, walking as if he didn't want his feet to touch the ground. But unlike the previous individual, this one had a blue jacket and a flat cap.

Was this a setup, a fluke, security, or nosiness?

Turgenev waited patiently, focusing on the gate to The Wardrobe.

Nearly ten minutes later, a figure appeared, but this one hadn't come out of The Wardrobe; he seemed to have come from farther back, perhaps from Friars Lane. Turgenev watched, focusing on the details: the same blue jacket and flat cap, same height, same build, same gait, same apparent need to ensure his steps were silent.

Turgenev smiled. Same man. And not a soldier. Sure, he was cautious—to a certain extent—but he wasn't observant. If he had been, he would have noticed the parked car with Turgenev sitting in it, and he would have avoided it or investigated.

That left two options: bad security or press. Security wouldn't bother changing their clothes, so this man had to be press.

He waited for the figure to pass behind his car, take the road leading to the river, and disappear. Once the man was out of sight, Turgenev silently slipped out of the car, keeping low, and slunk, cat-like, following the probable journalist.

He turned into the narrow lane leading to the river and followed the road as it then bent to the left, straightening to point at the Thames. The properties on this side road were different. Where there had been large, grand Georgian townhouses set back from the road around the Green, the houses on this side of the road were more modern—or rather, less old—and were much closer to the road.

The first few were semidetached brick-built houses set over three floors. These gave way to two-story, white stucco-fronted terraces, and then to smaller cottages. Every step down the road was a step cheaper and a step less impressive. There were a few older houses on the left, but these ended shortly, being replaced with a high brick-built wall.

The road was wide enough to fit two cars. On the left was a row of parked cars, with the right side being left free for driving. As Turgenev came out of the bend, he heard a car door close quietly and he stopped, looking for any sign of movement.

The parked cars on the left all seemed to be empty. Some way down the road he thought he could see a light inside a car, or perhaps his eyes were playing tricks.

He ducked behind the row of parked vehicles and slowly moved forward, using the cars as cover while he worked his way up to the end car. There was a break and the next car was parked in shadow, but within that car he could see an outline of a person and a faint glow as if someone was illuminated by a phone. He looked around; there was no other cover and only one choice.

If he was right that this was a journalist, then he would be safe. If he was wrong or plain unlucky, then his next move could be fatal. He dropped to the ground and dragged himself along the asphalt under the last car, resting when he had a worm's-eye view of the probable journalist's car.

The glow was extinguished and the shape started to move, causing the car to jiggle slightly. A man got out, now wearing a khaki trench coat and a fedora. The new wardrobe additions didn't go well with his frayed blue jeans and sneakers.

Turgenev watched as the sneakers came toward him—each step silently placed—before turning to take a path to the right. The silent footsteps moved away; he tried to listen but couldn't hear them over the sound of his own heartbeat.

He pulled himself along the asphalt; rolled into the shadow at the side of the road; stood, wiping off the grit; and then cautiously walked to inspect the path where the journalist had just disappeared.

On the left-hand side of the path was a high wall. To the right were some houses, newer than those on the street where he had been lying. And in the middle, walking his quiet walk, the journalist. Turgenev followed, remaining silent and keeping in the shadows.

The Russian noted the houses on the right, which had given way to a set of smaller, more compact properties, set farther back from the path. He looked back to the journalist, who had disappeared.

Turgenev increased his pace, ducking slightly to lower his height. The path ended sooner than he was expecting, and he found himself in an area with buildings on all sides and a small tear-shaped green area enclosed by a low fence.

He looked at the biggest house and guessed it must be Sherborne's. To the left was the arched gate with a khaki trench coat disappearing underneath. He went to follow, then hesitated, turning to look at the largest building in the enclosure and the row of buildings on the far side, which looked old—perhaps as old as Hampton Court, but he couldn't be sure.

The large building stood in stark contrast to the old buildings. It was taller and a different style. Best of all, it had sash windows.

Turgenev returned swiftly along the path, back to the journalist's car, a faceless Ford with an indistinct color in the darkness and no identifying features. You could forget about it while you stared at it. The perfect car for a journalist.

He cast a swift glance at the terraced cottages on the other side of the road. All were painted a uniform white; the only distinguishing differences were in the small pieces of land between each house and the road. All were paved, but some had made more of an effort to create a courtyard garden.

Two doors up he saw what he was looking for: shrubs. Two shrubs opening into a broad-leafed canopy at a height of about four feet. Turgenev quickly hid and waited; if the journalist stuck to his routine, he would be returning to his car at any moment.

He didn't hear him; the footsteps were still silent, but he did see the flickering change of light as the journalist moved. Turgenev fixed on him like a bird of prey hovering, waiting for the journalist to enter the shadow by his car. As he saw him go for his keys, Turgenev moved, taking advantage of the distraction.

The Russian reached the journalist before the journalist noticed his approach. Placing one hand over the journalist's mouth, he grabbed the back of his neck with the other and twisted. He became aware of the sound of the journalist's neck reacting to the violence as he broke the fall of the lifeless body, at the same time looking around for signs that the noise had been heard by one of the residents of the street.

He took the car keys out of the journalist's dead hand and checked his pockets, pulling out a phone, a notepad, and some cash.

The body was heavier than he expected, but not so heavy as to slow Turgenev in stowing it under the canopy of the shrubs where he had waited a few moments earlier.

Cautiously, he laid the body on the ground, stood, and turned toward the river.

fifty–four

The trunk lid flipped open, and Boniface could see Turgenev's outline silhouetted against a streetlight.

"Okay, Mister Talkative. It's time for you to do your job. I don't care if you tell me he's not your friend—you're going to get us in to see Sherborne."

Turgenev stepped back, keeping his stare fixed on Boniface; Boniface remained silent, feeling Ellen's breath against his face, her breathing becoming shallow and faster.

"In case you don't understand, let me be clear..." Turgenev's eyes met his and locked. "You will get inside the house. At each step, you will give me"—he held up a phone that Boniface hadn't seen before—"a running commentary. If you fail, she dies. If I think you have failed, she dies. If you say anything unhelpful, she dies. If there is any period of silence, she dies. Clear?"

Boniface nodded.

"And please remember, not only is her life now in your hands, but also the manner of her death. If you make me angry, it will be a very unpleasant, lingering death, and you never know what could happen before she finally expires." He stared straight into Boniface's eyes, slowly rubbing his crotch. "And if she dies, then I'll go and find Montbretia."

Neither man moved.

"So are we clear?" Boniface nodded. "Do you understand?" Boniface nodded. "Is there any room for doubt? Any?"

"No, we're clear. I understand." Boniface's voice was soft, but he still couldn't hide the cracks. He looked at Ellen, trying to reach her through the fear in her eyes, and whispered, "It's gonna be okay. Really. It's gonna be okay." He turned to Turgenev. "What do I do when I'm in?"

"Keep talking. Make sure everyone focuses on you and Sherborne, and I'll send you a signal when I'm ready."

Turgenev reached into the trunk, rolled Boniface toward Ellen, and removed his handcuffs. Slowly and cautiously, Boniface began to lift himself out of the trunk, slipping and taking a few steps to regain his balance as he reached the road. As he stood up, he saw that the trunk had been closed behind him. "Come on. Make her comfortable."

"No."

"It will help me...focus." Boniface kept his gaze on Turgenev. "I understand my mission, but you need me to succeed. You don't want me to be distracted. And if you just say yes to this one thing, then I'll shut up and we can start."

Turgenev exhaled, laboring the breath, and flipped the trunk open. Boniface watched as the Russian rummaged inside the trunk and found an old tartan blanket, which he placed under Ellen's head. His raised eyebrows asked the question as he indicated the academic in the trunk. Boniface pulled his mouth tight, and Turgenev shut the trunk.

"Here's your new phone," said Turgenev, reaching into his pocket and pulling out the phone he had just shown to Boniface.

"That's not mine."

"It is for now. Don't worry; I'm still keeping your phone safe."

"You remember that we're expecting a call?"

"And you will remember that you're on your best behavior."

Turgenev reached into his jacket pocket and pulled out a small Bluetooth earpiece before dialing a number on the phone. He touched the earpiece, then slipped the phone into the breast pocket of Boniface's jacket. "Now say something."

"Testing, testing. One two," said Boniface flatly.

"Now walk and talk, and remember that I'm listening and you know what happens if you fail."

Boniface walked 50 yards around the edge of the Green, then crossed to follow The Wardrobe, soon passing under the arched gateway. "Right, I've just come under the arch, and I'm now in the...well, I guess you might call it the courtyard, there's sort of a bit of grass in the middle with a road around the outside."

He looked around, then recommenced, willing his voice loud enough that Turgenev could hear but not loud enough to draw attention. "Er... Well...I guess you know what's here, but given that silence on my part is bad, let me give you a commentary. I've come through the arch, but I've told you that already. In front of me is a teardrop-shaped piece of grass. On the left, some very old buildings; they look like they were built around the same time as Hampton Court, but I'd like to see them in daylight. To the right, there are some garages. I guess they're attached to the houses out there. There are also a few cottage-like houses on the right, facing onto the teardrop of grass."

Boniface took three steps. "I'm starting to move now; I hope you can still hear me. So, on the right, beyond the cottages, we've got a gap. I guess there's a path that leads out of here."

He continued walking. "In front of me, there's the house. Three floors...no two, I think what looks like the top floor might be the loft—there's only a window in the center block. More modern than the buildings on the left, but I'm still guessing it dates from around the 1700s. It's what I think is called English Baroque or maybe Queen Anne style. I'm sorry; I never was an architecture student. The roof slopes at a gentle angle, mock columns, rendered exterior in the center, brick wings outside that, sash windows. On the right, there's what looks like a separate stable block, but that could be something to do with the next set of houses. I don't know; it's too dark to see them from here, and I'm not going to have a look."

There was a white car parked with its nose against the gates. Rust was starting to show around each wheel arch, each door lock, and every joined seam—rust that was visible even in the poor light of the courtyard. "I'm at the gates now. There's a car parked up against them. It's old and showing signs of rust. If I were Sherborne, I'd call the police to come and move it, so I presume whoever drives it is inside." He laid his hand on the hood. "The engine feels warm. Not hot, but warm."

He looked up at the gates. "Okay. Gates. Tall, metal, iron I think, two of them. The one on the left is partially blocked by the car, and the one on the right has the knob to open it. Both seem to open inward, so the car shouldn't be a problem. Inside the gate you've got a few cobbles, then the door. Well, I say cobbles, more like stones set in concrete. I'm going to try the gate now." He twisted the knob, which had lost the definition of its decoration through layers of paint over the years, and pushed.

The gate swung comparatively freely, making a smooth swishing sound from the hinges as they twisted.

"Gate opening." He gingerly stepped, his eyes scanning. "Gate closing, but I'm leaving it balanced on the lock, so all you have to do is push it open. I'm on the cobbles now." He took four paces before reaching the steps to the door. "Big door. I dunno, seven feet high, three feet wide perhaps. Maybe more. Probably more. Anyway, big, solid letter box, door knocker, no obvious windows in the door, but one over the door, and sash windows, two panes wide and full height, to either side of the door. Several locks visible from the outside. I can't see any sort of CCTV cameras. Nor can I see any other bell or buzzer, but it's pretty dark around here, and I can't see anything through the windows; it's dark in there." He grasped the knocker and banged twice. "Let's see what that does. We're going to replace the commentary with some whistling while I wait."

Before he could purse his lips, a light came on inside, and there was the sound of movement. "Right, I've got something. There's movement."

A few more lights came on, and finally the door opened. A tall, solid man in his late twenties answered. Boniface looked him up and down. The dark-blue blazer over a white shirt with a dark single-color tie and charcoal pants suggested his role. The severe haircut reinforced the assumption. "Evening, sir. How can I help you?"

"I didn't realize Mister Sherborne had taken on additional security. Are you alone, or are there more of you prowling the grounds?"

"Sir. Please."

"I'm sorry, I'm a bit shocked. I came round to see dear old Dickie and wasn't expecting to see a large chap like you. What are you six-three?"

"Sir." The guard was becoming insistent.

"Oh, I'm sorry," said Boniface, giving his best disarming smile. He offered his hand. "I'm Alexander Boniface, I need to see Richard as a matter of urgency. He's expecting me, and if he isn't, he should be. There may have been a few crossed wires in the communications tonight."

The guard remained impassive. Boniface took a step forward and was stopped by a large raised hand.

"Ask Dickie. He's expecting me."

"One moment, sir." The immovable object seemed unwilling to yield and pulled a radio from his outer jacket pocket, flexing awkwardly as he reached across while he kept his other hand holding Boniface in his place. "I've got a Mister Bon... I'm sorry, sir, your name?"

"Boniface. Alexander Boniface."

"Mister Boniface. Seems to think he's expected. Could you check?" There was static and a mumbled voice.

Boniface looked inside the jacket, under the arms as the poorly fitting garment twisted with the guard flexing. "So how long has Dickie had armed guards looking after him?" Boniface tried to sound casual.

The guard held his pose, seemingly listening to the static.

"It's a nice night to be out, but it's getting a bit chilly. Any chance I could step inside while I'm waiting?" The hand did not waver. "How many of you guys are there here? Is Dickie looking after you properly? Has Ada made you a cup of tea yet? If you were unannounced, then she probably died of embarrassment and started baking immediately."

The verbal war of attrition launched on the guard was broken by a voice at the other end of the radio. Boniface couldn't make out what it said. "Apparently you're not expected, sir."

"I think I am." Boniface was calm. "He had a telephone conversation with one of my associates earlier this evening. He may not have known I was involved, but he is expecting a visit. Check."

The guard's stare, pure cynicism, didn't waver.

Boniface met his gaze, locked on, and waited, calculating how long he could remain silent without Ellen being harmed.

The guard pulled up his radio. "Sorry, Harry. Could you check? The gentleman says an associate of his spoke to Mister Sherborne earlier this evening and that a visit is expected."

There was a static-filled pause followed by some more mumbling.

fifty–five

"Hey! This is an impressive entrance hall. I wasn't expecting it to be so grand. What is it...twenty feet wide and maybe thirty feet deep? Is that about it? And wow... that staircase going up the middle. That's impressive. It must be five feet wide, and the ceiling is, er, ten, maybe eleven feet. And that desk over there on the right..." Boniface leaned his head in the direction of a small, old but not antique, dark wood desk, its top empty apart from a small monitor screen and an out-of-place cheap telephone, its cord twisting over the floor, with a worn leather chair behind. "I didn't see the CCTV when I was outside—where are your cameras pointed?"

"Please sit down, sir," said the guard with an over-articulated accent, indicating the sofa in front of an empty fireplace. "Mister Sherborne will be with you in a moment."

"What? Sit on this dark-green leather scroll-armed Chesterfield-type sofa on the left, with all the greenery behind it?" said Boniface softly but swiftly. "Beside the fireplace, opposite this club chair. Do you ever light this fire? It must get quite cold, what with this marble floor."

Boniface sat as the guard turned, walking toward the desk. "As I said, Mister Sherborne will be with you in a moment."

The guard sat and Boniface stood. "Anyway. You haven't told me. How long have you been working for Dickie?" The guard's face was frozen in a look of interminable anguish. "And how many of you are there working tonight? Perhaps I should go and say 'hi' to your friend on the other end of the radio? And where is the indomitable Ada? I'm dying for a cup of tea."

The guard stood, knocking his chair, which rolled backward, hitting the wall. "That won't be necessary, sir. Please." He indicated the sofa. "Please have a seat." His jaw tightening. "Mister Sherborne will be with you very shortly."

Boniface sat on the green sofa.

There was a sound of activity on the next floor up. Slow, heavy, but irregular footsteps made their way to the top of the stairs and started to descend.

Boniface turned to see highly polished brown shoes appear from the ceiling, pausing at every step, with the same foot lowered each time. He watched as slowly and uncomfortably the obese figure of Richard Sherborne appeared: fatter, older, and closer to death than he remembered. In fact, on first look, it appeared that he could be reaching death at any moment.

With Sherborne creating a distraction, Boniface looked around the hall and hurriedly whispered a commentary. "As I said, large hall. Two suits of armor inside the door I came through. There's some other military hardware on the walls—pikes, spikes, and stuff like that. There are also a few muskets and other gun sorts of paraphernalia—Sherborne has always been interested in armaments. A few pictures, mostly maps and what look like treaties. I'm sure they're all part of the Sherborne family history and that Mister Sherborne will be more than happy to give you a guided tour."

As his host puffed his way to the bottom of the stairs, Boniface stood. Pausing for the first time since he had entered Trumpeters' House, he looked down at his own appearance. In the light he could see his suit was crumpled and muddy. He felt his top button undone with his tie loosened, his face streaked with mud mixed with a few cuts, and a glance at his reflection in one suit of armor told him his hair was styled by a subtle combination of mud, car-trunk fluff, and sweat.

"Well, this is a surprise. I was expecting someone else altogether." Sherborne looked Boniface up and down, sneering at his appearance. "I thought I had seen the last of you, Boniface." The two men faced each other, neither offering a hand.

"Come, come, Richard. Why would you have seen the last of me? You weren't that close to death last time we met."

"Ah, Boniface. Always the cutting tongue. Always a bit too quick with the jibes and too slow with the manners."

"Ah, Sherborne. Always the complete ass." Boniface sneered sarcastically. "You look like you need to sit down."

Sherborne pulled out a handkerchief from his top pocket to mop his brow and dry the moisture in the loose folds of skin around his chin as he waddled to the club chair. He turned and dropped, wedging himself into the seat.

Boniface returned to the green sofa. "So this is Trumpeters' House, where many a young lady has been invited to appreciate your horn performance. Or is that why you've got the guards now? To make sure they don't run away? How many guards have you got to keep those poor women from bolting?"

"Boniface, Boniface. You never could behave like a civilized human being. You always had to take it too far."

"I lack civility? Me?" Boniface couldn't keep the incredulity out of his voice. "You do remember why it is I..." He mentally searched for any word except hate. "Why I...have a problem with you? You do remember what you did to me?"

"And you do remember what you did to the rest of us, especially your poor wife?" Sherborne struck Boniface with a look of patrician disappointment.

A quiet fell over the room as the two men stared at each other, apparently content with the deadlock.

Boniface broke the still slowly and tentatively. "I remember. I remember and I regret. I hurt people—most of all I hurt Veronica—and I let people down. Any cliché going, that was me. And that's part of the reason I have to ask my few friends and old contacts to help me find scraps of work."

"You did more than hurt people, Boniface." Sherborne's look of disappointment remained. "You were always good at your job, but you didn't respect yourself for what you did. I'm guessing you're good at whatever it is you do now, but you still don't respect yourself. And if you don't respect your work, then your clients will think you don't respect them. You can't blame me for your situation."

"Can't blame you!" snapped Boniface. "I blame you for taking me from unemployed to unemployable. I know I was a mess, and I can't believe how many people didn't fire me—and I'm sure I kept several jobs only out of kindness to Ronnie—but once I was down, you didn't need to come in and give me such a good kicking."

"You deserved that for the way you treated Veronica."

Boniface hung his head, his eyes misting, his voice soft. "I did." He stared back at Sherborne. "But not from you. Not from you, Richard. All you did was to hurt Veronica by hurting me."

Sherborne winced. "How is darling Vron?"

"All the better for not working for you." Boniface paused, then carried on in a less strident tone. "But you will always look petty to her, and she blames you for the breakup of our marriage…" Boniface wasn't sure if it was true, but looking at Sherborne's reaction, he knew the comment stung.

A quiet fell across the room again. The guard moved in his chair, the creak of old leather breaking the trance as Boniface continued. "Anyway, I'm not here to talk about the failure of my marriage. I've come to Richmond Palace for a reason. This is Richmond Palace, isn't it? Richmond Palace, home for discarded Queens."

"Not quite, but close. Richmond Palace was…"

"History later, Richard. Let's talk about your newspapers." Boniface cut Sherborne's explanation short. "If I asked, I'm sure you would tell me you don't interfere in day-to-day editorial matters with your papers."

"And I don't," said Sherborne definitively, but somehow still managing to sound huffily defensive and confused about where Boniface was taking the conversation.

"But everyone knows you do, and I know that you will personally review any matter relating to the royal family." Boniface ignored the annoyance in Sherborne's face. "Some people, not me of course, but some people—you know those nasty, crude, gutter-inhabiting scumbags of the press—well, some of them might suggest this interest in the royals is due to your alleged friendship with Princess Heidemarie."

Boniface sat back squarely on the sofa so that he could look directly at Sherborne. "Some think that because of your *friendship*, you are keen to support the royals. Me, I'm the skeptical sort. I'm also the sort that likes a good rumor, especially a rumor about royalty and illegitimate children. And you know there's always been that rumor—the rumor that now gets regularly photographed falling out of all the nightclubs in London and occasionally playing polo. That's when he's not being caught by the newspapers trying to sell access to the royal side of his family."

"Oscar," said Sherborne gently. "He has a name, and it is Oscar."

"Oscar." Boniface looked conspiratorially around the room. "Now I wonder; is your motivation misunderstood?"

Sherborne frowned, like a bad actor without a speaking part, exaggerating the confusion he was intending to communicate in the hope of getting noticed by the director. "You're perplexing me, Boniface. We've had our differences—I know—and you've written some beastly things about me in the past…"

"Which were true, Richard."

The fat man grumbled under his breath. "That's a different conversation, Boniface. But what you have never done is behave like those—what did you call them—gutter-inhabiting types. Unlike many of your contemporaries, you never went after Oscar. Even when you were a drunken mess, losing jobs, and had a reason to disagree with some of my actions, you never took out your anger on Oscar." He softened his voice. "You have always been very principled in that way. Very honorable. And I respect that and hope you aren't about to change."

Boniface flushed and nodded his acknowledgement of the thanks before continuing. "And I'm still never going to go after Oscar as a way to attack you, but I do wonder with all this talk about a referendum whether you have a game plan that no one has twigged yet."

Boniface stood and looked down at Sherborne. "Kuznetsov's game is easy. He wants to become president as a power grab. For him it's pure greed—he thinks that if he achieves a referendum, then there will be a clamor for republicanism, and he will be best placed to stand as president. In truth, he wants to be a Tsar to legislate for his own benefit, primarily to take control of the banking system—or at least the regulation of the banking system."

Sherborne looked up.

"But for you, it's different. Theoretically, you've had power and influence for years. Whenever they publish a list of movers and shakers, you're there, Richard."

Sherborne grinned. "I don't move and shake any more. I'm more of a wobbler."

"Okay, so wobblers talking cobblers. But, if you've got the power—and I think it's fair to say that you do have some power by virtue of your publishing interests and not as a result of your royal connections—then there's only one reason that makes any sense for you to continue to support the royals in the way you have."

Sherborne's face kept his patrician concern. "You know there are many reasons to support the monarchy, Boniface."

"You might want everyone to think you're an old duffer, but you're smart, Richard. Really smart. Kuznetsov hates you. I understand that as a basic proposition—it saves the time getting to know you. But he doesn't understand how ruthless you are. I do. I've lost out to your ruthlessness. And there's only one reason you would play this game. You're not playing it for yourself. I mean, look..." Boniface took a step back and looked Sherborne up and down. "You're a coronary waiting to happen if your skeleton doesn't disintegrate under the mass of blubber first."

"You always did say the sweetest things, Boniface."

"Shhh. I haven't even started yet. I haven't told you where I think you're being clever, so pay attention."

Sherborne sighed, his mass sinking back into his chair.

"What I think is instructive, Richard, is the attitude of your paper. Kuznetsov calls for a referendum...and how do you react?" Boniface let the question hang, his voice echoing off the hard surfaces in the hall. "You don't say, 'Rubbish, we don't need one.' No, you say, 'Bring it on.' You're actively encouraging a referendum."

Boniface sat and leaned back in the sofa, relaxing. "Now to be clear, your newspaper has taken a very firm line, supporting the monarchy without question. It is a basic matter of principle that there should be a monarchy as far as the paper is concerned."

Sherborne looked squarely at Boniface. "And if you ask the British people, Boniface, the vast majority will support the monarchy. There's no shame in reflecting public opinion, as my readership is one-hundred percent monarchist."

"You're right, Richard. And by the way, just between us," Boniface dropped his voice, "I do agree about the outcome if there is a referendum. But you're smarter than that. You've finessed the proposition, and there seems only one reason for what you're doing."

fifty-six

Boniface had been mumbling since the moment he had started walking toward Trumpeters' House, and the commentary was becoming a persistent bee buzzing in Turgenev's left ear. Still, at least the commentary made Boniface focus on something, distracting him from the fact that he had been pushed into the wilderness to clear a path through any landmines.

And as far as Turgenev could tell, having to give a commentary also meant that Boniface hadn't figured that he was being followed. Turgenev was perhaps 30 feet behind, but presumably Boniface thought he was still back at the car, dreaming up new torments for the professor; and while that fear was etched into Boniface's brain, he would comply with Turgenev's instructions.

Turgenev watched Boniface hesitate inside the archway crossing The Wardrobe, and tried to ignore the Englishman's incessant over-description.

Boniface started moving and Turgenev mirrored, moving from shadow to shadow without being heard. He watched the other man stumble; clearly, he had never been a soldier. From the way he walked, he hadn't even been a Boy Scout.

Boniface turned and stood in front of the wrought-iron gate, twisted the knob, and pushed. From where he stood, Turgenev couldn't hear the gate opening; the only sound was the inane babbling. The Englishman proceeded across the cobbles, two cameras looking down on him, but somehow he hadn't seen them, according to his commentary.

He reached the front door and banged on it with the knocker. Never a sign of good security: Even if they don't stop you at the gate, they should be waiting by the time you get to the door. The Russian counted. How long would it take after knocking for there to be signs of life? One, two, three, four, five, six, seven…a light came on. So they don't pay attention, they're slow, and no one was near that door.

The door opened. Turgenev looked at the man who answered. He knew the type: He had probably once applied to join the army, maybe had been to some sort of activity day when he was a teenager, had perhaps spoken to a Marine or a Commando, but that was it. Not a soldier, but he definitely talked a good game at the gym, and if you didn't know any better, then you might be impressed. That is why the Russian Army would always be better than the British Army.

Turgenev smiled. This was a guard offering security for someone who didn't know better and who didn't know what real security meant. He chuckled; Boniface could be a pain in that guy's ass.

Boniface babbled as Turgenev edged around the outside of the courtyard and followed the path that led to the journalist's car near his impermanent resting place. He turned left off of the path; passed the car, instinctively checking his pocket to confirm the journalist's car key was still there; and followed the unlit narrow road down to the river, where he turned left again onto the broad path. It was a pleasure to be able to walk on a path by the river without Boniface constantly asking what the strategy was and without the professor in her heels slowing them both down.

He had first walked up this path after he had dealt with the journalist, and although his reconnaissance had been rushed, it had been long enough to get the lay of the land. He knew that up ahead was an iron fence, much like the wrought-iron gates that Boniface had passed through. When Turgenev had passed earlier, he had wondered about the security measures but had been unwilling to give them any real scrutiny for fear of tripping an alarm. Seeing how Boniface's approach had gone unnoticed, he was confident: There wouldn't be a trigger mechanism if he climbed the fence, there wouldn't be any alarms tripped as he went up the ornamental garden, there wouldn't be any guards outside, and if there were CCTV cameras, they would be attached to the house and would be static, so all that was necessary would be to walk around their field of view.

A quick look each way confirmed he was alone. He was over the fence in less than three seconds and able to follow the clean lines of the gardens funneling him toward the house. Even in the darkness he could tell that Sherborne had spent more on one day's gardening than he had on one year's security.

As he got close, he moved to the side, taking cover behind some rose bushes. Boniface was still talking; it sounded as if he was now inside and expecting Sherborne to appear at any moment. Turgenev smirked; from the few grunts that the phone could pick up, it also sounded as if the guard was ready to slap Boniface.

This rear elevation of the house seemed far more impressive than the entrance where Boniface had gone in, and it offered many opportunities for entry. On each side of the central door, there were six sash windows on each floor—twenty-five windows in total, including a central window above the door. The first two windows on each side sat under the huge portico supported by four Doric columns. The end windows were semicircular, and the roof ridge above these windows was turned 90 degrees, pointing front to back, unlike the main roof ridges and each wing, which went left to right.

From where he crouched, the guttering along the edge of the roof was hidden, but it must be there, because something fed the four rain downpipes set between every other window.

The most obvious access point would be through one of the windows on ground level. All the windows were sash windows where the panes slid vertically; it was a case of flipping a lock with his knife. If any of the windows were going to be locked or alarmed, it would be the ground-floor windows. Given Sherborne's lack of attention to security, the upper floors were unlikely to have these distractions, and if Boniface and Sherborne were on the ground floor, the height of the upper floor would give him an advantage.

Light spilled out of several windows, making it harder to see the exterior of the building. The room to the far left on the lower floor was lit by an exposed bulb hanging from the ceiling. He guessed this was the guards' room, but was this the location of the other person who talked to the guard that allowed Boniface into the building?

Several of the other rooms downstairs had light spilling into them, probably from the hall where Boniface was now incessantly chattering to whoever would listen—and if they didn't listen, then he would probably talk with the suits of armor he had mentioned.

On the left of the upper floor, the first window at the end—the semicircular window—was largely dark, but gave off a faint green/blue flicker, as if a television might be on. Windows two, three, and four on the left were lit, suggesting they were all part of a single room, and windows five and six emitted a dull glow, so again they were probably part of one room, and that room was probably getting some light from a passageway. The window over the central door was lit, but poorly.

He paused and listened to Boniface. There was another voice. Turgenev found it difficult to differentiate between English accents, but this had a different resonance. He seemed very full of himself. This was probably Sherborne, and if Sherborne was in the hall with Boniface, and Turgenev was right about the low-quality security, all eyes would be focused on guarding the principal. Looked at another way, it was now time for him to move.

The right wing of the house was in complete darkness. Turgenev ran to the second downpipe and tugged it. As he suspected, it was sturdy, cast iron, and securely attached to the wall. In other words, it was a near-perfect climbing aid. It took a moment to reach the upper floor, where he extended a leg and pivoted onto the brick windowsill. It took longer to open his knife than it took to open the window lock; it then required considerable force to slide the top window sash downward, breaking through years of bad maintenance and poor paint work, but once it did move, it created an opening that was large enough for him to get through without any effort.

fifty-seven

Boniface sat on the green leather Chesterfield sofa, camouflaged against the screen of plants behind it.

He had been angry at Sherborne and had not held back in expressing his ire at the way Sherborne had treated him in the past. But now, as the two men spoke, probably speaking frankly for the first time, he was starting to feel sorry for the older man.

Perhaps it was the result of a much too long day, perhaps it was seeing several people murdered in front of him, perhaps he had spent too long stuffed in the trunks of two cars, perhaps he had been handcuffed for too long, perhaps it was his concern for Ellen and her fear for Montbretia, perhaps for the first time he could see Sherborne's misguided motives, or perhaps it was his age leading him to get in touch with his feminine side.

Whatever the reason, it was undeniable; he had sympathy for the fat man.

He wondered if something had changed for Sherborne, too.

The man had always been fat—no, obese—but now he was starting to look close to death. The weight of his body and his enthusiasm for socializing were killing him, and he was dying in front of Boniface. The mass of his body compounded with the weight of his ambition—which was always so far reaching that it was doomed to remain unfulfilled—took their toll on his skeleton and organs. His heart had to work three times as hard as it should, his liver was always clearing gallons of alcohol, and all of his joints were worn down from years of carrying excessive bulk.

But beyond his morbid obesity, Boniface thought he could also see a man who was living on his nerves, having his worry fueled by paranoia. Where he had once seen the way Sherborne surrounded himself with women as pitiful—and it was true, he liked to have women around—he could now see that Sherborne had blanketed himself with people who would be kind to him, and to whom he could return the kindness without seeming weak.

While he was starting to feel sorry for the man, he still wasn't ready to trust him nor to give him a full explanation of the events of the last few hours. "So, as I say, that's the short version of the story... I've left out the really dull bits, but that's how I got to where I am. Nigel got shot, Ellen—who isn't dead—and I went looking for the papers, and everything has pointed to you."

"Quite an eventful evening you've had, Boniface. But you're sure that Ellen's alright—she must have had a dreadful shock, and with the loss of her friend..." His voice faded in a mixture of emotion and shortness of breath.

"She's as secure as she can be, given the circumstances," said Boniface, nodding cautiously.

"Good, good." The fat man muttered, wiping the sweat out of a fold that made its way down his cheek and ended in his third chin. "I'll call her in the morning to offer my condolences and see if there's any help I can offer."

Sherborne seemed distracted with his mopping as Boniface continued. "Now let me get back to the subject and tell you how I think you're being clever with the call for a referendum." He watched Sherborne twitch and wedge himself further into his club chair. "Oscar is a young man who doesn't seem to have a place in this world."

Boniface hesitated, calibrating the other man's response. "I'm sorry, that sounds critical of Oscar. That is not my intent. Let me rephrase."

"You don't need to rephrase, Boniface. We don't need to change the subject. For once we're having a civilized conversation; it seems such a shame that you want to spoil it."

"I'm sorry, Richard, but after the night I've had..." Boniface exhaled, wearily, his voice resigned. "Let me at least express my comment in a way that is less critical of Oscar."

Sherborne snorted as Boniface carried on. "Oscar is in royal purgatory. He is neither within the inner circle of royalty—if you will, he's not at the top table of royalty—nor is he able to function with the freedom of a non-royal. Would you agree with this very broad proposition, Richard?"

"I don't know where you're going with this, Boniface." The fat man seemed to be annoyed.

"I'll take that as a yes," said Boniface, continuing without looking for agreement. "And while Oscar is in royal purgatory, he will never be happy. He will never have his place in the world, because he's neither one thing nor the other."

Sherborne remained quiet, apart from his labored breathing and the gentle mopping of his pooling sweat.

"Oscar can't cease to be royal. There's no mechanism to set him free from the burden of his birth—and you have realized that. Of course, it's worse because Princess Heidemarie always tells everyone that she's the most royal of the lot of them, what with the Habsburg connection. I mean, she even gave Oscar her maiden name because she thought she was more royal than the family she married into. Not to mention that she hadn't changed her name because they were still on their honeymoon at the time of the accident, and it didn't seem worth it after the husband died." Boniface smirked. "Or is the rumor true, Richard? She didn't give her son her husband's family name because her husband wasn't the father, and he wasn't the father because he had been in a coma for a year when the child was born after that skiing accident on their honeymoon? That would be one way of making Oscar un-royal."

Boniface paused, letting the old rumor swirl as he avoided making eye contact with Sherborne before continuing. "So the sole option for you—as a friend of the family, as a parent, as whatever—is to craft a place for Oscar within the inner circle and hope that with the weight of civic duty comes a degree of maturity, coupled with the royal machine to apply some level of control to those influences that may otherwise lead him into the tabloid headlines."

Sherborne remained impassive.

"Princess Heidi wouldn't be against the idea of Oscar having a greater role, would she? It would vindicate her position, and for her it would give Oscar something to do beyond getting drunk and using his allowance to pay off all those debauched hussies, as I guess you would call them." Boniface relaxed back into his sofa. "How am I doing, Richard?"

"It's all nonsense, Boniface. A great piece of fiction, but nonsense."

"No. It's a great strategy of yours. You're marshaling public support, and you know the monarchy will be supported, but at the same time you're planning a future for Oscar. That's brilliant!"

The room was hushed apart from the sound of Sherborne's labored breathing and the security guard fidgeting in his seat, each man looking at the other. "Well, I hate to disappoint you, Boniface, but I've got something far more interesting to think about at the moment." The fat man's tone was triumphal.

"Well, it would be interesting, Richard, but I hope you don't think my appearance here is coincidental."

fifty-eight

Turgenev slid up the top half of the sash window, returning it to the position it had been before he entered, and stepped back on the soft carpet, looking around the room. Two two-seater sofas, upholstered in flowery fabric, faced each other, both perpendicular to a fireplace. A few pieces of fragile, dark-wood furniture had been carefully placed around the room, and a three-cornered cabinet sat in the corner farthest from the door, which was shut. Above the fireplace, a row of silver-framed photos sat next to some porcelain figurines.

The door fitted tightly in its frame with no light coming in around the edges. The Russian lay on the floor, straining to see through a gap between the door and the carpet where he could make out light on the other side. He knelt and leaned forward, twisting his head to look through the keyhole. There was definitely light, but not a bright light.

He stood and put his ear to the door, listening. Delicately, he twisted the knob and pulled the door back, waiting for his eyes to adjust to the electric glow.

Cautiously, he edged into the corridor—lit by a single uncovered low-energy light bulb—which was featureless apart from the four other doors, all closed. The door to his right at the end of the corridor appeared to lead to the end room. He dropped to his knees and looked through the keyhole. Nothing. He crawled to the two rooms on the other side of the corridor, looking through each keyhole in turn, finishing with the keyhole in the door next to the room through which he had entered.

Nothing. All dark.

The end of the corridor led onto a landing that was poorly lit, but light floated up from the floor below, mingling with the sound of voices rising to the higher floor. By the sounds of things, Boniface was in full flow. He seemed to be getting into personal territory, talking about his drinking and his failed marriage. Turgenev sneered.

He put his ear to the door to the left of his entry room and pushed. It opened into gloom, the only illumination the ambient light coming through the window and the dull bulb in the corridor. He stepped in and looked around the room, a bedroom, but with an old-fashioned, stale, flowery smell. "Old woman's perfume," he muttered, scanning the room. Unable to pick out any distinguishing features in the dark, he closed the door as he left and tried the room opposite. Again a featureless bedroom, but without the smell. The room next to that was a bathroom with a bath, a sink, a toilet, and a small medicine cabinet. In the dark, the room was featureless.

He paused outside the room at the end, listening, then entered suddenly. It was narrower than he expected but ran from the front to the back of the house with windows at each end. He couldn't make out its main function, but he was drawn to the river end of the room, where a spiral staircase plunged into darkness on the floor below.

He left the end room, carefully shutting the door behind him, and moved silently along the corridor, pausing where it joined the landing. Boniface and Sherborne were engrossed in conversation and battering him from both sides—in his earpiece and with a momentary delay from downstairs. He couldn't tell whether they were enjoying the argument, trying to destroy each other, or both.

Grateful for the distraction the two created, he eased across the landing, past the top of the broad staircase, and, reaching the passageway on the other side, reflexively checked behind him before moving forward.

This corridor had four doors, and two of those were open. Turgenev weighed which door to choose first. The one at the end would be last: Given that he hadn't seen any signs of human habitation in the other corridor, if there was a guard upstairs, then he would likely be in the room that had given off the flickering glow Turgenev had seen from outside.

The first room on the left had its door open but no lights switched on. He stepped inside. Bookcases lined the walls to the left and right, and at the front of the room a scroll-armed sofa sprawled on the floor. Beyond the sofa was an imposing desk with a large leather chair behind it. A few papers lay on top of the desk along with two tumblers. A third tumbler, still half full, sat on a table next to the sofa.

He turned and, standing inside the room he had entered, faced across the passageway. Where there were two doors in the other wing, here there was only one. He stepped forward and knelt to check the light. Seeing nothing, he tried the door and slipped in, returning the door behind him to its previous position.

His eyes strained to see in the darkness, but this was a bedroom. Without his night vision he had to rely on his sense of smell, which was unfortunate. There was an indistinct bitter tang—he wasn't sure what it was, but he didn't feel the need to get a definitive answer. Adjacent to the farthest corner was a door into the next room. Turgenev took five paces to get to the door, at each step finding his feet impeded by soft objects on the floor—bedding, clothing perhaps? Hopefully.

He pushed the door, cringing at the low squeak of the hinge, until he could see enough to know that it was a bathroom. Guessing that there was no one in there, he returned to his exit. He stepped out, closing the door on the smell, and took a few silent strides to the next room on the other side.

The door was ajar, with light streaming around the gap. He listened, then opened the door without hesitation, keeping hold of the knob so that the wood didn't swing free. There was no one in sight as he stepped inside, returning the door to its previous position.

Like its neighbor, this room had bookcases filled with books along both walls. Unlike its neighbor, this room seemed more ordered. On the wall behind the door there was a long, thin, modern table with a light wood-effect top and a modern typist's chair facing it. The combination looked out of place, as did the computer and printer sitting on the table. The modernity was thrown into sharp contrast by the array of vintage flintlocks displayed on the wall above the desk. His soldier's interest in the craft of the gunsmith kicked in, and he had to shake himself loose, recommencing his survey of the room.

As he had seen from his external inspection, there were three windows. Against the two pillars between the windows, back-to-back bookcases stood, creating small bays. On the inside of the bays, a large, solidly constructed stand-up desk was placed so the reader could study while keeping his back to the windows. In front of the desk, with its back to the desk and facing the door, was another scroll-armed sofa.

The room at the end of the passageway was the only space unchecked.

Turgenev crouched at the door, trying to look through the keyhole. There was a blue/green light dancing around like the Northern Lights, but no obvious sound. He stood, flipped the earpiece out and placed his ear against the door, feeling with the tips of his fingers for any vibrations.

He took a deep breath and opened the door swiftly, looking around for any sign of movement. "So have you had enough of the old man yet? Is he still convinced we're going to be invaded at any moment by a gang of crack mercenaries?"

Turgenev turned to the voice. There was a man—wearing a white shirt with epaulets, sitting on a flimsy typist's chair in front of a computer screen—leaning forward as if trying to urgently pick up something on the floor with both hands. The Russian moved briskly; he could see the man's bare legs and dark pants around his ankles. On the table next to the screen lay a dark-blue blazer and an upturned cap with a gun and walkie-talkie nestled inside.

The Russian moved to stand behind the man and, without a word, placed one hand under his chin and the other just back from the crown of his head, then twisted. There was a dull cracking, and the body went limp, falling to the floor.

Turgenev remained motionless, staring at the computer screen, which was now visible and showing a woman, naked apart from her stockings and stilettos. Somehow she looked familiar. He read her name, Kristalle, and shrugged. It probably should mean something, but he wasn't sure why.

From the light given off by the image of Kristalle, he looked at the gun. The magazine dropped out easily; he checked it and returned it, then slipped the cold steel into his jacket pocket before he picked up the guard's blazer and checked the pockets. Nothing. He looked down at the body, naked between the waist and the ankles, and shook his head.

Across the landing, he walked to the room at the far end of the other corridor and entered, quietly shutting the door behind him before he descended the spiral staircase.

fifty-nine

Boniface sucked in air through his teeth, pausing as he tried to find a way to phrase his next question to Sherborne. There was a rustling in the greenery behind his back. Across the hallway, the security guard jerked his head to look toward the source of the sound without moving the rest of his body. "Hey!"

Boniface turned to look in the direction that the bullet traveled, realizing that he had instinctively flinched away from the blast behind his head. The guard had disappeared, being replaced in Boniface's line of sight by a spatter of blood, gravity starting its slow descent down the wall.

The reverberation seemed interminable, but as the silence began to assert its presence over the room, Boniface turned to look at the origin of the shot. "That was the signal, was it?" He sighed. "That's how you're going to tell me you're coming in?"

Turgenev stepped forward. Unlike the last time Boniface had seen him, he now had a gun in his hand, and a broad grin was spreading across his face. "I would have called, but I got all teary-eyed when you two girls kissed and made up. You know, I'm going to sell that story to Hollywood and retire on the earnings."

"Who are you?" bellowed Sherborne, remaining wedged in his club chair. "Boniface! Call the police."

Turgenev caught Boniface's eye. Boniface flopped back on his sofa as confirmation that he had heard, understood, and complied with the unspoken command.

"That won't be necessary, fat man." Turgenev kept moving, lifting his gun and transferring his gaze to Sherborne.

In three strides he was on the other side of the hall, crouching behind the body of the recently deceased guard but still facing the fireplace between Sherborne and Boniface. He checked the guard one-handed, the other hand keeping his gun trained on Sherborne.

As he stood, he slipped a newly liberated pistol into his pocket, then walked to the fat man and squatted beside him, positioning the gun that had just killed the guard an inch away from Sherborne's head, but sufficiently forward so that the fat man could see the end of the muzzle. He paused. Boniface watched as Sherborne's rate of breathing started to increase. He began to tremble visibly and sweat even more profusely than normal.

Turgenev began in a low, quiet voice, the sound barely traveling across the room. "Right, fat man. I've got a few questions."

"I...er...well...I..." Sherborne looked to Boniface.

"Just answer, Richard." Boniface felt the look of resignation crossing his visage. He continued, his voice was subdued. "He's serious."

"I...er...understand. W-w-w-what do you want to know?" Sherborne pulled his handkerchief from the top pocket of his jacket and started vigorously mopping the sweat from his face.

"It's very easy," said the Russian, his voice barely audible. "How many other people are in this house?" He let the barrel of the gun kiss Sherborne's temple; the fat man let out a muted scream. "It's a simple number. How many?"

"Three. Me and the two guards," blurted Sherborne. "There's one guard over there, and the other one is upstairs."

Turgenev looked at Boniface. Boniface closed his eyes momentarily; the Russian didn't react when he heard about the other guard.

"You and the two guards, you are certain?"

"Yes. Absolutely certain." His voice was higher and trembling.

"You're an Englishman. Don't you have a butler somewhere? I thought all Englishmen had butlers."

Sherborne simpered. "I don't have a butler. I have a housekeeper, Ada, who is staying with her sister tonight."

"Alright then, second question. Are you expecting any more visitors tonight?" Turgenev stood swiftly and moved in front of Sherborne, keeping the gun on him.

"No. Yes...yes, I am expecting one person. But I was expecting him hours ago, and I'm not sure where he is."

Boniface interrupted. "He's not coming, Richard. He's dead."

Turgenev spun and looked angrily at Boniface. "What are you talking about?"

"The guy Richard is expecting is the long-haired one who was shot in Trudgett's house." He tried to keep the disdain out of his voice but failed.

Turgenev swung the gun to point at him. "Is this another trick, Boniface, or is this something else you haven't told me?" Boniface shook his head. "How do you know he was coming here?"

Boniface contemplated the gun. "Remember, I met the guy; I spoke to him. I was speaking to him when..." Boniface imitated a gun firing with his hand. "He said he had someone ready to buy the information. Everything he told me fits with the details Richard has given me, and all roads lead to Rome, or is it Richmond?"

"You're guessing." Boniface could see Turgenev's grip around the gun's handle tightening.

"I like to think of it as making reasoned deductions. I would go and ask the guy to clarify, but you'll remember that someone put a bullet through his brain."

The room fell quiet again, apart from the sound of Sherborne's labored breathing while he mopped the sweat collecting in his jowls. "He's dead, Boniface? What else haven't you told me?

"Yeah. There's quite a lot I need to tell you, but now is not the time," said Boniface.

Sherborne wiped his face again as he maintained his questioning. "So what happened to the papers or documents or whatever it was that this chap found, Boniface? Did you get them before...?"

"No." He turned to face Turgenev. "No, we didn't get the papers or whatever it was he found. And that is why we need Professor Armstrong here, now, to help us."

Turgenev remained impassive as Boniface continued. "I've stuck to my side of the deal. I've given you the running commentary." He removed the journalist's phone and offered it to Turgenev, who snatched it. "Added to which, you need her to interpret whatever we can get hold of. She was the person who knew Professor Trudgett best and stands a chance of seeing what he was thinking. The sooner we can decode the documents when they come through, the sooner you can start your retirement."

Sherborne looked shocked. "I thought you said Ellen was safe."

Boniface sighed. "I lied, or rather, I allowed you to form the wrong impression." He looked sideways at the Russian. "Remember, I was being listened to."

Boniface felt the almost imperceptible movement of his head and watched the other man's confusion. "So where is she?" Sherborne seemed almost angry at the revelation.

"Locked in the back of a car outside," said Boniface, turning to Turgenev. "At least, she was when I last saw her." He stared at Turgenev.

Turgenev stared back, both men remaining silent.

Boniface cracked first. "Come on. We need her help, and it gets you out of here sooner."

"But why do we need her now? You haven't heard from that hacker yet." Turgenev took out Boniface's phone and waved it at him.

"But once we do, you don't want us wasting time while you go and get her." He turned to Sherborne. "We're going to need a computer, Richard. Have you got one of those in this museum? With an internet connection?"

"I've got one. I got a new one last month. It's quite a good one, they tell me. My secretary uses it. Not a clue how it works, but I do have one. It's upstairs in the library."

"Shall Richard and I go up to the library, and you can go and get the professor?"

Turgenev took a step, straightening his gun arm. "No."

sixty

It took nearly fifteen minutes for Sherborne to get out of his club chair and then reach the top of the stairs.

It felt longer to Boniface. Much longer.

"You know you can get gadgets to help? Things to lift your seat as you get out of a chair. Stair lifts so you can get up and down without difficulty."

"Thank you, Boniface. I'm not ready for the nursing home yet." Sherborne seemed to be annoyed at the reminder of his physical deterioration. "While I can stand, walk, wash myself, feed myself, pour my own drink, drink it, and most importantly wipe my own arse, I will not be fitting a stair lift, grab handles, or any other hideous contraptions in this fine, architecturally listed building," he snapped, ending the conversation.

Turgenev seemed to find the process of moving Sherborne beyond infuriating. Initially he appeared to think that Sherborne was bluffing and held a gun to his head. When he put a bullet through the ceiling, he found that Sherborne probably was being serious and did move even more slowly than one would expect a fat man like him to move.

Boniface felt compelled to help him out of his chair. The stairs, however, were pure frustration. Sherborne took one step, always with his right foot, and then stopped. Every third step, he took a longer break, and halfway up he behaved like a man with altitude sickness.

There was no elation when they reached the top, no planting of flags, no cracking of champagne. Just a fat, sweaty man, wheezing and looking as if he was about to have a heart attack. Then there was the slow, lumbering walk to the library.

"Sit." Turgenev indicated another dark-green scroll-arm sofa, this one in front of a stand-up desk constructed with what looked like oak tree trunks. "Your hands." He indicated the hands nearest each other as he moved behind their seated position to the other side of the desk. "This way." Sherborne and Boniface each held up a hand, looking slightly confused. "Toward me," said Turgenev, grabbing the hands when they were pushed backward without enthusiasm, one on each side of a substantial leg of the desk.

Turgenev grabbed Boniface's wrist first, returning the handcuffs that had been present until he was let out of the car, and attached the other end of the restraint to Sherborne's thick wrist. Moving around to the front of the sofa, he cuffed their ankles together, struggling to get the restraint around Sherborne's swollen leg.

The shaven-headed man stood back to admire his work before he turned to Boniface. "You remember our arrangement."

"I do." There was defeat in Boniface's tone.

"If I am in any doubt about what you are doing, Professor Armstrong..." He drew his finger slowly across his throat. "And she will die here, in front of you. You will watch her last hours but be unable to do anything to help. And if the fat man tries anything, it's the same story."

"I understand." He continued tentatively. "Will you leave my phone in case the hacker guy calls?"

Turgenev snorted. "You? With a phone?" He spun and left the room.

Sherborne and Boniface sat in the draft created by the vacuum of the Russian leaving, listening to the sound as he took the stairs three at a time and jogged across the marble hallway. The fat man broke the silence. "What the devil is going on, Boniface? Why are you working with this thug?"

Sherborne looked over at Boniface, who ignored the questions, and instead busied himself looking behind the sofa. "You don't happen to have a key?"

"What are you talking about, Boniface?"

"Handcuffs. Key. Get out. Call police. Get back before psychotic shaven-headed Russian comes back." Boniface tugged at his wrist and ankle, reminding Sherborne that they were manacled with a large desk preventing them from starting a three-legged race.

"Of course I haven't got any handcuff keys. I'm not into that sort of thing."

Boniface ended his visual reconnaissance and slumped back on the sofa, his right arm still behind him. "Well, you've got all those museum pieces." He waved his left hand at the flintlocks on the wall above the computer. "Why not a key?"

Sherborne frowned at the question as Boniface kept talking. "We don't have long. And I'm sorry about..." He exhaled. "I'm sorry about a lot of stuff. I don't have time to prove it nor to explain how sorry I am. But once this is over, perhaps we can have a cup of tea. Yes, tea, not booze for me anymore, and I can explain all the unpleasantness that has occurred tonight. But for the moment, the thing that's worrying me is Ellen. I want her here, with us, and not locked in the back of a car. If she's here, then she has a much better chance of staying alive."

"But who is he and what does he want?"

"This afternoon he was Kuznetsov's head of security, and when I met him, Kuznetsov seemed to trust him absolutely. Now? Now, I don't know. He seems to have left Kuznetsov's employment and gone freelance. He seems to have gone off the rails and spent the last couple of hours killing people or getting people killed. His man killed Trudgett—which mistake is enough to mean Kuznetsov wants him dead—and I'm guessing his man also killed our light-fingered document-acquirer."

"He's dead, Boniface? Really dead?"

"If we're talking about the same guy, then yes, he's very dead. His brains are spread all over Trudgett's living room wall."

Sherborne winced, picked his handkerchief from his top pocket with his free hand, and mopped his brow. "But you seem to have promised this chap that you will get him something on the computer. Or am I missing something?"

"No. You're right, Richard. That's what I've said I'm going to do."

"And what does he think you are going to give him?"

"Photographs of the documents that the guy who got shot was trying to sell to you."

Sherborne leaned forward, his eyes wide. "So they are real? These documents do exist?" The fat man's eyes were alive, boring into Boniface, eagerly questioning.

"Yes."

Sherborne's face lifted; a look of hope started to form but then fell from his face. "But if the documents are to be believed, based on what that chap told me on the phone, doesn't it rather undermine the campaign by my favorite Russian oligarch?" Boniface bowed his head slightly. "Won't that cause a problem for you with Kuznetsov?"

"At the moment we don't have any options, Richard. I've been playing for time for the last few hours, hoping something, anything, would turn up, but now I'm out of ideas." He paused, continuing softly. "I really hope I didn't get Ellen brought here just to die."

"So what's the idea? They always said you were good with strategy; that's probably why the Minister hired you."

"The strategy is that you, me, Ellen...we all play along with this and do whatever we can to give him what he wants. No heroics, no messing around, we just do what we can do."

"But shouldn't we..."

"No." Boniface turned to the fat man, using the handcuffs to exert enough discomfort until Sherborne looked directly at him. "Richard, listen. No heroics. This guy is a killing machine. He's probably killed half a dozen people with his bare hands this evening, and now he's got a gun, so don't try anything." Sherborne exhaled. "He's like an angry wasp. If you annoy him, he'll come back and sting one of us. And if he can't get one of us, well...he's scared the shit out of Ellen by telling her he'll go after her sister."

Boniface kept Sherborne in discomfort, waiting for his agreement. "Oh alright, Boniface. Whatever you say."

The room fell still apart from Sherborne's labored breathing. Boniface spoke first. "Oscar."

"Really, Boniface! This is neither the time nor the place." Sherborne's tone was sharp, but there was no energy behind his rebuke.

Boniface reinstated the pressure on the handcuffs and waited. "For pity's sake, don't be a stupid old man. This is your one opportunity to talk. Don't you get that there's a good chance we won't get out of here tonight? It's not as if you have a lot of leverage with our shaven-headed tormentor in this negotiation. You can be collateral damage, and the Russian won't care and neither will his former boss. In fact, I suspect Mister Kuznetsov might be secretly pleased if a stray bullet hits you."

"Well, if you release the pressure on my wrists, I might consider it."

Boniface held the tension, then relaxed. Sherborne shook his arm loose. "Jolly inconvenient. He could have chained us in a more comfortable position."

"Please hurry, Richard," whined Boniface. "Get to the point: Oscar is your son, isn't he?"

Boniface watched Sherborne deflate. "You have to understand, Boniface. Things are not always as black and white as you would like them to be. There's room for subtlety, nuance, understanding, and dare I say, compassion."

"I can do compassion," said Boniface in a gentle voice with a reassuring tilt of his head.

"Attitudes were different. My close friendship with Princess Heidemarie is well known and is fully accepted now, but when it first became clear that we were close, there was that awful business, of course."

"Awful business of you screwing a new bride when her husband was in a coma?"

"Boniface. We were friends, and she needed comfort—it was an awful time for her, and that bloody family did nothing to welcome her. They were all about stoical duty. And then she got pregnant. At that time it would have been incredibly uncomfortable for Heidi to admit that she had cheated on her husband to whom she had only been married for eight days before the accident, and she was my friend."

"And so you protected her." Boniface soothed.

"And so I protected her and denied any improper relationship. I always maintained that the boy's father was her husband. In fact, at one point, when the press started talking about the immaculate conception—there being no father who would stand up and claim responsibility—I even gave the impression that I was resentful that I hadn't had a fair crack at the whip, so to speak."

"I'm sure you cracked a whip like a good 'un, Richard."

Sherborne stared into the distance, as if looking at a far-off time.

"And not only did you crack the whip, but you fathered the child."

Sherborne nodded slowly. "Yes. I am Oscar's father. And for the record, he has always known I am his father, and I have tried to do the best I can for my son. I really am incredibly proud of him, Boniface. He is a gentle, sweet, thoughtful young man. Nothing like the loathsome hooray or borderline criminal that the tabloids paint him to be." He smiled. "And nothing like his father."

The room was quiet, neither man speaking. Boniface started, calmly. "So, if what the dead guy said is true, Princess Heidemarie, who has always claimed to be more royal than the present lot, may ironically have a child who genuinely has the better claim to the throne."

"It's almost Shakespearean." The fat man took on an exaggerated deep voice. "Thou shalt get kings, Sherborne, though thou be none."

sixty-one

A door—almost certainly the front door—slammed on the lower floor. From where Boniface and Sherborne sat, the sound wasn't loud, but the reverberations traveled through every beam in the structure of Trumpeters' House.

There were two sets of footsteps. One set dull, heavy, thumping. The other alternating between the sound of a small, sharp, loud heel and a soft shoe scraping on the marble; the alternation between the two sounds suggesting smaller, more frequent footsteps. The two distinct sets of footsteps gave way to the sound of people walking on the stairs, with neither set of feet being distinguishable, but the sound of a female voice, clearly in some discomfort, rising above.

At the top of the stairs the party started moving toward the library where Boniface and Sherborne were manacled.

When Boniface and Ellen had been arrested in Nigel's office, she had been exhausted but still fired up and excited about seeing her sister in a few hours. Sure, she wasn't quite as well presented as she had been on the television earlier in the day—her skirt had a small rip, the blouse was creased, her hair was windswept, and the green/black lines under her eyes were starting to show—but that was nothing that a bath and a good night's sleep wouldn't cure.

But now she looked different.

She still wore the same clothes, but instead of the well-tailored business suit, all Boniface could see were old bits of torn fabric loosely fashioned as garments, apparently held together by copious quantities of mud. Mud seemed to be quite a significant theme in the look Ellen was modeling. As well as holding her clothes together, mud was also acting as her makeup, to color her hair, and to keep her hair in place, which didn't seem to be the place Ellen had intended it to be the last time she had brushed it.

The mud also seemed to be acting as a first-aid supplement, covering her cuts and scratches, and soothing the bruises.

Ellen stood, shivering, her hands still cuffed behind her back. The remnants of her clothes still damp from falling into wet grass and mud, chilled further in the trunk as the temperature outside had continued to decline.

"Dear God. What happened to you?" Sherborne hollered, then lowered his voice as Boniface yanked his handcuff when he saw the shock on Ellen's face. "Are you alright, my dear?"

She flinched. Where a few hours earlier there had been passion in her eyes, now Boniface could see fear. Fear she had never known before. Fear that she didn't understand. Fear of physical violence that she was not equipped to deal with. Fear that the only person that mattered to her was being physically threatened. Fear that the only two people who could help her were an overweight, aging, would-be Lothario who could barely walk and a self-confessed physical coward whose mouth seemed to run wild when he was thinking. Fear that the two people who might help her seemed to be manacled together, unable to stand from the sofa on which they were sitting.

Boniface tried to communicate some form of reassurance. Any form of reassurance, but he failed with the subliminal messages. "It's good to see you." Her mouth moved as if she was trying to show human emotion but failed. He looked to Turgenev. "Could you at least let her wash her hands and face? Please."

"No." Turgenev was unyielding. "Sit." He turned to Ellen and placed a hand on each shoulder, twisting her so her back faced the sofa, and pushed. Ellen took two stumbling steps backward and fell, wedging herself between Boniface and the arm at the end of the green sofa, with her hands still behind her back.

"It's good to see you. I was so worried," whispered Boniface. Ellen blushed slightly.

"I've told you before. Shut up." There was no hint that Turgenev was taking a negotiating position. Boniface stiffened and complied.

A phone rang from inside Turgenev's jacket. "That's our man. Let me talk to him." Boniface held out his free left hand.

Turgenev remained impassive.

"We're not going to go through this shit again, are we? The only one that loses is you. The rest of us can go back to our day jobs tomorrow, but if you don't get the documents, then you're not going to have any leverage."

Turgenev stared at Boniface.

"Fine. Don't do anything. But if you're not going to do anything, then stop dicking about and let us go home."

Still no response.

"What's the calculation? Are we going to screw you?" Boniface saw a flash of recognition, a brief involuntary twitch above the eyes. "You're scared of us, and you don't know how to get out."

"No." Turgenev sounded defensive, his pride slightly pricked.

"Then give me the phone." Boniface was feeling argumentative.

The phone stopped.

"There goes your pension. Happy now?"

Turgenev moved forward, standing on Boniface's left foot. "Final warning. Shut. Up."

The phone rang again. Boniface remained motionless and fixed his face.

"Yes." Turgenev answered. He muttered a few words in Russian, then looked at Boniface. "Give me a credit card."

"Come on, Dickie. You're a man of money; you must have a card or two in the wallet that's always in your pocket." Boniface flashed a quick look at Ellen, raising his eyebrows. Ellen's mouth formed an "O" shape, half in surprise, half in acknowledged conspiracy.

"Well, I..." Sherborne began.

"Give. Now." The Russian held out his hand. Reluctantly, Sherborne reached into his inside jacket pocket with his free hand and pulled out a worn brown hide wallet. One-handed, he flipped it open and eased out a credit card with his thumb, grudgingly handing over the piece of plastic. Turgenev read the details, grunted, and flipped the phone closed, dropping the card on the floor.

He stood, staring at the phone in the palm of his hand. After 30 seconds it beeped. He opened it and read the message. "This is goodbye."

Boniface looked up to see the pistol pointing at him. He raised his eyebrows, questioning, but remained silent.

"Why so quiet, Mister Boniface?" Turgenev pulled his mouth tight, articulating each word individually.

Boniface waited, moving his head from one side to the other as if holding a conversation inside his skull. "Because I don't get it. You've really confused me this time."

The Russian cocked his head and opened his eyes more widely.

"You've got the password now, so you can get into Professor Trudgett's file storage account or whatever it is. You can look at the photos…assuming they're there."

The Russian stared at Boniface. A look practiced over years.

"But what are you going to do next?"

The Russian frowned.

"You haven't got a clue what's there, have you? More to the point, you won't know what's important and what isn't, so you're going to need somebody to help you. By the time you find someone who knows their way around this stuff, it's not going to be worth half what it's worth now, and somewhere, while you're trying to find someone who can help you, you're going to get ripped off. What are you going to do if someone simply publishes the documents you send them?" He paused. "Shouldn't we take a look for you? We do know something about the subject."

The Russian pondered. It was his turn to appear to have a conversation inside his head. "Remember who's got the gun." He tossed the phone to Boniface, who reached out his left hand, catching it as it spun toward him.

"And now if you would be so kind…" Boniface tugged on his right wrist and right ankle, jerking Sherborne.

Turgenev walked behind the stand-up desk and released Sherborne's left wrist, leaving the handcuff on Boniface's right. Both men shook their arms to reinvigorate the circulation. "That feels better," muttered Sherborne as the Russian moved in front of Boniface, taking the cuff he had just removed from Sherborne and attaching it to Boniface's free wrist.

Boniface held his manacled wrists up to the Russian, who looked at him and shrugged. "You can still use a computer."

Turgenev squatted to remove the restraint shackling the two Englishmen at their ankles, and pointed the younger man to the computer. "Computer… Password on the phone. Go." He looked to Sherborne. "I don't need to tell you not to move, do I, fat man? But just in case." He squatted and attached the loose cuff to Sherborne's other ankle.

Boniface got to his feet awkwardly, pushing on his knees with his handcuffed hands to give himself enough leverage from the low seat; walked to the computer; and delicately positioned the typist's chair, which spun wildly at his slightest touch. "I'm going to need her help."

Turgenev jerked the muzzle of the gun to indicate Ellen to join him.

"She'll need a chair, too," said Boniface.

Turgenev stepped back out of the library. There was a sound of a door opening, some banging, a door closing, and the Russian returned with a typist's chair. "There." He pushed the chair to Ellen, who was now standing.

"She'll need to use her hands," said Boniface, turning back to the computer and starting to type. Several screens came up before he flipped open his phone and entered the details that the hacker had sent.

Ellen turned and leaned to push her hands toward Turgenev. He unlocked one bracelet, leaving the cuffs hanging from her other wrist, and pointed to Boniface. "Help him."

The academic wheeled the chair next to Boniface and sat. "What have we got?" she asked huskily.

"Nine photos. Not sure what, but they're downloading now—either the photos are huge or this connection is slow." He turned to Turgenev, who was standing a few paces back, keeping the three within a tight firing arc. "It's going to take a minute or two, but there is something here." Turgenev snarled, allowing the room to fall silent apart from the quiet hum of the computer and the occasional squeaks from the typists' chairs.

The first image finished downloading, and Boniface hit the print button. The printer shook itself into action, vibrating, squealing, and rumbling, outputting the page millimeter-by-millimeter. As it finally spat out the paper, Boniface passed the page to Ellen.

She read in silence, then looked up, expectation on her face. "This is it. Well, not everything." She pointed to the printer. "Hurry up, next page...but this is it." Boniface hit the print button for the next page, and the printer began shaking itself into a frenzy again. "This is the proof we need; we now know where Henry is buried, which leads to the logical conclusion that it was murder." She held up the page.

Boniface read it slowly. "You mean...? That its only function is to cover up the...?" His sentence trailed off with the realization of what he was reading.

A large smile had broken out across Ellen's face. "What Nigel always believed after those TV people visited; here's the instruction." She picked up the next page coming out of the printer. "And look at this," she whispered. "FitzRoy."

Boniface turned to Turgenev. "This is going to take perhaps five or ten minutes, so why don't you sit down? What we'll do is put all the images together in a single file along with a few words giving an explanation of what you've got here, so you don't need to read everything now. It will all be together in one file."

Turgenev grunted dismissively and moved to the sofa, sitting on the arm farthest away with his feet on the seat. As the documents printed, Boniface and Ellen quietly muttered between themselves with Ellen dictating and Boniface typing. After some minutes, Boniface turned to Turgenev. "We're nearly done. Get a thumb drive or something, and we'll transfer the file for you."

"Why?" asked Turgenev.

"You need to get the files off this machine," Boniface slapped the computer on the desk, "and you don't want to leave the details on Nigel's storage account, which has been accessed by a hacker." He waited as if to emphasize the point. "Do you want to rely on a system that you know has been compromised? By someone you can't go and threaten with a gun?"

The Russian grunted.

"You must have some thumb drives sitting around somewhere, Richard. You know, the things people send to you that you give to the secretary and she plugs into the computer?"

"Oh, those. Yes. I've got some; they're in my desk." Turgenev stared at Sherborne. "My desk in the next room. Do you want me to go and get one?" The Russian removed one cuff from around Sherborne's ankles, returning to his position on the arm.

"Get two," called Boniface, now facing the screen again, typing rapidly. "One's always bound to be faulty."

Sherborne slid forward on the sofa, twisting as he went, landing on his knees and facing the sofa. He lifted one leg, placing his foot flat on the floor, and then levered himself up using the arm of the sofa. Straining to breathe, he eventually reached vertical. "I'll go and get those thingummies."

Turgenev watched him moving—glacially—toward the door. "Is there a phone in that room?"

"Of course," said Sherborne, seeming to lose his breath with the exertion of talking and standing simultaneously.

"Then I'm coming with you." He jumped off the sofa; in two paces he was behind Boniface and reached to pick up his phone. "Don't want you making calls while I'm out of the room, do we, Mister Boniface? And remember, I'm going to be standing in the corridor you need to come along to get out." He held the gun up, lowering it when Boniface nodded his acknowledgement.

sixty–two

"You understand that there's a lot I want to say—need to say—but at the moment, my focus is on getting all three of us out of here alive?"

Ellen nodded, her muddy hair following the movement of her head but not showing any bounce as her head came to rest. "I don't care about anything apart from doing whatever he says so that Montbretia stays safe."

Boniface reached to touch Ellen's hand. "Richard moves so slowly that we've got a minute or two and before we do anything else, I need something I can lob. It needs to be small and light, but with enough weight that it will carry."

"Small?" asked Ellen, pushing her chair back as she stood, turning to the book-shelves behind her.

"About the size of a thumb drive. About the weight of a thumb drive. Makes the sound of a thumb drive if you drop it."

Ellen scanned the shelves. "And you. What are you doing?"

"Me. I'm trying to make sure that whatever goes onto the thumb drive that we give to Turgenev looks like the real thing but has no value and can't do any damage to Mister Kuznetsov. I'm playing with fire if I leave Kuznetsov open to blackmail. These words you've dictated say a lot, but I've made a few edits, and as for what I've done with the photos..." He trailed off.

"No, Boniface. It's too dangerous." Ellen turned to face him, her lower jaw trembling as she tried to speak. Her voice was quiet but insistent. "Give him what he wants. I'm not going to put my sister at risk by lying."

"He won't realize—he won't have seen the original, so he won't know that the quality of the images has been degraded—he'll think Nigel took bad shots with his phone." Boniface kept eye contact.

"No, Boniface. It's too dangerous. You're putting my sister's life at risk."

"All of our lives—including Montbretia's—are already at risk. That risk magnifies if we cross Kuznetsov." He held her gaze. "If there was another option, I wouldn't be doing this."

"You're sure?" Boniface tried to seem relaxed. "Promise me, Boniface. Promise that you're really sure this will work."

"I promise," said Boniface.

Ellen held his gaze and then returned to her investigation of the bookcases. He watched as she pushed the third one, rocking it toward the wall, and flicked something loose with her foot. "I've got three choices for you. A wooden figure."

"An unpleasant wooden figure," said Boniface, rotating the object Ellen had passed him. "What is it?"

"A caveman? A tiger? I don't know... No, look, it's a walrus. And to go with that walrus, here's a one-pound coin and a small wooden wedge. By the way, that third bookcase is a bit wobbly. Someone removed the wooden wedge that was keeping it level, so don't try climbing it."

She passed the other two objects to Boniface, who inspected each in turn, looking at it, feeling its weight in his hand, and dropping it on the table, listening to the sound as it fell. After contemplating the three items, he pushed them to the back of the table and returned to the computer.

Ellen sat on the edge of the desk, looking through the papers Boniface had printed. "So if you're going to give our shaven-headed tormentor something with no value, by accident, of course, what are you going to do with the real version? Email it to yourself?"

"Not enough time—this connection is too slow. Turgenev will catch us." Boniface looked at Ellen; she didn't seem to share his conviction in the plan. "If you want me to email it to you, I'm more than happy to as soon as I've got a fast connection and no Russian with a gun."

Ellen's face remained fixed, then softened. "No, you're right. It's too risky. How are you..."

Boniface cut her off. "No time. Just go with it. What about the documents? What else have you seen?"

"Not much more, certainly nothing revelatory," said Ellen with a slight note of caution in her voice. "Several references to John Stephens—remember, the name on the family trees in Nigel's case—and now..." she held up one of the sheets of paper Boniface had printed, "we know how he fits in." Ellen pointed at two of the sheets on the desk.

sixty–three

"So the documents show Richard is the heir."

Boniface leaned back in the typist's chair, contemplating. "But there's a more immediate issue for him."

A silence hung. "Tell me, Boniface," snapped Ellen.

"Oscar." Boniface looked around furtively as Ellen leaned forward conspiratorially. "Dickie *is* the daddy."

"Does Richard know?"

"Does he know that he shagged Heidemarie? I guess he'd remember a night of passion with someone claiming to be the most royal person in Europe."

Ellen was getting impatient. "Does he know that he's the heir to Henry and so Oscar will inherit the claim?"

Boniface sighed, releasing a stream of air through his nose. "He found out something. Mister Longhair called him, trying to get some cash. But he doesn't know *how* the family connections link him to Henry, and without these documents, he has no proof to substantiate the claim." Boniface turned back to the computer screen, awkwardly trying to type and simultaneously use the mouse with his wrists handcuffed in front of him while he kept talking with Ellen.

"So Longhair tried to sell him the documents that are still in some police station somewhere."

Boniface chuckled softly. "Yeah. Our architectural-whatever-he-was was trying to scam Sherborne until he could find his way back into Hampton Court."

A noise came from the corridor. Not so much a single noise, but a collection of noises: the sound of Sherborne's labored breathing and of his shuffling walk, the sound of Turgenev's military footsteps expressing frustration at Sherborne's slowness, the sound of Turgenev moving to check his surroundings, although Boniface suspected that anyone who might be watching him was probably already dead. "And for the moment," Boniface dropped his voice, speaking rapidly, "to preserve Richard's failing health, I don't think we should highlight his claim to our Russian friend."

The two men entered the room, Sherborne first with Turgenev following, casting a final paranoid glance down the short corridor. Ellen stood up and took two small paces away from the desk as Sherborne staggered the last few steps like a man who was only moving forward in order to ensure that he didn't lose his balance. At the last moment he turned and sat on the computer table with his back to his collection of antique flintlock pistols. The table quaked as his weight made contact with the horizontal surface, then groaned as it accepted his weight. He wheezed, still gasping for air from the exertion of having walked from the next room, and took out his handkerchief to mop his brow and between the folds of skin around his jowls, which were acting as gutters for his sweat.

"Did you get the drives?" asked Boniface.

Sherborne tried to speak but instead wheezed, pointing to Turgenev.

"Sit over there, fat man." Turgenev waved his pistol in the direction of the sofa. Sherborne wheezed and nodded vigorously, patting his upper chest as if to communicate some sort of excuse to the Russian. "Now."

"Let me get my breath," rasped Sherborne.

"While you two are sorting out the seating arrangements, could I have the drives, please?" asked Boniface, holding up his manacled wrists with his hands cupped in the expectation of delivery.

Turgenev reached into his pocket and dropped the two drives into Boniface's hands, then stepped back, sweeping his weapon through the narrow arc covering his three possible victims.

Boniface pushed the first thumb drive into a port on the front of the computer and restarted his clumsy ritual of trying to operate the keyboard and mouse with his hands chained, but now with the fat man overwhelming the desk space. He watched the screen and waited while a file transferred, then yanked the drive out of the computer. "See. I told you: This drive is crap."

Three sets of eyes followed the flight of the unidentifiable small object Boniface launched; the pound coin and the figure of the walrus remained on the desk.

With the eyes distracted, as the wooden wedge hit the far wall and fell out of sight, Boniface twisted awkwardly, slipping the first thumb drive into his pocket. "They always go wrong; that's why I told you to get two," he said, pushing the second drive into the port on the front of the computer and dragging the file he had hastily doctored onto the drive.

The file transfer completed, and he turned to Turgenev. "Let me show you what you've got here."

Boniface opened the file as the Russian moved to get a better angle on the screen while keeping the gun trained on the three. "As you can see, there is a single file with all the photos of the documents. Here's the list of documents that Professor Armstrong has prepared, with a brief summary of each. Here's the first document from five hundred years ago, the second, and so on, until the last." Boniface flicked through the images in a blur, coming to rest on the final photograph taken by Nigel in the police station.

"Happy?" Before Turgenev could answer, Boniface yanked the drive out of the port and held it for the Russian, who grabbed it and stepped backward.

"So explain to me what I've got here."

"Really?" said Boniface. "You've spent the whole evening telling me I talk too much, and it's a really long story."

"Give me the short version. As you said, having a bunch of documents isn't much use. It's like having a gun without knowing where the trigger is."

"Okay," said Boniface starting to stand. "But let me sit over here." He stood and moved to the scroll-armed sofa, falling backward to sit.

Ellen moved to the space vacated on the desk and sat next to Sherborne. She turned to him, placing one hand on his shoulder and the other on his back, and in a soft voice asked, "Are you alright? Can I do anything for you?"

"I'm fine, my dear." The fat man's wheezing slowed. "I'm quite looking forward to this story."

"You two. Shut up. You." Turgenev turned to Boniface. "Explain."

"Well... Where to begin with the story of Henry VIII? At the beginning, I suppose... Henry was married to Catherine of Aragon. She gave him a daughter,

Mary. Catherine got pregnant on several other occasions, but none of those pregnancies led to a live birth of a baby that survived. Henry had affairs, and there were probably lots of bastards; however, the one that he acknowledged was Henry FitzRoy, the fruit of his union with his teenage lover, Elizabeth Blount." Boniface snorted. "And they say unmarried teenage mothers are a post-war phenomenon... The infant's godfather was Wolsey."

"Everyone knows that, Boniface," blustered Sherborne.

"Maybe. Maybe not. But for our friend here," he tilted his head toward the Russian pointing a gun at him, "I'm keen to include all the details."

Turgenev grunted. "Continue. But get to the point quickly."

"Professor Trudgett put forward his theory that Henry was murdered by Wolsey, probably with help from Anne Boleyn, or at least the Boleyn family, sometime around 1532, give or take. Wolsey assumed Henry's identity, continuing to act as King, and proceeded to systematically eliminate anyone who didn't accept him as King. Many courtiers and nobles accepted the situation and survived. Those that didn't...died."

"This was the basis of Nigel's book," said Ellen. The Russian stared at her; she blushed and fell silent.

Boniface directed his story to Sherborne. "But Wolsey's cover story is brilliant. It's so good that it's still an intrinsic part of English history." Sherborne frowned. "Henry was a slim man when he became King. But Henry, or as we now know, Wolsey, was morbidly obese when he died. We all know the story, but have we ever seen the transition? Have you ever seen an in-between Henry? Is there a slightly overweight Henry?"

Boniface looked at Sherborne, who was pondering the question. "No." The fat man shook his head slowly. "No, I have never seen a picture of a slightly overweight Henry, or a fat but not obese Henry."

"But you know the stated reason for the obesity?"

Sherborne straightened. Boniface was sure the fat man sucked in his stomach before he started talking. "Of course. Everyone knows this. It was a jousting accident. Henry was unconscious for two hours, but after that he never regained his fitness, and instead put on weight."

"The man was brilliant, wasn't he?" Boniface shook his head in disbelief. "That was Wolsey's cover story to explain how a thin man became fat, effectively overnight. And look at the detail: We all know he was out cold for two hours. No story with so much detail could be a fake, could it?"

"But that must have taken..."

"This process of inserting himself as King took years. Well, in many ways, it took the rest of his life—he just killed everyone who he thought could be a threat."

Sherborne shook his head in wonderment. "All that was a story concocted by Wolsey?" He laughed, a deep throaty laugh, which turned into a cough. He rocked with the rhythm of the cough and started to try to stand.

"Can I get you a glass of water or something, Richard?" Ellen's face showed concern. "Anything."

The fat man continued to try to stand. He lifted his weight, wobbled, and threw his hand forward for balance. "Sit." The command from the shaven-headed Russian was free from ambiguity.

Slowly Sherborne toppled backward, thrusting his other hand toward the wall where his flintlock collection was mounted, and with an uncharacteristically swift move he grabbed the nearest pistol, swinging it round to point at the Russian.

"Richard, no!" Ellen stepped in front of the antique gun, holding her hands in front of her in a mini I-surrender pose. "Richard! It's too dangerous. If he doesn't get what he wants, he's going to hurt other people. He's going to hurt…"

"Drop your gun now," said Sherborne, ignoring Ellen's protestations and pushing her to the side with the flintlock so that it pointed at Turgenev. "This gun might be old, but it's deadly, and I'm close enough to death not to need to worry about the consequences of killing you."

"No, Richard! No. We need to do what he says. My sister…" She laid a hand on the flintlock.

There was a thunderous crack. Ellen screamed and fell to the floor. Boniface looked to where she had been standing and saw a cloud of black smoke and Sherborne spattered with blood. He rolled forward on the sofa and started to lift himself but was knocked to the floor by the Russian approaching Sherborne.

Turgenev grabbed the flintlock from the fat man's loose grip and threw the gun across the room. It hit the bookcases on the far side at the same time as he landed a single punch in Sherborne's solar plexus. Boniface got to his feet, moving toward the heap of humanity as the man he blamed for so much doubled over and fell to the ground next to Ellen.

The academic lay silently, the smallest motion confirming she was breathing. Boniface knelt beside her, looking at her face and torso, a mixture of soot, blood, burned flesh, cuts, and shredded clothing. He reached out his manacled hands.

"Time's up," said Turgenev, yanking Boniface by the hair to a standing position and pushing him out of the door before he could gain a sure footing. In the corridor, he kept Boniface in front of him, holding the back of his collar and locating the barrel of his pistol in the small of Boniface's back.

The two moved slowly, the Russian accelerating with the gun and braking with Boniface's collar. As the corridor gave way to the landing, they paused before moving to the stairs, where they gracelessly descended to the marble-floored lobby, each step echoing around them.

"I just need to do one thing," said Boniface.

"No."

"One thing."

"No."

"One thing, and that's me done with arguing. You've got a gun in my back—and I know I'm only alive because you've decided I should be—so I'm not going to be stupid." Boniface pulled Turgenev toward the guard's desk. The guard's lifeless corpse lay where he had fallen, with a pool of blood now congealing.

Boniface stood by the old phone, picked up the receiver with his shackled hand, and dialed three numbers before lifting the receiver to his ear. He felt the cold steel as the Russian pressed the gun into his temple. The phone was answered and he uttered one word—"Ambulance"—before placing the handset on the desk, leaving the line open as he started moving toward the front door, pulling Turgenev with him.

The shaven-headed Russian reached around him to open the door onto Old Palace Yard, Boniface feeling the other man's sour breath on his neck as he looked out, keeping Boniface as a shield as he pushed the Englishman until they were both outside.

The first light of the morning had cracked the cover of night. There was no sign of the sun, but the sky had turned from black to a deep blue, mottled by the passing clouds. The birds were equally unwilling to face the day, but some of their braver number were tuning up for the dawn chorus with all the grace of an orchestra warming up.

The two men stood, expelling the odor of burned gunpowder and scorched flesh as they felt the morning breeze being blown from the river.

Turgenev broke the trance first, pushing Boniface down the path in the opposite direction of the gatehouse. They reached an indistinct Ford, and Turgenev flipped the trunk. "You know the drill."

sixty-four

Once in the trunk with the lid shut, plunging him into complete darkness, Boniface lost any sense of direction. Logically, the car would have returned to Richmond Green, but even then he couldn't sure, and the route after that was a complete mystery. By the stop/start nature of the driving, at times the route might have been a mystery to Turgenev as well, assuming he was still driving.

At first, the driver seemed to have a destination in mind. The car was driven hard and then parked for a few minutes before returning to its journey. After a second stop, something was loaded onto the back seat.

Following the second stop, there was some fast driving over poorly maintained streets. After that the driver seemed settled on his route, with one or two stops, until he got near to the end, when again the route became more erratic.

It had been a couple of minutes since the driver had killed the engine, although for Boniface, in the chill of the morning and having had his body pummeled throughout the journey, it felt like hours. In the front of the car he could hear Turgenev talking, probably on the phone—he didn't think anyone else had got into the car during any of the stops.

He didn't know where they were, but there seemed one logical destination. From the trunk he could hear planes flying over—they were low and, he guessed, passing at the rate of about one every minute—and the only place Boniface knew where you got that many planes at that height was Heathrow. Added to which, the shitty, twisty, poorly designed road layout suggested the airport, and the confusion over which direction they were going when they got close told Boniface that Turgenev had—like everyone else—been confused by the roundabout at Hatton Cross. Who designs a big roundabout with little roundabouts around the edges and then tells traffic to go both ways around the big roundabout but only one way around the small ones?

Someone who hates humanity. Even Turgenev wouldn't design that roundabout as torture for his worst enemy.

The talking stopped, and one of the car doors opened. Then shut. Another door opened, then shut, and Boniface could hear the sound of heavy footsteps, Turgenev footsteps, behind the car. The trunk flipped open, and Boniface blinked into the half-light. It was still early and the sun wasn't visible, but there was more light outside than in the pitch-black trunk.

He shivered. It had been cold in his prison, but he had built up some comparative warmth, which was now spilling out into the cold English spring morning. In place of his own personal fug, the unmistakable, irritating smell of aviation fuel was pouring. Another plane flew over with its undercarriage positioned ready for landing. If planes were landing, then Boniface knew it was after 6 AM, but from the light and temperature, not much after.

He remained motionless as Turgenev stood over him, looking around the trunk. "Your hands, please." He pulled his hands from under his head and held them toward the Russian, who snapped another handcuff around the chain connecting Boniface's hands, pushed his hands back over his shoulder, and attached the other end of the restraint to the small metal child-seat hook at the back of the seat forming the rear wall of the trunk. "I love your European safety standards. They keep small children very safe and make it so much easier to make sure people stay where I leave them."

Boniface groaned, trying to roll onto his back to relieve some of the tension on his wrists.

The Russian stared at him, indifferent to his discomfort. "You are staying alive for one reason." Boniface suddenly became alert. "You are staying alive to pass a message to Kuznetsov." Boniface nodded. "It is a simple message. You know the information I have." Boniface nodded again. "Mister Kuznetsov can be assured of my silence; that information will not go any further than me, and I will never approach him again, provided I am left alone." Boniface nodded more confidently. "You understand. I am not a problem for Mister Kuznetsov, and I will not be a threat to him, provided I am left alone."

"Got it," said Boniface.

"Good. Because if he doesn't understand the message, then I'm going to come after you first to make sure he understands how serious I am." Boniface flinched as the Russian's stare bored into him. "Make sure Mister Kuznetsov understands that I will destroy him if I even suspect that I am not being left alone."

"I will," said Boniface. "Now, can you undo these cuffs, and I'll go and tell him?" He tugged at the cuffs and found no slack.

Turgenev had the bored look of a schoolteacher who would rather be having a drink than dealing with a child who didn't understand some sort of rudimentary natural law.

"How long will you leave me here? I need to get out if I'm going to pass on your message. Will you call the police when you're about to board your plane?"

Turgenev laughed. "Who says I'm flying? This might be a convenient place to change cars." His face showed no emotion. "Don't worry, they'll find you soon enough. You might be here for a few hours. Maybe days. But they'll figure out soon enough that this is a stolen car...that is, once whoever owns it figures it's missing."

Boniface sighed.

"But to show you how much I care, I've got some presents for you." His tone was sarcastic. His face a confusion of staring eyes and a forced smile. "Yes, you, Mister Boniface. Some presents just for you."

He reached into his pocket and pulled out a key ring. "The policemen at the university gave this to me." He flicked through the keys and held one up. "Here's the key to undo your handcuffs." He laid the key ring about 12 inches in front of Boniface's nose with one key separated.

Boniface tugged at his restraints.

"I know you're enthusiastic to get to your present, but you're going to have to be patient. And anyway, you haven't seen what else I've got for you."

He took the car key and laid it next to the handcuff key. "Now I've heard that you don't drive, what with..." he mimed drinking from a bottle, "but once you're out of here, perhaps you can find someone else to take you home. And lastly." He laid a parking ticket next to the car key. "Your ticket out of here. I'm sure you can charge that expense back to Mister Kuznetsov."

The Russian stepped back and checked his pockets, dumping the detritus he found into the trunk. "One last thought for you. Don't bother shouting: You're parked in a distant corner of the parking lot, so no one will hear you, and no one is going to be passing because there are no empty parking spaces." He slammed the lid, leaving Boniface in darkness, trapped with the smell of aviation fuel and cold air.

The trunk flipped open again. "Silly me. I almost forgot." Turgenev held out Boniface's phone. "In case you need to make any calls. Here you go." The Russian slid the phone into Boniface's inside jacket pocket, patting it in position.

He slammed the lid again. Boniface listened as the steps became softer, then louder.

The trunk flipped open for a third time. "There's one thing that's nagging at me—you seemed too ready to give me that thumb drive."

"You had a gun," said Boniface without emotion.

"But still, taking the time to make sure I had a working thumb drive and throwing that broken one away..." The Russian leaned into the trunk, thrusting his hands into Boniface's jacket pockets, then into his trouser pockets.

He stepped back, grinning and holding the second thumb drive for Boniface to see.

sixty-five

Sergey Krylov felt a buzz in his crotch.

The music was pounding—Def Leppard's "Pour Some Sugar on Me"—and the dancers were working, each throwing the same shapes as the others, each thrashing in a way they thought was sexy, and if not sexy, well, they were doing what they knew would generate tips. The Russian relaxed as he felt the pleasure of the buzz, then jolted and reached into his jeans.

His pleasure prematurely interrupted, he yanked his phone out of his pocket and looked at the screen. He didn't recognize the caller, but from the number it was someone inside the Silver Spike. He hit the answer button, pulled the phone close, and shouted, "Wait while I go somewhere quiet!"

He stood, pushed his way through a few drunk businessmen—their ties at half mast, their suits crumpled and stained—groping any female flesh they could reach as the bouncers encouraged them toward the rear exit and the privacy offered by the back alley, where Krylov knew the CCTV cameras always seemed to be in need of repair.

The barman stood aside as the Russian walked behind the bar, leaving the flashing lights and stepping through a door into a concrete corridor, lit by a single flickering strip light suspended from thin chains. The door moved slowly behind him as the spring closer narrowed the gap to about four inches, then slammed the heavy door shut, muffling the sound outside.

"This is Krylov." He straightened and put his finger in his ear away from the phone, and pushed the phone closer to his head. He nodded, hung up, then called another number. "Grigorii. Get a car and meet me outside the club." He paused. "Now."

The rotating spotlight caught his line of sight as he pulled the door and headed back to his seat. Putting on his leather jacket, he headed for the exit, taking the wide spiral steps up to the ground level—with each step, feeling the transition from the desert-dry air conditioning to the gentle damp of a breaking English morning in spring.

As he stepped into the early morning light he took a deep breath, substituting the odor of other people with pure air. From the service road running down the side of the club, two men in suits walked unsteadily. Krylov smirked; when he had last seen them, they had been far friskier with their hands, and they didn't have the red scuff marks on their faces nor the blood on their shirts, and their suits were only crumpled, not ripped.

He straightened his jeans, slipped off his jacket, and pulled his T-shirt straight as the gunmetal grey Vauxhall Insignia pulled up, skidding the last few feet as the driver leaned over to push the door, which Krylov slammed behind him. "Drive. The boss has a job for us."

"What does Turgenev want us to do?"

"Not him, *the* boss. And I don't know—all I know is he wants us to get to Heathrow airport. He's going to call, so drive." He pointed, indicating to then turn left, and fell back in his seat as the car tires squealed and dug into the road.

Krylov pulled down the sun visor in front of him and looked at his visage in the mirror: dull, pockmarked skin, sunken on his skull, and maybe ten days' growth of hair on the top of his head. He slapped his cheeks, but failing to encourage any signs of life, he turned to compare his complexion with his driver's. "Did you shave this morning?"

"An hour ago," said the driver, feeling the smoothness of his chin. "My father was Greek—at least, the man my mother thinks was my father was Greek—and so I spend my whole life looking like I need to take a blade to my face."

The older man grunted, fixing on the crescent-shaped scar behind the swarthy man's ear.

"So why are we getting instructions from Mister Kuznetsov? Why is he getting up early to talk to us?" asked the driver.

"I don't know; I spoke to his secretary, who told me he needs us at Heathrow. And as far as he's concerned, this isn't early. He gets up at five every morning and then spends at least an hour with his trainer."

The driver snorted. "Pretty girl in Lycra, big butt, big..."

Krylov cut him off. "You remember when you were first assigned to the unit and joined the training battalion?" The driver grunted. "You remember those trainers—sergeants who did anything they could to break you?"

The driver talked quietly, as if trying to force grit out of his throat without scratching. "Bastards. They treated you like a dog, pushed you beyond your limits, made you want to kill them, and if you didn't kill them, you wanted to kill yourself. In the end, they left you filled with rage. You go to war because it's preferable to the training camp and less violent."

The older man mirrored the driver, slowly nodding. "That's who trains Mister Kuznetsov. One of the training battalion sergeants." The driver turned to face Krylov, who remained impassive and pointed back to the road. "Focus. He needs us alive."

sixty-six

Each time his phone rang, Boniface pulled at the cuffs chained behind his head, giving up the struggle in the dark when the pain around his wrists won the battle.

Reflexively, he reached for his phone to check the time and winced as the cuffs again bit into his raw flesh. With the pain subsiding, he tried to estimate the number of planes that had arrived since Turgenev had left him. Best guess? Perhaps one hundred and fifty? If there was a plane landing every forty-five seconds, perhaps every minute, it might be around two hours since the Russian had departed. Two hours, which—assuming there was a convenient flight—was enough time for the shaven-headed thug to buy a ticket, get on a plane, and leave. And after that, if the plane had a phone and Turgenev used it, then Boniface would be free. If not, he didn't know how many hours, or days, he would be waiting in the dark.

The sound of the planes passing a few feet overhead masked other sounds, and several times he became aware that someone had been close but that he hadn't heard them until it was too late. Perhaps there was a car door closing in the distance, or some footsteps that were sharp enough that they couldn't be too far away, or maybe a car passing.

As a door slammed, he became aware that someone had closed the door of the car next to him. He shouted. The response was the engine coming to life with the driver revving until the engine gained some rhythm. And in case Boniface could be heard, the driver made sure his CD—some misguided 1990s dance music—was loud enough to induce permanent hearing loss.

Boniface lost heart as he heard the driver grinding the car into gear and pushing the engine. The motor roared, and suddenly his prison was jolted sideways—the violent lurch accompanied by the sound of metal fighting metal.

The noise of torture ended, and Boniface felt his car rock back to the level. The engine of the other car stalled, the music stopped, and a door opened. Footsteps. "Ah shit!" A slurred, angry voice.

Boniface opened his throat and screamed; a deep, throaty roar, partly in fear, partly in desperation, until the trunk flipped open, blinding him with the light of a bright spring morning.

He fell silent and looked up. Where previously there had been a shaven-headed Russian, now a man of average height stood, a bit pudgy around the edges from too many expensed dinners, a decent but crumpled suit, unshaven with dark rings under his eyes, and in need of a few hours' work on his hair. "Jesus Christ, man. What the hell happened to you?"

Boniface exhaled slowly. "Long story. See that key there..." He pointed to the handcuff key with his nose. "It undoes these handcuffs, if you would be so kind." He threw his head backward, indicating his cuffed hands.

The man stood with his mouth open, looking around Boniface's prison.

"Please," said Boniface. "It's not the most comfortable position I've ever been in."

"Sorry," said the man, still staring at Boniface as he picked up the key before he leaned into the gaping hole. Boniface recognized the smell of whisky. If he hadn't been so desperate, he would have sneered at someone who could drink the swill they hand out for free on airplanes; this guy was a drinker, not a connoisseur.

"Just got off a plane?" asked Boniface.

"For my sins they put me on the red-eye," said the man, fiddling to remove the cuffs that locked Boniface to the child-seat hook. "There," he said triumphantly as Boniface flopped his arms flat in front of himself.

"That feels good. Thank you. Now if you could help me get out of here, then perhaps you can get these cuffs off my wrists. It'll be much easier for you when I'm out."

Boniface rolled over, pushing himself up to a kneeling position. "That hurts."

The disheveled man offered Boniface a hand and put his other behind his head. "Careful. You don't want to knock yourself."

Boniface leaned on the man while half standing in the back of the car and jumped, landing gracelessly but finding his feet. He held out his hands, and the other man removed the restraint, standing back as Boniface started to vigorously shake his arms and stamp his feet, slowly rotating on the spot.

As he completed a full rotation he stopped, took a deep breath, closed his eyes, and exhaled, bowing his head. The other man remained silent. Boniface raised his face, opened his eyes, smiled broadly, and held out his hand. "Pleased to meet you, savior. I'm Boniface, Alexander Boniface, but please call me Boniface."

The other man looked befuddled as he shook hands. "Clive Barratt. Slightly shocked, but very pleased to meet you...Boniface."

"Really good to meet you, Clive," said Boniface, reaching into the car to grab his phone and check the time. "It's a really long story, and I'd love to explain, and I *will* explain, but first, could you drive me to the terminals—terminal three, I think."

"Shouldn't we call someone?"

Boniface shook his head slowly. "The guy that did this has probably already left the country. But if he hasn't, then there's someone else who might be in danger, and I need to get to her."

Barratt remained motionless, his eyes growing larger.

"Please." Boniface pursed his lips and cocked his head, waiting.

"Oh, of course. Of course. Get in." Barratt turned and walked toward his door, allowing Boniface a view of his car, a four-door black Mercedes—one of the lower-priced models—gouged down its length. Boniface turned to the Ford he had traveled in, looking at the crumpled rear quarter with scrapings of black paint flaking off, grabbed the car key that had been left in front of him in the trunk, slammed the lid, and walked to the passenger door of the Mercedes.

As Boniface enjoyed the feeling of being softly held in a car seat rather than thrown in the trunk, he turned to his driver. "Please don't think I'm being rude, but I've got a call I really need to make. As you saw, I've been a bit tied up."

"Sure," said Barratt, firing up the engine. Nineties dance music bombarded them from all directions. He smacked the off button. "Sorry about that." His cheeks went slightly red. "The kids love it." Boniface nodded, unconvinced, and pulled out his phone. The driver slapped the car into gear and stepped on the pedal, throwing both men back in their seats as the vehicle zigzagged to the exit.

"On the perimeter road outside Heathrow airport." His call answered. "I'm... yeah, I'm fine. Had a bit of trouble, which is why I..." Boniface watched as the car drifted to the left, Barratt corrected, and then drifted to the right. Boniface checked his seat belt, braced his legs, and then looked away from the road. "Sorry, slightly distracted... Anyway, I had a bit of trouble last night so I couldn't call you back, but I'm fine. I don't have time to explain, but I need you to do something."

The car nudged the curb, a squeal of rubber and a jolt. "Sorry about that," said Barratt with a slight look of surprise on his face.

"You need to get someone, no make that several people, to Sherborne's place...yes Trumpeters' House. Real people, good people, people you trust, people who will ask questions and follow leads—and find out what happened there last night." Boniface listened to his former wife, then continued. "It was bloody. We left Sherborne and Ellen Armstrong there. They didn't look healthy, but I called an ambulance as we left."

Barratt jerked the car into the right-hand lane and followed the filter onto the slip road leading under the runway and into the airport.

"You had a reporter down there? Really? Nope. Didn't see the guy, but I'm guessing he's dead. Was he driving a Ford?" Boniface stared into the distance, not focusing on anything in particular as he listened. "Three things I know about Turgenev: He tries to be cautious, he's scared, and he's very good at killing people. Bring those three together, and if your guy was bumbling around outside Trumpeters' House, our Russian friend would have seen him and killed him. Probably killed him with his bare hands."

Boniface's eyes came into focus, and he shot out his hand to set the steering wheel straight. Barratt looked at him, his mouth open. He shook himself back to consciousness. "Sorry, Boniface, I er..." The car straightened.

"I'm about to lose you as we go into the tunnel," said Boniface. "Find out what's been happening and call me back when you have spoken to someone you trust. Last night's headline had enough mistakes for this week."

The phone went dead.

sixty-seven

Krylov answered before the second ring.

Grigorii Belotserkovsky, the swarthy driver, kept the gunmetal-gray Vauxhall Insignia moving swiftly, but with little finesse, toward Heathrow airport, passing along an anonymous strip of asphalt cutting between Victorian terraces built from sandstone-colored bricks, blackened through years of proximity to passing internal combustion engines.

"Yes Mister Kuznetsov, this is Krylov." Krylov sat up straighter in his seat and pulled his shoulders back. "Nikolay. Yes." The swarthy man turned to Krylov, with a questioning look. The older man drew his finger from his nose across his cheek as if to indicate a scar.

The swarthy man raised his eyebrows, mirrored the finger across his cheek, and mouthed "Nikolay," then returned his focus to the road.

Krylov listened, then continued. "Yes. I saw Nikolay leave yesterday. Mister Turgenev told me that I might have to send some items home for him." He jolted in his seat as if he had received an electrical shock. "My understanding was that Nikolay was going home... I didn't get a reason or an explanation. Yes... That was Mister Turgenev. Yesterday. Early evening. Maybe six PM."

The remaining color drained from the passenger's dull, pockmarked face, and he opened his eyes wider. "Gone? Turgenev disappeared... No, sir, I haven't heard from him since we spoke about Nikolay."

The swarthy man pointed to himself—the sound of his index finger hitting his chest audible above the sound of the engine. Krylov looked to him, and the other man mouthed, "I saw him."

"Sir. Grigorii saw him after that." He turned to the swarthy man. "You were behind the desk in reception were you, Grigorii?" The other man nodded. "What time was that?"

"He went out on his bike at around eleven. I don't know—we don't note his movements. Said he would be back soon, but he hadn't come back when I left at midnight."

"And you haven't seen him since?" The swarthy man shook his head. Krylov pulled the phone closer to his ear. "No, Mister Kuznetsov. Grigorii last saw Mister Turgenev at about eleven PM and hasn't seen him since."

A plane passed overhead, its undercarriage dropped, ready for landing. Krylov acknowledged the other man's questioning look, pointed in the direction of the plane, then pointed back at the road, which had now broadened into a three-lane highway with light industrial buildings—most displaying the logos of international freight couriers—set well back from the road. In the distance, a row of hotels sat, each looking the same, only differentiated by the neon sign displaying the name of the chain. The pockmarked man waved his hand in their direction, and the driver accelerated.

"Yes. We're close to the airport now, sir." He listened. "Maybe five minutes... Boniface. Boniface. Right. You'll send a picture... I understand. Not in public. We will, sir."

Krylov hung up and cracked his window, taking a lung-full of oxygen infused with aviation fuel, then turned to his driver. "Well, Grigorii Belotserkovsky. You may have only been working with us for a few days, but there has been a significant change. Apparently, as the cowboys would say, Turgenev walked off the reservation yesterday. It seems you were the last person to see him."

"But that was only a few hours ago. Isn't it a bit early to be worrying? Hasn't he found a woman or something?"

"Grigorii. You're young, and you don't know better, so I'll forgive you this once." He scrunched his face, then released quickly, his image returning to its usual lifeless state. "When you were in the army, loyalty was a matter of life and death. For Mister Kuznetsov, loyalty is more important than that. You do not, and will not, have a disloyal thought. Turgenev understood that."

He paused and looked out the window, then turned back to the driver. "If Turgenev has been gone for this long, then he's either dead or gone. And if he isn't dead, then he will be dead as soon as Kuznetsov knows where he is."

A silence hung between the two men, broken by the pockmarked man's phone beeping. He looked down at the phone, then back to the driver. "The boss is angry, and we must fix it. He knows we didn't cause the problem, but he'll blame us for not fixing it. There's no one else to hold responsible—Turgenev has gone, Nikolay is missing. His session with his trainer must have made him even angrier, and he's taking all his rage out on us."

"So why has he sent us to Heathrow?"

Krylov sighed. "He thinks Turgenev might be there."

"But we'll never..."

"I know. And Kuznetsov understands. But he wants us to be close. He wants us to look, and if it goes wrong and we're here, then we've got a problem." The driver made a noncommittal sound, acknowledging that an order had been given. "And he also wants us to look for someone called Bonny-something." He looked back at his phone. "Boniface, that's it."

"Who?"

"Someone with expensive suits and soft hands who was doing something with some dead professor that Kuznetsov is upset about. Kuznetsov seems to think this Bon...Boniface...is with Turgenev or has helped him to escape."

The driver snorted. "Turgenev? Take help from someone who works in an office? Someone who uses hand cream and probably moisturizes?" He shook his head, sneering.

"I know. But he wants us to look for him, and all we've got is his photo." He held his phone out. "Turgenev will be expecting us, and so he'll hide. Kuznetsov reckons that this Boniface man will be much easier to find, so we'll go after him."

"Let me see the picture," said the driver, pulling Krylov's hand holding the phone into his line of sight. His eyes flicked to the screen. "I know him." He released the other man's hand. "I saw him yesterday. He met with Mister Kuznetsov. I'll recognize him."

sixty-eight

"That lane."

Having given the order when the gouged black Mercedes emerged from the tunnel and joined Heathrow airport's inner ring road, Boniface pointed in the direction of the terminal three road. The car drifted across two lanes as Clive Barratt moved without looking and without noticing the chorus of angry horns behind him.

The car jerked to a halt in the drop-off line outside the terminal, no apparent effort having been made to pull up to the curb. "Well, sir, thank you. You saved me; you got me here. Give me your card, and I'll call to arrange dinner, where I can explain the whole story." He offered his hand, the two men shook, and Boniface was out of the car and into the terminal building.

He was scanning across the rows and down the columns of the arrivals screens when his phone rang. "Montbretia, hi. Where are you?" He turned away from the screens, nestling the phone into his shoulder. "Passport control... In a long queue... Not an EU National... Right then, I'll get a cup of tea... Yes, very English... Call me when you're in the baggage hall... No, I'm sorry, Ellen...couldn't make it. She says 'hi,' but she had a life or death issue that needed to be dealt with... No, everything's fine." Boniface scrunched his eyes shut. "Anyway, you've got me as your host this morning, so give me a call when you're sure you're not going to be deported."

He hung up and sighed deeply, bowing his head, lost in silent contemplation. A small pink plastic suitcase on wheels knocked his ankle. His eyes followed the lead from the case to a small girl, no more than four years old, with blond hair tied back in a neat ponytail, pulling with both hands to free her luggage from his ankle. "I am so, so sorry," said the woman standing next to the child. Her look was similar, but her shade of blond tried too hard and seemed to suggest envy of the child. The iron grip around her collection of itineraries, booking details, and passports, coupled with a mis-buttoned blouse, all pointed to someone who wasn't a natural organizer.

Boniface squatted down and looked directly at the girl, unhooking the case while keeping a look of deep concern on his face. "I'm sorry. Did I get in your way?" She pushed out her bottom lip and nodded vigorously, her face breaking into a smile as she took back control of the case. He stood and looked at the mother's apologetic face. "It's not a problem. Really, it's fine," he said and then turned back to grin at the child, trying to ignore his vision of how her mother would spend the next several hours transferring all of her pent-up stress to the little girl. He couldn't, so he turned away, looking to see which of the cafés offered internet access.

Ye Olde Londone Coffee House seemed to fit the bill, even if the name made Boniface cringe with embarrassment for his city. At the top of the stairs he turned into the café and found himself looking at the food. Picking out a shrink-wrapped bacon sandwich, he joined the queue. "Cup of tea and this...please." He grabbed a tray, dropped the sandwich onto it, and placed the two next to the cash register.

One of the servers sneered, filling a cup of hot water and dropping a tea bag onto the surface. Boniface felt the unique disappointment that comes from the expectation of poorly made tea. "Heated?" asked the man behind the register, wiping his nose on the back of his latex-gloved hand.

"The tea?"

"The sandwich."

"Oh. Sorry. Please. Yes."

The disapproving tea-maker placed the cup with the floating tea bag onto the tray and picked up the sandwich, ripping open the plastic and flipping it into a microwave. Boniface looked at the water in the cup; a small trail of brown was starting to seep from the tea bag, but without any apparent desire to impart any flavor.

The nose-wiping cashier put a small stand holding the number 17 on the tray. "Seven pounds thirty."

He tried to hide his shock as he offered a £10 note. "Milk?" The nose-wiper tilted his head toward the end of the counter, dropping the change and a receipt onto the tray as he turned to address his monosyllabic question to the next person in line.

Boniface picked up two small plastic milk pots and three sugar packets from the end of the counter and made his way to the row of two old and battered computers standing against a wall at the far end of the café. He picked up one of the coins from his change, dropping it into the slot while he continued to unload his tray. He squeezed the tea bag, placing it on the tray, then added milk together with twice his normal amount of sugar.

He flipped his phone and checked the message received a few hours ago. With a few clicks on the computer, he was back in Nigel's online storage, downloading the photos. He took a sip of his tea, winced, and put it to the side. It was at least twelve hours since he'd had anything to drink, but even he couldn't drink that.

"Number seventeen!" a voice shouted across the room. Boniface contemplated whether he was brave enough for a second sip. "Number seventeen." The voice seemed weary.

"Here." Boniface raised his hand. Surely a premade bacon sandwich had to be better than a bad cup of tea. The nose-wiper carelessly dropped a plate with his sandwich in front of him. Boniface spent a moment or two assessing the risk of food poisoning before the need for food kicked in. He took a large bite and stared back at the screen.

With a few clicks, he opened his email. He had last checked his messages shortly before he had left for his meeting with Kuznetsov. Since then, he had received around five hundred emails, and only about half of those were spam. He could deal with the technology, but he needed someone to help him with the organization. He ignored the unread mail and started a new message. After attaching the photos he had downloaded from Nigel's online storage, he hit the send button.

sixty-nine

The gunmetal-gray Vauxhall Insignia sluggishly crawled past the long-term parking lot on Eastern Perimeter Road and turned onto Northern Perimeter Road, leaving the row upon row of abandoned motor vehicles, and followed the high barbed-wire fence around the runway, which was surrounded by young men in cheap weather-proof clothing carrying binoculars, cameras, and notebooks, all pointing excitedly at each arriving plane. "You don't think this guy will be camouflaging himself as a plane spotter?"

Both men scanned their surroundings like paranoid owls who had drunk too much coffee, the driver gripping the steering wheel with his left hand and scratching his nose with his right.

The phone rang. Its owner answered it before the second ring. "Krylov." He stiffened. "Sir... Terminal buildings. Fast!" He pushed his phone into his jeans as the car sped up, moving into the right-hand lane. "Boniface's phone signal has been tracked in terminal three."

The driver held the wheel tight, throwing the car to the right, then cut across two lanes to get to the left lane, took the ramp down, and turned left at the scale-model Airbus to follow the road to the terminals. "Hurry up!" he shouted at the bus in front of him as a minicab blocked him on the other side. "Are we sure this is Bonny-whatever-his-name-is?" He hit his horn and veered toward the minicab beside him. The minicab driver responded with his horn, but when the swarthy man didn't seem to yield, braked to allow him into his line.

"We're sure it's Boniface's phone." He sighed, grimacing. "And even if we're not sure, we're sure—Kuznetsov has told us we're sure. It could be Boniface, it could be Turgenev with Boniface's phone—we don't know anything except that we have orders to look."

The car shot out of the tunnel into the jumble of roads that fanned in front of them, before then contracting as the inner ring–road traffic joined the flow. "There." Krylov pointed at the sign for terminal three, and the driver accelerated, cutting across the traffic, daring anyone to get in his way as he followed the road.

"If you've seen him, then there's a chance Boniface can recognize you, so go to a gift shop first. Buy yourself a hat and some sunglasses. Look like a tourist, not like..." He looked the driver up and down. "Well...do anything but look like you. We want to find this guy and figure what he's up to. We don't want to scare him and make him run."

"But we can scare him later?"

"Oh yeah. Scare him a lot. It'll be easy—I'll rip his suit a bit. That'll make him cry. But first we need to know what he's been doing. Other people have made mistakes... big mistakes, so we can't afford to. This is all about being quick and quiet. We need to find and follow—if he's dead, then we can't ask him questions. But once we've got his answers...then we won't need him alive."

The car continued to accelerate, tires screeching through the next bend. It pulled up with a skid, throwing both men forward and then back into their seats as the vehicle stopped. Each rolled out, slamming his door behind, and started jogging toward the terminal.

seventy

As the email he had promised to send to Ellen started to lazily pass its cargo across the wires, Boniface picked up his bacon sandwich and took another bite. Given its provenance, it was surprisingly good and was consumed in three further bites as the email finished sending.

The nine photos on Nigel's online storage stared back at him. He created a new email addressed to himself and then stopped, falling back into his seat and softly muttering, "Don't need to do that—I've got a copy of the email I sent to Ellen."

Staring at the nine thumbnails as he chewed. "Gotta do it," he muttered and selected the nine photographs before hitting the delete button. He watched as the online storage showed a graphic display dragging each individual photo file to a bin until eventually the folder was empty.

He logged out and then went to the files he had copied to the local machine, deleted them, opened the recycle bin, located the nine files he had just deleted, and deleted them from the recycle bin. "Vanya will be pleased," he said softly, standing.

As he reached the bottom of the stairs he walked to the arrivals area, looking for somewhere to stand where he could see and be seen. He wondered whether he should make a sign so that Montbretia would find him.

The contemplation was disrupted by his phone. "Hi. How are you doing?" Boniface stopped walking. "You've got your luggage and you've just come through customs. That was fast...you're nearly here." The flood spilling from arrivals walked around him as he talked. "So what am I looking for?" He listened, repeating fragments. "Five-nine, shoulder-length brown hair, rucksack, white shirt, jeans, desert boots, pretty scuffed, phone in hand, standing in front of me if I lift my head..."

Boniface's vision found the sandy-colored desert boots laced up above the ankles, disappearing under the end of a pair of jeans, faded and close-fitting without being skintight. As he lifted his head he saw the white cotton shirt, which looked incredibly fresh, a tailored fit with brown buttons and sleeves neatly folded back. His gaze passed the rich brown hair lying over the rucksack straps and found the broad grin, the strip of freckles over the small nose, and the dark-green eyes. "Good to meet you, Boniface."

"But..."

"I recognized you from your website, although...you did seem to have a better suit on for those photos." Self-consciously, Boniface looked down at himself, pausing to notice his scuffed, dirty shoes, the large patches of mud on his suit, the shredded tie, and the crumpled shirt. "Rough night?"

"Rough night, long story, and needing a dry cleaner and a good bath are the very least of my problems. Let's get out of here."

"Sounds good to me." Montbretia was still grinning.

"Can you drive?" asked Boniface.

"Of course."

"Then let me take your rucksack, and follow me," said Boniface, turning and bumping into a tall man with about ten days' growth on his head, wearing jeans and a leather jacket. "I'm..." Boniface stopped, mouth open, color draining from his face as he took in the pockmarked skin. He looked again. "I'm sorry...I...I thought you were...someone else."

"No problem," said the stranger in an accent with a distinct Russian flavor.

Boniface took the rucksack. "This way, Montbretia. Let's go somewhere and get you a decent breakfast, and I can start to explain."

The bus followed its circle route between terminals, finally dropping them at the long-term parking lot. After some time looking for the parking ticket in the trunk and then paying the equivalent of what it would cost for dinner in a Michelin starred restaurant to get out of the parking lot, Boniface handed the keys to Montbretia who cautiously drove the Ford with Boniface sitting silently to allow her to concentrate. His only communication was the occasional hand gesture to suggest direction and a few ambiguous comments when Montbretia asked about her sister.

"I hate stick shifts."

"It's a family failing," said Boniface. "Left at the end here."

Montbretia pulled out and joined the flow of traffic. "Is that the Thames?"

"Yes."

"And do people live in those houseboats?"

"On some. But it gets a bit cold in winter." Montbretia's head flicked to look at the river before she returned her concentration to the road. "So where to?"

"Our destination is in sight," said Boniface.

"I see a wall. Bit of an old wall, if truth be told."

"Beyond the wall." He paused. "At the roundabout, turn right, then take the entrance on the left with the animals on top of the pillars."

Montbretia followed the instructions, slowing as she turned into the gateway. "Wow. I mean wow, wow, wow! This is proper, proper England. Is this..."

Boniface felt like a proud parent, keen to brag to all his friends about his child's achievement. "Yup. Hampton Court Palace." He turned to Montbretia. "And by the way, it never ceases to amaze, however often you come here." The car behind honked. "Park up... It's on the left here."

The two stepped out of the car into the sun. "Do you want to start taking some pictures while I get the tickets?" Montbretia opened the back door and rummaged through her rucksack while Boniface stood at the back of the car, admiring the rear wing refashioned by Clive Barratt.

"Ouch," said Montbretia, walking around to join him.

"Mmm." He continued, his voice distracted. "I'll get the tickets and find you somewhere around there."

"I'll be waiting."

He watched Montbretia walk toward the Great Gatehouse, her camera swinging from her hand, before he turned into the ticket office. It was an old building—new by Hampton Court standards, but old by everyone else's. The inside had all the lack of charm of a heritage center that could be found anywhere in the UK: large, dark porcelain stone-effect tiles on the floor; varnished oak tables that were still oak-colored, resembling the contents of a Swedish furniture store catalog, not having had the time to darken like the blackened, untreated oak in the Palace. Each table was covered with a range of cheap and dog-eared publications highlighting other English heritage locations for the uninspired tourist. Boniface bought two tickets and winced at the price.

The ring of his phone told him that Veronica was calling. He answered, slinking into a corner of the room, looking to confirm he wasn't overheard. "Talk." The color slowly drained from his face, dragging his soul and spirit with it. He felt himself go weak and started to wobble, landing in a nearby cheap oak-framed chair with fabric-covered padding, his head resting on his knees.

seventy–one

Boniface sat up. Feeling his eyes burn, tears streaming.

He wiped his eyes with the back of his hand, unsure of how long he had been sitting in the ticket office or who had been watching him.

After several deep breaths, he slowly got to his feet, taking his first few steps with the precision of a dizzy child. There was an exit sign above the door. He fixed his sight on the sign and tried to walk with purpose, picking up speed until he was outside and able to breathe fresh air again.

He took several gulps of clean oxygen, tugged his lapels to straighten his jacket, tucked his shirt in, and ran his hand through his hair, picking out grass, mud, and cow shit before wiping his eyes again and going to search for Montbretia.

Turning the corner he saw the figure: desert boots, jeans, immaculate white shirt, shoulder-length chestnut hair recently cut, engrossed in capturing the majesty of Hampton Court palace from every angle and in the changing light as the clouds moved across the fresh spring sky.

Boniface stepped onto the main drive leading up to the Great Gatehouse, relieved to be able to stroll along the length without urgency. Even more pleased that he wasn't being chased by a homicidal Russian.

He caught up with Montbretia. "Hey Boniface. Why the police cars and the crime-scene tape?"

Boniface looked back to the guard hut, now surrounded by police crime-scene tape vibrating in the breeze. He didn't want to lie, again, so he did his best to brush off the question and shrugged nonchalantly.

Montbretia, looking irrepressibly happy, like a puppy, seemed content with the unspoken answer. "I've got a load of photos. They'll be great for the blog, and Ellen will love what I'm going to say. So where does the tour begin?"

Boniface cocked his head and pointed away from the Great Gatehouse. "This way."

They followed the path through the kitchen garden—going against the flow of tourists heading for the Great Gatehouse and Anne Boleyn's Gate—and then along a quieter path.

Montbretia looked at the sign. "What's a tiltyard?"

"Where they tilted," said Boniface flatly. His companion looked confused. "Jousted," he added, leaning forward as if holding a lance.

Silence fell between them again. Boniface pale, his eyes still stinging, feeling sick, but not feeling anything that couldn't be blotted out by taking up drinking again.

"You look like shit." Montbretia broke the wordlessness as Boniface let his eyes point to the path they should follow. "No...I mean, when you met me at the airport, you looked like shit, and that hasn't changed. But there's something more now; you look worse, and more than ten minutes worse. And you've gone quiet—I know you were quiet when I was driving—but this is break-up-with-your-girlfriend quiet. What's up?"

Past the end of a wall, they moved out of the direct sunlight into a quiet, secluded area, away from the main features drawing the visitors. Boniface ignored the keep-off-the-grass sign, walking until the two were a distance from the path in a corner formed by two Tudor walls. He sat down on the grass, still damp with the previous night's dew, unworried by his wet ass or any damage to the suit, and motioned for Montbretia to join him.

"You do know that it's humor that gets a girl into bed, not wet grass," said Montbretia, sitting opposite him, resting against an old twisted tree. Boniface looked up, allowing her to see his bloodshot eyes with tears starting to flow. Her face fell, taking a look of concern.

"Your sister and I had a bad night last night. We saw things that we never wanted to see."

"Long story," whispered Montbretia.

"Long story." Boniface nodded. "Let me get to the important part that you need to hear." He wiped a tear that was trickling beside his nose. "You've heard of her publisher, Richard Sherborne?"

"The fat one with the harem? Is it still a harem when all the members post-menopausal?"

"That's the one." Boniface paused. "After you spoke to Ellen last night, we went to Sherborne's house. Again, long story. While we were there, we were held at gunpoint by a man called Turgenev."

"You're just making up Russian names to make your story sound more adventurous." Montbretia smirked, dropping the mirth when Boniface didn't reciprocate.

"The guy is dangerous." Nothing registered on Montbretia's face. "The crime-scene tape around the guard hut inside the gate?"

Montbretia bobbed her head once, seemingly apprehensive about agreeing.

"I'm guessing he killed a man last night. There." Boniface watched the shock on her face turn to fear. "And that wasn't the first nor the last person he killed yesterday."

"This man was holding you at gunpoint?"

Boniface flicked his eyelids closed to acknowledge.

"You and Ellen."

"Yeah." Boniface's voice faded, his words communicated through aspiration. "Sherborne took a chance. He has a collection of antique flintlock pistols. I don't know where he got the gunpowder or when he loaded it, but he tried to defend us. Ellen tried to stop him. Turgenev knew you were coming and threatened you. She wanted to protect you."

Montbretia trembled.

"The gun misfired."

Montbretia gasped, putting her hand over her mouth. "Tell me Ellen's alright."

Boniface slowly shook his head. "Ellen was hurt, badly. She was taken to hospital. She didn't recover and died two hours ago."

She laughed. "This is a great joke. Awful joke, but I almost believed you. Russians... Antique guns..."

Boniface shook his head, tears streaming down his cheeks. He reached and grabbed Montbretia, holding her while she sobbed.

seventy–two

"Where is she? I need to be with her." Montbretia pulled back from Boniface and tried to stand, falling back to the ground, clutching at Boniface and sobbing. "I need to be with my sister. She can't be alone."

Boniface awkwardly reached into his pocket and pulled out his handkerchief. Before last night it was clean and white. Now it was creased and stained with mud and blood, and Ellen's tears. He offered it to Montbretia. "I'm sorry, it's all I've got."

She took it, looked for a less dirty patch, mopped her eyes, and then looked up at Boniface, two sets of bloodshot, tear-stained eyes making contact. "I want to be with my sister, Boniface. I want to be with her."

"I know. But she's being looked after now." He lowered his head, his voice a whisper. "And there's a legal process...but she's being looked after."

"It was an accident, can't we just..."

Boniface wiped his eyes with his thumb and gently shook his head. "I'm sorry. There are legal processes. But I've talked to a friend who's a newspaper editor, and she has got some of her journalists on it—they'll be able to find out much quicker than we could. She'll make sure that you're the first one to know when anything happens."

Montbretia contemplated Boniface's dirty handkerchief, rejecting another dirty patch. "Tell me the whole story. Tell me how this happened. Why are you alive while my sister is dead?"

He could see the rage and the impotent frustration building. "I'm alive because I was on one side of the room, and she was on the other. If we had swapped places, I wouldn't be here. You can't even blame the Russian; it was simply an accident."

"An accident? My sister's dead, and you say it was an accident." Montbretia stared at Boniface, silently accusing him as the tears flowed, her voice breaking. "Why didn't you stay with her?"

Boniface hung his head, tears rolling down each side of his nose. "I wanted to. Really I did. But I was in handcuffs, and Turgenev had a gun. I didn't have a choice. The only thing I could do—the thing I did do—was call the ambulance."

"And what about Sherborne? Is he dead, too?"

"Not yet. But he wasn't that far from death before we began." He looked up, with the slightest hint of a twitch at the edge of his mouth. "Sherborne is fat. Not just a bit overweight. Not cuddly. But out-and-out obese. That's one of the main reasons why he was already so close to death." He shook his head slowly. "Turgenev punched him. If Richard hadn't been so fat, the blow would have killed him, but as it is, his blubber provided some sort of padding."

Montbretia smiled. "Well, can we go and see him?"

"Soon. I'm sure the redoubtable Ada is with him, tending to his every need." He looked up. "But there are other things that need to be done, and you're not going anywhere without me being there next to you."

"I'm a big girl, Boniface. I can handle myself."

Boniface could hear the offense in her voice. "I know, but..."

"It's a long story. I get that. My sister spends a night with a homicidal maniac, and all you can say is it's a long story. Well, I'm ready for the long story now, Boniface."

The silent expectation, laced with anger and blame, froze both of them. "You will hear the story. I was there, I saw what went on, and I want you to hear everything, and you will hear it from me." He weighed how to phrase his next remarks. "But there's something I need to do first. We're both still in danger."

Montbretia jolted. "Why am I in danger? I've only just arrived."

"Because your sister was in danger and you were threatened last night." Boniface bowed his head with a small smirk. "Long story…"

"Now you're being silly, Boniface. There's no danger."

"Perhaps you're right. In fact, I hope you are, and that I'm wrong. But I've seen too many people die in the last few hours, and I'm not taking any risks. I'm going to the source to make sure that I am safe and that you are safe. The order of priority for me is one, deal with the danger, then two, explain." He held her stare.

Montbretia broke first. "Then I'm coming." She went to stand.

"Nope." Boniface left no room for discussion. "You are going to stay here where I know you're safe. I can't think of a better place to be: There are loads of cops around, and Mister Turgenev certainly won't be returning to this crime scene for a while. And if you're here, you won't get caught in any crossfire."

She still looked unconvinced as he continued. "Ellen wanted to bring you here; we talked about it last night. It's one of the most gorgeous places in the country. Take some time, walk through the grounds, have a look in the buildings. Here…" He reached into his pocket and pulled out a ticket. "I did get the tickets, before… before…before I got distracted." He looked at her. "You've had awful news. You've had news that I don't know how you ever deal with." He saw a tear start to form in her eye. "Take some time, sit with your memories of Ellen. Be patient. I'll be back as soon as I can."

Boniface started to stand. "How long will you be?" asked Montbretia.

"An hour there, ten minutes meeting, an hour back? Maybe some delay—I've got to get the train. Certainly less than three hours. I'll be here for lunch. And after lunch we can check out the Maze. I'll race you to the middle, so no cheating and checking out your route while I'm gone." Montbretia tilted her head. "Deal?" He held out his hand to shake.

"Deal," she replied, taking his hand and pulling herself to her feet.

"You've got my phone number, so call if you've got any problems, but I'll be back as soon as I can." He reached into his pocket and pulled out his wallet, handing her all his cash apart from one bill. "Just in case."

seventy–three

Grigorii Belotserkovsky remained at a distance, scratching his stubble and watching the man called Boniface with the younger woman he had met at the airport.

Boniface had taken the woman to a secluded area and had made her sit on the grass with her back to a tree before he talked to her. From the way she reacted, it had been bad news.

He then went to leave, although she appeared to not want him to depart. But he had, and before he left he took something from his pocket and gave it to her—the swarthy man guessed this was cash. But why bring her here, upset her, then give her cash?

Her blouse—which had been white when he first saw her at Heathrow—was now marked with mud and grass stains, but that didn't seem to concern her as she sat on the damp ground, weeping.

In the quiet between the passing airplanes, and when there weren't any children running around shouting, he could hear the occasional sob and snivel, punctuated with gasps for air before she put her head down, wailing, with her whole body shaking.

He watched, waiting.

Slowly she lifted her head and looked around, wiping her nose on her sleeve. He started walking toward her, careful to make enough noise that his approach would be heard.

"Please. Sorry disturb. You are lady with Mister Bonny?" Inwardly he cursed his lack of fluency with the English language—he was a soldier; he had never thought diction or translation would be important. She looked up at him, staring blankly through bloodshot eyes. "Please, Mister Bonny need you help." He held out his hand to her. "Quickly."

She remained impassive, staring up at him. "Who are you?"

"Mister Bonny need you help, now." He reached forward, putting his hands under her arms, and gently lifted. Reluctantly she stood, wiping her eyes and contemplating the Russian.

"What's happened?"

"Please now." He tried to keep the aggression out of his voice.

"I'm calling him," said the woman, reaching into her pocket and pulling out her phone.

Belotserkovsky took one step to stand square to her and smashed his arm down just behind her ear. As he made contact she wobbled, then started to fall away from him. He took two quick steps, lowering his back, then grabbed her, pulling her weight over his shoulder.

He stood straight, his victim flopping over his back, and started to walk with intent, scanning to make sure he wasn't being watched.

seventy-four

Boniface left Montbretia sitting on the damp grass, resting her back against a large tree. Her formerly crisp white blouse was now far from pristine, having become muddy when Boniface held her as she screamed, and grass stained as she lay on her side sobbing.

He walked back from the far side of the Palace grounds to the Great Gatehouse, turning onto the central drive leading to the outer gate. The memory of driving along the track last night with Ellen was clear, but he couldn't remember anything since he had left Montbretia. Logically, he knew where he had been and the route he would have taken. He was sure that he would have seen other people, but he couldn't bring the image of the route to mind or recall any faces he might have seen.

He had been running on autopilot, lost in a trance.

He stopped abruptly. Someone was blocking his way. He looked up and recognized the form—highly polished boots, jeans, well-worn leather jacket—but couldn't call to mind a name attached to the lifeless pockmarked face glaring at him.

"Mister Boniface."

Boniface stared. A flick of recognition. Of course, this was one of Kuznetsov's men—the dress code, the military stance, the invasion of personal space, and the accent told him that, but there was something more. Sure, he had more than a passing resemblance to Turgenev, but probably so did half of the former Spetsnaz members now working for oligarchs around the globe.

"Mister Boniface. Alexander Boniface."

Boniface gave up trying to remember where he had seen this face. "Just Boniface." He took half a step backward. "I'm sorry, I can't remember your name."

"Mister Turgenev has been your guardian angel. He's rather busy today so has asked me to come and have a word with you." The Russian pointed in the direction from which Boniface had just walked. "Please. Walk with me."

Boniface remained impassive, swaying on his feet, unable to assess what was being asked of him or whether he should oblige. He took a deep breath and held it before he started to talk. "Look..." He was lost again in contemplation. "Look. I've gotta get to see Kuznetsov. There are some things he needs to hear...directly...in person...you know, confidential stuff."

He started to step forward. The pockmarked Russian did not yield, but leaned toward Boniface and quietly mumbled, "Don't make me upset Mister Kuznetsov by killing you in public." He pointed back in the direction from which the Englishman had walked.

Boniface slowly turned and started to walk, the Russian immediately behind and to his right, talking into the Englishman's ear. "We're going somewhere quiet for a pleasant little chat, and if you don't want to chat..." Without looking, Boniface could feel a grin spread over the other man's face. "If you don't want to chat, well... let's get away from these people, and I'll explain."

The two proceeded, turning out of the main flow of people converging on the Great Gatehouse, and following the path through the kitchen garden, through the outer grounds of the palace, toward the tiltyard.

"So this is where Henry VIII lived? He was the big fat one? He liked eating but was less worried about CCTV cameras."

Boniface stopped. The Russian's shoulder knocked into his. "Stop. Stop playing. Stop trying to intimidate me."

The big man's face maintained its palsy-like state. His unblinking eyes locked on Boniface. "Very brave. But remember, you're here because Mister Kuznetsov didn't want us to spill blood in his office. Now walk."

The two men held their stare. The Russian threw his head to the right, and Boniface started to walk in the direction indicated. "And as we walk, Mister Boniface, you talk." The Russian walked in lock-step diagonally behind and threw his shoulder forward to knock Boniface's. "Understood?"

"Understood."

"So start with your friend, Mister Turgenev."

Boniface stopped, spinning to face the larger man. "He's not my friend."

"And yet you spent so much time with him yesterday and you're still alive. What other conclusion am I meant to draw?" The Russian stepped forward, his glare fixed on Boniface, grabbed the Englishman's crotch, and squeezed. "I'm sure your friend Turgenev—or would you prefer me to call him your co-conspirator, Turgenev—led you to believe that we're all pussycats."

Boniface felt the growing pain. Unable to twist away, he remained motionless.

The Russian didn't deviate. "If that was the case, then I'm sorry for the misunderstanding, but I'm not cuddly like he was, and I've got a much more volatile temper." He increased the pressure in his right hand—Boniface whimpered. The Russian leaned closer, assaulting Boniface with his raw breath. "There's no point pretending you don't know what I'm talking about when I know that you do."

Boniface tried to make a sound.

The Russian continued to grip Boniface, who tried to speak, tears starting to form in his eyes. "But I don't..." The pressure increased. Boniface whispered. "I didn't..."

The Russian lifted his hand, and Boniface stood on his tiptoes. "So why has Mister Turgenev let you live? That's Turgenev who's on his way to Paraguay, by the way."

"Because," yelped Boniface. "Please." He flapped his hand, and the Russian loosened his grip slightly. "Because I lied to Turgenev." His speech became a fast hiss. "He had a gun on me. I had to get out. So I told him a lie. I let him think that I was giving him something to barter with Kuznetsov. Something that he could use to guarantee his own safety and retire. If he's sitting on a plane to Paraguay, that means he hasn't reached a computer and found that what I gave him was..." Boniface modulated his voice, "junk. A few low-grade, blurry, underexposed images that no one can read."

The large Russian smirked. "You fooled Turgenev?" Boniface gave the smallest of nods, trying to blot out the memory of the second thumb drive that Turgenev took. "He'll kill you when he finds out. You do know that?" The Russian released his hand; Boniface fell to his knees, taking large gasps of breath. "Keep talking." He lifted Boniface by his collar—there was a soft ripping sound as Boniface raised up. "And keep walking. Now explain about your girlfriend. Remember, if you don't talk, I'll hurt you, and then I'll hurt your pretty little friend."

Boniface stopped. "Leave her out of this. You've done enough to hurt her and her family. Take me, but leave her."

The Russian's face fixed again in its palsy-like state. His unblinking eyes locked on Boniface. "Very brave. Very honorable. And if you want, we can talk about it. But by the time we've finished the conversation it might be too late. My friend Grigorii was never a sensitive lover. Enthusiastic, yes. But far less tender than I am. He's a very vigorous young man."

Boniface stiffened. "Who's Grigorii? What's he doing to her?"

The pockmarked Russian remained impassive. "I don't know. You're the one that wants to spend his time talking."

Boniface started to sprint toward the tree where he had left Montbretia.

"Where is she?" he gasped to the Russian jogging behind him as they reached the tree.

The Russian raised his eyebrows and started walking. Boniface followed, running to catch up, his breathing becoming labored. The Russian left the path and headed toward a groundsman's shed—a rough shiplap-clad building with reinforced metal corners holding it together like an overstuffed packing crate, except this would probably fit two cars.

He held back as they reached the double doors, as if to allow Boniface to enter first.

Boniface looked at the padlock. The lock was fastened shut, but the screws holding the hasp in the second door had been forced out. The Russian pulled the door with the padlocked attached: "In."

Boniface stepped in front of the other man and felt a blow on the back of his head.

seventy-five

There was a rasping sound. Not fast. Stone scraping on metal. Slow, consistent, deliberate, focused, with a regular rhythm.

The grinding fought its way through Boniface's ears, stabbing into his brain as he started to come around. His head throbbing and bones aching, reminding him of the physical beating his body had taken over the previous 12 hours. Cautiously, he opened his eyes, keeping his focus narrow, wincing with the pain at the back of his head as he tried to locate the sound of scraping. With each rasp he felt an involuntary spasm, and the pain of movement as his body jolted.

He tried to focus in the gloom inside what he presumed was the shed he had been led up to, but movement was hard now; his wrists and ankles had been bound, and his body seemed to have been thrown on the ground with his hands bound behind his back.

The grinding was relentless as his blurred vision flicked around the shed. Gardening tools hung on the walls—forks, spades, several bow saws, hand saws, pruning saws, loppers, and shears—and the shelves were stacked with string, tins, and packets. On the floor of the shed were two lawnmowers, a roller, and several other pieces of large gardening machinery that he recognized but couldn't put a name to, along with piled bags of fertilizer, grass seed, and old sacks.

In the half-light, as his gaze moved toward the door, he saw a man sitting on an upturned wooden crate with a shovel laid across his lap. The swarthy man was focused on his task, rubbing something in his hand over the edge of the shovel. Boniface shifted his weight, scraping the floor as he moved. The man looked up from his shovel. "Sergey."

There was a low groan from the hinge as the door moved. Boniface struggled as his eyes adjusted to the light now streaming in. Regaining focus, he could see that the pockmarked man who had persuaded him not to leave Hampton Court was now in the shed and had picked up the shovel that the other man—a swarthy man Boniface thought he might have seen at the Silver Spike—had been crafting. The pockmarked man ran his finger across the shovel's newly sharpened blade as if he were stroking a newborn kitten and turned to Boniface. "It's like a compulsion for Grigorii. He's like one of Pavlov's dogs—you give him a shovel, and he sharpens it. He won't stop until it's sharp enough for him to shave, and as you can see, he needs to shave very often."

He turned to the swarthy man. "This is good work. Are you going to shorten the handle?"

The other man stood, took the shovel, and walked over to the saws. He selected one and rested on the wooden box he had used as a seat as he started to cut the handle.

"It's his training. The only weapon you ever need is a shovel." Boniface frowned. The taller Russian moved another crate closer to his captive and sat before continuing. "Every soldier in the Russian army has a shovel, but he relies on his gun. In the Spetsnaz, you have a gun, but you rely on your shovel—it is your weapon."

The other man finished his cutting and passed his handiwork to his senior. "I'll be outside," he said and left, pushing the door behind him, returning the shed to gloom. The pockmarked man tried the weight of the short-handled sharpened shovel in his hand, then tossed it several times, spinning it and catching it by its handle.

"You see, this is sharp. Sharper than an axe. You can use it as an axe, but the sharpness makes it more effective than a knife. A knife might be, what, twenty or thirty centimeters long? This is fifty. For hand-to-hand combat that extra reach gives much better range than a knife. Plus it's heavier, so if you hit someone, you can do more damage. Hit them right..." he stared at Boniface, resting his thumb on the blade, "and they lose a limb if you're being kind. If you feel unkind, you split their head like a log. And, of course, you can throw it." He snapped the shovel back, ready to throw, and laughed, watching Boniface flinch and wince in pain as he moved.

"Why not use a gun?" asked Boniface, his voice straining.

The Russian dropped the shovel back onto his lap. "Guns are for amateurs. Guns run out. Guns miss. Guns make a noise. You don't miss with a shovel, and if someone shoots at you, you can defend yourself."

He watched Boniface, seemingly letting the implicit menace distill into fear before casting a look of disappointment. "We had our fun and games outside, but now, if you don't tell me what I want to know, then I will give you a demonstration of what I can do with this shovel that Grigorii has so kindly crafted for me."

Boniface tried to sit up but found it too hard to move—his head throbbed and his limbs ached from too much travel in the trunks of cars.

"I need to pee." It was a female voice.

Boniface spun his head and looked into the dark corner of the shed behind him, beside a pile of grass-seed sacks. "Monty? I didn't see... What... How...?" He turned back to the Russian. "You've done enough to hurt her. Let her go; I've told you everything you've asked, and I'll tell you exactly what you want. Just let her go."

"Oh, Mister Boniface. I know you'll tell me what I want to know. While she's here, you will tell me everything." He lifted the blade of the shovel, again admiring the result of the other man's labor.

"At least let her piss. Then we can talk."

The Russian stood. "Grigorii." He stepped toward Montbretia with his shovel and pointed to her knees. "Open." She pulled up her knees and spread them, separating her ankles by a small amount and putting the tape binding the bottom of her legs under tension. In a blur, the Russian struck with his shovel, cutting the tape before returning to his seat. She held her taped wrists in front of her. The Russian looked, then shook his head.

The swarthy man came into the shed. "Take her for a piss." He jabbed his finger. "Round the side, then straight back here." The swarthy man turned to face the young woman who had rolled onto her front and was trying to stand.

Pulling her knees under her, she pushed herself up, reaching an unsteady standing position. She took an uncoordinated step backward to steady herself, and—with her wrists taped together—she continued to move, lifting her right elbow, jabbing it into the swarthy man's nose.

Boniface heard the crunch and saw dark liquid flow. Unbalanced, the man threw his leg to steady himself as Montbretia turned, lifted her foot, and stomped on the side of his leg, her boot connecting directly with the side of his knee, projecting her full weight through her foot.

There was a dull crunch, a muffled shout from the Russian, and he fell to the floor.

Before she could stand straight, the pockmarked Russian knocked her to the ground, pulled a roll of tape from his pocket, cut the tape holding her wrists, then bound her hands behind her back before rolling her over to bind her legs.

Boniface caught her eye. "He hit me. A girl's gotta get even. If I'd had more space, his days as a father would be over." The Russian finished binding her legs and tore off a short strip of tape, which he slapped over her mouth.

The crunch of cartilage in her nose was audible as his hand made contact.

He turned and shouted at the swarthy man in Russian. The swarthy man blushed and tried to move away. He shouted for a second time, and the other man was still.

"Mister Boniface. Now we talk." He stood up. Montbretia's body spasmed as he kicked her while moving back to the wooden box in front of Boniface. "A few more simple questions."

"I'll talk. But there's a lot of stuff that happened last night, and all you're doing is delaying the information getting to Kuznetsov. I was going to see him when you stopped me."

"Boniface, Boniface. You've got an answer for everything, haven't you? You're not going anywhere until I'm happy that you've told me everything. That way, if you have, shall we say, an unfortunate accident, then I will be able to tell Mister Kuznetsov the details you want him to know. It's much safer that way, isn't it?"

"But..."

"These images you gave to Turgenev."

"You mean..."

"I mean you don't answer my questions with a question of your own." The pockmarked Russian stood and kicked the elbow Boniface was leaning on. He fell, cracking his head on the concrete floor before the Russian placed his boot over the Englishman's throat. "Has anyone ever told you about our interpreters in the Spetsnaz?"

Boniface opened his mouth, gasping for air. The Russian rocked back and forth, adjusting the pressure exerted by his boot.

"Our interpreters aren't like the interpreters attached to Western armies. They are soldiers. Proper soldiers who fight with us. And why, why are these well-educated men integrated into the army?" He paused, staring into Boniface's eyes and holding the pressure through his boot. "Because they can speak the language of any...guests... we find along the way. If they can speak the language, then they can make them more comfortable."

He released his boot, dropping to sit astride Boniface, facing him, and crushing his bound arms under him. "So that means our interpreters are experts in motivating people to talk." He sneered. His hand flashed forward, coming into contact with Boniface's mouth, which opened as the Englishman went to scream at the pain of his head slamming back onto the concrete floor.

The Russian pushed his hand into the open mouth, reached, and grabbed Boniface's tongue, holding it firmly. With Boniface's jaws wedged open by his fist, the Russian felt in his pocket with his other hand and retrieved a pair of pruning shears. He opened and closed the shears, the spring squeaking and the blades scraping.

"Let me tell you something I learned from our interpreter friends." Boniface tried to pull back. With each movement, the Russian pushed his hand farther into the other man's mouth and gripped his tongue more firmly. "To help people talk, our interpreter friends like to make a snake." He pulled Boniface's tongue and thrust the open shears into his mouth, one blade above and one blade below his tongue, and started to squeeze. "Do you want a forked tongue, Boniface?"

Boniface tried to scream but was only able to expel air.

There was a click, and the shed darkened as a figure entered, pointing a gun at Boniface's tormentor. "Enough."

seventy–six

Montbretia tried to twist, delicately, feeling each bruise as she struggled to control the pain caused by her spine flexing over her wrists, which were taped together behind her back. She rolled—her back spasmed, and she flinched in pain, coming to rest with her spine jamming into her wrists, bone-on-bone-on-bone on something else really hard and uncomfortable that she was lying on.

She ached.

Her spine ached—each and every vertebra. Her wrists ached. Her arms ached. And her nose ached. She snorted, forcing drying blood out of her nose to ease the sole passage of oxygen while the piece of tape—so unceremoniously slapped in response to the demolition of the swarthy man's knee—remained firmly over her mouth.

The man by the shed door was dressed incongruously. From the waist down he was dressed as the two Russians: jeans and once-shined boots that were now muddy and scuffed. The top half of him was different—a red woolen sweater, which looked new and still had a price tag attached, and an improvised blue bandana.

Ignoring his sartorial choices, his intent seemed clear from the gun he held across his chest—pointing in Boniface's direction—as he peered around the edge of the door, apparently watching the two men he had just sent away.

He came inside and started fiddling with the phones he had taken from the two Russians. He pocketed the SIM cards and dropped the remaining electronics to the ground, crushing each under his boot, then grinding the pieces as if he were milling flour.

There was a sound of shuffling and moaning, and Boniface slowly levered himself into a sitting position, rocking forward with his hands behind his back. "Mister Turgenev. This is a pleasure; I wasn't expecting to see you for at least a few weeks."

There was no attempt to conceal the sarcasm, even though this was apparently the man who had held him and Ellen at gunpoint for much of last night. The man whose actions had led to a situation that brought about her sister's death.

The man she now knew as Turgenev ignored Boniface and continued to grind the phones with his heel while keeping the gun—the obvious indication of his violent tendencies—loosely trained on the Englishman.

"Why did you let them go?" There was incredulity in Boniface's voice. Almost anger in the slap-back echo of the shed. The Russian knocked the last few pieces of pulverized phone from his boot and ignored the question.

Boniface exhaled loudly. "Can you let them live? I mean…"

"They're not in a good state," said Turgenev, raising his head to look at Boniface and removing his bandana, his skull backlit by the ajar door, the sunlight halo around his features contrasting with the scowl they lit. "They are not a threat to me."

Boniface cocked his head.

"Once you tell Kuznetsov that I let them go, he won't be able to trust them. If he can't trust them, then they're not a threat." The Russian seemed pleased with his logic, or perhaps he was even more pleased that he intuitively understood something that Boniface didn't.

"Why the wooly jumper?" asked Boniface. "Is that what they're wearing in Paraguay these days?" He had a look of distaste as he surveyed the Russian.

"So they did know," muttered the other man. "Disguise. You think I'd dress like this for any reason but disguise? This was all I could buy at the airport, and I knew they wouldn't look for me dressed like this."

Boniface waited a beat. When he continued, his voice was quiet, his attitude approaching conciliatory. "So why are you back here? Why did you disguise yourself, then come here?"

The Russian looked straight at the other man. "I saw you walk into Sergey, and then they followed you." The Russian seemed almost friendly as he recounted his decision. "They were at the airport, so they must have known I was there. That means they would have someone waiting for me in Paraguay, so I couldn't get on the plane, and I needed to make sure you stayed alive long enough to pass on my message to Mister Kuznetsov." He paused. "And while I'm here, I can get my bike."

Turgenev ducked his head out the door, then stepped back in. Taking a step to Boniface and grabbing the tape holding his wrists, he lifted. Boniface let out a low yell as his shoulder joints were flexed, but leaned forward to release the tension on his arms as he reached his feet.

As Boniface found his balance, the Russian grabbed the shears on the floor and cut the tape around the Englishman's wrists, then stood back, training the gun on him again.

Montbretia watched Boniface as he shook out the tension in his muscles and examined the marks around his wrists, and turned to the Russian who was holding—for Boniface to see—what looked, in the gloom of the shed, like a small cylinder of plastic.

In his other hand, the gun was now pointing directly at her.

She tried to scream with her mouth still taped.

Boniface's head spun to look at her, then flipped back to the Russian.

"I never trust computers." The Russian's voice was heavily accented but calm and controlling. "We're at Hampton Court—go and find me some original documents. Fast." He moved his gun toward Montbretia.

Boniface lunged, making a grab for the piece of plastic the Russian was holding.

He missed but knocked it out of the Russian's hand.

Montbretia watched as the plastic spun toward her, bouncing on the ground and coming to rest about 12 inches from her feet. She lifted her legs—taking the weight of her body through her back onto her tied wrists underneath—and dropped her feet onto the plastic, listening to the satisfying crunch as it shattered.

Boniface and Turgenev stood silently, looking at the site of the destruction.

"Whoops," said Montbretia with no sincerity.

Slowly, a goofy grin spread across Boniface's visage.

When he spoke, there was anger in the Russian's voice. "You'd better run and find those papers."

"Not going."

Turgenev turned and pointed the gun at him.

"You need me alive," said Boniface.

The Russian stared blankly.

"That thumb drive that just landed under Miss Armstrong's boot was the last copy of the photos."

The Russian kept his stare fixed on Boniface.

"I doctored the pictures on the original thumb drive I gave you. Have a look—all you'll see are blurry images of some old documents, and the text doesn't make sense if you actually read it."

"Give me your phone." It was a command from the Russian.

Slowly Boniface opened his jacket, reached into his inside pocket, and pulled out his phone. He held it between his fingertips, offering it to Turgenev. "If you want the password, there's no point. You saw me at the airport, so you should know that I went to the internet café, where I deleted the online photos." He smirked. "They're all gone."

The Russian snatched the phone and pocketed it, keeping the weapon pointed at Boniface.

The Englishman's tone was controlled. "Here's how it goes: There's no evidence anymore, but I know what you know. Kill me, and Kuznetsov doesn't know why you need to stay alive. Let us live—both of us live—and I can make sure Kuznetsov understands the danger in not leaving you alone."

The Russian stood in silent contemplation.

Turgenev's fist connected with the side of Boniface's skull, a bright slap jerking his head. The Englishman's body fell backward, slamming into the side of the shed, making the wooden panel creak and the whole structure vibrate, before collapsing where he had previously been tied.

"I've wanted to do that for hours. That man talks too much." The Russian looked away from Montbretia, stepped toward the inert mass of humanity lying in a heap, and checked his throat for a pulse.

He stood and moved toward Montbretia. "You understand that I can't have you following me." His voice softened. "I hope you will agree to hand over your phone without complaint, and that you will accept a few pieces of tape to restrict your movements until Mister Boniface comes round."

seventy–seven

"Ow." Boniface looked up from his tea. "My tongue hurts, and this tea is hot." Unconsciously, he touched the bruise on the side of his head.

"Stop being such a baby!" snapped Montbretia with mock exasperation, as she picked up a napkin to wipe a drip of blood that fell from her nose onto the easy-wipe plastic surface of the café table.

"But he cut me," said Boniface. "Look." He let his tongue flop out of his mouth.

"He cut you because he was clumsy taking the pruning shears out of your mouth when Turgenev came in with a gun. He didn't actually…" She opened and closed her first two fingers as if snipping with a pair of scissors. "He didn't make a snake. You don't speak with a forked tongue."

She looked at his tongue, which was still hanging out, and winced. "But that is an unpleasant cut. When did you last have a tetanus shot?" He shrugged, replacing the lump of flesh in his mouth.

He gingerly sipped his tea at the side of his mouth, shifted slightly, and winced as his back twinged. "I don't think I've got a muscle that doesn't hurt." He looked up to Montbretia. "And you must hurt more. He hit you pretty hard."

"But that Greek-looking one is going to need surgery. I'll take a broken nose for the pleasure of hearing his knee crunch." For the first time since he had told her about her sister's death, Boniface saw Montbretia smile.

"Are you sure your nose is alright?"

Montbretia delicately repositioned the ice wrapped in a tea towel. "Do you think they…" she flicked her eyes to the counter, where two disinterested teenagers were serving a group of mothers with small children, "bought the whole I-tripped-and-hit-my-nose thing?"

Boniface leaned back; looked down at his suit, noting each rip and tear, the bloodstains on his shirt, and his grimy tie; then looked to Montbretia, who looked like she hadn't washed either herself or her clothes for several weeks. The only thing fresh about her were the duck tape adhesive residue around her mouth and her new cuts, bruises, and gashes.

"Do I think they bought our story?" He felt the muscles in his face relax. "No. Do I care? Even less. Am I glad it's over?" He slowly nodded, careful not to cause himself any further pain.

Small children, with the joy of being alive, ran up and down the broad passages between the tables. The boys mostly imitated noisy cars, and the girls pushed their dolls in miniature baby buggies, while the more boisterous of both genders raced each other on scooters. The mothers clustered around the room, all overweight, badly dressed, and stressed. All seemed desperate for any human contact; the noise of happy children sufficient to ensure their primeval instinct to protect didn't kick too hard.

"So what just happened, Boniface? How did we get out?"

"We got out by luck, and we got out because we need to strike a deal. Or rather, we got out because Turgenev needs to believe that we're going to make a deal that will keep him safe."

"So you literally talked our way out of there?" Montbretia frowned. "Talk. That's all you did?"

"For the record, I've got skills. I didn't want to hurt those guys in front of you. I felt you had humiliated Russian manhood sufficiently for one day. That's the only reason I let Turgenev punch me." He delicately felt the side of his face, touching the swelling where the Russian's fist had most recently connected.

"Well, I'm in a weakened state at the moment, Boniface, so if you can keep your skills under wraps, that would be appreciated. But tell me, are we going to do a deal?"

"Oh yeah... We're going to do a deal," said Boniface calmly. "Just not the deal Turgenev wants."

"What deal are we going to do?" She began hesitantly and then changed tack before Boniface could answer. "And why do you keep saying *we* are going to do a deal? How does this involve me?"

Boniface took another sip of tea and winced as the hot liquid hit his injured tongue. When he started talking, his voice was somber. "Last night, Turgenev threatened you. That may have been an empty threat to scare your sister, but it was a threat."

"And now he's gone, Boniface." Montbretia seemed ready to move on.

"Now. But what about tomorrow?" His tone invited no response. "Mister Kuznetsov's employee threatened you. If Mister Kuznetsov wants our future cooperation—and I'm sure he will—then I require that Mister Kuznetsov extend the courtesy of his protection to you."

Montbretia stared at Boniface but made no sign that she wanted to demur.

"The second reason you're involved is that I'm presuming you can access Ellen's email."

With a small nod of her head, Montbretia affirmed.

"When I arrived at the airport this morning, I emailed copies of the images to Ellen." He waited, watching Montbretia's seeming internal confusion. "In other words, you've got everything that Turgenev wanted, so you're as dangerous to Kuznetsov as Turgenev thought he was. The difference is, you have the photos, and since you broke that thumb drive, all he has are some doctored images."

"Yeah, I'm sorry about that," said Montbretia, seemingly trying to stop the look of a naughty schoolgirl spreading across her face. "It seemed like a good idea at the time. You grabbed for the drive, he dropped it—my boot stopped you squabbling."

"Unfortunately, there is a price that comes with this information." He grimaced. "We have to do a deal with a rather dangerous oligarch." Boniface kept his face still, calibrating Montbretia's response, then softened. "The price is simple: silence."

"Silence about what? Ellen's death?" She frowned, twisting her head away while keeping her eyes locked on Boniface's.

"No. The police already know about that, and Kuznetsov had nothing to do with that."

"So what am I keeping quiet about? Whatever it was is connected with my sister's death." She dropped the volume of her voice. "I've been taped up and beaten by three Russians. Are you saying that my reward is a cup of coffee? I think I deserve more than that."

"You do." He sighed. "Kuznetsov is pretty mercurial, more so when he thinks people have let him down."

Montbretia laughed. "Don't patronize me, Boniface. I told you I'm a big girl. I can look after myself." Her eyes bored into him. "Ask the guy with the snapped knee."

Boniface flushed. "I'm sorry... I'm..."

"It's alright," she mouthed, her face softening. "Tell me what I'm keeping quiet about."

Boniface pondered for a moment or two, his mouth moving, silently beginning sentences, until he sat still. "Kuznetsov's weakness—which even he doesn't know about yet."

"Which is?"

He cocked his head and began. "I'm sure Ellen explained the basic history behind Nigel's book."

"Mmm."

"So you understand the basic idea—Wolsey, in collusion with Anne Boleyn, killed Henry." She bobbed her head. "When the murder happened, Henry had an illegitimate son, Henry FitzRoy, who was about twelve—he was Wolsey's godson. The first thing Wolsey did—and there was already plenty of historical evidence to substantiate this before Nigel came along—was to arrange a wife for young FitzRoy. At the behest of Anne Boleyn, FitzRoy married Anne's cousin, Lady Mary Howard. This was 1533 or sometime around."

"So they were both dreadfully young," said Montbretia.

"Fourteen," offered Boniface, looking at Montbretia's shocked face. "Maybe thirteen." She twisted her face, looking as if she had tasted something unpleasant. "But it kept FitzRoy occupied while Wolsey did whatever it was he did and Anne was occupied being pregnant with Elizabeth, who was born around that time. However, three years later everything had changed, and Anne Boleyn was starting to cause trouble for Wolsey, so she was beheaded."

"A very efficient way of dealing with the person who knows all your secrets. Let's hope Mister Kuznetsov is kinder with us."

"Precisely." Boniface hesitated, realizing what Montbretia had suggested. "But, Wolsey didn't kill FitzRoy. I'm going to start speculating about his motives, but maybe Wolsey did have some scruples and couldn't kill his own godson. However, he needed him out of the way to ensure there would be no competing claim on the throne. So two months after Anne's beheading, Wolsey arranged for FitzRoy to be disappeared."

"I thought he died from tuberculosis. Was I told the wrong story?"

"TB would be far too routine for Wolsey. No, Wolsey arranged for FitzRoy to change his name to John Stephens and to disappear. The story about the illegitimate heir dying of a childhood illness was concocted by Wolsey as a cover. John Stephens, as he became, grew up and became a wealthy landowner and happily lived out his days doing whatever it was that wealthy landowners did."

Montbretia's mouth fell open. "Oh, Wolsey was good. Do you ever feel you could have learned something from him, Boniface?"

"A lot. If nothing else, I would love his administrative skills. I've got about a thousand unopened emails, all mixed up with spam offering me length and girth enhancements, not to mention several weeks of bills piled up, and I haven't filed a single piece of paper since I took my new office. But I digress..."

"You do." Montbretia tilted her head, seemingly waiting.

"John Stephens, FitzRoy under his new name, lived out his life, doing all the things that rich landowners did, including getting married and having children. Those children had children, and with each successive generation, the family mythology grew that they were not only connected to royalty, but that they were royal."

"Which they were."

"They were. But no one had records—Wolsey made sure all the documents were hidden—no one could prove anything, and over time it became part of the family story, and no one took it seriously. Well, no one took it seriously until two nights ago, when a small-time thief found some papers somewhere in Hampton Court Palace."

"Really! Where? Can we go and have a look?"

"I wish I knew where the document store is, but Turgenev's man shot the thief in front of your sister and me before he could tell us."

Montbretia's mouth fell open. "What were you two…?" A tear trickled down her cheek, washing a clean path as it descended. "What did you…?"

Boniface continued. "The man had been arrested by the police, and because Nigel was getting some publicity about his work with the publication of the book, the police called him when they needed a Tudor expert to assess some documents that someone had tried to steal from Hampton Court. So that's how Nigel met Pete." He paused. "Pete was the thief's name."

Montbretia picked up a napkin and wiped the tears trickling down her cheeks, leaving parallel clean tracks streaking across the dirt on her face.

"Nigel's life's work was Henry, and he was particularly interested in an idea he had that Henry had been murdered. Murder-and-replacement was the most plausible way he could find to explain how the intelligent, articulate, thoughtful Henry at the age of seventeen became the obese tyrant in the history books. Obviously, he was interested in all aspects surrounding Henry and the other lesser-known descendants, but Nigel's focus had been on Henry and the murder, and this was the book that Kuznetsov had commissioned him to write."

"Makes sense," said Montbretia.

"Nigel wasn't shocked when he found that FitzRoy lived. However, he was surprised to find out about the change of identity and was then able to quite quickly trace the descendants because they were a family of good standing—it's just no one had made the link with Henry."

Montbretia listened intently, nodding as Boniface recounted the story.

"What stunned Nigel was the identity of the descendant."

Montbretia sat silently, patiently waiting, then snapped. "Come on, Boniface. Who?"

"Patience. It gets better. Your sister and I followed the trail and found that not only was there an heir, but the heir has a secret love child." He looked up, scrunching his face as if trying to recall a detail. "Do we still say love child, or is it becoming an archaic term?"

"Boniface. You know I can kick." Montbretia grinned. "Spill."

"Sherborne."

"No shit!" Montbretia slammed her hand over her mouth and whispered. "The kids didn't hear that, did they?"

Boniface shook his head. "Sherborne is the daddy, and the interesting detail is that Oscar von Habsburg is his son. You know Oscar? Son of Princess Heidemarie."

Montbretia sat with her mouth open.

"So there's the real irony. By pursuing the truth about the murder of Henry in order to show that the current royals have no legitimate claim to the throne, which was part of the mood music to kick off the referendum campaign, Kuznetsov has led to the uncovering of a true blood heir. And even worse for Kuznetsov, the heir is the man he has been butting heads with since he came to this country."

Boniface fell back in his seat to allow Montbretia a question she seemed to be intent on asking. "So why doesn't Sherborne make a noise about this? Has Kuznetsov got a hit out on him? Is that where those two guys have gone now?"

"In a word, proof."

"Really? I thought he owned a newspaper. Can't he make them print a story? Why not start a rumor on the internet?"

"He could, but there's a problem—or two problems—and those problems are Princess Heidi and Oscar. If the story breaks, then there's going to be quite a furor. For a start, Oscar's paternity will be made public. Sherborne's proud of his boy and wants to publicly acknowledge him. But for Heidi, there's the issue of lies that were told to cover a scandal twenty-plus years ago."

Montbretia frowned.

"When she became pregnant, her husband was in a coma—a coma that began about a year before Oscar was born and ended a few months before the birth when the poor fellow died. Newly widowed Princess Heidi claimed that there was no possibility that her friend Richard could be the father. She suggested that perhaps the coma hadn't been that deep all the time, or hadn't reached certain parts of his anatomy."

"Oh," said Montbretia. "So if the story breaks, she's got to admit that she lied."

"And if they admit Oscar's parentage but can't prove his direct link to a murdered King, then she will have lost twice: his royal connection by virtue of the man currently claimed as his father goes, and her reputation is trashed. So they need documentary proof before they do anything."

"Can't Sherborne get hold of the documents or whatever they are? He's a rich guy; he's got friends, hasn't he?"

Boniface sucked air through his teeth. "Too political. Too close to the bone. If he draws attention, there's a chance someone will leak the story—or half the story, the wrong half—to another paper. Plus, he can't be seen to have links to criminals, especially as the story relates to Heidi."

"So what's stopping us from going public?"

"Fear."

"Fear?"

"Yup." Boniface met Montbretia's stare. "You're one person. However many knees you fracture, Kuznetsov will always find more people to hunt you and kill you. And if he can't find you, then he'll hunt those that you love and will kill them instead. So we shut up and hope that he loses interest in the referendum. When he does, we're out of trouble."

"That's crazy. What happens if this gets out?"

Boniface looked down, then back up at Montbretia. "It won't. Apart from us two, Kuznetsov, Turgenev, and Sherborne, there is no one who knows about, and can explain, the documents. If the story leaks, Kuznetsov will know where it came from."

"What about the police? Don't they hold the documents as evidence?"

"Sure. But they don't understand what they've got. They think they've got historical artifacts. They don't understand the evidential value. And they're not going to." He chuckled. "Once we've explained the story to Kuznetsov, he'll set his lawyers loose so that they can rain down chaos. They'll tie everything in legal knots so that nothing happens. That way no one will do anything rash, like try to return the documents to their rightful owners. Or read them..." He exhaled. "And that is it. That is everything."

Montbretia looked accusingly at him. "Are you sure that's everything? There's nothing else I should know, is there?"

Boniface wrinkled his nose. "Well, there is one thing I haven't told you." Montbretia held her glare. "But we need to be in the middle of the Maze for that." Boniface stood, picking up the change. "Come on."

"Can't we go and search for some more papers?" Montbretia kept her face straight, the edges of her mouth starting to involuntarily lift as she caught Boniface's stare. "Alright, later, perhaps?"

They walked the short distance to the Maze. Boniface took out a coin and flipped it. "Call."

"Heads."

He showed the coin. "Heads it is. Your choice: Do you want to go left or right?"

"Left."

"That leaves me with right. Let's see who gets to the middle first."

seventy-eight

Boniface sat on the wooden bench in the middle of the Maze, enjoying the spring sun near the peak of its travel, undisturbed by the ebb and flow of children finding their way to the middle and then losing themselves on the way out. Oblivious to the shriek of their excited voices as they closed in on their target, unworried by their return to tell their valiant tale of far-off lands in the middle of the Maze.

"Hey! How did you get here before me?"

"Cheating." Boniface smiled. "How else would you expect me to win? Ellen said you would beat her, so I had to think a bit laterally."

"Uh huh..."

"All you have to do is say to a parent 'I've lost my kids; could you let me through the emergency-exit barriers?' and they'll rush you straight through, no questions. It's a nice sunny day, my legs hurt—who am I kidding? All of me hurts—and it seemed a shame to waste it walking around when I could be sitting here with the final piece of the puzzle." Boniface stretched back, soaking up the sun's warmth.

Montbretia made a sour face. "I'm still strong enough to punch you, and I won't feel any remorse."

"Then I won't explain." Boniface shielded his eyes and looked up. "Sit down and relax in the sun while I finish the story."

She sat next to him on the wooden bench.

"There's one thing that's missing. One thing unaccounted for. The cornerstone of every good murder mystery."

Montbretia looked at Boniface, frowning.

"The body." Montbretia relaxed her frown as Boniface continued. "Without a body there can be no real proof of murder. And equally, by finding the body, you can prove murder. So how did Wolsey dispose of Henry's body?"

"I don't know." Montbretia screwed up her face. "He dug a hole?"

"He probably did dig a hole, but you're missing the point. If you've just murdered the King of England and you're trying to convince everyone that you are actually the man who you've just murdered, then you never, ever want the old King's dead body to turn up. It would raise too many questions."

Montbretia nodded at Boniface's logic.

"Now if you're Wolsey, pretending to be the King, you can't simply dump the old King's body, because then it might be found. And anyway, where do you take it? The only answer is to hide it. And hide it somewhere close so you can keep an eye on it and make sure it's not disturbed. And as the owner of Hampton Court Palace, Wolsey had ample space to bury a body in his grounds."

Montbretia brightened. "Of course."

"But if you're Wolsey with all these grounds, you also have a lot of gardeners." He paused. "But hopefully not the sort of gardeners who try to cut your tongue in half." He paused again. "You see, gardeners are the sort of people who habitually dig things up, like dogs looking for bones, so you need to put the body somewhere where they won't dig. Today it's easy; you bury someone in concrete under a road, and the body is effectively lost forever. But in Wolsey's day, it was harder. Particularly when Wolsey kept expanding Hampton Court and building new buildings."

"So what did he do?" asked Montbretia.

"As you've probably heard from your sister, the official version as they will tell you on the guided tour around Hampton Court is that this Maze was planted in sixteen-hundred-and-something, maybe even early seventeen-hundred, for William of Orange."

"And?" said Montbretia, exasperated.

"Possibly to replace a Maze that Wolsey may have planted while he still owned the Palace."

"That sounds like a rumor."

"It wasn't." Boniface was definite. "There was a Maze."

"Boniface, you're like an over-excited child who's about to wet himself. Where is Henry buried?"

"Here." Boniface spread his arms. "The Maze was planted on top of Henry's grave. That way Wolsey could be confident that Henry's grave would not be disturbed. Your sister and I saw the proof last night in Sherborne's house."

A huge grin broke out across Montbretia's face. "You are kidding me, Boniface. You're making this stuff up to make me feel better."

"Apparently Nigel had his suspicions years ago. Historically, it didn't make logical sense to him that there was a Maze here, on this specific spot. It made even less sense to him when he looked at the size of the Maze. So he did…I don't know, he did something that made him even more suspicious."

"Very scientific," sneered Montbretia.

"Anyway, whatever he did made him certain that there was something under here, and then a few years ago he found that there were bones." Montbretia looked slightly shocked. "They were doing an architectural history program for the telly, and the crew were using radars, or whatever they use to check out buried foundations. Nigel played nice, and one of the guys scanned this area for him, and hey presto, he knew there were bones."

"That'll teach me for being such a skeptic."

"Now, of course, he didn't know whose bones they were or when they were buried, but he already had his murder theory kicking around, and so he put two and two together but only got three because he couldn't prove anything. And because he couldn't prove anything, he was unwilling to go public and push for a formal dig. If he'd been wrong…"

"He would have looked like a complete…" Montbretia half-finished Boniface's sentence.

"Yeah, a complete dingbat. And it would have completely undermined his reputation. So he spent years looking for any evidence to prove that the bones were Henry's, and two nights ago, when a long-haired man got stuck in a hole, Nigel found his proof."

Montbretia looked over at him. "Nigel was patient."

Boniface's tone was gentle. "He was. And that is the end of the story. When your sister and I were chasing down Nigel's leads yesterday, she said she wanted to bring you here. She couldn't, but I'm pleased that I could."

He reached into his pocket to pull out a handful of clean napkins he had taken from the café and wiped his eyes. He turned to Montbretia, whose eyes were welling, and passed her several napkins. "When you're ready, we had better go and talk to the police. They're going to need our help, and I've got some explaining to do."

Montbretia nodded, wiping her nose.

"And there's the slight matter of the stolen car you've been driving, which needs to be returned to its owner."

"That car was stolen?"

"Yup. But don't worry; I'm fairly sure I know who owns it... Fairly sure."

Pollute the Poor

one

"German efficiency," Boniface spat under his breath, yanking the outer door and launching it like a trebuchet, the hinged piece of wood arcing into the side wall as he started to jog toward his office. His teeth stayed together as his lips continued moving: "Next time I'm getting a client who understands that people are asleep until the sun has risen and should have time to shower, shave, and read the morning paper."

Through the second door on the left—his corner office—the phone was ringing. Behind, with another dent added to the wall, the door stay squealed as it progressively released its load before dropping the weight through the last few inches to slam shut.

As Boniface picked up speed, with each step the smell he had noticed when he opened the door but had tried to ignore was tugging at his nostrils with newfound vigor. A bitter, acrid smell—ammonia fused with filth, fused with never-washed human. It wasn't rotting food or decaying household waste or forgetfulness to apply deodorant or a broken-down heater meaning a missed shower. It wasn't that Montbretia had left something in her trash or that the cleaner hadn't been through last night or the night before, and it definitely wasn't the smell of the new carpet. It was more like a municipal waste dump in the heat of summer to a factor of ten.

Boniface turned into his room flicking the door behind him as he ran to grab the phone. Two steps across the room and he snatched the handset as the door clicked shut. "Guten morgen, Chlodwig. Wie gehts?" He straightened and walked slowly around his desk, careful not to catch the phone cord as he moved to the window. "No, that's pretty much the limit of my German, I'm afraid. So if we can stick with English, I'd be grateful. Anyway, how are you this morning, and how is business in Hamburg today?"

He leaned to rest his head against the cool glass of the window and looked down on Wimbledon Hill Road, his breath misting the pane. From his vantage point two floors up, the perspective of the street was squashed. Everything looked its regular size but somehow flatter, and through the tinted glass, under the dull light with the sun still under the horizon, everything took on a monochrome hue.

The smell wasn't improving.

A bad smell can be acceptable—as much as any smell can ever be acceptable—if you can get away from it and breathe clean air, but for Boniface, the smell wasn't shifting. If anything, it was holding tighter and working its way farther up his nostrils and scraping down into his lungs. He stepped back from the window and looked around as if he would be able to see the source of the smell or at least see the smell floating across the room, then reached for the trashcan under his desk. Seeing a fresh liner in it, he shrugged, replaced the bin, and sat on his desk, pulling out his bottom drawer to rest his feet.

"Greta wanted me to bring you up to speed on an issue we've got and to walk you through our strategy to handle it." He nodded, made some vague noises of affirmation, and continued. "Greta wants me to brief you. Fully. She wants you to hear the problem and the solution together. She wanted to tell you herself and she would have done, but she's in Malta today to sign the deal for the bulk carriers."

Boniface listened. Nodded. Made more noises of affirmation as if to imply he was paying attention to Chlodwig rather than wondering about the smell and being frustrated about the early hour.

"The problem is with the Montenegro Shipping Line." He paused, listening, and then sighed with a knowing acknowledgement, his tone resigned. "Yes, it's always a problem with the Montenegro Shipping Line."

As the German responded, Boniface stood, gently kicked his drawer closed, breathed in slowly as if that might reduce the pungency of the smell, and pulled back his shoulders, still not paying much attention. He had already heard the arguments, and given what he was about to disclose, he wished that Chlodwig's voice had been heard more forcefully before the purchase of the Montenegro Shipping Line was completed.

Feeling the I-told-her-so homily dissipating as it worked its way down the line, Boniface continued. "It's a bit more serious than we might have expected, and the issue is likely to become public any day now. We don't know how or where it will become public, or even when, but we're fairly sure it will."

Boniface stared out of his window again. In the distance he could hear a siren. The monochromatic light of the street below, now with a steady flow of traffic, was illuminated by a gentle flickering light at the lower end of the hill. One, then a second police car came into sight from the bottom end of the hill, their flashing lights bouncing off the storefronts. As they reached Boniface's building, the two cars turned into the road bounding the second side of his office. He watched as they turned, their sirens attenuating as they disappeared from view, and stayed gazing at where he had last seen the vehicles.

"There's a problem. It's a big problem. We reckon there are photos. There's definitely a trail back to the Montenegro Shipping Line. There are dead bodies, but we haven't got a definitive number." Boniface paused, shaking his head as he waited for the question he knew Chlodwig was about to ask. "We don't know. Tens, at least. Probably over fifty. Maybe over one hundred."

He caught sight of his reflection in the window—his face, gray like the street outside, with all signs of joy drained—and registered the tremble in his voice as he tried to say out loud that his client might have been responsible for the deaths of more than one hundred people. One hundred innocent people. Men. Women. Children. He hadn't mentioned the other people who might be hurt: not only those who were visibly injured, but those who would be ill for years to come. Those who might contract cancer. The birth defects. The people whose lives would be blighted through polluted drinking water and living next to a toxic-waste dump.

"Somalia." He tilted his head away from the phone. "Yes, Somalia, and no, we don't know..."

His door opened. Two police officers—uniformed and wearing stab-proof vests—entered the room: a man in his mid-thirties with a younger officer, almost certainly fresh from the Peel Center, the Met's training college, standing nervously behind. They both stood at the far end of the room, apparently unwilling to step forward.

"Alexander Boniface?"

"Hold on a moment, Chlodwig." Boniface put his hand over the mouthpiece. "Could you give me a couple of minutes, say ten minutes, to finish this call? I'm sure Montbretia can fix you a cup of tea or something while you wait."

"Would you end the phone call, please, sir?" It sounded like a request, but Boniface understood that the officer was giving an order.

"Chlodwig, something's going on. I'll call you straight back in a couple of minutes."

Boniface placed the handset back in its cradle without making a noise. "You're looking pale, sir."

"Death is never easy." Boniface exhaled.

"So you admit..."

The younger officer looked admiringly at the older officer as Boniface's voice took on a new urgency. "Admit what? I was... Never mind, different conversation. Why are you here?"

"We've had a report of a murder."

"A murder?"

"Yes, sir. A murder."

"Where?

"Here."

"Who has been murdered?"

"I was rather hoping you could tell me, as you are apparently the murderer."

Boniface let his body fall into his chair back and waited for the room to stop spinning. "Here? Murder? Me the murderer?"

"Yes, sir. You. Alexander Boniface." The older officer took a step farther into the room; the younger man jumped, apparently to keep his human shield in place. "We had a phone call," he glanced at his watch, "thirteen minutes ago, informing us that you had committed a murder in your office."

two

"There's no dead body here," mumbled the man who appeared to be Alexander Boniface.

The sergeant pulled out a notepad from under his stab-proof vest and checked his watch before starting to make some notes. He surveyed the man who was sitting as if he had been dropped into his chair, his tie cocked, his eyes looking tired. "A few preliminaries, please, sir. You are Alexander Boniface; that is correct?"

The sergeant watched as the man slumped in the chair nodded, his mouth still slightly open.

"This is your office?"

The seated man nodded again, as if the effort to move his head required all his energy.

"You say there is no dead body here?" The sergeant made no attempt to moderate his volume. The young constable beside him stood up straighter, nodding as if to affirm his agreement with the sergeant's approach.

Boniface's head jolted and he stared up, pulling his tie straight. "There is no dead body." He sounded as if he was explaining a simple fact to a child. "I'm sure Montbretia told you the same thing."

"Who is that, sir?"

"Montbretia. The lady who let you in."

The sergeant relaxed his posture. "I'm sorry, sir, it wasn't a lady who let us in. It was a gentleman."

"A man? No man works here."

"It was definitely a man, sir. Unless this Mon-whatever-her-name-is has a thick, bushy beard." The sergeant scowled at the constable, whose mouth wriggled like an overexcited child telling a silly joke.

"What do you mean? There's no man here and definitely no one with a beard. Did you stop him? He's an intruder. If there's any murdering..." Boniface's voice became strained and the pitch rose. He leaned as if to stand up.

"Sir. Please. Let's start with the basics." The officer kept his tone calm but commanding. "We've had a report of a murder, and so we're under a duty to make some inquiries."

"But Montbretia." Boniface sounded nearly panic-stricken.

The sergeant stepped forward, positioning himself squarely in front of Boniface, and waited.

"Yes. Of course." Boniface leaned back in his chair. "Where do we start?"

The sergeant sniffed, flaring his nostrils.

Boniface was oblivious or ignored the implicit criticism. "The smell? I haven't got a clue. I noticed it when I opened the door, but my phone was ringing so I ran for that, and then you arrived. I thought it was the new carpet or perhaps some leftover food, but I've been here for..." Boniface made an exaggerated movement to see the time on his phone, "eighteen minutes, and it's not getting any better. I haven't had a chance to sniff out the source yet. Shall we go and have a look?"

Boniface leaned forward but rocked back when the sergeant remained motionless. "Questions first." He waited for Boniface's affirmation: a slight nod of the head.

"Are these offices all yours?"

"This suite, on this floor. Yes."

"What have we got here? In terms of rooms in the suite, sir?" The sergeant emphasized the word *suite*.

"There's this office." Boniface held his hands up and looked around the corner office, bare apart from his desk, the table with three chairs on each side, and the coat rack. "Montbretia's office is next door, and then there's the reception area at the end, next to the door you came through."

The officer stepped back, twisting in the direction of Montbretia's office.

"Next door, in the other direction, we've got the conference room, and across the passage there are two smaller rooms for clients to use, and the kitchen area."

The officer's eyes followed the direction of Boniface's hands as he pointed toward the other rooms. "Nothing else, sir?"

"No. The washrooms are communal: Go out through the door, and they're next to the elevator."

"Well, let's take a look around, shall we? See what we can see. If you would care to follow us, sir." The younger officer moved swiftly out of the office, followed by the sergeant, turning to walk backward and fixing his gaze on Boniface as he followed into the corridor where three other officers—their white shirts covered by dark stab-proof vests, each with a radio attached at shoulder height—spread across the hallway at the far end.

"Some might suggest that's a rather poor use of taxpayer resources for a bad smell," said Boniface, his voice calm, his posture straight. He had the look that the sergeant would expect from a business professional—tall, slim, wrapped in a blue suit with a subtle stripe, topped by dark brown hair, well enough cut to know that it had been cared for, but not so much effort that he would own a manicure set if they searched his home, and finished by a highly polished pair of black shoes. While Boniface had the full business armor, the sergeant knew that the best criminals went to the same tailors these days.

"Shall we look in Montbretia's office first?" Boniface reached for the handle and pushed the door open. "Aaaahhhh." He took a handkerchief and covered his nose. "I think we've found the source of the smell. You boys can go home."

The sergeant held up his arm, pinning Boniface in place without needing to touch him or utter a word, and stepped into the room. Where Boniface's office was bare, this was crowded. On the walls were framed newspaper articles. There were stacks of paper on the desk and table, and a large potted plant sat in the corner, leaning toward the window that ran the length of the far wall.

On the left, a body lay on the floor. A man, with a long, unkempt gray beard streaked with food, wearing a knee-length dirty green hooded coat held closed by several pieces of string knotted around his waist. Trousers that might once have been brown or perhaps blue, but now were dirt colored, poked out from the coat but didn't quite reach the two old shoes with holes in the soles. Under the shoes, the man was wearing one sock. Over his left eye, the weathered face tanned with dirt was broken by a gash, the top of his head now looking crumpled.

The sergeant turned to find Boniface had followed him in. He pointed toward the corridor and followed Boniface out. "I think we had better call this a crime scene, Mister Boniface." He looked to the tallest of the three officers lined across the entrance. "Call it in."

three

The lawyer removed his steel-rimmed glasses and laid them on the table, an imitation Swedish furniture store piece, its cheap blonde veneer darkened through wear and chipped to match the gouges in the gray steel legs.

He glanced up at his new client, Alexander Boniface, who was slipping his blue suit jacket over the back of the thinly padded chair. The meticulous tailoring of the jacket with its subtle stripe was in stark contrast to the factory-made, one-size-fits-all chair on which it was being hung. He understood why Boniface presented himself in this manner and appreciated the understated sophistication, which allowed his client to become invisible when he needed. He also knew that the police would not recognize the utility of Boniface's appearance, but would instead see someone they thought they could bully.

"How long will this take, Stephen?"

The lawyer kept his reply gentle. "A while."

"Quantify."

"Hours, definitely. At least eight hours. Overnight, perhaps, but unlikely. Almost certainly you'll be out within twenty-four hours, thirty-six if an inspector agrees to an additional twelve hours, and longer still if they apply to a magistrate."

Boniface flinched, slowly starting to pace across the anonymous room. "Can't you make it go faster? You're a criminal lawyer, you're used to dealing with this sort of thing—there's got to be a way to speed things up."

The lawyer kept any emotion out of his tone. "Plead guilty. Plead guilty, and we can all go home." He waited a beat. "Well, I say *all*. Of course, I mean all of us apart from you. You'll go to jail for fifteen or twenty years. Maybe more."

The lawyer felt his face twist as he suppressed a smirk while Boniface turned, pacing like a frustrated caged wild cat.

His client turned back to face him, his tone warmer, more conciliatory, perhaps. "I wasn't specific enough. Forgive me. Is there any way…"

Stephen cut off his client. "Let me make this simple. The cops' perspective will be that either you are responsible for the body, in which case they've got their man, or you know something about how it got there." He watched his new client, calibrating his responses, before continuing. "The idea that the body was dumped and it was bad luck that it was dumped in your office won't sound like a plausible explanation."

The lawyer replaced his glasses and looked over the lenses to fix Boniface with his stare before he continued. "If the body was dumped, then that's one thing and it's harder to link you, but if he was murdered in your office, then you've got a whole heap more explaining to do."

Boniface spun to face his lawyer. "What do I do, Stephen? What do I say when the truth is that I am ignorant about how the body got there, who he was, or how he died?" The anger ripped through.

The lawyer's tone remained calm. "Despite what you see on the TV, homicide detection is usually simple. Most people are killed by someone who knew them or was close to them. It usually is the husband, the wife, the boyfriend, the spurned lover, or whoever. You were in the room next to the body—in their eyes, with no other explanation, that makes it virtually unquestionable that you did it."

Boniface stared back at him, incredulous. "You're saying I'm guilty by proximity?"

"No. I'm telling you how the police will see things. I don't like how they will think about your situation, but I prefer that you understand the battle we're fighting."

"This is crazy." Boniface's voice was rising to a crescendo. "You're seriously telling me I'm guilty because I was close and in most cases that would mean I'm guilty?"

Boniface loosened his tie and dropped into his chair. The last time the lawyer had seen the man who was now his client was after a mutual client had been arrested. Boniface had been a man on a mission. He had listened intently, asked some questions—smart, insightful questions, questions that showed he was thinking not one step ahead, but at least three or four, as if he was playing games of chess simultaneously with a range of people, each with a different playing style—and then when he had a grasp of the facts, he had taken control.

A few relaxed conversations, full of humor and kind words, and the press soon concluded that there was no story. Or rather, there was a story—it had taken three phone calls by Boniface to find a far more interesting, and true, story for the journalists who gleefully turned in this new tale to their somewhat surprised, but nonetheless delighted, editors.

But now as he viewed the man in front of him, he could see that the initial disorientation of being taken to a police station was wearing off, and all that was left of the adrenalin surge that came with the shock was the gnawing little voice in his head saying, "What if I never get out? What if I go to prison?"

He observed more closely, trying to divine the other man's feelings: fear, confusion, panic as he tried to get enough information to understand the parameters of his situation, but not having the experience of his predicament to know what question to ask. Boniface rested his elbow on the table with his hand over his eyes, his thumb and middle finger massaging his temples. "Why can't they question me and get this over with? I'm here. I've got my lawyer. What's stopping them?"

The lawyer began slowly. "It doesn't work like that. All murder, manslaughter, and infanticide offenses are dealt with by Murder Investigation Teams from the Homicide and Serious Crime Command."

Boniface sat back in his seat. "So where are they?"

"Could be anywhere, but I'm guessing that the forensics guys will be taking your office apart piece by piece, and the detectives will go there first."

"These detectives are the murder whatever people?"

"The Murder Investigation Team, yes. They'll go to the scene—your office— first, and see what they can find. But there's a good chance the crime-scene guys won't let them in unless they've managed to create a safe path." Boniface frowned, questioning his lawyer. "They must ensure that the detectives don't contaminate the scene, so they'll get them into bunny suits, like all the SOCOs..."

"SOCOs?"

"Scenes of Crime Officers. The CSIs. The forensics guys. Whatever you call them, they'll always be SOCOs to me."

"These are the sensible shoes and practical haircut types?"

"Scientists is the term you're reaching for, I think, Boniface. And the SOCOs won't let the detectives onto the scene unless they're sure there will be no contamination, so normally they won't let them in until they've taken their samples."

"So why do the detectives bother going there?"

"The SOCOs will have done some field tests and have got those special 360-degree cameras that let them record the whole scene so the detectives can look at the output, and they'll want to have a look around outside."

Boniface sighed.

The lawyer continued in his matter-of-fact tone. "To be honest, you're also being left sitting around to soften you up. The cops know it's disorientating and unpleasant to be held in a police station."

He paused, making sure he still had Boniface's attention before he continued. "They'll make sure you're looked after—you can have refreshments and food. You've got access to a lawyer. When they start the questioning, they'll let you take breaks when you need, and everything you do will be recorded on their computer so they can prove they have discharged their duty of care. But it's still their house. They have a psychological advantage if you have to ask permission to take a piss."

Boniface sat fixed in his position, his eyes locked on his legal adviser. As the lawyer paused, Boniface leaned back in his chair with his hands behind his head, the sides of his mouth pushing upward. "I was a complete numpty. I followed them meekly like a lamb. When I got here they took my fingerprints, which is when I panicked and decided I needed a lawyer—I didn't know what else to do."

"You did the right thing." The lawyer followed down his scrawled notes before looking up. "Getting back to the body: You're sure that you have never seen the dead guy before?"

"I barely saw him this morning. They were so busy bundling me out of there. I smelled him more than saw him, and as for what I saw, I only remember the gash over his eye."

"A gash. How big? Was there blood?"

Boniface moved his hands as if positioning the scene. "Look. I saw the body for a moment. Yeah, there was a gash over his..." He looked up, his eyes flicking from left to right. "Yeah. A gash over his right eye. The whole area looked a bit...flattened? Like someone might have hit it."

"Was there blood?"

"In the wound. I think."

"Anywhere on his face or on the floor. Was there any blood there?"

Boniface slowly turned his head from side to side. "Not that I can remember seeing." He shook his head once. "No. I don't think there was any blood. At least none that I saw."

The lawyer nodded, scratching a few notes on a yellow lined pad. "Montbretia?"

"I called her. She called you."

"That I know," said the lawyer. "So she wasn't in the office when this all happened."

"Correct."

"The body was found in her room?"

"Also correct."

"And you don't see a link there?"

"Don't be stupid." The lawyer could hear the anger behind Boniface's assertion, and if this was insufficient to convey his client's disgust, the sneer was unambiguous.

He put down his pen and stared at Boniface, waiting for his client's annoyance to ebb. "Listen. You are my client. You, not Montbretia, and I'm making sure your best interests are served." A blink affirmed Boniface's acknowledgment.

The lawyer paused before continuing. "Can you trust Montbretia? The body was in her room—she doesn't have some axe-murdering secret that she's keeping from you?"

A mildly amused look spread over his client's face. "No. I'm fairly sure she doesn't keep an axe in the office, and she doesn't murder people as a hobby."

"Now be serious, Boniface. Can you trust her?"

Boniface stared straight, dropping the pitch of his voice as he quietly intoned, "I can trust her."

"Can you be certain that she's not involved?"

Boniface's voice kept its somber tone. "I trust her."

The lawyer sat motionless.

"I trust her. I work with her. I've seen her under stress. I've seen her in pain. I saw her when I told her that her sister had been killed. I've seen how she reacts. We lived under the same roof for five months, so I know something of how she thinks and feels, although I know enough to know that there's much more going on inside. But her thought process, her decision making, her values, her beliefs, her priorities all tell me that I can trust this person."

The room fell still, both men staring at each other. There were raised voices outside the room, what sounded like banter between two colleagues at opposite ends of the corridor. A rumble of traffic outside and trains passing nearby.

Boniface broke the stillness, his voice scarcely above a strained whisper. "I trust her. If there was anything else, anything, I needed to know, she would have told me."

"Okay," the lawyer mouthed. "Who else should we point the cops at? For instance, which clients are you presently working with?"

"They're off limits." Boniface didn't seem to offer any option for discussion.

"Still, it would be good to be assured that no client of yours is involved in all of this."

Boniface exhaled. "You don't get it, Steve, do you?" Stephen continued to take notes as the room again fell quiet again. He glanced up to see Boniface staring straight at him, apparently waiting until he had his full attention before continuing. "If this story gets out, my business is dead."

The lawyer frowned.

"Think about it. If you were a potential client, would you hire the guy who may or may not have killed a bloke and then left the dead body in his own office?"

"But you're innocent, Boniface."

"I know that, you know that. But think about it from the client's perspective— they ask me to represent them, and the first thing the press will say is 'Company A, represented by Mister Alexander Boniface, who was accused of killing a man and dumping the body in his office.'" Boniface relaxed, almost as if all his physical strength had drained from his body. "Would you hire me if you knew that's what the story would be? It's hardly a declaration of innocence or an illustration of good judgment."

He started to speak, but Boniface continued. "If I blab about a client—even once—then whatever tattered reputation I still have will be incinerated." His breathing seemed heavier. "Whatever happens, if news seeps out that I'm involved it will kill my business. Stone dead. Immediately. That means I lose everything—my business, my home—and I end up in a deeper financial hole of debt. Plus, it's not just me: Montbretia loses her source of income, and the people who have relied on me, the people who have helped me financially, they lose too."

"I hear you." The lawyer picked up his pen. "But you do realize that the cops will ask about your clients?"

Boniface returned to the standing position, stretched, and then leaned against the wall, the fine blue stripes in his white shirt highlighting its crispness against the dulling white of the wall.

"You're sure your current client has nothing to do with this whole situation?"

"My client wouldn't do this kind of thing. It's not as if they've got a chief killing officer on the staff. No one has 'disposing of dead bodies' on their job description."

The lawyer scribbled.

"I know that the next thing you're going to advise me is to keep quiet." Boniface pushed away from the wall with his shoulder and started to pace. "I know the general idea here: Police and press, say nothing and it will go away. Can't be misquoted, can't unwittingly give them a lead. I know. I've told enough clients not to say anything. I was a journalist long enough to realize that opening your mouth is often enough to hang you. But I don't want ructions. I'm innocent and I need to be free—I've got a client with a problem—so I want to be as helpful as possible and get this over with."

Boniface rested both hands on the table. "I can see the disappointment in your eyes when I tell you that, but I need to get back to work."

The lawyer sat up straight, facing Boniface directly, and began, "You've never done this before."

Boniface winced.

"I was forgetting. Sorry."

"It's not you that should be sorry, Steve; I was the one driving the car. I was the one who had been drinking. But the difference then is that I was drunk, so I didn't notice what was going on around me, and second, I was to blame, and I knew it. So you are right, this is my first time: the first time I've been interviewed by the police when I'm sober, and the first time when I was innocent of whatever it is they might think I've done."

"But are you happy to submit to questioning about a possible murder charge without preparation?" He fixed his gaze on Boniface. "What would you say if a client told you they wanted to talk to the press without preparation?"

Boniface's visage softened. "I don't need practice. I've got you by my side. What can go wrong? They come in. I tell the truth. We all go home."

"You don't get it, do you? What they want to do is to get a chronology of what happened. Their aim is to lock you into your story. They don't care what the story is; they want you to commit to it. Once you've committed to your story, that's it; then they'll pick at it and keep picking."

"I get it."

"No you don't." There was exasperation in the lawyer's tone. "In the last half hour you've changed your story—you've added, you've clarified—call it what you will, you've changed your story."

"I'm trying to tell you everything."

"Sure. But once they've locked you in your story, every change will be used as a weakness to lever you open. Any minor error or discrepancy will be a lie as far as they're concerned. Any lie proves your guilt. Any assertion without proof infers guilt. It's a one-way street. You can't clarify without saying you lied. If they have any evidence that contradicts your story, then they'll think they can prove their whole story, however fanciful or inaccurate it may be. Remember, you have no evidence to prove your innocence, do you?"

"What?"

"You can't prove that you didn't kill the guy. You can't prove that you didn't dump the body. Think about it and stay quiet, please."

four

"Hello boys!" Montbretia let the glass door swing behind her as she stepped into the street-level office two floors under Boniface's. Mentally she reminded herself: The Brits call them estate agents, not realtors.

"The delightful and fragrant Miss Armstrong. Your radiant beauty casts us poor wretches in the shadow of the misery of our meager subsistence without your dazzling looks and charming personality to shine light on our impoverished living." The man behind the first desk stood as he spoke, moving out and rolling his left hand as he made an exaggerated bow.

"Oh, Charles, you are full of shit, but do carry on. It makes a girl feel good." A broad grin broke across her face as Charles stood from his reverential Elizabethan bow.

"See. You're full of shit, Charlie boy." The second man turned to face Montbretia. "So when you coming out with me, Monty-girl?"

There was a hardening in the older man's voice. "Zahir, I…"

Montbretia cut them short. "Now boys, let's not get in a fight. Two scrapping estate agents isn't pretty." The joy on her face now felt forced. "You know I love you both equally." Her tone was of a mildly exasperated parent.

The warmest part of the not warm day had passed, and the plate-glass windows on two sides of the room let the gray light seep in. The property details hanging in clear folders suspended in straight rows acted like blinds blotting out any chance of brightness, and the strip lights in square blocks between the ceiling tiles seemed to cast shadows inside the office, not bring light.

Montbretia stood in her fitted, faded jeans and white shirt with a tailored brown jacket. Her eyes flicked between the two men. Charles, with his blond, subtly wavy hair, in his blue chalk-striped suit with a red silk handkerchief in his top pocket, and Zahir, in his less well-fitting suit. But you wouldn't notice the poor fit; all you would see is the dull green open-weave fabric with an electric blue lining, the chunky gold watch, one of many similar gaudy pieces, and the chunky rings, all topped by the rough-cut spiky black hair.

Zahir broke the silence. Keeping his arm by his side, he twisted his hand to point upward. "So?" His eyes followed his finger to indicate Boniface's office. "What's Mister Grumpy been up to?"

"He's not grumpy, he's preoccupied."

"He doesn't like us."

"Doesn't like you," said Charles under his breath.

Montbretia laughed, bringing her hand over her mouth, then paused as she tried to regain her composure. "No. He's got a business to run and clients with problems that need fixing. He's serious about what he does." She hoped she had sounded sincere. "He's one of the good guys, Zahir."

Zahir's left eye twitched, pulling the rest of his head around: an involuntary spasm that Montbretia had noticed always followed a disagreement. "Think about it. When my sister was killed, he was the one that gave me a place to stay—he gave me the keys to his front door, emptied everything out of his spare room, and told me to stay as long as I wanted and refused any rent. Even though I've got a place."

"You mean the place where you haven't invited me?"

"I mean the place where no one is invited—it's my home. It's the first home I've ever had, and I never planned to own a home, but the way it came about..." Montbretia's voice trailed off.

"Of course. Of course. What with your sister and that awful business," offered Charles in the voice Montbretia recognized as intending to be reassuring.

Montbretia bowed her head for a few moments in contemplation. "He was a real help—the only one to give me the help I wanted—when Ellen died." She looked to Charles for support. "You know that Boniface was the one who told me that Ellen had died?"

The only sound was the noise of cars passing outside the window and the buzz of a light in the ceiling. "In the weeks after Ellen—not just the immediate few days—as well as giving me a room rent free, he gave me money. Gave, didn't lend, and won't let me pay him back, and he's given me work when I want it."

Zahir had the look of someone desperate to say something. "Yeah, but I bet he's got spy cameras filming you, Monty-girl."

"He doesn't have spy cameras."

"You looked!" Montbretia felt her cheeks light up like two beacons. "See! You looked. You knew he let you have the room so that he could spy on you. Mister Grumpy is also Mister Pervy-cam."

"I looked, and there was nothing." She lowered her voice from the defiant tone she had used to respond to Zahir. "Within a few weeks I had figured that he didn't have the knowledge to install cameras and wasn't that sort of guy anyway."

Zahir gave an uncommitted sneer, half lifting his shoulders in apathetic acceptance. "Okay, so he's a saint, and he's not into women." He took a moment to take in Montbretia. "At least he's not into *hot* women, so what has he been up to?"

"Yes, we thought we had all the news for you," said Charles, stumbling over his words like a five-year-old with a new secret to divulge. "What with the burned-out van up on the Common, but it seems that you have the biggest story. What's happened? They say the police arrested Boniface."

Montbretia sighed and stepped backward to rest on the edge of the desk opposite Charles. "I don't know. What Boniface said didn't make much sense: He was on the phone, and the police came in and said there had been a report of a murder. When they looked, they found a dead body in my room."

"Wicked." The younger man in the unpleasant suit had a self-satisfied smirk. "I'm gonna ask those crime-scene dudes if I can have a look when I next meet them for a ciggie."

Charles flashed a look of anger at his younger colleague. "Gracious, that's quite shocking."

"So did Boniface do it? Is that why they've arrested him? Don't worry, I'll look after you when he's gone." Zahir seemed barely able to contain his enthusiasm. "So when you gonna come for a ride in my car?"

"I'm sure Mister Boniface will be touched with your concern, Zahir." Charles turned to Montbretia. "That sounds dreadful. Is Boniface alright?" Montbretia looked down. "What can we do to help?"

"You've got cameras here," began Montbretia.

"Sure. We've got CCTV."

"Can I have a look?"

Zahir looked up. "You look after the shop, Charlie-boy. I'll take her out the back."

Montbretia stiffened, and Charles continued. "It's alright. Thank you, Zahir. I think we'd all be better served if you keep your killer sales presence here, just in case a customer comes in."

"He's jealous because I sold three houses last week." Zahir held up three fingers, saluting like a boy scout. "Three. Two of those were big sales, 2.5 mill and 3.8 mill." He dropped his fingers and clenched a fist, holding it over his heart. He beat his chest twice with his fist. "Boy from Bangladesh sold well. One week, over seven million pounds in sales." He turned to Charles, raising his eyebrows. "What did you sell?" He waited expectantly. "Yeah. You're right, better keep the salesman in the shop, and when you're ready, Monty, you can come out with me. I'm the one that can afford to treat you right."

Montbretia gave a weak smile and continued her conversation with Charles. "Where are the cameras?"

"That's a secret," said Zahir. "If I tell you that..."

"You'd have to kill me," said Montbretia, trying to keep the tedium out of her voice.

"No. I could never hurt the woman I love." A self-satisfied look spread across his face. "No. You'd have to marry me, so I knew I could trust you."

"We've got two that record outside," said Charles, stepping between his guest and his overly pushy colleague. "The first one is there." He faced the door on the front elevation of the property and pointed to the top-right corner. "That looks across the door, pointing up Wimbledon Hill Road."

He pointed in the diagonally opposite corner. "That's the second one; it points along the Mansel Road window toward the junction."

"You mean it points away from our door?" Montbretia's voice was deflated.

Charles paused and flushed slightly. "Mmm."

"You don't have one on that outside corner? Pointing in our direction? Or anything else that might help?"

Charles sounded apologetic. "We're worried about people breaking the window. He twisted through 180 degrees and pointed up at a black bubble in the ceiling. "We've got a third camera there, but that records everyone who comes through the door, so I don't think it will help much."

Montbretia chewed her bottom lip, lost in contemplation. "Okay, well, let's see what you've got. Take me to the recorder."

"This way." Charles held out his arm, directing Montbretia to the door in the rear wall.

"See you later, babe." Zahir flashed a lascivious grin as Montbretia passed. "I better make some calls. Someone needs to bring in the cash to keep those cameras running, and it ain't gonna be you, is it, Charlie-boy?"

Charles led Montbretia down a short corridor and into a small, windowless room. "I'm sorry about him. I try...but you know." He gave a what-are-you-going-to-do shrug.

"It's alright. I can handle him, and despite the bluster, he's quite respectful. I spent an hour and a half across the road this morning. That was..." she searched for the word, "wearing."

Charles grimaced, pulling his chin back. "You mean you spent time with Jason, Declan, and Trevor."

"I think you mean J-man, D-man, and T-man." A mock admonishment. "Anyway, it was only Jason and Declan, although I can never remember which is which. One's taller and the other's heavier. Both have got bad haircuts that they think are trendy. Each wears a cheap, rather shiny suit they think is catnip for the ladies. One suit was more silver, the other more pewter in hue. Each wears chunky gold-like and platinum-like jewelry and probably sourced it from the same..."

"...online retailers that Zahir patronizes," Charles finished.

Montbretia's face reddened subtly.

"But you didn't break any fingers today." Charles looked slightly shocked, as if he had surprised himself by making the comment, and was even more surprised that he hadn't been punished.

"I only needed to do that once, and the lesson was learned; they've all been very wary about physical contact since then. It's the puppy-dog helpfulness that got to me." Charles frowned, waiting for Montbretia to continue. "I was going through their CCTV, and every three minutes one of them would be in. Did I want a cup of tea? How about coffee? A Danish? Lunch? Did I want company or cheering up? Did I want to take my mind off...? Well, I'm not sure exactly what I was meant to take my mind off, but there you go. And when that didn't work, they started with their stories and the brags about the houses they've sold, and..." She sighed. "As I said, it was wearing."

Charles's face took on a look of concern. "Did you find anything on their CCTV?"

"A man with a beard leaving the building. The significance of this man is that he left after Boniface arrived."

"So Boniface saw him?" Charles beamed as if he had solved an ancient mystery.

"That's rather the point; he didn't." Montbretia watched his face fall and continued. "But the police did."

Charles's face registered horror. "The police." A flicker of hope passed across his face, and the horror turned to enthusiasm. "So they arrested this fellow?" Montbretia shook her head once. "But they at least know what he looks like?"

"They were concentrating on looking for a dead body and were scared about the dangerous murderer who was still on the premises. Apparently the guy held the door open for them, and that was the last they saw of him."

"Gracious." Charles appeared to be back to his normal bumbling self. "So did the cameras across the road give you a good look at this man?"

"No—that's what I'm hoping to do with your cameras. To be honest, I only know the man's a man and bearded because Boniface said so; their cameras were too blurry to see much more than a figure leaving around the relevant time."

"Well, then, welcome to the beating heart of our empire." He gestured around the room, highlighting the table, several four-drawer filing cabinets, the stacks of papers and brochures, the computer and printer, and the single chair, triumphantly finishing like a game-show hostess revealing the monitor screen split into four with the first three quadrants showing the live feed from the three cameras.

"Show me how it works, and then you can go back. Zahir needs some adult supervision, and it's going to be a long, tedious process to watch not much happening."

five

"Are you alright to get started again, Mister Boniface?" Standing just inside the door, Detective Inspector Raymond Talbot looked for affirmation from Boniface and then looked to his lawyer, Stephen Holding, sitting next to him.

The lawyer nodded once. "Let's go," said Boniface. "But I'm afraid the story won't change." He stared at the detective, overweight, over forty, and over confident of the effect of his own force of personality, while being underpaid and underwhelming in the sartorial elegance department.

The supermarket suit was an unfortunately chosen shade of gray: If he splashed when he washed his hands, it would look like he wet himself. The polycotton easy-iron but never ironed shirt was thin, starting to wear and, despite being labeled white by the same supermarket that supplied the ill-fitting suit, was showing the ghost of too many stains, mostly from food eaten by hand or dropped from a fork as he gesticulated while eating. A polyester tie, ineptly tied, served to draw attention to the messy ensemble. Only his well-polished but cheap shoes suggested any sign of discipline.

Boniface passed a glance at his lawyer: cheap suit, cheap shirt, and cheap shoes. If he didn't know this was a show, put on so that people would underestimate this unprepossessing and otherwise utterly modest man, then Boniface would have reflexively sneered at his appearance in the same way that he now sneered at the detective inspector.

The detective inspector appeared to be enjoying himself much more than he had been when they broke. "While you've been enjoying a cup of our very finest tea, I've been having a chat with our scene-of-crime guys."

Boniface stared down at the half-finished and now abandoned plastic cup holding the swill the station's vending machine labeled as tea. In his disgust, he almost missed his lawyer speaking: "You will be making a full disclosure of everything you have found at the scene." Clearly the lawyer had also picked up on whatever was lifting the inspector's mood.

The policeman nodded his head, a look of smugness spreading across his face. "It will be my pleasure," he said as he sat down. The second officer, younger but with less hair, slimmer, and dressed equally—if not more—cheaply but with better-fitting clothes that had been cleaned more regularly, assumed his seat beside the boss.

He hit the record button. "Interview recommencing at seven-fifteen PM. Present are DI Raymond Talbot and DS Kevin Hitchcock."

"Stephen Holding."

Boniface sighed audibly. "Alexander Boniface."

"So, Mister Boniface. Shall we start again, from the beginning?"

Boniface sighed, again. "I arrived at my office a minute or two before seven. No, I didn't have a watch; I didn't check a clock. It was gray; it was after dawn. I reached the door to my office on the second floor at seven AM precisely. I know it was seven AM precisely because as I started to punch the security code, the phone in my office started ringing. My client is a stickler for punctuality: If they make an appointment to talk at seven AM, then they expect to talk at seven on the dot. Not at six-fifty-nine. Not at seven-oh-one. But at seven."

"Okay. We've got it. It was seven AM. Who did you speak to?"

"That's not material. As I've said, I will not disclose the name of my client, nor the name of the individual with whom I was speaking, without first discussing the matter with them and getting their agreement in writing. However, I can assure you that my client is a well-respected company that operates on a global basis, and I was talking with one of the board members who has an unquestionable reputation."

The inspector rolled his eyes. "You arrived, and there was no one in the office?"

"That is correct."

"You're sure, Mister Boniface?"

"I didn't do a full search of the office; I was running for the phone. But it was dark in the office. The central passage has no natural light. The lights are on motion sensors, and none were on when I arrived. There was no light coming from the rooms with open doors, and no light coming from under the doors that were closed. From that I made the assumption that I was alone, but as I said, I didn't check because I was running to answer the phone."

"So was the light on when you went into the office where you found the body?"

Boniface paused, thrown by a question he hadn't been expecting. "I can't remember." His eyes fixed on a point in the distance, even though the room was a small box with not quite enough space for the four occupants. "No, I can't be certain. Instinctively, I would say it came on when the door opened and the sergeant stepped in, but that room has a window, so the contrast between the light being on and off is less noticeable. To be honest, I was more worried about what we might find in there."

The policeman sat back in his chair. "You know what, Mister Boniface?" Boniface met his interrogator's gaze. "I don't find your story plausible."

Boniface remained subdued as the detective inspector continued. "Sure, you come across as a nice enough kind of guy. A bit of a problem with your drinking in the past, but you say that you don't touch the stuff anymore, and you haven't blipped on our radar since that, shall we say, unfortunate incident. In fact, that incident is the only record of you that we could find—you don't even seem to have a parking ticket."

"Not that I could get one of those at the moment," interjected Boniface.

The inspector looked momentarily confused before continuing. "True. But I still don't believe what you're telling me." He leaned forward. "I'll give you, you don't look like a murderer. But I've been wrong about murderers before, and just because you don't look like a murderer, that doesn't prove your innocence."

Boniface remained still.

"I accept your logic that it would be crazy to dump a body in your own office. But again, that's hardly proof-positive of your innocence. And you're right that there is no obvious link between the body and you, and again, that lack of a link does not give us any suggestion as to your innocence, especially as we have yet to confirm the identity of the deceased."

The inspector leaned in, his voice becoming quieter. "But here's the thing: You do have someone who you suggest could vouch for you, and yet you won't tell us who he is. You say it's a client, but you won't tell us the name of the company or the name of the individual you were speaking to. If you can give us a name, we can speak to them and get confirmation that you were talking the whole time. Sure, it's not irrefutable proof—you could have been murdering and talking—but it's the only evidence you've offered up."

The detective inspector waited.

He sighed and slumped back in his chair. "I get the notion of client confidentiality, but you understand we can get a warrant and check your phone records." The detective inspector looked to the lawyer as if seeking his agreement. "You recognize we'll be able to trace this person, and so that leaves me wondering why you're not being more forthcoming. Why don't you give us a name, and we'll all go home?"

The detective inspector drew his hand back through his hair, roughly combing it. "You assert that someone unknown to you must have dumped the body of someone else unknown to you in your office—in the room next to yours, which you say is usually occupied by your associate, Miss Armstrong."

Boniface felt his head involuntarily moving to nod.

"Are you offering nothing to back this suggestion?"

"The man with the beard," said the lawyer.

"The accomplice with the beard?" The inspector softened his voice so it was more of a whisper you would use when trying to comfort a child and regarded Boniface with soft eyes. "Look. Maybe it wasn't murder. Maybe it was the other guy: You were there, but it was an accident." He stopped talking, apparently hoping for a response. "But if it was an accident, this is your opportunity to tell me now."

Boniface relaxed in his chair. "As I've said before, I can't explain how a dead body got into my office. All I can tell you is that I have no idea who he is, and I had nothing to do with whatever happened."

"Alright, then. We tried. Now let me tell you what we've found." The edges of the detective's mouth twitched vaguely upward. "We've had the crime-scene people in all day going inch by inch through your office. I don't have the full details at the moment, but once I do we will make a full disclosure." He stared pointedly at the lawyer. "But for the moment, let's stay with the big picture."

The lawyer nodded.

"The crime-scene programs on TV where the forensics guys find the villains? It's different here; our forensics guys stay at the crime scene, and we do the detective work. But where the TV does get it right is with the spray. You must have seen it when they spray a surface and hold ultraviolet light over it. If there are blood traces or traces of any other human fluids, it lights up."

Boniface softened his stare.

"Luminol. That's what it's called, and as you might expect, they sprayed luminol around looking for blood." Boniface looked to his lawyer, who was scratching notes on his yellow pad. "The body was found in Miss Armstrong's room. Next door, the corner office, is yours?"

The inspector paused, looking at Boniface as if expecting a response. "That is correct." Boniface's voice was quiet but firm.

"Well, when the crime-scene guys sprayed the carpet in your room, it lit up like the Blackpool illuminations. No, this wasn't Blackpool; this was more like Las Vegas. A whole great strip, about eight feet long."

Boniface remained impassive.

"You know what I think?"

With a small movement of his head, Boniface confirmed that he did not.

"I think that's where you killed him, and once we've analyzed that piece of carpet we'll be able to tie you to the murder scene."

six

She watched as her knuckles made contact with the door.

The door of her ex-husband's apartment.

A delicate, controlled impact—enough to make a noise, but not enough to wake a sleeping person or to hurt her hand. Again, skin on dark wood. Again, silence with no light under the door to suggest human occupation.

She turned her ear toward, but not touching, the door and pressed the doorbell, startling herself with the vulgarity of its ring, which decayed, leaving the sound of movement within.

Veronica stepped back, smoothed her fitted dark-green dress, and checked her reflection in the window over the stairwell. She flicked her head, watching her dark auburn mane pulse over her shoulders, then stood squarely facing the door as it cracked open.

"Hi."

The face of a younger woman looked through the slit. Her body, wrapped in shades of pink, was positioned with her weight behind the door.

The older woman made eye contact and smiled. "Montbretia?"

The tension in the younger woman's face released, breaking into a broad grin. "Veronica?"

"That's right."

"Call me Monty." The younger woman stood back and opened the door. "He's still not back, but do you want to come in?" Veronica took in the faded fuchsia sweatshirt and dark-pink sweatpants as she stepped forward—the click of her heels silenced as she passed over the threshold and onto the carpet in the hall—turning in the direction suggested by Montbretia's look.

The hall was dark and became darker as the door shut. Stepping into the living room, the sole source of illumination was the light pollution forcing itself from outside. Reflexively, Veronica turned on the lights as she passed the switch inside the door, dimming them as she started to scan the room.

It was as it had been last time she was here. Two perpendicular sofas: The one on the left had a crumpled triangle of cushions—probably a sign that Montbretia had been sitting there, and given the lack of light, probably in deep in contemplation. A cup of coffee—cold, Veronica guessed—sat on the low table shared by the two sofas.

"Can I get you something?"

"A tumbler, please," said Veronica, slipping her bag off her shoulder and reaching inside. "He doesn't stock what I like." She slid out a bottle of whisky and placed it next to Montbretia's cold coffee, then sat on the sofa, keeping her ankles and knees together as she delicately lowered herself.

"Won't you join me?" she said as Montbretia placed a crystal tumbler on the table.

"I'm fine, thank you. Water? Ice?"

Veronica looked up at Montbretia, pulled a mock frown, and shook her head imperceptibly. "This is the good stuff. You don't dilute it." She released the frown. "Are you sure you won't have a sip? You look like you could do with a drink."

The younger woman dropped onto the pile of cushions on the opposite sofa, pulling her knees under her chin and wrapping her arms around her legs. "I can't drink anything at the moment."

"Come on, dear." Veronica's expression was one of concern. Her head tilted, her mouth half open. She leaned in. "This is Boniface. He will be fine. He's at the police station, and he's probably only still there because he's boring them with his stories." She smiled softly and slid around the table to sit next to Montbretia, putting an arm around her shoulders. "He'll be fine." She felt her lips twisting. "But he might break a few things on the way to being fine. You know Boniface."

Montbretia sat up straighter and dropped her feet to the floor. "I'm only here because I don't know where else to go or what else to do. I can't go to the office, I don't want to go home, and I figured he'll come here as soon as he's out. I've called him, and there's no reply,"

Veronica took a sip and placed her tumbler back. "I'm the same," she whispered. "I didn't know what else to…" She let her words fade to silence without finishing her sentence.

The older woman took another sip and disturbed the quiet. "I know it's been a few months, but I was so sorry about your sister. It was dreadfully shocking."

Montbretia bowed her head, biting her lower lip, and whispered, "Thank you."

The room fell still, noiseless apart from the sounds from the road outside. Veronica walked to the window, felt behind the curtain for the drawstring, and closed out the night. She tapped the dark fabric to knock out a few wrinkles, then walked back to the table, poured herself another whisky, and returned to her seat across from Montbretia, who looked up, forcing a look of confidence across her face.

"You're living back at…"

"Ham Common. Ellen's old place. I didn't want to go there—at first I cried every time I went there, and when I stopped crying I got scared—but now I find it comforting having Ellen all around me." Montbretia's voice trailed off, the only sound the noise of Veronica lifting and replacing her tumbler. Montbretia looked straight at the older woman. "Did you find anything?"

"No." Veronica kept her voice soft and tried to let her slight Scottish burr resonate. "It's hard to ask questions when you realize that by asking you're tipping off journalists. But I found nothing—no one seems to have picked up the story." She took another sip. "What did you find out?"

"I spent all of my time in the realtors'—sorry, if I don't use the English, someone who's not here will correct me—I mean estate agents' offices."

"Oh. Are you thinking about selling when you get probate?"

"No, it's just that Wimbledon… What is it with Wimbledon?" Her voice became more inquisitive. "Before I came here, I'd heard of Wimbledon because of the tennis. But now I've lived and worked in Wimbledon for a few months, I realize I was wrong: It's the land of tennis *and* realtors."

"Not forgetting the Papal embassy," offered Veronica.

"Tennis, realtors, and the Pope's London home-away-from-home on the Common," said Montbretia, her body relaxed as she continued. "There are three realtors in the storefronts under the office, two right across the street, another two further down the block, and they all seem to have CCTV."

"That sounds like fun." Veronica made no attempt to keep the sarcasm out of her voice as she raised her eyebrows. "Which was worse, watching the CCTV or dealing with the estate agents? I presume they all fit the stereotype?"

"So much testosterone. So much need for a public sterilization program," said Montbretia, exasperated. "But at least they don't grab. One tried it once during the first week I was with Boniface. He put his hand on my ass."

The older woman grimaced.

"So I told him, 'Touch my ass, and I'll break a finger.' He thought he would be funny and said, 'What, like this?' and placed his hand." Montbretia twisted to indicate where she had been touched.

Veronica sighed, still nodding.

"I didn't mean to break his finger. I only meant to twist it back and make him look a bit foolish." She held her hands out, palms turned up. "But I misjudged it." She became more serious. "In the end it was quite useful: I made my point, and no one has touched my ass since then."

"What happened to the guy with the broken finger?"

"Same as the other guys, he moved on to another job, but he moved on a bit more quickly than normal. He had lost face by getting beaten by a girl, and as it had happened in public, there was no way for him to deny it. But the rest of the guys love me for it, and so it was easy when I wanted to see their CCTV."

"And?"

"And it's very boring. But I did see a few things."

"Do tell." Veronica sat forward on her seat.

"I can do better than tell." Montbretia put her hand through her sweatshirt collar and pulled at her shoulder, dragging out a blue lanyard with a small oblong piece of silver plastic at the end. "I can show."

seven

Boniface looked across the road and up at his office. Under the street lighting, the yellow/beige 1970s brickwork layered between the brown-framed tinted windows had lost any sense of color, instead becoming lighter and darker stripes.

The estate agent offices on the ground level were empty: Apparently Charles and Zahir had sold enough houses for one day. Or more likely, Zahir had sold, and Charles had fussed and soothed the upset customers who were never intending to buy a property in the first place.

There was one light, somewhere in the heart of the building, on the floor between his and the street level—and that was likely a faulty sensor—but apart from that, as far as Boniface could see, the building was in darkness.

He crossed Wimbledon Hill Road, turned into Mansel Road and followed the side of the building to the parking lot behind the office, where he stared at the rear elevation. "How would you get a body in?" he muttered under his breath, looking up at the fire escape. "Or did they go through the front door?"

Boniface pulled out his key and entered the lobby from the parking lot side, locking the door behind him. A small, faceless lobby with magnolia emulsion walls, concealed lighting, and enough space for a tiny security desk that was never used, probably explaining one factor in keeping the rent down.

He looked back at the back door—a single aluminum-framed glass panel—then at the front door, two brown aluminum-framed glass panels; then he gave rear door a firm shake. He wasn't sure what he expected. A final scan of the lobby, and he started on the stairs, ignoring the elevator.

Two flights, turning at an intermediate landing next to a floor-to-ceiling picture window, and he arrived on the next-floor landing, which was a facsimile of his landing. Two further flights, and Boniface was outside his office. "Good evening."

"Good evening, sir." The officer looked to be around the same age as the young constable who had been in Boniface's office that morning, and if she was charged with standing outside his office overnight, there was every chance she was equally lacking in experience.

"What happened here?" asked Boniface.

"There was an incident, sir."

"An incident?"

"An incident." The officer was definitive, offering no apparent hope of elaboration. Perhaps she wasn't as guileless as the constable this morning.

"Can I go in?" Boniface tried to peer through the reinforced safety-glass panels in the door.

"Mister Boniface, I presume." She had evidently paid attention when she was briefed.

"That's right."

"I'm afraid you can't."

"And if I wasn't Boniface?"

"Unless you're a scenes of crime officer, then you're not going past." Her delivery remained emotionless and her message absolute.

"What about the fire exit, or should I say the non-fire entrance? Can I go through there?"

The officer's voice had an edge of exasperation. "I'm sure that any fire exit will have been sealed, sir. But please remember that this is a crime scene—do you want to leave your fingerprints and DNA in all the places that you know the SOCOs will be looking tomorrow?" She reached under her stab-proof vest, pulled out a notebook, checked her watch, and started to make notes, looking up at Boniface as she continued. "Procedure, sir."

Boniface raised his eyes. "What have they found? These scene-of-whatever people."

"I don't know, sir. You would need to talk to the senior investigating officer or one of the officers involved with the investigation, such as Detective Inspector Talbot."

"We're acquainted," said Boniface. "What about the carpet?"

The officer frowned. "Was there anything else I can help you with, sir?"

eight

Boniface fumbled as he pushed the key into the deadlock in his front door and twisted. The lock didn't move. He twisted the key counterclockwise. It moved. As he twisted back again, he could hear feet running inside. He tugged the key out of the lock as the door swung open and two women embraced him.

"So this is my welcoming committee to celebrate being sprung from jail? What have you got lined up for me? There are things an incarcerated man misses. He has needs, he has wants."

Veronica let go and stood back, looking up at him. "You're trying to tell us that the tea in the cop shop was awful?"

"That's about it," said Boniface kissing the top of Montbretia's head as she clung to him and leaning to kiss Veronica. "Shall we go inside?"

Boniface moved slowly, with a lump of varying shades of dark pink clinging to his side. "Why didn't you call when you got out?" asked the pink bundle.

"Because the nice, kind policemen escorted me out of the office this morning before I could plug in my charger," replied Boniface, reaching into his pocket and tossing his inert phone onto the sofa. "If you've ever seen the sort of person who doesn't carry a phone, you'll understand why I didn't go looking for a phone box." He grimaced. "Added to which, I didn't want anything to slow me from getting to see my two favorite gals."

"Even though you didn't know we'd be here," said Veronica.

"But in my heart, I did know where you were," responded Boniface lightly. They sat, Montbretia still hanging on to Boniface and Veronica, on the perpendicular sofa, reaching for her bottle of whisky. "You were expecting a long wait, I see."

"Preparation," said Veronica. "Anyway. Tell us. How did you manage to escape?"

"I dug a tunnel."

"Alexander." There was a sharpening of Veronica's tone as she held her tumbler away from her mouth.

"Horseradish."

"Will you stop with the horseradish-gate! Don't bring up that story—just tell us how you got out." Montbretia let go of Boniface and leaned back to stare at him.

"I'm being serious," said Boniface. "I'm free because of horseradish."

Montbretia continued to stare.

Veronica took a sip. "Let's get past this horseradish thing, then you can tell us about the police."

Boniface leaned back and relaxed. "It's good to be in a relaxing seat. The chairs at the police station are bloody uncomfortable."

"Horseradish."

"Right. Background. When I was sorting out my head," Boniface made quote marks with his fingers, "last year, I was friendly with a guy called Quentin. I got out and set up my own PR agency; Quent got out and decided to start making organic horseradish. Two months ago he called me. The first batch of organic horseradish was ready, and he wondered if I could give him a few pointers or a few suggestions for how to market it."

Montbretia leaned, like a sprinter getting ready on the stocks.

"I made a few phone calls and suggested a few other people Quent could call. Literally, I spent fifteen minutes. Anyway, long story short, Quentin's organic horseradish got mentioned in an article in the *Daily Mail*, and as a result, everything went wild for him. His internet server got swamped, crashing his website, but that didn't matter because he sold out the whole year's supply in under ninety minutes. So Quentin is hugely grateful and thinks I'm a marketing god, and to express his gratitude, he sent me a box of horseradish."

"But he sold out his supply. Also, horseradish doesn't come in boxes."

"That's why you're a journalist," said Boniface to his former wife. "Quentin sent me a box with 12 jars of horseradish. The horseradish was fine, but the jars were the test packaging."

"Which had some issues," interjected Montbretia.

"I had this box of jars sitting in the office for a few weeks, and I figured we should try this stuff, so about ten days ago Montbretia and I decided to have roast beef sandwiches. That way we could try the horseradish in its intended context." Montbretia seemed ready to butt in as Boniface continued. "So Montbretia offered to go to the sandwich shop while I finished something off."

"When I got back," said Montbretia, picking up the story, "he was in his office, ready for my return—he had two plates, a teaspoon, and the roll of paper towels. I walked into the room with the sandwiches, freshly made, and he's there like a simpering little kid, whining that he can't get the lid off."

"It was the test packaging. There was a fault with the lids. They were tight, and she distracted me."

"Distracted you!" Montbretia's voice rose in pitch and volume. "You were being a whiny little kid. 'It's too tight. Help me. Help me. Help me.' He was holding the jar up near his face and getting all red and angry."

"Which is when you distracted me."

"Which is when the seal gave way."

"You distracted."

"The seal."

"Move on." Veronica was firm.

"She distracted me, the lid flicked off, and I lost my grip on the jar."

"There was no distraction. I happened to be there when he let go of the jar of horseradish, which flipped up and then headed toward the floor."

"So there's a jar of horseradish heading toward our new carpet, and I reacted instinctively."

"He tried to catch it on his foot."

"I tried to break its fall so it wouldn't smash."

"Note how he says 'tried'. Because what he actually did was catch the corner of the jar with the edge of his shoe. Now, I'm no physicist, but I believe what he did was convert linear vertical motion into rotary motion. So instead of going down, this jar was now spinning like a wheel and going horizontally." Montbretia laughed loudly.

"End result," said Boniface, "we got an eight-foot streak of horseradish across the carpet."

"So how did this get you out of jail?" asked Veronica.

"Well," said Boniface. "On TV cop shows you get the science people coming along, and they spray stuff that shows blood trails."

"Luminol," said Veronica.

"That's the stuff," said Boniface. "Apparently it gives a false positive when sprayed on horseradish. So we're going to find a new cleaner, because when the crime-scene guys sprayed the carpet, they found the murder scene. Or at least what they thought was the murder scene. When I told the detective inspector about the horseradish, he was pretty deflated. Five minutes later, I was out the door with some gruff words to behave myself." He clapped his hands together once. "So that's my story. What have you two been up to?"

"I've been at work, Boniface," said Veronica. "However, Montbretia has been very busy on your behalf."

Boniface turned to Montbretia. "Did you get into the office and see the damage? I got the impression that the carpet in my room has a big horseradish-shaped hole in it now."

Montbretia twisted her head like a lighthouse, arcing left-to-right-to-left-to-right. "You can't get in. There was yellow crime-scene tape everywhere with a policeman at our door."

"There was no tape at the front when I went past, but there was a rather stern policewoman outside our suite."

"So in your heart you didn't know we were here, and instead you went to the office before coming here," said Veronica, looking disapprovingly at Boniface.

Boniface ignored the comment as he continued. "What next?"

"Next?" Montbretia rolled her eyes in an exaggerated manner. "Next, I went and talked to your favorite people."

Boniface shut his eyes. "I'm sorry for the suffering I put you through. I understand the sacrifice you're making."

"They're not that bad, Boniface."

"They're an indistinguishable morass of under-educated, ill-disciplined liars with no concept of their own ignorance or limitations. They all wear the same awful suits, nasty jewelry, and drive those appalling cars as if the laws of physics and death don't apply to them."

"They're not all like that."

"True. Charles is different, but he's even more ineffectual than the rest. I still don't get why you talk to them."

"Charles is sweet and the rest of the guys are fine. I talk to them because they're friendly and they show me around properties that I could never afford. I'm not taking risks or making compromises. None of them knows where I live—my house is still registered in Ellen's name—and they all move on to new jobs every couple of months."

"You didn't make any compromises today?" With a single turn of her head, Montbretia confirmed the negative. "And have you bathed in disinfectant since you saw them?"

Montbretia raised her eyebrows. "Relax, there were no compromises, and the only thing I flashed was a smile. I have had a shower; I did feel the necessity to wash myself down after swimming through all that testosterone. You don't think I went out dressed like this." She indicated the mismatched shocking-pink ensemble.

"What did you find?"

"CCTV and a burned-out van, which probably carried the body to the office—it's in the Caesar's Camp parking lot on Wimbledon Common."

Boniface turned to Veronica. "Have you got a driver?" She nodded, taking another sip. "Then let's go and have a look. You can tell us about the CCTV on the way up."

"There's not much to see up there," said Montbretia.

"There may not be, but I'd like to have a look, and then we can grab something to eat."

"You go," said Montbretia. "I'm in for the evening—I'm not dressed for dinner."

"It doesn't matter how you're dressed," said Boniface. "We're not going anywhere fancy. Wear what you wore today."

Veronica made an exaggerated sigh. "Bring me out here only to say we're not going anywhere nice." She sighed again, the extremity of her lip lifting as she winked at Boniface.

"You've got catching up to do," said Montbretia, "and I'm tired."

"But you're the one with the knowledge," said Veronica. "And you can't leave Boniface on his own. He needs adult supervision."

nine

"It's the obvious place."

"Why?"

"It's the closest isolated location and has the clearest access. Given the direction the van left the office, pretty much every permutation of any possible route avoids CCTV cameras." Montbretia stepped back from the burned-out Mercedes Sprinter van and held out an arm, rotating in a circle. "Standing here you're in the middle of a one-mile radius of the major road into and out of London, not to mention you've got five train stations, four subways, three hospitals, a cemetery, several supermarkets, a windmill," she smiled at Veronica, "and the Papal embassy, all within easy walking."

"Some of those are quite a distance," said Boniface.

Montbretia sighed. "If you've gone to the effort of lugging a dead body into an office, driving up here, removing the plates, and torching the van, then walking a mile or two, even in the dark, isn't going to cause you the sort of stress you need to talk through in therapy."

"Can't argue there," said Boniface. "So which way did they go?"

"A guess," said Montbretia, "would be that anyone would have walked toward the bypass—it's the major road into and out of London. If you go the route we came, then you're into a residential area pretty rapidly. But if you go that way," she pointed into the wooded area, a mass of shadowy black shapes in the nighttime, "then you've got the cemetery, a supermarket, and student accommodation blocks."

Boniface exhaled, nodding to suggest he knew where Montbretia was taking her logic.

"In other words, you've got an area where you will be unnoticed, and if you sit by a bus stop you're invisible, even to people standing next to you."

"And once you're on a bus, you're gone," said Boniface. He pointed back along the road they had been driven along. "Is that the only access?"

"For a van this size, yeah. There are other tracks, but they're gated, and you would want a four-wheel drive or a bike."

"Is this your route?" asked Boniface.

"You come through here?" Montbretia could hear the disquiet in Veronica's voice.

"Often—once or twice a week. It's the shortest route from home."

"But you live on Ham Common."

"Yup. And if you draw a straight line between my house and the office, you go straight through Richmond Park. There's a slight kink because there isn't a convenient gate, and apparently I'm not allowed to knock down the wall and go through people's backyards."

"The English are like that," offered Veronica, her Scottish brogue thickening.

"But when I get out the gate, I go over the bypass, and it's straight through." Montbretia kept her back to the road that led to the parking lot, holding out her arms in a V-shape. "There's the shortest track, but that's pretty bumpy." She indicated with her right arm. "Or," she indicated with her left arm, "I take the longer route, but it's a much better track and there are usually people around—dog walkers and horse riders."

"So which route did you take today?"

"I took the long route and was about 500 yards over there." Montbretia felt the disappointment tinged with hope in Boniface's and Veronica's looks. "I saw nothing." She watched as the hope left them.

"Question," said Veronica, startling Montbretia. "You reckon the van driver went away from the approach road. Away from the office."

Montbretia moved her lower jaw from left to right, contemplating. "It's a guess and a pretty weak guess."

"The guy you showed me in the CCTV with the fake beard went up the hill."

"That's the direction he appeared to be heading," said Montbretia. "But we're extrapolating from there. He could have jumped out of the camera arcs, ripped off the beard, put on a jacket, then turned back, and we wouldn't be able to recognize him. He could have kept the disguise and walked around the block, doubling back on himself—there's too much CCTV footage and only one of me."

"But he was last seen coming in this direction?" Montbretia nodded, allowing Veronica to continue. "If he did come in this direction, then why would the driver walk in the opposite direction?"

Montbretia lifted her shoulders, keeping them raised as she started to respond. "As I said, I'm guessing. Also don't forget, there was nearly two hours between the van leaving the office and the guy with the beard walking out. And to guess even more, I guess that the driver got here, set the van on fire, and left. I doubt he saw any necessity to hang around, especially as he won't have known when his fake-bearded buddy would be free, if that guy was waiting for Boniface to arrive."

Veronica hugged herself, apparently feeling the chill as she contemplated.

"There's one other thing," said Montbretia. "In fact, there are three things."

"Three things, and then let's get something to eat," said Boniface.

"Point one," said Montbretia. "We don't know what the driver did. We can speculate, but that doesn't take us forward. All we can hope is that someone saw him, so I'm coming back here tomorrow morning to find anyone who's here at the same time every day."

"That's crazy," said Boniface. "This isn't a good place to be alone in the dark, and that sort of sniffing should be left to the police."

"The police who haven't put a 'police aware' sign on that burned-out wreck? The police who think you had something to do with the body dump?" said Montbretia, not managing to keep the annoyance out of her voice. "Someone, somewhere must have seen something."

"There's..."

Montbretia cut off Boniface. "Point two. The driver and the bearded guy seem to have a different approach. The driver doesn't get seen. By contrast, the bearded guy waited until the police turned up and then left, crossing the arc of a CCTV camera."

"She makes a good point, Boniface," said Veronica. "These are professionals, and if a professional is happy to be seen on CCTV, then there's a reason for that." She turned to face Montbretia. "Point three?"

"We've discounted any notion that they might have left a car here." She looked up at Boniface and Veronica; both seemed confused. "It's not a smoking gun—I'm just pointing out that there are even more permutations, and the only way we're likely to find anything is by finding someone who actually saw something, which is why I need to get back here in the morning."

ten

"Nothing, until six-fifty-eight when you scamper past. Then at about ten-past-seven, two police cars scream round the corner, and two minutes later a guy with a big bushy beard crosses from our side of the road and turns up the hill."

"Can you see his face?" Boniface raised his voice over the sound of talking and cutlery clinking on plates as people ate.

"This is the best view." Boniface reached over the starched white tablecloth, now spattered with yellow grease stains, as Montbretia passed her phone. He squinted as she continued. "If you flick through to the next picture, you can see the top of the beard coming off under his right ear. He's trying to push it back as he walks."

"I see," said Boniface.

"But that's not the interesting thing," said Montbretia. "As he lifts his right hand, the sleeve drops and you can see a tattoo poking out. Not enough to see what the tattoo is, but there definitely is a tattoo and not a bit of wrist decoration."

Boniface squinted, then looked up. "I'll take your word. On this size screen it could be a smudge."

"Zoom in," said Montbretia.

"What, to see a smudge of a tattoo?"

"The previous shot—where he's pushing back the beard." Boniface fiddled with the screen. "Zoom in on the hand that's pushing the beard."

Boniface felt the muscle in his jaw lose tension. "Is he missing a finger?"

Montbretia nodded. "Still doesn't tell us where he went, but if we ever see him, he should be pretty recognizable." She held out her hand for her phone and continued. "That's pretty much it for the CCTV."

"Where does all this leave us? You've worked hard and risked your physical and mental safety spending time with those horrible children who are desperate to sell any property in Wimbledon, all to give us zero leads that we can follow." He read the disappointment on Montbretia's face. "Don't misunderstand: What you've done is helpful—you've chased every bit of evidence you've found to its logical conclusion—all I'm saying is where do we go next?" He surveyed the near-empty plates, the debris of saffron rice, near orange-colored chicken, and thin unleavened bread, all interspersed with serving dishes containing potato, cauliflower, chili, green peppers, onions, and other vegetables Boniface had difficulty recognizing. "More food for anyone?"

"It leaves us with a simple question." Veronica spoke as if she hadn't heard Boniface's offer. Her voice was measured, her focus fixed on her former husband. "Who is trying to get at you, Boniface? You don't leave a corpse unless you're trying to make a point. It's not a lighthearted April Fool."

Boniface remained quiet, letting his gaze fall on the dark-red flocked wallpaper.

Veronica continued. "Let's start with the people you've upset."

"That's a long list." Veronica narrowed her eyes as she always did when she didn't get a straight answer. "Where do you want me to start?"

"At the beginning." Boniface knew this look. He had been evasive, and so Veronica had flipped into interview mode. She had stopped asking questions and was now expecting answers.

"You probably know better than me," said Boniface. "You remember who I turned over when I was a journalist—you were married to me. People might have hated me, but the stakes were never big enough to get at me like this."

"Start with the simple guesses," said Veronica. "Your story forced Stan Gadson to resign as an MP, and his researcher went to jail for six months. Do you think it could be him?"

"Nah. That was far too long ago. Also, he had a heart attack the year after, and when I last heard, his health wasn't great—not that it was good when he was in Parliament."

"What about the researcher who went to jail?" asked Montbretia.

"Again, too long ago, and he never had the brain power to think things through, which is why he ended up in jail rather than Stan."

"He still mentions you on Facebook," said Montbretia.

"Really?" Boniface snorted. "You're kidding."

Montbretia gave a firm shake of her head in response to Boniface's grin.

"If it's not something you did when you were a journalist, then is it something to do with your time working with Gideon?" asked Veronica, still in interview mode. "You did some unpleasant stuff then—did you upset someone enough that they would send you a cadaver?"

"I upset people, but I didn't have any power." Boniface felt like he was whining. "I was handling the press, Gideon was the minister making the decisions. Someone might have wanted to get back at me for being a smart-assed pain, but a dead body seems rather extreme."

"You might think you were an angel, albeit an angel with a loose tongue, but does everyone else see it that way? The Honorable Gideon Latymer, Member of Parliament for some metal-bashing corner of the West Midlands, was involved with fairly dubious decisions. Contracts were canceled, new contracts put in place, and there was lots of cash getting passed in brown envelopes." Veronica sat back in her chair, plainly with a mild distaste in what she had said.

"Gideon was clean, but he was naive and made some bad decisions. There's a reason his political ascent stalled."

"Sure, but is there anyone who thinks that you were captaining the ship, even if you were taking orders?"

Boniface exhaled as if trying to blow out a candle across the room. "Politics is a contact sport and I was an enthusiastic team player, but why me and not Gid? Why now? It doesn't make any sense, but I'll call Gideon in the morning and see if he's heard anything."

Veronica reached down to her bag, pulled up her bottle of whisky, refilled her tumbler, and returned the bottle. "It's alright," she said to Montbretia. "We have an understanding in this restaurant. As long as I don't let other patrons see, then I'm not creating a precedent." She turned to Boniface. "While we're talking about alcohol, what about your fellow rehab inmates, Boniface?"

He chuckled softly. "Yeah, there are some pretty obsessive-compulsive, angry guys there. None that could get their life together sufficiently to organize this. But more to the point, they all loved me there."

"If it's not your past, then it's your present and it must be an angry client." Veronica took another sip of whisky. "Who is your current client?" She dipped her head, looking up at Boniface, and spoke in clipped tones. "By the way, I was a good girl. I didn't put matchsticks under Montbretia's fingers to make her reveal."

"It wouldn't have done any good," said Montbretia, her voice very matter-of-fact. "He doesn't tell me what he's up to unless he wants me to get involved." She flicked her head to face Boniface, her eyes sharp, her tone surprisingly bright. "What about the rapist?"

"What sort of clients are you taking on, Boniface?" asked Veronica, staring at Boniface. "Is money really that tight?"

"I didn't take on a rapist." He broke eye contact with Veronica. "I spoke to a rapist's father."

"And he was big and incredibly scary." Montbretia indicated height, width, and depth and started pushing and pulling her face into grotesque shapes.

"Yeah. He scared me, too, and nearly broke my hand when he shook it. Anyway, he threw down his business card, and I was too busy looking at his description of services—metal recovery and recycling, ferrous and non-ferrous including brass, lead and copper, domestic and industrial, nuclear decommissioning..."

"Stop."

"Seriously, nuclear decommissioning." He paused. "Then I read the name and twigged."

"So who was he?"

"Tommy Newby."

Veronica's voice took on an urgency. "Tommy Newby? Tommy Newby, father of Angelo Newby, who beat that poor girl to a pulp?"

"Yes, that Tommy Newby. That Angelo Newby who was found not guilty." Boniface fell back in his seat, his voice timid as he continued. "There was a delay in the trial, so Tommy got his driver to bring him down to see me. He thought it was time for a bit of PR input."

"What did you say?"

"There wasn't much I could say. Angelo had already been crucified in the press; anything I would have put forward would have made things worse. Added to which, I was busy and I don't take clients who pay in used fifty-quid notes."

"So you turned him away."

"I told him that my services wouldn't help. I suggested he hire a lawyer to start suing anyone in the press who might defame his mild-as-a-lamb son and to make a conspicuous donation to a women's refuge to show how seriously the family regarded the issue. You know the line, violence toward women is terrible, but our Angelo is a little angel who loves his mother—just look at his tattoos. In between the picture of the devil and the stripper who gyrates when he flexes, there's her name."

"So you turned him down."

Boniface grimaced. "I thought I gave him a more positive course of action, and I didn't charge him."

"This isn't about you, Boniface. This is about Tommy, the hand-crushing father of a violent rapist." Veronica fixed him with a stare as she continued. "Did Tommy Newby think that you refused to help his son at the very moment when he thought you were the one person who could help? I'm not asking whether you did the right thing, or even whether you made the right decision for yourself. I'm asking whether Tommy thinks you refused to help him."

Boniface deflated. "I don't think so, but I couldn't read the guy. He's used to getting his own way. He doesn't often hear the word no, or at least when he does, it is conventionally followed by the sound of breaking glass and breaking bones."

"You don't think it's Tommy?"

"I doubt it's Tommy. Look what happened next."

"You mean the witness didn't turn up and hasn't been seen since? Or you mean the case had to be dropped because of the lack of said key witness, and then Angelo went to Saint-Tropez, where he is currently in jail, having been accused of raping and murdering a hotel chambermaid?" She sighed and continued, her volume soft but the tone sarcastic. "Remind me again, how did that all work out for Tommy and Angelo?"

"What I mean is that Tommy took my advice to make a charitable donation." He watched Veronica's reaction: Without a doubt, she was disgusted by the notion of the man. "Tommy's a leg-breaker. Leaving a body would be far too much of an ambiguous communication."

Boniface scrutinized Montbretia and his former wife, who was refreshing her tumbler again. Montbretia broke the silence. "Is that it?"

Boniface squirmed. "No. I'll speak to Tommy."

eleven

Montbretia led into the entrance hall and waited for the reassuring click as Boniface closed the front door behind them. "Isn't it a bit weird?" She turned, trying to keep him in position without taking an aggressive stance.

"What? Having a new person in the office who's been sleeping on the job? Sleeping in your office." Montbretia's feet remained stationary, her head swiveling as Boniface walked past her into the lounge. He checked his phone that he had put on to charge before they left for Wimbledon Common, then reached for a CD. "Music I think."

He hit the play button, unleashing guitar power chords over the speakers.

"That joke wasn't even funny the first time. And don't you know that people don't use CDs anymore, grandpa?"

"People may not, but CDs still sound better than MP3s." He twisted his face. "I would have preferred vinyl, but a good dose of Dutch prog rock on CD keeps me happy."

"Really?" Montbretia could feel incredulity mixed with frustration in her voice. "You really want to go through the pain of listening to a whole album of this stuff?"

Boniface sighed. "No. Not really. This lot only did two tracks that are worth listening to."

"You mean this and that piece of yodeling shit?" Boniface had a wide and sometimes eclectic selection of music. Most dated from the 1970s. Most was tolerable if you were in the mood, but trying to use music as a joke was annoying Montbretia.

"Yes, this track, and the name of the other piece is 'Hocus Pocus,' I think you'll find."

"So, the yodeler's delight and 'Sylvia,' and that is it?" She glanced as Boniface gave a single curt nod, like a defiant child. "Well, 'Sylvia' isn't funny."

"No, but it is a great track. Listen to the melody: so much joy, hope, expectation, elation, but underneath it's tinged with melancholy. There's heartbreak and sadness. It's a whole story in one melodic phrase. Without using words, you understand exactly what the guy's telling you." He let the track continue, listening. "The world is always different after listening to this track."

"And its title is my middle name." She regarded the crumpled mound of cushions on the sofa where she had sat, deep in contemplation, in the fetal position—her knees under her chin and her arms tightly wrapped around her legs, with a cup of coffee that she let go cold as she waited for Boniface to return.

But he hadn't returned when she expected him to, and it had been dark when Veronica had arrived and rang the doorbell, rousing Montbretia from her numbed inaction.

She dropped into the spot where she had sat earlier. "Great. I've got the joke. Can we go back to no music and you promise never to play 'Sylvia' again? Or at least can we turn down the volume so we can talk like civilized human beings? If you don't want to answer the question, you can say so."

"What question?" said Boniface.

Montbretia tilted her head—the social-worker look, as Boniface called it. "I'm not trying to pry or be judgmental, but you and the ex—don't get me wrong, I like her—but isn't it a bit, well, weird?"

Boniface flopped onto the sofa where Veronica had sat earlier in the evening. "What? You mean it's weird that my former wife and I are not scratching each other's eyes out?"

"Sort of." Montbretia wished she had planned this conversation before asking the question. "But isn't it a bit weird that she arrived without prompting. You could have had a chick here—that would've been embarrassing."

"She rang the bell, though, didn't she?"

"How do you know that?"

"Because although she's got a key and could have let herself in, by ringing she makes sure that there are no embarrassing incidents."

"She's got a key?"

"So have you."

"But we weren't married."

Boniface's tone was dismissive. "Is that important? Am I required to cease to trust everyone from whom I'm divorced?"

"Don't be like that—that's not what I'm trying to say," said Montbretia. She continued, hesitant. "Shouldn't you be...over? Finished? No longer involved? It's not as if you've got kids."

Boniface paused, looking as if he was weighing what he wanted to say and how he intended to present his perspective.

"Our divorce was different." He sat forward. "We didn't split because we hated each other, and we never fell out." He stopped talking, his hands still moving as if giving directions in a conversation he was having with himself.

"There was a time when it was bad. Very bad. We shouted. A lot. Before that there was a time when we drifted, like two separate ships on a desperately foggy night, each seeing the other on the radar, but not getting close enough to see or touch. Something like that or some other cliché. But ultimately, we can't be married to each other."

Montbretia frowned. "Explain."

"The split was the final step before I went over the edge, not the cause. When I sorted myself out and had stopped drinking, things changed. Veronica can handle her drink, but I can't, and I can't remain in control when alcohol is around. That's why there's no alcohol here and she brings her own bottle and takes it away."

"But you wouldn't drink it if she left her bottle here."

"Probably not. But she understands the risk—it's rather like leaving a knife on the floor. Sure, the baby probably won't stab itself, but if it did, how would you feel?" Boniface fixed Montbretia with a stare, breaking as he continued. "So yes, it's kinda strange, but we're both big enough to work it out, and we both still care for each other, which is why she came around here."

Montbretia nodded tentatively.

"Does that make some sort of sense?"

Montbretia nodded more firmly. "I didn't want to intrude, it's just...well, you know..."

"Weird."

Montbretia snorted. "Weird. But okay weird, I guess." She put her hand through her collar and pulled at the blue lanyard with a silver memory stick.

"Before you show the CCTV footage, there's something I want you to do tomorrow." She let herself sink back into the sofa, flicking her eyes from left to right.

"Sounds like I'm on a mission tomorrow. Do I get a disguise? Do I get a codename?"

Boniface narrowed his eyes. "No. All you have to do is do what you do well: talk to people and put them at ease."

"Sure. Who?"

"Whoever is taking our office apart."

"But you saw, Boniface: There's a police guard. How am I meant to find anything?"

"Clearly you were never a smoker."

"Neither were you."

"True. But I know many smokers—or at least, I did before they died or got nagged to stop smoking by their worried spouses—and one thing all smokers do is go outside for a cigarette during their break. All you have to do is stand outside our office and wait for someone in a bunny suit to come down and find out what they know."

"I'm not a detective, Boniface. What am I meant to ask them?" She felt an emotion that was somewhere between annoyance, confusion, and incredulity.

"Every employee feels overworked, underpaid, and that their boss doesn't appreciate them." He let out a small sigh. "It's a law...it's written down somewhere, and if you're a science geek scrabbling through crime scenes, you must feel very aggrieved. You're likely to be about a thousand times more intelligent and better qualified than the administrative people who run your lab, and your pay is decided by politicians you will never meet."

That seemed logical. Boniface didn't need to continue, but he did. "Find someone and say something that makes them know that you feel their pain, and you'll be in. Then follow up with some direct questions about the body—who is he, where did he come from? If we can't find who dumped the body, let's see if we can find out who the dead person is and work back from there."

twelve

Montbretia checked her phone. Seven AM. Two hours gone, one hour left.

It was lighter than when she arrived—it was now between dawn and sunrise—but she still couldn't feel any change in temperature. It wasn't so much that it was cold—in fact, it was a near-perfect temperature if she had been cycling—but it wasn't warm, and that mattered because she had been in the same place since she arrived. The farthest she had moved had been from one side of the lot to the other—that wasn't going to be more than fifty feet.

She stared at the burned-out van. It looked very much like a burned-out version of the van she had seen on the CCTV. The van that had entered their office parking lot at about 5:30 yesterday morning—it was the first thing to enter the parking lot after her and Boniface had left at around 10:30 the previous evening. Montbretia knew—she had checked all the CCTV that was available from the businesses up and down Wimbledon Hill Road.

Ten minutes after arriving, the van was gone.

It seemed a pretty standard panel van. A Mercedes Sprinter, white. A brief internet search yesterday had suggested the van was used by any number of delivery firms, construction firms, and wannabe rock bands on the road. The number of vans on the road and the uses the van was put to seemed endless. It seemed to be the van that was used by everyone for everything and anything. In short, it was ubiquitous and anonymous.

There was nothing else on the CCTV apart from a few pigeons, until 6:58 when Boniface hurried past on his way to the office. At about 7:15, two police cars had rounded the corner, and two minutes after that, the man with the beard had passed.

Except he didn't have a beard. But he did have a tattoo that was exposed as his sleeve dropped when he slapped the fake beard back into place, and the top half of his ring finger on his right hand was missing.

After they had watched the CCTV, Boniface's mood had hardened. He had never been happy about Montbretia coming up to the Common, but after seeing the CCTV footage last night he had become quite insistent: no risks, no danger, nothing stupid.

She had agreed: no risks, no danger, nothing stupid. However, Boniface hadn't clarified what constituted a risk or danger, and stupidity was only relevant if you were caught, so she was happy to agree to his terms. Or rather, she couldn't see the point in arguing with him when she would do what she wanted in any event.

Boniface would be busy today. He had two leads to follow and a client—a client whose identity Montbretia still didn't know—to resign from. While he was running around in the center of London, she agreed to see if she could find someone in a bunny suit, and since he was focused elsewhere, he wouldn't notice that she was first doing what he thought she had agreed not to.

During the first two hours of doing what Boniface thought she wasn't doing, Montbretia had spoken to six people and gleaned no useful information. She slipped out her phone to flick through the stills from the CCTV again. She stared, hoping for a new insight.

She zoomed in: a white van; it looked the same as the one in front of her, except that the one here was burned out. She had seen it in the dark, seen it at the time it was dumped and set alight, and she could see it now. Whatever might have been in the van was burned, and she was no closer to knowing who the driver was.

A few more flicks and she got to the pictures of the man with the false beard, the tattoo, and a partially missing finger. However hard she stared, there was no more detail—what was she meant to do? Show it to people and ask, "Have you seen this smudge?"

She walked back to her bike and rested on the crossbar, waiting. It was still chilly, misty, and being surrounded by woods on two-and-a-half sides made her feel halfway to being in the middle of nowhere. Another time check. Still not time to go.

Along the approach road, two headlights were bumping on the rough track cutting through the golf course. Eventually the car pulled up, a German station wagon, but Montbretia was dubious about the make.

A small man wearing a worn blue waxed jacket and a crumpled flat-cap got out. Montbretia was talking before he noticed her. "Hello there. I'm so sorry to bother you. Were you here yesterday morning?"

The driver appeared startled, then froze. The only visible sign of life was his still-moving eyes, looking Montbretia up and down, scanning nervously around as if he was expecting an elaborate practical joke. Finally he spoke. "Yes."

"At this time?" Montbretia tried to keep her galloping enthusiasm out of her voice.

"No." His face had a look of awe, as if he was about to relay a tale of biblical proportions and unimaginable, incomprehensible tragedy. "I had a flat tire. It took an hour for the guy to arrive to fix it." Montbretia felt the appropriate response was a series of facial expressions to convey the acknowledgement he apparently craved. "By the time the tire was changed, the dog was too upset and she had crapped on the carpet, so I had to clean that up."

"Gracious." In her few months staying with Boniface, Montbretia had learned that the word "gracious" seemed to be used by the Brits to imply some shared under-standing of suffering without needing to calibrate how much understanding. She waited a beat before continuing. "Was the van here when you arrived?"

"The van and the firemen who were blocking up the place. I turned round and parked over by the pub." He threw his hand loosely in the direction of the road he had driven along.

"So you didn't see what happened here?"

"No." His head twisted and his eyes narrowed. "Is that an American accent I can detect?" Montbretia felt a resigned smile cross her face. "Where are you from?"

"Virginia. Richmond, Virginia."

"Ha! You've come all this way to be near to another Richmond. Have you been to our Richmond?"

"I have," nodded Montbretia, raising her eyebrows to point at the old Labrador standing patiently in the back of the car. "It looks like your dog wants to get walking, so I'd better not delay you any further. Thanks for your help." She spun away—she was bored, but not sufficiently bored to waste the next five minutes of her life com-paring two places that just happened to have the same name.

thirteen

His phone rang.

He ignored it.

After the sixth ring, it stopped.

He stretched and felt his right leg kick out the sheets and fall over the frontier of the bed. Strange. Sheets tucked in. He stretched his left leg: There were no sheets to hold it as it fell over the opposite extremity of his berth.

Still tucked-in sheets, and he could reach both sides of the bed without going full starfish. Something was wrong.

Then he remembered: It had been a good night last night. A very good night. But however much fun you might be having, if your companion's husband's company owns an executive jet and he's the CEO, you can never be sure what time he'll get back. So while you can rationalize to yourself that it was acceptable to entertain his wife—and she was a game girl who liked her entertainment in so many and such varied ways, all so pleasing to him—and that it was quite acceptable to choose one or two of the best bottles from the CEO's hand-picked wine-cellar (read, wall full of climate-controlled cabinets in the basement), it simply wasn't appropriate to still be there if said CEO arrived home before he was expected. So when the mutually beneficial activities came to a close, he was packed off in a cab and had spent the night in his club.

Hence the bed that had been made before he got into it.

Hence the single bed.

He yanked the sheets over his head and tried to get back to sleep again.

His phone rang again. His phone, not the phone in the room. He ignored it again, pulling the sheets tighter over his head, trying to stop the noise and keep out the traces of daylight that had made their way around the curtains.

The noise stopped, then started again.

"What?" Clearly the only way to get rid of telemarketers trying their luck this early was to shout. His face relaxed into a smile. "Boniface, my dear fellow. Where are you?" He glanced around but couldn't see a clock. "Here? Now? Where? Reception? Never heard of me? Definitely not staying? Pass me over to Brenda. It's bound to be Brenda; she always looks after me." He heard some mumbling and the sound of the phone being bumped as it was handed over. "Brenda, darling, I most humbly apologize. I should have told you to wear your best silk knickers. *That* is the famous Mister Boniface standing before you. He's quite harmless—you can send him straight up." He rolled onto his side. "By the way, and exclusively as a matter for the record, Boniface is rather Church of England in his tastes, so I'm pretty sure he'd be grateful even if you're wearing your comfortable old cotton knickers."

He dropped his phone, turned over, and tried to get back to sleep.

There was a knock on the door. Firm contact between wood and knuckles. Gideon pulled the sheets tighter. Another knock—this one more vigorous. Gideon threw the sheets back, leaving his trailing foot still on the bed as he took the half step to the door, which he opened without checking the peephole first, and stood, naked, to greet his guest.

"Boniface!" He watched as Boniface took in his state, then flicked his hips, his nakedness allowing skin to slap against skin at the top of his thigh. "You're lucky I don't have a boner; otherwise I would be pointing you in the wrong direction. Come in. Sit down." He pointed to the lone seat in the room, next to the bathroom door, then closed the door to his small room and walked past Boniface into the bathroom without closing the door behind him.

"First stream in the morning. Isn't that best to check whether I'm pregnant?" Gideon stood, leaning forward, arms outstretched, hands at roughly head height resting against the wall, aiming straight for the center of the bowl in front of him. "Sounds like a mountain stream in full flow, doesn't it, Boniface?"

Gideon shook, tore off a few sheets of paper, wiped, dropped the paper, and flushed before he moved to the sink. As he dried his hands, he caught sight of himself in the mirror and looked down at his wrists. "She was considerably more enthusiastic than I expected."

Boniface grunted from his seat outside the bathroom.

Gideon continued to examine his wrists. They may have been silk scarves, but he wouldn't be rolling up his sleeves today. At least not in public. "Have you got a comb there, Boniface?"

"Sure."

"It's this chocolate, stuck in my...well, look..." Gideon walked out of the bathroom, head down, both hands pulling apart pubic hair like he was the first explorer in a newly discovered jungle.

"Gideon, please." Gideon could hear Boniface's distaste as he replaced his comb in his pocket, looking away. The host remained standing at the extreme of Boniface's line of sight and continued to explore, his hands at the height of his former press-man's head.

"She was a game girl."

Boniface sighed expressively. "Is there some new law that I'm not aware of which obliges me to listen as you tell me about last night's exploits?"

"I'm sure there is, Boniface." Gideon slapped him daintily around the cheek, his feet unmoving as he placed his hands on his hips. "You know how much you enjoy hearing about my fun and games."

Gideon paused and watched Boniface as his head turned cautiously. "It's too early in the morning to have your cock pointing at me."

Gideon hoped there was a glint in his eye. "You're in a dilemma, aren't you, Mister B? You are desperate to ask me to put some clothes on—and you probably want to make some disparaging comment about my awful behavior—but you recognize that means you first have to acknowledge your discomfort at my nakedness..."

"You're in your own room," muttered Boniface without conviction.

Gideon continued, "You also know that asking me is likely to provoke me to take a step closer to you. And you're weighing up whether I'm staying naked to provoke you or if I'm lacking clothes because that's the state you found me in."

Boniface remained still with his head turned away.

"Really, Boniface, for such an old lush, you always were far too buttoned-down... or was it buttoned-up? I never got to figure what your kink was, and I always thought it would be bad form to ask the delightful Veronica to illuminate. How is dear V, by the way? Still the ex? Still haven't found a way to be sober and married?"

"Still haven't." Boniface looked Gideon in the eye, his voice slightly strained. "Try some clothes, please."

"There's no pleasing you, is there, Boniface? Anyway, I haven't told you my tale of last night." Gideon stepped into the bathroom, grabbed a toweling robe hanging behind the door, and returned to the bedroom where Boniface was sitting. "You're not playing this game very well."

"I didn't realize..."

"Shhh." Gideon finished tying the belt around the white robe as he walked along the narrow passage around the bed. "My story." He sat on the bed and faced Boniface. "You remember that Swiss guy with the aluminum company?"

"Moritz Leisy." Gideon nodded as Boniface continued. "You introduced us. I pitched for business. He decided he didn't like me...which wasn't so bad because I found him to be a truly tedious individual."

Gideon tightened his mouth and furrowed his brow as if contemplating Boniface's assessment of the man whose wife he had spent most of the night with.

"You boffed his wife." Boniface dropped his head into his hand and massaged his temples.

"Boffed. Really, Boniface. You're so animalistic. For you intimacy is about ejaculation. One spurt and it's the end of the story as far as you're concerned. But yes, Allegra and I enjoyed each other's company, and to be honest, I don't even remember whether there was coitus. There may have been, there may not have been. But what I can tell you is there was much nakedness, a huge amount of fun over a long period of time, and the dear lady was very satisfied by the time I was packed off."

Boniface glanced up, then dropped his head back into his hand.

"She was very enthusiastic—much more enthusiastic than I had expected. Marks for enthusiasm. Bonus credits for willingness to participate. Gold stars for being open about what she wanted to try. But she lacked finesse. Look at my wrists."

Boniface raised his head as Gideon pulled back his sleeves to show the friction burns around his wrists. "There's something sticky in my hair, and of course the chocolate stuck..."

"I get it. There was food, including melted chocolate."

"That's my point. You're not meant to put melted chocolate on your partner's cock...or near anywhere else where hair grows. Jam, cream, whatever, but nothing that is liable to set. Nothing that won't come out in a quick shower." He pulled down the shoulder of his robe. "I was already nursing a war wound: I don't require any more problems."

"Ouch. What happened there?"

"Hot wax that went a bit too far on the night before."

"Allegra again?"

"No, that was a far more adventurous young lady who really enjoys pain."

"Jesus, Gideon. You're going to break the internet if you create any more perversions. You do know that at the banquet of human sexuality and experimentation, you don't have to try every dish."

"Relax, Boniface. I haven't tried all the dishes." He paused, hoping for dramatic effect. "But I do have a to-do list."

"Is Allegra on that to-do list again tonight?"

"Oh no, no, no, no, no. You would never go to the same restaurant for two nights running. You would never go to the ballet two nights running. Especially not when you live in London and can go to the theater or the opera the next night. So why would I limit my activities on consecutive nights to one person? Besides, my allure is the new, the daring, the outrageous." He sighed mournfully. "The forbidden fruit ceases to be forbidden if you can get it on demand."

Gideon leaned forward before continuing. "I also get the impression that the husband is a bit like you. She's got to be lying at a right angle before he can begin. There are rules to be followed. Minimum standards to be met. If that's the case, then a bit of tedium will make her even more keen."

"You know how they warn teenagers about risky sexual activity?" Gideon could hear the disappointment in Boniface's voice. "Every time we talk, I feel like I'm becoming your disapproving mother telling you that your been-there-seen-that-done-her list will present, shall we say, issues for you at some point."

Gideon pushed out his bottom lip and waited for Boniface to notice. "You didn't wake me up with the sole purpose of telling me off." He brightened. "Come on. Why are you here, Boniface?"

"I'm here because I need to talk, but I can't talk when you keep flopping out. Get the chocolate off your gonads, and I'll be back in an hour."

fourteen

A few more people came through in the last hour Montbretia spent in the parking lot watching the burned-out Mercedes van. By the time she left, she had spoken to fifteen people.

No one had seen anything apart from a burned-out van and what the Brits liked to call the fire brigade. One person had seen the fire burning—or at least the end of the fire; that person had made the call to the emergency services—but they hadn't seen anyone around.

Before she went looking for people in bunny suits she needed to go home. The route out and the route back gave her two opportunities to check the paths that the van driver may have followed.

It was a long shot, and the track she followed from the parking lot gave her no clues—she would try the alternate on her way back. When she got to the main road, she crossed at the horse crossing before heading into Richmond Park. As she liked to point out to her friends who visited from New York, this was a proper park: three times the size of Central Park. For that matter, even Wimbledon Common was bigger than Central Park. She felt herself bristle at her friends' assumptions; then she realized how much she was going native, siding with the Colonists. She put the thoughts out of her head and made for the main path bisecting the park.

In just over three miles, she exited at Ham Gate, followed the road around the perimeter of Ham Common, past the church, and was home.

While it was home, it still didn't feel like home. Her house had become hers when her sister was accidentally killed five months earlier, and technically it still wasn't Montbretia's house and wouldn't legally be hers until the formalities of probate had been completed, which, according to the lawyers, would take another nine months or so. Until then, it was still owned by her sister's estate, of which Montbretia was the sole executor.

The house was still decorated to Ellen's taste, furnished with Ellen's furniture, the kitchen filled with Ellen's kitchenware and cookbooks, and the closets filled with Ellen's clothes. It was a comfort having Ellen still around, but it also made it harder to accept that she had gone, and would make it harder to ever move on from here.

It was also the site where Ellen's friend, and Boniface's client, Nigel Trudgett, had been murdered. Apparently there had blood spattered across the front of the house after he had been shot. Montbretia hadn't seen it, but according to Boniface, Hilda Longthorne, her next-door neighbor, had cleaned the whole area the minute the police had told her she could.

Montbretia walked up the path between the two homes with entrance doors on the side of each house facing the other, and leaned her bicycle against the wall. She opened the door and picked up the mail on the mat, flicking through the pile before she threw it on the side next to the answering machine with its red flashing light.

She hit the play button. "Hi Monty, it's Nathan…"

"He sent you flowers last month."

Montbretia hadn't heard Hilda behind her. She turned to see her next-door neighbor standing outside the open door. "Hello, darling." Montbretia jumped down and embraced the older woman. "How are you?" She stood back, beaming at her neighbor, who was straightening her faded green cardigan, pulling it tight over her brown floral dress.

Hilda's voice was stern, rising above the burbling message from Nathan, which was still playing. "You need to ensure that you are clear with these young men. They must understand that while I'm very grateful to receive their flowers, and I do love the flowers—but you should take them because they were sent for you—my acceptance doesn't mean that I have agreed to have sex with them."

Montbretia let out a short, surprised burst of laughter at her septuagenarian neighbor's comment, as she looked at the wrinkled skin and colorless gray hair, which disguised a youthful vigor and biting sense of humor. Nathan's voice droned on in the background. Montbretia wasn't quite sure what he was talking about, but she understood enough to realize that if he hadn't understood the word goodbye, then she had insufficient time to call him back. Ever.

Hilda returned Montbretia's smile. "I've had some more flowers."

"From Nathan?"

"No." She held the edge of a card with the local florist's logo. "One bunch was from Russell." She handed the card to Montbretia. "The second bunch was from Oliver."

"No card?" said Montbretia lightly.

"No card," affirmed Hilda. "No card because Oliver hand-picked the flowers and then delivered them in person. I promised I would pass them to you the moment you got in."

"Such a wuss," said Montbretia under her breath.

"It's sweet," said Hilda.

"No. It's annoying. I told him if he ever picked me flowers, wrote poetry, cooked me anything more than a boiled egg, or did anything else designed to show me his emotional side that I would puke. On him."

"Doesn't the car suggest some manliness?" asked Hilda. "When I was young enough to care about those things, I would have said yes to any man who drove a TR6"

"It's a lovely car," said Montbretia. "But it's forty years old, and he's such a simpering girl about it. The primary purpose of a car is to get from A to B, in the warm and in the dry. You can do that in a TR6 if it's a warm and dry day. If it's not, then you get cold and wet in that car. The car belongs in a museum, not on the streets of London."

"The flowers are lovely. Won't you take them?" Hilda's face almost begged. "Please?"

Montbretia sighed, trying not to be annoyed. "I like flowers, but I kill flowers and I'm never here, so I would rather they went to a good home. Your home. It's a favor to me and a small thanks for being such a super neighbor."

"I think these are meant to be special," said Hilda in an almost apologetic voice, a slight reddening coming to her creased cheeks.

"He didn't, did he?" Montbretia could hear the annoyance in her own voice.

Hilda's face softened as she gracefully conceded.

"You're telling me that Oliver hand-picked a spray of montbretias," said Montbretia. "I told you he was sickening. Now do you see my point?"

"I do," said Hilda.

"What did Russell send?" asked Montbretia.

"Stargazer lilies."

"Now that would have been a good choice," said Montbretia, "if I actually cared about Russell." The answering machine beeped behind her. "But like Nathan and now Oliver, he too is history. I've got other more important things to do."

Hilda had an inquisitive look on her face, but Montbretia knew she would never let her curiosity intrude, and at the moment she didn't have time to explain.

"I need to pick up one of Ellen's suits and get back to the office." She stepped inside, turning to face Hilda. "If any more flowers arrive, please give them a good home."

fifteen

Boniface walked down the creaky and uneven stairs, wary not to catch his foot on the thinning carpet, before he passed through the reception area. Dark wood and old marble—wipe-clean surfaces seemed somehow appropriate for Gideon.

Gideon who, while remaining a Member of Parliament, was now taking full advantage of the end of his Cabinet responsibilities by leading a campaign fired by his passion. On first blush it might seem strange for Gideon to be the leading campaigner for victims of sex crime, but when anyone heard him talk on the issue, there was no doubt of his commitment. For Gideon, a sexual omnivore with a biological need for frequent and varied stimulation and many experiences with many partners, sex crimes were an abomination.

Gideon's campaign embraced all such forms of sex-related crime. He wasn't only a supporter of the more obvious victims that the press could relate to—primarily women who suffered abuses on a spectrum from verbal intimidation, through groping, all the way up to rape and murder—he was concerned with male rape, with a focus on the victimization of rent boys, the exploitation of children in all the forms it took, people trafficking for sexual exploitation, and the least trendy area of all: the sexual exploitation and sexual rights of the vulnerable and mentally challenged, in particular, their rights around pregnancy.

To Gideon, in all its forms, however Clinton-eque one wanted to be in the definition, sex had to be a consensual shared act, and having shared a consensual act last night, he had then slept at his club, which Boniface was now leaving, and from where Boniface usually would have been quite happy to take the first cab.

But not this morning.

The first cab had what he didn't want: one of the younger cabbies with a bluetooth headset stuck in his ear who spent all day on the phone and never remembered to switch off the intercom, forcing his passenger to endure half a conversation around the details of the boy his fourteen-year-old stepdaughter had slept with and how if gun laws in the UK were like gun laws in the States, he would have put her honor beyond doubt.

In the third cab he stopped, he found what he wanted: short, fat, old, gray cardigan, flat-cap. Old school. Someone who would not only know all of the back doubles but would have the temperament and the patience to go up every back street, happy in the knowledge that he was racking up his fare.

The downside was that rather than listening to tales about potential bastard children, Boniface had to hear about the cabbie's wife's "women's problems, you know" in graphic detail. He was grateful when Tommy's vintage Bentley came into sight.

"Is that a Blower?" the cabbie asked as Boniface stepped out of the cab.

"Definitely a Bentley. Definitely authentic, but beyond that, I'm never sure what differentiates a Blower from a conventional Bentley." Boniface pulled out his wallet and pulled out two notes, which he handed to the driver.

"Thanks, gov." The cabbie continued to stare longingly at the Bentley. "Didn't know there was a difference; thought all vintage Bentleys were called Blowers."

"I know even less," said Boniface, "but if I find the owner, I'll ask him and let you know when I next get in your cab."

Recognizing the unlikelihood, the cabbie winked and started to pull away. "Cheers, gov. You have a good day." The diesel engine throbbed up the street as Boniface started walking past the Bentley, taking his time to admire the immaculately restored vintage machinery. He tilted his head in acknowledgement to the driver, who had been polishing the front headlight with a handkerchief—nursemaid and guardian of the antique while it was on the public highway.

As Boniface passed the front wing, the driver dropped his visual lock on Boniface, apparently now searching out the next potential threat to his responsibility. As the driver dropped his stare, Boniface became aware of his own apprehension: pounding heart, tightening in the stomach, and a loosening in the bowels. He stepped through the café door and stopped, scanning the rows of Formica-topped tables bolted to the floor, interleaved with bench seats covered in dark red leatherette as immobile as the tables, filled with people engrossed in eating.

He was grateful for the cabbie's wife's problems. If she had been a normal, healthy woman, Boniface's mind might have wandered, and it would have wandered to think about Tommy. But thanks to a middle-aged woman with a middle-aged problem married to a middle-aged man who liked to moan at great length, there hadn't been any space left in Boniface's mind.

Then Boniface saw him. He knew he had seen him because he could hear his breathing: fast and deep. He held his breath for a moment, then breathed out slowly and in slowly.

Boniface watched as Tommy lifted his paw up to his mouth. It was probably quite a large sandwich that he was eating, but in his hand it looked like a delicate cucumber sandwich with its crusts removed that a well-to-do Edwardian lady might consume at tea. As the food went into his mouth, Tommy saw Boniface. The big man's brow furrowed.

He replaced the sandwich and stood, wiping his hands. As he reached his full height, the only term that came to Boniface's mind was "bear." This was truly a bear of a man—a rather overweight bear wearing a sober charcoal suit, but a bear nonetheless.

He unknitted his brow, and the light of recognition sparked in his eyes. "Mister Boniface, what a coincidence." The bear smiled and offered his hand to Boniface, who felt his right hand get swallowed by the bear's paw. "Please." He pointed to the bench on the opposite side of his table. "Join me."

Boniface slid in, nervously watching Tommy sit down, very aware that he was in a place he hadn't been before, sitting with his back to the door, with a man who may have dumped a carcass in his office just over 24 hours ago. "And it's Boniface, not Mister anything."

Tommy nodded. "Have you had breakfast?" His voice was soft, concerned, reassuring, like a grandfather with his grandson. "Have a bacon sandwich. The best bacon sandwich you'll get in London."

The big man twisted in his seat to face the stainless steel and glass counters at the end of the café. Three men, all southern European in appearance—Turkish, Boniface guessed—with swarthy skin, hairy arms, and very dark hair, apart from the older boss man who had gone gray on his head and arms. All three looked like they could handle themselves in a fight, but at the moment, the younger men were busy cooking over a griddle. "Another bacon sandwich for my friend," said Tommy to the older man. "And could you make him a fresh pot of tea with boiled water, not that warm stuff that comes out of the tank?"

"Coming right up," said the older man, ripping a page off a small notepad and passing it to one of the cooks.

"I remember that girl of yours. Monty, is it? She gave me a pot of tea...said you liked proper tea, properly made."

Boniface acknowledged as the older man came across the red-and-white-checkered floor carrying a bacon sandwich. "That was quick. Thank you."

"For my favorite customer." He winked at Tommy, who managed to communicate his thanks without using words. "He can wait." He cast a lazy glance across the room at a man wearing a misshapen sweater, engrossed in the sports pages of a tabloid.

Boniface took a bite. "Good?" Tommy seemed in need of reassurance.

"Good," said Boniface, replacing the sandwich on its plate and dabbing his lips with the paper napkin that came with his breakfast. He stared straight at Tommy, who met his gaze. "I'm one of those people who prefers to meet face to face. If there's a phone call or any other interaction that doesn't involve two people in a room, I'll avoid it if I can."

"You're sounding like me. I always want to look someone straight in the eyes." Boniface could hear the softening of Tommy's accent, the gentle Derbyshire tones smoothing the edge of his big voice, making him sound almost like a modern BBC television announcer: correct pronunciation but with a regional accent.

"It leaves less of a trail. Electronic communications leave a nasty mess that can be sold to the press." The big man nodded but remained quiet. "Tommy, I've got to know. Did I upset you?" He scrutinized Tommy—small creases fluttering across his weather-worn brow. "If I did, I need to make things right."

"Upset me how, Mister...I mean Boniface?" Tommy's eyebrows lifted, emphasizing that he was asking a question. "You were the only one who treated me with any sort of dignity when Angelo was arrested. You didn't take my money, you understood my son was suspected of the crime—not me—and you weren't intimidated by my reputation. You gave me advice—and it was good advice that you gave me in about three minutes. I respect that, and I respect you."

The two men sat facing each other, the only sounds around them the noises of quiet conversations and people banging their cutlery against their plates as they ate.

"Why the question?" The big man waited, continuing when Boniface was not forthcoming. "I presume today's meeting isn't a coincidence?"

Boniface took another bite of his sandwich before continuing. "It's not a coincidence, Tommy, although it is a pleasure to see you again. I wish it was under better circumstances...for both of us."

The big man leaned in, his voice lower, his tone richer. "I know what my problem is: my boy. But what's your problem and what is it that brings you to me?"

Boniface paused as a teapot, milk jug, and mug were delivered to the table. He thanked the older man and proceeded to pour his tea, waiting until he was out of earshot. "It's a problem, but you should focus on Angelo today."

"Come on, Boniface. You're here, you might as well tell me. A problem shared and all that."

Tommy's voice was hypnotic. Boniface felt himself being drawn while still trying to hold back. "I've got a problem." Tommy nodded as Boniface forced himself to continue. "I can't be certain, but I think someone's trying to send me a message."

"How?" Tommy tilted his head. The concerned grandpa, not the angry bear.

Boniface hesitated. "Let's just say they led the police to my door for a crime I didn't commit."

Tommy nodded, after a while raising his eyebrows. Boniface sat mute, pursing his lips and giving a single, staccato nod in reply to the question raised by Tommy's eyebrows.

"You're not going to tell me what the problem is, but it's the sort of thing you think I might have been capable of if I had been angry?"

Boniface felt his cheeks redden slightly. "It's not that I'm refusing to tell you. It's that it's questionable as to what the problem is, and if there isn't a problem between us that needs to be sorted, then I don't see the necessity of boring you with my issues."

Tommy sat back, but his voice remained low. "Let me lay it on the line for you, Boniface. My boy did a bad thing: I've never said otherwise. When I was in trouble, everyone was happy to help. Everyone. But they didn't look at the help I needed—we needed as a family—all they saw was a guy who didn't have the greatest education, who didn't work in the most glamorous of industries, but who had done reasonably well for himself. And when they saw me, they had only one thought: money."

Tommy took a last bite and finished his sandwich, then washed it down with a slurp from his mug of tea.

"But you didn't take my money, even when I wanted to pay you there and then. Instead, you sat down with me, talked to me like a real human being, and gave me some advice. Good advice, which we followed. It's a shame that Angelo..." His voice became wistful. "Well, here we are fighting so that he doesn't get extradited back here." He voice trailed off as he stared into the distance. "That girl of yours. I shouldn't call her a girl, but you know...Monty?"

"Monty is what she calls herself. Short for Montbretia."

"Montbretia? That's..."

"Yup. A flower." Boniface clocked a look on Tommy's face that he took as bafflement. "Hippie mother," he offered by way of an explanation. "One daughter called Hibiscus, the younger Montbretia."

"I suppose I got away lightly with my wife insisting we call the boy Angelo." His tone was rueful. "Anyway, Montbretia was a true delight, even if she didn't realize."

Boniface tried to keep the astonishment out of his face, but failed as Tommy continued. "I know that with my size and my reputation I can come across as a bit scary, but she looked after me while you were busy."

"I think I was on a call," offered Boniface.

"You might have been; all I remember is talking to her and being impressed. She didn't judge me based on my reputation or based on what Angelo was accused of. She didn't judge Angelo based on the stories that had been in the papers. But she didn't ignore the seriousness of the case. She wanted to hear the facts, and she understood that there were two truths in the room on the night of the incident."

Tommy paused. "For that I am grateful to her. She also made a great cup of tea," he pointed to Boniface's pot, "which is where I learned about how you like your tea." He lifted his head and stared straight at Boniface. "So it's cards-on-the-table time. You know I've got a number of skills and that I was a bit of a boy when I was younger. I behave myself now, but I've got friends I can call on, and I reckon it would always be good to be owed a favor by you. So how do you need me to help?"

sixteen

Montbretia laid the headband and the plastic hairclip on the counter, and pulled her towel tighter, re-tucking the corner under her right arm.

She wasn't sure why, but somehow a hair accessory felt necessary. More proper. Isn't that how people who work in offices dress? A not really practical suit and something ugly and plastic to hold your hair in place. She felt like a twelve-year-old on bring-your-daughter-to-work day, trying to dress like someone else's image of a grownup.

And in her image, you needed something in your hair.

And a suit.

In her case, one of Ellen's pantsuits.

She had been there when Ellen bought the suit. Ellen had clearly felt put-upon by her younger sister and had been unsure in the shop, but when they got home she had been thrilled.

Montbretia went to her bedroom—the spare bedroom in his apartment, as Boniface would likely see it—and blow-dried her hair before putting on the white cotton blouse, hers; and the blue pant suit, Ellen's. She pulled the pants around her waist, breathed in, pulled each side together, fiddled with the button, and released her breath.

This was a level of discomfort she hadn't expected.

Ellen was shorter, with bigger boobs. Not much—a cup size, perhaps—but enough to notice, not that Ellen was aware when guys noticed. But surely bigger boobs equated to a bigger waist. It was a basic law of nature, wasn't it? Indisputably, it was the law of natural justice.

They had lived apart for years, not that they had been the kind of sisters to swap clothes when they lived together. When they had gone shopping together during Montbretia's visits to London, she never understood the English way of sizing—and to be honest, she didn't fully understand it now—but she had always assumed that Ellen had the larger waist.

But apparently not.

And now Montbretia was left with a pair of pants that were too tight, not quite long enough, and which rubbed at the top of her inside left thigh.

The choice was no choice: the ill-fitting pants, her jeans, her sweaty cycling gear, or her mishmash of pink gym clothes that she had yet to move from Boniface's apartment. The pantsuit would let her look like she might work in an office, so she slipped on the jacket and a pair of Ellen's sensible wear-all-day-in-the-office low-heeled pumps—the wrong size, but who cared; she was only going to be wearing them for a short while—before returning to the kitchen and picking up the headband.

She looked in the mirror as she combed back her hair and systematically fitted the headband, the burgundy arranging her chestnut hair in a way that made her look about eight years old. She would have preferred a headband with Minnie Mouse ears, but that probably didn't fit the office-worker look.

It was 10 AM, and she was clean, no longer sweating, refreshed, and dressed in a way that suggested, to her at least, that she might plausibly work in an office. She walked from Boniface's apartment down Wimbledon Hill Road to acquire her last few props.

It felt weird for Montbretia, buying her first pack of cigarettes in her mid-twenties. Somehow she still felt like a kid doing something forbidden, not that much had ever been forbidden when she was growing up. Their mother was what others liked to call a free spirit, which was something of a euphemism for a hands-off parent who felt she had two younger sisters and not two children. But some conditioning kicked in: It would have been less stressful to buy porn.

She paid for the cigarettes and left.

Two minutes later, she returned when she realized she would need a lighter.

Two minutes after that, she wondered whether it would be easier to start a conversation if she didn't have a lighter.

Then she figured she wouldn't be smoking anyway, so it wouldn't matter.

As she waited in the coffee-shop line, wriggling with the poor fit of her blue suit, she toyed with the cigarette packet and pulled off the cellophane. Flipping back the lid, she picked out the paper to expose her props. Would it look better with a less full packet, she wondered.

"You no smoke here." The barista's accent was thick Eastern European. "It's the law. You smoke outside." He pointed to the tables outside the door.

"I..." I what? I don't smoke? I'm holding these for a friend? "I...I'll have an Americano."

seventeen

"I almost don't recognize you with clothes on." His guest faked a look of shock. "Look at you: suit and tie, polished shoes—I expect no less—and you've even coordinated the handkerchief in your top pocket with your tie. A bit 1980s, but I appreciate the effort."

"Boniface." Gideon stood to greet his guest. "I thought the library would be best. The old duffers either aren't awake or are still getting breakfast so we won't be disturbed, and I've got a pot of tea for you. Sit down." Gideon indicated a wing-backed chair, positioned to mirror his own, forming a triangle with the unlit fireplace. He watched his former colleague across the room—uncharacteristically looking somewhat hesitant—then turned to a small side table and poured from a silver teapot.

Gideon placed a cup of tea on a side table next to Boniface. "Whatever your question, dear Boniface, I'm sure we can find the answer in this room." He pointed to the expanse of bookshelves covering an entire wall of the narrow room. The shelves were old and showing signs of wear, especially at ground level, where the frequent scuffing had chewed holes in the uprights. But the shelves were packed with books. Old books, new books, hardbacks, paperbacks, English, foreign language, literature, reference.

No two books were the same size. "Anything you want, but exercise some vigilance if you want any books from that end column."

Boniface frowned.

"Woodworm met wet rot. Some of the books still smell a bit, and it's all rather precariously balanced. If you lift one end, the other is likely to fall apart. They were ready to fix it, but some of the longer-serving chaps were unhappy with the minor addition that would be levied through the annual fee, so it's a rather make-do-and-mend solution at the moment. Very wartime spirit, which puts the old boys in a good frame of mind." Gideon vigilantly lifted over his own cup of tea and sat across from his guest. "What occurrence demands that we talk so urgently?"

"I've got a problem."

"Ointment."

"A serious problem, Gideon." Gideon watched Boniface squirm in his chair, seeming to find it impossible to achieve a comfortable position.

"Lots of ointment." Boniface's mouth tightened. Gideon felt a small pang of guilt, unsure whether he might have misjudged his reaction. "Sorry." His voice was straining to be more than a whisper. "What's the problem?"

"Someone is sending me a message." Boniface paused. "Maybe I'm being dramatic, but it feels like someone's trying to destroy me."

The only movement in the room was the breathing of the two men. Gideon broke the impasse, raising his eyebrows and tilting his head in an inquisitive manner, hoping to encourage Boniface to elaborate.

"I don't know." Boniface's speech was rapid. "It may be nothing. But it might be something, and if it is something, then I wonder why it's not your problem too—and if it's nothing, I don't want to waste your time."

Gideon smiled sympathetically. "For an articulate man, you can lose your powers of communication at quite a pace." Boniface mouthed the word "sorry" as Gideon continued. "You don't wish to elaborate—that's fine, but a few questions."

Boniface's mouth twitched—not quite a fully formed emotion, but enough to imply the affirmative to Gideon.

"Are the police involved?"

A nod.

"You're the suspect?"

Another nod.

"So this is something going after your reputation. Could this put your name into the public domain?"

"That's what seems to be happening." Boniface shifted in his seat. "Whoever has done this is smart: If this leaks, people will always remember me for the story. They won't remember that I was innocent; they'll simply attach my name and the event."

"With a click of their fingers, your reputation is trashed."

"Precisely. I can't be the behind-the-scenes adviser if my attachment to every client will lead to a news story linking that client to me, and me to this case."

"You're here because you think it might be related to some of the stuff you pulled when you ran my press and media at the Department?"

Boniface's voice was rising. "I'm here, Gideon, because I'm in freefall. Messages are usually signed or have cards. This one had neither: The first I knew was when the cops showed up at my office yesterday morning."

Boniface stood and took a few steps away from his chair.

Gideon kept his tone soft. "I get that something bad is happening. I get that you think I can help or might be a target too. But what task do you want me to perform?"

Boniface sighed, keeping his back to Gideon. "If it's not you and me, then it's me. Me alone." He started to pace beside the tables arranged along the central spine of the room. "If that's the case, can you call in some favors? Keep your ear to the ground? See if anyone's heard anything?"

"You recognize that I'm..."

Boniface regarded Gideon from the far end of the room. "I know you're not a minister, because if you were I might have a job with you." There was a ringing echo as Boniface stopped talking. When he continued his voice was calmer. "I know it's hard to call in favors, but is it that much of an embarrassment for a guy who's happy to dance naked around his bedroom while I sit there?"

"Boniface, you know..."

"I know everything you're going to say. It's hard. It relies on personal relations— which in your case is doubly hard because, as a rule, you've shagged the wife of virtually everyone who might be useful. You're not a minister anymore, so you don't have the same influence." He continued his path around the central tables. "But do you think it's easy for me? I've been to see you twice, and it's not even 10 AM."

Gideon kept his tone soft. "Alexander, you're going red in the face." Boniface's head twitched reflexively at the use of his first name. "Come and sit down and quietly tell me how far you've got so I don't waste any effort."

Boniface walked slowly up the room. Apparently lost in thought, his feet dragging along the thin carpet, hand to his face, holding his chin. As he sat, Gideon said, "If we're looking for people who don't like you, then I suppose we've got to begin with Stan Gadson."

Boniface released his locked position slightly, the trace of a pleasure showing. "Dear Stan. My first big scoop." His tone conveyed a tinge of melancholy. "Already ruled out him, and the researcher."

"So who else?"

"No one. There is no one from my time as a journalist that I can think of who would have a hunger for destroying me like this. There are a few of the old-time politicos and their hangers-on who still pull faces at me, but nothing more. Have you got any ideas?"

"You had a certain reputation while you handled the Department's press. To understate how you were described, some might have thought of you as pugnacious."

"Committed?" Boniface's tone was light.

"Committed." Gideon lowered his voice. "But you were a mess and you made mistakes. Not that I'm criticizing as I sit here is this glass house making sure there are no stones lying around."

"I think the end result is sufficient proof of how much of a mess I was. But can we get to the point here?" There was agitation is Boniface's voice. "Sure, I pissed people off, but I didn't have any power. I was handling the press; you were the minister making the decisions. Someone might have wanted to get back at me for being a smart-assed pain, but ultimately any decisions were yours, not mine. So why would they get at me and not you if this is a political problem?"

"That would be my assumption, but that only leaves one option, doesn't it?" Gideon paused for dramatic effect. "It must be beyond question that one of your clients is trying to mess with you, and since you haven't been in business for that long, I must congratulate you on upsetting someone so completely and so rapidly. I know upsetting people was once sport for you, Boniface, but you have exceeded all of your previous records."

"I'm ahead of you on that one. My first thought was Tommy. Tommy Newby."

"Tommy Newby? Tommy Newby, father of Angelo Newby, who beat that poor girl to a pulp after…" Gideon recalled Tommy Newby's name.

"That Tommy Newby. That Angelo Newby, who was found not guilty."

Gideon's voice had an angry edge. "Was found not guilty after a delay in the trial because they couldn't find that afternoon's witness." Gideon felt his eyes drawn to Boniface, trying to suppress the feelings of disappointment. "Was money such an issue, Boniface, that you needed to make these compromises? Is that what's making you so highly strung?"

"Hold on. Let me explain." Gideon took a deep breath before nodding for Boniface to continue. "The afternoon that the witness didn't turn up, Tommy got his driver to bring him down to see me. He thought it was time for a bit of PR input."

"A bit late, but what did you say?" Gideon could hear the incredulity in his own voice.

"There wasn't much I could say. He was already crucified in the press; any active PR campaign would have made things worse. Added to which, I was busy."

"So you turned him away." Gideon grimaced and held his arms in a gorilla position while talking in a deep voice. "I'm Tommy, and I let some southern softie in a suit turn me down."

"I told him that my services wouldn't help. I suggested he hire a lawyer to sue anyone who might defame Angelo, and that he make a conspicuous donation to a rape-crisis charity to show how seriously the family regarded the issue."

"So you turned him down."

"I turned him down, but I thought I was at least pleasant about it, and I thought my advice had been taken when a sizable donation was made to a charity."

"So it's you we have to thank for thirty pieces of silver going in the right direction."

"I didn't think about your work; I suggested a solution for Tommy." He continued, his voice softer. "You know what came next: Angelo went to Saint-Tropez, where he is in jail, having been accused of raping and murdering a chambermaid, and there's an application to extradite him back here to face numerous other charges, most relating to violence toward women." Boniface threw his hands in the air as if surrendering. "I offered some advice, for free, but given the way events turned, I wondered whether Tommy was upset with me, and whether he took it badly because his son is going to spend the rest of his days in prison."

"So when will you be meeting Tommy?"

"I've been. He's in court every day with the extradition hearing. I had breakfast with him while you were scraping chocolate off your cock."

"And?"

"And I'm his new best mate. I was the only one who didn't take his money. If I've got a problem, he can help, and if he can't help, he knows people. As in *people*."

"Do you believe him?"

"That he knows people, yup." Boniface tilted his head from side to side. "That he didn't do it, probably. But I'm not sure I could trust him, and I absolutely don't want to be under any obligation to him."

"So if it wasn't Tommy, then who? Which lowlife client has been causing you problems?"

Gideon could make out the slightest shake of Boniface's head. "Not a clue. Most of my other work has been corporate strategy and general communications. You know, media training, how we want others to see us. Nothing in the least contentious."

"And your present client?"

"It's not them." Boniface shook his head vigorously, relaxing as the subject moved from Tommy. "They're in it, deep. As in deep, deep, deep, deep. The last thing they need is me and the police causing them any grief."

"Who is the client?"

"Big problem, big secret, I'm afraid."

"How long have you been working with them?"

Boniface defocused, as if the answer were written where the far wall met the ceiling. "About nine months."

"That's quite a while; that's long enough to upset someone. Who knows about the work you're doing for this mystery client?"

"Me. The CEO. I was literally telling the first person outside of us two when the cops walked in yesterday."

"Has Montbretia done any work for the client?"

"She's done lots. But she doesn't know who she's been working for."

Gideon frowned. "How is the delightful Miss Armstrong, by the way?"

"She's fine. She sends her regards."

"Regards and nothing more?"

"Nothing more."

"Do you think...?"

Boniface cut him off. "I don't think. I'm not her boyfriend; I'm not her pimp. I have no influence over her choices."

"Oh." Gideon felt the disappointment. "The delightful Miss Armstrong must have seen a bill or some sort of financial transaction for this client."

"Nope. No bills. No paper trail."

"Montbretia must know who she's working for."

"Nope. Not a clue."

"Come on, Boniface, she's not stupid."

"She's anything but stupid. She turned you down—that must say something about her level of common sense and understanding of risk. But that still doesn't mean she knows who she's working for. She thinks we're being paid—and hence her work is funded—by an overseas charitable trust, and indeed, that's true. What she doesn't know is the arrangement our paymaster has."

"I'm intrigued. Explain."

"My client has a charitable trust, which is ostensibly their Hail Mary pass to wave when they are called to account for their sins. Added to which, it looks good in the corporate social responsibility report."

"What? You think no one will make the link from the charitable trust to the associated company?" Gideon scowled, incredulous. "You do know that the charity will lose its tax status when that comes out."

"I do, or at least, I would. That's why we're not being paid by the charitable trust." Gideon sat back as Boniface continued. "Our CEO has a friend who is CEO of a packaging company in Spain. That packaging company also has its own trust and was about to make a donation to an infrastructure project in Chad, to help with the refugees from Sudan's Darfur region."

"So they swapped projects?" Gideon felt the realization showing on his face. "Two strangers on a train."

A slight smirk of self-satisfaction formed at the edge of Boniface's mouth. "Absolute disconnect. Timing and amounts are totally unrelated. Two people—two friends—had lunch in Madrid nine months ago, end of story. No investigative reporter could spin any inference, but we get paid."

"What happens when you turn up at their offices, or are the meetings all secret squirrel?"

"They think I'm the CEO's life coach. And on that happy thought, I will leave you."

"I'll be in touch," said Gideon, rising and shaking hands.

eighteen

Montbretia scanned, hoping not to see Zahir.

When she passed, he didn't seem to be in the office, which would mean he was in one of three places: in the back rooms of the office, out having a smoke, or haranguing a client into considering a property he was forcing them to view.

Feeling guilty about the poor soul who would have to endure Zahir's sales pitch, she hoped it was the third option as she continued to wonder whether to have a full pack or to remove one or two cigarettes as she stood outside the office.

She put her coffee on the sidewalk and took out the cigarette packet. She didn't even know how to hold a cigarette. Holding a short tube isn't that difficult, but how did smokers hold these things? Was it between the thumb and first finger? No, that seemed like pantomime villains who always sucked too hard. She pinched out a cigarette and tried it in the V between her first and second fingers, the tip of the filter a small way above her palm.

She had only met Gideon twice, but with him meeting Boniface today he had taken up residence in her head, and why was this? Both times they met, he had propositioned her. Each time she had declined, politely, and he had accepted her rejection without question, carrying on the conversation as if he had asked whether she would prefer red or white, only to be told that she would prefer a glass of water. As for the stories Boniface had told, they sounded like urban myths, until she met the politician. After that, she suspected Boniface underplayed Gideon's past and his tastes.

"Light?"

Montbretia glanced up, surprised. "I'm sorry?"

"Do you want a light?"

A tall, thin, somewhat unhealthy-looking man was talking to her. It was another moment before she realized he was wearing a white plastic one-piece suit, like a baby's romper suit, zipped up the front and with elastic cuffs and an elastic hood that he slipped back. Boniface's comment made sense now: She had found someone in a bunny suit. She had found her target, a scientist.

She gave her best slightly-shy-so-as-not-to-scare-the-geek smile. "Thank you. But I'm trying to quit."

He frowned, the new information not computing in his scientific brain.

"I come out here, and I follow the ritual for the bit of smoking that I enjoy—the break from the office, the fresh air—but I try not to smoke." She smiled softly. "Day two and I haven't cracked." She gazed up at the scientist. "I might have done it if you hadn't stopped me. Thank you." She bobbed down, bringing back her coffee. "But coffee. Some addictions can't be cured."

"Oh...well...umm...er... You're welcome." He put his lighter away and zipped up his bunny suit. "You're right. We should all smoke less."

"I haven't seen you before, so I'm guessing you're one of the crime-scene guys."

"The bunny suit didn't give it away?"

"You mean this isn't your best suit for work?" She sipped her coffee, watching as the scientist mirrored, sipping from his thin plastic cup of indistinct brown liquid.

"This is business casual," said the scientist. "If it was best, I'd be wearing a tie."

"Of course." Montbretia was mindful to ensure her voice was solemn before she continued. "Dreadful business in there."

"Mmm."

"They say he was murdered. Is that true?" Her voice still solemn, her heart pounding.

"Don't know." Montbretia looked up, hoping he sensed her question. "It takes a few days, longer if there are chemicals—drugs and the like—that require analysis."

Montbretia wondered how good the scientist was with uncomfortable silences and waited, staring expectantly.

The scientist cracked first. "But we do know he was alive two days ago."

Montbretia stepped closer, cocking her head. "How do you know that? Is there some clever scientific technique?"

A vaguely nervous look spread from his lips. "I would like to say there is, and when they took the body away there was no noticeable decomposition that would come with someone being dead for longer, but the truth is far more mundane: He was arrested in Tilbury two days ago. That's why his prints were on file and they were able to identify him."

The pitch of his voice dropped, and he spoke with less haste. "That's why they think it was murder. But as I said, the autopsy won't take place for a few days, and the real difficulty is that we almost certainly don't have the murder scene, so it's hard to tell whether he died and was bludgeoned, or whether he was bludgeoned and that killed him. I mean, common sense says you don't beat a dead body, but they dug up Oliver Cromwell's corpse so they could hang him."

Montbretia calculated: Was there more he could tell her? Probably not. "Where is Tilbury? This place where you said he was arrested?"

"You're not from around here, are you?"

"You found me out, science boy," she said, cracking a broad smile, hoping he had some sort of a sense of humor. For the first time, the nervous look lifted from his face, and she saw a hint of a goofy grin. "As you've guessed, I'm from across the pond. Virginia. Richmond, Virginia."

"Richmond? Like..."

What was it with the Brits? Two places, one name. "Like Richmond up the road, but I haven't been to Richmond in the U.S. for quite a while. I was travelling, and I've been here since..." Her voice trailed off. She caught herself with another memory of Ellen. "So, yeah, I'm a foreigner. Where is this Tilbury place?"

"You've got London." The scientist held his fist in front of him at chest height, turning toward her as if showing her a map. "With the River Thames going through the middle." He drew a horizontal line across his fist with his other hand. "Then you've got the M25, the big motorway that goes round London." Montbretia watched as he drew a circle in the air around his fist. "Where the M25 and the Thames cross in the east..." he started making hand gestures, one crossing the other, "if you go about two or three miles further out down the river, you get to Tilbury. It's part of the Port of London."

"So it's close?" Montbretia tried to keep the excitement out of her voice.

"Physically, yes. But speaking as a scientist in terms of evolution, no, it's not close." Montbretia reached into her pocket and pulled out her phone. "That was a science-boy joke, by the way," he said apologetically. "I've never actually been to Tilbury."

Montbretia gave a quick flash of her teeth to acknowledge the attempt at humor. "You're right, it's close. But it seems to be in the middle of nowhere. It's totally separate from London; all that connects it is a train line."

The scientist leaned, trying to peer at the screen, then snapped upright as Montbretia slipped the phone back into her pocket. "Not smoking makes me want more coffee. I've wasted enough of your time, and I can see you want to get back to work. There's a mystery that needs solving." She held out her hand. "It's been a pleasure."

He shook her hand weakly and started stammering. "Perhaps...coffee...later..."

Montbretia hesitated, then reached for her phone, unlocked it, and handed it to him. "No promises," she said firmly. "Put your number in, and I might call."

He tapped and tutted, then handed the phone back. "I put it under 'science boy' so you'll remember who I am."

"Well, science boy, thank you," said Montbretia, turning to leave, knowing that she would almost certainly never see him again unless she needed something more from him.

nineteen

Leaving Gideon's club for the second time that morning, Boniface followed the side streets through St. James's, heading north, and had soon crossed Piccadilly, diving into the warren of streets that was Mayfair.

He never enjoyed visiting Mayfair.

Each property in Mayfair was, without exception, gorgeous: lots of old town-houses, many examples of perfect architecture crafted in Portland stone several hundreds of years ago. What wasn't to like? In a word, Mayfair itself, and what it had become.

But for Boniface, the problem was more practical: Mayfair was sandwiched between Oxford Street and Piccadilly, with Park Lane and Regent Street stopping the filling from spilling out from each end. Even before you started getting snooty about the Bond Street divide—and Boniface didn't care whether it was east Mayfair or west of Regent Street—the space comprising Mayfair was finite. On the Monopoly board, Mayfair had always been the most expensive location, but when you started cramming prime London real estate, a fixed resource, with hedge-fund managers and corporate headquarters in between some of the choicest residential locations in Western Europe, you made money the condition of admission.

Large piles of money were not enough. This wasn't the place for professional soccer players or rock stars, although Jimi Hendrix did live there almost fifty years ago, when the location was still considered faintly bohemian, but now it was the place where the super-rich—those for whom a billion was a mere rounding error—kept their London houses. This was now the land of the oligarchs. The place to find the people who controlled the world's energy supplies.

With the heritage of the architecture, planning laws had evolved to severely limit any external alterations to any properties, which gave the super-rich only one option: renovate internally, and if they wanted more space—if they needed a gym, sauna, Jacuzzi, or swimming pool—then dig.

Never mind the nightingale singing in Berkeley Square, all Boniface could hear and see as he threaded through the narrow streets of Mayfair were the signs and sounds of construction workers. White vans delivering, trucks being filled by hand with dug-out soil because there wasn't enough space to get proper machinery in, scaffolding and safety hoardings all covered with notices proclaiming how considerate their construction workers were—those acclaimed staff all wearing dirty high-vis jackets and hard hats but seemingly incapable of finding a pair of jeans to cover their ass cracks.

Boniface passed a group of workers chatting on the street, none speaking English, as he began the gentle slope up to the Weissenfeld Shipping global headquarters. It sounded grand. In reality, it was a converted house in Mayfair that was rumored to have once been the home of a famous sailor, but no one was quite sure who he was or which battles he might have won. As far as Boniface was concerned, it was a good-sized house but a comparatively small office.

He walked beside the red-brick wall, stopping to hit the intercom button before looking up at the camera. A buzz confirmed the unlocking of the wrought-iron gate, which clunked shut behind him as he passed over the stone path crossing the small garden—the raised beds, manicured shrubs, and trimmed mature trees a green oasis in the heart of the West End. For some reason, he couldn't stop himself from wondering how Greta Weissenfeld would get on with Gideon Latymer: There was something in the domination of her personality that would make her such a challenge, and such a thrill, for Gideon.

Stepping through the front door, Boniface crossed the black-and-white marble floor and jogged up the stairs, two at a time.

"Mister Boniface. I thought you'd abandoned us when you didn't turn up yesterday."

"I wasn't scheduled, Lennie. The lady wasn't here."

"That's true, but you could have come to see me. My life could do with some coaching." The security guard's manner matched his appearance: sixty-something, 5-foot-9, heavyset, graying and thinning on top, but still military smart. "She's got Mister Regenspurger with her at the moment."

"Oh." Boniface felt the tension is his jaw as he grimaced. "Whose kneecaps is he going to break today?"

The security guard remained impassive, then conspiratorially whispered, "She's got *another* new secretary."

"It's something we're working on," lied Boniface as he started on the next flight of stairs.

"Mister Weissenfeld wants to see you," he said. "Immediately, he told me to tell you."

Boniface stepped back down the stairs. "Mister Weissenfeld? As in Chlodwig."

"Him." Lennie nodded definitively. "When I mentioned you were expected, he said he wanted to see you when you arrived."

"He's here?" Boniface could feel the tension in his voice.

"In the conference room."

Boniface heard himself swearing under his breath. He hesitated, collecting his thoughts. "What does he want?"

"I guess you'll find out when you see him."

"I guess I will. Catch you later, Lennie."

As far as Boniface had seen, every room in Weissenfeld's London office was awkwardly and inconveniently shaped. This was not all that surprising, given that the building had been designed as a family home more than 200 years ago.

Two hundred years ago, all houses in London had fireplaces: it was that or get cold. Fireplaces required chimneys, and chimneys took up lots of space as the pipes from the lower floors traveled through the upper floors, eventually finding freedom through the roof. Every room had a fireplace standing proud on the wall, and every room had chimneys passing through, so no room had four flat walls.

Couple that with the changes since the house was built—walls moved, bathrooms added, back staircases repurposed, plumbing for central heating, gas lighting added, gas lighting removed, electricity—and you ended with a situation where, depending on your attitude, each room was either unique or inconvenient. The conference room was even more inconveniently shaped, with the addition of an overweight German who looked close to tears.

As Boniface came through the door, the German stood, apparently trying to speak but making stammering sounds, which were muted when he moved a shaking hand to cover his mouth.

"We killed those people, Boniface. Us...we... It didn't just happen. We did it."

Now standing, the German remained immobile: an overweight statue covered in a crumpled beige suit with hints of yellow and green, but somehow avoiding brown tones.

"I keep thinking that I should have done something. I could have done something." Boniface felt ashamed to witness the soft, puffy face exaggerated by the swollen red eyes, the neatly trimmed near-white goatee quivering as the German tried to articulate his thoughts. "If I had acted, those people would still be alive. I could have stopped Greta."

Boniface tried not to show any shock on his face. The notion that someone could stop the unstoppable, that a force of nature could be controlled or managed, didn't sound plausible. "It is my fault. I should have stopped Greta, but I behaved like our father."

Boniface remained still, like a birdwatcher observing a rare species, watching as Greta's older brother tried to recover some dignity. He tugged the lapels of his suit jacket, the fabric tightening around his shoulders before he straightened his tie. Boniface made a small turn of his head to encourage the German to continue.

"Whenever Greta would come home, father would always sigh. He disapproved of how she behaved, but he would never tell her because he couldn't stand the argument. If you tell her she's wrong, she will keep arguing until you apologize and tell her that actually it is you that is in the wrong and not her. When she has bullied you into submission, she will then tell you about all your faults and how much you have hurt her by criticizing her, and you must be wrong in criticizing her because you have just admitted you are in the wrong."

He sighed. "Father spent four hours one night after he challenged Greta on one little matter. Somewhere in those four hours, she told him that he clearly loved the rest of us more than he loved her." There were tears again in the big man's eyes. "She was the baby—she was his favorite, and this broke his heart. He never argued with her again."

He inhaled, almost a sob, his physique again crumpling like his jacket as he sat down. "When Greta told father she should become chief executive, he didn't argue, and he accepted it when she removed him from the board two years later. It was his own fault, he said. He let her get like this. He had indulged her, so he must pay the price."

Chlodwig rested his elbows on the table that dominated the room while he held his head. Boniface couldn't figure whether the table was too big or the room too small—either way, the light-colored wood with an open grain pushed the surrounding chairs against the walls.

He squinted against the autumnal sun, sliced into julienne strips as it pushed its way through the single sash window. "What are you doing here, Chlodwig?"

The other man looked up, surprised. "You told me about all those people dying, the police turned up, and I couldn't get hold of you..." His voice trailed off. "What was I supposed...?"

Boniface turned away from the damp eyes; he knew what was waiting for him when he saw Chlodwig's sister.

"So I came, and I bought Sophie to help Greta."

In other words, Greta would be annoyed that Chlodwig was here, and that annoyance would be compounded by the imposition of a new secretary.

"Chlodwig, I think you should know that I will be tendering my resignation. I will tell Greta face to face: That's the reason I'm here today."

The puffy face nodded, a look of confusion forming. "Why, Boniface?"

twenty

Boniface ascended to the top floor and followed the maze to the secretary's desk outside Greta Weissenfeld's office. A head bobbed up—it took Boniface a few moments to realize that she was standing.

She came out from behind the desk, holding out her right hand to greet him. "I am Sophie Driesdorfer. Pleased to meet you, Mister Boniface."

As Boniface shook her hand he checked: She was short. Shorter than Greta, and if he was being brutal, dumpier. As she walked back behind her desk, he tried to guess her age but failed, settling for somewhere in the range of twenty to fifty.

"It's Boniface. Not Herr Boniface, not Mister Boniface. Just Boniface." He tried to convey reassurance, tilting his head and softening his smile. "You must be Greta's new..."

"Yes." Boniface hoped she was as efficient as her response. "You started today?"

"Yes. Herr Weissenfeld... Do you know Herr Weissenfeld?"

"We've just been chatting."

"Herr Weissenfeld thought I would be suitable to work with his sister. She doesn't trust English secretaries." Realizing what she had said, she started gabbling; her English was good, but with a rip of a German accent cutting through. "Herr Weissenfeld feels that it would be beneficial for Fraulein Weissenfeld to have a secretary who understands her language and the work ethic that she is accustomed to." Satisfied that she had given a good account of why she was hired, she jerked her head forward to emphasize each word. "So I am here."

There were voices in Greta's room, and the door opened.

A figure exited. Slim, dressed darkly, marginally shorter than Boniface. He moved without making a noise, and Boniface suspected if he walked through water, there would be no ripples and no wake.

Boniface had heard the rumor, ex-Stasi, but had never felt able to ask a direct question from anyone who might know—after all, why would a life coach care?—and so had to be content with throwaway lines and odd adjectives: "sorts problems," "practical," "on the ground," "local knowledge, local contacts," "no nonsense," and Boniface's favorite, "pragmatic." The figure continued to pass; dull skin hung loosely over the skull, contrasting with the two dark eyes that fixed Boniface, igniting a primeval urge to confess every secret he knew.

Sophie had stepped into the room and was holding the door open. "Fraulein Weissenfeld, Herr Boniface is here."

"Boniface, I need you to start talking to people. Today. Now." Boniface had yet to enter the room, and orders were being given. He knew Greta would be sitting behind her desk—her Louis XIV reproduction desk, an abomination in Boniface's mind, showing a Mayfair victory of money over taste over practical function—reading from a list in her notebook that she carried with her everywhere, gold pen checking off each task as she gave her command without looking up to ensure the instruction had been received. That she had uttered the words was sufficient to absolve her of responsibility. Failure on your part to hear did not constitute an excuse or even reasonable grounds for a delay in implementation.

Boniface advanced into the room, the door shutting as the secretary left.

He had one option to slow the oncoming torrent: distraction. "That's new." She looked up. "Stand up, let me see."

As Boniface warily positioned himself in the uncomfortable Louis XIV–styled guest chair, Greta stepped out from behind her desk.

The dress was a simple design. The skill was in fitting it to her figure, and Greta's dressmaker showed formidable skill in cutting and stitching the lemon-gold fabric, which stopped half an inch above the CEO's knees. Boniface assumed that, as was usual for Greta, the dress would be sleeveless, but that detail was hidden under the embroidered, almost metallic gold jacket edged with three-color twisted piping: one line matching the gold of the jacket, one a deeper coppery gold, and the last a more ivory tone. If he were feeling less charitable, Boniface would have described the shoes as slut-wear, but given that she was still the client, he felt he could be more generous and acknowledge to himself that these heels were probably most suitable for the bedroom and could only be worn outside the bedroom if your chauffeur dropped you at your office door.

Boniface never knew what to say in these situations: He didn't care for her dress sense, but he appreciated that she had very distinctive taste. Over the last few months, he had learned that he needed to openly notice what Greta was wearing if he wanted her to feel good about herself and so be in a reasonable mood. He had also learned that an earnest look on his face accompanied with a measured nod of the head would communicate the appropriate response, even if he didn't understand the full extent of what he was communicating.

Irrespective of her talents, Chlodwig had made a wise selection of secretary for his sister. The uncharitable would describe Greta as being squat. She addressed the issue through her attire. By contrast, Sophie was shorter, stockier, and far less well groomed. She wore sensible shoes and a dress that you would forget while you stared at it. Chlodwig instinctively knew—with his sister's compulsion to compare and to calibrate her emotions through comparison—that Greta would always feel good about herself when she saw Sophie.

"Before you..."

Greta silenced Boniface, her approach strident. "First tell me what Chlodwig is doing here. He says he spoke to you yesterday, and because of that conversation, he got on a plane and came straight here. And he bought me a present: a fat present that dresses badly." She paused, continuing with more measured tones. "But she's only been here for three hours, and already she's done as much work as that other useless girl did in three weeks, so maybe she can stay."

"I need to exp..."

"No, Boniface." Her voice was hardening again. "What you *need* to do is to make Chlodwig go home." She continued, striking the desk with each word for added emphasis. "You created the problem. You, Boniface. You! You need to fix the problem."

She seemed tired from the exertion and exasperated from needing to explain, but still she continued. "You spoke to him, and as a direct result of that conversation, he is here."

She fixed a glare on Boniface, as if encouraging him to acknowledge that she was correct. "I'm not missing something, am I Boniface? It's not my fault that he's here, is it? It's not that I did anything?"

"No, but…"

"You're right, Boniface. No buts. Fix it. Make him go home." Her tone became more conciliatory. "Take him to dinner tonight. It's not a problem; he's on German time, so he'll be in bed by 10 PM. Let him stay a night so that he knows his ugly little girl has got settled, then he can go home tomorrow morning."

"I'll do it," said Boniface. "But there's something I have to say first." His voice was timid, almost apologetic. "I am tendering my resignation."

There was a twitch as Greta's head turned to face him. He noted that her straight blond, shoulder-length hair moved as one helmet-like structure. It was expensive to have such a simple look—and Boniface was sure that one afternoon in the salon would cost more than he spent on his hair in a decade—but all he could see was a Wagnerian Brünnhilde character. He could readily imagine her standing in her helmet with horns, gold body armor shaped to her figure, carrying a big stick and singing very loudly.

He tried not to let any emotion register on his face.

"You're not resigning, Boniface. There's work that needs to be done. First, you've got to make sure Chlodwig goes home."

"I'll deal with Chlodwig. But the last thing you need is to be represented by someone who has been arrested for murder. It won't support the right image for the context in which we're trying to present the events in Somalia."

Boniface explained the events of the previous day, starting with his phone call with Chlodwig. Greta listened impatiently, becoming increasingly frustrated.

"But this is all a problem for you, Boniface. Not for me. Why are you resigning at the time when I need you?" Boniface ignored the rhetorical question as Greta continued. "I've been paying you for nine months with nothing going on, and now that this issue is about to break…now…now that we are putting your plan—*your* plan, not my plan, *yours*—into action, now you decide you want to resign."

Boniface thought she was pausing, but he was wrong. "You told me you could handle the press. You told me you were an expert in public perception." Boniface squirmed in his uncomfortable chair. "Now you're saying that there's a dead body in your office and that it's going to affect me. How stupid do you think I am? You're like a little girl"—she affected a squeaky voice—"I don't know how he got there, I don't even know if he was murdered." She dropped the affectation and reverted to her normal voice with added thunder. "Of course it's murder, Boniface. You don't find a dead body in a street and decide to dump it in some stranger's office."

"I…"

"No, no, no. You are not resigning, Boniface." She started pointing, a disapproving finger was being waved. "Get out your notebook and write this down—you need to brief all the executives today. The story is about to go public, so you need to make sure they all understand the strategy and are following it without deviation."

Boniface reached into his pocket and pulled out a small notepad. He clicked the button on the top of his pencil to extend the lead and readied himself to take notes, aware of the contrast with his principal: Where she recorded detailed notes, written with archival ink containing carbon particles—ink designed to be read in 1,000 years—in a notebook that contained all her records and was always with her, he wrote with a pencil, as many left-handers did, and once actioned, he tore and shredded his used pages for additional security.

"Task one, Boniface." Greta's voice was clipped and fast. "Meet with each executive individually: Jeremy Farrant, Joanna Baines, and also for these purposes, Brad Phipps. Explain the background to the Somalia issue—broad strokes, avoid details. Tell them your strategy. Tell them what the line is we're taking and what they're doing next. When the story breaks, it must be minimized, and there's no scope for confusion through conflicting accounts."

"I saw that Mister Regenspurger is here. Should I brief him?"

"No. Why would you? But get a hotel. I want you close, and I don't want you to waste time traveling. And before you send Chlodwig home, make sure he understands the situation. This time, I want no confusion and no blubbing big brother."

Boniface scribbled and lifted his head.

"You've wasted enough time today, Boniface. Stop discussing, stop asking. Go. Do. Don't talk, just do." Boniface put his notebook into his pocket as he stood. "You had the police visit you yesterday. Is there anything else I need to know, Boniface? Is there anything you haven't told me? Are there any more surprises that you should tell me?"

Boniface reflexively tightened his lower lip.

"What is it, Boniface?"

"It's..." He sighed. "The question is not so much as to whether there's anything else." He spread his hands. "I mean..." He clasped his hands together. "We've all got a history. It's more a case of how far they'll look, how deep they'll dig, and how much they'll attach my name to what they dig up."

Greta nodded, holding the silence. "That sounds like a yes to me, Boniface."

Boniface mirrored her slow nod. "I suppose it is."

twenty-one

The full extent of Montbretia's knowledge of Tilbury had been based on the maps of the place she had consulted on her phone during the train journey and science boy's comments—and he had never been there.

After talking with science boy in his bunny suit, Montbretia had walked to Wimbledon station without delay: She had covered the less than half mile walk in eight minutes. In less than five minutes the train had arrived, which dropped her at Waterloo Station seventeen minutes later. It took a similar amount of time to get across London on something Boniface called the Drain, but which seemed like "the Tube," as she was learning to call the subway. Whatever they wanted to call it, she changed at Fenchurch Street station, where she got on a very slow train that resentfully dragged itself out to Tilbury.

Total journey time: about 90 minutes. Final destination: the 1970s, apparently. Change in Montbretia since leaving Wimbledon: one headband left behind, blue pantsuit still intact and rubbing, annoyingly. Reason for visit: That was where Montbretia wasn't sure. If she was honest, she had acted on impulse; it was probably because she didn't know what else to do, and it was the only lead she had.

She stepped off the train and saw one other passenger disembark at the same time. She followed the path he took through the station, coming out onto what she presumed, having squinted at the map, was a main road. Her fellow traveler had already disappeared.

On sight, Tilbury was the most depressing place Montbretia had ever visited. It was desolate. It was a wasteland. It was as if the aliens had come, killed all the humans and all the vegetation, and then departed, leaving behind concrete, tarmac, and steel but no forms of life.

She looked left. She looked right. Blacktop. Closed stores. No people. No trees.

She looked again. This was wrong—she needed to find the details, she needed to perform a mental inventory.

Three cars, parked. No signs of drivers.

John's Leather and Casual Wear. Shutters down. Notices posted on the shutters. A Chinese takeout. Shutters down. A faded sign. Shutters down with posters stuck to the shutters. Another Chinese. Another shutter. A mission, probably Christian. Shuttered. Even God had given up on Tilbury. Shipping agents. Shuttered. A car-parts store with a dropped curb at the front. Shuttered. Another Chinese. Yet another shutter. Dental surgery. Shuttered. A social club. No shutters to shut, but a closed notice pasted to the door. A combined post office/travel agent. Shuttered. A tattoo and body-piercing parlor. Shuttered. Beauty salon. Shuttered. Liquor store. Shuttered. Chicken, pizza, burgers. Shuttered.

There were more shuttered stores on the right than on the left, so she followed in that direction, passing seven more cars, all stationary, all without drivers. The variety of stores expanded: fish bar, community center, taxi office, drugstore, all shuttered. The shuttered commercial properties turned into blocks of apartments as she continued. Comparatively new blocks of apartments, but still all without any sign of life.

The new blocks gave way to older properties, mostly houses, the transition marked by a flophouse. This had been out of commission for a long time. Unlike the storefronts, there were no rolled-down metal shutters; instead, this had been boarded and was thick with posters offering cash for gold and check cashing.

Apparently someone had once thought human beings might pass this way, but that must have been a long time ago.

Montbretia kept walking, remaining on the road with the familiar sights of humanity—houses, cars—but without any signs of human inhabitation, even though this was meant to be a comparatively busy time for human beings: lunch time.

She had walked little farther than half a mile when she decided to head back to the station—there had to be some humanity there. Added to which, she wasn't comfortable with what she was wearing: Ellen's pantsuit wasn't her style, and their different body sizes meant that there was chafing. And while the shoes were sensible wear-all-day-in-the-office low-heeled pumps, they were the wrong size and were really beginning to pinch.

The walk back felt longer than the walk out, but as she approached her destination, she saw a small café tucked in the side of the station. If you knew it was there, it was obvious. If you were walking out into Tilbury and looking around, it wasn't.

Montbretia stepped in. It was small: four Formica tables crammed into a tiny room, and behind the counter the kitchen area, with what looked like a side window opening onto the main route out of the station, which would explain why she didn't see the place as she passed through. An old gated wooden sign leaned against the wall: "Trev's fried chicken—7 PM 'til late." It at least implied that some form of humanity might pass this way at some point.

The man behind the counter—the second human Montbretia had seen in Tilbury—leaned with his back against the counter, reading a newspaper.

"You must be Trevor." Montbretia was pleased to find someone to quiz about Tilbury.

He turned and nodded, a graying goatee hiding any emotion.

"I'll have an Americano."

"Coffee comes out of tin." He dropped one side of his paper and clumsily lifted a catering tin of instant coffee. "The only question is, do you want milk?"

"Coffee with milk, please," said Montbretia meekly, feeling chastised.

He grabbed a white mug, tossed in a teaspoon of coffee, opened the tap on the boiler, then splashed in a slug of milk and banged the mug on the counter as he put it down. "One pound twenty."

Evidently service was extra. Montbretia reached for her cash, feeling Trevor's eyes appraising her. She placed a few coins on the counter and turned, picking up her mug. "Thank you."

"I'd go home now." He nodded as if that affirmed the wisdom of his opinion. "Drink your coffee, then go."

twenty-two

Boniface had already been in one gentlemen's club that morning, and stepping into Jeremy Farrant's office was like stepping into a second. Crossing the threshold at his office door was like crossing the threshold into a time when Great Britain was the sole global super-power and Britannia really did rule the waves.

He hadn't been into all the individual offices in the building, but those that Boniface had visited—including the CEO's—possessed a single door. Farrant's opened through a double door, giving the feeling of a room that required a servant for each door.

Office carpets had never interested Boniface—or at least they hadn't until the SOCOs apparently cut a big hole in his. They were things you had because you couldn't *not* have something to cover the floor. What was the alternative? Bare wood? Polished metal? Floating on air? In his experience most floors—except in the executive suite—were either covered with mismatched tiles with a high nylon content, delivering a static shock whenever you earthed yourself, or by a single piece of carpet, which was then ripped up and shoddily refitted when someone decided that the ethernet cabling needed to be upgraded.

Boniface had never paid attention to the carpets in the Weissenfeld office, which was another way of saying that nothing in the carpeting had ever drawn itself to his attention. The carpet was a flat piece of fabric, well laid and with no bumps or wrinkles, clean, and without any marks where furniture had been. Thinking about it now, its color was a lemon/yellow/gold that was not dissimilar to the color of the dress Greta was wearing today.

He wondered whether that was intentional and whether he should have mentioned it. Probably not.

But walking across the carpet in Farrant's room, Boniface noticed the difference. It was as if he had rolled off a bed of nails and onto a mattress of feathers. With each step the carpet enveloped and supported his foot, making sure it wasn't too much effort or too much of an inconvenience to walk across it.

The feel of the carpet distracted Boniface from noticing that a different-color carpet had been fitted. Instead of a lemon gold covering, this was the color of crushed green olives with a broad border, about eighteen inches deep and expertly fitted, having a dark red and burnished gold pattern.

Boniface's eyes followed the border, watching how it followed the irregular features: the old fireplace, the alcove, the next room jutting into this. He noticed the border going around the bookcases. "He can't have done..." Boniface walked over to the bookcases and looked down the side.

The wall bowed—the building was several hundred years old, and every wall bowed—but the bookcase had been fitted perfectly to the wall with the far flank of the upright carved to reflect the imperfections of the wall. At the foot, the baseboard had been fitted around the front of the bookcase, and only then had the carpet been added.

Boniface moved in closer to appreciate at the handcrafted piece of furniture. It was impressive: one single structure, constructed in situ. He examined the end panel—there were no joins, and the only ornamentation was some exquisite rosewood fretted inlays. Either this was a single plank or a good piece of veneer. Boniface laughed at his own stupidity: He was starting to get a feel for Jeremy Farrant—there was no way this would be veneer.

He was right; the end panel was a single solid piece of mahogany: The corners gave him the proof he needed. There was neither the join of two pieces of veneer, nor the unnatural grain when veneer is rolled around a corner. Instead, you could see the grain crossing the corners where the wood had been cut. He twisted his head to peer under a shelf, then under the next, and under a third. If you bought a bookcase in a store, the shelves were adjustable. These weren't. These shelves had been positioned in full knowledge of the library they were to hold.

Boniface surveyed the library, which covered the whole wall on either side of and above the double doors, acting like insulation against the rest of the company. From floor to ceiling the shelves were lined with leather-bound law books, labeled by year, an unequivocal statement that the resident in the office was a lawyer.

Boniface sneered.

In the twenty-first century, legislation was so extensive, complex, and changeable that all lawyers referred to online sources when reviewing legislation. This allowed members of the legal profession to know they had the most up-to-date reference, with all changes tracked so they could see what legislation was in force on any day in the past. Not only that, but computers allowed a lawyer to follow links—legislation made frequent cross-references. For a computer-based lawyer, a cross-reference was as much of a challenge as clicking with a mouse. For Farrant, a cross-reference would require that he stand up, go to his library, and pick out the next book, which would then likely be out of date.

This wasn't convenience. This was risk. Using paper—even leather-bound paper—meant this man's knowledge would go out of date. "Dangerous," muttered Boniface under his breath.

The light from the two sash windows on the outside wall drew his attention to a small collection of framed pictures on the side wall behind the desk. He walked past a wall safe—which appeared to be of the same nineteenth-century vintage as everything else in the room—to have a closer look at the paintings. Two were portraits of family groups; the third picture showed a large gray-stoned house, the sort of building that was now used for period dramas on TV and hired out for corporate bonding sessions. Boniface had heard that Farrant owned a castle in the Scottish borders—he wondered if this pile was it.

He turned from the wall, glancing at the desk as he passed. Unlike the bookcases, this looked genuinely old—if it had been commissioned, Farrant would almost have got something more in proportion with himself and the room, thought Boniface. It looked sufficiently battered to be at least 200 years old, with drawers out of alignment and not fully closed. This explained the safe.

Crossing the room, he reached the seating area: a club chair and a sofa, both scroll-armed with buttoned dark-green leather, angled toward each other. Boniface dropped into the club chair, which faced toward the far corner past the desk. It was good to sit in a comfortable chair—the one at Gideon's club had been thin and old, the one in Greta's room had been designed for looks rather than comfort, but this was comfortable.

Boniface felt a vibration inside his pocket and reached for his phone. "Gideon." He listened. "I know it... Late lunch... Sure." He took the phone away from his ear and checked the time. "I can't be there until at least three, maybe later." He closed his eyes, listening. "Where would we be without your juvenile sense of humor? I'll see you later."

He stood and slipped the phone into his pocket as the door opened. A man, perhaps six inches shorter than Boniface, entered. He was older—he had the appearance of a spritely 80-year-old—but Boniface pegged his age as late sixties. Slim and well-dressed in a dark gray pin-striped three-piece suit. "Mister Boniface, I believe. So good to meet you." The voice sounded like a caricature of a BBC radio announcer from the 1950s. Exaggerated Received Pronunciation tones, but in this case slightly high pitched.

He pulled a small silver box from his pocket, flipped the lid, took a pinch from the contents, held his fingers to his left nostril and inhaled. "I'm sorry you've had to wait, Mister Boniface, but I'm afraid any conversation will have to wait until tomorrow. Say first thing tomorrow morning?"

Boniface kept his tone calm. "The matter that I need to talk about is both urgent and highly important."

"Oh, I'm sure it is—that is why I will see you so expeditiously."

twenty-three

She wasn't quite sure what she had expected when she left Wimbledon, but she hadn't expected unconcealed hostility. She hadn't expected to be told to go home when she only wanted a cup of coffee, which was now on the first Formica table where she was intending to sit.

"You're not the first social worker, researcher, do-gooder, or whatever you want to call yourself to come around here telling everyone how sorry you feel while you try to boost your own career." Montbretia found she had lost the ability to talk as he continued. "You look around and say, 'Oh, the depravation, the docks have gone, what will the poor people do?' Well, the docks are still here, and they're busier than ever."

"I know," said Montbretia.

"But it's the work that has gone..." He paused, apparently catching on that Montbretia had replied.

"You're talking about the impact of containerization." She kept her approach calm. "People say it's globalization and they're wrong, it's containerization. Where it would have taken days to unload a ship and would have required an army of stevedores, TEUs can carry more cargo, and that cargo can be loaded and unloaded faster and requires less skill."

"You know what a TEU is?" The man behind the counter had a slight crack in his goatee where Montbretia guessed his mouth might be.

"I do," said Montbretia.

"Seriously, you know what a TEU is?" A bemused look had turned to outright cynicism.

"I'll call them intermodal containers if you prefer," said Montbretia, straining to keep the satisfaction out of her voice. "Intermodal containers, TEUs or twenty-foot equivalent units, or shipping containers; shipping containers that you see everywhere on ships, on trains, dragged behind tractor-trailers, by the side of the road, for storage, and in any number of uses. How do you want me to describe them?"

She sat, twisting into the hard plastic behind the table and turning to better see her inquisitor before continuing. "If you want me to talk about the economics of containers and shipping, I'm happy to. I'm happy to talk about bigger ships, which can carry more cargo more efficiently, meaning that the fuel footprint per ton of cargo is reduced. Or maybe you'd like to discuss the paradox of the huge benefit of global trade while local businesses—particularly businesses around ports—are destroyed?"

He came out from behind the counter, wiping his hands on his stained red-and-white striped apron and grooming his goatee. "I think I had you wrong, didn't I? I'm sorry." He offered his hand. "I'm Trevor."

Montbretia stood and accepted the handshake. "Monty."

She sunk back into her seat. Trevor mirrored at the next table. "Why the interest in shipping?"

"My job."

"Come on, girl. No one takes a job in shipping unless they've got no other options."

Montbretia gave a soft laugh. "Well, I'm not in shipping as such, and the shipping link was a fluke." Trevor frowned as Montbretia continued. "I was traveling and came to London. Long story short, I've been staying for longer than I thought I would."

"I sense a man," said Trevor jovially, his face falling as Montbretia felt her breath leave her body and her heart slow.

He started stammering: "It didn't work out. I didn't mean to put my foot in it." He held his hands up as if holding back her sadness.

Montbretia felt her eyes misting. "Sorry. I wasn't expecting this conversation." She dabbed her eyes with a tissue from her pocket. "It wasn't a man. It was a death." She wiped her eyes again. "My sister."

"My dear God, I'm sorry."

The two sat in silence, Montbretia taking the occasional sip of coffee. "I had to stay to deal with—I'm still dealing with—probate, and to be honest, after Ellen...I couldn't keep moving. I wanted to spend a few months reflecting...remembering..."

"Mourning." Trevor's tone was smooth, comforting.

Montbretia continued, her voice still strained. "There was this guy who was with my sister at the end, and he's been great. Boniface, that's his name. He had set up his own business a few months before, and he needed someone to help, but he didn't want the hassle of an employee. I needed money but didn't want to be tied down with a job and didn't want to work in a bar, so the arrangement works for both of us."

"So he's in shipping?"

"No," shrieked Montbretia, moderating her volume as she continued, shocked by her own reaction. "Definitely not. Boniface isn't the physical labor sort. No, he's...if I call it PR it would give the wrong impression. He's not the issue-a-press-release, get-a-pretty-girl-to-stand-next-to-your-product kind of guy. He's much more into strategy, big messages, crisis management—that's a big thing for him. He's an ex-journalist, ex-government press guy, so he's got a lot of contacts, a lot of experience."

"I don't see the shipping link."

"That's because it's not that obvious," said Montbretia, her face softening. "When I started working with Boniface, I did the easy stuff. Week one I sorted his filing. Tedious, but he gets scared by paper." She hung her head, shaking it in disappointment. "Such a wimp. Then week two, I sorted out his technology—made him use a phone that was built in this century, taught him how email can benefit his clients. Week three I sorted his website, which was when he figured I could help his clients, and so I did a bunch of websites for his clients, which is how we come to shipping."

Trevor sat stroking his goatee as Montbretia continued. "One of Boniface's clients...well, it's not so much a client as a group of concerned companies all somehow associated with shipping, are worried about the reputation of businesses involved in global logistics."

She took a sip of coffee before continuing. "He figured that each organization had similar public perception issues, but he also saw the irony that a public which disapproves about shipping companies moving toxic waste is the same public that wants cheap consumer goods. Boniface's argument was that if you want your iPad or whatever, then there will be consequent chemical waste that needs to be disposed of safely, and a public discussion was needed about the two sides of the coin—his point was if you don't want the nasty chemicals, don't buy the electronics, but since consumers want gadgets they should take some responsibility for the consequence."

"He sounds like a bright guy."

"He is," said Montbretia. "But he's also practical—he helped set up what's called the Global Logistics Forum, which is meant to be a place to discuss these issues."

"I'm with you so far, but how did you get involved?"

"The website—I set it up. Boniface wanted a place where respected and identifiable individuals could put forward their perspective and other people could discuss the matter in a dignified manner. The way we started this discussion was by setting up a website and encouraging academics and experts to submit papers on their subject."

Montbretia felt the enthusiasm for her work as she explained. "I'm a go-with-your-gut, go-with-your-heart kinda gal, but pretty soon I was reading a wide range of papers from an even broader array of very clever, very informed, and very experienced people, and I got to know the subject. So I started asking people to contribute. For instance, I found a chemist in India—she's a PhD—to talk about the challenges of managing production but also the ethical considerations around the chemicals that are involved in production. She got a grip on the difficulties with noxious substances in countries where the infrastructure isn't in place to deal with the amount of waste that is created."

Trevor's head nodded.

"In a roundabout way, that is how I came to know about TEUs."

"What brings you to my humble establishment? Are you reviewing the economics of running a greasy spoon where the only passing trade goes through the station or is white van drivers delivering crap that people have ordered from the shopping channels?"

"I'm afraid not. I'm after a bum." Trevor's eyes opened wide. "A vagrant, a tramp, one of the homeless..."

Trevor sat back. "Got a few round here, and when they come I tell 'em to..." He stopped himself. "I tell them to go away. I mean seriously, do I look like a charity?" He lowered his voice, his tone questioning. "Why do you want a vagrant? What's it got to do with shipping? It's not some clever new strategy of your boss?"

Montbretia felt a sharp intake of breath through her teeth. "It's quite bizarre. We had a dead body dumped...near where I live." She didn't like blurring the truth, but she couldn't think of a better excuse. "Nobody knows much about the bum. In truth, there is only one fact of which we're certain: He was arrested in Tilbury two days ago, and I figured he might have..." Montbretia realized she wasn't quite sure why she had come to Tilbury or what she was hoping to find. "I dunno. The police are doing nothing, and I wondered if he had friends or someone who knew something about him. Someone, somewhere must care. Someone must want to know that he's gone."

Trevor let out a slow breath. "Asking about one guy is a bit like asking about a raindrop. We get a lot of outsiders through here, and no one has a home. Sailors don't have a home; they're always on the move. People you might think of as vagrants are often sailors who've been stuck in port for too long. Usually they'll find another ship and the next tide will take them away."

"What happens to the ones that don't get back on their ship?"

"Most of them move on—that's what they've done all their life; that's what they keep doing. Most head for wherever they think of as home, and the rest go to London—we're close enough, and that's a much better place to be homeless. There's a better passing trade if you're out begging."

"What about the ones that don't move on?"

"They die." Montbretia couldn't hide her shock. Trevor's voice softened. "They don't stop-die." He clapped his hands loudly as if to emphasize the speed and finality of death. "But soon they're gone. It's Darwinian: The strong ones get back on a boat, and the weak stay here. You see them around—sometimes there are small groups of them around a fire. Nobody knows them, and without the structure of being part of a crew—without a captain giving out orders—they drink too much, don't wash, don't eat enough, get ill, and die. For men who are used to hard, physical labor, it's sad. Most don't make it through their first winter."

"You said they sit round a fire. Where?"

Trevor raised his shoulders, shaking his head. "It changes. They move on. Wherever they are, they'll be out of sight. It'll be somewhere that can't be seen from the road and somewhere that they won't be noticed. But honestly, Monty. Leave them alone. You're a lovely girl, so go home. They won't talk to you, ever. They hate strangers..."

He grinned. "And they'll know you're not a sailor."

twenty-four

"Mister Pitcher for Mister Catcher."

Gideon's puerile humor hadn't improved over the years, especially when he was seemingly trying to add a veneer of discretion, although it wasn't evident to Boniface why Gideon would want a meeting with Boniface kept off the radar.

At least for the acne-ridden juvenile—forced to wear a clean white shirt and waist coat, or vest as Montbretia would insist on calling it, then made to stand behind the reception desk and be helpful—the innuendo, weak as it was, made no sense. He grunted in a manner that the French seemed trained for from birth and waved his hand with Gallic disdain, leaving Boniface to find his way from the faceless dark wood and marble reception to room four.

Room four was up the stairs and along a corridor. It was easily recognizable: It was the room with an open door with Gideon sitting in view. "Boniface, old chap. Come in, come in, but do shut the door."

The door clicked as he shut it, the sound bouncing off the hard surfaces in the room, and his feet echoed on the floorboards as he walked to greet Gideon. "Still or sparkling?" Gideon pointed to the two bottles on the circular table covered in a crisp white linen cloth.

"Sparkling." Boniface pulled back the free dining chair and sat as Gideon poured.

"You old hell-raiser. Sparkling mineral water, and during school lunch time. Are you going to amp yourself up a bit more and have a small herbal tea later?"

"What's with all the codenames, Gideon?" Boniface surveyed the small, feature-less room—his attention drawn to the view of St James's Park, the park the Queen looked over when she pressed her nose to the front windows of Buckingham Palace.

"In clubland there are certain standards. Discretion is understood. But we're in the jungle here, Boniface: We're in Westminster. We may be overlooking the Palace, but we're looking from the jungle. Normal rules of etiquette don't apply; I mean, they let journalists become members of this establishment." Gideon beamed at his self-conscious attempt at levity. "When you have staff who don't understand discretion, then I'm afraid precautions are called for."

All humor evaporated from Gideon's voice as he continued. "I've made some enquiries: You've been associating with very bad types, and you've got yourself in a dreadful pickle, Boniface." Any remaining mirth fell from his face. "This is hard, Boniface, but I'll come to the point: I can't be seen with you until this whole thing blows over."

Boniface felt like he had been punched. In the space of six hours, Gideon's attitude had changed.

"This isn't goodbye, Boniface, but it is definitely *au revoir*." Gideon took a sip from his glass. "It took me two phone calls, Boniface. Two phone calls to find that the earthly remains of a recently departed derelict have been left in your office and that you're the prime suspect." He paused, continuing when Boniface made eye contact. "You, Boniface. You are the prime suspect. Do they think you did it? Probably not. But are you involved? Do you know more than you have told them? Definitely. Do you know why the body was dumped in your office—which is not an easy feat, by the way? They don't know, but they suspect you probably have a good idea."

Boniface fought to quell the anger, feeling every sinew tighten as he tried to maintain his outward composure.

"You told me you had a problem. You told me that you thought someone might be trying to destroy you. I get it. I guessed it was something financial or grubby—photoshopped pictures of you in rubber, something like that. But no…murder."

"You know…" Boniface began, but was cut off by Gideon.

"I know you didn't do it. I know you're innocent. I know you're being set up." He slowed, looking around as if he might find instructions for what he was trying to say written on the walls. "But you've been a royal pain in the you-know-where. You've come up with some cock-and-bull story about a mystery client whose details you won't disclose on a project you can't talk about. That's the sort of stuff that annoys cops."

Gideon had a pained expression. "You understand my big problem. I'm leading a campaign against all forms of sexual violence. You've even suggested ways we can make sure the campaign has more resonance—how it can matter more—to the average person. And I'm grateful." Gideon sat back in his chair, his voice becoming more animated. "I'll give you a practical example. I'm talking at a conference," he checked his watch, "in forty-five minutes, about child prostitution."

Boniface listened.

"You know my view. There is no such thing as child prostitution. No such thing." Boniface knew and agreed with the argument. "What there is, is horrific exploitation of children by adults. Whatever you think about prostitution and the social, gender, and political issues around it, there can be no doubt that a child does not have the capacity to make an informed decision to work as a prostitute. Your high-end call girl is quite an entrepreneurial young lady, and this is more so since the days of the internet. Your so-called child prostitute does not get self-motivated; they are always, *always* forced into the life by an adult who then takes their earnings. Call it what it is: It's child sex slavery and nothing less."

Gideon paused. He had been emphasizing each point by banging on the table with a single finger. When he continued his tone was modulated. "So look at it from my point of view. How can I be anti–sex crime but pro-murderer? How can I take a public position of support—or even association—with you without the discussion in the press moving from extreme child exploitation to whether Gideon Latymer supports murder if it's committed by his friends? You were a journalist, you remember how it works."

Boniface, his head lowered, became aware of his breathing.

"I'm all for fair trials, most particularly in the court of public opinion, and innocent until proven guilty. But here's the thing: I don't want my day in court. It's little comfort to be proved innocent when you are wrongly accused." Gideon continued, his tone almost apologetic. "All this and you're working for a client where you're covering up your money trails, which makes it sound like you're into international money-laundering. Are you staying on the right side of the street with this one? It's one thing to take a risk when your business is spotless, but it's a whole other thing when you're accused of murder…." His voice trailed off.

Boniface stared out of the window, through the lush trees and across St James's Park. He didn't notice when Gideon continued. "If there's a chink of light, as a former minister, I am due a certain amount of respect, a limited number of privileges, some courtesy, and I can beg a few favors. But there are scores to settle against me. Also, with some of my tastes, I have a few acquaintances with shared interests on whom I bring pressure, although the irony is that they might enjoy it if I play rough. Having pulled those strings, I'm satisfied that it's not us."

Boniface frowned, questioning.

"It's not MI5. And for the record, it's not MI6 or any other of our lesser-known and somewhat more furtive and off-the-books chaps that you can think of. This is your foul-up, not some establishment conspiracy."

Boniface sat quietly. When he spoke, his voice was hardly audible. "Thank you."

"I know this sounds cruel, but I know you understand: I can't be associated with a murderer. I know that if you were doing my PR you would tell me to do what I'm doing." He stood and stepped to the door. "Come out to the country when this dreadful business has blown over." His face lit up. "Bring Montbretia."

He had half stepped out of the door when he turned around. "You will remember to leave by the back door."

twenty–five

"Have you come to give me a blow job?" Montbretia felt herself tremble and her face burn. "Then fuck off. If you're gonna call yourself a social worker, then be social," he started as if to unbutton his trousers, "and get to work. If you're not going to be social and you're not going to work, then fuck off."

The man with a thick Glaswegian accent sneered to the second man standing behind a burned oil drum, as if giving him a cue for the correct emotional response.

"Fuck off, lassie. We're not a project for you. And for future reference, I prefer my girls with bigger..." He held his hands as if holding a basketball to his chest with each.

"He's very picky about his ladies." The other man's London accent cut through. "I ain't..."

Montbretia had relented and accepted a second cup of coffee from Trevor. It was no better than the first, but it was tolerable—and this time free.

Most of the cup of coffee had been spent with the café owner urging Montbretia to turn around and go home. In the end, he had agreed that he couldn't stop her walking along a public road. For her part, Montbretia had agreed to check in with him before she left Tilbury.

Before beginning her walk, she had used his restroom. It wasn't a public restroom, but it was what he used. It was filthy and the door didn't shut, which was less of a problem because the light didn't work. However, the greasy floor—it felt easier to assume the floor was greasy when she considered the alternatives—or rather, the mechanics of using a restroom with a greasy floor when she was wearing pants and using one hand to hold the door half closed while still letting enough light in, was a problem.

After she finished scrubbing her hands in the café's sink, she looked at Trevor's first-aid kit and found only a two-pence coin, which apparently was what used to work with public phone booths. There being no Band-Aids, she padded her shoes with some paper napkins she found. It didn't stop the shoes rubbing, but they dug into her feet in a different place so she had a different discomfort to distract herself from the minor pain she already felt.

As she walked, the discomfort had itself become a pain.

But then again, that was expected. Trevor had suggested she continue down the road she had walked earlier. It led to a footbridge over the railway line. Montbretia demurred; she wanted to cover the ground she hadn't seen, and so she had turned left and walked up to the roundabout where the Tilbury town road and the main road to the docks joined. Trevor had said the roads were disinteresting and not designed for pedestrians.

He hadn't lied.

He hadn't exaggerated.

Having walked for a mile or so, all Montbretia had achieved was to draw parallel with the station, but on the other side of the railway line from the café. During her walk she had seen lots of blacktop roads, ugly shuttered cement walls around Tilbury docks, and lots of tractor-trailers pulling TEU containers—lorries, as

Boniface always called them. Lorries speeding to and from the port, every lorry that passed kicking out black clouds of sooty diesel fumes.

Despite having covered some distance, she hadn't seen any signs of humanity. Sure, there had been people in the many lorries and the few cars that passed, but apart from that there had been no signs of any human habitation. Before coming to London, she had been traveling for two-and-a-half years. She loved cities, the buzz of people, and the mix of cultures. She also loved getting away from everything—following a trail for days and being totally isolated.

But the road to the Tilbury docks gave her neither of these experiences. She was on her own but she wasn't alone. It wasn't like being in the city with lots of people around, providing safety in numbers. It wasn't like being the only person following an old trail when there's security because there's no one else around to be a danger. Here she felt the worst of both worlds—no crowd for security, but lots of individuals passing, any of whom could be a predator and would be out of the country in hours.

She thought about the pantsuit again. This was dangerous. As well as bad shoes, which would stop her from running away. She looked so anomalous that she might as well be wearing a target. If she was to get in trouble, these clothes offered no defense: They could be quickly and easily ripped by an attacker.

At least if she had jeans on, they couldn't be ripped. And if someone tried to attack her, especially when she wore a belt, it would take too long for an attacker to get her jeans off—and even longer than that when she was fighting. And she was prepared to defend herself—boots were good for kicking people.

But a pantsuit—a pantsuit that rubbed the top of her thigh—gave no protection.

She made up her mind to walk for another ten minutes before she turned around and went back to Trevor, the train, and home. After seven minutes, she saw two men, both roughly dressed and dirty, flanking a burned-out oil drum.

As the Scotsman greeted her and encouraged her to get on her knees, she realized the danger she was in. It was the Londoner talking now. "So if you're not up for a blow job, how about a hand job? Two of us, one of you, and a nice time skiing." He let the implicit threat hang in the air.

Montbretia stepped back.

"How about a cup of tea?"

It was the Scotsman who spoke. "I'd prefer a blow job."

"And a bacon sandwich," offered Montbretia. Neither responded. "Perhaps while you have your tea and bacon sandwich, we could talk about the guy who was arrested two days ago. I know what happened to him."

The Scotsman stood up quickly. "You know, you really are starting to piss me off."

twenty-six

"I'm sorry to say, Boniface, but I'm very disappointed." The gentle German voice was as a kindly uncle delivering a rebuke; it was caring, helpful even, but firm. In reality, it was a body blow to Boniface. The tone was light—the gruffness and the lower frequencies were naturally filtered out of Chlodwig's voice—but the sadness was unmistakable. "Honestly, Boniface, I thought more of you."

Boniface remained still, sitting across the overly large conference table in the too-small conference room watching the German as he continued. "What is so upsetting is that I like you and respect you. You are bright and engaging, and you are an honorable man with the highest moral concerns." He paused before continuing. "This morning you told me that you were resigning, but now you tell me that you didn't follow through, and indeed, it is your intention not to resign."

Boniface had recounted the events of the previous twenty-four hours—from their telephone conversation to the arrival of the police, the discovery of the body, and his becoming a suspect for murder—when he talked with the CEO's brother that morning. It hadn't been an easy conversation, but it was clear to both men that it wouldn't be tenable for Boniface to represent Weissenfeld Shipping.

He looked up into the puffy eyes of the German, no longer red as they had been this morning, but the disappointment was wounding. "I understand your reaction. Really I do, Chlodwig. I understand what I'm saying is a turnaround, but that's why we should talk, and talk somewhere away from the office."

So far, so Greta. He was doing what he had been instructed to do, he just wasn't sure in his mind that he was here because he had been bullied by Greta or because he was looking three steps ahead and was concerned about the damage an angry client could create.

It is one thing to deal with bad publicity surrounding a corpse: Boniface could at least try to explain the situation to any potential new client. A slim hope, but some hope. However, trying to find new work when your last client publicly criticizes you for walking away from the project that you were hired for and had been paid for, at precisely the moment when your talents are required, is a whole other issue.

It was time for the textbook negotiation opening. Unfortunately, this textbook was being rewritten by a man who was negotiating his way into doing what he didn't want to do, what he had specifically set out *not* to do this morning, and which would upset Montbretia when he told her that he wasn't yet able to devote all his time to trying to find who had left a cadaver in his office. "I, too, believe you are an honorable man, Chlodwig, so I hope you will hear me out and will consider my suggestion, which I think might have advantages for both of us."

It was low calling to his sense of honor, but Boniface was running out of options, especially now that Gideon had severed diplomatic ties. "As I said, it would be good to chat somewhere away from the office. Could we have dinner tonight?"

twenty-seven

"When the ship took the cargo to Rotterdam, the payment was to have been made electronically, company to company."

"Standard payment practice," said the CFO.

Boniface continued, "But when the ship left Brindisi for the second time, they were carrying dollars—sports bags stuffed with greenbacks."

"Who signed off on the cash payment? Who signed off on them even carrying cash?" Joanna Baines, Weissenfeld Shipping's chief financial officer's speech was deliberate, considered, some might say aggressive, but punctuated by odd pauses: She eschewed the usual errs and umms that often filled spoken communication, choosing instead silence, as if she would be charged for each wasted sound. When she continued, her manner was quiet, small, cautious, as if using the minimum energy necessary to convey her point. "It's not practice for crews to carry this much cash." Her tone became insistent without any increase in volume. "There are policies in place to ensure no unauthorized cash payments are made, and how did they get that much cash?"

Boniface was content to let her continue: She was repeating what he already knew, but in accountant-speak. He rocked his head forward as if he might care, but in all honesty, he never got excited by anything the bean counters said, particularly the bossy, controlling types like Joanna Baines.

"Is this so hard for these people to understand? I mean, it's not like this was a mistake—someone consciously decided to take the dollar bills. Even Regenspurger understands the process."

"Regenspurger?" Boniface's post-lunch stupor and post-Gideon contemplation was immediately forgotten. "How is Regenspurger involved with money?"

The CFO paused, apparently not expecting a question. Boniface looked on as the rather hefty, somewhat inelegant woman repositioned herself. She made a few hand gestures, like a nervous actor mentally rehearsing her cue, then began. "You've probably heard about his reputation."

Boniface tried not to appear too sheepish. He had heard rumors, nothing more, and nothing that could be substantiated.

"Some of it is almost certainly true, and that reputation can be useful."

"So he does...?" Boniface held up his fists as if going into a fight.

"No. But as I say, his reputation is useful." The woman's voice was calm and definitive as she got into the rhythm of her explanation. "We're a big company in the world of shipping, and we go to many places where the rule of law is not implemented in a way that we might hope."

Boniface let his head nod, degree by degree, and he tried to bring some levity. "What we might loosely categorize as lawless hellholes."

She mirrored Boniface's nod. "You might say that. I couldn't possibly comment." Her face took on a more serious air. "These places present a challenge—again, being euphemistic, the challenge might be termed local culture and custom." She rubbed her fingers against her thumbs, seemingly becoming more circumspect.

"If I understand what you're telling me, Joanna, you are seen as the big, rich shipping firm, making you an easy target for someone looking to raise an additional bit of local taxation."

"Precisely."

"And Mister Regenspurger?"

The CFO leaned forward. "We have legitimate interests to protect, and it's important—staying within the confines of local law and ensuring compliance with international non-bribery laws—that we send a message that we are not a firm to be messed with. Time is money and all that, and if we offer a bribe once, then we'll be on the hook every time we pass through that port. And even if we don't pay, we'll waste time; that delays shipping, and we get fined." Boniface could see the pain at the thought of spending money with no equivalence in return. "Mister Regenspurger's skill set is in negotiating between the locals and our crew in order to find a mutually acceptable solution, which doesn't cause us any problems down the line."

"A fixer," offered Boniface.

"On a logistical front, he fixes problems." The ungainly woman dropped her voice. "I'm not trying to say that there has never been a situation where a couple of bottles of scotch were accidently left behind five minutes before one of our ships was cleared to leave port, but most of the time all you need is a big lad or two to stand there. If the locals know they can't push the crew around, they'll go and pick on someone else."

"So what happens? You get a problem and Regenspurger jumps on a plane?"

"Rarely—we only unleash the big beast if there's a big problem. More often there's a niggle that needs to be sorted then and there, and we don't have time to waste, so it's a case of getting local ad-hoc help. Reliable help that won't cause problems for us down the line. It's a specialized market: You need people who have an incentive to drop whatever they're doing and go and help our guys."

Boniface winced. "What's the issue with cash and Regenspurger?"

"Bluntly," she looked like she was trying to stop her eyes from involuntarily rolling, "think of the services that Regenspurger acquires for us as being a twenty-four-hour call-out service. These people must be paid in cash, and we are obliged to pay a retainer in expectation of future services."

Boniface felt the tension drain out of his body. He had been sitting with the CFO for he guessed about twenty minutes, and he was becoming increasingly fixated on the furniture, starting with a 1960s linoleum-topped desk. Linoleum topped so the surface could be replaced. The 1970s office chair Boniface was sitting on, fashioned from a single tube of steel with a thinly padded seat and backrest, each covered with loose nylon covers, which could be removed for washing. The only good thing he could find about his chair was that it rocked—it was sort of like an adult rock-a-tot for the office. But what had been taking almost all of Boniface's attention since he arrived were the filing cabinets. Two walls were covered with cabinets of different vintages and different shades of brown, gray, and green. The bottom layer, four-drawer cabinets; the top layer placed atop the bottom layer, two-drawer cabinets. Every single cabinet had a flaw—a patch of rust, a drawer not fitting, out-of-kilter corners.

Boniface drew his gaze away from the filing cabinets to find Joanna Baines staring at him, a look of stifled excitement in her eyes. "How much?"

"I beg your pardon?"

"How much do you think I paid for all the office furniture in this room: the filing cabinets, my chair, your chair, this desk?"

Boniface pushed out his bottom lip, slowly shaking his head. He didn't care, but he felt he should make a show of considering the question. "Go on. Tell me, Joanna."

"Fifteen pounds."

"Fifteen quid?" Boniface could hear the barely disguised shock in his voice as he nearly shouted.

"I had to pay a man sixty-five pounds to collect the furniture, which was quite a bargain, what with him having to bring it up two floors and the load not fitting in the van, meaning he had to do a second run."

Boniface wasn't sure whether to be impressed or horrified. "This looks ex-Civil Service, ex-government."

"That's where I got it, Boniface—government surplus."

Boniface looked up and down the cabinets, then back to the woman, her brown suit jacket not reaching her wrists. "You've heard of computers, right?"

"Computers don't give you the advantages of paper. I have everything, *everything* available to me. There's no waiting for it to boot up, and nothing's as compatible as paper. We run a global business, Boniface, with hundreds of different offices all using different standards, formats, and languages. Everyone understands paper. Nothing is quite as compatible as paper: You never have to worry about converting data into one format from another. My paper is never incompatible with your desk."

Boniface didn't know what to say.

"Paper can't be hacked and altered. If someone changes one of my files, I can see the change—I don't have to pay some IT geek to tell me about digital signatures or electronic fingerprints." A look of smugness spread over her face. "Plus, I can start checking the records—or rather Brian and I can start checking the records—as soon as you leave here, and we'll be able to see what cash the Montenegro Shipping Company has paid out."

Boniface tried to restrain himself, knowing he would regret asking the next question, but he couldn't hold back. "Why spend fifteen pounds on furniture when you could get something..." He tailed off, thinking of the lawyer's office. "New. Different. Better. Custom built."

The CFO pondered before answering. "Me? I don't care about my office. One desk is the same as the next. One filing cabinet the same as the next. I honestly see no difference between a brand-new filing cabinet and one that might be forty years old and rusty. If you look at the function that they've got to perform, they are the same."

Boniface faced the woman square on, listening as she continued. "I bring people here when they are trying to spend company money. The conversations are always the same: They talk about 'investment,' which is their code for vanity spending. But when you're sitting here looking around my room, it's hard to argue that you absolutely have to spend 10,000 pounds on a mirror to go in a bathroom. I don't have to argue; this room makes the case."

"So why didn't you bring Jeremy Farrant in here to talk about his shelves?"

Baines half-laughed. "I did. Surprisingly, those shelves weren't that expensive. If you know a good cabinetmaker and he has a good source of wood, then the job is done to a much higher standard and much swifter than if you get a bodger in who breaks things. I'm not suggesting the guy was cheap—simply that in the context of the finished product and the extent of the work he undertook, we got incredibly good value. The carpet, however…" She shut her eyes, shaking her head. "I wince whenever I walk on it, knowing how much it cost and how much we wasted pulling out the old carpet, which was three months old."

She opened her eyes. "The desk has been in his family for generations, ditto the seats, which he had reupholstered at his expense about six months before he was hired. But he's not here for the law; he was hired for his contacts, and his office is like his suit. He has to present a certain image. You see, Boniface, it's all about form and function, and form can have function in context, so that was money I was happy to spend." She relaxed, her tone changing from that of a crusading missionary. "We didn't accidentally spend the money on Jeremy, and we won't have accidentally passed cash to someone in Somalia."

"So are you saying this is fraud?" asked Boniface.

Baines pointed to the filing cabinets. "I doubt it, but that's why I've got the paper, and you can be assured I will check before I do anything else."

twenty-eight

Boniface stared through the plate-glass window onto the poorly lit emptiness of the street outside. The occasional passersby passed by; most looked in their early twenties and on their way to seek out cheap alcohol and the company of others who couldn't stand their own company either. They would reach the end of the night drunk and unhappy, but tell themselves they were having a great time with lots of friends.

"Your bratwurst, gentlemen." The owner of the deli meticulously positioned a plate before each diner. Her German accent was thicker and her tone far more assertive than Chlodwig's. "Can I get you anything else?" As Chlodwig thanked her, Boniface scrutinized his dinner: bratwurst, coleslaw, and a crusty white roll.

The deli was empty apart from the two men and the owner. Any sound—a moved chair, a glass replaced on the hard table—reverberated on the hard surfaces without any human or other soft object to damp the resonance. Anything above a low voice ricocheted around the room, and a whisper became a sibilant snake sneaking into sunlight-starved recesses. Without the usual background noise providing anonymity, Boniface felt exposed.

The German looked up and gave a nervous smile. "I very much appreciate the opportunity to talk, and I'm sorry if this food is not what you're used to. If I change my diet too quickly, my stomach..." He pulled a face. "Let's just say my stomach can be a bit delicate."

Something changed in the German's tone; he seemed to be beginning a story or maybe a moral fable. Boniface continued to eat. "When Greta removed Father from the board, it broke him. He was a proud man, a resourceful man. After the disaster for our country of the Nazis, who Father always hated, and the war, he built up his own small business, which became a very successful shipping company in the Baltic. It was small, well managed, and efficient. It generated good income, which supported the family and paid for all of our education. Losing his business—even to his daughter, but particularly in the way that she snatched it—broke him."

Boniface scanned the room: three tables lined against the window with a counter separating the cooking area. Chlodwig and he were still the only customers, and he suspected that as soon as they left, the deli would close for the evening. Five minutes to finish the meal, five minutes to tell Chlodwig what he had to say, and he could be gone.

A wistful look came across the German's face. "I know everyone remembers their childhood as being perfect, but we really did have a perfect childhood, and much of that happiness was because we had a successful father who was well-respected in the community, and we all loved him dearly."

Chlodwig fell quiet, gazing into the distance, apparently looking back over fifty years. Boniface continued with his dinner, not wanting to interrupt.

"This wasn't enough for Greta. She didn't want small, however successful. She wanted a global business. She had a vision of a fleet. Different ships for carrying different cargoes: grain, coal, even wine or beer. You name it, she wanted to carry it. Once she had all these cargo ships, she bought Regal International Cruise Line, which, quite naturally, had to have the biggest passenger liner. Have you seen the pictures of the ship? It has seventeen decks; it's bigger than an aircraft carrier."

Chlodwig paused. "As a businessman, I understand her strategy. She had a vision for the business and grew Weissenfeld Shipping by buying other shipping lines and then running the combined fleet more efficiently. And you know what? She realized her vision, and she has built a global shipping empire that is hugely successful. But it is nothing like our father's old business. Without her, we would still be running boats across the Baltic."

He hesitated, then continued weakly. "Without her, our business probably would have crumbled because we wouldn't have taken advantage of the efficiencies that are necessary to succeed in business today." He nodded as if agreeing with a conversation going on inside his head. "But this is not the business that Father set up, and it is not that business because Greta's will must prevail. She will always be that spoiled child who was indulged because she was the baby. Because of that force of will, we bought the Montenegro Shipping Line, and those people are all dead."

He stopped, a slightly self-conscious look across his face, his eyes reddening. "I'm sorry, Boniface. I'm going on rather, but my point is simple: Greta gets what Greta wants, irrespective of the costs to others." He fixed his stare on Boniface. "I hope your change of heart isn't because of pressure Greta has put on you."

Boniface sized up the man across the table. There was ten years in age difference between him and his sister. In attitude, it felt like ten generations.

"Of course Greta wasn't happy with me resigning. But, in the very short term, there is a job to be done, and I felt I couldn't walk away from that." Boniface paused, making sure the German had processed the information before he continued. "I will resign. I will resign as soon as I can, but until everyone understands their roles, until the strategy is in place, I can't leave the job incomplete."

He looked to the German, waiting for his confirmation that he could deliver the final line of this argument. "Say this whole thing explodes tomorrow. Half the people implement the strategy, half don't. What have you got? Chaos." He softened his voice. "I'm only there to coordinate—I'm not the one in front of the camera—and I'll be gone in days, not weeks, not months."

"I'm not sure, Boniface."

Boniface tried to keep his voice calm, knowing he was about to take a risk. "Maybe we should bring in Greta? I would suggest we go and see her to discuss this, but I saw her heading out five minutes before we left. From the way she was dressed, I guess she's on a date."

"That was over an hour ago," Chlodwig lifted his wrist and deliberately looked at his watch, "so it will be over by now, and the gentleman will be history."

Boniface was shocked to hear this patrician man become so dismissive. Chlodwig appeared to notice. "It will not end well. She does not respect any man that shows her kindness—all she sees is the weakness that can be exploited, and she detests that." He softened his voice before continuing. "On a Darwinian level, she knows that a kind man would never protect her, so he's no good for her. But if he's the sort of man who does not show that level of kindness—if he is the sort of man who will not bend to her will—then in her mind he cannot love her."

Boniface listened, processing the double negatives. "That's an unwinnable dilemma. What man could ever be good enough for her?"

Chlodwig's voice became very soft, almost a whisper. "When our father died, it was a terrible time. We were all very upset, but Greta—the baby—was in pieces."

He stopped, composed himself, then continued. "Greta was in a terrible state when she heard the news and tried to get hold of her husband, Wolfgang, who was locked in negotiations. He was doing a huge deal with his company. Literally, the doors were locked—the negotiators cut themselves off from the outside; there were no phones, no messages until the deal was sealed."

Boniface finished his last mouthful and listened as Chlodwig continued. "Greta hated that Wolfgang was not available to her. She shouted and screamed at all of us, at the people where the negotiation was going on. We were already hugely upset, and this made everything worse."

"No messages were passed?"

"None. But a message was left at reception, and as soon as Wolfgang heard the news he came home to be with Greta. He was a good man—a kind and loving husband. But when he arrived home—it was a three-hour car journey in winter—all Greta could do was berate him for not staying behind to keep looking at the details of the deal." He took a sip of water. "So you see, it will not end well. She will end the relationship tonight, it will be his fault, and she will line up another man, any man, for tomorrow evening. Poor fellow, as you English would say."

"This is all men?"

Chlodwig paused, looking as if he were making a shameful admission. "There is one person who Greta has yet to dominate and exploit by her force of will, and I'm not convinced that he will win."

Boniface raised his eyebrows.

"Her pet, Regenspurger." Chlodwig spoke with a tightened mouth. "I cannot abide having Stasi thugs on the payroll. Father never would have hired such a person; he's nothing more than a Gestapo man with a different uniform. I understand the necessity for practical people on the ground to sort out problems, but I disapprove of having thugs."

The two men sat in silence as their plates were cleared. Boniface waited until the owner was out of earshot. "Chlodwig, there's a noticeable tension with your sister. Perhaps if you were to go home tomorrow, it would de-escalate the situation?" The flash of tension across Chlodwig's brow passed. "I could be your man on the inside for the next few days."

The German didn't respond.

"Will you at least consider the situation please, Chlodwig? I know you're not happy with me remaining, and I hope you can see that I'm not happy with the situation either. But perhaps, as a short-term fix..."

Chlodwig spoke in measured tones: "Boniface, you are unmistakably trying to persuade me of something—that is your job. But while you are doing that, I think you are missing the simple message that I'm trying to communicate in my slow and ponderous manner: You need to protect your own best interests, and I'm not convinced you're doing that."

twenty-nine

"What do you mean you didn't resign? You need to resign, Boniface." Montbretia looked up at him. He was getting bored with other people's disappointment, but at least Montbretia had the courtesy to show some annoyance in her eyes, scolding him like he was a child. "Phone them now and tell them."

"I can't," Boniface felt himself mumbling. "Not now."

"Can't? Can't!" Montbretia seemed to be moving from exasperation to anger. "Boniface, slavery has been abolished. Nobody can force you to do something." She relaxed, seemingly trying to be more understanding, or perhaps conciliatory. "I thought we agreed. You would see Tommy and Gideon, and then you would resign, leaving you free tomorrow. Or did I not understand this correctly?"

He knew he was in for a pounding. It was almost as if she was tag-teaming with Chlodwig, even though she had never heard of him. It was best to sit back and take a few punches, then when she was tired he could try to explain.

Montbretia's annoyance finally appeared to ebb.

Boniface started gradually, trying to keep his demeanor calm, reassuring, engaging. De-escalate, move past the provocation, get to a better place. "To be honest, I thought they would want me out. Immediately. For them, there is huge potential reputational damage in having me there."

Montbretia flicked out a hand as if saying, "Of course!" Her eyebrows raised—the look of a teenager, but a paragraph of argument communicated without the necessity of speech.

"I was wrong." Montbretia's fixed face fell as Boniface continued. "I can't walk away."

"Do you want me to show you how, Boniface? It's not difficult."

When he had spoken to Montbretia before he left for dinner with Chlodwig, she had said she was in Tilbury, which in itself was surprising. They agreed to meet and talk—the story she told sounded quite alarming. Knowing what he would tell her, he suggested somewhere that wouldn't annoy her—somewhere she would feel comfortable—and undoubtedly, she felt comfortable expressing her disapproval here.

He had chosen well.

A traditional pub in the heart of London's West End, one block north of Shaftesbury Avenue, the London street best known for its preponderance of theatres. The pub was small, with an L-shaped bar giving two ends where customers could find relative seclusion, but it was still big enough for there to be background hum wrapping you like a warm blanket, unlike the Teutonic austerity of Chlodwig's favored bratwurst deli.

The brass fixtures, dark wood, patterned burgundy and blue carpet, and brown leather furniture with alcoves and screening all said "relax, kick your shoes off, and make yourself at home—you're not on display here." He shuddered to think of the reaction if they had met in a hotel bar. Montbretia was allergic to bar nuts, light jazz, and interior design executed on an industrial scale. He knew what she would have said: "It's like the Apple Stores—they bring me out in hives: all that uniformity, all the conformity. I can't stand rooms designed for a cult and filled with smiling dead-behind-the-eyes automatons."

Boniface leaned closer to start his explanation.

"Don't say that it's more complicated than I understand."

Boniface wasn't sure whether Montbretia had issued a threat or an instruction, but he tried to keep his voice light. "Am I allowed to say there are things you don't know, because I haven't told you?"

Her eyes brightened for the first time since he told her that he hadn't resigned. "Yeah. You can say that, Boniface."

Boniface relaxed into his seat. "I've been working with this client, as in getting paid by this client, for about nine months now. Before we met, I was working with the client. While you were still in Turkey and wherever you were before that, and while Ellen was still"—he faltered—"they were paying me."

"This is the same client that you won't tell me who it is?"

Boniface grimaced.

"And for whom there is no documentation in the office?"

"You looked?" Boniface's calm was broken.

"Mmmm." Montbretia stared down, a slight warmth appearing to radiate from her cheeks. "Is this the same client you said you would go and see this morning and resign?"

"I did offer my resignation." Boniface could hear his desperate indignity. "It was the first thing I did, and it was rejected, but believe me, the first thing I'm going to do tomorrow is offer my resignation again."

Montbretia sat with her mouth half open. "Now you're sounding pathetic. How hard can it be to resign?"

"You don't take the money and then resign because it's inconvenient to you." He sat back and exhaled through his nose. "We're ninety percent done. We've rehearsed, and show time is any day now. If they want me to stay, I can't walk away without making them very upset, and an upset client potentially kills the whole business."

"But when we talked you were going to resign. Now you tell me you've been to dinner and that you're staying in a hotel so you can start early. All with a client whose identity I don't know, and apparently can't know."

Boniface opened his mouth—Montbretia held up a finger, commanding him to stop.

"What use are you to your client if you're in jail? Won't it be far more damaging to your client if this whole dead-body-in-the-office issue blows up and spatters onto them? If you've sorted it, then you've immunized them against damage."

She dropped her finger, keeping Boniface fixed in her gaze.

"Let me tell you about Tilbury." Boniface remained still as she continued. "I met science boy in his bunny suit outside the office."

"Science boy?"

"To my shame, I didn't get his name." She brightened. "I got his number."

"Science boy?" Boniface felt able to take a sip of water for the first time since he had begun his conversation with Montbretia.

"He put it in my phone and he put his name as science boy so I wouldn't forget." She looked down. "I don't think anyone has ever cared enough about him before to give him a nickname. I felt like such a cow taking his number. It gives him hope—I could see it in his eyes—hope that will never be fulfilled. If I call him, it will only be because I need something."

She met Boniface's gaze for assurance before she continued. "I started at the Common—I went early."

"I said..."

She shushed him. "I know what you said, and you also said you would resign. Anyway, I took care and didn't get murdered. After that I went to the office, where I met science boy. It sounds like it's going to take a long time to analyze the place, but what he did tell me was that the guy whose body was dumped was alive two days ago. They know that because he was arrested in Tilbury. So I went to Tilbury."

Voices, indistinct but clearly conversations punctuated with the sound of glasses, creaking and squealing doors, and the occasional laugh all faded as Boniface listened to Montbretia telling him about her trip to Tilbury.

"I don't like you taking these risks, Monty. It scares the hell out of me."

"I'm a big girl, Boniface. I spent over two years traveling around the world on my own. I think I know how to look after myself."

"You're missing my point." There was a sharpness in Boniface's retort. "You can do what you want to do—that's fine with me. On the whole, London is one of the safest places you can go. It's not dangerous to walk down a street. It's not dangerous to walk on the Common. But when you go and poke people with a stick, when you seek out dangerous people who may have committed murder in order to poke them with a stick, when you seek them out in isolated places and come back and tell me that some aggressive vagrant asked you for a blow job while you were wearing clothes that could be ripped off and shoes that you couldn't run in, when the only reason you went was to help me—then I get scared, and I think I'm allowed to ask you not to take any risks on my behalf." He fixed her with a stare. "Take risks for yourself, not for me."

"You need to get off your ass. You don't get to change the rules, Boniface. Not when you're ignoring the rules and when you're not defending yourself." He sat straighter. "I do have a stake here. Whose room was the body left in? Are you sure that it's you they're after?" She pointed a finger apparently for emphasis, continuing in a calmer manner. "I would have gone with you. It would have been fun to take you along to the god-forgotten hole that is Tilbury, but, oh yeah, you were working with your special client."

"You make it sound as if I've done nothing all day."

"No. *You* make it sound as if you've done nothing all day. You don't get credit for doing the complete opposite of what you said you would do, no matter how much you try to spin it."

"But I did go and see Gideon and Tommy—Gideon three times, once without clothes on."

"Yuck!" Montbretia sat open-mouthed.

"For the whole conversation, while he was telling me about his exploits with last night's paramour, and picking chocolate... Anyway, I left and came back when he was dressed."

"Yuck, yuck, yuck." Montbretia shuddered. "Please tell me you got something useful from these two."

"I did." Boniface leaned toward Montbretia, looking left to right, and whispered. "Tommy loves you."

"What?"

"Tommy loves you. Seriously. Thinks you're a charming lady who treated him well and didn't judge him on the basis of how he looked or because his son is a murdering rapist."

"Gideon? What did you get from him apart from an image burned into your brain, which they'll find if you donate your brain to medical science?"

"Good news, bad news. Which do you want first?" asked Boniface.

Montbretia thought for a moment. "Shall we start with the good?"

"Gideon has offered his body for your pleasure."

"I thought we were starting with the good news." Montbretia had the look of someone who had just eaten something unpleasant and was looking for somewhere to discreetly spit it out.

"The good news, as much is it's good, is that he's pretty sure it's not political."

"How's that...?" Montbretia stopped herself. "So what's the bad news?"

"The bad news is he's backing off. The cops think I know more than I'm telling, and with his sex-crimes campaign he wants some distance." Montbretia frowned as Boniface continued. "In short, he can't be portrayed as being anti-rape but pro-murderer."

"But..."

Boniface stopped talking and waited for Montbretia to play the scenarios in her head. When she relaxed back into her seat without offering any argument, he continued. "I think we both need some sleep. Do you want me to get you a room at the hotel?"

"Nah. I prefer my own bed." She waited for a beat. "And I really want to wear my own clothes tomorrow. There's a reason why you don't see me in pantsuits."

"You can stay at my place if you want."

"Thanks, but the only clothes I've got there are my pink gym clothes, and I won't be seen in public wearing those."

"What? You've got photographers following you?"

"No. But I have standards, Boniface, and there's stuff I've got to get for tomorrow."

Boniface let his eyelids affirm his agreement. "Will you at least let me pay for a taxi to take you home?"

"Deal," said Montbretia.

"Let's have dinner tomorrow night. Hopefully the situation will have moved forward by then."

thirty

The dark blue Mercedes, approximately the size of a Dutch barge, wallowed up the road, drawing to a halt outside the Weissenfeld offices. The driver got out and held the door open for the passenger with very high heels, who exited without acknowledgement as she continued her phone conversation while passing through gates and doors that automatically opened, subsuming her within the building.

Within thirty seconds Boniface was at the gate. The gate was closed, the car gone, and there were no people to usher him inside. He waited for the gate to unlock, passed through the garden, entered the former house, and took the stairs two at a time. "Morning, Len. I need to catch the lady; I'll be back for a chat in two minutes." Reaching the top floor, he followed the winding passage to Sophie's desk.

He stretched for the handle to Greta's office. "She is on the telephone."

Boniface straightened and turned to see Sophie's unsmiling face. Beside her desk a tall, skinny man in his early twenties stood, his eyes unnaturally open like he had a permanent surprise. His brown suit camouflaged him against the office furniture, and the large stack of files he clutched, like a mother holding a baby who had been pulled out of the rubble after a natural disaster, offered some sort of protection.

"I'll wait." Boniface moved away from the door, becoming aware that he could hear the otherwise noiseless man breathing in but not out. With each inhalation, his head twitched.

"She is busy today," said Sophie in a flat voice.

"All day?"

"Yes, Mister Boniface, all day." Sophie looked down at a day planner, running her finger over each appointment listed. "All day." She raised her head from the planner, her eyes looking away from Boniface and toward the stranger who turned, noiseless apart from his inhalation, and started to walk away from them, his steps uneven beats as if he were about to break into a canter.

"No gaps? No slivers of time?"

"No." Sophie was using vocal sounds but without attaching any emotion. Boniface wasn't sure whether that was a "no, I'm sorry" or maybe a "no, let me see what I can do" or even "there's loads of free time, but Greta doesn't want to see you."

"Can we change her schedule? Slip in five minutes here or there?" As the words fell out of his mouth, he realized he was suggesting something Sophie knew to be impossible. Boniface was the person telling the Nobel Laureate that, in truth, gravity doesn't exist.

"Why would we do that? What do we do with the meetings that have already been scheduled?" Sophie slipped along a path between baffled and bemused.

It was too early. Boniface had done what was expected—he stayed in a hotel and was at the office at 7:30. That was enough drama for the day. "Can you tell her I want to talk to her as soon as possible? If she's looking for me, I'll be with Brad Phipps."

He dropped down the steps to the security desk. "Lennie."

"Boniface."

"I'm looking for Brad. Where would I find his office?"

The guard pointed downward. "But he's not there yet."

"Could we?" Joanna Baines, the joyless CFO with the £15 filing cabinets, ascended from the floor below, a finger pointing Boniface in the direction of her office.

thirty-one

"Boniface." Joanna Baines had her back to the door and hadn't turned around when Boniface entered. "MV Paranoid."

"I beg your pardon." Boniface wasn't sure whether he was more surprised by the CFO's utterance or by the gangly youth Boniface had last seen with Sophie Driesdorfer, but who was now sitting at Baines's table, his pile of files looking ready to fall and crush him.

"Motor Vessel Paranoid," said Baines.

"You've lost me," said Boniface, looking between her and the acned face of the young man who was still twitching as he inhaled.

"The previous owner—indeed, the founder—of the Montenegro Shipping Line was a big fan of Black Sabbath."

Boniface wasn't sure whether she had finished speaking or if she had paused for dramatic effect. He watched as she rounded her desk, then met his gaze.

"He christened each ship in his fleet after Sabbath albums, so we've got MV Master of Reality, MV Sabbath Bloody Sabbath, and MV Sabotage, which is a really stupid name for a ship that you are intending to insure through Lloyd's of London." She gave a look that he took to be embarrassment, the first time Boniface had seen her express any emotion. "MV Paranoid is the ship that went to Somalia."

"That's good, isn't it?" asked Boniface.

The muscles in Joanna Baines's face faltered. "We've only been able to go so far through the records since we spoke yesterday." Her head swiveled to look at the thin man sitting at her desk before turning back to Boniface. "By the way, have you met Brian? Brian Singleton."

"I saw you up..." Boniface stopped himself—better to remain diplomatic and not mention where he saw the younger man. "I've seen you around. Good to meet you."

The younger man mumbled something and continued to twitch as he breathed in noisily.

"You can blame Boniface for not going home last night," Baines addressed Singleton before she turned back to Boniface. "To confirm, the dates you told me yesterday were?"

"Leaving Brindisi on 10 October, dumping in Somalia on 15 November."

Baines glanced at Brian Singleton and nodded. "We've been through the papers we've got here, and the Paranoid was definitely in Somalia—there are expenses recorded." She extended her arm, waiting until Singleton put a piece of paper in her hand. "The full itinerary that we can reconstruct from our records is: 21 September leaves Brindisi, 30 September stops in Rotterdam, 10 October back in Brindisi, 25 October Ivory Coast."

Boniface glanced up from his notepad, where he was busily scribbling the details as Baines recounted them. "Ivory Coast?"

"Correct, Ivory Coast, the last stop before they arrived in Somalia on 15 November."

"So that's it?" asked Boniface. "That's the proof that the Montenegro Shipping Line sanctioned the dumping?"

"Quite the opposite," said Baines, her voice strident. "That's the evidence that MV Paranoid visited those ports. We have transactions that can be traced to each location. What we have no evidence to suggest was that there were any substantial cash transactions."

Boniface inhaled sharply through his teeth. "In that case I had better get out your way and let you do some more digging."

"I think you misunderstand, Boniface." The CFO's voice was firm. "I'm telling you that we are not the source of the dumping. Our ship may have carried the waste, but we didn't pay for the waste to be taken."

Boniface put his notebook back in his pocket before he continued. "You carried the waste. You dumped the waste. It's enough to crucify the company, and this is why I need us to get to the position where everyone understands what happens next and how we run this thing in a way that minimizes the damage for the business."

"This, I'm afraid, is where I have a problem," said Baines.

"Go on," said Boniface, trying to keep his tone measured.

"There are several aspects here. First, the strategy you outlined yesterday is to essentially throw our hands in the air and say, 'Yup, we did it.'" Boniface raised his eyebrows slightly as the CFO continued. "In other words, you want us to legally admit guilt and assume an open-ended liability. When I hear the words unquantifiable loss, I come out in a rash. I also know that as an officer of this company—a publicly listed company—I am required by virtue of my directorship to ensure that we make an immediate report to the Stock Exchange because I have information that may have a material impact on our share price."

"I don't think you've got the strategy quite right," said Boniface. "Can I explain?"

"Hold on a moment," said Joanna. "Before you explain, could I bring up my second point?"

"Please." Boniface sat back and listened; out of the side of his eye he caught Brian Singleton pushing himself back into his chair, his unnaturally wide eyes making him look shocked at the objections coming from his boss.

"We've got a marketing and PR guy. You've probably heard; his name's Brad."

"I was on my way to see him when you diverted me," said Boniface.

"The point of Brad, if you will, is to be a central resource to remove duplication and to bring efficiency. As you can guess, it was my idea to create the role."

"Makes a lot of sense," said Boniface.

"I'm not sure how much work you've done to date, Boniface, but going forward it should be Brad that handles these issues. It seems like you've glossed over some of the fundamentals, like the necessity to talk to the Stock Exchange, so why don't you go and have a chat with Brad and leave us to it? Send your invoice directly to Brian, and he'll deal with it without delay."

thirty-two

After five minutes Boniface gave up listening.

The call had come in; Brad had answered.

That annoyed Boniface, but he could tolerate a brief interruption—he wasn't sure whether the tall, slim All-American kid who was in reality Canadian had an assistant who would take messages, and voicemail can be very impersonal. He was more annoyed when Brad didn't ask to call back, instead launching into the conversation as if there wasn't someone else he was already talking with.

Boniface might have been more accepting—perhaps it was a genuinely important call. However, apparently Brad took all his calls on speakerphone and, while talking, walked around the room playing basketball with the small ball that seemed to live on his desk and the matching small hoop—which Boniface was sure was meant to go over a wastepaper basket as a weak joke—that was attached to his door, which the Canadian closed with a hefty kick.

After the first minute, Boniface was convinced Brad was talking to a friend. By minute three, Boniface was sure it was a supplier to Weissenfeld—someone who had to suck up to the company to keep getting paid. By minute four the stomach-turning realization hit him that this was someone who Brad was trying to positively influence. This was someone on whom Brad was unleashing his full marketing and PR arsenal.

Boniface was used to conversations with nouns and verbs. Sometimes adverbs and adjectives could be thrown in with more sophisticated audiences, but when he got away from nouns and verbs, he became twitchy. By contrast, Brad's conversations used words he didn't understand, punctuated with a number of vocal noises and with a regular supply of words that didn't mean anything. "Yo" was employed both as a greeting and as a replacement for the word "your"; "awesome," "dude," and "bro," which appeared interchangeable; along with the equally flexible "yer feel," "cool," and "alright." Except Brad didn't say alright. Instead, he tended to say alllllll-riiiiiii-ide. He pronounced Ts as Ds, but then again, so did most country singers.

He knew it would be a painful experience when the conversation began. "Yo, man! You're that Boniface guy, right? Good to meet you, man." But when Boniface started to explain the problem and Brad called it "awesomely gruesome," Boniface felt himself begin to die inside.

Boniface felt no more enthusiastic about the discussion that would follow. As he tried to ignore the phone conversation assaulting his ears, he looked around the room, paying attention to the details, but couldn't find a space larger than three inches square. The rest of the room was covered with sports memorabilia—Brad was manifestly both a keen participant and an enthusiastic follower, particularly of hockey.

Boniface made a mental note to call it ice hockey. He knew it would upset Brad.

Between the autographed hockey sticks and many pucks, there were several basketballs, all autographed and in glass cabinets, awards, and photos, most of which were autographed, and those that weren't had a man who looked remarkably like

Brad growing up over the years—tall, blonde, slim but fit, with clear skin that always had a slight tan from being outside.

The phone call ended, and Brad continued without a pause. "Look Boniface, I'll be honest. In this company they're a bit...I don't wanna say slow, but y'know...they're kinda old school." He inclined his head as if concluding after deep cogitation—his sign, a hint to Boniface: professional-to-professional, chewing the fat. "They don't get how you do business these days. I told them we need to get the company name on soccer jerseys. The premier league—the English league, right—is the biggest league in the world, right? We should be there, right?"

"When you say we, you mean Weissenfeld Shipping?"

"Who else could I mean, Boniface?"

"The people who charter ships go to the subsidiary companies, like the Montenegro Shipping Line, so they have no knowledge of the Weissenfeld brand."

"Precisely, Boniface. They don't know the brand, which is why we need to be on soccer jerseys."

Boniface was figuring out how to respond to the basic *who's your customer— which brand do they recognize* misunderstanding, but Brad was continuing. "You try telling them about search engine advertising—you know, keywords when people search Google—and it's like you're speaking a foreign language."

"But aren't there a limited number of shipping companies, and a limited number of people who charter ships, so everyone pretty much knows everyone already?"

"Precisely, Boniface. So when someone searches for shipping, they should find us, and if we don't advertise, they won't find us. I mean, it's obvious, isn't it? But apparently not to them upstairs."

It wasn't obvious to Boniface what the benefit to Weissenfeld would be, so he let it slide and tried to get back on track. "So, Somalia."

"Yeah. Like bad. Just *the* worst." Boniface marveled at how the English language could be mangled by a man who seemed to have a total lack of any real empathy beyond a slogan.

"We're still clarifying details—"

"Whatever, dude. There's a boat in Africa, I get it." Brad was back in his chair, spinning and rocking. Boniface suspected he was medicated for ADHD symptoms as a youngster, whether he needed the treatment or not.

"No one knew what the cargo was—and still no one knows what the cargo was. No one cared what the cargo was, so the locals—as far as we can tell—unloaded it and moved it from the port and left it where they drop all their other waste, right next to a squatter town."

"So why don't we say 'Yo! Yo deal with it!' and come home?" He thrust his chest forward and shoulders back, swaggering.

"Well..." Boniface counted to ten, then continued. "It's a tricky legal situation. There is culpability, there is a money trail—although there is some dispute—and there are photographs. Also, let's not forget the dudette-in-chief." He noticed Brad's eyes flick as he tried to mimic the other man's language. "There is the desire on Greta's part to do something, but it's not as easy as reaching into her pocket. There are implications. You can't say 'We're responsible for ten percent of the problem' or 'We only killed eighty-six people.' It doesn't work like that. As soon as you admit any liability, you open yourself up to all liabilities. Those liabilities could bankrupt the company or tie it up in incredibly complicated and tedious litigation for years, and no one knows what reputational damage that would do."

Brad looked blankly.

"So that's the background. But we didn't want to force the problem prematurely into the open, and we can't be flat-footed if the story breaks, so we've been working to provide context around..."

"What context is there?" Brad seemed agitated. "People died, right?"

Boniface stopped himself from sighing. "People died. But dangerous chemicals don't happen in a vacuum. People don't say, 'Hey, let's go and find some nasty chemicals to move around the world.' Noxious chemicals are a byproduct of the manufacturing process, so what we are trying to do is reinforce the causal link between consumer consumption and waste products."

Brad frowned. He had the look of a confused man who didn't know what question to ask.

Boniface continued. "In short, we want to say, 'If you don't want the nasty chemicals that require disposal, then stop buying electronic gadgets.'"

Brad nodded, as if he was pleased to see that Boniface had reached an understanding that was self-evident to him.

Boniface tried to hide his annoyance as he continued. "We've also done a lot of work to manage the information people will find when they search."

"What? Like when they Google?"

Boniface wondered whether he could have his head fitted with an exasperation valve. "We wanted more than that. What we wanted was a central forum where all the issues associated with globalization could be discussed. All the issues: the manufacturing process, economics for the producer countries, economies of the countries exporting jobs, the logistics, the product benefits, and so on. The first manifestation of this forum was a website, but naturally, the intention is to build into the real world starting with conferences and some high-level summits."

He saw nothing in Brad's eyes. Nothing. No spark. No recognition. No understanding. No thought about how this tool could be exploited for his own advantage. Nothing. Whatever was there before had slipped away.

"The first step has been a website where we have encouraged some interesting discussions, and I think we've also been able to demonstrate a level of independence by coordinating criticism of the industries and calling on academics to submit papers, but we've also made sure there are enough realists that the necessities and the pragmatism are seen."

The word "website" elicited a response in Brad in the same way that a loved one's voice might elicit a response in a coma victim. But as with a coma victim, you never knew whether they were responding to the stimulus or having a dream.

"Now, because the website is so authoritative since it has leading experts contributing and linking to it as they discuss the issues, the site has been gradually rising up the search engine rankings. As it has risen, more people have linked to it—so now, for instance, we have links from the BBC, the FT, CNN, and The Wall Street Journal. With those links we're now showing in the top two or three listings in the search results for all the major search engines, in all territories."

"Big whoop. You set up a website. That's like, what? An afternoon's work?"

Boniface contemplated the hockey sticks: It wouldn't be the first time that one had been used in a murder, and he was already suspected of murder, so why not be accused for one he *did* commit?

"It's not like selling widgets. We're trying to do something with a lot of moving parts. First, we've created a forum with a network of experts discussing the issues. Some are more disposed to us, others more against, but if the press contact them, they will give a rounded view of the issue. And that's the other half of the story: If you search for any related issues—so if you drop Somalia, toxic waste, and Weissenfeld into a search engine—what pops up at the top of the list? So we don't just get found: The right message with all the complexity around the issues and a bunch of sympathetic experts gets found. It ranks way above any conspiracy nut-job site."

Brad sighed. "Man. You are making it way, way, *way* too complicated. "SEO— y'know, search engine optimization—ain't rocket science, Boniface. You get an agency to buy links."

"Which get blocked by Google for trying to pervert their system." Boniface heard his snappiness. "This isn't search engine optimization—this is about creating a sympathetic community of experts to push our case."

"Man, I hear what you're saying. But, y'know, you're starting to sound old school—there's a much faster way to solve this problem." He picked up his mini basketball. "I should be leading this, right? I do PR around here, yeah? I'm the new broom brought in to shake stuff."

He turned, dropping the ball. "I mean, like, when something goes wrong, I know who to call." His eyes moved to his unnaturally tidy desk, from where he picked up a plastic folder. "See. I've got a list of all the people I can call at newspapers." He brightened. "Joanna paid some dude on the internet like twenty bucks to research this list, so we're covered."

thirty-three

Boniface stepped into the corridor, closing the door on the Canadian.

He tried to keep his feet firmly placed on the black-and-white-checked marble tiles running across the floor as he felt the tension at the back of his head—the anger boring into his brain stem—and waited, willing the pain to subside. When he felt he could turn the pain into an ache, he swore under his breath, and kept swearing as he walked up the stairs to the security guard's desk.

He stood in front of Lennie, motionless, his eyes wide.

Lennie nodded.

Boniface's look became more aggressive—his head lowered, and he continued to fixate on the guard, his eyes looking up.

"I'm an old soldier. I was hired to take orders. Orders come down from the lady general; I pick up my weapon, attach the bayonet, and go over the top into battle. I don't ask questions."

"But he's a..." Boniface let out an infuriated sigh, his eyes drifting up to the next floor, where Sophie and the rather odd man he now knew to be Brian Singleton were standing at the top of the stairs facing each other—as far as Boniface could tell, neither social misfit was speaking.

"I follow my orders." Lennie winked. "But in the fog of war there are accidental casualties." He let out a long and heartfelt sigh. "You can be assured that I would carry out my duty and bury the dead." A look of satisfaction had appeared across his face, which fell away as Boniface's phone rang.

"Boniface." He answered. "Tommy." He felt surprise in his voice, becoming aware he was talking too loudly. He moved away from the security guard, holding his phone closely, talking in a soft voice. "I can. I'll see you there."

A cantering step and the sound of inhalation caught Boniface's attention, and he nodded to acknowledge Brian Singleton as he walked past, his head twitching as he inhaled. Boniface replaced his phone in his pocket, turning back to Lennie as he continued. "What's your take on him?" He tilted his head in the direction that Joanna Baines's galley slave had cantered.

"An odd one, but he's meant to be very good at his job and incredibly detail focused, which I guess is what you want in a numbers man."

"Odd how?" asked Boniface.

"Lives with his mother, who makes him sandwiches. Fixed routines—has to go for a walk at twelve-forty-seven each day, always leaves the gate and turns left, returns after precisely twenty-six minutes." The security guard stepped back and looked from side to side before leaning toward Boniface to continue. "I've never had a conversation with him, but as I say, odd with routines and probably harmless."

Boniface took in Lennie's comments. "Catch you later," he said, moving toward the staircase.

For the second time that morning, Boniface wound around to Greta's office, managing to touch the door handle before he heard Sophie's sharp tones. "Was I not clear? She is busy all day." Boniface had not seen her behind her desk.

"I need to see her. You will let her know." The dumpy German made eye contact with Boniface and continued with her work. "I'll be with Jeremy Farrant, but I want to get a breath of fresh air first."

"In London?" Her head oscillated slightly as she laughed to herself, and seemingly having answered her own question, she looked up at Boniface. "Why are you telling your movements? Fraulein Weissenfeld doesn't want to see you. Do you think I am responsible for you?"

thirty-four

"I'm like you; I like to speak face to face."

Boniface scanned the café. It hadn't changed since yesterday. In truth, it probably hadn't changed much in the last 50 years. Some of the clientele might be different, but the red-and-white-checked tiles, the Formica tables with bench seating, and the stainless-steel counter, they were definitely unchanged.

Tommy's suit had changed—Boniface noticed the different belt, which led him to see a fractionally different fabric color.

Tommy whispered. "I had a word. You know, *a word*, with some of my former associates who may—not saying are, but may—be on the wrong side of certain lines from time to time, and who know people who definitely are. That's why I thought we should, you know, face to face."

Boniface mentally calculated the time he had wasted getting a cab halfway across town to listen to Tommy's tales from beaten-down criminals who didn't have the sense to get out of the game. "Thanks, Tommy. I appreciate it," he lied.

"Anyway," Tommy was still whispering, although Boniface couldn't figure why. "I've had a word, and they all say that this is an outsider job. No one has been asked to do any work in Wimbledon." He continued, louder but with an almost apologetic tone. "If I knew what had happened, I could ask more direct questions."

Boniface sat back and took a sip of tea—Tommy had ensured a freshly drawn pot was delivered between the time Boniface entered the café and when he sat down. He exhaled, then spoke quickly and lightly. "A dead body was dumped in my office."

Tommy looked visibly shocked. "A dead body—your office?"

"Montbretia's office, actually. But definitely a body. Very definitely deceased."

Individual muscles in Tommy's face twitched as he seemed to process what he had just heard. "That's serious. You don't leave a body unless you have real need to say something." He had another thought. "The cops think you're involved?"

Boniface exhaled again. "Yup. I am their prime suspect, and if I didn't do it, then I know more than I'm telling them."

"Do you know who he was? The dead bloke."

"All I know, Tommy, is that he was dead in my office, but he was alive and well, and arrested in Tilbury, two days before we found him. He was a vagrant."

"Tilbury? Town or docks?"

"Docks, I think. Does it matter?"

"No, but you've got big trouble, Boniface." Tommy sat back, visibly shaken, as if someone had given him a diagnosis that he had three months to live. "I said this was an outside job. It is, and it's professional." He stared straight at Boniface, his voice low and measured. "Who do you know with connections to shipping?"

Boniface let a silence fall between him and Tommy. The rest of the café still resonated to the sound of cooking, chinaware, and conversations about sport, but an icy chill surrounded Tommy and Boniface.

"You're being crazy, Tommy." He caught what he had said. "I mean that in the nicest possible way. But surely you're exaggerating."

"I know Tilbury docks, Boniface. One of the reasons why I moved down from Derbyshire was because there was good scrap-metal business going through the London docks, and you know I've done well out of my business. I've done well because I've got to know the people at the docks. Some of them are lovely lads... some of them..."

"Really, Tommy? Is it that bad?"

"It's like anywhere. Most of it is fine. But around the edges, that's where the problems come, and Tilbury has more edges than most places." He took a mouthful of his bacon sandwich and continued. "You see, Tilbury has vast numbers of people coming through—they're either coming or going. Nobody ever stays in Tilbury—they're always passing and passing quickly."

"That's what Montbretia said," offered Boniface.

"Why does she know Tilbury?" There was concern in Tommy's voice.

"She went there yesterday."

"You idiot, Boniface. I thought you cared for that girl." Tommy's face reddened. "It's not the sort of place for someone like her."

"She's tough," offered Boniface.

"I don't care how tough, she ain't a criminal, she won't think like a criminal to avoid getting in trouble." Tommy looked up. "I'm serious, Boniface—you look after that girl."

Boniface mumbled some sort of affirmation. "So people come, people go. That doesn't make it bad."

"No. But it makes it easy. Say you decide to send someone a message. Say you drop a stiff in someone's office." Tommy lowered his voice. "If you know someone who can get people in and out on a ship without paperwork, you import a couple of guys from East Europe or somewhere. Give them an old van. They pick up the first vagrant they see near the docks and beat the guy over the head." Tommy looked up at Boniface. "The body was beaten over the head, wasn't it?"

Boniface felt his lower jaw hanging loose.

"Beat them over the head. Take them to wherever. Drop the body. Take the van somewhere. Burn it. Get back to Tilbury and get on a boat. They'll be out before the cops have found the body. Whoever dumped the body will be gone by now."

Boniface still couldn't speak.

"And if they want someone to disappear, having access to a boat is a great way to dump a body. They don't last long on the North Sea, and any sailor who might witness what went on ain't British and will be out of the country for months, if not years or forever."

thirty–five

He flipped the small silver box out of his pocket, opened the lid, took a pinch, put his fingers up his left nostril, and sniffed. Then repeated with his right nostril. As he had been yesterday, the small man was immaculately presented, wearing another tailored three-piece suit, this one charcoal with a narrow herringbone stripe, and a silk handkerchief in his top pocket. However, this piece of silk was worn with more of a peacock flourish than Gideon would have welcomed, having a lighter shade than the politician would have settled on.

"For you?" Jeremy Farrant held his silver snuffbox between his thumb and his index finger and looked over his half-moon glasses at his guest. Boniface declined. He was sitting on the same green leather scroll-armed club chair that he had sat on yesterday, but today he contemplated the room in a different light. Remembering what Joanna Baines had told him, he somehow felt less uncomfortable knowing he was sitting on Farrant's family furniture. But he also recalled the often-used definition of new money: Someone who bought their own furniture.

"You're an interesting old chap, aren't you, Boniface? Far more interesting than I expected after our brief exchange yesterday." He took out two green files, dropping one on the far side of his desk and opening the closer one as he sat down behind the huge lump of old wood.

"Soooooo. A journalist. Made your name with the Stan Gadson affair. Your research led to the MP resigning and ultimately his researcher receiving a jail sentence, and as their stars fell, yours rose and there followed ten years of what can only be called great success. You were a very well-regarded journalist, and through that time you were married to another journalist: Veronica Rutherford, now the editor of the *European Daily Herald*, owned by the charming Ivan Kuznetsov."

Boniface could hear the attempt at sarcasm as his host said the word "charming."

Farrant looked up, keeping his finger on the page. "But this isn't news for you."

"It's only news that you care about what I did fifteen years ago."

"It behooves me to check. It's important that we know who we're dealing with, wouldn't you agree, Mister Boniface? Telling you what you already know is hardly useful information, but it does give us an opportunity to have a discussion." He lifted the side of the file that was closer to Boniface. "Here. This copy is for you."

"Thanks, but I don't feel the compulsion to read the file—I was there. I saw the movie; indeed, you may say that I was the author and the screenwriter."

"Quite so." The small man gave a patronizing smile, wrinkling his nose and narrowing his eyes. "So you are expecting that the file will cover the end of your marriage, the meltdown, the alcoholism, the time with Her Majesty's Government, that unfortunate incident and the brief relapse, and the establishment of your own business?"

Boniface sat up straighter, twisting to face Farrant. "If when you say 'unfortunate incident' you mean the one with the car, the solid object with which the car came into contact while I was in charge, having more alcohol than a distillery in my veins—indeed, I think it would be more accurate for you to say I had blood in my alcohol—with the resulting and continuing driving ban, and the additional treatment, then yes. That seems a fair summary."

The older man wrote a few notes on his file as Boniface continued. "But that was the day when everything changed, and since then I've been a good boy with no relapses."

"I must say, for an alcoholic—sorry, for a *former* alcoholic—you are incredibly well presented, Mister Boniface. Good skin, no weight problem—as you know, there is a tendency to balloon or wither, depending on the chosen poison—and you can unequivocally dress yourself and have found yourself a good tailor."

Boniface's eyebrows flicked.

"Your belt, Mister Boniface. Or rather, the lack of a belt and the absence of belt loops. Always a definitive giveaway. But also, the suit fits you. You can see it when you move—there are no odd wrinkles or pulls as you flex."

Boniface relaxed as the small man continued. "If I may make a suggestion, however. Your shoes. Beyond doubt you bought those in a shop...and they look like a suitably stout pair of brogues, but you would appreciate the difference if you found yourself a decent cobbler. A small luxury, but worth it. I'll get my assistant to give you details of mine."

Boniface found himself almost ready to thank the man who had refused to talk to him yesterday and in the intervening period appeared to have carried out a detailed background check worthy of the security services. But as Farrant continued, Boniface lost the urge.

"Now you have your own firm." He stopped scratching notes and returned the lid to his pen. "I thought public relations, whatever that means, was the domain of well-mannered young ladies who went to a good school before being finished, but who would never amount to much in the employment field, and yet had a yen to prove—however fallaciously—that they weren't wholly dependent on daddy's money before they married into the role of breeding the next generation of the aristocracy and the moneyed classes."

The lawyer stood, leisurely starting to walk around his desk toward the windows. Boniface gazed at the hand-stitched leather on his feet gliding over the olive green expense that upset the CFO so desperately.

"I looked at your website, and I saw that PR is so much more than well-turned-out girls and press releases: There's crisis management." He held his hands up, his mouth open, aping a cliché of a shocked person. "Communications." He pulled a serious face. "Strategic advice." He held his chin in his hand as if thinking. "Apparently we're living in the electronic age where stories can't be squashed, so we should all embrace engagement and openness." He shook his head in a theatrical flourish. "It's all quite beyond me, which is why our glorious leader called you, I presume."

"If you've finished patronizing," muttered Boniface without bothering to move his eyes toward the small man. "That's how it started."

"I spoke to Joanna last night. She briefed me after you had your little chat. Then I told her I wanted to spend fifty pence." The lawyer moved the muscles in his face as if trying to express happiness. "She's like a boring grandparent. A boring grandparent who doesn't want to spend any money but feels we are obligated to immediately report this matter to the Stock Exchange."

He turned and looked out the window. "Let me be sure I've got this right. Dollars were paid, and there are photographs."

"Dollars paid, but Joanna disputes their source," said Boniface. "The photographs and documentary evidence of a Montenegro Shipping Line vessel having been in Somalia are beyond disputable."

He seemed peeved at Boniface's interruption but continued. "We have Weissenfeld—one of the biggest global shipping concerns—and we believe there are people who assume we have very deep pockets from which they can extract money due to the apparent facts."

"That's about it," said Boniface. "But there is an ironic twist." The lawyer turned to face him, apparently intrigued. "The irony is that most dumpers drop their waste into the sea off Somalia. For all their faults and foul-ups, our crew at least tried to do the right thing and pay for their waste to be taken. If they had dumped it, we wouldn't have this issue."

"So, quite literally," the lawyer spoke evenly, "we have people with enough brains to be dangerous." He paced forward and sat on the sofa opposite Boniface with the same caution he would employ if he were wearing a short skirt. "Now, Boniface. Your approach?"

"My strategy is the long game. In short, avoid any flash points so the issue can be managed."

Farrant nodded.

"The difficulty for Weissenfeld is if the story suddenly blows. If there are headlines saying Weissenfeld has killed hundreds, the reputation damage would be immense and lasting." Boniface relaxed, feeling able to explain with greater detail. "But if a story breaks about a company standing up and taking responsibility in an industry with a high death rate, working in a country with an incredibly high death rate, well...it's not news. Also—and this is the bit you'll like—it changes the definition of loss, so it immunizes you against court action."

The lawyer continued to nod.

"There are other benefits to this approach," said Boniface. "By having a process which you are proactively managing, you are keeping your hand on the cost lever. It's the ongoing nature of that cost which has upset Joanna. She's far more in favor of determining—and paying out—the cost now and amortizing it, ironically, over the future life expectancy of the victims."

The lawyer pursed his lips. "That's a very detailed and well-thought-through strategy, Boniface. Take a problem, morph it into something else—something else that greatly reduces the risk of court action and makes you look like the good guy over a sustained period. Very smart." He sat back in his chair, his voice becoming snappy. "But we can't do it. It's not practical."

Boniface jolted.

"Look, Boniface. We appreciate your hard work thinking about possible solutions, but this is incontrovertibly a legal matter. The determination of whose liability it is and of the amount of liability...those are all legal matters which fall within my purview, so I'll take it from here. I think the first thing is to get an injunction to prevent any publicity. I'll instruct counsel on the matter this afternoon; there is no reason to delay."

"But in the age of the internet..."

The lawyer cut him off. "In the age of the internet, the law of the land still applies." His tone became soothing, reassuring. "Look Boniface, I like your strategy—it's very clever in theory. But we don't have the time to wait. We can't keep implementing that program over years—over years where there are no guarantees about the amount of our liabilities. No, the only solution is to get an injunction and to cut this off in the courts."

thirty-six

Boniface's back was toward the corner of Weissenfeld Shipping's London office as he contemplated the buildings across the road intersection.

He slipped out his phone. 12:43. He cast a glance up the hill to the entrance gate to the office before returning his gaze to the central London streets.

Mayfair, where business and residential overlap, is a strange place at lunchtime. Residents either are inside eating or have gone out to eat. In either case, they're not on the street. Construction crews tend to sit in a line on the curb to have a smoke and share a two-liter bottle of warm soda.

The executives in offices need to support the conceit that they're too busy to be away from their desks, even for the time it takes to pee. They can scientifically prove this assertion by bragging about the cost of rent for their office. The only group of people who go out to find something to eat are the administrative staff from the offices, in particular, those sent by their too-busy bosses to get them some food.

Since the administrative staff will walk to the nearest sandwich bar, there is little requirement for motorized transport, which means that apart from a few delivery drivers, the only vehicles on the road are those passing across Mayfair or taking advantage of a shortcut to avoid the jams on the four main roads bounding the rich man's ghetto.

Boniface checked his phone again. 12:46. He watched the second count, clicking over to 12:47. Thirty-eight seconds later, the lolloping figure in the brown suit came out of the gate and started walking down the gentle hill. Boniface tried to pace his steps: one long, one short, one long, one short. He lightly tapped his hip with each step and found himself tapping a classic shuffle rhythm, as Brian Singleton drew toward him.

"Good afternoon, Brian." Boniface relaxed his face, trying not to intimidate the accountant. A sound dropped out of Singleton's mouth, but nothing Boniface could understand as English.

The interaction did nothing to slow the younger man's pace as he passed Boniface, crossing the street and heading down the hill. He continued without breaking pace, without looking back. Boniface observed, sensing the rhythm—long stride, short stride—as Singleton moved, not limping, not showing any disability.

He had covered about 20 yards before Boniface started to jog, slowing as he drew level, and matching his pace. "I heard you like to walk. Mind if I join you?"

A noise came from the other man. Nothing specific, only a noise, but enough to suggest to Boniface that his swift-cantering companion had not dissented.

They reached the next intersection and crossed diagonally, turning right into a small mews-style road with street-level garages under townhouses on one side, and bijou terraces on the opposite. "I've got a bit of a delicate matter to discuss," said Boniface. "I think you've got an admirer in the office."

The younger man continued, his rhythm steady.

"It's Sophie."

Boniface listened as the accounting galley slave's rhythm missed a beat, quickly recovering and continuing at its brisk pace.

"I need your help. Could we slow down or pause for a moment?"

The accountant slowed, then stopped. Boniface felt his heart thumping as he pulled in extra oxygen, pleased that the physical exertion was over. He turned to stand face to face, not quite sure where to focus as he looked into the over-open eyes.

He paused for a few moments, gathering his thoughts, making sure he put forward the most compelling argument he could. The truth could wait for another day. "She likes you, but she's too shy to say, and she can't compromise or jeopardize her position in the office by being seen wasting time with you."

The wide eyes blinked. Boniface took that as a positive sign.

"So what we require is a reason for you to spend time with her. She's far too nervous to go on a date and she's only been in the country for a few days. But I can find a way for you to spend time together, where she will feel safe."

The eyes narrowed, inquisitive.

"It's her feelings we need to think about," said Boniface.

Singleton dipped his head once as Boniface contemplated how to lay out his proposition. He stepped back and turned, gesturing to the accountant. "Walk. But walk slowly, as I explain."

The skinny man followed Boniface's lead as they paced along the street. Boniface caught the younger man's eye, then pointedly flicked his eyes at three construction workers standing outside their site's hoarding having a cigarette. Singleton nodded and the two continued in silence, rounding a left turn before Boniface spoke. "They tell me you're very good at what you do."

The accountant looked blankly at Boniface, his eyes over-wide again as he gave a single nod and mumbled something. Boniface didn't understand what he said, but this was definitely an attempt at direct communication.

The left turn turned again, doubling them back and funneling the two men onto a road wide enough for a single car to pass and no more. "You've been looking through the files," said Boniface. "The files about the Montenegro Shipping Line."

Boniface fixed eye contact with the junior accountant. A blink was sufficient acknowledgement.

"You must have noticed something odd."

Eye contact was broken.

"Look. I'm a PR guy. My strength is not in detecting problems with the accounts. But I know there's a problem." Boniface made sure he still had his companion's attention. "Do you know how I know there's a problem?"

The other man's head vibrated. Boniface was hesitant about whether he was encouraging Boniface to continue or inhaling.

"I know because Greta told me."

The accountant stopped, confusion across his face, vague syllables falling out of his mouth.

"This is quite simple," said Boniface. "At some point, someone will figure where the problem lies. When that happens, you're either with the angels or with the devils." He waited a beat before continuing. "I think you're on the side of the angels, but I would hate to see someone keeping something from you and then blaming you for a problem."

Singleton muttered.

Boniface leaned closer so the other man could hear. "We can't identify where the problem lies and I'm not blaming anyone. However, until we can identify the problem, we can't trust anyone. That's why Greta has involved me, an outsider."

Boniface waited while the accountant balanced the ledgers of risk and reward, and weighed the numbers.

"Joanna's paper is a great haystack to hide a needle, and as she said herself, it's hard to audit a handshake." Boniface continued. "My interpretation of what she said is that she agrees that her records may not be complete."

The accountant mumbled. Boniface wasn't sure, but he thought he said, "That's one explanation."

"I need you to go back and review this Montenegro issue with a critical eye. Get forensic. Find out whether there is a paper trail from Montenegro Shipping to Somalia. I don't care how obscure, how well hidden the trail is, you need to find it. When you've found it, come to me first."

Boniface calibrated the accountant's look as suggesting reluctance.

"You come to me first because I'm the outsider. You come to me because I make sure it gets taken directly to the person who hired me—Greta." Boniface stepped back, trying to keep his body loose. "You come to me, and I'll make you a star in Greta's eyes. I can't take credit for your work—I won't understand what you're telling me, and it will have more credibility coming from someone who understands all the detail—but I will get you in front of Greta to help clear up the mess."

The accountant didn't seem to have twigged what Boniface was suggesting.

"Once you're a star in Greta's eyes, you will spend all of your time going in and out of her office. That means lots of waiting outside with Fraulein Driesdorfer, and it means the chief executive will be telling Fraulein Driesdorfer how smart you are."

Boniface watched as Singleton's skepticism gave way and the look of an over-excited schoolboy spread across his face.

"If someone wanted to pull this off," said Boniface. "How would they hide the paper trail? When you're doing double-entry bookkeeping, do you put a nod in one column with a corresponding wink in the other?"

thirty–seven

"Is it nature trek day at school?" The Glaswegian barb was as inviting as it had been yesterday, although she wondered if she could detect a tiny reduction in the aggression of the delivery.

Montbretia felt much more confident this morning: She had dressed in a way that was comfortable and practical. A shirt with a jacket for warmth, jeans for comfort and added protection, and her boots—if anyone wanted to fight, she could kick, and if that didn't work, she could run. She was still going somewhere secluded with people who hadn't shown much respect or didn't have any idea of boundaries, but at least today she was prepared.

And there was no chafing to annoy her.

"You look different today." The Londoner spoke. "See. It's much easier for her to get on her knees."

Montbretia ignored the comment and took off her backpack.

"Look, Angus. She's changed her hair. Yesterday it looked as if it had been held in place by a band. Today, look. She's washed it and it's free-flowing." He nodded knowingly. "Women communicate through their hair."

"What?" Montbretia exploded.

"Well-known fact, love, even if you won't admit it."

"You are communicating shit." Montbretia squatted by her backpack and pulled out a small stove.

"I think she's communicating to you, Angus, that she's up for it. Her hair is saying if you want a blow job, it will erotically caress and stroke you as she longingly accepts your shaft down her throat."

Montbretia had lit the stove under a dented cooking pot into which she had poured a dark-brown liquid with solid lumps. "It can't simply be that this is how I usually have my hair?" she asked.

The Londoner, taller and more gaunt than Angus, stood and stretched, then pulled his dirty gray coat tighter. "See how her hair swooshes, Angus. It's thick and rich, a gorgeous shade of chestnut, cut to about shoulder length, looks naturally straight, but with a slight inward curl at the end—it's like she came out of a shampoo advert." The Scotsman nodded as his companion continued, now addressing Montbretia. "Each time you move your head, your hair flicks. But you move your head in a very definite way. As you turn your neck, you slow until your hair catches up."

Montbretia stirred the soup with a wooden spoon, lifting and inspecting a carrot before returning her focus to the broth. "As I said, this is how I have my hair."

"So you usually have it ready for giving blow jobs, and yesterday you flattened it to tease us." The Londoner had a victorious smirk. "You're a little minx, aren't you? But I respect that—much as I enjoy a woman that will drop 'em on command, I always feel a bit...I dunno, dirty, afterwards. Chase is better than the catch and all that."

Montbretia threw the spoon into the pot and raised herself from her squatting position, taking a step toward her tormentor. "Can we be clear? The only sexual contact that will ever occur between you and me is my boot and your bollocks. Anything beyond that is in your dreams."

The Scotsman laughed loudly as the thinner man blanched.

Montbretia reached into her backpack and took out three mugs and a brown paper bag. "What's this?" asked Angus.

"Breakfast? Lunch perhaps," said Montbretia.

"You think that heating up some tins of soup will make us your friend?"

"It's not tinned. I made it myself, and I'm not asking for anything in return. But if I may pick you up on a point of etiquette, I haven't actually offered you anything yet."

"Well, hurry up and offer," said the scolded Londoner, stretching his neck to look in the pot.

Montbretia stirred her pot and took a step back, wooden spoon still in hand. The Londoner moved closer, reaching his hand toward the pot. Montbretia tapped him on the back of the hand with the spoon—he jumped and stepped back, as if realizing that Montbretia was looking for their attention.

"Gentlemen. I think we got off on the wrong foot yesterday, and I feel that sad state of affairs is my fault for not introducing myself properly to you." She glanced left and right, making sure she made eye contact. "My name is Montbretia, and it would be my honor if you would join me for some soup." She half paused before continuing in a less formal tone. "As I said, it's homemade soup—beef with some vegetables. And I've also got some bread, some nice rolls...but unfortunately they're not home baked."

"I hope the vegetables are organic," said the Scotsman, noticeably trying to keep his face straight. "I've tried to keep all pesticides out of my diet since I made my lifestyle choice to pursue outdoor living."

Montbretia appeared slightly embarrassed. "They are."

"Well in that case, I'd be pleased to break bread with you. I'm Angus, pleased to meet you, Montbretia."

"Gerbil," said the Londoner. "They call me Gerbil."

"It's my pleasure to meet you gentlemen; please call me Monty." She stirred the soup and tasted it. "Now, if someone would be kind enough to arrange something for me to sit on, I'll sort the soup."

Gerbil returned dragging three palettes, which he stacked and offered to Montbretia as she handed him a mug of soup.

"This is good," said Angus. "You can come back tomorrow and bring us some more." He put his mug down and pulled his coat tighter around him. "Think of it as your entry fee to this very exclusive club."

"A very exclusive but kinda chilly club," said Montbretia, feeling the rawness of the day as she cooled from her brisk walk from the station.

"Chilly?" The Scotsman continued in his nearly indecipherable twang. "We're at the docks. That's the North Sea out there. What do you expect?" He softened, giving Montbretia a reassuring glance. "But there is a bit of a bite to that wind."

A lorry thundered past, dragging a container behind it, shaking the three soup drinkers. "An exclusive club in such a pleasant location." Montbretia mirrored the Scotsman's joviality.

"Aye." He said, his eyes looking over the scrubland where they sat, past the road, and over the concrete wall enclosing the docks. "I've been in the middle of the ocean and found it less desolate than sitting here. It's like an urban desert with the mechanical camel trains passing." He gestured as another lorry went past, moving at about forty miles per hour, but with the size and bulk of metal traveling at that speed, bumping and rocking over the worn-out road, looking as if it were traveling at the speed of a spaceship.

"I'm sure our next location will be even more salubrious," said Angus, winking. "We like to move the club every two or three days...so the riffraff don't get in."

"And so we don't get hassled," said Gerbil, coming back to life.

"Is that what happened the other day?"

"What?" Gerbil's reaction was reflexive.

"The guy who was arrested...was he hassled?"

There was a rasp of annoyance in Angus's tone. "Why are you so interested in this guy?"

"Because he's dead and his body was dumped in my office."

"You're serious?" Gerbil spoke and Angus stayed motionless.

"Albie was telling the truth, then." Angus looked across to Gerbil—an unspoken conversation passed between the two. He looked back to Montbretia. "Sailors tell stories. You travel the world, you see a lot of things, most often in cheap places where people with few choices do anything for a few dollars, so you see some wild stuff. Wild." He paused, lost in silent contemplation. "But then you spend weeks on a ship with nothing to do but talk, and that's where you learn to embellish your stories. That's assuming you can talk. Most of the crews are Filipino these days. I know a few words—enough to say 'where's the brothel' and 'where's the beer'—but not enough to have a proper conversation."

Gerbil picked up the tale. "Albie came here. He was agitated..."

"It wasn't agitated." The Scotsman cut in. "He was fucking upset." He turned to face Montbretia. "Albie and this other guy were sitting there when this van pulled up. Two guys got out and bundled Albie's mate into the back of the van."

"What sort of van?" asked Montbretia.

"A white one," said Gerbil. "Albie ain't so good with the lingo. That's why he was with this other bloke: They both spoke the same language."

"Which is?"

"Albanian, I presume," said Gerbil. "I get by with English, French, German, Polish, and like Angus, some of the Southeast Asian languages, but I never understood when those two were speaking. Anyway, these guys gave Albie a good kicking."

"Who..." Montbretia paused, unsure what to ask.

"You need to speak to Albie," said Angus. "He saw what happened, and if you give him enough alcohol, he might remember something. If you get him enough alcohol, he'll tell you that the two guys were acting on orders."

"Albie? Short for Albert," asked Montbretia.

"Just Albie." His speech slowed as he lost himself in thought. "I haven't seen him since that night."

thirty-eight

"Where have you been, Boniface?" It wasn't a question as much as a full frontal attack. Boniface pulled out his phone, glanced at the screen, and Greta exploded: "Sophie looked and you weren't here."

"I…" Boniface tried to find the right way to start his sentence.

"I run this company. I paid for your hotel, so you are here when I need to speak to you. I'm not here to fill a space in your schedule." Her voice was forceful; her German accent became stronger when she was angry. He moved to the Louis XIV chair. "Don't sit—you're not staying. Brief me and then get back to putting your makeup on or whatever it is that you do while I'm paying you to work."

Boniface stiffened as Greta continued. "Why is Chlodwig still here, and why is Chlodwig still very unhappy? I gave you a simple task, Boniface, and you have failed." She looked up. "Have I failed to pay you?"

"No," said Boniface, his voice a movement of his jaw and a weak aspiration of air.

"Good." She was firm. "Now tell me the execs all understand the strategy. Tell me they all understand what they must do."

Boniface took a calculated risk and sat. "There are a few jitters."

"Jitters?"

"Nothing long-term…it's people getting used to a new idea."

"Did they understand the strategy, Boniface? Yes or no. Either, or. Black, white. Answer without gray, without maybe, or perhaps. Answer in a way that I understand, and which gives me confidence that you are money well spent."

Boniface checked his notebook and was returning it to his pocket as he started. "There are jitters—they're focusing on their own responsibilities instead of looking at the broader issue, so Joanna wants to know who authorized the payments and to ensure any future payment over five-hundred bucks is countersigned by her, and she wants to tell the Stock Exchange; Brad is upset that he's not running the PR operation; and Jeremy thinks you should be focusing on strategy and leaving him to handle what he sees as a legal matter." He paused. "What was the question? Yeah, I've told them, and none of them like the strategy, but I'll give them twenty-four hours to mull it over and take another run at them tomorrow morning."

"Another run at them tomorrow?" Boniface could hear the anger dripping, like molten lead burning holes in the carpet. "We don't have time. Sort the problem. Earn the money I've already paid you."

Boniface hesitated. "Who do you want me to deal with first?"

"Don't test my patience, Boniface. You get like a whiny little girl." Her voice took on the tone of a young child. "You can't have two priorities; you can only do one thing at a time and you have to do them in order." Her regular voice returned to pierce Boniface. "This isn't a joke, Boniface. Sometimes I think I'm the only one taking this seriously."

"I'll get straight on it," said Boniface. He brightened his voice. "By the way, how was your night last night?"

"You're changing the subject, Boniface. You only ask that question because you can't compliment me on my dress because it's the afternoon. But since you ask, he wasn't the man I expected. And since we're talking about last night, tell me why Chlodwig is still here."

"He's cautious. If I'm honest, I think he wants to be supportive but doesn't know how to show it."

Greta threw her head back and cackled. "You are funny, Boniface." She grabbed a breath and continued, her voice deepening. "Chlodwig wants to appoint a COO. That's madness. A chief operating officer. Who do you think looks after operations at the moment? If he paid attention, he'd see that's what I do. I know more than any COO ever would about this company, and I care more than some outsider would. He's looking for me to make a mistake, then he can act."

Boniface frowned. "I got the impression that…"

"Stop there, Boniface. You're making excuses. Go." She pointed to the door. "Get rid of him. Get the execs sorted. I've been paying you for nine months, and the progress is going backwards, and everything I ask you to do ends in failure." She sighed. "Have you even sorted out the mess in your office yet?"

"It's not been my focus."

"Why not? How difficult can it be?"

Boniface sighed. "The police haven't released my office yet. But we do have a lead on the body. Apparently the dead guy was seen alive in Tilbury."

"I can't see what's holding it up. Now go and sort the execs."

Boniface opened the door. A slight rustling at Greta's desk made him glance back to see her looking directly at him. "You're coming with me to the opera tonight. Covent Garden." She scanned up and down, assessing him, judging. "You'll need your tuxedo. Sophie will give you the details." Her head dropped and she was focused on the papers in front of her.

thirty-nine

"What do you mean where am I? I'm with Angus and Gerbil, of course." She felt an imp-like grin working its way across her face. "Gerbil." She beamed. "You heard me correctly. They're my new best buddies. It was a simple equation: Food plus the human touch equals men who are happy to spend time chatting. You're in PR—you should try it sometime."

She looked back at Angus and Gerbil, about twenty yards away, sitting and chatting. Having returned after going for a walk and to find somewhere to relieve herself, she saw that the two had broken up some palettes, ready to light a fire after the evening drew in, when the smoke would be hidden.

"I've spent most of the day trying to decode broad Glaswegian—I'm pretty sure it's Glaswegian mixed with a hefty dose of alcohol. Do you know what neeps and tatties are?" Her face was incredulous. "How do you know that? I had to do a search for it when I went for a pee, which, by the way, is not a pleasant experience if you're a girl wearing jeans and in this place that time and humanity forgot." She felt sheepish. "I did go and use the restroom in the café by the station that I went into yesterday. I felt I had to order a cup of his awful coffee—but I learned after yesterday and got it to go, then poured it down the first drain I passed."

Another lorry rattled down the road. Each truck had its own signature defect that manifested itself as a subtly different noise. This one had a low squeak, but the squeak didn't seem to be synchronized with the movement of the truck or have a regular rhythm. Montbretia struggled to hear Boniface as the squeak squawked into the distance.

"What do you mean, 'Are these guys that relevant'?" She unclamped the phone from her ear and held it in front of her as she pulled a face. "Boniface, it's not that the guy who was murdered was a vagrant and these guys are vagrants too..." She tried to keep her voice calm, but she could feel the annoyance rising. "Boniface, Angus and Gerbil actually met the guy who was murdered."

Another two trucks went past as Montbretia strained to hear Boniface. "Angus and Gerbil met the guy, but there's another vagrant around here who was on good terms with the guy who was murdered and who tried to help him. He got a good kicking for his efforts by the sounds of things." She listened. "Albie. Albie the Albanian."

She removed the phone from her ear for a second time and pulled an even more grotesque face. "I'm with a homeless man called Gerbil. Do you think I asked for identity papers to confirm Albie the Albanian is his real name? They call him that because he is Albanian and they can't remember what his birth name is. He said it once and they didn't understand what he said, so now they call him Albie and he answers to it."

The temperature in Tilbury felt ten degrees colder than it had felt when Montbretia left home that morning. Montbretia figured the temperatures were similar, but with the constant sea breeze and the damp from the river, what had been a nip in the air was starting to become uncomfortable. It had been worse when she was sitting, but now that the sun was dipping, she could feel the temperature falling further.

She hunched her shoulders against the chill. "Look, I don't care what his name is. All I care about is that I find the Albie guy and see what he can show us. I don't know if he'll tell us anything useful—and for that matter, I don't know whether Angus and Gerbil have uttered a word of truth today, but I'll hang around for a while longer and see if I can find Albie. So I might not have found anything, but I thought I should tell you what I've been up to and that I'll head out of here in about an hour. Where are we meeting for dinner?"

She strained to hear. "I can't hear you, the wind is getting up. Where are you, anyway? It sounds like you're standing in the middle of the road." She listened. "In a car. Near your apartment. But what about dinner?"

Montbretia had found that anger had warming properties. "So you're going somewhere tonight—dropping me without actually bothering to tell me—and you're going somewhere secret with your secret client who you said would be your ex-client by now."

She found her breathing becoming fast and heavy as she listened to Boniface.

"No, Boniface. No. You don't get to make recommendations. Get here and help; then you can recommend to your heart's content. But you're not here, and while I'm doing all the work, I make the decisions. I'm a big girl—I've got myself out of plenty of scrapes." She held the phone by her side, shaking her head in disbelief, then continued. "I know there are risks, and of course I'm concerned. But what makes me scared is that you don't seem to get that what you're doing is much more dangerous."

forty

Detective Inspector Raymond Talbot put out his hand to slow his bag man, as he liked to call him. "Wait. Watch." Detective Sergeant Kevin Hitchcock nodded to acknowledge that he had seen the object of their observation as Boniface got out of the large chauffeur-driven Mercedes that had swept into the drive around the front of the block.

The two officers paused under the canopy at the front of Boniface's apartment block, standing back on the dirty white stone porch, disappearing into the camouflage offered by the unlit hall on the other side of the dark wood-framed glass doors behind them.

Boniface held his phone in his hand and leaned into the window of the dark blue Mercedes to talk to the chauffeur. "Notice that?" asked Talbot.

"What? That they seem to be arguing?"

"No. Big car, clearly a chauffeur from the way he's dressed. But he's a chauffeur giving Boniface some lip, and he didn't get out to open the door."

"You mean Boniface has pissed him off, too?" asked Hitchcock, pulling out his notepad and recording the car's plate. "Someone else's car and chauffeur. Do you want to bet it's got something to do with that mystery client?"

"Precisely. Gives you the warm fuzzies about the national computer, doesn't it?"

Boniface waved his hand in the direction of the rear of the block as the car drove in the direction indicated, leaving Boniface walking toward the entrance, head down, phone clamped to his ear. "Hi Monty." His tone seemed subdued. "Look, I'm sorry, I was...I was out of... Look, I was wrong. Could you call me when you stop being angry at me?"

Boniface glanced up to see his way blocked. "Detective Inspector. Detective Sergeant. What a pleasant surprise." His eyes were dull, bags starting to form underneath. The vigor he had shown during his interview two days ago seemed to have deserted him.

"The pleasure is all ours, Mister Boniface, isn't it, Sergeant?" He looked to the younger man, not sure whose fake bonhomie would crack first; he suspected Boniface's, looking at his condition. "We were just having a look around your office, and I said to the Sergeant, 'You know, Sergeant, that nice Mister Boniface lives up the hill—why don't we go and have a look and see if there's anything to see,' and so we walked up, not thinking that we might have the good fortune to bump into you."

"I'm pleased you did, and I look forward to the next time the stars align and our orbits collide." Boniface moved, seemingly intending to walk past the two.

"Ah, Mister Boniface, are you not going to stay and have a chat with us?" Talbot liked to adopt unusual speech patterns; he felt it unsettled suspects, giving them two issues to consider simultaneously: the question and why the officer was talking in a strange manner.

"I'm..." Boniface indicated along the driveway around his brick-built block in the direction the Mercedes had driven. "I'm in a hurry, I'm afraid. Apparently if I'm one second late, I turn into a pumpkin and my carriage will depart without me, so if you don't mind."

"Mister Boniface, that's not a chat." Talbot exaggerated a frown, turning his head. As his head twisted, he could feel the connected muscles in his back rubbing the jacket of his overly tight suit. "That's you not telling us what you know."

"Again," offered the Sergeant.

"Come on, Boniface. We're all reasonable men. Can't we have a reasonable chat? Out here. In the open air. No nasty tape recorders or anything like that." Talbot sniffed, damp air mixed with the fumes of the traffic up and down Wimbledon Hill Road, getting increasingly heavy as the afternoon moved into the rush hour.

"Alright Detective Inspector. I'll begin with a question," said Boniface. "When can I have my office back?"

Talbot held his hand open, as if suggesting everything was beyond his control. "You know those scientists."

"You mean the ones who have difficulty differentiating between blood and horseradish?"

The Detective Inspector tutted. "Mister Boniface, I thought you were better than that. But if you want the scientists to finish all of their tests before they release your office, it might take a little while longer. But it's funny that you bring up your office." Talbot struggled to contain his joy that Boniface had set up his next line. "We've had a lovely chat with some friends of yours."

"At your office," added Hitchcock.

"Well, they said they were friends of yours, Boniface, but you know me, plodding old policeman, I get suspicious." Talbot puffed up his chest and rested his thumbs in his belt. "They didn't dress like you, and to be honest, we thought they were sizing up your office, which is why we had a chat, and as we talked, they told us they were your friends." His face cracked and he exhaled while sneering—a technique he had spent long perfecting. "Actually, the big guy said he was looking for Mister Bonnington, but his comrade-in-arms corrected him. So I'm guessing they weren't friends, but what? Business acquaintances? Clients?"

Hitchcock turned to his detective inspector. "You know what, gov, I've been thinking. You remember we were suspicious about Mister Boniface's clients because he wouldn't tell us anything about them, and this made it sound like they were a bit, you know...maybe not on the right side of, you know...legal."

"Mm hmm."

"Well, I was wondering. Did he refuse to tell us about his clients because they're all, you know...complete knobheads, and he's ashamed to be seen in public with them?" He turned to Boniface. "Knobheads is a technical police term, Mister Boniface. It means..."

"I think I understand the gist of what it could mean," said Boniface, his tired, featureless face cracking.

"Interesting gentlemen," continued Talbot. "And d'you know what, Mister Boniface? It was very lucky we turned up, because they were criminals." He made two small emphatic nods.

Hitchcock jumped in again. "I love the police computer, Detective Inspector. She makes me feel happy inside."

"I haven't got a clue who those two could be," said Boniface. "Can I go now, please?"

"Relax, Mister Boniface. This is far more interesting than having a conversation with that chauffeur..."

"And whoever owns the car," added the younger officer, scratching at his notebook.

"We've got so much to talk about, and I know it will interest you: There have been lots of calls to the station about you. You're a popular guy, Mister Boniface," said the detective inspector, scratching his stomach as he remembered it was at least two hours since he had eaten.

"I know I'm meant to do the whole poker-face thing, but this is news to me," said Boniface.

"Funny thing. Very next morning after we had our last little chat, within three minutes of getting in, I had a call. Assistant Commissioner. For me. Directly. Wanted to know about you and the case. Didn't make any suggestions, just wanted details. Funny that. Don't often get the brass calling, and definitely don't get the third most important man in the Metropolitan Police Service calling with no reason. But here's the odd thing—I couldn't make out whether he was a friend or an enemy of yours."

Boniface's lips twitched at one end. "Never met the man. No clue why he would call."

"Then this afternoon, we started getting these calls from newspapers. Calls plural. Asking lots of strange background questions—nothing specific, and no one knew what the right question was to ask." He waited, letting the revelation sink in before continuing. "But here's the odd thing—it was like we got called by the work-experience kid each time. By the third call we realized that they were all asking the same questions in exactly the same order."

"Exactly the same?" Boniface was frowning quizzically.

"Exactly," said Talbot. "No derivation from the script. No intention to get further details or even listen to the answer. Just a list of questions."

"Now, Detective Sergeant Hitchcock and I are exceedingly vigilant." Hitchcock nodded in an exaggerated manner as Talbot continued. "We're very keen to make sure the good name of an innocent man isn't besmirched by an unintended conversation with the press. Having read a bit more about your background, I think you know something about the press saying bad things.... But it does seem to me, Mister Boniface, that you have a very interesting group of people—diverse in their concerns—who have an interest in your well-being."

forty-one

He watched as Boniface was raised up. A solitary figure ascending from below—bleary-eyed with his head slowing turning to scan his environment. Tired, but he still had some innate sense to present himself in a way that was simultaneously professional, believable, but at the same time sufficiently uncontroversial to allow him to fade into the background like a chameleon.

Boniface stepped off the moving staircase and walked over to his table, pulled out a flimsy metal seat that twisted too much to give any support and yet didn't bend in the right places; he sat without waiting to be asked and talked without paying attention to his host. "I've had a gutful of Gideon's cloak-and-dagger shit. Can't we have a normal meeting like normal people? Do we have to meet in a train-station café?"

"Did you enjoy the opera last night?" He indicated across the round metal table—its surface fashioned like a piece of engineered steel, which only served to catch the dirt—to the second cup of tea.

"What was that?" He heard a rasp of annoyance in Boniface's voice.

"You went to the opera last night. I asked if you enjoyed it. This is what people call conversation."

"No. This is what people call..."

"Shhhh." He sat calmly, waiting for the fire in Boniface's eyes to show some sign that his head wasn't about to combust. "Gideon went to the opera last night. He didn't know that you would be there, and indeed, he was as surprised to see you as you are that you were seen."

Boniface had fixed his host with a blank stare.

"Gideon saw who you were accompanying and felt it best for all three of you that he stayed in the shadows. But you will understand—with the company you have been keeping recently—that Gideon was very concerned when he saw who you were consorting with, and wondered about whether one could find a connection with your current...challenges."

"Really? This is your excuse?"

"Shhhh, shhhh, shhhh." He held a finger over his lips. "Inside voices. I'm speaking. You'll get your turn when I've finished." He pointed at the tea he had bought for Boniface. "You can drink you tea and listen."

Boniface returned to his sullen teenager look, steadfastly ignoring the tea.

"Will you let me finish?" He waited for Boniface to make eye contact before continuing. "You've had a rough couple of days, Boniface: dead bodies, police think you're a murderer, association with a known criminal who has the ability to dispose of bodies and his dangerous son, and a client with big problems. Gideon understands, but he's worried. Worried that people may take advantage of your good nature, worried that people may exploit your short-term needs in a way that damages your long-term interests. I could go on, but can we accept that Gideon is worried?"

"You know this because you're your own little one-man Gideon Latymer tribute band." Boniface's voice was calm, but his words spat fire. "You wear his clothes, but you lack his natural charm, flair, wit, and intelligence. In other words, you lack everything that makes Gideon, Gideon. If you want a career in politics—which I presume you must if you've got yourself up a few rungs to being Gideon's personal flunky—then if you want to take that next leap, you need to become you. Reach inside and find your inner you, however unappetizing he might be."

"And find my own personal Boniface to do the Machiavellian string-pulling behind the scenes?"

"Wouldn't hurt, would it, Benedict?" Boniface paused. "It is Benedict, isn't it?"

Benedict nodded.

"Surname?"

"O'Reilly."

Boniface continued, his momentum moderated. "Don't get me wrong, you're clearly a smart boy. But if my experience over the last few minutes is anything to go by, then the first step for you is to learn some serious presentation skills. And I don't mean *can use PowerPoint* presentation skills, or TV interview skills, I mean being able to connect with people. The ability to find the message and focus on it. Get to the point before I die of boredom."

Boniface kept his focus as he continued. "Drop the pitch of your voice—get some power and take elocution lessons for the timbre. All I can hear is this nag, nag, nag, nag sound in my head. Power. Authority. Gravitas. Humor. That's what you need. You have to be the kind of person the public want to identify with. Even if you're not one of them, they need to like you and think you understand them—they need to know your name is Benedict and not say 'that bloke who hangs around with the sexual deviant.'"

O'Reilly paused, giving Boniface a chance to finish his monologue.

"A voice like a squeaky flywheel will never make you likable." He sighed. "See what happens when you deprive me of sleep by calling me at 4 AM? I get annoyed and give you some free advice." Boniface's gaze focused, his face looking quizzical. "Why did you call me at 4 AM if you knew I'd been out late?"

"Be grateful. You at least got to bed." O'Reilly took a sip of his tea, again indicating to the cup across from him. "Me? I got a call from Gideon when he saw you at the opera. I've been doing the background research for you since then."

He held up a manila folder and tapped it.

"We must assume that this trip to the opera wasn't pleasure—no one actually goes to the opera for pleasure. Even Gideon. This suggests an obligation on your part, and the logical extrapolation is that you were required to play the role of the gracious consort to someone who has a hold over you. One person who might have such a hold, at this time, is a client. When Gideon saw you with Greta Weissenfeld last night, he put two and two together and assumed that Weissenfeld Shipping is your client with 'a bad thing' waiting to break."

Boniface growled. "You're doing that pain-in-the-ass condescending talking again. Cut it out or I'm off."

"I'm sorry, Boniface, but Gideon is worried: These are not nice people." Boniface went to say something, but his host continued. "You're a big boy, we know. We reckon you've got a pretty good idea about what you're dealing with. Gideon is concerned that Weissenfeld's resources are greater than yours, and they could literally spend you into the ground with their pocket change."

Boniface held his hands over the table between the two men, turning them. "See that." He carried on slowly turning his hands, like a small-scale oscillating fan. "I know I'm playing with fire, but I haven't burned myself. Yet."

"Yet… And while it's not a good reason for you to listen, I have spent the whole night pulling this material together, so, as well as being polite, it might be useful to make sure I haven't found anything that you don't already have a detailed knowledge of."

"Go on. Let me hear it." Boniface sat back in his chair, sweeping a hand through his hair.

"I'm sure it goes without saying that Greta Weissenfeld is highly talented and highly driven." He looked for Boniface's confirmation before he continued. "Many who have dealt with her are less complimentary; the word 'sociopath' seems to be a common choice." Boniface seemed ashamed as he wrinkled his nose in acknowledgement. "But what about the lawyer, Jeremy Farrant? What do you know about him?"

"Pompous ass," said Boniface. "Likes to spend money, mostly on carpets it would seem. Thinks he's it. Owns a castle in Scotland. Is there more?"

"He's dangerous. It not that he's a shark, it's that he brings an unfortunate combination of competence and incompetence, mixed with greed and ruthlessness, all polished off with that pompous arrogance you have noticed."

"Thinking about it, he also did a background check on me. It was pretty thorough."

"No, he didn't." O'Reilly paused, trying to inject some dramatic effect in a dreary station café. "Tamsin Smales-Mainer, his so-called secretary, did."

"So-called?"

"Yup. She's not a secretary."

"We're talking about the same woman—triangular with narrow shoulders and a 1980s big-hair perm that looks so odd that it must be natural."

O'Reilly reached into his manila folder and pulled out a photo, which he showed to his guest.

"That's her," said Boniface. "So if she's not a secretary, what is she?"

"She's a lawyer. Young, but very well-regarded lawyer. Will be going places if she passes the Jeremy test."

"Why would a lawyer work for him and pretend to be his secretary or assistant or whatever she is called?"

"Most young lawyers get all the grunt work, Jeremy's grunt work is at a much higher level. The grunt work is the top-level stuff that Jeremy should be doing—it's great experience for any lawyer." He considered the situation for a moment. "How many junior lawyers get to do a background check on Alexander Boniface? Working for Farrant, you get all the introductions and the contacts you could ever need, and everyone knows that if you survive Jeremy, then you really are good. So after two years, Jeremy gets a new slave, and the one who has survived the ordeal by fire and kept Jeremy out of jail gets rewarded with gold."

"Does he," Boniface twisted his hips forward awkwardly in his chair, "give them practical lessons in how to interface with senior lawyers?"

O'Reilly turned his head. "As far as we can tell, Jeremy is asexual. He keeps these people around so he can look good and puff his chest out."

"But Jeremy must do more than hire good staff," said Boniface.

"Jeremy's main role is his contacts. That's where the castle helps: He takes those who need to be influenced hunting, shooting, fishing, or for a few rounds of golf, all within his very private and very exclusive estate with ample and sumptuous accommodation, lots of good food, and lots of very pleasant alcohol. In the long run, it's much more persuasive that kneecapping."

"Good people skills," said Boniface, his tone flat.

"Indeed, but Jeremy isn't an idiot. He's smart man: street smart—which is odd given that he hasn't been on a street since the late 1960s—but not intellectually smart. He simply does not know the law. His arrogance is his Achilles heel, and that Achilles heel is where we started digging the dirt on him." O'Reilly tapped the manila folder. "Botched work—covered up by the old boys' network, trips to his castle, work to other law firms, you know the score. In the end he was ousted as partner from his old law firm because he became too much of a risk." He dropped the manila folder, making the table rock. "It's all in here."

Boniface stared at the folder on the swaying table.

"There is one other thing you should know about."

Boniface's gaze lifted from the folder.

"Lots of journalists—from different news outlets—have been calling Gideon for background on you. The basic story is the same, and it all ties back to your time with Gideon."

"Did it seem like they were all asking the same questions?"

"Funnily enough, Boniface, yes. They all posed the same questions in the same order. Why do you ask?"

"That's what the police told me yesterday."

"That's interesting," said O'Reilly.

"What's more interesting is that my client..."

"You can say it, Boniface: We know it's Weissenfeld. By the way, it's only me and Gideon who know about that detail, and you can rely on us to remain mute on that issue."

"Thanks," said Boniface. "Anyway, what is interesting is that Weissenfeld—most notably, their PR guy who takes all the calls from the press—hasn't mentioned the issue."

The two men sat in wordless contemplation.

"This is for you." O'Reilly picked up his manila folder and laid it on the table before Boniface. "Now, you do understand—and it saddens me as much as it saddens Gideon—but this is the end of your relationship with Gideon, at least until after the next election. This research is your going-away gift."

Boniface's tone was incredulous. "What do you mean my going-away gift, you little turd?"

"This is a token of the esteem in which Gideon holds you, or rather used to hold you and hopes to hold you again, but not in this decade. Not until you are far less radioactive. He's disappointed about your choice of friends, and the choices of those friends' friends. Because of those friends, he cannot be friends with you. In short, Gideon cannot be seen with you and cannot communicate with you. He would have liked to tell you himself, but it's the whole being seen talking with you that he has to avoid."

"This is..." Boniface stood, pulling out his phone. O'Reilly reflexively grabbed it.

"Gideon has been courteous." O'Reilly stood, returning the phone to Boniface. "Please extend the same courtesy to Gideon."

Boniface snatched the phone and walked off. O'Reilly made out his first few words above the hum of the station. "Monty. Can we meet?"

forty-two

"Nothing?"

Boniface was standing in an office he hadn't known existed in Weissenfeld House.

From the size of it, he guessed the windowless box hadn't been an office until recently, when it had been converted from a storage space. The walls and ceiling had been painted white, a piece of standard-issue corporate carpet—Boniface wondered if it had been recycled from Jeremy Farrant's room—had been thrown across the floor, and dark wood shelves went from floor to ceiling on two walls.

Brian Singleton sat behind his desk—or what Boniface assumed would be his desk underneath the stacks of files—and shook his head.

"Nothing?"

Singleton grunted and mumbled as Boniface scrutinized the office, looking for any detail to deflect his frustration. The shelves looked familiar. "Did you and Jeremy get a job lot of shelves?"

Another series of grunts and mumbles—Boniface was getting better at translating; he was sure he heard the words "off-cuts" and "same carpenter."

Boniface reflected on the shelves in a new light. "He really has done a good piece of work." He examined the detail of the carpentry before flipping back to the junior accountant, unable to contain his frustration. "Could someone else be funneling cash and so misrepresenting the transactions?"

Singleton remained behind his desk, staring at Boniface with his overly wide eyes silently saying, "I'm an accountant; do you think I haven't considered that option already?"

Boniface met the stare and locked eye contact, breaking when he realized the younger man's slightly shocked, somewhat sarcastic look wasn't an act he was feigning—that was how he looked.

"What...?" He felt the constriction in his throat as he rasped. He lifted the stack of files on the side of the desk, placed them on the floor and sat in their place, resting his right foot on the pile. He leaned toward the younger man and spoke slowly. "You've done me a favor, and I'm grateful."

He waited for some acknowledgement from the accountant. "I'm grateful, but we need a story for public consumption. You have one task: Slay a dragon. They don't make movies about the really nice guy who was good at mathematics and went looking for a dragon but couldn't find one."

Boniface calibrated the response on Singleton's face: a slight twitch at the edge of his mouth masked by the twitch when he inhaled.

"We're all agreed there is a problem. You, me, Greta," continued Boniface. "But if you can't find something, then I can't make you look like a hero in front of Greta, and if I can't do that, I can't get you next to Sophie."

He mumbled—Boniface leaned to hear better, becoming aware of the changes crossing the man's face. He wasn't sure what he was reading between the acne. His best guess was fear and anger—at least, that was what Boniface hoped. If he was right, these emotions would make the accountant work harder and faster.

"I need you to understand, Brian, this isn't about me. It's helping you, too." Boniface leaned back, making sure the younger man was paying attention. "There's a difference between no evidence of fraud and evidence of no fraud."

The other man thought, then looked up at Boniface, a look of hope forming in his eyes. "You understand your basic challenge—either find the money trail or confirm that there is no money trail. Don't confirm that you haven't found a trail—confirm that one does not exist."

The younger man picked up a file and started flicking through.

"Remember," said Boniface. "We know there's a problem, and if you don't find something, then you're the one being set up by Joanna."

forty–three

Boniface closed the door as he left Singleton's office on the middle floor of Weissenfeld House, meeting Brad Phipps as he descended from the top floor.

"Brad, hi. How y'doing?"

"Cool, bro, cool." Brad's lazy, non-specific North American accent, coupled with his inability to construct even the most basic sentences without adding the words "yo," "dude," "bro," or "awesome," challenged Boniface's ability to divine meaning where there probably was none.

Boniface stopped and walked back to Brad, facing him across the open space that was more of a four-way intersection next to Lennie Watkins' desk. "Have you had any calls over the last few days? Odd calls? Perhaps several calls from different people, but all asking similar questions?"

"That would be, y'know, like, weird."

"You mean no?"

"No, dude." Brad's head flopped from side to side. "Why?"

It was the first sensible question Boniface had heard Brad ask—ever—he thought he would have longer to prepare an answer. "Just, like, y'know. Sometimes these things. Y'know."

"Sure, dude. No probs." Brad turned.

"I'll see you around, Brad. I've got to find Jeremy." Boniface stepped, expecting Brad to move.

"He's not there, dude."

"What?" Boniface moved back to face the large Canadian fidgeting awkwardly in his beige chinos and blue button-down shirt, looking even taller than normal as he balanced on the bottom step.

"Not there. He's gone to court, or is it Counsel? I dunno, it's like…" He seemed incapable of standing still or applying any focus.

Boniface felt his fists clenching. "Why has he gone to Counsel, or court, or whatever?" He slipped his hands in his pockets to get some control.

Brad's face tightened up as if the pressure would help him think better. "He's applying for one of those, y'know things. With the…"

"An injunction," said Boniface, straining to keep his voice calm.

Brad snapped his fingers and pointed at Boniface. "One of those."

"Who authorized this?" Boniface tried to sound nonchalant…casual, even conversational.

Brad blew air out of his mouth, his lower lip flicking open.

"Does Greta know?"

"You mean the dudette-in-chief?"

Boniface regretted using the term yesterday.

"Not a clue, man. Why would she care?"

"Because she runs the company? Because her name's on the letterhead?" Boniface felt the back of his skull throbbing.

"I've got stuff to do, man, I need to call people about this…"

"Injunction?"

"Yeah, I've got to call people about the injunction."

Boniface couldn't keep the rage out of his voice. "Why are you calling people about the injunction? Isn't the point of an injunction to stop people talking?"

Brad stood, eyebrows raised, mouth half open, his head almost shaking. "Dude. The point is to stop *other people* talking."

"No, an injunction..." Boniface stopped. He continued in a lighter voice, but aware that his question was barbed. "Why are you calling people, Brad? It wasn't part of the strategy."

"It wasn't part of your strategy, man. But now I'm running PR. I told you yesterday."

forty-four

Montbretia rested on her crossbar, balancing against the additional weight strapped to her bike. The autumnal chill was catching her after her physical exertion to reach the rendezvous. Her eyes scanned in an arc as she zipped up her fleece, hunching her shoulders against the cold.

At the north side of the park, coming down from the Mayfair edge Boniface appeared, dressed in his trademark suit but with his hair looking disheveled. He usually only displayed this look after he had spent the day sitting at his desk, resting his head on his hand, intermittently gripping his hair as he tried to focus. It was barely 10 AM, and already his hair had given up on the day.

He loosely balanced the handles of a small brown paper bag on his fingers. As he stepped closer, she could see his eyes were having difficulty focusing and his facial expression looked forced. "You look like shit."

His face relaxed. "Thank you and good morning to you." He held out the bag. "Peace offering."

"A muffin? You hate muffins, Boniface."

"They say these are the best muffins—the bakery is in all the tourist guides, and at that price, I hope it's good."

"Am I really a muffin kind of girl?" She kept her tone soft, trying gentle mockery to keep the atmosphere light. "If it were a cupcake you'd be in serious trouble." She took a bite, keeping her lips together as she chewed. "Why here?" she said, trying not to spit food, as she pointed around with her eyes.

"Green Park? I like it. Piccadilly over there; you've got the sweep of green leading down to the Palace. Good morning, Your Majesty, if you can hear me." He bowed his head in the direction of Buckingham Palace. "You've got these gorgeous old houses here." He vaguely indicated the properties a few hundred feet away on his left. "You've got Spencer House—the historic home of the Spencer family." Montbretia frowned, waiting for him to elaborate. "Spencer as in Diana Spencer." Montbretia's frown remained. "You young people know her by her married name: Diana, Princess of Wales."

"Oh," said Montbretia.

"It's owned by a hedge fund manager or something now. That Australian newspaper tycoon lives somewhere over there, and then there's Lancaster House—where the agreement was signed giving Rhodesia independence and thereby creating Zimbabwe."

"And?" Her voice was muffled as she chomped.

"And it's not that far from the client's office."

"For crying out loud, Boniface." Half-chewed muffin fired out of her mouth. "Why haven't you got out of there?"

Boniface was like a scolded child. When he started speaking, his voice was quavering. "I came to apologize and to try to..." His hands circled as if he was trying to communicate but couldn't recall any commonly understood body movement. "Let's say clear the air, because I can't think of a better term. I know you're angry. I know you're upset. But please, I hate arguing with you. I want to...to get past whatever this is."

Montbretia put the last lump of the muffin into her mouth, wiping the crumbs around her lips.

"What's all this?" Boniface pointed to the load strapped to Montbretia's bicycle.

"It's some of Ellen's old stuff—blankets and a few old pieces. It's cluttering the house, so I'm giving it to the hobos in Tilbury." She fixed Boniface, sensing that he wanted to caution her but was holding back. "They were helpful yesterday—and I... we, still need their help."

It was Boniface's turn to question with a frown as two people on rollerblades wobbled between them, the his-n-hers matching black helmets, red jackets, and padded elbows proclaiming their coupledom as they passed through the green space following the path toward the Palace.

"The guys know Albie...Albie the Albanian. They're out looking for him."

"Can we rely on this Albie?"

"I've never met him, so I can't answer that." She inhaled, pondering. "I can't say with any certainty that we can rely on any of them: It's like drunk Chinese whispers trying to have a conversation with them. But Albie saw what happened and understood what the guys in the van said."

"So they spoke in Albanian?"

"Maybe." Montbretia made an exaggerated shrug, throwing up her hands. "All the sailors speak a little bit of lots of languages. They know how to get a drink and..." She stopped, feeling her cheeks faintly redden as she remembered the scope of Angus's linguistic requirements. "But it beats me how they understand anything—I don't understand most of what Angus and Gerbil say, and they're speaking English, apparently. So I'm getting this secondhand tale about Albie, and they keep talking about some guy called Reagan."

"Reagan?"

"Reagan. As in the president." She flapped a hand dismissively. "He's like some ghost or big scary ogre or something. According to Gerbil he sent the guys in the van. It doesn't make sense to me, but maybe once I've seen Albie it will."

"It sounds dangerous, Monty. You make sure you take care."

Montbretia kept her voice soft. "If it's so dangerous, why don't you come with? You can hear what Albie has to tell us, directly from the horse's..."

"I would but I've got to..."

No longer feeling any necessity to attempt to be conciliatory, Montbretia blurted. "You would but your super-secret client has clicked their fingers and so you've got to go running."

Boniface remained motionless, looking down at the ground. He started talking without looking up. "Gideon sent his flunky to talk to me. Benedict. The guy called me at 4 AM."

"No wonder you look so rough."

"Thank you again for the compliment."

Montbretia pushed forward. "Where was Gideon?"

Boniface hung his head. "Gideon doesn't like my friends, so he won't play with me anymore." She scrutinized his face—she wasn't sure whether she was reading shock, disappointment, or anger. Maybe it was acceptance? "He thinks my friends are bad people."

"Are we talking Tommy and Angelo?" A multicolored dog with a piece of cloth tied around its neck scampered up to Boniface and dropped a stick at his feet. When Boniface didn't seem to notice or care, the dog picked up his stick and ran off.

"Yes," nodded Boniface, "and he's very twitchy that I've been talking to Tommy when the extradition case is going on, but he's also made a guess as to who the client is, and he doesn't like it."

"The client whose identity I'm not allowed to know?" Montbretia fixed Boniface. "You're saying that Gideon knows who the client is?"

The side of Boniface's mouth twitched involuntarily. "He's made a guess."

She laughed, a single, joyless exclamation. "So who is it?"

"You don't need to know—and once I've resigned it won't matter."

"So this client is important enough that Gideon has broken off diplomatic relations, but I'm not important enough to know who it is." Montbretia couldn't look at Boniface.

Boniface sighed. "That's not the case. If I don't tell you and something goes wrong for the client—which I expect to happen, very soon—then I can put my hand on my heart and say, 'Montbretia definitely didn't know. Montbretia was not the source of the problem.' I'm not suggesting this benefits you, but it makes me feel better."

Montbretia turned her head and tried to make eye contact at Boniface.

"Benedict, Gideon's flunky, was pretty damning about the client. Nothing much that I didn't know—or couldn't extrapolate." His eyes focused into the distance. "But the information he gave me—the direction I'm being pointed—all seemed a bit simple, straightforward. Packaged with a bow on the top."

"Do you trust what you were told?"

"Yes. No. Perhaps. But I don't know why I'm being given this information. Is Benedict trying to break Gideon's relationship with me? Or is this Gideon protecting himself?"

Montbretia watched Boniface, a man who always seemed so confident in his analysis, so sure of his next step, even if he knew that he didn't know where the next step would lead. Now, standing in a public park in central London, he seemed able to figure all the permutations, he seemed able to grasp his options, and yet he seemed unable to figure how to move forward.

"Come on, Boniface. There's more. What aren't you telling me?"

Boniface chewed his bottom lip and started talking, his lip still held between his teeth. "The cops came round last night."

"Why didn't you tell me?" Montbretia asked.

"Because, honestly, it doesn't matter—they were yanking my chain. It was an exercise for their enjoyment. Something they do when they're bored."

"But still."

"And you shouted at me on the phone..." Boniface straightened. "They did say one interesting thing. They've had calls from the press about me."

"I suppose that was to be expected," offered Montbretia.

"It was. But what surprised them was that the questions were the same—it was as if they were being read from a script." He squinted at Montbretia. "And nobody asked about the body."

Montbretia went to talk and was cut off by Boniface. "Then when I saw Benedict this morning, he said Gideon had received similar calls—low-grade journalists reading questions from a script."

Montbretia felt her jaw hang loose. "So that means…"

"Still not finished." Boniface half lifted his hand. "That alone doesn't mean anything, but here's the interesting bit: When I told the CEO that I was quitting, my resignation was refused. We talked about the situation, and the last thing the CEO said was, 'Is there anything else I need to be aware of?'"

"What does that mean?"

"The CEO wanted to know whether there was anything else from my past that could be negatively connected with the company. As we know, my past is not without blemish."

"But it's all in the public domain?"

"The varnished truth, yes. The less varnished truth, no. The less varnished truth is known by people who were there or who know me—you, Gideon, Veronica, and now the CEO."

"Okay, I get why you told the CEO, but where's the link to these journalists?"

"These scripted questions all seem to be pushing toward the less varnished truth that I discussed with the CEO." Boniface looked down, kicking an invisible stone. "It's not proof, but the coincidence is interesting."

Montbretia sighed loudly, trying to make sure Boniface noticed. "Are you paying attention, Boniface?" She glared at him: no response. "You need to get out now. They're the source of your problem. Your client is killing you, Boniface."

Boniface raised his hands to his face as if in silent prayer. "One last attempt to explain. They've been paying for the last nine months, so if they're genuine, I've got some sort of obligation not to walk away."

"No," said Montbretia. "You've got an obligation to sort yourself out. Then you can fix your client. Remember, a dead man can't administer first aid."

"But if they're dirty, then I've got to stay on the inside and figure out what's happening."

"Okay," Montbretia tried to sound reassuring. "If you won't come to Tilbury, then let me come with you and we'll sort out this client."

Boniface's mouth twitched.

"Come to Tilbury or I come with you now," Montbretia was resolute. "We fight this together."

"I…" Boniface was motionless apart from his eyes, flicking.

Montbretia counted to ten in her head, and counted to ten for a second time, then threw her leg over her bike. "It's obvious you don't want me involved. I don't understand why, but it hurts like hell."

forty–five

Boniface wondered whether she was born with an asbestos mouth, throat, and gullet or if some specialized, albeit very cheap, treatment had been applied. Or maybe she drank gallons of water or was oblivious to pain.

He was sure he could feel his hair starting to singe while she pinned him into the corner with fire spilling out of her mouth as she roared. "You didn't trust me. In fact, you positively suspected me of fraud." He was sure the flames were licking him as she bellowed.

Brian Singleton looked embarrassed as his boss continued to shout at Boniface, but it wasn't clear exactly what the source of the young man's embarrassment was. Boniface was grateful for the conundrum to run around his head as he tried to distract himself from Joanna Baines' onslaught. The simple explanation was that Singleton had blurted and was embarrassed that Boniface now knew that he had blurted—that knowledge being gained by Boniface as a consequence of the metaphorical thrashing he was now receiving.

He tried to figure—as much as he was able to concentrate with the fire-breathing woman berating him—if he could tell her that he never suspected her: Boniface had only told the younger man not to trust her to give him an incentive to carry out his task in secret and without delay.

He couldn't, so he continued to distract himself while trying not to draw Baines' attention to the fact that he was looking for clues from the underling sitting behind his desk. Perhaps he was embarrassed because he didn't like displays of emotion. That would be very English and would fit with Singleton's rather inelegant social dysfunctionality.

"You didn't trust Regenspurger." Boniface was confused by her statement; he struggled to find a reason why he, or any sensible person, would ever trust Regenspurger to do anything other than inflict pain. "We've got the records—you gave us the dates, he wasn't spending money in Africa. We've checked the travel expenses—he wasn't there."

As his ears prayed for relief from the barrage they were receiving, Boniface let his eyes sweep the room in the search of any exit from the tiny box, or any pretext he could use to divert his tormentor. There wasn't enough space for one person to exist in comfort, let alone three, especially when one was snorting flames and the preponderance of wood and paper made the room highly combustible, while its origin as a closet meant that no one had thought to invest in extending the sprinkler system.

"But more significantly, Boniface, you didn't trust the system and the processes in place. You didn't trust the company—your client." Boniface was beginning to regret not spending more time with the CFO figuring out her dragon-like tendencies. If he had, he would have revised his investigative strategy, but as it was, she had now given him enough time to make another guess about Singleton's embarrassment. It was clear that he was embarrassed to be watching someone being pounded as much as he would be embarrassed to be caught watching pornography.

Boniface relaxed, pleased that he had found a plausible explanation to the conundrum that only served to distract him during the unpleasantness, while growing increasingly aware that the CFO appeared to be running out of breath. Her speech was becoming measured, almost calm by the standards of the last few minutes. "Your conspiracy theory that Regenspurger was running an operation off the books or that I'm trying to set up Brian is daft. No, it's not daft, it's offensive."

She stopped and picked up a file.

"Bookkeeping is simple—it's addition and subtraction. There's no multiplication or division. There's no projection. We take facts—provable facts—then add up and subtract numbers."

She seemed to be waiting. Boniface felt an involuntary forward movement of his head. Singleton gingerly looked up to witness the interaction between the two visitors in his cell.

"We know what we started with. We did an audit—we counted. That's what bean counters do."

Another involuntary nod. There was a perceptible cause-and-effect link between his nodding and her calmness of delivery.

"We know what's come in." She hesitated, but not long enough for him to appear to give consideration before nodding. "We know what's gone out."

A nod.

"We know what is left—what we started with, plus what came in, minus what went out."

A further nod.

"Brian told me he was trying to prove that the money trail didn't exist, not to prove that he couldn't find it."

At the mention of his name the younger man looked away.

"He didn't rat on you—he didn't have to tell me anything. As soon as I heard those words, I heard your voice." She opened the file she was holding and laid it in front of him. "Here is the summary of our records—they give you the proof. If you think the records are wrong, then call the police and tell them we have been the victim of an elaborate fraud."

Boniface heard the words but couldn't break from his trance: Now he understand Singleton's embarrassment. He had been caught for the schoolboy error of copying; he had copied Boniface's words. Now the embarrassment made sense.

"Stick with doing what you do, Mister Boniface." Joanna Baines was moving toward the door. "And why are you still here? Brad should have taken over by now."

forty-six

Veronica clamped her phone between her ear and shoulder and pulled at the bridge of her spectacles, drawing them farther down her nose as she stared over the half-moons to see the person her assistant had led to her office door.

Montbretia hesitated in her doorway, looking slightly flushed as if she had been exercising. Her jeans and fleece said otherwise; only her running shoes suggested she may have endured any physical exertion, and they were hardly the sole preserve of gym junkies. Then again, maybe she cycled.

"Mmm. Um hmm." She raised her eyebrows, looking at Montbretia, who stood uncomfortably in the doorway, clasping her hands together, her shoulders hunched like a meek child who needed to ask to go to the bathroom.

Montbretia swayed in and out of the doorway, then mouthed "It's okay" and turned. Veronica snapped her fingers and pointed at the leather armchair across from her desk.

Tentatively, the younger woman crossed the room, her eyes darting from corner to corner, looking at the meeting table, the potted Japanese maples, and the television on the wall. Veronica watched as she sat, balancing on the front of the seat, before turning and then looking past her and out of the window, raising herself up to better see the view. Veronica knew that Montbretia was looking over her left shoulder at the sight of Big Ben 500 feet below them.

"I'll call you back," said Veronica, hanging up the phone. "I'm sorry to be so rude and click my fingers at you." She released her frown. "How are you, Montbretia? It's good to see you again."

"Boniface said you had a good view, but wow!" The self-assurance, the poise, the attitude, the confidence of the other night were missing.

"It *is* quite something, isn't it?" said Veronica. "I never get tired of the view."

"I shouldn't be here; you're busy." Montbretia stood: again, the cowering, jumpy girl. There was no power in her voice, and its pitch seemed higher than Veronica remembered.

She softened her face, her eyes asking to the younger woman to sit.

"I feel like the kid who says she's getting bullied," said Montbretia, still standing. "But actually nobody can be bothered with her because she's a whiny little bitch, and so she keeps going to the headmistress to get attention."

Veronica tilted her head and tried to bring some warmth to her eyes—the typical journalist's pose whenever you're interviewing the subject for a human-interest story. "Well, speaking as your headmistress, is there anything you feel you should tell me?" She looked up at Montbretia, peering over her half-moons.

Montbretia moved toward the door. "This was a bad idea—I'm wasting your time."

Veronica flicked her eyes back to the leather chair facing across her desk. "Sit." She kept the instruction ambiguous, allowing Montbretia to interpret it as an instruction or an invitation, but her continued eye contact hinted strongly. Almost imperceptibly, Montbretia rocked back and forth before turning and gradually walking back to the chair.

"You wouldn't be here if something didn't matter," said Veronica, trying to keep her voice gentle, her tone reassuring. "You don't go to someone's office, without an appointment, without calling ahead, and you don't go to see the ex-wife of the guy who you work with and who is happy for you to use the spare room in his apartment, if it doesn't matter."

Veronica watched as Montbretia sunk into the chair, almost as if she was hoping it would hide her. She continued, "This must be something to do with Boniface."

Montbretia's cheeks lit up and she bowed her head, hiding her face.

Pleased to have hit her target—not that it was a hard target—Veronica continued. "Shall I talk a bit and tell you where I stand? Perhaps I can tell you a few things Boniface won't say or doesn't know."

A small face poked up in front of her. A delicate movement of her lips suggested agreement.

"We're never going to be the kind of girls to sit around doing each other's nails. We're never going to go out on the lash and have a dare about who will pull and sleep with the ugliest guy, who she will then dispense with in the most cruel manner the next morning."

"True." Montbretia's voice was little more than a breath.

"I could be wrong, but I get the impression that you're the kind of lady who would get bored hanging around when I'm enjoying my favorite hobby."

Montbretia frowned.

"My favorite hobby is drinking whisky." Montbretia's mouth formed a perfect circle. "By the way, would you like a drink?" asked Veronica, reaching into a drawer and putting a half-filled bottle of whisky on the desk.

"No thanks," said Montbretia hesitantly. "I'm on my bike...hence the clothes. Not my regular office getup." She smiled, apparently trying to hide her embarrassment. "Who am I kidding—it's not that far off."

"We don't really know each other, but I like you and hope we can be friendly, perhaps even friends." Montbretia tilted her head as Veronica continued. "However, there are...boundaries."

Veronica paused, waiting for Montbretia to make eye contact. "Boniface is off limits as a subject matter."

Montbretia's face paled, her shoulders tensing.

Veronica tried to keep her voice reassuring. "I'm sure you didn't come to talk about Boniface, but I think it helps to make sure we're clear."

The visitor visibly relaxed.

"I'm not sure how Boniface and I describe our relationship now, but he didn't stop being smart, witty, intelligent, and funny just because we divorced. He didn't lose his integrity or stop believing what he believed because we divorced." Veronica paused. "That's where I stand."

Montbretia's head seemed to be involuntarily acknowledging what Veronica said.

"Boniface is off limits, but let me tell you this: With the divorce and the meltdown, things changed for him. He's become darker on the outside, more mournful, but he's happier on the inside now that he's not fighting his demons." She sighed. "The thing to understand about Boniface is that when he worked for other people, he was an introvert trying to behave like an extrovert, but now he can behave as an introvert, so he's happy. He's happy inside his own head, which is where it matters."

The room fell quiet.

Montbretia's eyes seemed to brighten. "Is Gideon setting him up?"

"Gideon?"

Montbretia pushed her eyes up, questioning.

"What? As a sex slave to keep Gideon's women warm in between courses?"

Montbretia grinned, swiftly pulling her hand to hide her emotion. "No. More serious. I don't really understand. It's...I don't know... It was something Boniface said."

Veronica pondered the question before answering hesitantly. "I have no reason to believe that Gideon is acting against Boniface, but that doesn't mean much." She drew her mouth tight.

"What about strange calls from journalists?" asked Montbretia.

"All the time," said Veronica. "However, they work for me."

"Of course," said Montbretia. "But has there been anyone asking questions about Boniface? Anyone reading questions from a list?"

"A list? No." said Veronica. She passed a business card to the younger woman. "I'm not being much help, but put my numbers into your phone, and if you find out more, call."

forty-seven

Boniface positioned himself in front of Sophie Driesdorfer's desk as the dumpy secretary, wearing a different but shapeless and forgettable dress, burned through the pile of work beside her.

The male voice inside Greta's room moved to the door, which then opened. Regenspurger ghosted out, his gaunt figure clothed in darkness, moving without creating a breeze as he passed. "Fraulein." He dipped his head to Sophie, a half bow; Boniface noticed as she drew in her elbows, shivering as the figure disappeared.

He tried to give her a reassuring smile as Greta's voice, coming from her office, pierced him like a shard of glass. "Boniface, come here and stop wasting Sophie's time."

Greta was running down the list in her notebook as Boniface entered, concerned that he would now be required to explain that his ascribed task—a simple task, get the executives to understand the strategy—had yet to be completed. The question was how to present the issue to Greta. Ironically, for a man whose career was built on presentation, he couldn't figure out the best way to present the topic to his principal.

He became aware that he was speaking, but didn't know what he was saying. His mouth was on autopilot while his brain was in freefall. In his hand, his notepad and pencil were furiously making notes.

"According to Brad, Jeremy is applying for an injunction."

"He's a lawyer, Boniface. Isn't that what they do?"

"But if we're trying to prevent people from talking, it confirms that there is something worth investigating. Once we've stated in writing for the courts what we don't want people to talk about, we can't later argue we didn't know about the problem."

"You're talking in riddles, Boniface." He could hear the nib of her pen dragging over the page in her notebook.

"Joanna refuses to discuss the funding aspects until there has been a statement to the Stock Exchange."

Boniface was relieved that Greta's head was still down as she wrote notes—his facial expression may have hinted that Baines had other issues.

"Brad wants to do something that I don't understand. He seems to want a campaign when the injunction will prevent any public comment."

"An injunction wouldn't apply to us, would it, Boniface?" Greta looked up, her piercing blue eyes framed by her helmet-like hair. "You're making it sound like everything is our fault and nothing is your fault, Boniface. You remember when I hired you, I told you that was a conversation I never wanted to have. We're committed—you need to do what you said you would do."

Boniface sat mute as Greta glared.

She broke the silence. "The other issue, your office. Is that sorted?"

Boniface relaxed. "It's not sorted but there's progress. Montbretia has found someone who knew the dead man who can also identify the two guys who picked him up at Tilbury. It should all be sorted this afternoon."

"That's good," said Greta, standing and walking to the door. "I must just give something to Sophie."

Boniface pondered: Maybe Montbretia was right. Maybe he should resign and live with the consequences if Greta wanted to go public and let all future clients know he had walked away when the going got tough.

"Is there anything else?" Greta returned, closing the door behind her.

"A few strange calls, but nothing specific."

forty-eight

Boniface closed Greta's office door behind him.

"I need somewhere to sit and do a bit of work. Is there a free desk somewhere?" he asked Sophie. Her fingers were moving at a speed that Boniface was sure was a fire risk.

"The cubbyhole. Is that how you pronounce it, cubby?"

"It is," said Boniface. "Sounds good. Where is it?"

"Back here," said Sophie. She moved backward, alerting Boniface that she was standing. She took two steps and pointed to a space that would be a storage area in a normal office but was a makeshift office here. White painted shelves lined the far wall, and an expertly cut plank had been fitted as a desk across one of the side walls, with a drawer underneath.

"Herr Regenspurger usually sits here, but he left immediately after Fraulein Weissenfeld spoke to him."

"When?"

"Just now. While you were in with her." She turned toward her desk, allowing Boniface to pass. "Don't touch anything. It makes Herr Regenspurger angry." She involuntarily pulled her elbows in. "He gets very angry."

"He's a bit territorial, is he?" offered Boniface, his pencil already in his hand as he took out his notepad and started to flick through the pages.

Sophie shook her head. "It's not like that. He…" Boniface glanced up from his notepad as the highly efficient woman shrank before him, her voice a whisper. "He scares me."

"I'll be careful. Very careful." Boniface ripped three pages out of his notebook. "Could you shred these, please?"

"Yes," said Sophie, taking the pages and turning.

Boniface clicked his pencil to extend the lead as he sat at the narrow desk. He glanced down—the lead had stopped extending. He pulled the end of the lead out of the pencil and clicked to load the next lead. Nothing. He rattled the pencil. Nothing. He cursed under his breath and then pulled the drawer under the desk, looking for something to write with.

It was a matter of lore, and Boniface was prepared to argue it was a matter of law, too: When you find someone's passport, you are required to laugh at his photograph. Boniface's arm moved, even though the voices in his head were shouting not to pick up the passport that was sitting in the drawer before him.

Boniface hesitantly leaned out of the cubbyhole. No Sophie. He opened the passport: The lifeless eyes of the unsmiling Regenspurger stared out at Boniface. Accusing, interrogating, disapproving, preparing revenge…

Boniface flipped the page to hide the photo; he felt like a child hiding under the pillow, as if closing his eyes would make the monsters go away.

He surveyed his find. Stamps: passport control stamps and visas. He flicked a few pages, taking in some of the locations Regenspurger had visited: Panama, Venezuela, Mauritania, Liberia, Equatorial Guinea, Argentina, French Guiana, Yemen,

Georgia, Lithuania, Philippines, Iran, Vietnam, Indonesia, Somalia, Iraq, Djibouti, Ivory Coast, United Arab Emirates, the stamps and visas continued.

"Shit. Shit, shit, shit. Shit, shit, shit, shit, shit, shit, shit, shit." Boniface could hear himself cursing under his breath. "It was Regenspurger."

He flicked back through the passport, checking the stamps, looking at the dates. His route was clear: The first stop was the Ivory Coast, arriving on 17 October. 19 October his passport was stamped in Mauritania. The next day, Liberia. The following day he was in Equatorial Guinea, and then on to Somalia, arriving on 22 October and departing on 24 October, when he returned to the Ivory Coast.

Twenty days later, on 13 November, he was back in Somalia. The date wasn't lost on Boniface. MV Paranoid with its toxic cargo had arrived on 15 November. According to his passport, Regenspurger then left the country on 17 November but had returned since, his last visit being ten days prior.

There was the sound of footsteps. As he hurriedly stuffed the passport back into the drawer, Boniface leaned out of the cubbyhole to see Sophie. "I made confetti," she said.

Boniface frowned. This unmarried, wedded-to-her-job-and-probably-never-would-be-married lady might have something of a wedding obsession.

"The pages. I shredded them…it gives you confetti," said Sophie, returning to her desk.

"Thank you," said Boniface. "I wonder…could you get me a cup of tea, please?"

"Certainly," said Sophie, already back on her feet. "Milk and sugar?"

"Milk, one sugar," said Boniface, pulling out his phone and opening the drawer as Sophie left.

He fumbled, holding Regenspurger's passport in one hand and his phone in the other as he photographed the pages with the passport control stamps. He put the passport back into the drawer, lying on top of a blue folder, and shut the drawer.

He paused, leaned out of the cubbyhole, and ducked back, opening the drawer and taking out the blue folder.

The icy chill of the Stasi put its fingers around Boniface's heart and gripped tightly, stopping its beat.

He was breathless, winded, feeling physically sick.

He glanced down again at the open folder. Photos printed by a black-and-white laser printer, circles drawn by hand with a thick red pen to identify individuals in the photos.

The building was immediately recognizable. When he saw his own face circled, he knew it wasn't an amusing coincidence: His initial reaction had been right; it was his office.

He turned to the next photo and felt his heart kick. Montbretia. Circled in red. Montbretia. Identified.

He flicked through the remaining photos: His office, people coming, people going, which was to be expected in a block shared with other tenants, but only he and Montbretia were circled.

The sound of footsteps jolted him, and he flipped over the pictures. "Your tea." Sophie put the cup down on the small surface, next to the papers Boniface had flipped over.

"Thank you," said Boniface, realizing the sound he was making was the aspiration of air with no vibration of his vocal chords, which were paralyzed.

He turned back the pages as Sophie spun back to her desk. Surreptitiously, he held his phone, snapping pictures of the photos with red circles. He winced with the sound of the shutter, cursing that he'd never learned how to silence the phone as he held it tightly to muffle the sound, and then replaced the pictures in the folder, slipping it back into the drawer.

"Monty. It's Boniface," he whispered, using both hands to hold his phone. "Call me. Call me immediately."

He stood, hastily scanned the space where he had been sitting, making sure he had left no trace before walking past Sophie's desk without a word.

forty-nine

Boniface strolled down the two flights of stairs, mock saluting to Lennie as he passed his station on the middle floor. With each step he felt his phone—each step a knock against his chest, a reminder of the photos it contained and a distraction when he needed to focus.

At the bottom of the stairs he headed left, following the black-and-white marble tiles. Reaching an open door, he took a breath before entering—a cursory knock as he stepped into the room, hanging just inside the door. "Hey, dude."

The big Canadian looked up, his face sullen.

"I was a bit of a jerk earlier on: I'm sorry. Could I take you to lunch...as an apology?"

Brad went to speak, tilting his head as you would when disappointing a slow child with a basic fact. Boniface continued speaking. "To be frank, I've got something and I'd like to get your advice. It needs your expertise."

Brad's eyes sparked. "Well sure, dude! Of course! I'm always delighted to help."

"Cool, bro." Boniface felt he had exhausted his supply of Brad-isms already. "Are you good to go now?"

"Sure," said Brad, gathering up some papers as Boniface moved fully into the room. "Where are we going?" He dropped the papers into his desk, locking it as he stood.

"There's a great pub down the road," said Boniface. "It's a proper English pub, good food, proper English beer as well as the chilled stuff in bottles. Or if you want something with a bit more flounce, there's a nice French restaurant that I haven't tried yet."

"The pub sounds great," said Brad, reaching up to place something—the key that locked his desk, guessed Boniface—on top of a small glass case containing a hockey puck. "Let's go."

Boniface followed the Canadian. "You like good food? Proper home-cooked food, not something out of a packet or slung in a microwave?"

"Of course I do, dude."

"Of course you do. A big guy like you needs to eat, right, bro?"

They walked through the courtyard garden and out of the gate. Boniface tilted his head to the left, leading his companion down the hill and turning right at the second crossroads. "There we are," said Boniface, pointing to a pub about 100 yards down the street, dropping the pace and wrapping his arms around his stomach. He groaned—a low moan, animal-like—and pointed a contorted face toward Brad.

"What's up, man?" asked the Canadian. "You look in pain."

Boniface looked around, checking they were not overheard. "I got the squits, dude." He winced. "You go find a table, order yourself a beer, and check out the menu. I'll duck back to the office and empty my stomach."

"I'll come with," the big Canadian started.

"No, dude. I'll be fine." He grimaced. "I don't need you holding my hand when I'm...you know... Go and get a good table—I'll be with you in a few minutes, but now I've got to run before I leave a nasty stain." He turned, then looked back at Brad. "Make sure you set up a tab—it's my treat, remember."

Boniface clutched himself, gracelessly lumbering to the corner, checking behind to make sure the Canadian was still heading toward the pub. Around the corner he released his grip on his stomach, stood up straight, and jogged back to Weissenfeld's office. He saluted to Lennie via the CCTV camera as he passed through the outer gate and went straight to Brad's office, reaching to his full stretch to get what was, indeed, the key. He dropped into Brad's chair, unlocking the top drawer and lifting the contents onto the desk.

The top loose sheets of paper were handwritten—at a guess, Brad's fitness log.

He opened the green file below the loose pages. The sheets were neatly clipped inside and had never been turned. The first page was a handwritten note.

> *Brad*
>
> *Mr Farrant wanted you to have a copy of this dossier.*
>
> *T*

Boniface noticed the handwriting—he had seen it in Farrant's office. Presumably T was Tamsin Smales-Mainer, Jeremy Farrant's indentured servant cum lawyer.

He opened the next file, a buff-colored piece of card with a few loose sheets with typed notes. He recognized the handwriting:

> *B*
>
> *Your copy*
>
> *T*

Then he noticed the heading: Greta briefing.

The note was dated two days ago. Boniface skimmed the contents: a near-verbatim record of his discussion with the CEO about issues from his past that could cause Weissenfeld embarrassment.

Issues that could cause Boniface embarrassment, too.

Boniface pulled out his phone and photographed the pages scattered over the desk before moving to the next file. This was thicker, stuffed with unclipped paper, but with several batches of stapled sheets.

The first was labeled: key talking points. Boniface scanned it. There were two columns. In the first was a list of some of the key dubious behaviors in Boniface's past. The second column appeared to suggest a retort to anyone disagreeing with the "fact" in the first column. Boniface photographed it and placed it face down on the opposite leaf of the folder.

The second sheet was in a different format from the other documents. There was no heading, no footer, no file reference, no date, and the font was one that any modern word processor would default to. All the document contained was a list of questions—questions that had become very familiar to Boniface since the police first mentioned them to him yesterday.

Next was a stapled bundle labeled "people Boniface has upset." The list started with Stan Gadson and his researcher. Boniface flicked through the pages, photographing each one, briefly scanning for details. Some names were familiar. Some he knew had once borne a grudge. Many he didn't recognize.

The next stapled bundle was much thinner: people for background. He recognized a few names as he photographed.

The list of journalists was two pages long and looked more like a spreadsheet printout with columns for name, outlet, phone number, and email address, with a few hand-scribbled annotations that Boniface couldn't figure out. He photographed the pages, then scanned the column of names: not one name he recognized. A similar trip down the outlet column: again, nothing he recognized—there was no BBC, no Times, no major news outlet. Instead, these seemed to be small shipping and transport-related journals.

He placed the list on the left, leaving the final document: a single-page document, dated tomorrow, with the word "draft" stamped in red at the top and bottom. Boniface started to read: "We are hugely disappointed to have been let down…"

fifty

Boniface and Brad walked across the courtyard garden and through the front door of Weissenfeld's office. They stood facing each other at the foot of the stairway to the middle floor.

"So I said, 'Dude'!" Brad threw his head back, laughing out loud.

Boniface laughed. It was the laugh he had honed through several thousand non-funny situations where he was still expected to show empathy and not reveal his true feelings. His true feelings that Brad was the most obnoxious, juvenile misfit it had ever been his misfortune to encounter and all he wanted was never to be in the same room as the overgrown child again. Boniface wasn't even sure what he was laughing at: He'd stopped paying attention ninety minutes ago, when he forced himself to ask Brad an inane question that he knew the dimwit would be able to understand sufficiently so he would think he had given Boniface some good advice.

"They've been looking for you," Lennie stood at the top of the stairs, disappointment in his eyes. "They've gathered in Mister Farrant's room, I believe."

"Dude. I've got work—let's do it again soon." Brad bear-hugged Boniface before turning toward his office.

"Both of you," said Lennie in a flat tone.

"After you," said Boniface, following Brad as they ascended, giving Lennie a pained look, followed by a wink as the pair passed.

Boniface walked behind Brad as they entered Farrant's office to find Greta seated in the club chair and Joanna Baines on the sofa. Boniface indicated to Brad the seat next to the CFO before turning and resting on the overly large desk spanning most of the right wall. As he rested on the desk, Boniface noticed Tamsin Smales-Mainer standing, sentry-like, just inside the door.

"Thank you all for coming." Jeremy Farrant strutted like a professor—an exquisitely and expensively clothed professor—preparing to deliver a lecture to a group of eager students. "I am pleased to tell you that we have been granted an injunction. I won't bore you with the details, but broadly it covers all matters in connection with the Somalia problem, and its scope prevents the UK press from publishing details about the matter."

"Why only the UK?" Boniface was surprised to see Brad asking a question.

Farrant smiled, a thin smile with no warmth. "The UK courts—or should I say, the Courts of England and Wales—can only require parties within the jurisdiction of the United Kingdom to refrain from publishing details. Unfortunately, we can't go round telling those foreign chappies what they should do."

"But isn't that sort of the point that Boniface made?" Brad turned to Boniface. "You don't mind me asking this, do you, bro?"

"Please continue," said Boniface, resting more securely on the desk hewed from ancient wood.

Brad turned back to Farrant. "So surely what we've done is told everyone that we've got a problem—we wouldn't want an injunction otherwise—and now all the foreign papers can print the story, citing us as their source, and we can't do anything to stop it?"

"We can." The lawyer's tone was sharp. Dismissive. "We apply for an injunction in their country."

"Every country? Like, there isn't a central place in Europe or something we could go to?"

Farrant's tone remained sharp. "But you're missing the point. We have applied for, and been granted, what in tabloid parlance is often called a 'super-injunction'." A look of pride crossed his face. "This is an injunction where, in addition to restraining the publication of certain allegations, the existence and details of the injunction may not be legally reported. So there's no source for your foreign newspapers."

"What about the interne…"

The lawyer cut off Brad. "But we've also gone further and included Mister Boniface within the scope of the injunction."

"I beg your pardon," said Boniface. "You've done what?"

The owner of the castle in Scotland frowned, tilting his head. "I think it's quite plain to everyone else, even if it's not apparent to you, Boniface, that there must be a connection between your work for Weissenfeld Shipping, the human reliquiae in your office, and this whole sorry issue in Somalia. Manifestly, there must be a leak or something in your organization, and so for belt-and-braces protection I have made sure there will be no stories about you in the press."

"That's crazy." Greta was standing, her notebook snapped shut. "Do you mean we can't say anything about Boniface and the dead body?"

The lawyer's tone was soothing. "No, it just means the press can't report it."

"So we can't protect ourselves?" Greta turned to Boniface, her tone almost apologetic. "No offense, Boniface, but we might need to throw you to the wolves if you become an embarrassment."

"No offense taken," said Boniface lightly, wondering how painful it would be to be chewed by wolves.

The CEO continued. "The point of an injunction is to ensure that Weissenfeld will be immunized against any publicity during the period if, or when, Boniface goes down." Her attitude became more conciliatory. "But you are certain that there's no way for anyone to get around this injunction?"

"A question in Parliament," offered Boniface.

Greta turned to Boniface, frowning.

"Members of Parliament are covered by parliamentary privilege, which means they can't be prosecuted for breaking an injunction in Parliament, even a super-injunction, and the press can report what happened in Parliament, as long as they don't deviate from what was said. That's right, isn't it, Tamsin?" Boniface stared at Farrant's assistant, who nodded her affirmation.

"That's not what we agreed," said Greta quietly to no one in particular.

"Now I'm sure there's no necessity to remind everyone to make sure everything is locked away." The senior lawyer walked behind his desk and tapped his safe, a smug grin spreading over his face. "The last thing we want is any sort of leak from this office that undermines our case."

fifty-one

Boniface let the other meeting participants leave the lawyer's office before him.

As he closed the door behind him, he saw two eyes fixing him. Two eyes, radiating hate. Two eyes alive in a dead face of loose gray skin, balanced on a body wrapped in nondescript black clothing.

Boniface could feel no warmth from the man, could smell no odor, could feel no movement of air as the figure approached. All he knew was the two orbs locking him in position.

The figure lifted his hand. "I believe this is your pencil, Mister Boniface." Regenspurger paused before continuing. "I understand the Fraulein instructed you not to touch anything, and yet..."

"I didn't," said Boniface, his throat contracting.

"And yet, I found it. In my drawer. Under my papers." His voice was soft, almost reassuring, and calm—Boniface had never known such menace as the former Stasi officer, and now apparently international jetsetter between some of the most ungoverned regimes, let the silence hang.

"I have put my papers back in order, Mister Boniface, and now I think it's time for you to leave." The eyes pointed to the stairs and Boniface felt compelled to move, walking down the two flights in silence, through the front door and across the courtyard.

The gate slammed shut, and the two men faced each other on the street. The former Stasi agent stepped forward, stopping when their noses were twelve inches apart.

"I believe you have a notebook," he said, snapping the fingers of his outstretched hand.

fifty-two

Montbretia sat on the leather sofa: too low, too uncomfortable.

Somewhere at the coffee shop's head office, someone had decided that this sofa had the look they were after, and then a finance director had pointed out that the unit cost multiplied by the number of outlets gave a big number and so they had bought something that looked similar but could be sourced for one third of the price. Now in every store in the chain—like this one in Fenchurch Street station—there were customers sitting on uncomfortable brown sofas, wondering why the table in front of them was a little too high and worrying that it was quite difficult and rather undignified to get out of the seat.

As Montbretia wondered about moving to a more sensible seat, Boniface came in. She noticed his tie first. He didn't always feel it appropriate to wear a tie, but when he did—as he had been while working with his current client—the tie was always perfect: a symmetrical half-Windsor knot, tightened to his collar, hanging straight, the point reaching a small way over his waistband.

Now his tie was pulled down and hung to one side.

She tried to catch his eye. His usual sharp glint was gone. The usual penetration with which he would inquisitively scan a room was missing. His eyes were moving but not seeing. Montbretia inelegantly rolled out of the sofa to stand and took two steps, positioning herself to obstruct his unfocused gaze. "You looked rough this morning, but you're looking a whole lot worse now."

He looked up, a widening of his eyes suggested recognition.

"Sit down. I'll get you a cup of tea."

She walked to the counter and ordered a tea, looking back at Boniface, now trapped in a seat from which he might never be able to raise himself, at least not without the help of a crane. His hair—short and neat, styled so that you don't notice but you somehow remember, cared for sufficiently that the rules of basic hygiene are met while never being washed more than once a day and never becoming an obsession—was now messy, even more messy than it had been when they talked in Green Park. That wasn't the problem. The problem was that Boniface didn't seem to notice and, more worryingly, didn't seem to care.

Montbretia tentatively placed the tea before Boniface and sat down as he mumbled something that she assumed to be thanks. Feeling like a young child on Christmas morning, she started. "I found Albie...Albie the Albanian."

Boniface's visage remained impassive.

Montbretia tried again. "Albie the Albanian. He saw the two guys.... I've spoken to him.... I would have got more, but your message," she smiled, "all three of your messages, sounded important so I came here. I'll go back and talk to Albie and see if I can video him so that we've got something we can show the police." She held up her camera to show how she intended to video the vagrant.

Boniface sipped his tea, his eyes now starting to move as if under control of his brain, but still he wouldn't make eye contact with Montbretia.

He exhaled through his nose, the air stream rippling the surface of his tea. "I know who dumped the body."

Montbretia was struggling to speak, trying to form a question.

"I can't prove it yet. But all the pieces are there." Montbretia held him in her gaze, eyes wide, nodding for him to continue. "His name's Regenspurger. Garen Regenspurger."

Montbretia fell back in her seat. "Reagan. They all said Reagan-something." She sat straighter. "So who is he and why did he dump a body?"

"He's what you might call a fixer. A troubleshooter. He makes problems go away."

"But he doesn't seem to have made this problem go away—he seems to have created the problem."

Boniface pushed a hand through his hair. It didn't return it to its usual state, but at least the top of his head looked slightly less wild. "You're looking from the wrong end of the telescope. We're the solution to someone else's problem."

Montbretia listened, still not sure what question to ask, but keeping her focus on Boniface.

Boniface met her gaze. "Let me try and explain. I was hired by the client..."

"The super-secret client," Montbretia could hear the grit in her voice. "Are you saying it was them?"

Boniface remained impassive. "You need to hear this. Shouting won't help."

Montbretia shrank. "Sorry."

"I was hired by the client. I was hired before I met you, before I met Ellen, before Nigel, before everything. I was hired for many reasons, including my political connections, and—I like to hope—because I am good." He straightened his tie halfway and continued. "The client had a problem: The story could be newsworthy, but from a business-reputation point of view, it would be poison." Boniface snorted and whispered "poison" under his breath.

"This wasn't your usual sort of corporation in trouble—this wasn't a fire that needed extinguishing, this was a potential problem that would last over years. Five years, ten years, twenty years. Importantly, they didn't think the story was about to break, so what they wanted to do was take control of the situation and have a strategy in place so that when the story did break, they could demonstrate they were already proactively managing the issue." He waited, looking Montbretia straight in the eye. "They were doing the right thing in a difficult situation and wanted me to help ensure that the right message got out there."

"So, Saint Boniface, what was the problem?"

Boniface snorted. "They're a shipping company. A big shipping company who move a lot of stuff around the world. Somehow, a load of toxic waste was taken to Somalia and dumped. Except, it wasn't just dumped—they paid to dump the waste, and the locals they paid moved it to where they drop all their other waste, right next to a squatter camp. Our guys didn't know where it went—they didn't care; they were glad to have got rid of their waste—and nobody in Somalia knew or cared what they had: The people in the squatter camp don't have the internet, and the people who took the cash were busy getting drunk and paying for hookers. You can get a lot of hookers when you're dealing with dollars."

His face turned gray and his speech became strained. "What no one realized was this waste had radioactive materials and all sorts of chemical nasties that got mixed together." He paused, apparently deep in thought. "When it rained, all the poison got washed into the water supply." His eyes misted. "People died. Men, women, children. Some died quickly, some slowly. Some have had their lives blighted—people are blind, there are birth defects…. It's awful."

Montbretia stared at Boniface and started gently. "That's awful, but why are you so cut up?" Then, becoming aware of what she said, with more urgency and even less thought. "It's not that you shouldn't be upset, but you look like it's your fault."

A woman with large gold dangling earrings came into the café and recognized a bleached blonde across the room. Montbretia struggled to hear Boniface's quiet voice over the two women screeching. "The story I was told was that it was beyond doubt that the client was at fault. After all, they paid for the waste to be accepted. But the line was always that no one knew who made the decision. The inference has always been that it was the captain or maybe someone from the local company." He hesitated. "So I was working with the owners, who privately acknowledged their corporate culpability and wanted to make things right."

"Why do I feel there's a however?" asked Montbretia.

"Because there is." Boniface held out his phone. "I've got the evidence. Photographic evidence. Someone knew what was going on. Someone sent the ship to Somalia and then flew there, arriving a few days before the ship and leaving after the waste had been dumped." His voice a whisper. "This wasn't an accident. This was premeditation."

They sat without speaking, becoming consumed in the noise of the café with the train announcements intermittently breaking through from outside.

"That someone," began Montbretia. "Who?"

"Regenspurger."

"Regenspurger? The guy who's looking down the telescope from the other end?" Boniface made no movement as Montbretia continued. "The guy who's responsible for the dumping the body in our office?"

Boniface flicked his eyelids in acknowledgement—apparently tilting his head was too much effort.

"I don't understand."

"That doesn't matter." Boniface hesitated. His voice faded and he continued, his tone almost apologetic. "Some things are not quite as you thought."

Montbretia frowned. "You mean you lied?" It was a tentative question, not a statement.

"No. I told you the truth. But not the whole truth. There are gaps in what I told you, and you've had the impression that things are different to how they really are."

"You had better explain, quickly."

"The work you've been doing for the Global Logistics Forum. Getting it set up, finding contributors, building the website, the benefits of global trade, ethical considerations…all that stuff."

Montbretia tipped her head forward warily.

"Through the work you've done, you know some of the big shipping companies? At least by name and some of the very broad details of their businesses?" Montbretia continued her hesitant affirmation as Boniface kept talking. "So you're acquainted Weissenfeld Shipping."

Montbretia's nodding became far more positive. "Big firm. Lots of different shipping lines with different specializations—have a ship for pretty much every job. Run by Greta Weissenfeld. She's built it from a small family business to what it is today. Determined woman, very smart, very savvy, but don't stand in her way." She wrinkled her nose. "I've seen some photos—always very well presented even if it's not how I would dress. Forty-something. That's about it."

"You know how the Forum has been largely funded by a Spanish trust?"

Montbretia nodded, feeling some foreboding about what she was about to hear.

"Weissenfeld is our client and Weissenfeld has been funding the Forum."

Montbretia thought for a moment. "That doesn't make any sense, Boniface. If they funded the Forum, then why did Weissenfeld make such a stink when that Norwegian guy wrote an article about foreign shipping crews? Surely they could have ignored it; I mean, it's not as if the piece even mentioned them."

"But they had a point: The article went too far. Read in a certain manner, it wasn't far off racist."

"Come on, Boniface, it was accurate, even if you didn't like the style."

"It had some points of fact that were correct, but how it was presented was misleading. It implied that foreign sailors are a safety hazard, where the truth of the matter is sailors from the Philippines, India, Singapore, Panama, Africa, Europe, or wherever are all uniformly safe. The nuance the article didn't bring home is that it's the range of different languages spoken that leads to reduced safety. It's not the fact that crews are foreign, it's the fact that they don't all speak the same language, which leads to misunderstandings and accidents, and against that background Weissenfeld put out a press release criticizing the Global Logistics Forum. But in reality, it was a very mild press release."

"Mild? Did you read the press release, Boniface?"

Boniface met her stare. "Read it? I wrote it."

"You."

Boniface nodded. "Yes. Me."

"But..."

A glint flashed in Boniface's eye. "But what? Tell me, what happened after that press release?"

"There was a piece in the *Financial Times*, a short article on the BBC website, some French sites picked it up. I don't know—there was a lot of shouting—what specifically are you referring to?"

"What happened to your web traffic?"

"It grew."

"By how much?"

"It spiked." Montbretia threw up her hands, almost to dismiss the comment. "For the first three days we averaged fifty times the normal traffic. After that died down, we stayed at about ten times the normal traffic."

"What about the links from other websites, like the BBC?"

"We got a lot."

"A few weeks later, what happened to your ranking on Google, Bing, and the other search engines?"

"We starting hitting the first page of results for key target search terms."

"So take me through this slowly. Where's the downside to you, to the Forum, to the website, arising from the press release issued by Weissenfeld?"

Montbretia sat, moving her lips but knowing that no sound was coming out.

"Can we do the painful bit and join the dots?" Boniface asked.

Montbretia remained still as Boniface continued. "Super-secret client. Weissenfeld. Employer of Regenspurger. Weissenfeld. You and I. Working for Weissenfeld.

The Global Logistics Forum. My idea to help as part of a process to manage the press reaction to an accident. In good faith, you thought it was an independent forum. In reality, Weissenfeld's motives may be to use the Forum to help cover up their willful dumping of toxic waste in Somalia."

Montbretia stood, wrapping her arms around herself, taking small gulps of air. "You lied. You lied about who was financing the Forum, you lied about its purpose. You made a judgment call—you didn't give me the information to make my own decision. In fact, you gave me enough information to lead me to one conclusion: the wrong one. Now you're saying that I've been working for a company that has killed hundreds of people by dumping chemical waste, and it's not your fault because you had the best of intentions."

She took a few more gulps of air and pushed her hair behind her ears. "Do you get it? It's not that I feel foolish—I feel like I've..." She stumbled over her words. "I don't feel like—I have been helping a murderer get away with it. The lies, I'll get over. The lack of trust..."

A tear slipped down her cheek. "What is it about you and these dysfunctional domineering women? They're like catnip to you—is it some form of new addiction to replace your old ones?" The people at the next table turned at the raised voice.

"There's one other thing," said Boniface, softly but firmly.

"I don't care."

"You need to. We've been under surveillance. Me and you. Regenspurger's got photographs of us—me and you, separately and together—going into and out of the office, red hand-drawn circles marking us out."

Montbretia felt like a truculent teenager. "Wow. You've put me in danger, too. I might get hurt by a red circle."

"This is serious, Monty. Regenspurger is a dangerous man. Whatever you do, for the next couple of days stay away from the office, stay away from Tilbury, stay away from my place, stay away from your house. Stay in a hotel, go somewhere—I'll pay. Just don't be found."

"What are you going to do?" She paused. "No. Don't tell me. I don't care and I wouldn't believe it anyway." She stepped away from the table and hesitated. "I'll come and collect my stuff—from your place and the office—sometime. But at the moment, I'm too angry to be in the same room as you."

fifty-three

"If I may summarize," Stephen Holding, Boniface's criminal lawyer, looked up. "In making these comments, I am, naturally, taking a harsh view. I don't wish to give you any false hope."

"Naturally," said Boniface without any commitment as he skulked in the corner of Holding's office, looking at the scuffmarks on the desk's modesty board and imagining the thousands of clients—all on legal aid, wearing their best nylon-shell suits—who had come into this room, sat in one of the chairs opposite the lawyer, and then tilted the chair back, resting their feet against the modesty board.

"The nearest you've got to material you could produce in court is some photos that were probably obtained illegally, meaning that they have little evidential value. However, if I'm wrong and we could construct an argument that these photos were legally obtained, then I'm not sure that they prove much."

Boniface frowned.

"Look, Boniface. If this goes to court, the other side would argue that they were fakes, and really, what have you got? Some blurred shots of passport control stamps and a few shots of printed pages. It's hardly proof of a criminal conspiracy. It's not like we've got sworn affidavits or statements from the lawyer—not that we would be able to get hold of them easily."

"But is it enough for you, Steve? Is it enough for the cops? Is it enough for some sort of negotiation?"

Holding leaned back in his fabric-covered chair and swiveled to meet his client's gaze. "Can I make sure I've got the remaining details correct? And then perhaps we can talk about the photos—and how they can be used—in context."

Boniface had his arms folded and rocked; his weight transferred through his left foot on the ground, his right leg bent back with his foot against the wall as he tensed and loosened his thigh muscle. "That sounds like a no to me."

"I'm dubious, Boniface, but maybe there are options." The lawyer picked up his steel-rimmed spectacles and looked down on his notes spread across the brown wood of his desk. "You have made some allegations. Let's start with the one that most directly affects you."

"Please continue," said Boniface, standing away from the wall but remaining with his arms folded as he started to walk along the path crossing on the long edge of the lawyer's desk, assiduously avoiding the two fabric-covered seats that Boniface was sure smelled of criminal.

"You say that this Mister Regenspurger ordered the murder of a vagrant who was picked up in Tilbury docks. The body is the one that was subsequently dumped in your office."

Boniface grunted his acknowledgement as he reached the wall that separated the office from the corridor running outside, standing to the right of the dark-brown wood door—the entrance and exit for the room. The wall was solid to waist height—plaster panels, sheetrock as Montbretia called it, which had been regularly repaired—topped with obscured safety glass to the ceiling. Boniface stared at the metal grid embedded in the safety glass before turning and leaning on one of the pillars between two panes.

The room went quiet. Boniface turned to see the lawyer had laid his pen on his desk and was apparently waiting until he had his client's attention. "Other than a few conversations between Montbretia and these vagrants, Angus, Gerbil, and Albie the Albanian, we have no evidence to prove Mister Regenspurger is involved in the murder, and even less suggestion that he was acting on the direction of a company director or officer."

Holding picked up his pen and continued. "Not to mention, we've yet to establish why you would be the target for such a body dump." He looked back at Boniface to acknowledge his next point. "I know you have a theory—and it's a plausible explanation—nonetheless, it lacks any evidence."

Boniface shifted his weight as the lawyer looked down.

"It seems to me that we may be able to prove that Mister Regenspurger has an extensive collection of frequent-flyer miles, that he may have dubious tastes in holiday destinations, and that he returned your pencil in a manner that you found to be intimidating." He turned a page, then turned back. "If Mister Regenspurger was in Somalia and the other African countries at the relevant times, then there may be a reasonable belief on your part that the chief executive, Fraulein Weissenfeld, may have lied to you, but that's not enough to even suggest a connection with the murder of the guy dumped in your office."

Boniface unfolded his hands and swept his hair back.

"How is Montbretia? How has she taken your revelations?" Holding seemed genuinely concerned.

Boniface felt every muscle in his face sag. "I think if we were to describe matters in terms of how one would present the issue to a court, you would say that our relationship—both in terms of business and friendship—has broken down completely and irrevocably. I mean, how do you build trust and get back from what I've done?"

"But you have made the risks—as you perceive them—abundantly clear to Montbretia. She is in no doubt as to the kind of people who are involved, and she understands that she appears to have been under surveillance?"

"I have tried, but she's angry and she's hurt. But she's sensible—once the initial rage has passed, she'll go somewhere she won't be found."

"So, Montbretia is safe." Boniface affirmed as the lawyer carried on. "As for the photos and this Regenspurger character, I'm glad for the information, but I'm not sure that there's anything we can do—at least, there's nothing we can do at the moment."

"Can't we go to the police?" Boniface felt the forlorn hope he was searching for.

A look of disappointment came over the adviser's face. "What? Lay it all out for them?"

Boniface became more enthusiastic—searching for the hope in the question that didn't seem to be present in his lawyer's tone. "Yeah?"

"You remember what I said that first morning about locking yourself into a story?" He sighed. "If you had said nothing, then we could have done something. But you were quite resolute in your defense of your client, and what you are now suggesting is that you change your story. In other words, you are proposing to stand in a police station and say you lied and wasted police time. Not only that, but you are considering going into a police station and saying that you have obtained information possibly by criminal means."

The lawyer continued tentatively. "We can do it. But there are consequences, and I'm not sure we'll get the results you want.

The two men sat in silence before the lawyer continued. "Go home and sleep on it, and if you want to talk, come and find me tomorrow." He pulled an appointment diary out of his suit pocket and started flicking through pages. "I'm free between 10 AM and 10:30."

"Thanks, Steve. I'll sleep on it."

He felt the office door slam behind him before he yanked out his phone, searching for a number as he followed the nylon carpet toward the stairwell. As he reached the street in the early twilight, crossing between angry taxis, motorcycle couriers running late, and frustrated van drivers, the phone picked up. "Tommy. Boniface. I want some manpower."

fifty-four

Montbretia stood. Head bowed, sobbing.

The keen bite of the estuary wind targeted her damp cheeks as she smeared a tear with her finger. In the early evening twilight, the temperature was falling rapidly, but the articulated lorries dragging their containers still thundered up and down the road leading into the docks, apparently unaware of the ending of the day.

Three figures stood on mud and grass next to smashed pallets, burned-out oil cans, and the detritus left by truckers on a strip of land bordered by the road and a steel palisade fence. Angus, Gerbil, and Montbretia in a triangle.

Montbretia sobbed again as she looked to the center of the triangle. "I would have been here. I should have been here." For the second time that day, she clutched herself, raising her head at the top of her sob, letting it fall as she expelled her animal-like pain.

"If I'd been here he'd still be alive, but instead I was wasting time with Boniface. I could have been here sooner." Her head fell and her shoulders quivered.

"If you were here, you'd be dead." Angus's mournful Scottish accent somehow seemed appropriate. "Whoever did this would have killed anyone who got in their way. If you tried to help, you would be lying next to him."

The inert body of Albie the Albanian lay in the middle of the triangle with the three standing guard at each corner. Even in death no one knew Albie's real name, but then again, no one knew what had killed him.

All that could be said with any certainty was that he had been bludgeoned.

The body was face down—half on compacted earth, half on grass—wrapped in a sand-colored raincoat, now spattered with blood. His right leg was broken. Even someone without any medical training could make that diagnosis—it bent midway down the thigh at approximately ninety degrees, with the bone cutting through the fabric of his trousers. His head was turned long past the point that the human neck will tolerate and was now looking down on his back. Or rather, it would have done had the face not been caved in. The eyes were closed and bleeding, the nose literally flattened, and the right cheekbone caved in.

"That's execution," said Angus. "Murder up close, by people with strength."

"I'm calling the police," said Montbretia.

"No." Gerbil spoke for the first time since the three had arrived at the body, his voice scrawny like him, but commanding. "No police."

"You can't leave his body here to get pecked to pieces by the seagulls. He deserves more than that." She wiped another tear as she tugged out her phone. "Much more."

"This looks like a guy who was bludgeoned in a hobo fight," said Angus. "The cops don't like us at the best of times. You think they're going to be friendlier when they have to pretend to care?"

"Then you go," said Montbretia, starting to walk around the body, taking photos. "And step back if you think that a photo might capture your soul."

She took her fifth snap and stood straight, flicking through the pictures, selecting the one that looked goriest. She attached the photo to an email and typed: "Boniface: This is what Regenspurger did" and hit the send button. "No signal. I'll walk up the road until I get some bars and then I'll call the cops. You boys had better scatter. I'll come and find you later. Where will you be?"

"Walk around—we'll find you," said Angus. "I've seen those guys once tonight; I don't want to be around if they decide they've killed the wrong homeless guy."

"You saw them?" Montbretia was concerned.

"They came looking for Albie. The guy with the missing finger looked ready to take a swing with that lump of wood."

"He had a missing finger?" asked Montbretia.

Angus nodded and indicated his right hand. "Half there."

"I'm going to call the police." Montbretia zipped up her fleece. "I'll come looking when I'm finished, but try and find me—I'm not too keen on being out here alone."

fifty–five

It had cost him 150 quid to borrow a cherry picker.

It was useful having an electrician as a mate. An electrician who worked for Southern Supply and spent every day in his cherry picker fixing broken bulbs in streetlights. Except he didn't call them bulbs—bulbs are what go in the ground, apparently. Lamps are what go in streetlights.

Reg Johnson didn't give a toss about whether they were lamps or bulbs, if he was being honest. He had transport with a lift on the back, and all he needed to do was to wait for this Boniface bloke that Tommy had told him to meet here.

Small job. Nice payday. Everyone can be tucked up in bed before midnight. He checked his watch: 9 PM. Right place: southwest corner of Berkeley Square, under a streetlight. Where was this Boni-who-or-whatever?

Three men walked past—each wearing tuxedos. Reg decided to hate them on sight—it would save time assessing all the individual ways he could find to hate them. A man walked past the three coming down the slope: good suit, hair had a bit too much effort but seemed slightly disheveled. He made eye contact and held it.

It couldn't be: Who wears a suit when you're breaking into a building?

Reg reached for the passenger door. The suited man opened it and got into the cab, holding out his hand. "Boniface."

"Reg." He shook Boniface's, feeling the other man's weak grip and small hands. "Reg. Not Reginald, only my mother calls me that, and definitely not Reggie. That's for the wife." He looked the suited man up and down. "You not got anything else to wear?" He indicated the green boiler suit he was wearing. "That's not a usual getup in my line of business."

"It is in mine." Boniface's face remained emotionless. "If I'm seen, I want to at least have a plausible explanation."

"Suit yourself," said Reg, smiling at his small humor as he turned over the engine, which soon found its rhythmic diesel chug. They took the first left, two-thirds of the way up Berkeley Square, followed the road across a crossroads, took the next left, and the next left, into a mews road heading back in the direction of Berkeley Square.

As they passed the corner, Reg said, "This it?"

"Yup," said Boniface.

They continued toward Berkeley Square along the narrow road of garages and upscale apartment blocks, following the next left and pulling up in front of two wooden garage doors, black, set into a white stucco-fronted house.

Reg looked through the windshield, straining to see the higher floors of the buildings, then opened the door, easing himself out to look behind before he killed the engine. He groped between the seats and pulled out something that he threw at Boniface.

"Put that on." As Boniface struggled to pull on a hoodie and a pair of jeans, keeping his polished black brogues, Reg continued. "Round the block once: We're looking for cameras on the building."

"Right," said Boniface, reaching for the door handle.

"Walk. Not fast, not slow. Be aware of your feet and make the minimum noise possible. Feel like you're gliding. Don't do anything to draw attention. You're a ghost. Don't wiggle. Don't walk funny. Put the hood up and keep your head down."

Reg watched him as he walked up the slope, disappearing as he followed the left-hand corner. Three minutes later, he slipped into the passenger door, closing it behind him without making a noise. "Tell me about the cameras," said Reg.

"Three. One on the gate. As you face it, it's up and right. One to the left of the gate, pointed downhill along the side face of the building. One on the lower face of the building, pointing along the wall covering the entrances to those garages. So if you stand on the bottom outside corner and look up, you'll get hit by two cameras covering the walls."

"Gotcha," said Reg, fumbling to stick a fake moustache to his top lip. "I'll be back in three—keys are in the ignition if you've gotta move."

Boniface was muttering something as Reg got out, putting on his sunglasses and a flat-cap to cover his shaved head. He walked the two sides of the block, then turned left down the hill to pass the target, slowing as he approached the building. Having turned the corner and got clear of the building, he speeded up.

"You missed one." Reg shut the door behind him, removing his disguise.

"Really?"

"Go through the gate and there's a little garden, right?"

"Yeah."

"There's a camera covering that," said Reg, holding his hand up and pointing at a downward angle, as if that explained the position of the camera.

He sat back in his seat, turning to Boniface. "This safe. Where is it?"

"Top floor, center and right window."

"Where's the guard?"

"On the middle floor, but he walks around, hence the suit." Boniface pointed at himself, a single flow from his shoulders to his feet.

"I reckon we should take out that camera on the back wall," said Reg, firing up the engine and watchfully pulling out. The cherry picker followed the route the two had walked, rounding the outside corner and turning in close to the former house which was now an office, drawing up as they cleared the end of the building.

He killed the engine and slipped on his hat again. "Keys are in the ignition," he said to Boniface. "I'm going to take out the camera. If we need to skedaddle, then drive, but remember that I'll be in the basket."

"I can't drive," said Boniface. "Well, I can, but it's illegal. I was banned."

Reg exhaled loudly. "Boniface, what we're doing is called criminal enterprise—we're about to break into that building, and I shall then break into a safe for you. In the scale of things, a driving offense is pretty much a civil matter." He paused. "If you want to piss your pants, we'll go home now."

"Sorry," said Boniface sheepishly, sliding into the driver's seat as Reg got out, reaching for a pair of gloves and a hammer in the door tray. He quietly shut the door before walking to the rear of the cherry picker and sliding into the basket once his gloves were on.

Reg looked around, then pressed the button to raise the basket, cringing at the sound of the motor in the quiet night. When it reached level with the roof he stopped, pleased at the silence, and leaned over, pulling off three slates.

Holding the hammer in one hand and the slates in the other, Reg had a quick look before hitting the descend button with the forefinger of his hammer hand. The motor broke the silence, and Reg dropped the slates, watching them shatter on the ground under the CCTV camera but not hearing the noise above the motor. Keeping his finger on the button, he took the hammer with his free hand and, as the basket passed the camera, he swung, knocking it to point at the wall.

The basket reached the bottom and Reg jumped out, pleased to be surrounded by silence.

He opened the van door. "Over there," he pointed to the far corner across the street from the target. "Sit on the ground like you're homeless and watch. Don't get seen and be grateful it's not raining."

Boniface got out and Reg jumped in. "I'm going to hide the wagon. I'll be back to find you. And put your hood up."

fifty–six

"Anything?" Boniface hadn't noticed or heard Reg approach, but now he was squatting beside him as he sat on the corner of the crossroad opposite Weissenfeld Shipping's London office.

"The security guard came out and looked. He saw the slate, threw his hands up, and went in. That's it; that's all that has happened."

"So in the last hour, no police? No additional security? No one coming or going?"

"A few people walked up and down the street. Maybe residents, maybe people from the offices. They were all in a hurry."

"Okay, let's go."

"We're going in?" asked Boniface, becoming aware that his throat was tightening and his pitch rising.

"I'll go and get the cherry picker. Back in ten. You keep watching here." The shaved head on top of a somewhat rotund dark-green boiler suit with splayed feet departed, walking as if he hadn't made it to the bathroom in time.

Reg and the cherry picker were back in ten minutes.

Boniface found himself like a wild animal, his head twisting in the direction of any noise as he walked over to the vehicle with the basket directly under the right window.

He removed his borrowed clothes and joined Reg in the cherry-picker basket. "Up, in, open the safe, out, down, gone."

Boniface wasn't sure whether that was an explanation or an order from Reg. He nodded anyway, and as he did the motor graunched across the night, lifting the basket to the window. As the basket stopped, there was silence, apart from the metallic creaks as the basket rocked.

Boniface noticed that in the split second he had become aware of the quiet, Reg had opened the wooden sash window and moved inside. He was now offering his hand to Boniface, who struggled through the window, reaching the floor and finding every creak in the several-hundred-year-old floorboards.

He walked to the wall on the left behind the large desk, the room dull with only the ambient light outside. With each step, a creak. Reg followed, each step as if his foot was held by a cushion of air. Boniface pointed to the safe on the wall. "That."

There was a sound outside: someone passing. Boniface took three swift steps, reached the light switch, and flicked it as the door swung open. "Mister Boniface."

"Lennie," said Boniface, trying to remember what normal behavior looked like. "I came in here for a kip," he pointed to the scroll-armed sofa, "but slept for a bit longer than I was expecting. I've just opened the window to get a bit of fresh air." He dropped his voice. "You won't tell them?"

"I thought you had gone," said the security guard. "When you and Mister Regenspurger walked out, he said that you had been suddenly called away and signed you out. I didn't know you were back—I didn't see your name on the log."

"Sorry, Lennie. I must have forgotten when I came back." He grimaced. "Long day and all that."

The guard nodded, pensive. "Did you hear anything? While you've been in here?"

"Hear?" asked Boniface.

"We've had a problem with the camera. Look, I can show you," said the guard, moving forward.

"It's alright," said Boniface. "I know the one you mean. The one just out here."

"Funny thing. It looks like some slates fell off the roof and knocked it. It's no use to man nor beast now." He chuckled to himself, plainly desperate to relay a witticism he had been planning for a while. "Scrub that. It's useful as a pigeon perch."

"Didn't hear a thing," said Boniface. "What will you do—get someone in tomorrow?"

"Tomorrow? You've got to be kidding. They've got a four-hour contract." He checked his watch. "But at this time of night, they're normally here in under two, so hopefully it'll be fixed within the next forty-five minutes."

"That's quick," said Boniface, trying to disguise the tension in his voice. "I guess I should get on—you don't want me still here when they come to fix the camera."

"I'll leave you to it," said the security guard as he closed the doors.

"Next time, Boniface, talk faster," said Reg, noiselessly extricating himself from under Jeremy Farrant's desk. "I'm too old to be hiding under desks—learn to say less." He stretched his legs, turning toward the safe. "But I've got to say, that is really soft carpet. I could sleep on that floor."

"Any idea how long?" asked Boniface.

"Looks old. Shouldn't take long," said Reg, reaching into his pocket and pulling out a bird's nest of pieces of metal.

Both of their heads jerked to face the door. "You carry on. I'll deal with it," said Boniface, straightening his tie and tugging the sides of his jacket to pull it tight around his shoulders. He stepped into the corridor, closing the double doors of Jeremy Farrant's office behind him, and stood where he had been when, several hours earlier, Regenspurger approached him to return his pencil.

"Hey Lennie," said Boniface, seeing the familiar shape of the security guard creaking up the old stairway.

"I thought you'd like to know that I've marked you as coming back into the office at about 5 PM, which is when I was on my break." He leaned in, frowning, his voice conspiratorial. "That way we've got the records straight, in case they check." He winked.

"That's good," said Boniface.

"Did I tell you what little Kayleigh has been up to now?"

"She's the youngest," said Boniface—questioning more than stating. The security guard nodded, standing up straight and beaming. "Listen, Lennie, I've got a few bits to finish. Can I tidy up and I'll come down? We can have a cup of tea and you can tell me then."

"Right you are," said the guard, turning. "You want to hear this story. She's just like her mother."

"I'll be right with you," said Boniface. As he got to the door, he turned back. "Lennie. Is there anyone else still here?"

"You're the last one. Sophie left about ten minutes ago."

"Thanks, Len," said Boniface, slipping back into the office and closing the door. "Sorry, Reg, he wanted to talk about his granddaughter. How's it going?"

"Beautiful safe. Lovely piece of engineering for its day, but someone replaced the lock."

"That sounds bad," said Boniface, pulling out his phone. "How long will this take?" He switched on his phone before looking up at Reg. "If they know I'm here, I might as well have my phone on."

"What do you mean how long?" asked Reg. "I'm in. The new lock is a piece of fluff designed to look good—there's more security on a kid's jewelry box. You could've got in with a wire coat hanger." He let the safe door swing open. "Do you want it all?"

"Let me look at what's there," said Boniface, moving to the open door.

"Pick it up and let's go," said Reg with some urgency. "You can read these at your leisure when we haven't got someone who will notice that there's already a cherry picker where he wants to put his cherry picker."

"We need to lock this back in the safe. Missing papers will cause a big problem." Boniface's phone pinged; reflexively, his hand moved toward his pocket.

"Ignore that," said Reg. "Start looking." He lifted all the papers out of the safe and laid them on top of Jeremy Farrant's desk.

Boniface opened the first file. The content was familiar: Tamsin Smales-Mainer's research on him. There seemed to be a bit more detail and more background, but no surprises. The next file contained a few notes on the application for the injunction. Boniface scanned the instructions to counsel, chuckling as he read the signature of the instructing lawyer, seeing Jeremy Farrant's signature, knowing the document was the work of Tamsin Smales-Mainer.

"Hurry up, Boniface." Reg's eyes burned into Boniface as he flipped over the last file. Boniface was no expert, but as far as he could tell, the documents he was looking at were the legal deeds for Farrant's Scottish castle and the surrounding estate.

"There's nothing here. Put it back and lock it up," said Boniface, pulling out his phone: one email from Montbretia. He felt like he had been punched in the stomach and only became aware of his legs giving way when he found himself leaning on the desk.

"Ready?" asked Reg.

"I've got to go this way," said Boniface, pulling himself together. Reg looked somewhere between shocked and confused. "They've signed me in so I've got to sign out...and Lennie...I've got to listen about his granddaughter." He slipped his phone back into his pocket and looked up. Reg was gone.

Boniface walked to the window and looked out. "You're sure you're not coming?" said Reg, standing in the basket.

"I'm sure I should pay attention: You've had more experience than I have when it comes to making a swift getaway." He offered him his hand. "Thanks. I appreciate the help."

Reg nodded his acknowledgement as he shook Boniface's hand through the window. "Tommy will settle up," said Boniface.

Reg nodded.

"Don't forget to submit a VAT receipt." Boniface winked, lip-reading a stream of profanities as Reg's voice was lost under the motor lowering the basket. Boniface pulled down the window and conscientiously locked it. You never could be too cautious—he had heard there were burglars in the area.

He followed the twisting corridor to Greta's office and entered without knocking. Lacking occupants, the Louis XIV furniture looked even more ridiculous than it did when the queen was in her hive. Without any occupants, it was a swift task to confirm that no papers were kept there, and why would they be—Greta kept all her records in her notebook, which was with her at all times.

Boniface pulled out his phone. "Tommy. One last favor." He reflexively looked around the room to see if he was overheard. "Have you got someone who's quick on their feet?"

fifty-seven

Boniface hadn't slept well. After one night in his own bed, he had returned to the hotel close to the Weissenfeld office, but this time he was paying, not Weissenfeld.

Lennie's chattering had seemed interminable, and Boniface was happy when the engineer arrived to fix the broken CCTV camera. Boniface had made some sort of interested noises—it did seem odd that three slates would fall off, and no, he wouldn't have expected that much damage either, but there you go—and then left, telling Lennie he didn't want to be in the way while the guard dealt with the engineer.

Boniface was sure that Lennie's stories of his granddaughter's exploits would send him to sleep, but with a combination of adrenalin following his first ever break-in, accompanying a professional thief who had served time for safe-breaking—in the good old days, when safe-breaking was an art, said Tommy, before everything happened electronically and you needed a degree in computers just to commit a minor robbery—and trying to figure why a corpse had been dumped in his office, Boniface's sleep had totaled under two hours.

The hotel charged by the night, not by the hours slept, unfortunately.

He checked the time on his phone as he stood up the hill from Weissenfeld's office. Diagonally opposite the office, almost at the precise spot where Boniface had spent an hour last night, watching the reaction to the broken CCTV camera, a figure stood. Looking like a workman waiting to be picked up—oddly anomalous in such a high-end neighborhood—he seemed relaxed but somehow managed never to show himself. All Boniface could make out were running shoes, jeans, and a hoodie with the hood raised. The only other detail: He smoked.

Cars, vans, and cabs passed up and down the hill at irregular intervals. At 7:29 precisely, a large midnight-blue Mercedes turned the corner and started making its way up the hill.

The man in the hoodie—apparently a uniform for associates of Tommy—stamped out his cigarette and started to loosen up like a sprinter readying himself. As the Mercedes passed him, the hoodie crossed the road, looking up and catching Boniface's eye, dropping contact as he started to pull on a pair of gloves. He knew Boniface even if Boniface didn't know him.

The Mercedes stopped outside the gate, which was opening apparently without human intervention, and the chauffeur was out of the car. Boniface recognized the face: Bertrand Scheidling. Despite his resentment at the imposition, Scheidling had driven Boniface to his apartment to pick up his tuxedo and then taken him to the opera, where Gideon had seen him and Greta.

As the chauffeur opened the door, the hoodie started to jog. The chauffeur helped his principal, taking her coat and bag as she stepped out—bedroom-wear heels, and a phone firmly to her ear while she gave orders. The hoodie began to sprint as Greta slipped her handbag onto her arm—the handbag containing her notebook, the book in which she wrote all her notes.

Boniface started to walk toward the Mercedes as the hoodie came level with the group, making a lunge for the bag.

Bertrand Scheidling wasn't young, but he was fast and, like any good driver, had predicted what was about to happen and was already taking evasive action. His kick was perfectly timed and perfectly aimed, squarely hitting the hoodie's ankle as the hoodie grabbed the bag.

The hoodie lost his grip on the bag as his ankle twisted and, slamming into Greta, he went down with the chauffeur jumping on him, hurriedly followed by the security guard who had apparently been behind the gate.

Greta, on her heels, spun and fell backward toward the gate, hitting her head on the corner of the brickwork surrounding the entrance as she went down. Boniface was kneeling beside her before she could scream.

Instinctively, Boniface reached to support her head. "Boniface," was all Greta said as she fell toward him, her arms around him like a long-lost lover, resting her head on his shoulder.

Sophie was there. "Fraulein Weissenfeld. Fraulein Weissenfeld." There was concern in her tone as she continued fast-talking in German.

Boniface released his hand, which had been supporting the back of Greta's head since she clung to him. He held it for Sophie to see: Little clean skin was visible under the blood. "We should get her to a hospital."

"I'll call an ambulance," said Sophie, her usual unflappable temperament flustered.

"Get a cab," said Boniface, twisting his head to indicate the passing taxis. "It'll be faster, and Bertrand is going to be here for a while." He made eye contact with the chauffeur sitting on Tommy's hoodie-wearing associate. "You don't want to move at the moment, do you?"

Scheidling sneered at the hoodie as if to convey his agreement with Boniface's strategy.

Boniface made a mental note to teach Sophie how to flag down a cab in London as he watched her bobbing up and down in the gutter, waving both hands in the air. "He wants to know where you're going," said Sophie as a cab pulled up.

Greta moaned, and Boniface held her head firmly, but not too firmly, as he turned to Sophie. "Tell him we're going where the Royal family goes."

Sophie looked back as if to question whether Boniface was sure. He gave a single nod, and she went to relay the destination to the driver before opening the cab door and returning to help.

"Greta. We need to stand up and help you into the cab and get someone to look at this gash." Boniface's voice was soft, reassuring, as he examined the back of Greta's head, her face still firmly nestled in his shoulder, her immaculately coiffed helmet of blond hair clumped and streaked with a spreading patch of purple-red.

Boniface gently untangled himself from his former principal, taking care that she was supporting her head before he moved away from her. He repositioned himself to squat beside her. "Your suit." Sophie had her hand over her mouth—the other was pointing at the left half of Boniface's jacket, now thick with blood.

Boniface gave a dismissive shake of the head. "Can you stand?" he asked Greta.

"We should call an ambulance and get a stretcher," said Sophie.

Boniface felt Greta cringe and shake her head. "No," he said. "It's far less undignified to travel in a cab. Hold her arm as we stand."

Sophie leaned, her rotund figure and shapeless dress making it hard to see which muscles and which limbs she was moving. Slowly, with Boniface and Sophie each holding an arm, Greta balanced, squatting on her heels.

She indicated to Sophie that she was fine, and the secretary let go of her arm as Greta continued rising, resting on Boniface for support. Greta reached down for balance with her free arm, dropping her handbag as she lifted herself further.

The CEO reached a standing position with Boniface supporting her on her right side as she balanced on her heels. She looked around and saw the hoodie-wearer on the ground by the gate, the chauffeur and the guard sitting on him. Scheidling was eyeing him and holding his arm behind his back, while the guard was making calls.

Greta lunged, aiming a kick at the hoodie's head. She missed. Missed by a long way and twisted on her non-kicking leg, losing her balance. Boniface grabbed her around the waist as she fell, walking forward to push her upright. "You can get him later," he whispered. "Let's get you to the hospital first."

"Boniface," pleaded Greta, gripping onto him. "Stay with me." She took two small steps before Sophie ran forward to hold her other arm, and together with Boniface they helped her into the cab.

"Call the hospital and tell them we're coming," said Boniface to Sophie, sitting next to Greta. "Give me her bag." He pointed to the handbag Greta had dropped, which was still lying where she had dropped it. "I'll make sure it stays with her while she's getting checked out."

Sophie passed the bag, and the cab pulled out as the blue flashing lights of a police car appeared at the bottom of the hill.

fifty-eight

Montbretia pulled the blanket tighter. It smelled familiar, but it wasn't what she was used to sleeping under. She also wasn't used to sleeping fully dressed and wearing a zipped-up fleece.

She tried to figure the time—it was early, but there was light so it wasn't that early. She couldn't see sunlight, so it probably wasn't 8 AM yet. All she could see when she looked up were a few seagulls lazily circling in the dirty sky. Another blast from the estuary, and she drew the blanket tighter, twisting uncomfortably on the hard ground.

She hadn't had enough sleep to make her anything other than tired and grumpy. But there was no way she could catch up on her sleep while she stayed in Tilbury, sleeping rough with a couple of bums.

By the time Montbretia had walked back from the place where she had found a phone signal, she could hear the sirens. The first police response car had arrived about a minute later. The two constables got out, inspected the body, made a few jokes that, in retrospect, were in poor taste, and then said they needed to preserve the scene.

Apparently, preserving a scene means asking the person who called you, and who was standing around the scene, to move about ten yards away. While the first officer moved Montbretia and started taking her details and some background about how she came to find the body, the second radioed in. Twenty minutes later, the cavalry arrived. It was perhaps two hours before Raymond Talbot turned up.

He introduced himself. "Good evening, you must be Miss Armstrong. I'm Detective Inspector Raymond Talbot, and this is DS Kevin Hitchcock." One look at their suits—even under streetlight—was enough for her to understand why these two annoyed Boniface. When they started talking, their forced officialdom and propensity to use words they apparently didn't understand the full meaning of, but that they thought sounded intimidating, was enough for her to agree with Boniface's assessment.

Between the attending officers, the backup, and Talbot, the conversations had been numerous and became repetitive. Talbot more than Hitchcock had difficulty with the notion that Regenspurger should be arrested. "Please. What evidence do you have for your assertion that this Mister..." he squinted at his notes, "Ray-guns-purr-gerr is behind this murder."

Montbretia tried to explain but couldn't seem to find a way to get him to understand. "I'm not disputing what you are telling me," he said. "All I'm saying is that before I knock on his door, I would like to have at least one single fact that I can present to him that suggests he has some responsibility for this murder, and for the murder of the man who was dumped in your office in Wimbledon. At the moment, the best I have is a weak story from the officers who attended Mister Boniface and found the body, some cock-and-bull from Boniface, and a bit of CCTV footage from that mouthy little brat in the estate agents office under your office."

Montbretia wasn't sure what time she finished talking to the police, but it was late and virtually all traffic on the dock road had disappeared. She walked around for approaching another half hour before Gerbil found her and took her to the place where he and Angus would be spending the night. It was as well appointed as their other residences, but this was farther from the madding crowd, being about five hundred yards past the end of the main dock road.

Angus built the fire, and they spent hours chatting. Talking about Albie, talking about Ellen, talking about the men's lives at sea. Gerbil fell asleep first, and by that time the last train had gone and Montbretia had decided she didn't fancy cycling all the way home, so she decided to stay: Sleeping rough in Tilbury was no worse than sleeping anywhere in Tilbury from what she had seen of the place.

When she went to sleep, she had been sitting, wrapped in her sister's old blanket, with a warm fire next to her. As she woke, the fire was out and she was lying on the ground. At a guess, she'd had three hours' sleep.

She sat, keeping the blanket wrapped around her, aware of how much she needed to pee.

Sluggishly she stood, kicking some life into her feet. Some vagrant reflex kicked in, and both Angus and Gerbil opened their eyes wide, searching for the source of danger. "Sorry," said Montbretia. Gerbil shut his eyes and rolled over.

"What are you doing?" asked Angus.

"I need to pee, and I'd also like to know where I left my bike," said Montbretia. "I know I locked it to a palisade fence somewhere, but it all looks the same to me, so I can't quite remember exactly where it is."

"It's back round there," said Angus. "I can show you later." He settled himself, keeping one eye open. "Find a bush to piss in, then go back to sleep—there's no point in being awake now; it's the safest time of the day to sleep."

"Yesterday was a big day for me. I thought I'd started to find my way, thought I'd started to get things on an even keel after Ellen, but everything kinda got shot to shit, and I found that I wasn't where I thought I was. Then Albie got..." She faded, staring up across the scrub ground. "I'm not sure I'm ever going to sleep again, and I need to...you know, head together."

Angus stared up at her.

"Most mornings, I get up and go for a jog or a bike ride, but I'm not...so I'm going to go for a walk and maybe have a pee at the café. Shall I bring back something to eat—a couple of rounds of bacon sandwiches, perhaps?"

"As long as that won't interfere with my macrobiotic diet," said Angus.

Montbretia smiled. "I'll see you later," she said as she traced the route that Gerbil had led her along last night.

Albie's death had reignited the memories of her sister and her violent death. Boniface had been the person who had told her about Ellen's death—he had been there when Ellen was hurt. Boniface seemed to be the one person who understood Montbretia's anger and the loss she felt at Ellen's passing.

He was also the one who understood that she was living—and enjoying living—a different kind of life. She had been traveling for two-and-a-half years, her financing coming from odd jobs and part-time work as she moved from place to place. He understood that she didn't suddenly want to be tied down and join the nine-to-five brigade, but he also understood that with Ellen's death there was a grieving process, which meant that she couldn't keep moving.

She had to stop and reflect, but she still had to support herself. With that under-standing Boniface had offered her a place to live, so she didn't have to stay alone in

Ellen's old house, and work when she wanted it. And not just grunt work—it seemed that it was work with real value.

But now it was clear that Boniface had lied to her and hadn't trusted her. Worse, the work she had been doing was a cover for toxic-waste dumping, and now it seemed that her involvement had somehow led to Albie being bludgeoned to death. Her choices, her judgments, Albie's death.

Everything collapsed yesterday. Everything she had built since she had lived in London. Even the memory of Ellen was now tainted because it involved Boniface. Now she was alone and nowhere felt safe, but she couldn't go back to traveling because she wasn't sure anymore that she could trust her own instincts: As yesterday proved, her instincts could be catastrophically wrong.

She felt a tear in her eye as she came to the small section of waste ground protected by a slither of yellow police tape flapping in the breeze and a police officer who, even to Montbretia, looked young. A van pulled up, and two civilians got out. Montbretia watched as they walked to the rear of the van and started putting on bunny suits. She thought of science boy and looked at her phone: lies she told because Boniface had lied to her.

She stared at the phone again—this time reading the screen—remembering how last night she had switched everything off that might drain the battery. Now the battery showed only seven percent left.

Hopefully Trevor would have a charger.

fifty-nine

He knew how to swear, get laid, and get alcohol in most languages.

Where he wasn't fluent, the international language of violence was usually suffi-cient to communicate his message succinctly and cogently, and with an appropriate nuance that translated perfectly into the local dialect.

At the nurses' station, they had been nervous about talking with him. A bit of subtle—who was he kidding?—a bit of less than subtle intimidation had got the necessary information, although he wasn't sure it was worth the hassle in getting it: Fraulein Weissenfeld had a nasty cut to the rear of her head necessitating stitches, and a twisted ankle. She wasn't in her room as she was being x-rayed. However, they thought that Mister Boniface—do you know Mister Boniface...very nice man—was waiting in her room for her return. Perhaps you Mister...Mister...would like to wait with Mister Boniface.

Regenspurger wasn't fluent in Albanian, but he spoke it well enough to be understood.

Standing outside Greta Weissenfeld's room, English would be overheard, and someone might speak German, but there was unlikely to be an Albanian speaker, and both the guys spoke Albanian. He thought about Vlach or Macedonian—one of those was their native tongue—but he was too weak on those languages, so Albanian was the way to have a conversation in public but keep the details confiden-tial. Then again, more than three hundred languages are spoken in London, so it's best to be somewhat oblique.

He looked at an angle through the window, then ducked under the square of glass to scan the remainder of the room. At about forty-five degrees, he saw Boniface standing, looking hesitant, shifty. He looked harder: Was Boniface hesitant or shocked?

He dialed, momentarily taking his eyes off Boniface but returning them as he put the phone to his ear, talking immediately when it was answered while he surveyed the blood covering Boniface's shirt, tie, and jacket. That would be upsetting for a man who dressed so particularly. It was time for a visit to the tailor—this wasn't something the dry cleaner could sort.

"Find the package. Take it into your possession."

Boniface surveyed the room, his head remaining stationary—his eyeballs doing the work—and then moved closer to the foot of the bed.

"Lock up the package securely, then leave it."

Boniface reached out to the table across the bed. Standing with his back to the table, he appeared to be trying to look inside the bag that was on the table.

"Call me when the package is secure. I need the leverage."

Boniface reached back and pushed the mouth of the bag open.

"If this works out, then I want you both on a ship this evening."

He hung up and dropped his phone back in his pocket, keeping his gaze fixed on his prey. Boniface had turned toward the bag and grabbed the bottom, giving it a quick yank so that some of the contents spilled before he walked away, apparently drawn by something outside the window.

Regenspurger watched as Boniface walked back from the window and helped a leather-bound notebook, which was half out of the bag, to be fully liberated.

The notebook lay on the table as Boniface appeared to scan the room again.

There was a swift movement. Boniface reached inside his pocket and pulled out his phone. He drifted along the side of the bed and flicked through the pages of the notebook. Stopping, he held the phone over the pages and tapped the phone's screen. He turned a page, held the phone over the notebook, and tapped the screen again.

He flipped the page again as Regenspurger pushed the door. "Mister Boniface. Good morning."

Boniface dropped his phone, which ricocheted off the table, landing on the linoleum floor with a single impact. His face went white—even through Fraulein Weissenfeld's blood smeared over his cheeks, it was still apparent that Boniface had lost his color.

Boniface reached for the contents of Greta's bag, spread over the narrow table. "It fell," he stuttered, clumsily trying to return the contents to the bag. He knocked some pieces onto the bed—keys, makeup—and looked down, trying to pick up the items with trembling hands.

Without much commitment, he swept the debris he had created back into the bag and stood it upright, shaking it as if settling sand in a bucket. He scrabbled on the floor, then moved toward the window—to all intents a passerby who happened to see a problem and tried to help.

Regenspurger remained impassive, standing inside the door, observing every move.

"Good to see you, Garen," offered Boniface, his voice still quivering as he slipped his phone into his pocket.

Regenspurger kept his glare on Boniface, who stepped backward as if pushed by the force of the stare, stopping when he hit wall. He put his hand to the back of his head, checking whether he was hurt. "Lucky that wasn't worse—we've already got one person with a cut head." His forced good humor faded as Regenspurger maintained his silence.

"We should have a conversation, Mister Boniface." Regenspurger's inflection was tender, reassuring.

Boniface stammered and stuttered. Regenspurger continued, appearing not to notice. "I am disappointed that you haven't behaved as we expected. I thought I was clear yesterday."

"I came to apologize," said Boniface.

Regenspurger raised his eyes and cocked his head.

"I hoped to get my job back..." Boniface was starting to babble, his speech running like a river in full flood. "I haven't been paid the last installment and hoped we could finalize matters."

Regenspurger took three measured paces across the room and stood, with his hand out, before Boniface. He stilled his breathing, looking into the Englishman's eyes, which darted around, fleetingly making contact but breaking it almost immediately.

He snapped his fingers, once, to draw attention to his outstretched hand.

Boniface's eyes still darted.

"Your phone," said Regenspurger.

Boniface's mouth twitched with small, stammering tics audible.

Regenspurger leaned his body toward Boniface—one or two degrees—relaxing his shoulders and feeling his head lift as his did. He locked eyes with Boniface and whispered. "Your phone, please, Mister Boniface."

Boniface fumbled to find his pocket. Slowly he withdrew the phone and placed it in Regenspurger's hand. Regenspurger broke his stare and returned to his position just inside the door, looking back at Boniface, who crumpled and was now wiping sweat with a handkerchief.

"The last thing Fraulein Driesdorfer said before we put her on a plane back to Hamburg was that she thought you were taking pictures of documents on my desk, but she thought that was too much of a crazy idea to be true." He glanced up from Boniface's phone, which he manipulated with his right hand. "However, apparently she was correct in her observation."

He continued to flick through the photographs. Sometimes frowning, sometimes turning the phone and zooming in. "Quite the photographer, aren't we, Mister Boniface? Maybe you can do it professionally in your next job."

He found what he was looking for—select all, delete, are you sure, yes—then watched as a timer whirred, ending on a blank screen: no photos.

"This morning?" Regenspurger looked up at Boniface: He had uttered two words. Two words that Boniface could interpret in many ways. Two words that he uttered as both a statement and a question.

Boniface stared back. Apparently he was aware of the technique Regenspurger was employing: Say something, leave an uncomfortable silence, and wait for the person you're trying to intimidate to deal with the social embarrassment by filling the gap. Regenspurger knew he was stronger mentally—he knew from firsthand experience that everyone breaks at some point—but at the moment he didn't have enough leverage and he didn't have time to waste, so he was happy to fill in the spaces and leave long pauses to keep Boniface unsettled, scared even.

"It was rather a strange place for you to be."

Boniface looked up, questioning.

The German spoke quickly, dismissing comments with a wave of his hand before the Englishman could say them. "I know, I know...you were there to beg and plead. But why were you there then?" He placed both feet squarely on the ground and faced Boniface. "Why not call and ask for a meeting to discuss these matters?"

"I tried to expl..."

A wave of the hand silenced Boniface. "The point I'm trying to get at, Mister Boniface, is why you were at that specific place at that specific time." He extended his arm with its upturned hand farther toward the mumbling Boniface. "A lesser man might suggest you were there to perhaps point out a target or to give yourself an alibi."

It wasn't a question, but Regenspurger let the thought hang.

"Don't you see how it could look, Mister Boniface?" He kept his glare focused on Boniface, as if to remind him that all questions were purely rhetorical. "The role you played seems odd."

Regenspurger shifted. "This man, who is dressed scruffily, is running fast in the direction of the person you say you wanted to meet. The danger must have been clear to you, but you seem not to have reacted." He snorted. "I can almost understand that: You have soft hands and make a living by telling lies."

Boniface remained impassive, held in place by Regenspurger's menace.

"This man runs up and attacks the person you have come to see while you are a few meters away. What is your reaction? All the men grab this vicious attacker, subdue him, and call the police." He sneered at Boniface, the blood drying on his jacket. "But you? You act as nurse and carry Fraulein Weissenfeld's handbag."

He let the room settle, the only sounds coming from the corridor outside.

Regenspurger snorted. "But here's the interesting part. Bertrand Scheidling, the chauffeur. He's a good man, a loyal man. I talked to him, and do you know what he said?" He glared at Boniface—he wasn't sure what he saw; it could have been anger, it could have been fear. "He said it was as if you knew the attacker."

The room was silent again.

"Tell me. Did you enjoy your visit to the office last night?"

The still was broken by the door opening. "I have insisted on a brain scan." Chlodwig Weissenfeld came into the room, talking to himself under his breath. "Since my sister has had a considerable blow to the head and is already in the hospital, she should be thoroughly checked."

He continued walking into the room and around the bed. "Boniface, I understand you were a great help, thank you." His eyes shifted toward the Englishman, his head moving up and down as if scanning his appearance. "We will reimburse you for the cost of a new suit."

Regenspurger watched as Chlodwig turned to him. "I want to understand how such a thing could have happened."

Boniface looked to the other men. "Gentlemen, matters of company security are beyond my brief, so I'll leave you to discuss those issues in private. And as you can see, I need to clean myself up."

He stepped forward and snatched the phone from Regenspurger's hand as he passed. "Thank you for picking my phone up when I dropped it," said Boniface, his hand reaching the door. "I will, I am sure, see you two later."

sixty

"Can we?" The man in the olive-green army surplus jacket clenched a tight fist, pulling his arm up. "Can we, you know?" He lifted his fist and bared his teeth.

"No."

"But did he say we couldn't?"

"No. But it's too early in the morning, and we need to find her first, and we don't even know if she's here."

"So we grab her, and we can come back later when she's tired?" The scrawny, rat-faced man in the green jacket turned to face the driver. "She'll be tired. She'll be grateful." He sat back in his seat. "Think about it: Have a screw, get on a boat, get something to eat, and have a sleep."

The driver, one hand on the wheel, the other supporting the chin of his greasy face, ignored his passenger.

"Who goes first? We'll flip a coin." He grinned at the driver. "That's not fair on you. You should go first—I've got the big cock. You won't touch the sides after I've finished with her."

The black van lumbered along the main road to the docks, bouncing its passengers with each pothole and rut in the road, its blown exhaust confirming to everyone it passed that the van was as cheap as it looked.

"There." The driver pointed with his left arm, which stretched out of his leather jacket, revealing tattoos up his arm.

Coming out from the pedestrian bridge across the railway was a lone female, dressed in well-fitted jeans and a blue fleece jacket, carrying two bags, which she tried to hold in one hand as she glanced down at her phone.

The van slowed, holding back as the woman followed onto the path beside the road. "Go past her," said rat-face, straining to keep his gaze on her. "Don't blast the engine or you'll spook her."

The van moved forward a short way, following the road as it wound around the docks. "We did well yesterday," said the driver as they passed the flapping yellow police tape enclosing two figures wearing white all-in-one suits. "But we should wait farther down or they might see us."

The rat-faced man kept his gaze on the woman as the van passed. He ran a hand through his dirty sandy-colored hair, nodding. "How are we going to do this? The normal way?"

"Yep," said the driver, accelerating.

"Far enough," said the passenger as the driver bounced the tire over the curb, craning to check oncoming traffic before heading back along the road they had just followed.

"She's not expecting anything." The passenger twisted his neck, trying to keep his prey in his sights for as long as possible. "Wait for her to get past—" he pointed imprecisely toward the taped-off area they were passing again, "where we did some beating last night, and then we move."

They passed the woman, still walking, and when out of her sight, the van turned, again bumping over the curb, and then followed the target. "Slow, slow, slow," said rat-face. "Keep far enough away that she can't hear the exhaust."

She stopped as she came to the taped-off area.

"What do we do now?" There was confusion in rat-face's voice.

"Wait," said the driver, bringing the van to a halt and looking in his mirrors. He slid the van into reverse, moving unhurriedly. "We back off and wait."

The woman whose face had been ringed in red on the photo they were given stood by the tape, watching the men in white all-in-one suits work. Something distracted her—she slipped out her phone, looked down at it, and tapped the screen as if rejecting a call.

"Not too far back," said rat-face. "I want to be able to see her."

They watched as their target slipped her phone back into her pocket and stood outside the tape, looking in. Contemplating. She exchanged a few words with the young police officer who, along with the yellow tape, was the sole protection for the area. "See that?" said the driver, pushing up the sleeves of his leather jacket, the tattoos on his right arm balancing those on his left. He pointed with his right hand—three-and-a-half fingers and one thumb—checking to make sure his passenger had seen. "The cop's aware of her. We need to be way out of sight, and you've got to get her mouth shut tightly, or else the cop will come running."

She pulled out her phone, seemingly in frustration. An exaggerated craning of the neck. An exaggerated stab to the screen, and the phone was straight back in her pocket. "She's moving," said rat-face, a shudder traveling through his body as the driver turned the engine over.

"Easy, easy," rat-face's voice was soft, but still tense. He lowered his shoulder, trying to crouch while he sat as the van glided, its trumpeting exhaust muted. "Slow it, then we can go faster once we're past the cop."

The driver eased the brake.

"Why are we stopping?" asked rat-face. The driver pointed with his head—she had stopped and was going through her routine of pulling out her phone, angrily hitting the screen, and dropping it back into her pocket.

They started moving as she began to walk again, increasing speed past the yellow tape, following until she was about 200 yards past the crime scene. "Are you ready?" asked the driver.

"Willing and able," said rat-face.

The driver pushed the speed up, and as he drew parallel with the pedestrian, cut-and-started, cut-and-started the engine, finally cutting it and then allowing it to drift, bumping across the curb and onto the path as it came to a halt. He got out, miming anger and frustration, and flipped the hood.

He ducked under the hood and watched as the pedestrian approached, apparently unaware of the van in her path. She glanced up, saw the van ahead of her, and continued without breaking step. "Can you see?" he whispered.

"She's in my mirror," said rat-face.

She looked like she had in the photo, although her face seemed worn, maybe tired, and her hair didn't have the sheen or the bounce he was expecting. She glanced at the van with less care than she had glanced at the people working the crime scene, not sensing danger, not slowing, not breaking her rhythm. He stepped back from under the hood, and she noticed him—her eyes completing a mental inventory—but kept walking.

He pushed up his sleeves as she drew level with the van. That was when she noticed: She was staring at his right hand.

She froze.

Rat-face was out of the van. He threw the tape to the driver, his hand continuing in a single movement until it was in place over her mouth. His other arm was around her waist, and he kicked out her feet, falling on top of her. The driver pulled a length of tape, ripping it with his teeth, and put three quick turns around her legs, then ripped another strip.

"Ready?" he asked.

Rat-face kept his weight on the woman and nodded as the driver watched for the other man to drop his hand so that he could place a piece of tape over their captive's mouth.

The woman screamed under the tape and twisted, getting an arm free and kicking the driver with both legs. Rat-face backhanded her across the face, allowing the full weight of his arm to transfer through his hand to her cheek, and then sat on her, one knee pinning each arm.

"Please," said the driver, knowing he was speaking in a heavily accented tone but knowing that he would be understood. "Please do not do that. You will find that while my friend may look scrawny, he is, in fact, stronger than ten men, and any compassion he may have had was brutalized out of him when he was in his army."

The woman struggled, writhing like a bronco trying to buck its cowboy. Rat-face leaned back, slapping his hand on the woman's ass and letting his fingers slide between her thighs. She stiffened as his hand lingered, drifting upward, a dark scream coming from under her taped mouth.

The driver observed his passenger, astride his new ride, and indicated their prisoner's arms, his eyes moving from one to the other. The passenger dragged his hand up, over the woman's jeans, moving it to one arm, and his other hand to her other arm. He moved backward, placing his crotch at the bottom of the woman's ass, grinding as he wrenched her arms together, allowing the driver to wrap tape around them.

With her arms tied, he fell on top of her, allowing his hands to slip under her body.

The driver jumped up and took the two steps to the van, closing the hood and firing the engine, and then backed the van to where the two lay. Leaving the driver's door open and the engine running, he opened the rear doors and turned back to the two on the ground.

The rat-faced man had moved and was now sitting with his legs over the woman, who was still face down in the mud. In his hand, a white-bread sandwich. He grinned as he chewed and offered one of the bags that the woman had dropped to the man in the leather jacket, nodding and looking at the sandwich as he took another bite.

The driver pushed his sleeves back and took out a sandwich, holding it between his thumb and three fingers as he bit. He focused back on the man holding the woman on the ground, nodded his appreciation at the food, before looking back into the bag and pulling out the remaining contents: two more sandwiches. He offered one to the man on the ground and kept one for himself, walking around the two on the ground at a leisurely pace as he continued to eat.

As he finished, he wiped his mouth on his arm and his hands on his jeans. He pointed to the woman on the ground—the dirty, sandy-haired man nodded, pulled his feet back, and squatted beside the tied body. He rammed one hand between her legs and unhurriedly slid the second hand, palm up, under her breasts and lifted her. He took two steps before briskly sliding her head first into the van.

The man in the leather jacket jumped in the back, and the doors closed behind him. A moment later, the man who had been the passenger jumped into the driver's seat and revved the engine, trying to take control of the bucking steering as the spinning wheels gained traction.

From his position of discomfort in the van's cargo bay, he reached to roll the woman. As his hand touched her she flinched, trying to move away from him. He moved forward to reduce her space and manhandled her onto her side before reaching into each pocket of her jacket.

As he put his hand into the jeans pockets, he could feel her trembling. There was defiance in her eyes, but he knew that was a mask for terror. He pulled his hand out of the first pocket and slipped it into the one on the other side before triumphantly yanking out what he had been looking for: her phone.

He dropped it beside himself and reached behind for the tape, adding more wrapping to her legs and arms. He then ripped the tape off her mouth. "Listen to that engine. There's no point in screaming." As if to emphasize the point, rat-face hit the gas to exaggerate the roar of the blown exhaust.

"You killed that man." The woman's accent sounded American. "Back there. That was you, wasn't it?" She started to struggle, like someone trying to demonstrate the butterfly stroke on dry land. He slapped her, knocking her head back against the floor.

"You killed that other man and left him in our office, didn't you?"

He placed a thick, dirty finger over her mouth. "Enough." He held it in place, staring at her, waiting for the blink of acquiescence. She sighed—a warm jet of air out of her nose to warm his hand, then the slight nod of her head.

He released his finger and reached for her phone, tapping the face. He held the screen toward her. "Code?" She blinked, her mouth not moving. "Code." He dropped the phone and slapped her again. "Code."

"Three-four-nine-seven," said the woman, a tear forming in her eye.

He looked at the screen. "Has Mister Boniface upset you? He's been calling you very regularly."

sixty-one

There were four newspapers on the counter.

Boniface tried to focus on the pages—forcing his eye to scan the columns, looking for his or Weissenfeld's name.

He had seen neither, but he wasn't sure he had looked hard enough. Each time he started looking, he thought of Montbretia.

Montbretia.

Boniface picked up his phone: Four minutes since he had last called Montbretia. He stared at his phone, watching the clock. It clicked past another minute. He hit redial—straight to voicemail. Until an hour ago the phone had rung—for varying lengths of time, suggesting Montbretia was hitting the hang-up button to forward the call to voicemail—but now, every call went straight to voicemail.

He left another message and tried to focus on the paper.

Instinctively, he reached for his tea—his disappointing tea. Tea is always disappointing in a coffee shop—it's part of the job description of a coffee house to make bad tea—but in between trying Montbretia and focusing on trying to read the newspapers to see whether either he or Weissenfeld had hit the headlines, he had let his tea go cold.

He checked the time again, too soon, but he called again and didn't leave a message again. He stood and looked in the mirror along the side wall and reached up to straighten his tie. As his finger made contact with the dried blood, he forewent the urge to smarten his appearance: How was a straight tie any better when you were covered in dried blood?

He left and started walking, following the backstreets of Fitzrovia toward Oxford Street, the burble of London—the cabs, people shouting, trucks from an industrial age negotiating streets that were built in medieval times following cow paths from centuries before that—failing to distract him.

The arm temporarily blocked his path.

Without looking up, he instinctively moved to go around the obstruction.

The obstruction moved and pushed him toward the railings surrounding the building he was passing, the roar of a van with a blown exhaust covered Boniface's mumbled apologies as he looked up.

The eyes that greeted him told him he was wrong to apologize. The same eyes that greeted him yesterday as he left Jeremy Farrant's office. The same eyes—piercing but held in a loose, gray-skinned face—that saw him this morning as he tried to find what was in the leather-bound notebook.

He turned.

Regenspurger pulled him back.

He turned again. His way was blocked by a thin man, the same height as him with a pointy rat-face; greasy skin; sandy-colored, unwashed, greasy hair with loose curls; and an olive-green military-style jacket.

"Don't be like that, Boniface," said Regenspurger.

Boniface leaned against the railings, grateful for their support, and stared back. He had no inclination to speak and no idea what to say.

"A few words," said Regenspurger, his light German accent piercing Boniface's ears.

Boniface stood straighter, releasing his grip on the railings, and felt the other man push closer behind him.

"I've said all I'm going to say." Boniface's voice was without emotion.

"Really? It seemed like you had a lot to say." He slipped out Montbretia's phone and delicately held it between his thumb and forefinger. "Perhaps I can remind you of what you wanted to say?" He tapped the phone and offered the screen to Boniface, showing a photo. "Your girlfriend. Wearing the very latest fashion in duck tape. About an hour ago."

Boniface grabbed for the phone to find himself gripped by the surprisingly strong man with the rat-face. He struggled, willing himself to stay mute, finally giving up his effort to be free.

The human barricade invading his personal space stepped away. "This way, please," said Regenspurger, his voice a menacing calm tone. Like an unctuous waiter in an overpriced restaurant, he indicated a black van with its near-side wheels on the curb, the man with the green army jacket now standing behind the back doors.

Boniface walked behind the rear entrance to the van—its roof at his chest height. Regenspurger nodded to the other man, who opened the doors. Boniface bent to look into the cargo area. "Monty?" He stood upright. "Where is she?"

"I didn't say she was here."

"Then I want to talk to her." The two men scanned the surroundings like hawks as Boniface became more agitated. "I want to talk to her now. I want to know she's safe."

The younger man landed a blow squarely in Boniface's gut, winding him. Boniface bent forward and felt as his head was shoved, slamming it against the corner of the van's roof, before his legs were kicked away. To finish, the rat-faced man in the green jacket shoved him through the open doors, giving a final push to make sure he was fully inside.

Regenspurger leaned through the doors, holding a roll of tape. "Miss Armstrong needed this. I presume you will remain as our guest without further argument?"

sixty-two

The van doors opened. Boniface felt above his eye where his head had been propelled into the edge of the van roof and wondered if he needed medical attention.

"Out."

Boniface started to slide himself along the van's floor.

A curse was spat out in a language Boniface didn't understand, and the green jacket grabbed his foot and yanked. Boniface reached, grabbing wildly for anything to slow his movement, gashing his hand but finding the door pillars to slow his horizontal motion as his leg was dropped.

His back twisted across the threshold of the van's cargo bay, acting like a pivot as his legs hit the ground and his torso was turned ninety degrees, bringing him to a sitting position as he landed on his coccyx. He flopped forward, putting down a hand to steady himself, where he found a film of oil covering the concrete he had landed on.

Regenspurger clicked his fingers and pointed—the rat-faced man in the green jacket reached for the scruff of Boniface's jacket, yanking it and lifting Boniface, who felt the jacket give way under his arms as it held his weight.

He stumbled, and like a baby animal born on the run, he was walking, taking his first few steps out of the garages under Weissenfeld's offices. The garages under the CCTV camera that Reg had adjusted with a hammer a few hours ago.

The van doors slammed. The wooden garage door creaked on its hinges, then banged together, and Boniface was jostled. Regenspurger led the way along the outside wall, setting a pace that Boniface found hard to keep up with—the green-jacketed man walked behind Boniface, ensuring that he achieved the necessary forward motion as they turned the corner and ascended the slope. The trio passed through the gate—with blood still showing on the brickwork to the left—crossed the courtyard garden, and entered through the front door before taking the first flight of stairs.

"Where's Lennie?" said Boniface as they passed the security guard's desk. A new face, without uniform, stared.

"Who?" said Regenspurger. "There is no Lennie working here."

Boniface cursed under his breath. Someone else who had got hurt because they were close to Boniface.

He followed Regenspurger into the conference room. The same room where he had spoken to Chlodwig three days ago—or was it two days? Boniface was having trouble remembering. Another snap of the fingers instructing Boniface to sit at the far side of the overly large conference-room table with his back to the window: one man positioned at each egress.

"You didn't seem surprised. You didn't seem concerned." Regenspurger stopped talking. He had tried this in the hospital—Boniface was starting to notice a pattern.

Boniface waited, then decided to speak. "Neither did you."

Regenspurger smiled. "That's the first clever thing you've said."

"It's better than saying 'when,' which is how you wanted me to answer."

"You know when." The German's voice was controlled. "When I found you in Fraulein Weissenfeld's hospital room this morning, you didn't seem concerned. You were worried when I came in and caught you, but you didn't seem concerned about her."

Boniface opened his mouth—Regenspurger raised a single finger.

"Spare me, Boniface. You're a man who is paid to lie, and you lie plausibly for a living, and to be honest, I don't need the truth out of you."

Boniface tipped his head, his eyebrows rising.

"Oh, Boniface. You're teasing me," said the German in a mocking tone that sounded more menacing to Boniface. "Look at the basic facts. You go through my desk, taking photographs. You photograph the contents of Mister Phipps' desk. I escort you off the premises, and then you are found, apparently asleep in Mister Farrant's office, around the time the CCTV camera is broken. Broken when a slate decides to dislodge itself from the roof for the first time in two hundred years."

He snapped his fingers again. "I missed the best bit. When the slate fell, you heard nothing, apparently."

Boniface left the silence for Regenspurger to fill. "It doesn't make sense to me. Does it to you, Mister Boniface?"

"I think you've made up your mind already," offered Boniface. "Rhetorical questions rather bother me. Can we talk about Montbretia, please?"

A look spread across Regenspurger's face—for the first time, Boniface saw him smiling with his eyes. "I have a proposition for you, Mister Boniface."

Boniface waited.

"We have a press conference later today. One of your specialties, I believe."

Boniface made no show of emotion.

"I would like you to lead the press conference and make a small announcement."

Boniface calibrated the slight twitch at the extremes of the former Stasi officer's mouth and waited for him to play his card.

"You chat at our little press conference: Miss Armstrong lives. You don't: She dies. One small announcement in return for her life. Five minutes' work, that's all I'm asking."

It was Boniface's turn to remain mute, leaving the other man to fill the awkward social embarrassment—or in this case, the frustration of not seeing an emotional response from Boniface.

Boniface knew the question Regenspurger wanted him to ask: What do I have to do? But it was more fun to imply another question—and the response could be more illuminating. He kept his intonation moderate as he looked up at the ex-Stasi officer. "We know your threat to kill Montbretia is realistic because you killed the guy who you dumped in my office and you killed that poor fellow at Tilbury yesterday."

The pride in Regenspurger's eyes was unmistakable, even with the confusion of the unexpected approach. "You give me too much credit, Mister Boniface. I didn't kill anyone." He took Montbretia's phone from his pocket, deliberately setting it in front of him. "Miss Armstrong seems to take my view: She believes that yesterday's death was your fault."

"My fault, but not my hand. I think that is the point that was being made." Boniface let the silence settle, looking at the man with sandy-colored hair across from Regenspurger. The man met Boniface's glare and locked on.

"As long as you understand that our threat is real, that is enough." Regenspurger's comment distracted Boniface, who broke his stare, turning back to the German.

Boniface went to speak but found no words coming.

"Our friend at the end of the table is a man who enjoys what he does," offered Regenspurger. "For him, what he does is more of a vocation. He doesn't see it as work, but as a pleasurable business with added bonuses." He picked up Montbretia's phone, holding it so Boniface could see as he flicked through to the photograph of her taken earlier that morning. His tone became sharper. "Would you like Miss Armstrong to become one of those added bonuses before she dies?"

Boniface felt his jaw tremble and his eyes moisten.

"You're not a punching and kicking sort of person, Mister Boniface. Even if you were, you don't know where Miss Armstrong is located, and all it takes is one call from me and..." he let his unfinished sentence hang. "Are we clear?"

Boniface wiped his eye. "We're clear."

"Good," said Regenspurger, a flick of emotion distorting the lifeless skin draped over his face. "So we're agreed: You will make a brief appearance at our little press conference this evening."

Boniface remained silent, his head gently bowed.

"Aren't you going to ask? Isn't that big brain of yours curious to know what the press conference is about?" Regenspurger's approach was like he was dealing with an upset child who he was trying to win over with kindness.

Boniface raised his eyes to the German.

"I lied a little bit." Regenspurger put his hand over his mouth. "I might have given you the wrong impression: You will be the star of our press conference. We need you to make a public confession."

Regenspurger sat back in his chair, twisting it in the narrow gap between the table and the wall to face Boniface. "A small confession. A public apology. That's all. You know the drill: I've let my friends and family down. I am truly sorry. I am going to the police station straight away."

Boniface lifted his head weakly as Regenspurger continued. "It's a small confession—you don't have to admit to murder or anything like that." He dragged his hand over his face, pulling the skin tight. "All you have to say is that the body dump was your idea. You didn't murder anyone—you just wanted to dump a body to create a stink."

"That's what you public relations people do, isn't it—create a stink? You say that you asked someone to drop a dead body, but there was an argument about money, and the person you asked to do the work dropped the body in your office."

Regenspurger waited before continuing. "You tell your story and say you are truly sorry for what you did, and that you are sorry you caught up Weissenfeld Shipping in this matter, making it appear that there was a link to their business. You will sit next to Fraulein Weissenfeld and apologize."

"I'll do it," said Boniface.

Regenspurger's head flicked to scrutinize Boniface—his eyes apparently searching for some sort of confirmation of what his ears thought they had heard.

"I'll do it," repeated Boniface. "But you know that the story won't stick. At some point, someone will figure that I'm not the murdering type, and however hard I protest, there won't be enough evidence to even take the case to trial."

"We will help," said Regenspurger. "Do you think we lack the ability to make someone look guilty? While you're talking, we'll fill in some of the gaps."

The German smiled. "A bloody knife in your apartment should help. Even if you do walk away after years of legal proceedings, because you made your full admission to the cameras while sitting next to the CEO, people will only remember that Weissenfeld hired a bad PR adviser."

Boniface sat up straighter. "And as I make the announcement, you flush something through the tubes." He hesitated, his voice softer as he continued. "I'm the chaff while you release details about Somalia."

Regenspurger made the smallest movement of his head.

"Got it," said Boniface. "I make an announcement, you make an announcement. Both announcements are covered by the injunction, making it hard for the press to report, but you put the information in their hands and give them two stories. One about dead people in Somalia, the second about a PR adviser dropping dead bodies as part of his strategy to influence people."

A slow sneer broke out across Boniface's visage. "If I'm a journalist—if I'm an editor—which story will I pursue? Which story can I pursue, being as it's difficult to get into and out of Somalia, and, let's be frank, the public don't care about a few more deaths in Africa? So even if the injunction falls apart next week, by that time, everyone will have stopped caring about toxic waste because they're far more interested in the corpse in the office in Wimbledon."

Regenspurger nodded. For the first time, Boniface thought he saw genuine pleasure reflected in his cold demeanor.

"I publicly sacrifice myself and Montbretia lives?"

"That is the deal, Mister Boniface." The German's voice chilled.

Boniface stood, untangling himself from a chair that wouldn't go back far enough for him to get out without wiggling. "I may not be in a position to negotiate, but may I make a suggestion?"

Regenspurger looked up and nodded once.

"Look at me," Boniface indicated his bloody suit. "My appearance may provoke interest in another story. Can I change? Perhaps have a shower?"

"Yes."

"A quick trip home to sort myself out?"

"I would expect nothing less. In fact, my friend here," Regenspurger indicated the green jacket, "will be pleased to drive you home and then make sure you are at the press conference—which will be held in the Methodist Hall in Westminster—at 5 PM."

"Five PM for a five-thirty news conference. Timed exactly for every news outlet whose lawyers feel they can run any snippets on the six o'clock news, which will alert the editors of the press, getting the story into the newspapers tomorrow morning." Boniface winked at the German. "Good strategy—what I would have suggested."

"In case you're wondering, our friend," Regenspurger nodded at the man opposite him, "doesn't speak English, so please don't try talking to him or negotiating any changes."

"How will I tell give him directions to my apartment?" asked Boniface.

"No need. He already knows where you live."

Boniface's voice was weak as he continued. "Is he the man with the beard?"

"No." Regenspurger bared his teeth, like a shark having his photo taken. "*He* is with Miss Armstrong in case you forget our agreement."

sixty-three

The lunchtime traffic was frustrating the rat-faced driver.

Boniface enjoyed watching his futile annoyance as the van sat motionless before moving a few yards, only to wait again. Each time the traffic eased, the driver gunned the engine, the blown exhaust shouted, and the driver moved swiftly to the next impediment to his journey.

They pulled through the rear entrance behind Boniface's block, an L-shaped building with the horizontal member facing onto Wimbledon Hill Road and the vertical stroke—with the cheaper apartments—overlooking the parking lot and the bins.

As they pulled through the entrance, instead of directing him to the front as he had done when Bertrand Scheidling had been driving, Boniface pointed to the service entrance at the back. "Put it over there."

The driver didn't respond but swung the van round, reversing into the area indicated by Boniface.

He slammed the door as he got out, looking across the low roof of the van at his driver, who seemed hopeful that Boniface would try his luck or upset him in some way so that he could unleash a few swift blows—perhaps do more and go back to Regenspurger to plead that he had no other choice.

Or go back and find Montbretia.

Boniface scanned the brick-built structure, white wooden frames surrounding the doors and windows, and white metal casement windows with three horizontal panes in each section. The man in the green military jacket was staring at him, a flick of his head unmistakably communicating impatience.

"This way," said Boniface, pointing to the rear service door. A lump of brown wood in another white frame with a single slit of wired safety glass running most of the length of the door. He pulled the door open, stepping into the dim hallway.

The rat-faced man in his olive jacket and with his unwashed hair followed behind, at just over an arm's-length distance as the two crossed the polished marble-chip flooring. The light—a dull light listlessly bouncing off the white plaster walls—came from the window over the intermediate landing, where one flight of stairs turned to meet the next, rotating those who ascended and descended through one-hundred-and-eighty degrees.

Boniface put his foot on the first marble-chip stair—the wear in the riser more pronounced than on any of the following stairs. He reached for the dull brass rail and started his ascent with the rat-faced man staying three steps back.

He slowed at the intermediate landing, then stopped, flicking his head back toward the service-entrance door like a wild animal startled by a noise.

Rat-face mirrored his move.

As rat-face began to turn back, Boniface kicked off the wall, aiming his elbow behind the man's eye. He caught his guard's temple, then watched as the other man's reflexes deployed. The man with the filthy hair swung his far arm, fist clenched, toward Boniface, turning his whole body and pivoting on the worn step. His foot slipped, and Boniface kicked out, transferring enough momentum to topple his captor down the stairs.

Boniface watched as the other man fell—his arms still trying to punch as his head hit the step, the next step, and the last two steps as his body slid down the stairs, stopping when his shoulders were resting on the entrance-hall floor.

Boniface exhaled, resting his hands on his knees, unable to look away from the crumpled heap at the foot of the stairs.

Olive-green jacket, jeans, army boots. The body seemed motionless. Boniface became aware of himself panting as he strained to hear over the noise of his pounding heart whether the other man was breathing. He held his breath and looked, too afraid to step closer.

He took two steps down and observed.

Lifeless. Silent.

He took another step and kicked a boot—the highest part of the static body.

No reaction.

Boniface swung his legs—one then the other—over the brass banister and slid down, jumping off before the rail curled at the end. He walked around the inert figure, staying outside the reach of the arm that flopped at a right angle.

He squatted. Studying. The top of the chest was moving rhythmically, but the breathing was light.

Boniface kicked his tormentor's right shoulder and jumped back as if he had received an electric shock.

The body remained unmoving.

Boniface looked down, leaning left and right to see under the head. He leaned down and twisted the head from left to right.

No reaction.

He glanced back furtively, his eyes covering every inch of the dull hallway, then lifted the head and strained to raise the shoulders. He used his knees to prop up the shoulders and reached his hands under rat-face's armpits, bringing his hands together over the man's chest. He gripped his hands together, pulling his body closer to the inert slab of meat on his hallway floor, and rested his head on the inert body's shoulder.

He inhaled and turned his head away. "You could do with a bath," he muttered as he inhaled and started to drag the body backward. The feet thumped down the last few steps, and Boniface found a momentum as he slid the body over the smooth surface. The body dragged over the doormat as Boniface hit the door, pushing it and taking three steps to the van, where he dropped the lump, leaning it against the back end.

Boniface felt the pain is his lower back and became aware that he was outside, in the open, visible to people who he couldn't see.

He scanned the parking lot and the balconies, then reached down, patting the pockets of the man in the green jacket. There was something is his right jeans pocket—Boniface pushed his fingers in, extracted a small bunch of keys, and opened the rear doors of the van, leaning the body forward as the doors swung.

Boniface squatted inside the van and reached, returning his arms under the other man's and his hands to their grip at the front of his chest. "One, two," he whispered, listening as the last few threads at the back of his jacket gave way. "Three." He hefted the torso up and levered it into the van's cargo bay, then slid it until the legs flopping at the knees caught on the threshold.

The body was half on top of him; Boniface pushed it off and slid out of the van to shove the legs in before jumping back in and pulling the doors closed behind him.

He sat, sweating, panting, feeling his muscles ache. Montbretia was right; he should go to the gym or do some exercise.

Boniface stretched out his hand and pushed his fingers into the side of the other man's throat. A pulse. Light but consistent. He hurriedly felt around the back of the other man's head. He could feel no bleeding—and he should be quite an expert on that by now, this being the second head injury for which Boniface could be held culpable that day.

He scanned the van—he knew there was some tape when he had been pushed in, and presumably since Regenspurger had threatened him with it, it must have some function.

He found the roll of silver tape.

Which first? Arms or legs?

He went for the legs, then stopped. Wrong. He contemplated the body—a curled S-shape half on its back. Boniface pulled the feet out the way so they wouldn't stop the body twisting, then reached over and grabbed the olive jacket on the far side, pulling it toward him, using his knees to ensure that the body didn't slide.

It flipped over onto his knees.

Boniface pushed the man off and again leaned over to release his right arm, which he was lying on. He yanked the two arms together and bound the wrists, putting four or five turns of tape around them. He pulled the feet and put five or so turns around the ankles before sitting back to admire his work.

"How much tape do you need?" he muttered under his breath and tried holding his hands behind his back, imagining they were taped. "More than that."

He tore off a strip of tape and pulled the elbows as close together as he could get them before wrapping the whole of the lower arms in tape. He admired his handiwork and then levered the body back across his knees, adding a few turns around the body, taping the arms against the back of the inert body.

He shoved his former jailer off his knees, flipping him onto his back. As he had done with the elbows, he pulled the knees together before encasing his legs in duck tape swaddling in the same way that Montbretia had been bound in the photo Regenspurger showed him, but with more tape.

Boniface grabbed a lump of hair and immediately let go, instinctively wiping his hand on his jacket. "You need a good shampoo, mate."

He sighed, then pulled the hair, lifting up the head so that he could slip a foot under to keep the skull elevated. He took the tape, laid the end of the roll over the mouth, and then wrapped several turns around his head, moving his foot as he was finished.

"Vomit? Suffocation?" He studied the body slumped in front of him. "Fuck you, you took Montbretia."

He felt the vertical bracing in the van, giving it a firm tug. It didn't move. He tore a long strip of tape and fed it behind the bracing several times to make a loop. He flipped the body onto its front again and created a similar loop behind the arms before pushing the body toward the bracing and joining the two loops with more tape.

"Enough," he said and jumped out of the van, slamming the door behind him before pulling out his phone and hitting a familiar number. He jogged into the hallway, scanned the bottom of the stairs—not a mark on the floor—then ran up the stairs to his apartment. By the time he got through the door, his phone was ringing.

"Tommy. One last favor—it's for Montbretia, not for me." He walked to his CD rack and flicked through, pulling one out. "I'll make her appreciate Dutch prog rock," he whispered, returning his phone to his ear.

sixty-four

"It's a bit fucking public here, Tommy." Boniface's eyes were darting like a fly trapped in a bottle.

From the moment Boniface had got out of the battered black van, he had looked agitated. No, not agitated, more than that—and angry. Distraught, frantic, perhaps. The man who was usually so smooth and relaxed was twitching, tightening his own spring, which seemed ready to release at any moment.

"What's the problem, Boniface?" Tommy took a bite of his burger.

"Problem? I've got a bloke tied up in the back of the van."

"Your sexual preferences are up to you," said the big man, trying to bring some levity to the situation.

"Tommy!"

"Did your boyfriend hit you?" Tommy pointed to a cut over Boniface's eye.

"Tommy, Montbretia's in danger, and you bring me out to a place like this to take the piss." Tommy looked around: It seemed like a good place, near the motorway, near to people he could call on, near to Tilbury—where they were going, apparently—away from CCTV cameras, and at a place where you could get a decent burger from a guy who was a mate.

But things were clearly not normal; this was the first time he had seen Boniface not wearing a suit. Business casual might be expected, but old jeans and disheveled hair seemed out of place. A sign that all was not well with Boniface if the phone call he had received ninety minutes ago had not already made the point.

"Calm down, Boniface," said Tommy, laying a father-like paw on his shoulder, stuffing the remains of the burger into his mouth with his other hand. "We're among friends. Talk to me, tell me what we need to do."

"They've got Monty."

"Who?"

"The people who killed that vagrant and left his body in my office." Tommy looked down at Boniface; he was trembling, tears in his eyes. "They killed another man last night. Pummeled him to death and left him. I've spent the last ninety minutes driving a van while I'm legally banned from driving; a van that I'm not insured to drive and that is probably stolen anyway." He wiped the back of his hand across his nose, straining to contain his impotent rage.

"Shhhh," Tommy kept his intonation delicate. "These are small problems. Do you want the van to disappear?"

Boniface nodded.

"The guy in the back." Boniface nodded again. "Alive or dead?"

Every muscle in Boniface's body tightened as he looked up at Tommy. The upset was replaced by shock. "He's alive and he needs to stay alive. He's my leverage."

"Okay," said Tommy, pulling out a phone and starting to dial. "Gary. Tommy. I'm at the burger stand on the A13... Yeah, that's right. Listen, there's an old black Ford Escort van. You can't miss it: beaten to shit with an RSJ for a front bumper. Can you make it disappear? Now."

He fixed on Boniface, who was twitching again. His head moving in small jerks.

"One minor problem—there's someone in the back. Could you keep him alive? Thanks, Gaz. I owe you." He flipped the phone back in his pocket. "Gary will be here in ten to sort the van." He held out his hand. "Keys."

Tommy walked to the van, opened the driver's door, and put the key in the ignition, then leaned over and looked in the cargo area. A figure wrapped in silver duck tape wriggled and groaned. Tommy looked up to see Boniface had opened the passenger door and was retrieving a suit carrier and what looked like a CD. "Who is he, Boniface?" asked Tommy, looking over the van as they slammed the doors.

"I told you," said Boniface with no emotion, "he's my proof, and he's the only leverage I've got, which is why I've got to be back in Westminster by five."

Tommy started walking to his van. "Five? As in 5 PM today?"

Boniface dipped his head once, biting his bottom lip, apparently concentrating.

"Today?" Tommy made sure Boniface understood it was a question.

"Yeah," said Boniface disappearing out of sight on the other side of Tommy's van.

Tommy faced Boniface as they opened their doors, the big man getting in first, rocking the suspension under his weight. "We'd better move." The wheels spun on the loose surface before Boniface was seated as Tommy threw the steering wheel to point the van at the exit.

The engine screamed as the van accelerated; when it reached cruising speed, Tommy shouted to his passenger: "Without wishing to sound rude, Boniface, but you're not much of a fighting bloke—and if I'm honest, you're not really great with the gaffa tape—how did you get that bloke in the van?"

"I figured my only chance was one-on-one on my own turf. I had to hope to get lucky, and I got lucky. I played like I was beaten, and they went along with it. I got onto some stairs, giving me the higher ground, and did that whole 'what's that?' look—he glanced back, I pushed him, he hit his head. Dumb luck. Nothing else."

"So why didn't you call the cops?"

"Because he's the only bargaining chip I've got, but I can't play him until I know that Montbretia is safe."

"About that," said Tommy, his voice sounding serious. "Whatever it is that you've got to do in Westminster, you go and do it. I can drop you at the station; you can put your suit on and go. I'll hang around here and look—I'll call some of the guys to come and help." He snorted. "We could even call the cops."

"Once I start talking in Westminster, there's no incentive to keep Montbretia alive," said Boniface, in almost a whisper. "Montbretia's in trouble because of me, so I've got to sort it out. She's far more cut out for this running and jumping, punching and kicking stuff than I am, but if she can't help herself, I can't leave her, even if I'm not sure what I can do. There is no option to walk away after what I've done."

"Are you sure, Boniface?"

Boniface deliberated, apparently trying to put words in the right order. "They've taken everything from me, Tommy. My business is dead because I'm being forced to admit to something I didn't do. Random strangers are being killed. I've kidnapped someone. I have one option, and that is to break them, and I'm going to break them with Montbretia by my side."

He stared out the window as he kept talking. "I need to find Montbretia. She needs to know that she's safe." His voice cracked. "And I need to say I'm sorry." He turned back to Tommy, wiping a damp smear on his cheek. "Once she's safe, I need to get back to London and..." He scrabbled for the right word. "Vengeance is an ugly word. They killed, they tried to destroy..." He inhaled. "I need to make sure there's no more destruction, and I need to make sure that what I thought I was working on—what Montbretia thought she was working on—is what happens."

Tommy exhaled. "So how do we play this one, Boniface?"

Boniface reached for his CD and held it up. "Dutch prog rock."

Tommy took his eyes off the road and flashed at Boniface. "Are you crazy?"

"We can't shout and holler—we'll draw a crowd, perhaps we'll get arrested, and maybe we'll find his friend."

"His friend," said Tommy, feeling the tension in his voice.

"I knew there was something I forgot to tell you," said Boniface. "We don't know what he looks like. But if we play 'Sylvia,' Montbretia will know it's me and will know it's safe. We can then get to her before anyone figures what we're up to."

sixty–five

"It's been an hour, Boniface. Are you sure this is a good idea?" He leaned up against his white van, pockmarked with rust spots. "Are you even sure she's here?"

Boniface strained, as if looking harder would help him to hear or would help the sound travel to Montbretia. He felt like he had seen every reinforced concrete fence, every piece of barbed wire, every steel palisade fence, every tractor park, every bit of scrub and wasteland, every chain-link fence, every collection of shipping containers—some in designated areas, but most, it seemed, left on any piece of unclaimed land.

Tommy had taken them to the top of the road leading from the docks, killed the engine, put in the CD, and cranked the volume. As the opening power chords of "Sylvia" spread, Tommy and Boniface would start looking—Tommy would then kill the music, and in the comparative quiet, broken by trains, lorries pulling containers, passing planes, seagulls, and any other number of noises, they would both strain, kidding themselves that all they needed to do was listen harder and they would find Montbretia.

"Are you sure she's in Tilbury?" Tommy asked again.

"No." Boniface was noncommittal. "But after the last twenty-four hours, I'm not sure about much. What I do know is that I messed things up, and because of that Montbretia came here, and because she was here they found her and took her, and the very minimum I can do, if I ever want to be able to look at myself in a mirror again, is to get her out of the hole I've put her in."

Boniface held up his hand, commanding Tommy to be quiet, twisting his head as if it would give him the hearing of a superhero. He dropped his hand, straightening. "This is the last place that I know she definitely passed through. If she's not here, then where? Where would they have taken her?"

They got back in the van, and Tommy fired the engine before driving two hundred yards without speaking. Tommy opened his door, reaching for the CD. "It's not that I'm not having fun, Boniface, but would it be easier if I asked Gary and some of his mates to persuade our friend who you so kindly gift-wrapped in silver gaffa tape to tell us where she is?"

"He won't talk and he doesn't speak English."

The melodic power chords played as both men began their survey of the surrounding area. "There was a moment that I thought I was starting to like the track," said Tommy as the melody started. "But now..." He continued scanning. "I get the point of playing *this* track, but is there really nothing else we could use?"

He stopped the music—Boniface was close against a rusty chain-linked fence, pushing his head against the slack as if trying to get closer.

Tommy walked over. "We've covered everywhere obvious."

"Then we'll do the not-obvious," hissed Boniface, sounding like an annoyed reader in a library.

"Sure you don't want to go back to London and do what you need to do there?"

"I want to be in London," said Boniface. "But I need to be here."

sixty-six

The music stopped. Boniface gripped the gray steel palisade fencing, staring through with the look of a man who had been in prison so long that he had lost everything that mattered to him, including his own sense of self.

"Play the music again." There was an urgency as Boniface shouted. "The opening chords."

Tommy half-jogged, half-lumbered the few steps to the van and leaned in. A momentary pause, and the sound of 1970s Dutch prog rock played through tinny speakers filled a small part of Tilbury docks. Boniface kept a hand on the fence, which was now a gilded cage protecting the jewel: Tilbury railway terminal. Anywhere else in Tilbury, and the land would have been a vacant lot, but the rail siding ended here and someone had laid cement so that containers could be stacked, and brought in a crane to move the containers onto the trains.

Nobody knew the value of the contents of the containers, but you don't move empty boxes, so whatever was there needed to be protected.

Boniface drew his hand across his throat, and Tommy killed the music.

Within the yard, quiet—far away, there was banging. A deep sound. Something hitting metal. A big piece of metal—something thick. But there was also a resonance: It wasn't just the impact of a solid object regularly coming into contact with metal; the sound continued to reverberate after the impact.

"Monty! I'm here, Monty," bellowed Boniface.

"Shut up," Tommy reached Boniface as three bangs rang out.

"M..." Tommy slapped his paw over Boniface's mouth.

"She's alive. Let's keep it that way." He released his hand. "She didn't get in there by accident. If the guys inside the fence know she's there, they were bribed. Even if they weren't, remember that we still haven't seen that other bloke you talked about." He wiped his hand. "I thought you didn't want to make a scene."

"You need to get me in there, Tommy."

"Now you're thinking straight," said Tommy. "And I'm glad you volunteered, because I'm not in a state to get over." He looked down at his gut, a gelatinous mass flopping over his jeans and stretching his T-shirt to the limit of the tensile strength of the fabric. "I'll get the van over."

The engine strained as Tommy bumped the vehicle over the curb, backing it parallel to the fence. "Sorry. Can't get it closer," said Tommy, pointing at the rutted ground around the fence as if that was sufficient explanation. "On to the roof, jump down, and you're sorted." He opened the back doors of his van and pushed the younger man's leg as Boniface hauled himself onto the roof.

"It's higher up here than you think," said Boniface squatting, the van rocking as he moved.

"That concrete will be harder than you think when you land on it," said Tommy. "If I were you, I'd get one foot on the top of the fence instead of jumping. That way you can slide rather than adding another big height to your fall."

Boniface moved toward the edge of the roof, the radius pulling away his support. "Have you got a plank or something?"

"Not in the van, but I can look around," offered Tommy.

"No time," said Boniface, focusing on the fence. He hesitated, then launched himself, his back foot sliding on the curve of the roof as he pushed himself, his front foot aiming to make contact with the spiked trident at the top of the palisade.

As his center of gravity passed over the fence, Boniface started reaching down, trying to grab anything to break his fall. One hand scraped the top of a trident defiantly standing guard on the top of the steel. His other made contact as Boniface ducked deeper, trying to roll but finding the fence was burying its spike into his left foot.

He pulled his trailing leg, feeling the pain with another trident spiking his calf, ripping flesh and fabric as he rolled, letting go as his body went into freefall. Boniface held the fence with the one hand that had gripped, trying to slow his fall, letting go as his foot slammed into the concrete, sending shockwaves through his spine.

A twist and his knee broke the rest of his fall, bringing his body to rest on the solid ground.

"Drama queen," said Tommy, standing by the fence, a look of shock registering across his face. "Could you do that again and I'll film it? I'm sure we could get a couple of hundred quid if they show it on the telly."

"Can you break a kneecap? Because I've never felt pain like this before," whimpered Boniface.

"I'll go and tell Montbretia that we won't be rescuing her today," said Tommy, opening the passenger door of the van. He returned, pushing his hands through the fencing. "Is your leg alright?"

Boniface examined his leg—his calf was a mass of ripped flesh, ripped fabric, and blood. "Doesn't hurt that much."

"It will," said Tommy. "That's shock stopping the pain." He pointed down to the objects he had stood on the ground inside the fence as Boniface tried stretching his knee. "A knife and something to drink."

Boniface rolled over to analyze the offering. "Beer?"

"I don't carry water," said Tommy. "This is a work van. The guys that use this van want to feel that they're being rewarded. Water—even your finest foreign water—doesn't say thanks like a beer does."

Boniface put his weight on his ripped leg, pulling himself up by the fence, then gingerly tried resting some weight on his damaged knee. He fixed Tommy with a glare and very calmly, very precisely said, "Ow." He grimaced. "That is my final word until I've found Monty."

"It'll get better as you walk on it," suggested Tommy.

He leaned to pick up the penknife and can of beer, slipping both into his back pockets. "I'll go find."

"I'll grab something to make it easier for you to get out, and I'll make sure we've got a good excuse for parking the van here."

Boniface limped, trying to figure whether it was his knee or his kneecap that hurt when it took his weight.

Stepping more fully into the yard, he surveyed the rows of containers—long rows, each with containers stacked three or four high. He walked to the row on the far right, checked on the passageways flanking each container, then hissed, "Monty."

He moved to the next row, again another shouted whisper. In the next row, he heard a familiar—but this time louder—sound. Metal being struck. He stared up: The containers were stacked three high in this row, all with door seals except the top container. The doors were locked, but the security strip of wire was missing. Keeping his voice low, he said, "I'm coming, Monty."

Boniface positioned himself in front of the stack of three crates, looking up. Montbretia had told him once—and with all the work she had done for the Global Logistics Forum, she should know—that crates were at least eight feet high, and sometimes over nine. He didn't have a tape measure, but he could see that they were above his head height, and when he tried to grab the top of the crate, it was higher than he could reach.

He stood back to observe his task. Before him, two doors, locked. For each door, two vertical bars ran from the top to the bottom, fitting into secure slots at each end. A small way off the ground—Boniface presumed at a reachable height when the container was loaded onto a trailer—was a handle for each bolt. Each handle had a padlock hole, which was empty. Instead, the four vertical bolts were secured by a massive block spanning all four, which was much newer than the container.

Boniface tried the vertical bars: They felt secure, and with some caution he could slip his fingers behind each bar. He lifted his foot onto the lock and pulled to heft himself up.

He glanced down: Two, maybe three feet up, and already he felt dizzy looking at the ground. He stretched—he could get his fingers over the lip of the container. He dug his foot into an indentation in the door and levered himself higher, throwing a hand to grip the top of the container in a slot in the roof's corrugation.

A half turn of his head, and he faced back to the container. "Don't look down," he mumbled as he threw his free hand to grab a vertical bolt on the container above. He grabbed and pulled, lifting his right leg until his foot found purchase on the bottom container.

He panted and felt the tremble in his leg as he slipped his hand along the bar and pulled himself farther, levering his body into a standing position, his toes on the lower container as he gripped the vertical bars locking the middle container.

It was official: He didn't care whether it was his knee or his kneecap—he had a pain in his left leg, and the calf in his right leg was pumping.

He lifted himself by the lock on the second crate, feeling the burning pain as he propelled himself with his right calf muscle. He took a breath, gripping the vertical bars with one hand as he felt behind him to grab the can of beer and then the penknife, moving the contents of his pocket onto the top of his crate.

He risked a glance across the yard and saw Tommy under the hood of his van, black smoke billowing out of the engine, then turned to face the crate and begin the final ascent.

As his toes embraced the second crate, he firmed his grip on the vertical bars, realizing it was him shaking, not the crates wobbling. He moved to the left, standing clear of the door on the right, and leaned across, reaching for the handle.

The handle pulled out to ninety degrees. Boniface then pushed it down, opening the bolts at the top and the bottom, and repeated the process with the second bolt before pulling the door against its tired hinges. The door refused to shift more than a few inches before Boniface gave up and pushed his arm through the door, barging sufficient space for him to slide in.

His steps echoed in the dark as he walked back to kick the door open, keeping firm hold of the locked door as his foot impacted against the unwilling, but slowly moving, metal.

He surveyed the contents of the crate, looking for Montbretia but finding his eye drawn to a fallen white plastic garden chair with a gray roll on it. It took a few seconds to realize he was looking at a person—mummified with duck tape—taped to the garden chair and tipped back, but with its feet against the outside of the crate.

"Monty!"

She moved her head and mumbled something through her taped mouth as Boniface ran over and hefted the chair to the sitting position.

Feeling his eyes moisten, he went back to the door, where he leaned out to reach for the knife and beer before returning to kneel next to Montbretia.

"Listen, I don't know if you're still talking to me." Her eyes crinkled. "I've got a plan, but do you want a beer first?" The silver roll of duck tape nodded as Boniface opened Tommy's knife.

sixty-seven

Montbretia couldn't watch, so she looked around the metal box that had been her prison for the last several hours.

Corrugated steel walls; they looked rusty, but it was dark. A floor that might have been painted once, but in the light that pushed through the half-open door she could see it was scuffed, scraped, and worn.

"Eeeee." A sharp intake of breath.

"Did I hurt you?" said Boniface, pulling the knife away.

"No, sorry. I'm not used to seeing you with a knife unless you're eating." She felt it impolitic to say "with a knife when you're nervous, shaking, and waving the blade near my arm." Boniface returned to his task: cutting diligently through the duck tape binding her right arm against her body—the unspoken assumption that he was taking care to avoid the flesh on either side and, if possible, without cutting the clothes she was wearing.

Oh, and all major organs and any arteries should also be avoided.

His attempt to cut a hole for her mouth had been almost successful. Almost. He only cut her top lip twice.

And her chin once.

But it's not easy trying to find a mouth when it's covered with duck tape and there's little light. Boniface had spent several minutes feeling the tape, trying to find the precise place to cut—he had been close when he plunged the blade, just not close enough. Maybe it was the cut over his eye that was distracting him.

Then again, maybe it was her fault. He had offered her the choice—he could pull all the tape off or he could cut. She went for cut, knowing the pain of taking sticky tape out of her hair.

"There," said Boniface, evidently pleased with himself.

Montbretia lifted her right arm from the elbow as Boniface shuffled on his knees to the left arm. "What are you doing?" shrieked Montbretia.

"Sorry, did I get you again?"

"No."

"You want me to do the whole of that arm before I do this one?"

"No, Boniface. Go!"

"Not until I..."

She cut him off. "Go! Forget all that stuff about revenge is a dish best served cold. If you don't serve it, it doesn't count. Give me the knife, and I'll cut my way out." She waved her now free hand, splaying and contracting the fingers. "I'll feel safer doing the cutting, too."

He stared into her eyes. "Are y..."

"Yes. Go. This isn't about matching punch for punch and landing a good blow. Revenge is about a knockout punch. I understand the plan; I'll get out of here. You get yourself gone." She pointed to the door with her head as Boniface self-consciously dusted himself off.

She watched as he cautiously sat on the threshold of the crate, dangling his legs outside. He gripped the door, then pulled himself back in and walked over, reaching into his pocket. "Phone," he said, laying his phone on the floor next to her. "Call Gideon and talk about really dirty stuff. We need his help."

He returned to his sitting position at the exit, gripping the closed door. "Are you're sure we can trust Tommy?" she asked.

"I'm sure. I'd trust him with my life. I'd trust him—I *am* trusting him—with yours. He thinks you're great, and he'll save you from any covenants you feel obligated to enter into with Gideon." The last thing she saw before he dropped out the door was a nervous smile.

sixty–eight

Boniface dropped, hitting the concrete and falling clumsily.

He lay where he fell, breathing steadily, taking a mental inventory. Head: hurts, but hit concrete last so probably hurts least, and anyway, was already cut above the eye. Shoulder: new pain from the fall, but probably more the surprise of hitting the concrete. Hip: ouch, but like the shoulder, this was a new injury, not one introduced by Regenspurger's man in the green army jacket, and not added when he slipped, landing badly as he came over the palisade fence.

He raised himself, resting on his arm as he continued his inventory. Having landed heavily, his knees could be filed under hurt-pain-ow, especially the left one, and his right calf, to use the best understatement he could call to mind, was throbbing.

Boniface rolled back toward the container and hauled himself up, using the vertical bars to hold his weight, reaching if not vertical, a sufficiently upright position that a long-ago extinct human ancestor would have been proud to adopt.

He took a few steps—capable of balance, but not yet used to the newly found pain in walking. Somehow the rat-faced man was now firmly in his mind. What would happen if he had got out before Gary reached him? What would happen if someone looked in the van or heard the groaning?

What if he got out? Boniface's head spun, with the pain in his neck it felt like it had turned through 360 degrees, but he knew he had looked left and right, scaring himself about who might be around.

He moved, barely lifting his feet as he followed a path through the crates, unable to get the rat-faced man out of his mind. What would happen if he got free? Would he know how to contact Regenspurger? Would he come back and look for him and Montbretia, and kill them? Was it safe to leave Montbretia here, even with Tommy?

Was this another stupid risk he was taking—this time even more reckless because he knew what was at stake? What chance did he have that his plan would work? He sighed. Too many moving parts, too much risk.

He reached the palisade fence separating the yard from the scrubland running along the dock road and followed until he drew level with Tommy's van, which was still smoking. He pushed his face against the vertical bars, looking for Tommy. Looking for whatever Tommy had found to help him get out of the yard.

It took a while to realize that the figure about fifty yards away was Tommy sitting on someone. Boniface stared: The lumbering old walrus appeared to be on top of someone who was struggling but still able to land blows from his horizontal position.

Tommy was in control, but he was taking a pounding, and the other guy seemed to have the energy and the incentive to fight.

Boniface focused on the rows of three-high containers running parallel to the trident-topped fence that had nibbled his shoe and chewed his leg, looking for anything to help him get over. Someone, somewhere—someone who wore a high-vis jacket—had undertaken a health and safety check and had ensured that all waste in the yard was cleaned up. Boniface was all in favor of reducing workplace accidents, but the lack of any wood or rubble lying around wasn't helping.

There was nothing.

He assessed the containers, trying to gauge their height relative to the height of the fence. The fence looked higher than one container. He positioned himself between one stack of containers and the fence, his arms spread. He touched neither, guessing he would need to extend each arm by around twelve inches to reach.

He cursed under his breath and looked up at the containers: two regular containers and on the top, a specialized brick-carrying container—the same proportions as its siblings below, but lacking a side wall to allow easy access.

Boniface cursed again, walking to the end of the container stack.

Practice makes perfect. It might have hurt more, but Boniface's second ascent of a container stack was swifter. Halfway up, he figured that the pain wasn't increasing and it was easier to climb without a can of beer in his jeans. He reached the top and edged his way around from the end doors, holding onto the reinforced vertical corner as he turned onto the open face of the brick container, leaning back to rest on the bricks and look at Tommy, who was still on top but was getting hit with greater frequency.

He leaned back, pulling at the heat-sealed plastic wrapping, and eased out three bricks, which he tossed over the palisade fencing, watching how they arced to the ground. He tried to calculate how far he would have to jump out so that he too could arc over the fence.

He lifted himself to a standing position, muttered "gravity, height, distance" and jumped, leaping as far away from the crate as he could. As he started to feel the effect of gravity, he began to wish he'd thought about a landing strategy as he frantically tried to recall the old war movies he had seen when the parachutists roll.

His contemplation was interrupted by his feet hitting the ground. His forward momentum pushed him, and he found his ankles bending, breaking the fall onto his knees, his hip, and twisting as he rolled onto his back.

Again he lay still, waiting for a new pain but not feeling it.

There was a muffled sound in Tommy's direction. He gathered up his bricks and ran to the big man. "Hey, Tommy," he said, holding out a brick.

"Afternoon, Boniface," said Tommy, looking up, a look a pride spreading across his face as he took Boniface's offering while the flailing arms remained weighted under the human ballast.

Boniface gripped a brick in each hand and scrutinized the flesh on the ground. He stepped on one arm, precisely positioning his foot at the elbow where the forearm protruded from a leather jacket. Boniface focused, waiting for the thrashing hand and arm to pause, and then slammed the bricks together, crushing the hand between the slabs of fired clay.

The man in the leather jacket bellowed as Boniface released the arm and walked to the other side. He put his foot down, trapping the right elbow, and closely examined the hand. Three-and-a-half fingers, one thumb. "Where's your beard now?" said Boniface, as the bricks came down on the hand.

Tommy held his brick as if ready to strike the man's head. "Enough," he said as the man lay still. "There's some webbing in the back of the van, Boniface."

Boniface jogged over and came back with the strapping. "Legs first, Tommy?"

"Legs first, Boniface," said Tommy, moving forward on his captive's stomach, still brandishing his six-sided oblong weapon.

"All done," said Boniface, admiring his newfound skill in wrapping.

"We're going to roll you," said Tommy to his seat, holding his brick above the man's face. "It's your choice whether you get hit."

The man nodded. Tommy started to stand, and his captive jerked violently to the left, pulling his legs up. Tommy dropped his weight back onto the man. There was a sound of air being expelled, followed by a thud as Tommy brought the brick into contact with his head.

Tommy stood, taking a second webbing strap Boniface offered. "Where's Monty? Is she okay?"

"She's fine—she's cutting herself free."

"So what are you doing here? Go," said Tommy, pointing toward the station. "I'll take care of her...and him."

sixty-nine

Boniface caught his reflection in the glass panel separating him from the cabbie: hair, shirt, tie, jacket, all straight. Cut over left eye, still nasty, but he had at least been able to clean his hands and face in the restroom at Fenchurch Street station before jumping in the cab, which then doubled as his dressing room during the fifteen-minute jaunt across the City of London, grazing the West End and finishing in Westminster: the heart of British political power.

Boniface kicked his bloodied jeans, T-shirt, and sneakers into the gutter as he opened the door, paid the cabbie, and walked swiftly around the corner to Westminster Methodist Hall.

Most people saw the word Methodist and figured church. Most people saw a church and figured religion. Most people didn't realize Westminster Methodist Hall had a whole range of rooms, from large to small, that could be hired by the day or by the hour, making it a perfect meeting and conference center.

Its proximity to Parliament—topping an oblong with the Houses of Parliament at the foot and Westminster Abbey and a purpose-built conference center along the sides—made it a near daily location for political press launches.

But today, this had been chosen as the site of Boniface's public execution.

"Where have you been, Boniface?" He was six-two and Canadian but had the temperament of a small, angry man. "I've been calling."

"But which phone?" asked Boniface. "I don't have a phone, so it can't have been my phone that you called."

"Boniface, I don't have time. We've got a press conference, and in case you haven't noticed, we're discussing a very serious issue. Now what was that issue?" North American sarcasm never works well on an English ear. "Oh yeah. You. You telling us how you thought you would dump a body." He exhaled. "Geez, Boniface, what were you thinking? This is a real mess I'm going to have to fix."

Brad had turned and was already walking. He hadn't said "yo" or "man" or "dude" once, and somehow Boniface missed that.

"Keep up, Boniface." He didn't look back. "Regenspurger has been intolerable. He thinks it's enough that you're here. He doesn't understand all the arrangements that need to be made. The people to be called, the..." Boniface stopped listening as Brad went through the oak double door into the central reception.

"We're back here," said Brad without breaking step as he led Boniface through a carpeted labyrinth threading around a series of small conference rooms. "We've got a room for the actual press conference with a room where we're meeting before."

"Can we have a look at the room where the press conference is being held?" asked Boniface.

"No time," the Canadian continued at his pace.

Boniface slowed, waiting for the figure in sandy chinos and a blue shirt to notice, slow, turn, and backtrack to where Boniface had decided to stop. "Come on, Boniface."

"Give way on this one thing, Brad. It'll make it much easier for you, and we'll all get wherever it is you're going quicker than if we stand here arguing."

Brad sighed and flounced down the corridor. "Alright. We were going that way anyway."

The tall Canadian pushed a door and led Boniface into a room. A long table, covered in a blue velvet-like cloth that reached the floor at the front and with three heavy leather-bound chairs behind, stood on a low stage. In the main body of the room, there was an island of gilt-framed chairs: four rows of interlinked chairs, each row split with five seats to either side of a central walkway.

A brief flicker of awareness rippled around the room as the two entered. Boniface scanned the faces, looking for anyone familiar, but saw no one. Three young-looking journalists chatted; two older journalists tapped furiously on their phones. Boniface scanned again. Why the recognition? Were they pleased to see anyone or had they been pre-briefed? Perhaps that was how Brad had persuaded them to come. A dumb move, but possible.

Boniface maneuvered himself into the room, looking around and muttering platitudes—"Hi...how are you doing...good to see you"—as he walked to the second row and sat.

Brad sat down beside him, leaning in close and straining to keep his voice quiet. "Boniface. What the hell are you doing?"

Boniface sat up straight, watching as another journalist came into the room. Looking concerned and unsure as she entered, her face burst into life as she recognized one of the older journalists, his head momentarily raised during a brief pause from tapping on his phone.

"If you want me to commit suicide in a religious building, then please let me sit and contemplate, and get a feeling for the room." No one heard apart from Brad.

"Keep your voice down," Brad's voice was air pushed through a clenched jaw. "We need to prepare."

"Then let us go and prepare," said Boniface. "I presume the charming Mister Regenspurger will be there."

"You bet," said Brad, standing.

"I want to come back here before we start," said Boniface as Brad shook hands with another journalist who had just come through the door. "What do these journalists cover?"

"Some are transportation and logistics specialists, like..." He inclined his head toward the man he had shaken hands with. "We also sent the invitation to the business desks."

"That explains why I don't recognize any faces. I used to know the politicos."

Brad led them out onto the corridor—a broad passage that ducked and dived around the rooms—his mop of light-colored hair flopping from side to side as they walked, every five feet passing a fire extinguisher, a health and safety notice, or an exhortation to worship.

Boniface slapped his pocket, his habitual check on his phone. The primeval instinct to panic was rapidly replaced by regret that he had given his phone to Montbretia. He felt his knee twinge as he tried to keep up with the Canadian, and the feeling of regret was washed away by a wave of relief for having made sure the right person had the phone.

"Have you got the time, Brad?" Boniface asked as he tried to keep up.

"Five. Five-fifteen. Something like that," said Brad, turning a corner into a darker part of the passage, then turning back on himself and pushing a door.

A small room. Like the press conference room, it was spartan: a plain but functional carpet and white painted walls. Unlike the larger room, this had no source of natural daylight and no raised stage.

"You see, Mister Phipps. I said he would be delivered at the time we needed him." Regenspurger turned to Boniface, continuing in his precise tone, the German accent scratching at the Englishman. "Where's your friend, Boniface?"

"Parking the van. There were too many cops around, and it's too much of a sensitive location for him to leave it on the street." Boniface paused. "I think he's staying outside. This isn't his sort of place."

Regenspurger nodded.

"I presume Greta will be here."

Regenspurger nodded again. "She is recovered from this morning, thank you for asking, Boniface." The German sarcasm seemed much more effective than the Canadian.

"One more thing," said Boniface without making eye contact. "I want all the executives to be here."

"That's not..." Brad started and was cut off by a look from Regenspurger.

"That would not be practical, Herr Boniface."

"Then make it practical. They're all within a mile of here." He moved farther into the room before continuing. "This has nothing to do with our agreement—and as you can see, I'm doing what I said I would." He waited for a flicker of acknowledgement to pass across the piercing eyes. "I want confirmation from all the company officers—from Greta, from Chlodwig, from Joanna, from Jeremy—that after today, our relationship is finished. I want to hear it firsthand from them." He faced Brad. "I apologize if this delays your press conference, Brad, but I'm sure Mister Regenspurger understands my perspective."

The German remained motionless, then flicked his eyelids, pulling out his phone.

"While you two sort that, I'm going back to the room."

seventy

Boniface didn't like to make presumptions based on appearance and stereotypes.

Who was he kidding? He loved to.

Then he'd spend the next five minutes revising his opinion as reality kicked in.

The journalists were starting to arrive with greater frequency now, but their entrance was always the same. The heavy wooden door would open, and the deer-in-the-headlights face would appear. After the initial shock, the eyes would then begin to sweep the room.

Some would skim in circles; others would scan along the rows. Some would alight on a friendly face, and a new playground clique would be formed. Those that didn't find a friend would feign cool professionalism—they didn't need anyone to talk to; they had work to do, and they had phones to tap and stare at earnestly as they hoped someone would come and sit next to them.

Boniface made an inventory—reviewing appearances against his mental library of stereotypes as he tried to assess which were the shipping and logistics journalists: His guess was the just-out-of-university types. The business reporters: His gaze alighted on three somewhat older journalists who dressed better but had that not-on-the-track-to-editorship look. Brad had also mentioned that he had called some crime journalists. Boniface made another assumption based on a stereotype: The guy with the 1970s tobacco-colored leather blazer, complete with belt, suggested Brad might have been successful.

He had been sitting for two minutes, and already the seat was starting to feel uncomfortable. A gilt-colored frame with seat and back padding wrapped in deep-red synthetic velvet may look stylish in the brochure and may be acceptable for a short while, but Boniface could find nothing to recommend the overly narrow human-hating contraption.

He shifted one seat to the right and leaned toward the journalist sitting alone at the end of the row. Young, wearing a suit that Boniface guessed he wore every day—it had that I've-only-got-one-suit-and-it's-a-cheap-suit look. "Could I borrow your phone?"

The acne-scarred face under the flop of greasy hair turned to look at Boniface. Shock registered, as if Boniface had suggested they wrestle naked in the middle of the floor.

Boniface pointed at the gash above his eye. "I got mugged." Some of the fear seemed to drain from the young man. "I just want to check the BBC; you know they're expecting the big one to break any minute now."

"I didn't," said the young man, reaching for his phone. "What have you heard?"

Boniface called up the BBC news website. Apparently nothing was happening: The president in a central Asian dictatorship was dead, the inflation figures had been seasonally adjusted, which made a 0.1 percent change—the leader of the opposition was trying to argue that this was a very, very, *very* bad thing—and yet another soccer player had been accused of assault. Boniface couldn't be bothered to check whether he assaulted his girlfriend or someone in a bar who supported the opposition.

"Who are you with?" asked Boniface as he refreshed the screen. He didn't listen to the reply or the justification about how, whatever job it was, was a step on the career ladder. "Thank you," said Boniface, handing back the phone and returning to his own scan of the room. Three more journalists had arrived and added to the pockets of tête-à-têtes vibrating in a hive of self-created intrigue.

The door opened again.

There was something familiar in her face.

He watched as she scanned—she was an along-the-rows scanner—waiting until her gaze passed him and then bounced back as some flicker of recognition triggered in her synapses. Her momentary look of confusion morphed into an inquisitive look—a question posed across the room as she frowned, tilting her head, but with her lips smiling.

At last, a familiar face.

The haircut had become less practical over the years. Boniface remembered when it was long. Now it was straight at the front, and as you looked around back the hair was cut up high on her neck, angling down to the straight edge. Very stylish. Looked great. She could carry it off, but it obviously required a lot of work to keep it looking that good and to stop it from going flat.

Boniface got to his feet as she started walking toward him. The clothes had changed, too. They were less fashionable now, but more stylish—classic would probably be the right description of the skirt and jacket combination—and with some more color. If he wasn't after a favor, he would have also noticed that she had added a few pounds. Correct that: a lot of pounds.

"Jennifer." He spread his hands.

"Boniface." Jennifer Quilley met his embrace, politely kissing him on each cheek.

"All grown up," said Boniface, stepping back to admire his acquaintance and putting into practice everything he had learned with Greta about paying a compliment without using words.

"Boniface the bullshitter," said Jennifer, flashing a mouthful of television-ready teeth. "It's rather rude to call you what we called you behind your back, but it does have a certain alliterative panache." Her grin was replaced by a flirtatious pout of her lips, seemingly intended to keep the atmosphere light.

"Alliterative charm or not, it wasn't really true."

"Oh Boniface, it was true often enough." She slowed, weighing her next line. "Alright, you told the truth except when you were protecting Gideon. How is Gideon, by the way? Still got the same...tastes?"

"You mean Gideon who, just this week, stood naked to answer the door to me and then picked chocolate out of his pubic hair?" She nodded, a slight hint that a story was being stored away for later retrieval. "Not a clue—haven't seen him for years." Boniface gave his best look of mischievous inscrutability, stepping back and offering Jennifer a seat.

Boniface sat next to her, his own tête-à-tête. "So you've fought your way out of the political trenches to become the business editor and on television?"

"Slightly more humane hours, or at least more predictable, and more time indoors. But it does lack some of the..."

"Thrill of the blood sport," offered Boniface.

"Thrill? Vicarious enjoyment, perhaps." She tilted her head. "What about you, Boniface. I miss watching your performances. You're...?"

"Sober," he said, cutting in before a question could come.

"Don't apologize," said Jennifer. "Some of my best friends are sober."

Boniface leaned toward the journalist, the muscles in his jaw tightening. "Jennifer, fun as this is, I need a bit of a favor, rather urgently."

seventy-one

Boniface watched the turquoise jacket cross the room. The sharply cut blonde hair seemed an age-appropriate improvement for Jennifer Quilley.

He looked across at Brad, who had been talking to some of the younger journalists—the shipping and logistics journalists, Boniface was guessing. The Canadian seemed desperate to try to keep his attention on the young woman he was talking with, but his eyes were drawn to Boniface's acquaintance as she crossed the room.

Before she could reach the door to the room, it opened forcefully. He watched as Jennifer's hair was caught in the draft. Instead of the normal hesitant journalist, an older man stepped in, immaculately presented in a three-piece suit and oblivious to the inconvenience he may have caused for anyone else.

Jennifer stepped to the right, ducking behind Jeremy Farrant as she left. Farrant had adopted the standard behavior of the journalists and was scanning the room. His eyes came to rest upon Boniface. He made eye contact and gave a sharp backward nod, leaving Boniface feeling compelled to follow the man, who had already left the room.

He was standing across the corridor, obliquely facing the door, scowling, as Boniface exited. "Why am I here, Boniface? I'm told you're making a public announcement."

"Boniface. Why did Jennifer Quilley leave?" Brad seemed unaware that Boniface and the lawyer were in conversation. "You were talking to her, and then she left. She's an important TV journalist—we need her here." He was looking down the corridor in the direction she had gone.

"She's an old friend of mine, Brad." Boniface didn't mind exaggerating somewhat. Well...exaggerating extensively, and without limitation.

"But we're meant to be starting now," the Canadian was whining. "You've been here for nearly an hour, I don't see any reason for the delay—you seem to be wasting time."

"Calm down, Brad. It's not a problem." Boniface held a business card so Brad could see it. "She's got to pop out for something. I promised her that I would personally call her five minutes before we start if she's not back."

Brad inhaled, looking ready to speak, then walked toward the room where the Weissenfeld executives were gathering.

"You were about to explain, Boniface," hissed Farrant. "Why am I here?"

"Good evening, gentlemen." Chlodwig Weissenfeld and Joanna Baines appeared behind Boniface.

"They are gathering in the room at the end," said the lawyer, pointing in the direction that Brad had gone. The two carried on walking, not breaking step—Chlodwig acknowledging Boniface, Baines staring straight ahead.

"There is one point of law that requires clarification before I speak. I am keen to make sure that my interests are protected and that the Weissenfeld interests are also considered." Boniface dropped his voice to a whisper. "More to the point, this demands someone with your...gravitas. I want to ensure everyone accepts your confirmation—I don't want an ongoing discussion based on ignorance of the law." He stood up straight. "Do you see why I *needed* you?"

"Gracious. I quite understand." Boniface watched as the lawyer took joy that someone had recognized his talents.

seventy–two

"This isn't the sort of car to pick up women. But it is the kind to draw a crowd," said Tommy Newby, pulling his vintage Bentley Speed Six onto Parliament Square. "Let's see how big we can get the crowd." He parped his horn and joined the five lanes encircling the green square fronting the Houses of Parliament.

"Notice how people notice," he said to Montbretia. "You don't get that with a Porsche or a Ferrari, and people don't hate me like they hate those bankers and their flash cars."

Montbretia pulled out Boniface's phone. "I'm going to make some more calls."

Tommy reached for the gear stick, flattening the clutch and praying that the gears didn't graunch in public.

"Political desk!" Montbretia shouted into the phone.

A cabbie drew level with the Bentley, apparently more concerned about looking at the car than he was with his or his fare's safety.

"You heard right," shouted Montbretia. "Gideon Latymer will break a super-injunction on the floor of the House of Commons. Within the next thirty minutes—if the Speaker agrees to an emergency question."

"How many journalists have you got coming?" asked Tommy as Montbretia ended the call.

"Who knows? But a crowd should help: Boniface wants it to make the news." She looked around and turned back to Tommy. "Are you sure you can manage it?"

"It's mechanical—it's easy."

"Remember," said Montbretia. "You need to break down before the barrier so we can get a crowd of people. If you're in the parking lot, then they can't get to you. I'll give you a whistle when your crowd has drawn enough people and you can send them over to us, and it should look good in front of the TV cameras."

"Gotcha. You ready?"

"Yup."

Tommy finished the circuit of Parliament Square, moving into the curbside lane and slowing the Bentley as it passed in front of the Houses of Parliament, the passersby all turning as they heard the thundering beast of an engine. He cautiously positioned the vehicle between the two crash barriers; Tommy knew that they might look inoffensive with their muted brown covering and fluorescent yellow highlighting, but underneath was solid concrete designed to protect Parliament from suicide bombers. In an argument with the barriers, Tommy's Bentley would lose, so he followed the road as the fortifications funneled vehicles into the Old Palace Yard parking lot, pulling up at the security gate and stalling the engine.

Montbretia turned to the police officer who had stepped out of the guard's box behind the gate, apparently unsure as to whether he could stop worrying about the safety of British politicians for long enough to admire the vintage British engineering.

"Gideon Latymer should have cleared us about thirty minutes ago," she said.

The young officer looked down at his clipboard. "He did. Straight through and park...you can park wherever you want with a car like that."

Montbretia started to thank the officer as Tommy turned the engine. It turned but didn't fire. He turned it again, but still it didn't fire.

"I'm off," said Montbretia, jumping out. Tommy tried to keep sight of where she was heading, seeing a cameraman and a sound engineer holding a boom with a long fuzzy microphone at the end, and a third person with the group—a woman, better dressed and checking her face in a compact.

"I'm sorry about this." Tommy acknowledged the policeman. "If you want a car to start first time, don't get one of these." He turned the engine again, shaking his head in disappointment when it didn't fire.

He got out of the beast, removed the leather straps traversing the long nose, and opened the right side of the hood.

"Look at that engine." There was a muttering on the far side of the crash barrier where a small crowd was gathering, apparently preferring to admire the vintage car rather than worry about their personal safety as they stood on the road.

Tommy put his hands onto the engine, pulling faces to suggest he was concentrating on adjusting the machinery, as he watched Montbretia scuttle around in her quest to find journalists and encourage them to gather around the Saint Stephen's entrance to the Houses of Parliament. It had seemed a bizarre plan that Boniface had concocted, but there were several TV cameras standing around, and he knew that some of the political bloggers that Montbretia had spoken with had promised to make sure there was maximum real-time publicity.

Gideon Latymer appeared on the steps outside the Saint Stephen's entrance. Surprisingly for a politician, he appeared not to be talking. Montbretia looked around before being swallowed into the crowd. It was Tommy's cue to move away—apparently Gideon was hesitant about appearing in public with Tommy. Tommy checked and could see the top of Montbretia's head as she emerged from the crowd she had created, walking up the steps and giving Gideon a peck on the cheek before standing next to him, gripping his arm.

Tommy stepped back from the car, closed the hood, and fastened the straps. He then turned to the small crowd admiring the car. "If there are any journalists here, could I suggest you gather over there, where I understand Mister Latymer is about to make a very important announcement?"

He pondered, then continued. "In fact, even if you're not a journalist, you may find the announcement interesting. For myself, I will move the car into the parking over there." He indicated the Old Palace Yard parking lot.

"If it starts," said a voice in the gathering.

"It will start. First time," said Tommy. He surveyed the crowd. "A small wager for anyone?"

seventy-three

A turquoise jacket appeared at the end of the passage.

Boniface watched as Jennifer Quilley proceeded along the passageway. "Can we start now?" asked Brad.

Boniface acknowledged Jennifer as she crossed toward the room scheduled to hold the press conference. She looked to Boniface, nodded her affirmation, and then twisted her head in the direction from which she had walked, returning to meet his vision before giving a slight questioning frown. He mouthed "thank you," feeling the ends of his lips lift involuntarily. She looked perplexed—having been involved in a whole conversation without words, it appeared she did not understand what she had heard.

Brad shuffled as Jennifer disappeared from view, like a teenager being told to wait.

"I want two minutes," said Boniface. "Two minutes with everyone else so that we are all agreed on what is happening."

"I think we know what's..."

Boniface cut off Brad. "Two minutes to make sure it's not a total cluster... To make sure we all give the same message."

"I don't see that it's necessary, Boniface," whined the Canadian.

"You stay here then; I need to talk to the decision makers," said Boniface.

"Well, if that's the case..." Brad followed and passed Boniface, hurrying toward the room where the executives had gathered.

seventy–four

Brad pushed the door and Boniface followed him into the box with no source of natural light, checking to make sure everyone was there: Greta, Regenspurger, Chlodwig, Jeremy Farrant, and Joanna Baines.

Greta stepped forward, swathed in a bottle-green dress, tailored to her preference to imply a full figure rather than suggest the necessity for a diet. Her shoes, also green, were high but not the height of her usual office shoes, reducing her stature by an inch or so. Her hair had returned to its flawless helmet-like shape, and when she spoke her voice was resolute. "What's the holdup, Boniface? Herr Regenspurger tells me that you will be making an announcement."

Boniface could detect no sign of any weakness after her injury that morning, and her reduced height had not translated into a reduced determination.

Chlodwig gave his slightly-disappointed-but-wanting-to-stay-encouraging half smile. "We want Greta to be next to you, receiving your apology, so that everyone understands that this morning's incident was minor. It's important for the share price that the markets understand that the CEO is in control."

There was a burble of agreement around the room. Boniface waited for it to calm and asked, "Before we start, does someone have a phone?" He surveyed the faintly unsettled, frowning faces. "Not for me—we should check the breaking news before we proceed. Brad, you must have a phone."

"Sure. But I don't..."

Boniface stopped him. "Call up the BBC news website and go to the live broadcast feed." Brad remained motionless. "Humor me on this: Let's see what story they're running."

The room focused on Brad as he tapped on his phone, then squinted at the screen with the tinny sound of the small speaker carrying the commentary into the room.

"Perhaps if you could hold the phone up so everyone can see what's happening?"

Brad held his phone with the screen facing outward.

"What is the relevance of all this?" asked Jeremy Farrant, looking at the screen over his half-moon glasses balanced at the end of his nose.

"Maybe nothing," said Boniface. "But could somebody who has got a better view tell me who the journalist is?"

"I can never remember his name," said Joanna Baines, "but he's the BBC's political editor."

"Political *editor*," said Boniface. "So not a regular journalist?"

Baines mouthed the word "no."

"Can someone squint and tell me what the ticker on the bottom is saying? Or perhaps you could turn up the volume, Brad, so we can all hear."

Brad twisted the phone back and stabbed a button. The volume increased, the tinny speaker distorting with each sibilant and plosive the political editor delivered: "Of course Mister Latymer will not be saying anything here—while he's outside the Chamber of the House of Commons, he's not covered by parliamentary privilege."

"That's interesting," said Boniface. "It seems that Gideon Latymer is about to do something newsworthy. Has anyone read the ticker yet?"

Brad turned the screen back; holding it close to his eyes, he started to mumble: "MP to break super-injunction." He stared out. "It says MP to…"

"We heard, thank you, Brad," said Boniface, pausing as he felt the tension drain from his muscles. "You know about my connection to Gideon Latymer. Indeed, that was one of the reasons for hiring me." He focused directly on Greta, catching a glance as she looked away, her eyes darting, searching elsewhere for reassurance.

He scanned the room: Regenspurger seemed calm, Baines looked angry, and Chlodwig appeared confused, but doing his patrician best to be supportive in a difficult situation.

"I'm seeing some confusion," said Boniface. "You're here because, despite the injunction, you want me to make some announcements to the press, knowing that the press cannot report what they are being told…because of the injunction." Jeremy Farrant stood straighter at the mention of the announcement. "But you also know that there is a sufficient legal gray area that the press will be able to mention my connection with a dead body and will push further because they know I'm one person, and as an individual I won't have the legal resources to fight the matter, especially if I'm in jail."

"Man, they really got you." Brad had a broad smile. "Now I get how it works."

"Don't you see?" Joanna Baines blurted.

Boniface ignored the two and continued. "When the Somalia story comes out, then it will have lost much of its sting because it will already be old news for the press, and you will always be able to remind people that you had bad PR advice."

He caught Regenspurger's eye—a self-satisfied aura possessed his face with the hint of a smile forming at the corner of his mouth.

"A calculated gamble," said Boniface. "One that I can respect, but I have an alternative proposition."

Regenspurger frowned, his voice soft. "But you are not forgetting our agreement?"

"How could I forget?" said Boniface, raising his voice as he continued. "I will not be making a statement this evening. I did nothing wrong. I was not responsible for the death of the man whose body was dumped in my office, and I had no connection to the people who dumped the body."

Boniface saw the confusion spread across Chlodwig's face as he looked to Regenspurger, his eyes asking for an explanation.

"As you can see on the news, Gideon Latymer is about to break your injunction." He glanced to Jeremy Farrant. "I'm sure Mister Farrant will confirm, a Member of Parliament can break an injunction, even a super-injunction, and is protected by parliamentary privilege."

Farrant puffed himself up, gripping his lapels. "That is correct, Boniface."

"The media is then free to report, without restriction, what has been said in Parliament," added Boniface.

"That is also correct," said Farrant. "Although they may only report what has actually been said; the injunction is still in place, so they can't extrapolate any further. But I think you're missing something, Boniface. It would be highly inappropriate for a Member of Parliament to take this action; it would be a complete abuse of his position."

"What? To tell the truth? To announce that Weissenfeld Shipping made a decision at an executive level to dump toxic waste in Somalia?"

"Greta?" Chlodwig turned his disappointment onto his younger sister, who was giving him her best indignant look.

Boniface continued. "As you can see, Mister Latymer is at Parliament, so he can't be diverted." He turned to Regenspurger. "Even you, Mister Regenspurger, with your extensive network of bullies, thugs, and intimidators. You can't stop Gideon."

Regenspurger's countenance remained unstirred.

"But you're thinking that you have some leverage." Boniface saw a momentary glimmer of pride. "Brad. If you look closely, there should be a lady holding tightly to Gideon's arm."

"She's hot," said Brad.

"Would you mind showing Mister Regenspurger the screen?" As Brad passed his phone, Boniface continued. "Some of you were unaware that as well as dumping toxic waste, Weissenfeld has also been involved in kidnapping. But let's not worry about that yet, because as you can see, Mister Regenspurger, Montbretia is free."

Boniface paused, watching Regenspurger's face twitch. "Montbretia free. Leverage over me, gone." Boniface beamed. "In case you're wondering...those pleasant young gentlemen...I've got some friends looking after them, and we'll deliver them to the police later this evening, when I'm sure they will be happy to explain the two murders they committed."

"Murder?" Greta shrieked, turning to Regenspurger, whose face had returned to its customary look of dead flesh draped over a skull.

"You authorized him to procure a body and dump it in my office, but time was short, so he got a body the old-fashioned way," said Boniface.

"Is this true, Greta?" asked Chlodwig.

"I'm afraid it is," said Boniface. "And they beat another man to death yesterday."

He caught sight of Greta: Outwardly, she had aged ten years in ten minutes. Once proud, once strong, she looked broken.

"We can talk over the details later," said Boniface. "First, we've got a press conference with people waiting."

"But we can't... Not if you're not..." Brad was jabbering. "This is very embarrassing, Boniface."

"It's alright, Brad. The press conference is still going ahead," said Boniface. "However, the agenda has changed slightly."

Boniface relaxed his shoulders and stood straighter. "First order of business: Greta, you are announcing, with immediate effect, your resignation."

"Absolutely not." Her retort was swift, but as Boniface observed the CEO, he could see no appetite to fight.

"Greta, there have been two murders." Chlodwig's voice was soft but definite.

"Chlodwig is correct, and that is why you will announce that he will be acting chief executive while a search is made for a long-term successor," said Boniface. "You can explain that regretfully, the head injury you suffered this morning will require surgery, and with the recuperation time you won't be able to devote your full energies to the role."

He looked at Chlodwig. "The first task for you as CEO is to acknowledge that Weissenfeld has been involved in dumping toxic waste in Somalia. While you're making the announcement, Mister Farrant will call the lawyers to have the injunction lifted. You can say that the injunction was sought to give Weissenfeld time to confirm some key facts, which have now been confirmed."

"But this is still…"

Boniface held up his hand to stop Chlodwig. "You will make one other announcement." The patrician German paused, waiting for Boniface to continue. "You're going to announce that Weissenfeld is establishing a foundation for Somali victims of any chemical dumping, and are endowing the foundation with one billion dollars, U.S."

"No, Boniface, you're going too far. We don't have that sort of money," said Chlodwig.

Boniface made an exaggerated shrug. "I'm sure if we ask Joanna and consider the alternatives, we can agree that is an achievable figure." He glanced at the CFO. "It's tax-deductible, too, and it's far less than other companies have paid for spilling oil into the Gulf of Mexico."

"No, Boniface. Absolutely not," said Chlodwig. "You are asking us to change our whole management structure and to commit a vast sum of money. We need time to think about this."

"You've got all the time you need," said Boniface. "But remember, your company has been responsible for two murders, and as soon as Gideon walks inside and reaches the floor of the House of Commons, your options all disappear."

seventy-five

"I do not know where you heard that story; I suggest you check with your sources. It would be highly inappropriate and highly unusual for a parliamentarian to interfere with the judicial process."

Boniface could hear Gideon's explanations to the last few journalists who were questioning him on the steps, framed by the Saint Stephen's entrance to the House of Commons, the splendor of the Victorian gothic architecture rising above him. He stood erect, aware that there could be cameras on him.

A face poked from the far side of the dark blue suit. "Boniface!" Montbretia dropped Gideon's arm, ran between him and the journalists, and threw her arms around Boniface.

Although having the air rapidly expelled from his lungs, Boniface could hear as Gideon continued. "I was not the source of this story. My office was not the source."

Montbretia squeezed tighter.

"I'm sorry," said Boniface.

"Shhh."

"I'm sorry and thank you," said Boniface. "If I'd listened to you, I never would have needed your help."

Montbretia said something that Boniface couldn't hear.

"I know your sex life is none of my business, but I hope you didn't have to promise Gideon too much to persuade him to take your call and to play ball."

"It's alright, he's had me clinging to his arm and staring up at him in front of all those cameras for the last hour. He has had sufficient reward," said Montbretia, looking up at Boniface.

Boniface continued. "I'm not going to make promises that I can't keep; I've learned my lesson. But while I was telling Greta that she was resigning, even though she didn't know it, I had an idea."

Montbretia let go and stood back, staring up at him, mock stern. "Don't you think you've had enough good ideas, at least for this year?" Two tourists walking past stopped and stared at Boniface and Montbretia.

"No, this really is a good idea. I thought, as well as making Greta resign and admit to dumping toxic waste, thereby ensuring that she lost all her power and authority and has had to publicly humiliate herself..."

"That was a good plan, Boniface. As I lay trussed up like a duck tape sausage, it did give me a certain pleasure as you explained what you wanted to do. It also distracted me from my fear of your knife skills."

"It gets better," said Boniface, watching the tourists start to walk away. "I suggested... Well, I told them that they are setting up a foundation to support victims of chemical dumping in Somalia. Doesn't matter who dumped, the foundation will support them."

Montbretia's face had a look suggesting she had just had a pleasant surprise. "That is a good idea, Boniface."

"Wait. That's not the good idea. I also told them that they will endow that foundation with a large establishing grant," said Boniface. "And they agreed."

"That's a very good idea. How much did you suggest?" She stared up at him, expectation in her eyes. "Please tell me you at least said something sensible, like ten million bucks?"

"I said one billion dollars."

Montbretia stood open-mouthed.

"I was thinking on my feet," said Boniface dismissively. "They won't end up paying that much, but they announced it, so it will be a big number."

He stared at Montbretia, her eyes starting to mist.

"Don't cry yet," he said. "I spoke to Chlodwig—he's a good man, and he has a conscience. I recommended that he get a range of people on the board. People who can ensure the money is spent on the people who need it."

"You were full of good ideas today, Boniface."

"I suggested you." Boniface observed as his words registered with Montbretia. "And he said yes."

Montbretia remained stationary. "Really?"

"It's not full-time work; it's board meetings and then supervising the distribution of funds to make sure that the money is making a difference, and that might mean some travel." He looked her straight in the eye. "Can you cope with some travel?"

She turned her head from side to side, as if weighing the question.

"So if it's not too much like a commitment to a day job, will you do it?" He hesitated, then gabbled, stumbling over his words. "Weissenfeld will meet your expenses and pay you a day rate when you're working for the fund."

Montbretia embraced Boniface again, sobbing.

"Don't cry yet," said Boniface. "Wait until everything's in place."

"But what about you?" Montbretia pulled back, wiping her eyes. "Haven't you still got a huge problem—a dead body, police, and all that?"

"Nah. Nothing that I can't lose with a more interesting tale of international intrigue and two foreign killers searching the mean streets of Tilbury, looking for vagrants to kill. As there's no evidence linking me, there's not much to print." He put his arm around Montbretia's shoulder. "Come on, let's go and tell Gideon about your new position. You're going to need all the political friends you can find."

There was the sound of heels behind them. "I thought I might find you still here."

"Veronica!" Montbretia dropped Boniface's arm, rushing back to embrace her. "Thank you, thank you, thank you."

Boniface could feel the involuntary spasm of muscles across his face and knew his former wife would read the confusion. "I was about to say that you should develop good relations with the press, but you already seem on pretty good terms."

"Congratulations, Boniface," said Veronica, embracing Montbretia and facing Boniface over the younger woman's shoulder.

Boniface mouthed "thank you."

"I didn't get it. I thought you let her off lightly." Montbretia turned her head to observe Boniface as Veronica continued. "Then we heard the rumor: They're getting ready for her at Biggin Hill."

"What's that?" asked Montbretia.

"It's an airport—it specializes in executive jets. It means Greta will be out of the country within an hour," said Boniface.

"So congratulations. When I heard she was running, I realized you had got inside her head." Veronica paused. "You bounced her, I take it? Didn't give her any time to think?"

A smirk spread across Boniface's visage.

Veronica tilted her head. "And now the admission that she made will chew away at her brain."

"It will keep chewing and chewing and..." said Boniface in a matter-of-fact tone. "Forever. But they tried to hurt Monty." He let the thought hang before turning to walk over to Gideon, reaching him as the final journalist left to file her story.

"Boniface." Gideon embraced the man standing two steps down.

"Thank you, Gideon," said Boniface. "Without you...well..."

"Me?" asked Gideon. "All I did was stand here with Montbretia."

"Montbretia who has got something to tell you. She's with Vron—go and ask her," said Boniface. "I'm off to chat with Tommy."

He walked across the Old Palace Yard park lot to the Super Six, which still had a small group of people admiring it and asking Tommy questions.

"Boniface." Tommy bear-hugged the thinner man.

"I can't begin to thank you, Tommy, but next time could you hurry up? I strained every sinew to slow things down so you had enough time to get here, and then I find you went home to get your favorite toy."

"I had to take the van back, as it had our friend in it," said Tommy. "I brought the Bentley because people pay attention to a Bentley, and that was what you wanted, wasn't it?"

"Next time, bring it faster," said Boniface with a wink.

Tattoo Your Name on My Heart

one

"You need to call the police."

Boniface leaned back in his chair, forcing his head and shoulders still as he softly spun his seat from left-to-right-to-left-to-right, twisting at the waist as he waited for his potential new clients to consider his advice.

"I'd call the police now." Boniface reached for the phone, clumsily grabbing it by the side and dropping it on the edge of his desk toward the bassist. The handset bounced out of the cradle and tumbled to the floor.

Boniface reached across his desk to pull up the handset by its cord and looked up at the bassist, hoping he wouldn't notice his nervousness. Hoping the other man was accustomed to fans being slightly on edge around him.

"No." The bassist's voice was quiet, but his opinion was clear, his decision definitive.

This was a man who understood how to project his presence. A man who performed on stage—Boniface had seen him perform with the band several times. And when the bassist stood on stage—an imposing, muscular figure in his black leather trousers and black sleeveless T-shirt freeing his arms as they exercised complete domination of his instrument—he had a clear understanding of how his audience would perceive his physical presence. He was patient and understood timing; he was a man who wouldn't play a note if it wasn't the right note at the right time.

He might not be the frontman, but he was the leader of the band—the general who always stood shoulder to shoulder with his troops and who understood cowardice in the face of the enemy. He understood that if you flinched, you failed—and you can't fail when people have paid money to see you perform.

This was the man who had said no, and had communicated no.

Boniface sat forward, his frown questioning. He made eye contact with the bassist and waited before raising his eyebrows to suggest he was hoping for elaboration.

"We can't."

The bassist appeared to have said all he was going to say. It was as if those two words were a full explanation. Boniface looked between the bassist and the bassist's wife sitting beside him, wordlessly cursing himself when he realized that as he stared at the outline of her now-clothed figure, he was remembering what she had looked like when she was modeling.

"We can't involve the police," said the bassist. His tone had changed. He wasn't pleading; it was more that he was trying to be conciliatory. "If we go to the cops, Boniface, it will take time for them to investigate." He snorted, his solid figure—still sitting—twitched with his indignation. "Seriously, Boniface, the cops have got better things to do. They're not going to jump just because I snap my fingers." His tone softened. "And before we make it official, we've got to acknowledge that some cops are bent, others are just plain incompetent, and some leak stories. There are huge amounts of poison being spilled about us, and we need to know what the problem is—we're not trying amplify the hate and the shouting." He seemed almost apologetic. "No. I'm sorry, the police aren't an option."

The bassist sunk back into the leather sofa, his right hand seamlessly joining his wife's left. The slightest tightening of his hand in hers conveyed reassurance, the only sign that the two lumps of flesh might not be of the same person.

"A private detective?" offered Boniface, standing and walking to the window, a brown strip that spanned two walls. He looked through the tinted glass across the side street and over the girls' school on the other side of the road, its inmates having departed several hours earlier along with most of their jailers, although the few remaining cars implied that some were still dreaming up fresh torments for tomorrow.

He turned to resume the conversation and sat on the broad windowsill with his back to the school. For the first time since Boniface had shaken hands with his prospective new clients, a suggestion of a smirk started to spread across the bassist's face. Not a look of joy, but a hint that he was amused by the absurdity of what he had just heard.

"Do you know a good private detective? One you could actually trust?" The bassist relaxed back into the sofa, as if he had decided that he had said all he needed to say to settle the matter—at least to settle that a private investigator was not the right option.

Boniface regarded the other man. It wasn't one simple detail that suggested he didn't work in an office, but more the combination: his off-duty bright shirt under under an old sandy jacket, the slightly too long but styled hair, and the almost waxy skin tone from rarely seeing daylight for thirty years. He tried to show some grace as he gave way to the potential client. "No. Not in this country. I don't know any good investigators."

The bassist continued. "I don't have time to go through the process of searching for a good one, only to find that we've hired a dickhead rather than a dick."

Boniface gave a charitable smile for the bassist's weak joke and changed tack. "You must know other journalists, apart from me—you've been in the game long enough."

"The ones I know are hacks."

Again, it wasn't what the bassist said, but how he said it that told Boniface this wouldn't be a fruitful line to continue, but he persisted. "I was a hack."

The bassist's wife noticed her husband's reaction, momentarily shutting her eyes as if preparing herself for a tale from the road that she had heard before. "Look, Boniface. When we were on the road, we'd set the journalists up with a groupie, perhaps several. They'd be so grateful we'd get a glowing review."

The bassist looked to his wife, as if silently acknowledging why the groupies that must have followed the band were always irrelevant for him. Without catching his gaze, the coiled spring inside her started to release, letting her body melt softly into his.

"Those journalists—if you can really call those sorts of people journalists—are not the sort of people I respect, and are not the sort of people I want knowing our problems." The bassist's voice took on a more businesslike tone. "Tommy rates you. He says you're the smartest guy he's ever met—and Tommy's no fool." He tilted his head forward so that he looked up at Boniface and pointed with an open hand. "You're the perfect cover: a serious journalist doing a serious biography."

As the two potential clients sat together, Boniface understood that the sofa had been a good decision. When he re-carpeted the office—for the second time in less than six months—Montbretia had suggested he dispose of the businesslike meeting table with chairs on either side and replace it with something more informal, in this case a sofa and low table. She had also persuaded him that filing cabinets just wasted space. It took her a few weeks to digitize his archive and a few more weeks for him to get used to accessing that archive through a screen rather than pulling out a stack of papers, but by the time he was ready to concede that she was right—and that he didn't need filing cabinets in his office—the carpet fitters were ready. One day while he was out at a meeting with a client, Montbretia supervised the carpet fitters and managed to dispose of all the filing cabinets in the office—apart from the one in her room—putting the matter beyond discussion.

Boniface pursed his lips, thinking how to word his next question.

The bassist grinned. "And don't suggest a lawyer—I'll shake hands and be counting my fingers, and I need my fingers." He mimed playing the bass guitar. Where most mimes are a crude indication of how a non-musician thinks an instrument should be played, muscle memory kicked in as the bassist reached for the neck with his left hand, the fingers on his right a blur of rhythm.

"You're the perfect cover, Boniface. A serious journalist writing a serious biography about Prickle. You have a history: If people google you, they'll know who you are, and you'll seem plausible—and Prickle were big enough to justify a decent biography. If we send in a detective, that suggests we think there's a problem, which will lead to more questions." He waited a beat. "You can go anywhere, find what the problem is, and figure what our options are." Another beat. "Find a way for whoever's got a problem to get out without losing face, and we're all winners."

Boniface went to speak but was cut off by the bassist. "Look. Just spend a day or two, and if you find nothing, we'll call it quits."

two

Montbretia stood by the conference room door, watching.

Boniface led his guests out of the office and to the elevator. The husband had the look of a confident man. He stood straight—not military straight, more *I'm used to being looked at* straight. His walk had the slight swagger of someone enjoying life, pleased to see every new person who came into his orbit.

When the couple arrived, Montbretia had been by the door receiving a delivery. The delivery guy recognized the man and mumbled "you're Danny…" before he crumbled. It wasn't clear who this man was, but the delivery guy seemed to think he was famous, and the probably famous man seemed accustomed to this reaction, offering a firm handshake and happily agreed to a photo—Montbretia as photographer, with the delivery guy's phone.

With the few words they exchanged, Montbretia could recognize his accent: south London, but slightly softened—it didn't quite have the full rasp. She had been living in London for nearly a year, and now she was able to differentiate between the nuances of south London, cockney, and Estuary English. Accents were so much easier back home in the States.

The husband threw back his head, laughing. His solid figure—stocky, but not overweight, wrapped in neat jeans and a patterned blue-red shirt held in by a well-worn sandy jacket—projected the sound of his laugh through the door as he slapped Boniface on the shoulder. She watched as the edge of a dopey grin spread over Boniface's profile.

The wife stood neatly, her feet together and her back—which was toward the doors Montbretia looked through—was perfectly straight, maximizing her height, but even with heels she was still shorter than Montbretia.

Shorter but more elegant, felt Montbretia.

She was dressed modestly: brown suede ankle boots, jeans that were fitted but didn't cut off her circulation, a white cotton blouse that followed every contour without any excess material billowing, and a light-brown suede jacket, matching her boots but fringed along each arm and across the back. Her jewelry was equally understated, with wedding and engagement rings, a single bracelet, and a small brooch on her jacket's lapel.

For all the elegant understatement, the one fact she couldn't hide was that her figure showed the perfection usually reserved for plastic dolls. If there was ever to be a sliding scale of zero to I-wonder-how-much-surgery-would-cost-to-look-like-her, against which every woman could find her place, then on whatever measure you chose to consider the archetype, she was pretty much at the top of the scale.

Boniface stood straighter, his hand raised to offer his guests the elevator, and Montbretia took her last look. Her final glimpse was of the woman's hair. Montbretia had looked closely when she arrived—she hadn't meant to, but she was taller and looked down on the other woman. Although she couldn't tell for certain, Montbretia was sure that perfection like that—blonde hair that didn't look bleached—would cost a fortune. But each strand seemed to be a slightly different color, and the color of every hair was consistent from root to tip.

And no one pays to have the odd gray hair, do they?

They had gone. Montbretia's vision remained fixed on the space where she had been staring at the blonde woman with the soft gray eyes. As she pulled herself out of her trance, she realized that Boniface had gone, too. Where he would usually say farewell to clients by the elevator, he had apparently decided to escort this couple to the parking lot.

She sighed noisily, continuing to stare.

Her line of sight was broken as Boniface walked from the elevator and through the door. There was a lightness to his step she hadn't seen before, but she did recognize his slightly embarrassed, over-excited teenage boy look.

"You disgust me, Boniface." She exhaled heavily, intending him to hear. "You were sickening."

Boniface's grin spread.

"You're besotted with her, and you're treating him like your best buddy ever. Honestly, Boniface. This is sad." His grin continued to spread. "Come on—eyes back in your head. Tongue off the ground and back in your mouth. You know you didn't take your eyes off her ass?"

"But I had my back to you." Boniface enjoyed his minor triumph.

"I don't need to be able to see your eyes to know where you're looking. I've been here for a year—I can understand how Londoners greet each other, and I can tell where you're focusing by looking at the back of your head." Montbretia stared at Boniface. "You're not going to say I'm wrong, are you?"

Boniface looked down, chewing slightly on his lower lip as he shook his head.

"Who were they, anyway?" asked Montbretia.

"My teenage fantasy."

"Which one?"

"Both!" said Boniface. "Danny..."

"You mean your new BFF."

"Danny Featherstone," said Boniface, his tone lower, "is the bassist in a band called Prickle."

"Never heard of them."

"They're not really your thing," said Boniface. "Melodic, hook-laden, classic rock. They started as a blues band in the seventies, but in the eighties the founding singer left and Danny took control. He recruited a new singer—much better than the original guy—and pushed them in a tighter, more commercial direction." He paused. "I saw them...twice."

"That probably explains why I've never heard of them," said Montbretia. "And your new sexual fantasy?"

"There's nothing new about that fantasy." Boniface seemed wistful. "Dawn was perhaps my very first fantasy. She is a gorgeous creature who comes from a time when we didn't have the internet, and the only way for a teenage boy to see young ladies who got the goods out was in the newspapers."

"What do you mean, Boniface? She's your age—what was she doing posing?"

"Think again—she's ten years older than me."

"Wow," said Montbretia. "Life has been kind to her."

"Maybe. Maybe not. She comes from a time when sixteen-year-old girls could appear topless in the newspapers." Boniface shrugged. "It was great when I was a teenager...but I'm older now, and now, in retrospect, it just seems like..."

"Child abuse," offered Montbretia.

Boniface bobbed his head as if trying to construct the next sentence. "Yeah, but even though girls have to be eighteen now, I'm not convinced that topless women in daily newspapers are, you know, a good thing." He smirked. "Which isn't to say I've fallen out of love with the female form."

"While we're behaving like grownups, what do they want?"

"Tommy sent them."

"Tommy as in Tommy Newby?"

"The same," said Boniface. "Apparently, Danny and Tommy bonded over a love of vintage Bentleys, and when Danny mentioned to Tommy that he has a problem, Tommy sent Danny to us."

"And the problem?" asked Montbretia.

"The problem is Danny and Dawn are being trashed on the internet." Boniface stood firmly, his feet apart, his arms folded. "Prickle are headlining a charity gig: Trying to sell tickets when you keep getting slagged isn't easy. After the gig, the band are taking a year off, and Danny and Dawn have been talking about doing some TV work."

"And the TV offers are sticky if the internet hates you," said Montbretia.

"Precisely."

"I get it, but what do they want you to do?"

"Not much, just talk to a few people, see if I can find what's going on." He pushed out his chin with an I-don't-know motion. "See if there's a problem that can be solved."

"But you're not a private investigator, Boniface, so please tell me they're paying us well." Montbretia watched as Boniface unconsciously flinched. "They *are* paying us?"

Boniface pursed his lips.

"Boniface?" Her question was more insistent than she intended. "What are we charging them? They're getting the full Boniface charm offensive, and this office doesn't come for free."

Boniface wrinkled his nose. "It's..." He exhaled. "There's..."

"Tell," demanded Montbretia.

"They've got a problem with the band's management." He paused, thinking. "They control the band's finances."

Montbretia shut her eyes. "You're saying we're not getting paid." Her voice was monotone. "You are playing at being a PI, and we're not going to get paid." She opened her eyes and watched Boniface, knowing he was mentally playing through every argument he could put forward, trying to predict her response.

"Two meetings. I can do it alone—I don't need you. By this time tomorrow, everything will be sorted." He stopped as if that was sufficient explanation, but continued when Montbretia remained silent. "And I'm not being a private investigator—there's a simple cover story: I'm a journalist researching Prickle's biography."

"So Prickle are some sort of rock gods—at least rock gods in your mind..."

"Prickle are headlining the Royal Albert Hall," said Boniface weakly.

"I still haven't heard of them." Montbretia shrugged, feeling slightly chagrined. "And she's something of a sleazy, low-rent former model—with a killer figure and great hair, if I do say so myself—and somehow they've wrapped you around their collective finger, persuaded you that all you need to do is meet two people under the guise of research for a biography of some band that no one else will have heard of, and the issue can be solved? That's it?"

She widened her eyes to indicate that she expected a response. Boniface seemed to assent, but with little conviction.

"And payment—at best—is goodwill of someone who has had a lifetime of lies from jerks, plus you get to stare at Dawn. If you honestly believe that this only needs two—or three or four—meetings, then we're going to be bankrupt by the end of the month." Montbretia turned into the conference room and sat at the large table, looking at the papers she had spread in front of her.

Boniface came as far as the doorway and stopped. "I...I promise not to involve you." He stepped into the room, looking at the papers. His tone changed: "You're working late."

"And getting paid. There's a novel concept." She softened her voice. "Some Weissenfeld work. We're about to award the contract to an NGO to deliver the second tranche of aid in Somalia—I said I'd look over these papers for Chlodwig and give him a call in the morning."

"Paper?" asked Boniface. "I thought no one used that anymore."

"Ah, the missionary zeal of the newly converted," said Montbretia. "People still use paper to communicate, Boniface. What we," she pointed between the two of them, "don't do is store paper. We receive, read, digitize if it's for the record, and then recycle."

"Say hi to Chlodwig when you speak to him. I'll be in after...you know."

"I know," said Montbretia.

"And now I'm going to research a singer from the 1970s, so that I know as much as I can before I bang on his door tomorrow morning."

three

Boniface looked for a doorbell.

There was none.

He looked for a knocker.

There was none.

There was a corroded chrome letter slot with mounts at either end where a knocker would usually hang, but clearly it had been yanked off many years ago.

He stepped back and surveyed the front door—the sky-blue paint, which had probably been applied in the early 1970s, was now faded and chipped, and from the wear marks at the bottom of the door, Boniface guessed the door was habitually kicked open when it stuck in the winter. He stepped forward, rapped firmly with his knuckles, then stood back so as not to be aggressively filling the space when the door was answered.

Not that the knock had aroused any signs of life.

As he had walked along Bethnal Green Road from Bethnal Green underground station, before he turned north up a side street, he had wondered how to start the conversation. He still wasn't sure—so much depended on the attitude of the man he hoped would answer the door.

In his mind he went through the details Danny had told him and the additional information he had gleaned from the internet. Graham Barrington—Gray, as he preferred to be called—had founded Gooseberry, a tight blues/rock band, in the early 1970s. Due to a similarly named band, they had quickly changed the name to Prickle and hadn't looked back.

With Gray Barrington and his gravelly voice at the front, the band worked tirelessly, gigging around the UK and Europe. Typically, they would play more than 300 shows a year in a range of venues up to 1,000-seaters. Every show sold well—even if it didn't sell out, it would break even—and every album sold in respectable numbers over time, but never in sufficient numbers over a short enough period to hit the top of the charts.

In 1979, Gray was impressed with a 17-year-old bass player's feel for the blues and offered him the gig when the band's previous bass player left. And so Danny Featherstone found himself a member of Prickle.

Boniface rapped on the front door again, this time harder, and then pressed his ear to the peeling sky-blue paint. Somewhere inside someone shouted. He rapped again. Another shout. He stepped back from the door and turned to look down the street as he waited.

Fashions change, and with the advent of 1980s hair rock, Prickle's blues-based sound was increasingly at odds with what the mainstream wanted. Album sales slowed, and as their contemporaries started playing theaters and stadiums, Prickle began a midsized club tour. Gray interpreted this comparative lowly status as the band holding him back, and after accepting a deal with a US-based management company, quit the band for a solo career on the other side of the Atlantic.

Danny had explained, the solo career didn't work as Gray expected. The record label enforced a contract term on Gray requiring him to deliver two further albums.

Having taken the US management deal but then being obligated to deliver two further albums in the UK, Gray had wrapped himself in legal red tape from which it took him three years to extricate himself. After three years, few people remembered him, and even fewer cared.

Even from two paces away from the front door, Boniface could hear the heavy footsteps descending the stairs. The heavy steps of the man who, as far as Boniface was able to divine, had spent the last 30 years in the musical wilderness, not earning very much money—or if he had earned money, apart from a few royalties from his 1970s recordings, it hadn't been from making music. There had been some gigs, mostly in pubs, some failed bands, some promises of work, a few irregular performances at small blues festivals, but nothing of any note as far as Boniface could tell.

A quick scan of their respective offerings on YouTube was enough to bring the distinction between Gray and Prickle into sharp relief. Gray had a few handheld videos shot in pubs, usual filmed on a mobile phone—in total seven songs. By contrast, Prickle—the band Gray had abandoned—had professional videos, stadium footage, bootleg videos of stadium performances, and a few TV specials.

The footsteps reached the door, and Boniface heard it squeak as it opened. "What?" The voice was raspy, angry, insistent.

Boniface turned, casting a gaze over the street. On each side of the street, the brick-built terraced houses—each adjoining both neighbors with no gap—formed solid walls with no front yard separating the residences from the sidewalk. The houses were what used to be called two-up/two-downs. Literally, two rooms upstairs and two rooms downstairs with the staircase from the lower floor to the upper horizontally bisecting the house.

When they were built, none of those four rooms was a bathroom. Then again, when the houses were built, Queen Victoria was on the throne, heating in houses was provided by fires, and electricity was an unheard-of notion.

During the Second World War, the Luftwaffe razed much of the East End of London. The terraced two-up/two-downs that remained were then labeled as slums—the lack of bathroom making them unfit for human habitation—and, in an irony not lost on Boniface the houses that survived the attentions of the Luftwaffe were demolished to be replaced by gleaming tower blocks, which soon became nests of deprivation and academies of crime.

Those terraces that weren't cleared as slums, now with indoor plumbing and gas-fired central heating, had become highly desirable, although as with everything from the Victorian era they required constant maintenance, and looking along the street Boniface could see that some of the properties were very well maintained. In short, gentrification was happening around—the incoming residents could afford to maintain and upgrade their houses. Those who had lived there for longer couldn't.

Gray's house fitted the latter category and was not maintained. Danny recalled that Gray had inherited his house from a grandparent, and it was probably that grandparent who had painted the front door sky-blue.

His house wasn't well maintained, and as Boniface finally looked at Gray, he could see that neither was the man who had first formed the blues rock band Gooseberry more than forty years ago.

Boniface knew that Gray was sixty-something years old, but as he pulled his thin toweling robe, which might once have been white but now wasn't, the short but wiry man behind the door looked seventy-something. What hair remained was dyed, cheaply. It had probably been dyed black but had faded to a dirty brown—its tone not helped by the lack of washing and the apparent absence of a comb in Gray's life.

"Gray? Gray Barrington?" The man might be Gray, but in none of the photos Boniface had looked at last night had Gray looked so old or been standing in a toweling robe.

The man behind the door grunted but didn't disagree.

Boniface put one hand forward to shake and held his business card in the other. "My name's Boniface...Alexander Boniface. I'm writing a biography about Prickle—I was wondering if I could buy you breakfast?"

Gray shook his head and let the door swing fully open as he leaned on the door jamb. Boniface looked through the door, which opened directly into the front room with a beaten-up sofa against the far wall, an old cathode-ray-tube television in the corner across from the sofa, and—piquing Boniface's sense of irony—a stack of paint cans, brushes, rollers, roller trays, dust sheets, and a stepladder spattered in many colors of paint.

"What's the chief prick and the little pricks up to now?" asked Gray.

"As I said," continued Boniface, "a biography of the band. I was hoping to have a chat since you are the guy who got the whole thing started."

"Honestly, Boniface," said Gray, looking down at the card Boniface had pushed in his hand, "you're less welcome than the Jehovah's Witnesses. You'd be doing me a huge favor if you'd just fuck off and let me get back to bed." He stepped back and started to swing the door.

Boniface put his foot on the threshold, blocking the motion of the aged wood. "Come on, let me buy you breakfast. Full English. A proper fry-up." He smiled. "Are you a tea or coffee man?"

"Seriously, you look like one of those poofy city-types that keep moving in around here and talk about how much *character* the street has. I don't like them and I don't spend time with them. I don't like you and I'm not going to spend any time with you, no matter what that kid Danny is up to." He seemed weary. "Just...just go."

Boniface removed his foot, and the door banged without closing properly. From the outside Boniface could hear soft flesh impacting the wood, followed by a squeak as the lower part of the door made its way fully into the frame, the latch clicking closed.

four

"We don't hold people by their ankles and dangle them out of windows."

Aaron Delcort chuckled as he sat across from the PR man who called himself Boniface, then winked at Fiona Aldred sitting to his left. "At least, not as a business practice. What we do for fun in our own time is a private matter, right Fi?"

He smiled broadly. The Boniface guy seemed to have a sense of humor bypass.

For a PR man, Boniface wasn't very chatty—there seemed to be no notion of that bonhomie he would have expected. Delcort pushed the corner of the other man's business card and scanned it again: *Alexander Boniface*, and immediately below, in smaller text, *Boniface Communications*, a company which apparently had an office in Wimbledon. It didn't give him much to work with.

He had never heard of Alexander Boniface—or Boniface, as he asked to be called—and he hadn't had time to check him out. Five minutes on the web would have been useful—even thirty seconds looking at a street-view of his office would have helped establish whether the address was kosher.

But you play the cards you're dealt, and Boniface had turned up and asked for a meeting about Prickle. Given the contractual difficulties with the band, he had asked Fiona to sit in with them—she was the lawyer; she could take over if there was no hint of any new business to talk about, no deals to be done. But if there was a negotiation, he was the man to lead.

"I'm sorry, you have us at a bit of a disadvantage. You know about us—we're PAD Management. I'm Aaron Delcort, the D in PAD; Miss Aldred, Fiona, is the A; and Haroon Patel..." He looked through the glass wall of the conference room but couldn't see his colleague. "Haroon Patel is the P in PAD, and we handle the affairs for Prickle—but we don't know about you."

An Asian man with rimless glasses, a pencil mustache, and the wisp of a beard perched on the peak of his chin passed. "Ah! That's Haroon, there. He handles the money, and Fiona looks after the legal matters." The lawyer by his side bobbed her head once, as if affirming his introduction.

Boniface was well dressed in a dark-blue suit with a subtle white stripe. He sat quietly on the other side of the table, seemingly listening intently. All he seemed to have brought with him was a phone, which he laid to his right. He inhaled softly and began. "There's not much to tell you beyond what I've said already. It's a bit of a labor of love for me...I'm writing a biography about Prickle." He paused, looking between Delcort and the lawyer. "It's in the very early stages, and I'm just gathering background information at the moment before I start interviews." He became hesitant. "Now, I know you've got some...challenges...issues, minor contractual snagging to work through. I don't how you want to describe it...but I was hoping we could open up some form of communication."

Delcort looked to his colleague. "Do you want to grab this one, Fiona?" He flopped back into his seat, hearing his bracelet clink as he dropped his arm, its satisfying weight gripping his wrist, then looked at Boniface, watching for the reaction he expected.

"Before we entered into our relationship with Prickle and Danny, we obviously undertook extensive due diligence." And there it was—Fiona had started talking, and from the slight shift in his facial muscles, Delcort saw that Boniface had reacted.

He liked taking Fiona to meetings with him. Other people always found her slightly disconcerting; she was never what they expected.

First, there was her appearance. She was tall, 6'1" he believed, but then there was her preference—no, make that consistent, unwavering choice—to wear heels, which gave her an additional four or five inches. Especially with what she called mega-heels. To him they looked like a throwback to the 1970s—the bastard child from a night of passion between a stack heel and a stiletto. While tall, she was skinny. Not left-to-right skinny—she seemed a normal enough width—but front-to-back skinny. If she turned sideways, the wind would blow past her.

Her hands were small and delicate. Framed by her brown shoulder-length hair with hints of red, her facial features, while mildly asymmetrical, were equally delicate. Apart from her nose, which was thin and protruding, with a prominent bridge giving it a near oblong profile.

But it was her voice that seemed to have got Boniface—it was not the sort of voice one expected to come out of that sort of body. It was deep. Very deep. But rich—suggesting a level of education and sophistication—and soft. Delcort watched as Boniface leaned forward at the siren call of that soft, rich, deep voice.

"We intended—still intend—this to be a long-term relationship with the band," continued Fiona.

Delcort sat straighter: It was time to add some detail that Fiona should have brought to Boniface's attention. "These guys aren't young anymore. We wanted our relationship to be like one of those houses you move into when the kids leave home. You know, there's still space for the kids to visit, but the house is more practical for your requirements as you age…because, you know, it's the last ever house you need to buy before you…" He shrugged. "You know…"

Fiona continued. "We sought warranties—basic assurances of facts—in a number of areas, and these were all readily forthcoming." This was the reason he made Fiona a partner—she was a great lawyer and went straight to the key point in any legal matter. He could hand her any document, and she would instinctively sniff out the weasel words slipped in.

She understood what was there for show and what was there to look crazy. She was the one who had explained to him why the riders in concert contracts specified a large bowl of M&Ms with the green ones taken out: If you turn up at a gig and there's a bowl of M&Ms with the green ones still there, then everyone can see that the contract terms haven't been met. And if the promoter doesn't bother with the simple conditions, then you can expect they won't have bothered with more compli-cated terms of the contract—for instance, all that stuff about the safety of the band while they are performing.

In addition to her awesome understanding, she was his secret weapon in any negotiation. She was happy to sit in a meeting and make sure every "i" was dotted and every "t" crossed. Send her in, and she would willingly lead the war of attrition, waiting for the other side to crack. She could read a contract and analyze it in five minutes, but she was happy to grind the other side down over five hours of negotia-tions, knowing their lawyer was on an hourly rate but that she was on staff and could wait all night.

"There's no need to get into the detail," said Fiona, "but let's just say these warranties are much of the root of our present discussions with our client."

"To repeat what I said before," said Delcort, chuckling and adjusting his diamond-studded cufflinks, "we don't dangle people out of the windows, but in this case we do have a legitimate grievance, and while this matter is outstanding we will comply with the contractual terms to the letter."

Delcort looked directly to the other man, who had pulled out a small notepad and was jotting. Boniface looked up from across the table. "And one of those terms allows you to freeze the band's finances because you control the bank accounts?"

Delcort twisted his cufflink the other way, playing back the words and the tone Boniface had used. There seemed to be no rancor, no angle or implication. It seemed to be a basic statement of facts, expressed as a question. He watched as Boniface made another note.

"This isn't doing you any good, is it?" Boniface sounded sympathetic. "You're paid a percentage, so if the band isn't earning, you're not earning. And if you're not out there hustling for more work, then your future earnings are going to be impacted." He paused, staring straight at Delcort. "I'm not missing a subtle nuance here, am I?"

Delcort went to speak and found himself cut off as Boniface continued. "If Prickle has ceased to exist by the time I finish my book, then I'm going to have trouble selling my book—it will have become as interesting as last month's newspapers." His voice brightened. "I'm talking to people—surely I must be able to put your perspective forward. If I could give a push...just to get things moving."

She didn't need to make a sound; Delcort had known her long enough to know that Fiona was silently groaning and was getting ready to stamp on Boniface's naïve stupidity. "I wish it were that simple, Mister Boniface, but you need to understand that our dispute is not simply about one little thing that needs to be fixed. We are dealing with so many contractual issues—contracts that date back many years before our relationship with Prickle ever began. Claims, especially by Mister Barrington, about issues from the 1970s where the contract terms were never documented and were not even mentioned during our due diligence. There are men turning up looking for payment in cash." She sighed; Delcort know these visits had distressed her. Heck, they had distressed him. "I'm not sure which is worse, these men or Luca's former wife. She is getting tiresome. Not that Luca seems to care—her behavior seems to amuse him."

"Look, I'm sympathetic to Luca's plight, but I'm not releasing funds," said Delcort, picking up where the lawyer stopped. "If he gets any gear, then that psychotic ex-wife of his will steal it again. She has no concept of *owned by Prickle*. As far as she's concerned, if Luca has touched or been in the same room as the gear, then Luca owns it, and so now after the divorce, it's hers."

Boniface grimaced and Delcort continued. "You're a wide-eyed optimist if you think you can sort this, Mister Boniface. There are just too many people and too many problems, and while this situation remains, we're not going to do anything to facilitate this biography."

five

"I've just been talking with the tallest lawyer in the world. Seriously, I've met shorter giraffes."

Montbretia stared at Boniface. They were standing at the corner of a residential street somewhere—Montbretia wasn't quite sure where precisely—in East London. The instructions Boniface had given were to get to Bethnal Green tube station and then walk. Walking wasn't usually difficult, but walking in brand-new, cheap, high-heeled ankle boots was.

As she came toward him, Boniface's eyes surveyed a side street—a solid wall of conjoined two-story houses with no front yards lined either side. "Let me get this straight, Boniface." She could hear the anger in her voice but didn't care. "All this job will take is two meetings, which you can handle—you don't need me involved."

She paused. He was looking down.

"But now you've dragged me across town—literally from Wimbledon in the west to Bethnal Green in the east—having instructed me to pass through some flea-bitten market on the way and deck myself out with what can only be described as 1980s hooker-chic. I'm not feeling it, Boniface."

He was still looking down, refusing to meet her glare.

"I told you this would go wrong, and now we're both working for a client that we shouldn't even call a client because they're not paying us. It's not good business." She waited a beat. "And to make things worse, it's one o'clock and I haven't eaten."

He lifted his head, his eyes scanning up and down, seemingly pausing and examining each separate item: the boots—-red, complete with buckles—that pinched and were hell to walk in, the short tight black skirt, the flouncy top made of something scratchy with lots of cheap nylon lace, the random neon patterned jacket, a collection of mismatched scarves dangling from one wrist, and enough cheap bangles on the other to permanently lengthen her arm, all topped with back-combed hair and huge dangly earrings that she remembered each time she moved her head as their momentum slapped her shoulders and tugged her lobes. Thankfully, there hadn't been time to get her hair streaked, otherwise Boniface might have insisted.

"I'm sorry." He faced her directly. "I've messed up—this is bigger than I thought."

Montbretia glowered at him, feeling her anger ebb as she calibrated his reaction. He was sincere in his apology. He was contrite—even if he was hiding it well. If she pushed it, he'd just get angry, and to be honest, she couldn't remember why she was so angry...it wasn't as if she was having her pay cut. "Is this what the 1980s looked like?"

Boniface nodded slowly. "I'm afraid so."

"I feel like a streetwalker." His mouth twitched as he tried to maintain a serious look. "When can I put my own clothes back on?" She held up a carrier bag holding the clothes that she had changed from at the market when she went back in time to the 1980s.

"Very soon," said Boniface.

"I wasn't sure whether to get legwarmers and fingerless gloves."

"No. No need. You're fine." Boniface reached for the carrier bag. "Shall I take that?"

"Why?" Montbretia could feel the bristle of suspicion creeping up on her.

"I need you to do something," he said. His mouth smiled, but his eyes didn't. "And since you're dressed and ready, it would be a shame if you missed out on the fun and games."

Montbretia shut her eyes and willed her voice calm. "Go on."

"Up there..." She opened her eyes, looking in the direction Boniface was now tilting his head. "Number eighty-seven is where Gray Barrington lives."

She wrinkled her forehead.

"Gray Barrington was the founder and original lead singer with Prickle." The wrinkle softened as Boniface continued. "He may...or may not—I don't know until I've spoken to him—be the cause, or at least one of the causes, of Dawn, Danny, and Prickle's problems. Until I've spoken to him in a civilized manner, I won't know."

"You *can* do civilized, Boniface. It just needs a *little* effort." She noticed he didn't respond. "You brought me all this way and made me dress up, just to give you some reassurance?"

He was quiet. She felt her head leaning forward in expectation of a reply to her facetious question. Boniface noticed, wrinkled his nose, and with a shake of his head, no more than a twitch, confirmed that wasn't why she had been summoned. "I need you to get me in." His tone suggested humiliation. She waited for the explanation. "I spoke to him, he told me to...to go away."

"Ah."

"So I need someone else, someone he doesn't know, someone who can get us through the front door, and you're good at this stuff."

"This stuff? You mean good at dressing like a hooker?"

"Good at talking to people. Good at putting people at ease. Good at not confronting them and putting your foot in the door when it's being closed on you." His voice had become a whimper.

"And again I pose the question—why am I dressed for a 1980s prostitutes' fancy dress party?"

Boniface shifted his weight from one foot to the other, his gaze looking down. "I just thought you should look as nonthreatening as possible."

"Well, I'm certainly threatening the eyeballs of the people of this street." Montbretia glanced down at the fluorescent orange, yellow, and green areas of her jacket. "But I don't see how this makes me less of a threat to him."

Boniface shifted uneasily again. "I just thought that this is a guy who doesn't... understand modern women. He doesn't understand current fashions—he sees them as threatening—so I thought it would ease the way past his front door if you dressed from an era where he actively participated."

"How old is he?"

Boniface pushed out his bottom lip. "Sixty-something, give or take."

"And he only likes women who demean themselves like this?" Montbretia held out her arms, looking down at her new clothes. "What are you saying? He's a misogynist?

For the first time since she had arrived, Boniface laughed. "Quite the contrary—he likes women as far as I know. His problem is they don't like him." His look became more serious. "Look, I'm not suggesting he's a feminist—simply that, like many men, he's putty in the hands of a smart, good-looking girl who gives off the right signals."

"And if it gets hairy?"

"If he makes a grab for you, kick him and run—I'll be outside the moment you go through that door."

"You?" Montbretia failed to hide her incredulity. "You're not really renowned for your street-fighting prowess."

"He's an old guy."

"You mean, I'm more likely to save you from him?"

"So you're agreed it's pretty low risk."

"As long as you discount the risk I've already sustained by dressing like this and the risk of my further embarrassment."

Boniface grimaced.

"So I knock on the door. What's my story when he answers?"

A slow grin clawed its way across Boniface's visage. "Gray made some decisions which—given what happened subsequently—may now be regarded as less than smart decisions."

Montbretia grunted. "So?"

"You need to understand the scale of these decisions," said Boniface. "Gray quit Prickle and headed for the big money in the States, but that got messed up."

"I thought you told me Prickle were big."

"They became...but when he left they were just a hard-working band not earning much money, and with a small fan base."

"Oh," said Montbretia. "So where was Danny when this happened?"

"He was there—he was in the band," said Boniface. "And like the other guys, he thought the band was dead, but this is where he stepped up and took responsibility. There were gigs the band was contractually obliged to play, and Danny doesn't like disappointed fans so he kept the band together."

"Good for Danny," said Montbretia. "But don't bands get new singers all the time?"

"It was a rough time: The drummer quit to join Gray for his first solo album, their management ended their relationship with the band, and the record label dropped them." Boniface waited a beat. "The record label dropped Prickle but enforced a clause against Gray as the frontman requiring him to record two further albums for them."

"The record label kept Gray but dropped Prickle?" asked Montbretia, noticing the wry smile spreading across Boniface's visage. "Given that Prickle still exist and you're star-struck by them, I'm guessing that things turned around."

"I think more to the point, *Danny* turned things around. It took about 18 months, during which time Prickle recorded a new album with their new drummer and their second new singer, just to stop the band from sinking. They also found a new record label and got new management in place. The first track off Prickle's new album was 'Tattoo Your Name on My Heart,' a song Danny wrote to impress a girl he'd met who he was trying to show that he could be responsible and provide a secure income and home life."

Montbretia waited expectantly as Boniface continued. "'Tattoo Your Name on My Heart' was Prickle's first international mega-hit and was the song that broke the band in the States, making Prickle one of the few bands from the UK to break the States in the 1980s. By this time, the British Invasion twenty years earlier was a distant memory."

"Stop, Boniface! Don't tell me about the band: What happened to the girl?" Montbretia was exasperated; he never focused on things that matter.

"You tell me," said Boniface. Montbretia went to speak but stopped as his face softened. "You met her last night at the office. They've been married for nearly thirty years."

Montbretia went to speak again but stopped, again, gently holding her lower lip between her teeth and feeling her eyes beginning to mist. Her lip released as the smile spread across her face. "Aww."

"And thirty years later, all the material Prickle has put out since Gray left is considered classic rock. And this is where the *quid pro quo* bites Gray in the ass: Danny and Prickle have had the success that Gray thought would be his when he left the band." Boniface tried to hide a smirk. "Seems it wasn't the band holding Gray back…"

Boniface had stopped talking and seemed to be looking expectantly, his eyes darting toward what she presumed was Gray's house. "So, again I ask," said Montbretia. "After I knock on the door, what's my story when he answers?"

"You say you want to meet Gray Barrington—you've been listening to his stuff forever. Tell him your dad loved his stuff—something like that—and make sure you tell him you don't like the direction that Prickle went after he left. Tell him you much prefer the blusier feel of the band's early songs. Once he's talking, tell him he should write a biography. When he agrees to that, you open the door and give me a shout, and your work is done. Within ten minutes we'll be having lunch."

"Really?"

"It's a plan." Boniface sounded slightly offended.

"A plan?" She sighed. "A plan says the man with the unresolved issues with his former wife, a hard-on for his current client's wife, and who's asking a girl in her twenties to act as bait for an old, lecherous, somewhat past-it rocker."

"You get a new wardrobe on expenses," said Boniface, winking as he turned toward Gray's house. "You're here and you're dressed for the part. Come on, it'll only take two minutes."

six

It's hard to know what is considered the front when you're talking about a circular building.

Logically, the front has the entrance that looks over the main road toward the Albert memorial; after all, this was the Royal Albert Hall. But Danny had qualified the front when he said "the steps," which implied the other front entrance, or as Boniface preferred to think of it, the back entrance. The entrance that didn't have the large hanging banners promoting the charity gig in two weeks, which Prickle would be headlining. Their first gig since Thad Stirling's untimely death.

Boniface understood why Danny and Prickle felt they had to perform. Thaddeus—Thad, as everyone had called him—had died three months previously from pancreatic cancer. He had been dead within a month of his diagnosis. When his widow, Penny, asked Prickle to get involved with the gig—a fundraising effort to support research into pancreatic cancer—there was only one answer, and so in two weeks Prickle would take to the stage of the venerable London venue, with a new singer, and pay tribute to an absent friend.

It might not have been the front, but the broad, shallow stairs leading up to the hall gave the best perspective of the building, and halfway down the stairs Boniface rested on the stone balustrade, watching as the figure of Danny Featherstone appeared, dressed much as he had been yesterday, but with a different, although equally loud, shirt under his old sand-colored jacket.

"How long did I take?"

Boniface pulled out his phone and checked the time. "Not that I was counting, but four minutes, thirty-six seconds. Thirty-seven. Thirty-eight."

Danny reached Boniface, the corners of his mouth twitching. "See, I said I'd be out in under five."

"You said under five, and a cup of tea." Boniface had meant to keep his jest light, but he felt a certain annoyance—he could have spent the last four minutes and thirty-eight seconds getting a drink for himself.

Danny's mouth twitched more noticeably, and he turned to look in the direction from which he had come. His head bobbed, as if scanning the far horizon, then after a moment or two he raised his hand and waved before turning back to Boniface, now grinning and saying nothing.

She appeared at the top of the steps, frizzy blonde hair, a crisp white cotton blouse, a short but not slutty black skirt with an apron, carrying a tray, heading toward Danny. "Your tea, Mister Featherstone."

"Thank you. And it's Danny." The bassist picked the teapot from the tray, poured the tea into a cup, and turned to Boniface. "Milk? Sugar?"

"Yes, and one, please."

He stirred, and then lifted the cup and saucer from the tray. "Thank you. I'll bring the cup back." The waitress turned and ascended the stairs as Danny passed the tea to Boniface. "It tastes better in porcelain." His goofy grin returned. "Where were we?"

Boniface sighed. "Don't I feel like a dick?"

"Tommy said I've got to treat you right. And I never disagree with anything Tommy says." He took two steps, turned, and rested against the balustrade, leaving space for Boniface to rest his saucer. "So. Where are we?"

"I've talked with Gray. You're right—he's an asshole and bitter and is causing problems, but I can't see that he's got the wit to arrange an internet hate campaign. He's not on Twitter, he doesn't have a website, and he's only got a dumb-phone." Danny slowly focused as Boniface continued. "That kid, Danny…"

"Everyone's a kid to Gray, but I find it hard to believe that you had a conversation with Mister Barrington without the words 'chief prick and the little thorns' spilling from his mouth."

"And I believe I have the honor of addressing the chief prick," said Boniface, distracted as a group of Japanese tourists ascended the steps, enthusiastically pointing at the building and pausing on every third step to take a photo. "The only time he said anything vaguely respectful was when he mentioned Thad. Seemed he really rated him as a singer, even if Thad was part of the conspiracy to brainwash *his* audience."

"How did you get in?" asked Danny. "I thought he'd tell you to do a range of physically impossible but sexually explicit activities."

"He did," said Boniface. "Montbretia got me in."

Danny continued. "I knew I liked her. So what else did Montbretia help you get out of Gray?"

"Not a huge amount. You're all unspeakable people. You were a joke for hiring Kit to fill his place."

"But Kit was only with us for five minutes—he didn't even record an album." He softened. "Five minutes, but we still get his fans turning up—they like to see where it started. We come on stage, and it's all a bit surprising for them."

"Well, Gray didn't like Kit. He thought you were smart replacing Kit with Thad, but apart from that, nothing." He took a sip of tea. "Well…there was one thing. He mentioned the name Billy Watkins. Does that mean anything to you?"

Danny paused, narrowing his eyes. "Never heard the name. What was the context?"

"Gray seemed to think that Billy Watkins—another kid—had something against Dawn and you."

Danny pushed out his bottom lip.

"That was what I got from Gray."

"I hope you thanked Montbretia."

"I did," said Boniface. "I took her to lunch."

The bassist stood, pulling up his shoulders to stretch his back. "What about PAD? Did they give you anything?"

"They're angry, if that's what you mean." Boniface paused. "They think you didn't disclose information." He felt a certain indifference to the overly pushy salesman and the tall lawyer he had met.

"They are angry." There was disappointment in the bassist's voice.

"Angry, but not trying to destroy you. That was my take," offered Boniface.

Danny rocked his head from side to side, seemingly contemplating.

"I could believe they might want to renegotiate your deal, but they didn't sound like they want to walk away. They're annoyed. They're frustrated. They hate all the claims that Gray has hit them with—claims that Gray didn't mention when we spoke—but apart from that, their big problem is Luca. What's happening with him?"

Danny relaxed. "Luca is perhaps the most talented musician I have ever worked with. Ever. His playing is sublime—he is technically brilliant, and his musicality is...I run out of superlatives." He paused, defocused, as if he was recalling the playing of the guitarist. "But everything else in Luca's life lacks structure. I think that's the polite way to phrase it."

Boniface felt a slight chill as the broad stairway funneled small gusts toward the concert venue. "Luca does the whole social media thing?"

Danny had the look of a slightly exasperated but still indulgent uncle. "There's only one way to get that phone of his out of his hands—give him a guitar. He's always holding one or the other."

"I'm just throwing this out there," said Boniface, hearing the caution in his own voice. "I got the impression from PAD that Luca had issues, and you know he does the social media stuff.... Is he the source of these stories that are out there?"

"No." Boniface was surprised at how definitive the response was. "Not his style. Luca is fearless—when he's got a problem, he tells me directly. Very directly."

"The wife," said Boniface. "PAD said there was a problem with his wife."

"Bing-Bing."

Boniface raised his eyebrows.

"Missus Parzani, Bing-Bing. Or Bing2, as it gets written." An amused look crossed his face. "Yeah. She's a fiery one, but she's not our problem. However, there is something you could help me with here."

seven

Boniface had the look of a boy with a new girlfriend who knew tonight was the night.

The night.

And he was about to have a shower and get out his best underwear. "I'm surprised you've got time to drag yourself away from your new BFF to come into the office." He didn't seem to notice. "Don't worry, I can carry on without you."

"Could you do something, please?" Montbretia could swear that Boniface had gone deaf since lunch. "It's Luca."

"Luca."

"Prickle's guitarist."

"Prickle, who are not our..."

Boniface cut across. "Prickle, our client." He still seemed unfeasibly joyful. "Prickle who have a gig in two weeks. A charity gig, and some organization is needed, and as you know, their management is refusing to undertake any work."

"Because of Mister Barrington, who likes to live in a time warp and thinks women forty years younger than him are impressed that he was in a band twenty years before they were born."

Boniface seemed to come down slightly from his high, but only far enough to be marginally empathetic. "Yeah, I didn't like him much either. But he was far more pleasant when you were there. Anyway..." He floated back to his high. "Luca has a problem and needs some help."

"Happy to do so," said Montbretia, watching to see if Boniface noticed the sarcasm, "once we have a contract in place and he's made his first payment."

"And there's our problem," said Boniface.

"Well, I'm glad you realize," said Montbretia, pushing her chair back from her desk, spinning to face Boniface, who stepped into her office. She was on home territory: back in her own office, wearing her own clothes—jeans, not as well fitting as Dawn's; white blouse, also not as well fitting as Dawn's; and sneakers—in combination, so much more comfortable than the streetwalker outfit Boniface made her wear to see Gray. And now, safely in her own comfort zone, she was happy to take on Boniface.

Boniface went to speak, then stopped. Waited. And then began. "Luca was made bankrupt two months back—he has no cash. So this thing with Prickle having their bank account frozen is hurting him the most. Danny and the other guys have got money in their own bank accounts—Luca doesn't."

"Well then, Luca should be the one chasing Barrington and that giraffe woman." Montbretia sat forward in her chair, readying herself to spin back to her work.

"Luca is a musician, not a businessman, and in any event, Luca has a bigger problem. Three months ago he got divorced..."

"Well, clearly you're the ideal person to counsel him, as I'm sure the former Missus Boniface would attest."

Boniface smiled. "Veronica and I divorced amicably—at least as amicably as you can when your heart feels like it has been torn out. Missus Parzani, however, has other problems." Boniface bit his lower lip, shaking his head. "At the time of divorce, a financial settlement was agreed. That settlement—not unreasonably—led Bing-Bing, that's the ex-wife, to have certain expectations."

"Why does this story sound like the story you told me about the managers?"

"Quite," said Boniface. "The trouble is, with his bankruptcy, Luca isn't in a position to meet his obligations."

"Ah," said Montbretia, sitting back.

"Ah, indeed. But where many people would get mad, Bing-Bing is getting even. She seems quite a feisty individual...and she's been looking for any asset that she can sell to generate the cash she believes is her right. It doesn't matter who owns the asset; if she can get hold of it, then she takes it and sells it."

"Oh."

"Luca had four guitars. Each was individually built to his specification. They took months to build—the tops were hand-carved from wood chosen for its resonance, the electrics were state of the art. I know nothing about guitars other than these cost about five thousand bucks each and were the tools of his trade."

"Were?"

"Yup. She bribed a crew member—ex–crew member now—and took possession. She sold the four for 250 quid each."

"Twenty-thousand bucks' worth of gear sold for one-thousand pounds?"

Boniface nodded mournfully. "All Luca now owns is the clothes he wears, his phone, and...well, that's it. She's taken the rest and sold it."

"And where do we fit in?" asked Montbretia.

"Luca needs help, but he doesn't want charity—he does have some pride—and Danny..."

"It's alright, Boniface, you can call him 'darling' or 'my true love.' I won't be offended. I realize you've moved on."

"Danny wants us to see if there's anything we can do to help the gear situation."

Montbretia flopped back in her chair, shaking her head. Boniface walked across the room and leaned on the windowsill with his back to the tinted glass. "We do PR, Boniface. Oh, and apparently you do a bit of private investigating." She felt her voice harden. "Since when do we do musical instruments?"

"This is simple PR," said Boniface. "The idea is to get some gear for Luca. The roadies think they can get some guitars, I said we'd see what we can..."

"We?"

"We." A look of smug confidence crossed his face. "See, you already think you're on board."

Montbretia sighed loudly and stood up, crossing her arms. Boniface didn't seem to notice and continued. "Spend five minutes on the internet—search for guitar amps—and find what the main brands are. Then call them and ask to speak with whoever does artist relations. Tell them that Luca Parzani is interested in their gear, and you'll find they will be eating out of your hand. It's a simple trade: They give him gear, he gives them publicity."

"Why am I doing this?" Montbretia felt her crossed arms gripping herself tighter.

In her anger, she missed the sotto voce comment Boniface made, but she could have sworn that he said "you virtually offered." By the time her gaze had burned out his retinas, he was more conciliatory. "Because you're good at it...and it's not going to take long."

"It's not what…" she muttered to herself, not even sure what she was saying. "What sort of idiot is Danny? I mean, I don't like being rude about your BFF, but why are we doing more when all we have done so far—if you look at what we've actually achieved—is fail?"

"Danny is trusting us because Tommy told him he should. And we're doing this because I feel we owe Tommy one, even if this is paying him back indirectly." He relaxed, his upright posture collapsing. "And Prickle are in a bind."

Montbretia dropped her crossed arms and leaned on the back of her chair.

"Besides, I get to hang out with rock stars and models. The fifteen-year-old boy who lives inside my head won't let me turn down this experience. Like every fifteen-year-old boy, I need to get it out of my system."

"Basically, you're a groupie, Boniface. And you know what sort of reputation groupies have?"

Boniface shrugged.

"And does the groupie understand the danger here?" When he didn't seem to be responding, she continued. "No one knows who's started this chaos. No one really knows the extent of whatever the problem is. Have you even checked to see whether we're just talking about a few drive-by posts on Facebook that the happy couple have taken out of proportion?"

"It's more than that," said Boniface. "Remember, we talked to Gray, and I talked to the managers. No one said there isn't a problem."

"But you still don't know exactly what the problem is." She spun her chair and sat down. "Anyway, what are you doing to help?"

Boniface looked sheepish.

"I'm taking advantage of my newly rediscovered independence and the generosity of my friend Gideon Latymer."

"You mean you're driving somewhere."

"Mmmhmmm." Montbretia raised her eyebrows, holding them until Boniface continued. "Danny and the band have found a new singer for the gig—they saw a video of him on YouTube fronting a Prickle tribute band and offered him the gig as a one-off. He's arriving tonight, so I'm going to listen to his first session with the band."

"Where?" Montbretia didn't even make an attempt to sound interested.

"Danny and Dawn's. Danny's got a studio where the band are rehearsing. And after that, I've been invited for dinner—Danny called Dawn while we were chatting earlier." He pushed up the ends of his lips with little sincerity. "It would be rude to let them down after I've already accepted."

eight

"The princess killer," said Gideon as he handed over the keys. "For your use. I retain ownership, so you can go bankrupt and it won't be repossessed. I'll also meet the cost of insurance—for you and any driver you nominate—as well as the maintenance, and I've had one of those bluetooth things fitted so you can use your phone...to do navigation or music or actually talk to people." He shrugged. "Montbretia will understand."

She understood, but she didn't love the car. "It's not a classic, Boniface. It's just old. But it is very sweet of Gideon." The night before Boniface's driving ban expired, there had been a knock at his front door. Gideon stood, holding the keys in front of him. He still felt a continuing need to apologize for his behavior when Boniface was implicated in a murder he didn't commit, and he hoped the gesture might demonstrate his contrition in a practical manner.

"Why princess killer?" said Montbretia slowly, when Boniface relayed the story the next day.

"It's the car—the same make and model, a Mercedes-Benz W140 with a 2.8 liter, straight six, petrol engine and automatic gearbox—that was carrying the then most famous woman in the world on the night she died in Paris." That alone was enough to ensure that Boniface always wore his seatbelt, and given that he had stopped drinking quite some time ago now, he could always be sure that he would be sober.

But he was still cautious about driving anyone who wanted to behave like a princess, and preferred to call it the barge due to the way that it wallowed. But the wallowing was not a problem; the car was comfortable and to date it had performed its intended function of transporting him from place A to place B with 100 percent consistency.

And this bluetooth thing was great.

One of the first things Boniface had done with Montbretia after they met was ask her to accompany him when he went to replace his phone. She had refused to let him buy a flip phone like his last model. Instead, she insisted that he buy one that could "you know, Boniface, actually do useful things."

And one of those useful things was maps and navigation. Danny had explained to Boniface that he and Dawn didn't so much live in a place—more at a GPS location, which happened to be near a narrow country lane. As they stood outside the Royal Albert Hall, he had put his finger on the map. "Navigate to here and you'll find us." As Boniface drove down the long, narrow, winding lanes of the Surrey Hills, he was pleased to hear the directions shouted out by his phone be relayed via bluetooth through the car's speakers.

He wasn't sure what route he had followed, since his phone told him to leave the main road, and he didn't know exactly where he was, but he knew that it was the Surrey Hills. There had been a big sign—*Surrey Hills, area of outstanding natural beauty*—and the road had then inclined upward, winding into a forest.

The directions had led him over the brow of a hill from where he could see the valley floor sweep below him and everywhere apart from the sky and a red-brick church was green. As he followed the road into the valley, he was directed from one narrow road, to another narrower, to one narrower still and with additional twists. And just to add to the fun, this narrow twisting lane was cut through its surroundings, leaving steep banks on either side. Steep banks with sandstone projections that had been smoothed by passing cars, and a canopy of trees enclosing the top of the route. It was nearly an hour and a half until sunset, but already Boniface had felt the need to switch on his lights.

Heading south, he reached a village. Shere.

Old is a relative term. In the UK, there are several measures of old—most are based around events in the history of the British Empire. There is, however, one measure of old on which all British citizens agree: Domesday.

With the Norman Invasion led by the man who became known as William the Conqueror, the British Isles were changed permanently. Having invaded and conquered in 1066, William set about assessing his new dominion. He wanted to know what was there so he could levy tax.

The survey, an inventory of the land, people, and assets—recorded in what the overrun population colloquially called the Domesday Book—was completed in 1086 and now stands as one definitive test of old. If your town or village is in the Domesday Book, it is old. If it is not, then you're just a jumped-up oik with new money and ideas above your station. If you can prove that your building is Norman—in other words, that it was a construct of the invading Norman hoards—then you can scrape a claim to being old. But younger than that, and you are just a kid, as Gray Barrington would call you.

Shere was officially old. However, while listed in Domesday, most of the architecture was a mixture of wood-beam Tudor and red-brick Victorian.

The tiny but picturesque village was only fifteen miles from the outer limits of London's sprawl, but Boniface knew it was the last recognizable waypoint on his journey. It took him 90 seconds to pass from one end of the village to the other, and only that long because the street was narrow and cars were coming the other way. As he left the village, he knew he had to rely on his phone to guide him, although, ironically, while the navigation system could still find the satellites in the sky that it needed for direction, he had long since left phone reception behind.

Relying solely on the voice of his phone, he followed the narrow strips of tarmac, occasionally passing driveways and once or twice turning at junctions. "In thirty yards, your destination is on the right," announced the navigator. Boniface took his foot off the accelerator and allowed the weight of the barge to slow his forward movement.

A stone-covered driveway came into sight, and Boniface turned right, crunching along the track, passing a brick house and drawing to a halt with a slight skid on the loose surface when he reached a cluster of cars.

He got out and stretched. "Come to where we're making music," Danny had said. Boniface looked around. In addition to the house, there were two barn-like structures: old brick footings with the main structure formed from blackened rough-cut overlapping planks. On the nearer, a row of LEDs gently winked around the eaves, reassuringly confirming that the valuable antique car—a passion shared with Tommy Newby, who had referred Dawn and Danny to Boniface—was under constant electronic vigilance.

He listened. Rock bands make noise, right? Surely that was half the point of being in a band, and Boniface couldn't see any neighbors who were likely to complain.

But all he could hear was birds chirping.

A door opened forcefully in the far barn, and a tall man with curly hair that reached halfway down his back walked out, stopped, and turned to face where he had come from. He shouted back in the direction he had just come from; with each syllable he gestured with outstretched arms to emphasize what he was saying. Boniface didn't recognize the language, but he recognized Luca Parzani from his photos and presumed the language he was shouting was Italian.

Parzani stopped, pulled the phone is his right hand closer, tapped on the screen, then started walking swiftly toward the cars. Every few yards he looked back over his shoulders and shouted something.

He reached the parking area and headed for an anonymous small beige Korean car. Boniface didn't know the manufacturer, but he recognized the type. It was the perfect rental car: totally anonymous—it would never annoy anyone so it would never get vandalized, and it always offered perfect reliability. He guessed that Danny was paying for it and had made the choice of model in case Bing-Bing tried to take possession.

Without acknowledging Boniface, Luca got in the car, reversed, spun the wheels as he began to move forward, and accelerated to the gate, turning left and disappearing.

Boniface followed the path Luca had just taken and stepped into the barn, taking a moment to get used to the dull light of the lobby. In front of him there was a small office-like alcove with a desk. Sitting, hunched over the desk, Danny was talking softly but quickly on the phone.

There was a sound of shuffling from the room to his left, and the lobby became darker as a figure stood between the large room and the lobby. "Boniface, right? Just Boniface. No Mister, no first name, just Boniface."

"That's it," said Boniface, looking up at the big black figure. He was shorter than the giraffe in her mega heels, but still about 6' 2", broad, and deep. In a fight, Boniface would want this guy on his side.

"I like your style, man. I'm Mel, and you know my brother Danny." He held a fist over his heart as he let his gaze indicate the alcove where Danny sat, releasing his fist and reaching forward to shake Boniface's hand.

He'd never put his hand in a vice, but Boniface reckoned he would feel less pain if he did. Mel was pure physical strength, but then again, he did hit things for a living. Typically, he would spend two or three hours a night hitting things, and hitting things constantly with all four limbs.

A heavyweight boxer, by contrast, might take twelve three-minute rounds. Thirty-six minutes. And much of that time would be walking around or hugging the other guy to stop him from throwing punches. Boniface would lay money on the drummer every time.

"Come in, man," said the drummer, turning back into the bigger room. "Have you been here before?"

Boniface shook his head.

"Welcome to where the music is made." Mel Grant led him into the room filled with instruments—Boniface surveyed his new surroundings, noting what seemed to be stations for five musicians arranged in a pentagon.

A drum kit stood on the farthest point. Boniface started counting the drums—there were at least fifteen, including two kick drums; at least ten cymbals; four cowbells; enough electronic pads, Boniface guessed; and what looked like an electronic xylophone.

He felt his feet hit the floor, but the sound was wrong. "Acoustic treatment," said Mel. "Listen." He clapped his hands. There was the sound of flesh slapping, but no brightness, no echo. "See the fabric?" He indicated the fabric-covered walls and ceilings, lit by small white lights on brushed steel rails. "Basically, there's a whole heap of rockwool behind there, which kills the reverb, so what you hear is the sound but not the slap-back that you're used to hearing in a normal room."

To one side of the drums, a row of five bass guitars stood in a rack next to a stack of black amps. On the other side, an old guitar was plugged into a small amplifier. The bassist's and guitarist's stations were each completed with a microphone with a long lead snaking across the room. At the fourth point of a pentagon was another microphone, its lead also running across the room, and no instruments.

"So where's the new guy?" asked Boniface. "I was hoping to hear him. Are you still waiting for him to arrive?"

"Ah," said Mel. He grimaced, looking away as if checking whether they were being overheard.

"Uh oh."

"Where had you got to in the story?" asked the drummer.

"You found a guy on YouTube...he was arriving tonight, but I guess not," said Boniface.

"Oh, he arrived. He arrived," Mel sighed. "It goes like this: We saw this guy on YouTube who was based in Auckland."

"Auckland, New Zealand?"

"Is there another Auckland?" said the drummer, for the first time starting to look weary. "We saw his performances on YouTube: He wasn't Thad, but he had power and a good tone, and he sung the songs with conviction. He knew the words, and he looked like he could handle an audience, so we thought why not get him in for the gig?" He sat down on his drum stool, his huge biceps threatening each kit piece. "You know we've got a problem with our management?"

Boniface nodded.

"Right, so we made the arrangements to fly this guy over and put him up at a hotel. Danny got it sorted and paid for everything. Anyway, as the arrangements are being made, the guy says that he'll be flying in from São Paulo. We didn't care where he came from, so we made the arrangements and today we sent a taxi to pick him up at Heathrow, take him to the hotel, and then bring him here at five PM once he'd had a chance to rest and have a wash."

Boniface stepped over to a stool by the rack of basses and sat.

"When he arrived, he looked whiter than the guy in the video, his hair was longer, and boy had he put on weight. But, y'know, we only saw a video on YouTube; people change, and we couldn't be certain when the video was shot."

"But he could sing?" asked Boniface.

"The guy in the video? Oh yeah, he could sing. This bozo?" The drummer looked down, shaking his head at the memory. "The lisp and the thick Portuguese accent we might have been able to deal with. We might have been able to work with the mumbling. But he didn't know what a tune was—seriously, there was no melody—and he thought he had a great falsetto: I can still hear the screaming now."

"I'm sorry, I'm not understanding," said Boniface. "You make it sound like this was a different person."

"It was! The guy had sold the gig on eBay. Sing at the Royal Albert Hall with Prickle. This guy from São Paulo is a complete Prickle super-fan; he paid ten-thousand bucks for the gig and was totally overawed at meeting his heroes. The pity is that he couldn't sing, his heroes were mightily pissed, and as you've seen from Danny, the search for a new singer is now pretty urgent."

"So what's happened to the guy?" asked Boniface.

"Newt..." Mel pointed to the three rows of keyboards stacked on a triangular stand, as if to indicate the keyboard player Newton Jubb at the fifth point on the pentagon. "Newt was so appalled with the whole situation that he took the guy back to his hotel and will then take him to Heathrow, pay his fare home, and wait until he is gone."

nine

Boniface sat at what he guessed was probably an interior designer's idea of a perfect table for a country kitchen.

If pushed—and in the same position—he probably would have made a similar recommendation: long, unvarnished oak, with wooden chairs on one side and at the head, and a bench on the other side. It married the basic requirements for form and function.

His biggest gripe, as he sat in one of the wooden chairs on the side of the table, was the lack of padding. Already his bum was feeling weary.

Not that he really cared about the discomfort of his bum; it was just that the discomfort was distracting him.

Distracting him when he had an opportunity to sit and look at Dawn.

She had been standing since he arrived, tending to the dinner that she was cooking, and as she walked around the kitchen—stirring, adding a pinch, looking and assessing, increasing the heat, decreasing the heat—Boniface sat back and did what the teenage boy inside told him to do: admire. Who cares if you're on a hard seat if you get to see your teenage fantasy up close?

Well...teenage fantasy but clothed.

As had been the case twenty-four hours previously, Dawn's choice of clothes was unfussy but stylish: jeans that fitted—a marginally different shade from yesterday—a white T-shirt that fitted without any stretching or bulging, wedding and engagement rings, and a single bangle, also different from yesterday's but equally unadorned. When she found him—chatting with Mel Grant in the studio—she had kissed him. It wasn't the kind of kiss that the teenage boy inside his head wanted—just a peck on the cheek—but it seemed to hold genuine affection. "Come and have something to eat," she said.

He didn't need to be asked twice. In fact, he probably stopped listening after the word "come".

"I'm sorry for dragging you away from the boys," said Dawn, turning toward Boniface. Something inside him melted as her gray eyes seemed to involuntarily open to express regret, while the smallest tilt of her head reassured. It was a simple enough gesture, but it left Boniface feeling that all his strength had left his body.

If Dawn was talking, that was probably a sign that he had been silent. If he had been silent, then that was a sign he had been staring. Staring when he should have been asking questions, trying to get to the bottom of...trying to understand what the problem was...before the latest problem.

"No worries," he brightened. "To be honest, I was glad to get out of there—it seemed pretty tense."

"They all looked so...serious, and I heard Luca shouting," said Dawn. "I've never seen my bear get so angry." Her voice was a whisper. "He was so hurt. You know, Thad..."

Boniface nodded, not saying anything, but keeping eye contact, knowing where his eyes would land if he didn't force them away.

There was the sound of a soft, moist plop on the range behind Dawn and she turned, grabbed a wooden spoon, and focused her attention back on the main pot.

"So while Danny and the others are in the studio making noise, what does a normal day involve for you?" asked Boniface.

She kept the spoon slowly stirring the pot in front of her as she turned her head toward Boniface. "A lot of the time, I'm off taking pictures." She tilted her head toward a large print of a Gothic tower topped with battlements, shot against a blue sky with puffy white clouds. The trees around the tower only seemed to reach one-quarter of its height, giving it a sense of size. "That's one of mine."

"Wow." Boniface stood and placed himself directly in front of the print, looking at the detail of the stonework edged with red brick. "Stunning building, stunning photo." Dawn flushed slightly, rapidly looking back to her pot and stirring with renewed vigor. "Where is this?"

"About four miles in that direction." She jutted her chin forward. "Four miles by foot or horse. Farther if you drive—all the roads go north/south; only the locals understand how to go east or west."

"Where did you get it printed?" asked Boniface.

"Here." Boniface felt his head twist too quickly, letting Dawn know that he was surprised at her skill. He stumbled to recover. "I didn't know the printing systems you could get at home were that good."

"They're not, at least not at the consumer end. But if you spend some money, then..." Her voice trailed off as she bent to look in the oven. "And I'll let you in on my dirty little secret." She wiped her hands on a cloth as she walked over to Boniface. "This wasn't the first time I shot this tower, and it wasn't my first print. In fact, it wasn't the second or the third or the fourth time—for either."

Boniface stepped to the side to allow Dawn to face the picture directly. "I'm sorry," he said as she moved closer than he expected, brushing his arm, and then wondered why he was apologizing.

"You see there?" Dawn pointed toward the top of the tower. "It's a bit noisy—I tried to balance the sharpening and the noise reduction. If you step back to here..." she put her arm around Boniface's waist and her other hand on his closest shoulder to softly move him back, "you can't see it, but if you move here," she glided him forward, "you can see it's just a bit overdone on the edge of the octagonal tower." She dropped her arm, returning to the range as Boniface wiped a bead of sweat from his forehead. "But there's an emotion in that picture—a vibrancy—that I love, even if it's not perfect."

He pulled back his seat, noticing a tremor in his hand, and sat. "So...your dirty little secret?"

Dawn giggled. "It's part photography, part exercise. I go out three, four days a week taking pictures. Sometimes I walk; sometimes I borrow a horse and ride. I can spend weeks taking the same picture every day, because every day the light will be different, the landscape changes, the plants change. You can never get the same picture—you always take a new and unique picture."

She reached into a cupboard.

"Fresh today." She placed a loaf of bread on a breadboard on the table. "And then I sort through the pictures and print my favorites, but there are so many choices—different papers, different inks, different settings—so every print can come out different. Many times I've taken a shot thinking it was the best I've ever taken, then I've come home and printed the picture. When you go from this," she held her fingers to indicate a small square, "to this," she held her hands apart, unwittingly thrusting her chest forward, "you notice things."

"You would notice," said Boniface, sliding his chair toward the table.

"I come home, I print out the picture, and it'll be great...I mean *really* good, but there will just be something. Something small, so I'll go back to the original image, process it a bit more, print it again, and it will be better, but..." She made an odd sound as she grimaced. "So the next day I'll go out again and take the same photo, then come home and go through the same process. It can be like a meditation—you just keep focusing on one thing, constantly repeating, and in the end..." she pointed with her eyes toward the picture of the Gothic tower behind Boniface, "in the end, you live with the imperfection."

"So where do you go to take your pictures?" asked Boniface.

"All over—I guess you'd call my territory the five-mile radius from here." She grimaced. "Funny. I was born twenty-five miles away, but it's like a different world. It was a different world—I never knew about this place. It was only when Danny and I got married that someone suggested the church at Albury. Do you know it?"

Boniface felt his head confirm that he didn't.

"You should," said Dawn. "If you go back to Shere, turn left and follow the path across the fields. You'll soon find it—it's in the grounds of Albury Park. It's old—very old, Domesday old—although like all old buildings, it's been added to. The last guy was in this sort of Catholic sect, and he didn't want the peasants near his house, so he built this new Protestant church in the village, then he built a Catholic church for his sect, and then he got Pugin—I looked him up; he's the guy who did the interior of the Houses of Parliament—" Boniface felt his eyebrows raise, "to convert one wing of this tiny Norman church into a mausoleum, and it's stunning. I won't describe it—you need to go. It's not used as a church anymore, but a charity looks after it so you can visit at any time. When you get there, you'll see why we fell in love with the place and had to get married there, and that's how we discovered this area."

She laughed softly. "The funny thing is, even with so many churches, this whole area used to be so lawless. All the old houses around here have disproportionately large cellars from the time when people would do a bit of rustling, do a bit of stealing, and then hang out in the hills. It was so remote up here that no one got caught." Her voice brightened. "Anyway, are you ready for some food?"

"Definitely," said Boniface.

"Well, cut yourself some bread—I told you, it's fresh, it didn't come from a supermarket."

"I'm sorry," said Boniface, flushing slightly. "You mean it's your own bread."

"I didn't grow the wheat and mill it, but I did make the bread today. And the vegetables in the soup were all grown here." She placed two large steaming bowls with carrots, peas, onions, and spinach floating in the dark liquid on the table: one in front of Boniface, the other where she sat.

"Thank you. It looks amazing," said Boniface. "And all grown by you?"

"Grown and cooked by me," said Dawn.

"Should I go and call?" Boniface pointed loosely in the direction of the studio.

"No need—they'll come when they're ready. When the boys are working, they never know when they're going to be finished, so I prepare something that's going to be ready when they say 'NOW!' but which won't spoil if they spend an extra hour rehearsing. Soup is good because it's not too heavy if they're eating late at night—there's nothing worse than fat rockers."

Boniface took a mouthful. "It tastes even better than it looks."

"Thank you." Dawn smiled. "I didn't know whether the new singer was going to be a vegetarian, so I didn't include any meat." Boniface matched her ironic grin. "Anyway. Tell me about your investigations—Danny mentioned you were busy today."

"Yeah. Strange day," said Boniface, leaning forward to cut a slice of bread.

"You can dunk," said Dawn, pointing between the bread and Boniface's soup. "So what made the day strange?"

"As you would expect, it's no one's fault, and everyone blames everyone else, and no one seems to know what they've done that's a problem. But the thing that's odd is this one name came up, and no one seemed to recognize it."

"Oh?" said Dawn.

"Billy Watkins," said Boniface.

There was a small crash as Dawn's spoon hit her bowl, splashing soup over the table.

Boniface looked up to see her face flush, her chin trembling. "I'd better go and check on the boys," she said as she stood, leaving her soup.

ten

Danny slid out of the black Audi A8 and stretched, feeling the stiffness that comes from a fitful nap grabbed on the sofa in the studio alcove. "I ache, Sven," he said, leaning on the car door and talking through the open window. "Really ache. I'm getting too old for this shit. All I had to do was walk to the house and up the stairs, but..."

The drum roadie, who was always keen to drive, nodded. "And if you hear anything from Reuben, call." Sven nodded again, the large stretched piercing in the center of his earlobe, lined with dark-colored bone, looking like a fulcrum on which his head moved. "I'll be back in five."

He took the stairs two at a time, both flights, reaching the landing outside Boniface's office, where he peered through the wired safety glass in the door. He lightly tapped with his index and middle fingers on his right hand—a brief rhythm resonated, and within a few seconds Montbretia's face appeared from a room on the left with a slightly confused look.

Her frown fell away, replaced by a broad smile as she recognized him, cantering for two steps and slowing as she reached the door. Cantering...he looked at Montbretia's ponytail, the ends flicking across the shoulders of her white cotton blouse as her head twisted.

"I was wondering who would knock like that," she said, pushing the door and leaning to hold it as he entered. "And now I know. Is he expecting you?"

"Nah, I just dropped by—it's only a flying visit." Montbretia left the door to swing as she turned toward Boniface's office. Her step was light but confident as she bounced three steps in front of him before leaning around Boniface's door and knocking once.

"Visitor for you." She stepped back and was gone before Danny had his foot into Boniface's office.

"We didn't have a meeting scheduled, did we?" Boniface stood up quickly—the look of confusion giving way to a businesslike greeting. "I haven't got anything new to tell you, although we're working hard to get something sorted for Luca, and there are a few people it would be good to talk with. Anyway..." he indicated the deep leather sofa facing across the room. "Please sit. Do you want a tea? Coffee?"

"No...no...nothing for me," said Danny, remaining standing. He caught his reflection in the window cutting through the center of two walls—if the band weren't going to tour for a while, then he was going to need to exercise. Who was he kidding—he already needed to exercise. "I just wanted to apologize for last night. It was a complete...you know...and I just ignored you and..."

Boniface visibly relaxed. "It's not a problem—really—you had quite a *challenge* to deal with." He paused and then continued, his voice darker. "Have you sorted things out?"

Danny snorted. "The first half, yeah. The big issue, no." He moved to stand more clearly out of Boniface's personal space. "Our would-be new friend is on a plane and should be in Brazil around now. Luckily, because of our dispute with PAD, a contract hadn't been drawn up for the guy, hence he had no legal claim against us. I paid for the flight here and the hotel, and Newt paid for the flight home last night." He sighed. "So that's done. The big problem is that I haven't found a singer for the gig, but I'm working on it."

Boniface said, "Well, if..."

"Thanks, man, but I really came here to say sorry," said Danny. "I'm on my way to the Albert Hall again. There's a lot of stuff that PAD would usually sort. I've got Sven—Mel's drum tech—driving me. He loves driving—and he loves people's reaction when they see him in the car."

The confusion crept over Boniface's visage.

"He's tattooed and pierced," said Danny, pointing to his ears, nose, and arms as if that explained the situation. "People don't expect to see a guy like that driving a dull businessman's car." His tone became more matter-of-fact. "And it's good to have him with me—he can check out the practical stuff for this gig."

Danny moved to the door and looked back. "What went on with you and Dawn last night?"

He could have sworn that Boniface blushed.

"When?" asked Boniface.

"I mean, did she seem alright to you?"

"Yeah," said Boniface. He paused, seemingly replaying something in his head. "But thinking about it, she did seem a bit...I don't know...there was an odd reaction."

Danny frowned and cocked his head.

"I mentioned that name to her: you know, Billy Watkins." Danny listened. "She seemed..." He shrugged. "Disconcerted?"

"What did she say?"

"She didn't. She went outside."

"That's probably when she came in," said Danny. "I was on the phone. She was cat-like, you know, nuzzling up against me. But that call took an hour." He looked up, feeling a small jolt. "You weren't on your own for all that time."

"No. Mel came in for some food. We had a good chat, and after that I left—I figured you were busy, so I didn't disturb you when I went." Boniface straightened, his voice slightly strained. "Why? What did Dawn say to you?"

"That's the thing," said Danny. "She didn't. I was on the phone—she just came and purred around me, then went." He rested on the doorframe. "By the time I had made all the calls I could make, I was so wound up that I didn't want to go back into the house and wake up Dawn as I thrashed around getting into bed, so I crashed on the sofa in the studio."

He stood away from the doorframe, pushing his shoulders forward to stretch the muscles in his back. "It's not the first time I've slept there, and the next morning is always a little bit less pleasant than the time before." He let his muscles relax. "I guess I must have kipped there for about three hours and finally gave up at about six, when I went inside. I made us some tea and took it up to Dawn, but she wasn't there."

Boniface showed a look of surprise.

"That's not totally unusual—it was after first light but before sunrise, and sometimes she goes out early to take photos. But it didn't look like she had slept in the bed, and she hadn't taken anything with her as far as I could see." Boniface frowned and Danny answered the silent request for elaboration. "She left her phone, which is not totally unusual—coverage is so spotty in the hills that sometimes all you're carrying is a heavy clock. She didn't seem to have taken any cameras." He exhaled deeply. "It's as if aliens came down and took her."

Boniface stood silent.

"So she didn't say anything to you?" Boniface shook his head. "I guess she'll be home by the time I get back, but I just wondered..." He stood up straight. "Look, man, I've got to shoot, but if you hear from her, give me a shout. Let's stay in touch."

As he passed, without breaking stride, he tapped a rhythm on Montbretia's open door. "See you, Monty."

eleven

Veronica Rutherford felt the pressure at the bridge of her nose and softly massaged the throb with a thumb and two fingers. She sighed as she released, opening her eyes to focus on her breakfast companion, her ex-husband.

He was doing that thing he did when he started to get excited—leaning forward, his head tilting forward and back imperceptibly, with his eyes opening wider. He wanted her reaction. He wanted her help.

She checked her watch. Ten AM. Far too early. She should have still been at home with a coffee and the papers, but instead she was in a restaurant that catered to the breakfast-meeting crowd. Or rather, in a restaurant where—since there would be staff preparing for lunch—you could get something to eat if you knew the manager, and because this was three minutes' walk from her office and served good enough food, Veronica knew the manager.

She resettled herself in her chair, giving a gentle tug to the seams of her dress just above her hips, feeling the material straighten around her shoulders. "Please tell me you haven't got the hots for her and this isn't some desperate attempt to play the hero."

Boniface seemed almost hurt; he had obviously been expecting a different response, and as he scrambled to deny the implicit accusation she continued. "From what I've heard, they're utterly devoted. It's not even the stuff of romance novels—there are no obstacles to their love."

Her ex-husband paused, then seemed to deflate, his tone slightly disappointed. "They talked about doing some sort of a reality TV show—you know, at home with…"

Veronica felt herself frown involuntarily.

Boniface's tone remained subdued. "I didn't know how to tell them it would be awful telly. Really tedious. After the first five minutes, you'd figure they were never going to fight—nothing like the Osbournes. And then they're class traitors. They've left their roots but haven't been fully accepted on the next social echelon. Remember, Danny is mates with Tommy Newby—he's not the sort of guy you invite 'round when you go and meet the Ambassador."

The restaurant sat where the top end of Shaftesbury Avenue met New Oxford Street at a 45-degree angle, and it mirrored that angle, with two glass-fronted windows converging toward the east of the building. The large windows let in light, which cast deep shadows but also meant that one diner would be framed by a halo of light. In this case, it was Boniface who was backlit, casting his visage into gloom—physically and metaphorically.

"But the TV series isn't today's problem. You're fiddling, and you're going to break something that isn't broken."

"No. It *is* broken." Boniface was cautious but firm in his assertion. "Dawn is missing."

"Dawn wasn't there when Danny woke up, you said. You also said that Danny said this wasn't unusual. And, to quote yet another fact you told me, Danny doesn't know when Dawn left because he was sleeping in an outbuilding. In other words…"

She took a sip of coffee, becoming increasingly frustrated with the delay of her scrambled eggs. "In other words, Dawn might have gone for a walk five minutes before Danny woke up, and could be home by now."

Boniface deflated further. "She could." He leaned forward. "But even if she does come back, you didn't see her reaction last night." Veronica remained silent—with the slightest twitch she indicated for Boniface to continue. "I mentioned this guy Billy Watkins, and it was like...it was like she had a seizure: She dropped her spoon—into her soup, which splashed halfway across the table...not that she noticed it—and she dashed out of the room. This wasn't a mild reaction; this was...I don't know...I don't want to say fear, but it was certainly a primeval reaction. This was something she couldn't control. This was something that made her react physically and emotionally." He sat back in his chair. "This is something that matters."

Veronica looked at her former husband. He certainly looked rational. He had dressed himself properly—but he always did wear good suits, and this was a good suit. He had obviously washed. He was feeding himself. Nothing seemed wrong or out of place, but one small incident with a woman he had only met 36 hours earlier seemed to be driving him.

"If it didn't matter—if it wasn't something to be worried about—then Danny wouldn't have turned up at my office this morning. He didn't need to see me in person—if he wanted to apologize, he could have called. He could have sent an email or a text. There's any number of things he could have done—especially since his time is limited at the moment. But instead, he went out of his way and came to see me."

Boniface could be laid-back. He could be trusting. Laid-back and trusting to the point that it seemed that he didn't care, but something seemed to be niggling him. "What do you want from me?"

Veronica had a sinking feeling as she heard the words drop out of her mouth. The dread dissipated as she heard his response. "A bit of common sense? Some thoughts about who might have some background on Dawn? She would have been modeling about thirty years ago, so have you got any ideas of someone who might have been around then who might have an idea about what's going on?"

"Thirty years ago, you and I were still at school, and dinosaurs roamed freely in the hills." She rested her head on her hand and defocused. "I guess the guy who would know about models would be a photographer."

Boniface nodded once.

"Do you remember the fat guy with the mustache who used to be on staff?" She hesitated. "Terry Meyerson, I think his name was?"

Boniface's grimaced. "I remember. Obsessed with his bowel movements; he couldn't start work until he'd had a good shit and then described his output in nauseating detail. Some people read the runes, others read tea leaves, but Terry predicted the future based on the texture, color, and shape of his bowel movements."

"And the contents of today's mustache would form the topic of tomorrow's bowel movements." She grimaced. "If you've got the stomach for it, he's probably the one to ask first."

Boniface pulled out his phone and checked the time. "He's a photographer; he won't be up yet. But that's a good idea—I'll go and see him this afternoon."

"My pleasure," said Veronica. "I'm just pleased to have a chat that doesn't end with you asking me to dig through our archives."

"Ah," said Boniface. "Now that you mention it, since we're talking about pre-internet history, dinosaurs, and all that, could you have a quick look and see if you can find anything about this Billy Watkins guy? See if there are any links to Dawn?"

twelve

Boniface left Veronica and walked down Shaftesbury Avenue, the main artery of London's theater district and the fastest route to find another person who was there when the dinosaurs were wondering about their continued evolution.

Gray had been pretty dismissive about Kit, but then he would be—Kit was the singer who had filled Gray's place and helped Danny when Prickle made good on their contracts after Gray walked.

Kit had a very powerful, almost operatic voice, but he didn't last long in the band—only about a year. There were no albums released with him performing, but there were a few TV shows and live performances that had been uploaded to YouTube. "Funny thing," Danny had said to Boniface as they chatted outside the Royal Albert Hall the previous day. "Kit was the first guy to sing 'Tattoo Your Name on My Heart'. We nearly recorded it with him, but when he told us that he wanted out, we felt it better to get the new guy in who could tour with us in support of the album he sung on. That new guy was Thad, so it turned out good for all of us. And Kit was there when it mattered—he was always honest with us, and we've stayed great mates."

According to Danny, Kit loved the performance side of being in the band but hated everything else—in particular, he hated being in a band that was constantly on the road. The touring fatigued, and so he quit. Instead of being in a band, he went on to perform on the West End stage, becoming one of the leading stars of musical theater.

Boniface reached the theater, named after a long-dead English actor, and a mirror image of the theater at the other end of the block. What had once been white stone faced onto Shaftesbury Avenue. Posters advertised the show and highlighted its star: Kit Flambeau. The name Christopher Edington, which his birth certificate still showed, was an otherwise forgotten memory following a suggestion by Danny when he felt the band wanted to reflect that their new singer had more fire than the last guy.

Boniface turned right, following the side street on the edge of the theater. Immediately the change was visible. No longer stone-fronted, the side and rear elevations of the theater were red brick with yellow painted concrete details around the doors and windows.

The street had also changed. He had left the bustle of the tourist trap and was now heading into the seedier side of Soho, at the seedier end of Soho, knowing that if he kept walking he would find the building that had housed London's first strip bar offering full-frontal nudity. Now this area was a magnet for low-rent brothels populated by trafficked hookers, sleazy strip clubs, and money exchanges. It was a strange convergence, but thinking about it, both areas probably attracted tourists equally.

Boniface turned right again to find the theater's stage door—a black lump of wood that was intended more as a fire exit than as an entrance for stars. He grabbed the scuffed steel knob and heaved the door, stepping into the gloom lit dimly by an exposed incandescent bulb.

"I'm sorry, sir," said a voice to his right. "The box office is at the front." Boniface looked to the voice: A small man with loose gray skin that had lost its elasticity, wearing a white shirt with small straps on the shoulders to affix epaulettes, dropped his newspaper next to a cap on the shelf beside him. He stood from his stool, as if this added authority to his implied instruction.

"Oh, hi," said Boniface. "I was wondering what time Kit Flambeau arrives."

"He's not here, sir," said the gray-faced man.

"I get that," said Boniface. "It's 10:30 in the morning, and the performance isn't until 7:30 this evening. What I want to know is when he arrives."

"He arrives when he arrives, sir." The guard was apparently being polite—he was certainly using the words a polite person would use—but he seemed unable to care about Boniface's question.

"Okay, thank you," said Boniface and turned, pushing the fire door to leave.

As he heard the door being yanked shut behind him, Boniface felt the stab of his eyes adjusting too quickly to the daylight and became aware of the noise of the city: people shouting, bicycle couriers blowing their whistles, black cabs driving past, construction workers thrashing masonry with mechanical tools, and a van with the word Gas on the side beeping every four seconds for no apparent reason.

He stood with his back to the door, letting his vision track along the stores with a view of the stage door: a Lebanese restaurant, a money broker, a convenience store, a euphemistically named massage parlor with a minicab office above, a betting shop, and directly opposite a bar with a sign advertising its suitability as a place for users of a high-profile gay hookup phone app to meet.

There seemed only one sensible choice, and he set off for the convenience store.

"Hi, how are you?" he said to the Indian-looking man behind the counter just inside the door, the whiff of burning incense filling his nostrils.

"Good morning you, sir," replied the man, his white-toothed grin like a beacon in the gloomy store.

"It's a lovely day, isn't it?" said Boniface.

"Good morning you, sir," said the other man. Boniface was sure the thick accent was Indian.

"It feels like spring," said Boniface.

The other man continued to smile broadly, nodding vigorously. "Good morning you, sir."

Boniface paused. "I wonder if you can help me?"

"You want newspaper?" asked the other man.

Boniface shook his head.

"Cigarette?"

"No. Thank you, no," said Boniface.

"Whisky?"

Boniface laughed, shaking his head.

The other man kept his head still, his eyes moving from left to right, exposing eyeballs bloodshot at their extremes before he ducked under the counter, returning a few seconds later. "Girlie girls?" He held up a magazine.

Boniface shook his head once, and the other man ducked back under the counter, returning a moment later. "Asian?" He held up a magazine with a naked Japanese-looking girl who appeared to be no more than twelve. Boniface felt a sickening feeling in his gut and pulled a sour face.

The man ducked again, coming up with another magazine. "Granny?" he asked, holding up a magazine picturing a thirty-something woman with sticky fluid around her mouth, the number 69 prominently emblazoned in the top-right corner of the magazine.

"I don't think it means that...oh never mind..." said Boniface.

The shopkeeper dropped the magazine to the floor and began flicking through the next in his stack. "Big girl?" He found the page he was looking for and turned the spread for Boniface to see. "Big girl," he said with some pride, puffing out his cheeks.

Boniface slowly shook his head. A look of shock started to cross the other man's face, and he ducked back under the counter. There was some rustling, and he returned. "Poo poo wee wee?"

Boniface shut his eyes, slowly shaking his head. He opened his eyes, pointed at the stack of magazines that had accumulated on the counter, and waved a finger over them while shaking his head.

There was the sound of plastic strips lightly slapping together and shuffling feet. A slightly older man, also Indian-looking, with the addition of a thick black mustache, came. "Good morning, sir."

"Morning," said Boniface, feeling slightly weary. "I wonder..." he addressed the man with the mustache directly.

"Yes sir, how can I help?"

Inside Boniface felt relief. He wasn't sure how he would mime this question to the first man, charming as he may have been apart from his interest in selling a wide variety of pornography. "The theater across the road—you can see the stage door."

"That is correct, sir," said the second man, grinning broadly like the first.

"So you see when the cast arrive? At least, you must notice when the big star arrives—there must be a crowd of autograph hunters, people wanting their picture taken with him..."

The man with the mustache nodded. "Oh yes, sir."

"What time does he turn up?" asked Boniface.

"Four o'clock, sir." His head kept nodding. "Lots of people."

"That's great—that's all I need to know," said Boniface, leaving the store and pulling out his phone. On the third ring it answered. "Could you set me up to write a piece about the theater?"

thirteen

The street was becoming familiar. This was Boniface's third visit in just over twenty-four hours.

The brick-built terraces lining each side of the street were unchanging, but this wasn't surprising. Little around here had changed for the last 150 years, and as he turned the corner onto Gray's street, Boniface expected Gray to be similarly unchanged.

He rapped his knuckles on the peeling sky-blue paint and listened.

Silence.

He balled a fist and beat the door three times. At times like this, he would like Mel Grant with him to do some serious hitting. There was a voice inside, muffled. Boniface remembered how long it took Gray to answer the door the day before and waited, expecting to see the no-longer-white toweling robe shortly.

Footsteps came down the stairs, and someone cursed under his breath as he fought with the door. There was Gray, looking like he did when he first answered the door yesterday. "Can't you just piss off, Boniface? I told you yesterday I'm not that sort of girl—I'm not going to sleep with you."

Boniface tried to keep his face straight but failed. "Can I come in?"

"No." Gray didn't even consider the question. "I've got my reputation to think about. What would the neighbors say? Imagine what would happen if I die in a car crash tonight—they'll say 'he would get friendly with anyone in a suit,' and I'm not having that."

"Yesterday's offer of breakfast still stands."

Gray wrinkled his nose, seemingly unconvinced but willing to be persuaded.

"Come on," said Boniface. "Come and have breakfast."

"Nah," said Gray. "What do you want?"

Boniface accepted defeat and moved to the right of the door, leaning on the front of the house so he could see the other man while he half-hid behind the door. "Something you said yesterday..."

"You mean when what's-her-name was here?"

"Montbretia."

"Yeah, Monty. Where is she?"

"Back at the office, working."

"Shame."

"You mentioned the kid. Billy Watkins."

Gray remained silent; his body language stayed quiet, too.

"Who is he?" asked Boniface, letting his gaze follow the line of the street and focus in the distance.

"Just some kid at the place I play poker."

"You any good?"

"What?" asked Gray.

"Poker? Do you win?"

"I'm on a streak I don't want to be on at the moment." Gray seemed to have offered more than he wanted.

"Perhaps get another game," said Boniface.

"I've got to win back what I owe here first."

"Gotcha," said Boniface. "So where is your game?"

"Haggerston," offered Gray.

"Yeah, yeah, yeah, Haggerston," said Boniface. "Is that the one by the…" he moved his hand as if drawing a straight line on a piece of paper in front of him. "Next to the…" he horizontally cut the air with four ascending cuts. "With the…" he twirled his finger in front of him. "You know, that one."

"If you mean is it the one next to the Halal butcher and the dog-grooming parlor, then yes."

"So this kid Billy, he's at the poker place in Haggerston. Does he play?"

"No." Gray was slightly incredulous. "No. He's like a junkie begging cash. I'm not sure why Ernie tolerates him."

"Oh, it's Ernie's place—why didn't you say?" said Boniface. He moved on before his bluff was called. "So what's Billy's beef with Prickle?"

"Dunno." Boniface waited. Finally, Gray relented. "He knows I used to be in Prickle, he knows big-tits Dawn is married to Danny, he thinks she's a whore. I mean, we're all whores—we all do stuff for money, he's doing stuff to buy drugs—but he seems to have a real problem with Dawn."

He stopped, seemingly having given up all he knew.

"Do I need to talk to him?" asked Boniface.

"What? Because he said something nasty about your new mate Danny? Or have you got the hots for Dawn?"

It was the second time Boniface had been asked that question that morning. It was becoming uncomfortable. He kept his voice soft. "I just wondered whether there's an angle for the biography. You know, I wondered whether he's significant."

Gray snorted. "He just a junkie kid, Boniface. Leave him alone. And leave the biography alone—I mean, who actually cares about the pricks? And now, if you'll excuse me…" He snorted. "Whether you excuse me or not, I'm going back to bed, but before I go, one request: Please don't wake me up tomorrow. In fact, I really don't think I need to see you again."

fourteen

When Boniface implied to Gray that he knew Haggerston, technically that was what people called "a lie."

Of course, he knew *of* Haggerston, but as far as Boniface could recall, having lived in London for his whole life, he had never been to Haggerston.

And he didn't have a clue who this Ernie guy was, but he was grateful for the information from Gray.

When he got to the end of Gray's street, he called up the map on his phone and found where the top end of Bethnal Green meets the bottom of Haggerston. He searched on Google for a Halal butcher in Haggerston, found one—actually, found several, but started with the one with several good reviews—and checked back to the street view. Sure enough, there was a dog-grooming parlor in the same row. He set the map to navigate and started walking. Expected distance: 0.8 miles. Expected time: 16 minutes.

The farther he walked from Gray's house, the farther into the sprawling mass of urban north London he walked. The less it appealed, the faster he walked, arriving in well under 16 minutes.

Boniface looked at the row. As Gray and his map had suggested, there was a Halal butcher. Looking through the window, there was a butcher dressed in a white coat and white hat who seemed to be concentrating on turning a large piece of meat into many smaller pieces with the assistance of a big blade.

Next to the butcher was a black wooden double gate giving access to an arch under a building. Then came the dog-grooming parlor that Gray mentioned, which seemed to be more of a general pet shop that also groomed dogs—whatever the case, it didn't look like an enticing place to take a prize pooch.

After the pet shop, there was a Chinese takeaway, presently closed, although whether it was permanently closed or due to reopen later in the evening was unclear. Lastly, there was a convenience store that seemed to specialize in toilet paper, cigarettes, and alcohol. Above this, there was the sign for a cab firm.

Nowhere looked like a gambling den run by someone called Ernie.

There were few enough people on the streets. None looked like they could be the "junkie kid" Billy.

Boniface played Eeny, Meeny, Miny, Moe and decided to start with the Halal butcher.

He was struck by how clean the butcher's shop was, how organized it felt. The man in the white coat and hat was still concentrating on the piece of meat, but it was much smaller than when Boniface had first seen it.

"How can I help you, sir?" The butcher put down a cleaver as he turned to face Boniface.

Boniface paused, not certain how to preface his question. "Do you know a kid called Billy who hangs around this area?"

Boniface thought he saw the butcher's eyes flick to his knives. "Billy? Billy who? Is he a customer?"

"I don't know," said Boniface. "I was told he hangs out at the...club...the gambling...and wondered if you might..."

Unlike Gray, the butcher didn't seem keen to want to fill in any gaps Boniface was leaving.

"You know, the club?" Boniface asked.

"If you're asking me about gambling, then you may have some misunderstanding about my faith, sir."

Boniface flushed. "Sorry—I'm not looking to gamble myself, I'm looking for someone who does. I'm trying to..." Boniface held his hands as if gripping a steering wheel and bearing left, "guide him away from gambling. Do you know the place?"

"As I said, sir, my religion."

"Thanks anyway," said Boniface as he left, heading down the street.

The pet shop/grooming parlor had a sign saying "gone for lunch, back at 2." The Chinese takeaway had a stack of flyers for other restaurants piled with the mail inside the door—it looked like more than a few days' worth of mail.

Boniface took a look at the convenience store and, remembering his last experience with a similar store across from the theater a few hours earlier, decided to check out the cab office first. Continuing around the corner, he found seven cars parked at varying angles and at different distances from the curb, all Japanese or Korean in origin, all a shade of brown, all with plates noting they were more than fifteen years old, all with a Christmas tree air freshener hanging from the rearview mirror—apart from the car that lacked such a mirror—and all showing dents, scratches, and bad repairs.

There was an open door that looked like the door you would find on a cheap residential property thirty years ago—brown wood, with a semicircular arc of glass at the top. From the look of the door, it had been fitted thirty years ago and had not been varnished since. The door opened onto a small lobby, no more than three feet square, the walls covered with woodchip wallpaper that had been painted—but not recently, as the dirt marks showed.

Boniface looked for a sign or some directions and, finding none, allowed his eyes to follow the dirty streaks on the wall, turning right onto a staircase. Standing outside the door, he leaned forward, craning his neck into the lobby. His nose was assaulted by the odor of chemical air fresheners, takeaway food, unwashed men, and poorly maintained plumbing.

He looked from the stairs to the street and back to the stairs. It seemed fairly obvious to him that—lacking any other handrail along the stairs—as people came down the stairs, they would slow themselves on the wall, and no one had ever bothered to clean where everyone steadied themselves.

Boniface pulled his head out of the lobby, took a deep breath of clean air, and stepped in, following the stairs to the top, where they turned awkwardly into a long, thin room. The blinds—probably the same vintage as the front door—were closed, but through the broken slats, sufficient light fought its way into the building. But it seemed that when it got there, the light became disheartened and died of disappointment, leaving all of the surfaces a murky, indistinct purple/brown color.

He took a moment to try to understand the architecture. He guessed this had probably once been an apartment or the upper floor of a house, but someone had seemingly adapted it to be the cab office. What he guessed had been the front room had the wall between it and the corridor at the top of the stairs removed. Clearly the wall had been structural, so it had been replaced by a beam to hold the roof.

On the far wall, across from a low table that was probably even older than the front door, was a row of chairs—the sort of chairs you would have found in a doctor's waiting room in the 1970s: square seats, thinly padded, covered in dull green vinyl, and interlinking with the seats to either side. The seats were worn, with the fire-hazard foam stuffing coming through the tears.

Boniface couldn't see all of the seats—three were occupied. Each occupant looked similar but with minor variations: small, dark-skinned, unwashed hair, thin nylon jacket, indistinct trouser color matching the wall coverings. They talked in a low but fast babble in a language Boniface didn't understand.

"Hi," said Boniface. The man on the right looked up—the other two continued talking. The man said something. Boniface wasn't sure whether he was talking to him or continuing his conversation with the other two.

"English?" asked Boniface.

The man lowered his head and began to engage with his compatriots.

Boniface looked at the wall separating the front and the back room, where a large window had been inserted. On the other side sat a man who looked similar to the three in front of Boniface—he held a microphone and was also talking in a language that Boniface didn't recognize. However, where theirs was a low, constant babble, this man was talking more forcefully—it sounded like he was angry.

The man put the microphone down. "English?" said Boniface, looking through the glass between the notes and postcards pasted on the other side. The man shrugged and looked down at the desk in front of him.

A phone rang. The man behind the glass reached out his hand and put a receiver to his ear. "Haggerston Cabs. Where do you want to go?" he said in a thickly accented voice, looking away when he caught Boniface's eye.

As the call continued, Boniface surveyed the structure. Where the front room had suffered a merger with the passageway, the back room, even with its window into the front space, still retained its separation and was accessed through a doorway from what remained of the passageway. Boniface walked to the door and waited for the call to end.

He felt his nose burn slightly. There had been an unpleasant smell when he first stepped in, but he had acclimatized to that. However, there was something more here—chemicals singeing the hairs in his nostrils. He turned his head to the bathroom with its door perpendicular to the back room.

The bathroom suite was the kind of pink that was only available in the 1970s—or the decade that taste forgot, as most people tended to think of it. There was a bath stacked with boxes, a sink with dust that Boniface could see from where he stood, and a toilet—with a white plastic seat that had yellowed. The yellow clashed with the pink. The floor in front of the lavatory pan looked as if there was a plumbing leak. At least that's what Boniface hoped the source was.

The phone clicked, and Boniface spun to face the controller. He seemed better fed than the other men and had washed his hair more recently. "Where's the poker club?"

"No poker club here." The voice was accented but softer than Boniface had expected.

"Sure, but where? It's up here somewhere." Boniface let his hand drift to point in the general direction of the street.

"No."

"How long since you had your last tax audit?" It was an immutable law that any business where most of the income came in cash would be twitchy about their taxes. Even the most honorable of businesses—and Boniface suspected this business might not fall into that category—would be wary of officers of Her Majesty's Revenue and Customs banging at the door. Even if they had done nothing wrong, there's always a room for error, interpretation, and huge amounts of time to be wasted.

"It's a bad place." Boniface was disappointed that the only card he could play hadn't elicited more, and he waited for elaboration. "Very bad place," continued the other man.

fifteen

Boniface had seen the black gates as he passed. He had assumed they were something to do with either the Halal butcher or the pet shop, which was still closed for lunch. But according to the controller in the cab office, this was where the poker club was.

And that was the limit of the information Boniface could force out of the other man, apart from being told again that it was a very bad place. It might be bad, but it wasn't as if Boniface wanted a game.

While not particularly well maintained, the wooden gates filling the arch had a certain look of solidity to them. Boniface pushed lightly; they moved but were clearly locked. He tried the wicket gate—the door cut into the right gate. Applying the same pressure he had applied to the main gate, he found that the wicket gate swung easily with a smooth swish of the hinge.

Careful to lift his foot and duck his head as he passed through the gate within a gate, Boniface found himself under the arch—a tunnel formed from the red-brick wall of the butcher and red-brick wall of the pet shop, and the roof from the floor above that joined the buildings. He felt his foot twist and looked down to find cobbles giving an uneven path leading out to a small courtyard with two figures: One had noticed him.

Boniface found his footing and proceeded through the tunnel—keeping to the right to avoid a stack of paint tins, dust sheets, and a stepladder against the pet shop wall—and walked out onto the small courtyard, a neat cobbled square open to the sky and extending behind the pet shop and the butcher shop with an iron rail guarding a concrete staircase leading under the back of the butcher's building. Two large wooden beer barrels stood outside a closed glass-paneled door, obscured by a curtain on the inside.

Now that he was closer, the two figures seemed bigger.

The guy on the left, maybe in his thirties, was slim and about the same height as Boniface, with black lace-up boots under his frayed, dirty jeans and a sleeveless denim jacket covering a shapeless bottle-green sweater. His hair was raven black—the sort of raven that finds a way to create his own dye, probably to cover another color failure—and his face scarred from acne that still exploded across his cheek. He drew heavily on a roll-up, pulling his lips around the cigarette before forcing the air out of his lungs.

He didn't move to look in Boniface's direction.

The other guy did.

As Boniface looked at the dark skin, he could see a young Mel Grant. He had the same basic bone mass and potential for muscle as the drummer—if he spent five hours every day hitting things—but at the moment, he looked less fit. However, Boniface didn't feel the need to test the streetfighting readiness of the teenager who was letting his stare silently judge Boniface.

"Hey," said Boniface, feeling slightly uneasy.

The black teen raised his eyebrows. He may have been the younger of the two standing outside the door, but he seemed to be the guardian.

Boniface weighed up which name to throw. "Billy mentioned I might be able to get a game."

The teen's eyes opened slightly, questioning. "Billy?" From the accent, this guy could definitely be Mel's son—or a cousin born a few streets away in South London.

He looked toward the white guy, still sucking on his roll-up, then back to Boniface. "I'm sorry, sir, there must be some mistake." He stood and as Boniface looked up, recognizing a figure as big as Mel Grant's, he understood the conversation was over.

"My mistake. Sorry for the intrusion." He took two steps into the tunnel, then turned, reaching into the top pocket of his jacket. "If Billy does turn up..." he walked toward the large black youth, holding his out his business card, "perhaps you could get him to call me. He won't be disappointed."

sixteen

Boniface wasn't quite sure what he had been expecting when he found that Terry Meyerson had a studio in Camden.

The word "studio" can be interpreted in so many ways, and Camden means different things to different people. To some, Camden means TV studios, internationally renowned markets, a range of hip gig venues, and a strong connection with the alternative culture.

To others, it's another part of London that you never want to go near.

Boniface wasn't surprised to find that Meyerson's studio wasn't in Camden Town, but instead was within the municipal borough, and so qualified as being in Camden on a technicality. The surrounding light industrial units suggested there would be a reasonable-sized studio but that it wouldn't likely be a high-end establishment.

A cheap but rust-proof plastic sign directed Boniface between two buildings—each lightweight corrugated steel. Up two concrete steps, the front doors were aluminum-framed with glass panels—two doors that met in the middle badly. Boniface looked at the doorbell with another plastic sign—"Please ring"—then back to the right door, which had not fully shut.

He pushed. It opened. He stepped in, letting the door fall behind him.

The lobby had the feel that it had been left by the previous resident. The blue nylon carpet tiles showed the trail of passing footsteps, and the Blu-tack on the wall reflected the extent of posters that had once hung. Now, the Blu-tack demarcated the limits of the less faded areas. And the desk at the front showed four corner holes around a similarly lighter-shaded oblong where a previous occupant's nameplate had been removed.

And the previous occupant's receptionist had also since departed. The dusty detritus left on the desk suggested no replacement.

There were two doors at the other side of the lobby. One led down a white painted concrete-block corridor, lit with a buzzing strip light. The other didn't. Boniface turned his head down the open corridor and, seeing only more blue nylon carpet tiles, returned to the other door, which he pulled gently, finding a small well on the side of a larger room. A male and a female voice were audible from within the main room.

Cautiously, Boniface stepped into the large room with a high ceiling, finding himself reminded of a school gymnasium without the wooden floor. At the far end was a white screen pulled from a roll at ceiling height and turned through 90 degrees as it met the floor. Two banks of lights focused toward the white strip, as did two space heaters. A fat man stood in the center behind a camera on a tripod at eye level, and a woman stood a quarter-turn further around, with a makeup brush in her hand.

Boniface felt his foot scrape against the floor.

The woman gasped, dropped her powder brush, and ran toward the door Boniface had just entered through, her heels clipping as she passed. The photographer slowly winched himself to an erect position and turned through 180 degrees as he walked backward in a small arc to reveal another woman—naked from the waist up, and if

Boniface was being honest, somewhat chubby—who let out a small yelp and crossed her arms over her chest, her eyes darting as if searching for somewhere to hide.

The photographer turned back to the model. Boniface could hear his low mumblings and attempts at reassurance as the chubby girl blushed. It took a few moments, but she was soon nodding with more certainty, although her arms remained firmly fixed across her chest.

He turned to Boniface as the makeup artist returned and, seeing the distress of the model, ran a few steps to her, turning to the photographer as she passed. "I'm sorry about that—the door's locked now."

"Didn't you used to be Alexander Boniface? Last I heard you melted down..." The belly was fatter than last time—the shirt no longer had any chance of circumnavigating the girth and reaching the top of his trousers, and the mustache had lost color and shape, but this was Terry Meyerson. As he stepped forward, Boniface could see that the other man had eaten a burger at lunch. "Terry," he said holding out his hand. "Good to see you." He flicked his eyes to the model who, helped by the makeup artist, was slipping on a blouse. "Can we have a quick chat?"

The fat man flicked his head up, pointing to the door through which Boniface had entered, and ushered him through the lobby, down the strip-lighted corridor, and into a side office. Like the corridor, the walls were whitewashed concrete block, but with a row of framed photos on each side.

Boniface glanced. He recognized some of the shots—some of the most iconic images that had accompanied the news over the last thirty years: a policeman dying in the streets, having been attacked when he tried to save a five-year-old who got caught in a riot; three grandmothers with tears in their eyes as Princess Diana's gun carriage passed; sportsmen—the England cricket team, Boniface thought—being driven around London in an open-topped bus. "Are these yours?"

"Mmm." His face softened. "I've been around for a long time, Boniface—if you wait long enough, you get lucky."

"These are good pictures. Really good pictures," said Boniface straightening. "I was..."

The fat man cut Boniface off. "I'm sorry—this girl's already paid, and she's on her lunch hour. She's got to go back to the office and tell them she went shopping." He raised eyebrows, shaking his head with a look of amusement. "Give me ten minutes to finish this thing, and then I'll be with you."

He reached the door and turned back. "There's a bottle of scotch in the desk drawer—help yourself."

seventeen

"What did he look like?"

Ernie Norton sat back in his vintage desk chair—deep green buttoned leather over dark wood—listening to the spindle squeak as he coaxed his chair from left to right, then rolled it back and kicked his feet on his desk as the seat slowly tipped.

"He wasn't a gambler," said Jojo. The big black teenager dressed in combat pants and a sweatshirt was thinking.

Jojo Brooks was young, and like many kids from what sociologists laughingly liked to call the wrong side of the tracks, he had no fear about using violence. But unlike his contemporaries, somewhere down the line Jojo had learned about consequences—this made him cautious. He didn't lose his bravery, but he thought ahead, which meant he didn't cause trouble except when he wanted to and when he was content to accept the consequences.

And he wasn't one for bravado. Where most teens brag—and brag about things they don't understand—Jojo listened. When confronted, he shut up and waited for the other guy to talk first. More often than not, the other guy found this intimidating—and it was—but in truth, Jojo wasn't trying to intimidate, but rather to find out.

"What does a gambler look like, Jo?"

Jojo paused, weighing the question. "There are two types of gamblers who turn up here, Mister Norton."

He was respectful too, thought Ernie, and he liked that.

"The first sort of gambler is the professional. The guy tries to do this for a living. They've got their whole story settled—they do whatever they need to do to look cool. It's like their heads aren't attached to their body."

"Huh?"

"Below the neck," continued Jojo, "they're still. There's no heartbeat. No movement. From the neck up, everything moves like when they show a bullet fired in the movies. It's all in slow motion. The neck moves slowly. The eyes move like they're on drugs."

"Like a swan, but in reverse," offered Iain Irvine, sitting in the corner behind Jojo, his high forehead in front of his slicked-back thinning gray hair reflecting the few beams of light that had got into the room, casting the contours of his face into deeper contrast.

"Nah, man," said Jojo. "They don't fly and crap on your head." He laughed with Irvine, then turned back to Ernie. "Swans have their legs going like this." He rapidly dog-paddled with his hands. "These guys are slow and dead."

"The others," said Ernie, tugging on his collar.

"The chancers. They're all swagger. They try to look like the big man—walk up all confident, like they've just ridden into town." He patted his shoulders firmly. "It's the shoulders and the hips that give it away. They put one shoulder forward and drop the other hip." He looked to Iain Irvine and carried on explaining. "It's like a chick, but a chick stands up straighter so her bum wiggles and her tits stick out further. And girls have shorter steps—these blokes stride."

Ernie dropped his feet to the floor, feeling the moment of the upward tilt push his body forward. He stopped its movement by resting his elbows on his legs. Clasping his hands together, he looked over his desk at the big teenager. "So this guy? This..." he looked at the business card on his desk, lit from the brass banker's desk lamp with the green shade. "This Boniface?"

"He just walked. Like a normal person. He had a suit; it was like he was going to the office."

"Maybe he works in an office?"

"No. It was his eyes. He was looking everywhere—it was like he was trying to take in every detail. He wasn't playing the big man." He paused. "It was like he was sizing the place up for a job."

"And what did he say?"

"Billy said I could get a game." He looked up. "Something like that. Definitely 'Billy.' Definitely 'get a game.'"

"And Billy was there?"

"Standing right beside me."

"Did Boniface recognize Billy?"

"No."

"Did Billy recognize Boniface?"

"Said he'd never heard of him."

"So this guy, Boniface, says 'Billy says I can get a game,'" said Ernie. "What did you say?"

"I'm sorry, sir; there must be some mistake."

"You didn't ask him anything?"

"Didn't want to give him a hint about anything."

"Smart." Ernie sat straighter and sniffed. "How did it end?"

"He said 'sorry to disturb you' or something like that and walked away. Then he turned back and gave me his card and said if Billy turns up, he won't be disappointed."

"What does that mean?" He looked around Jojo to the third man. "Do you know, Irv?" The two were silent, but he could hear them shifting slightly. "And how did Billy react to this?"

"You know Billy; he's a junkie. His eyes flashed, but this Boni-whatever-his-name-is didn't see. I told Billy it was nothing, and he went off looking for a score."

"Have you called the number here, Irv?" Ernie tapped his finger firmly on the card, the knock echoing in the darkened room.

"Yup." Iain Irvine stood up. Cypriot born to Scottish parents, he had a love of the sun, and when he couldn't return to the land of his birth, he worshiped sunbeds. His double-breasted light-gray suit with a heavy stripe showed a slim figure, and even in the low light, his white shirt contrasted against his tanned hide mottled with age spots. "They do PR. That's what the American girl I spoke with said. Boniface wasn't there—she could get him to call when he gets back if I wanted." He shrugged. "They usually get business by personal referrals, apparently."

Ernie sucked air through his teeth.

"It seemed like a lot of work and a lot of detail for a fake number, but I'll check them out on the internet tomorrow when I release my next torrent of shit about Danny and Dawn."

"But it still doesn't answer the question, does it?"

Jojo Brooks and Iain Irvine glanced at each other, then returned their focus to their principal. "Who knows about Billy? Who told this Boniface about Billy?"

The two seemed to relax.

"And my question is, has our little songbird been singing? I should probably ask him."

He looked at Jojo. "Just a hunch, but if this Boniface returns, I want a word with him. A *word*."

eighteen

"I'm sorry. It took longer to get her settled than I thought."

"Not a problem," said Boniface, sitting in the chair behind the desk. "She's not your usual subject." He indicated the walls, and a few prints he had found on the desk that he looked at while he waited.

"Unfortunately, increasingly this is what I'm doing," said Meyerson. "The world of the smudger has changed. Hell, we're not even called smudgers anymore, are we? There's that new breed: the paparazzi." He paused. "But you can't just blame those guys. It was coming—the paper got rid of the staff photographers, I got older and fatter, we went digital...it all changed."

He dropped onto a lime-green hessian-covered sofa. "I guess the biggest thing was that I didn't have the energy to keep getting up early and working late. So I started doing more studio work, and now you see my empire." He made a sweeping gesture. "In many ways it's better—I've got a lot of sources of income. I do a bit of teaching—you know, spend five hours in a professional studio with a pro photographer and a model—I've been digitizing my old archive, and a lot of that's now available through the photo libraries...."

"Good income?" asked Boniface.

"Not really." He stopped. "Well...it's not good if you compare it to what I might get paid for a day's freelance work. But if you think that it's a photo I shot thirty years ago that is still bringing in income when I'm asleep, then it's bloody good money! And it's consistent—it's a small amount every month, which balances out one of the other things I do: portfolio building."

Boniface frowned.

"Like the one that gave you an eyeful."

"My eyes aren't that great, Terry, but all I saw was an embarrassed chubby girl—and not chubby in a good way."

The photographer sighed loudly. "They come here thinking if they get their gozangas out, that's the way to change their life. They figure all they need is a portfolio, and the phone will start ringing. They dream they'll be rolling in dosh by summer." He dropped his voice. "Take that one out there. She's twenty-three and has decided her life is shit—she didn't work at school, and now she's in a dead-end secretarial job. The trouble is she's got too much facial hair, doesn't have a personality, and the body's gone, if it was ever there. There are girls of eighteen who are far better—and she's got the damage from an extra five years of bad diet, lots of drinking, and not looking after herself."

Boniface stared at the fat man.

He held up a hand. "Guilty as charged. I am living proof of how bad living robs you of your model-like figure. I tell you, put me on lettuce leaves for a week, and I look like Cindy Crawford."

Boniface raised his eyebrows, questioning. "Does shooting portfolios for these wannabes make money for you?"

The fat man snorted and his mustache wobbled. "It's break-even paywise, but some of them are useful if I need a model for the photography days here. Where I make the cash is on the occasional referral to agencies. I tip 'em the wink if I see a good one, and they slip me a few notes." He shrugged. "Supply and demand. In the old days, before silicon, the girls who could supply more were always in demand. But now, what they want in the business is really simple—a natural girl in front of the camera. Pretty, but not too pretty. Can't look too sexually aggressive. If I find one of those and make the referral, then it's pay day for me. Double if she actually signs up."

Meyerson stopped talking, seemingly thinking about how much he might get paid for his next referral.

"So baby-face Al is all big and grown up, and now calls himself Boniface. You got—not famous—what's the word…? Renowned. Notorious? What happened?"

"I got drunk. I embarrassed people. I went to work with Gideon Latymer handling press for the Department of the Environment. I got drunk. I embarrassed people. My marriage ended."

"I'm sorry. Vron was such a sweet girl," said Meyerson, with a note of regret that sounded sincere.

"Yeah. It's a tough one—but we're still on good terms. It was her who suggested I chat to you. You probably heard that after the marriage ended, there was that whole damaging-a-tree-with-a-car-while-drunk thing and the meltdown, so now I'm on my own."

"I heard some of it," said the fat man. "But it seemed pretty tame stuff in comparison with what we got up to in the seventies." Boniface was sure he pulled in his stomach before he asked his next question. "You said Veronica suggested me?"

There was hope in the question.

"I'm chasing something from the past," said Boniface. "I'm doing a biography—it's a bit of a labor of love, and I need some background." He paused, waiting until he was sure Meyerson was listening. "Do you remember Dawn Featherstone—Dawn Vickery, as she was then—and the group M-Stub8?"

A look slowly spread across the fat man's face, morphing into relaxed tranquility. "Dawn Vickery. The last of the torpedo-tit girls." His eyes were closed. "I remember Dawn. I photographed her—I've probably got those pictures sitting waiting to be digitized."

Boniface waited—he didn't want to think what was passing through Meyerson's mind.

"What can you tell me about the band?"

Meyerson seemed lost—floating in a bubble of bliss.

"And do you know where any of them are?"

Meyerson opened his eyes slowly, moving as if he were coming around from a general anesthetic. "What can I tell you? There were four girls; it ended badly."

"Tell me what you know," said Boniface.

"There were four of them—they all started off being photographed for the papers, and someone thought it would be a good idea to make them put on clothes and sing. It was just a racket—the rumor was they got session singers in and mimed the live performances." He shrugged. "Anyway, there was Dawn. She was the pretty blonde with…" He held his hands in front of him. "She was the one the men chased, but she was always…reticent."

"About men?"

"No. In general. She always stepped back." He looked up, a look of enthusiasm on his face. "I'd love to shoot her again. You know, I could do a then-and-now spread. Properly lit—really tasteful and arty."

He was lost again, his eyes defocused.

"Lorna. She was a sweet girl.... Such a pity about her death—that was what finally ended the band. Then there was Carmen. She was the really wild one, the man-eater, but she's probably drugged out of existence now. I heard she had been doing really filthy porn—you know, where they actually hurt the girl. Proper hurt, not acting hurt. But that was just a rumor, so don't quote me."

"I won't," said Boniface.

"And last there was Jilly. Jilly with the wonky headlights." He held his hands in front of him, then raised one and lowered the other. "You never could shoot her head on—the left one would be staring you in the eye while the right would look at your shoe. This was before Photoshop, of course, so you had to hoist up one side with a bit of sticky tape and shoot from an angle. Nice girl, though. Still sends me a Christmas card every year."

"Seriously," said Boniface. Meyerson nodded. "Where does she live? Have you got an address?"

The fat man levered himself to his feet and walked out of the room, turning right. Boniface could hear drawers being opened and closed, and Meyerson returned. "Leyton."

"Leyton, East London? Leyton five miles away?"

Meyerson half-smiled. "Yeah. There's the address."

Boniface stood. "Terry—it's been a pleasure. We really should get together soon."

"Don't forget, I'm always available for work—if you want me, or if Veronica ever has an assignment that could use my skills." He pointed to the pictures hanging around the walls. "I can do more than just flabby girls."

nineteen

"For crying out loud, Boniface." Veronica immediately regretted the sharpness of her tone, but from the way Boniface was loitering in the doorway—seemingly not wanting to commit to actually coming into the room and nonchalantly pretending that he was just passing—she felt justified.

Like you just pass the fifty-eighth floor in an office block. When you don't work there. When you've got no other friends in the office—and indeed, arguably, a number of enemies.

In short, he was after another favor; he knew he was chancing his luck. He knew he would get shouted at, and he knew that if he stayed by the door, he could run and avoid the conversation; but if he was sitting in front of her desk, there would be no avoiding the torrent of abuse that he knew she could heap upon him.

That's torrent of abuse as he would tell it—in reality, all he would be subject to would be a simple statement of the basic facts.

He half-stepped into the room and began, casually, as if he was mentioning the weather. "Did anything ping with Billy?"

Veronica felt a surge, an overwhelming desire to do physical harm. "Does our divorce not mean anything to you, Boniface? *Anything*?"

Boniface had the look he got when he was calculating the odds—when he was playing verbal chess, trying to figure out what he needed to say to make sure the conversation reached the point he wanted it to reach in three moves, rather than saying what he wanted to say.

Veronica knew that he knew she knew what he was doing, and given his hesitation at the door, he would be guessing that whatever he said would be criticized.

So he seemed to be choosing to do no wrong instead of trying to do right, and was waiting without replying.

Which, given how Veronica felt, was probably the right play. Boniface would never be a poker player—you could always read his tells—but he knew this, and he knew strategy, and he knew the tactics to deploy to achieve the strategy, so he didn't need to worry if people could read him.

He just needed to avoid poker players.

"I haven't had time, Boniface." She was angry that he was making her feel guilty for not having finished looking into this Billy Watkins.

Boniface had that look he got when he was about to be understanding.

"Don't tell me it's alright. Don't patronize me and say it's okay while you start feeling frustrated inside. If you want to help, tell me what I'm looking for and I'll find it. But just remember, as you said, this is before the internet age, at a time when we used—shock, horror—typewriters. Someone needs to look through files or fire up the old microfiche to find this stuff."

Boniface remained quiet.

"What's my priority here—apart from, you know, doing the job that I'm paid to do, and not abusing the resources of my employer? You know, I'm meant to be the editor of a national newspaper—the one who says yes, no, and that's a stupid idea, stop chasing it, now go and do something more productive...."

She looked around her office. Unlike her staff, who sat at their workstations in the middle of a big room, she got an office with some degree of personalization: a chair of her choosing, and not the latest in ergonomic design, which only confused her and broke her nails—no, a proper chair upholstered in leather and made for her comfort. She got a desk: not too wide—it was a charming piece of vintage cherry-wood, not some bombastic statement that was bigger than Boniface's car. She even got real plants—in this case, Japanese maples, which seemed to get exchanged every few weeks with very similar versions of the same species.

"I've got you into that theater," she said. "You've got an appointment at three-forty-five. Ask for Morag Sullivan."

"What do we know about Morag?" Boniface was keeping his tone light.

"That her name is Morag. That she was kind enough to agree to meet you this afternoon."

She looked over her gold-rimmed half-moon glasses: Boniface trembled like a scolded child. A shake of her head and she felt her auburn mane ripple. When it settled, she continued. "You do understand—you do remember, you used to work in the business—that we have deadlines here. I can't just say to my readers, 'Sorry there's no news today, I was sorting out some stuff for my former husband—here are some pictures of kittens that we grabbed off the internet instead.'"

Boniface shrugged one shoulder and muttered, "Might raise your circulation—kittens are very popular, especially cute ginger kittens."

Veronica waited for his smirk to fade. "I'll leave you to make your pitch for that new strategy to Mister Kuznetsov." She paused. "I'm sorry—my proprietor, your friend, Vanya." She continued, her voice softer, conciliatory. "How's it going? Did you see fat Terry?"

"I did, and he gave me a name and an address," said Boniface.

"Related to the theater?"

"No—it's another lead. I need to see this Morag Sullivan to get in there to see Kit Flambeau."

"But he's a musical theater guy—goes on TV when they need a rather camp but slightly vivacious guest. What's he got to do with all this?"

"He was a member of Prickle for a short time."

Veronica mouthed "oh" as Boniface continued.

"I figure he must know if there were any unresolved issues—he dealt with the aftermath of the original singer, Gray Barrington, walking away." Boniface sighed. "Danny thought...no, Danny doesn't think—Danny loves everybody. Danny wondered out loud who might be bitter and causing the problem, and Gray's name came up. I spoke to Gray, and even twenty-five years later he seems angry, and I get the impression he's got some unpleasant mates...so I'm just putting two and two together, and so far I've got thirty-eight. I'm hoping Kit can get me down to about thirty-six or thirty-five. I've just got dead-ends. All I want is some little hint."

He moved to stand outside the door but leaned in, a somewhat mournful look across his face.

"I'll call you if I find anything on this Billy," said Veronica.

Boniface mouthed the words "thank you" and was gone.

twenty

It was an odd haircut.

Rising vertically at the sides, but with tight curls on the top. And the brown-blond-silver looked dry, very dry—don't-touch dry, like twigs, kindling ready to ignite, somewhere that no bird would nest because there was no comfort.

Boniface was aware that Morag was talking, but he really hadn't been paying attention—the conundrum of the architecture of her hair needed to be resolved first.

She led him through a door—from the front of house to the back of house, public to private. He stopped thinking about the hair for long enough to take in the difference. Where the front of house was velvet-covered to the dado rail, well-tended dark wood, and soft carpet, this side was concrete, walls painted army-surplus colors with paint probably acquired as a job lot left over from the 1940s and bought on the cheap in the 1950s.

Which was probably when they bought their lightbulb. Boniface could swear there were still traces of paint on it—a wartime practice not to give the Luftwaffe any help. Post-war austerity had then dictated that the paint be scraped off rather than a new bulb purchased.

He checked the time on his phone and looked along the corridor. The fire door at the end looked familiar, as did its guardian, who didn't seem to recognize Boniface from his earlier visit.

Morag continued to talk.

Boniface wondered whether it was too soon to look at his phone again, wondered whether she might find it rude, which it would be. The door at the end of the corridor opened, and a figure entered backwards.

"Thank you, thank you. I love you all." The voice was light, affected. Some camera flashes bounced in the gloom, and as the door shut, the sound of excited voices was muted.

Morag leaned forward conspiratorially and muttered, "Kit's very theatrical."

Kit had the round face of a man who had lived the good life and had never missed a meal, and the cravat and handkerchief of a man for whom a certain panache was worn like a second skin.

"Darling Morag. How are you today?" He turned to Boniface. "I'd certainly remember you if we had met." His voice was rich, resonating, with slightly camp inflections that Boniface was sure he was effecting. "This is a very special treat you have brought, just for me. You are such a darling, Morag."

"Boniface," said Boniface. "And I was wondering if we could have a quick word before you get busy."

"Darling, Boniface. You can have a slow word." He pulled his shoulders back, forcing out his chest, fluttering his eyelashes as he looked down.

"Theatrical," mouthed Morag, giving Boniface a "told you so" look.

"Two minutes and I'll catch you," said Boniface to Morag, who looked slightly shocked as Boniface followed Kit into a room off the gloomy passage.

Boniface let his eyes take in the room. Utilitarian white paint had been uniformly applied within the last five years. The only color came from a spray of flowers where the plastic had yet to be removed and a rail of what Boniface presumed were the actor's costumes.

Kit caught Boniface's surprise. "Yes, darling. This really is what the star gets." The word "star" was laced with irony. "But it's much nicer than what the other poor souls are forced to endure."

"You're busy, so I'll get straight to the point: Prickle," said Boniface. Kit raised his eyebrows, then gave up. "I've been asked by Danny to write a biography of the band. I'm at the early research stage, and I'd like to schedule some time to sit down with you properly, but at the moment, there's something I'm missing."

Kit nodded.

"The bad blood with Gray. You were there. Beyond the obvious—Gray quit and left the band with a whole bunch of contractual engagements to fill—what happened?"

"Ah, Prickle in 1984," said Kit, the flamboyance returning. "They were the best of times. They were the worst of times."

He sighed and looked up. Suddenly, Boniface could see plain Christopher Edington talking to him. "I knew Danny was pissed at Gray, but I didn't see anything beyond that. It happened before I arrived. And to be honest, I had my own issues." His voice seemed to catch. "I was coming to terms with being gay."

"You make it sound like a bad thing."

"No, no, no," said Kit, brightening slightly. "But it's tough when you're eighteen—biology largely determines that we're brought up by heterosexuals, and no matter how loving and how supportive, heterosexuals tend to work with the basic expectation that their offspring will be...well, straight. And you're conditioned that anything not straight must be bad—queer never meant good."

The singer leaned against the dressing table as he continued. "Things were different then. When I was born, homosexuality was illegal."

Boniface felt a slight shock register over his face.

Kit continued. "Homosexuality was illegal until 1968, and after that the age of consent was twenty-one. When I joined Prickle I was eighteen, so if I wanted to be a gay man, I would have to break the law—and if you were caught you were regarded as a sexual deviant, not due any respect in the justice system."

He smirked. "It's funny looking back. A short while after I joined, Mel joined, so we had a black guy and a gay guy—we were the most politically correct band before they had even invented political correctness."

Boniface reflected on the other man's wistful recollection and tried to push the conversation back to the topic. "But was Gray mentioned?"

"The management grumbled occasionally but then decided to drop the band, so it was pretty irrelevant." He looked around as if a prompt on the floor might give him a hint. "I'm not sure what I can add—I joined when I was a kid. I was still living at home and hated being in a new place each night. We'd get to a grotty little bed-and-breakfast, and pretty much my first question would be 'where's the gay bar?' It was alright for the others, but I never found any gay groupies."

"What about Dawn?"

"I was there before Dawn." He looked at Boniface expectantly, stifling a joke. "Night. That comes before dawn, right? Seriously—she came on the scene when I was on my way out. She was lovely—if Danny had married her sooner, then I might have stayed. She was my friend—perhaps the only real friend I had—but she was damaged."

Boniface waited for elaboration, staring directly at Kit.

"Lorna. All that bad business." He shrugged. "I think Dawn was pleased to have someone who she could chat with who she knew wasn't trying to get into her knickers or exploit her." His face brightened. "I still remember when Danny first played 'Tattoo Your Name on My Heart.'"

Boniface cocked his head, silently asking for the story.

"He strummed it on that acoustic guitar he used to carry around." The thespian was lost in his memories for a moment or two. "I cried, Boniface. Big soppy tears. There's Danny—he's a very personable guy—but he's a guy. He doesn't do feelings—unless he's talking about vintage Bentleys."

Boniface waited.

"Danny had all these new songs, all these big choruses to get the audience on their feet punching the air, and 'Tattoo' had a huge chorus, but when you listen to the words, when you hear the emotion of a guy with an acoustic guitar spilling his heart—I lost it and blubbed." His voice was meek. "It's a boy telling a girl he loves her. And she believed him." His eyes misted.

Boniface watched as the other man blinked away the moisture, then straightened. "One last question. Does the name Billy Watkins mean anything to you?"

"William Watkins," said Kit. "I know lots of willies...but no William or Billy Watkins, I'm afraid."

twenty–one

Rafferty kicked his ball. Hard and without much skill, which wasn't that surprising when you are five and your football pitch is your grandmother's kitchen. That limited skill being further compromised by hyperactivity, currently provoked by the greenish-yellow sweets the man next door had given him about thirty minutes ago when he came to tell Rafferty's grandmother about his trip to Singapore, and which—unknown to Rafferty, the traveler, or the grandmother—contained quinolone yellow, or E104 as the Europeans liked to call it.

The ball knocked a vase on the window containing a single fluted daffodil, and the flower, vase, and water headed for the floor, with glass smashing and small fragments radiating like an army of dagger-wielding ants.

As the glass hit the tiled floor, two-year-old Jade, Rafferty's half-sister, screamed, then through her tears started to tell Rafferty how naughty he was. Savannah, seven months, Jade's full sister and Rafferty's half, continued crawling from the hall into the kitchen, and when Jade went to slap Rafferty for his naughtiness, got caught by her older sister's swing and started screaming too.

Jilly turned off the gas, removed the pan from the heat, and resisted the temptation to tell Rafferty that he was a little bastard. Even if he was, literally and metaphorically. That could come later—first she needed to get the kids away from the glass, and second, she needed to clean up the mess.

"Stay there!" Her voice was loud enough to give Rafferty a reason to pause, but only pause. Jilly could see his eyes focusing on the football—the football that had rolled to the other side of the room. She took three small steps and reached the siblings. With each step, she felt the grinding of glass between the floor and her slippers.

"Naughty, naughty, naughty, naughty!" Jade ensured blame continued to be ascribed to the guilty party. Savannah just kept screaming.

Jilly reached and grabbed the crawler, pulling her close and inspecting her hands for any slivers. Not seeing anything, she pulled the baby's hands over her cheek, feeling for anything more dangerous than dirt.

She looked down at the other two: "Out!" She threw her head in the direction of the hallway.

"Football, football, football." Rafferty was jumping up and down. "Football, football, football."

"Naughty, naughty, naughty, naughty!" Jade hadn't paused.

"Stop. We will have quiet in this house," said Jilly. The baby screamed. "Including you, miss," she said softly, pulling the baby closer and kissing her. "We'll feed you in a moment." She looked down at the two siblings standing in front of her: "Come on, out. It's very dangerous in here."

Rafferty moved to pass his grandmother. She held out a leg to stop him. "No, Rafferty. You two stand there," she pointed to the carpet in the hall, ending at the edging strip where the kitchen tiles began. "Come on, both of you, now."

"Can I get..." began the five-year-old boy.

"No. I'll get it for you—it's very dangerous with the glass. Now come on, both of you, onto the carpet."

Reluctantly, the two moved the short distance, turning to face into the kitchen, leaning and trying to maximize the portion of their bodies that was in the kitchen while keeping their toes behind the edging strip. "You stay there," said Jilly, feeling that it would be easier to train a sheepdog as she took a soft brush from the closet and pushed the glass fragments to the side, clearing a path for her to retrieve the ball.

She grabbed the ball and returned to the two who seemed—with the exception of their toes—to be completely in the kitchen. She shooshed them back and squatted, looking from one to the other. "It's very, very dangerous in here, so no coming in here until I've cleaned up. Alright?" Rafferty made a grab for his ball—his grandmother was faster and held it behind her, releasing the firmness of her grip on the baby to balance. "Is that clear?"

Both children nodded.

"Now, Rafferty. You can have your ball back—but no more football in the house. Alright?" The five-year-old cracked first and nodded his reluctant agreement to the deal before his grandmother returned the untethered wrecking ball. "Now, both of you go! I need to clean up."

As the kids turned, the phone rang. Jilly looked at the caller's number and sighed. "Hi babe, are you on your way?" She looked at Savannah and said, "Yes, it's your mother—she's calling me to say she's coming home soon...yes she is."

The baby gurgled as Jilly stepped into the hall, closing the door on the half-swept broken glass and other Rafferty-induced chaos that was keeping her from feeding her charges. She turned away from the closed door, passing the pictures of her children when they were young.

A lot had changed since then. The older, James, was now traveling, as they liked to call it. As far as Jilly could tell, that was a way of having an excuse for getting really drunk, taking a lot of drugs—most of which would be illegal in the UK—and, during those periods when the drugs and alcohol didn't have a detrimental effect, having a lot of sex with anyone who wouldn't say no. She looked at Savannah and frowned—some other mother would have to look after the results of their daughter's stupidity, even if her son had been equally culpable.

She and Pete, her now ex-husband, had named Kayleigh after the song. It was a favorite of both of them. She had been an incredibly cute kid, but as she grew up she found she had inherited her mother's figure, but super-charged through the growth-hormone-rich diet that everyone unwittingly ate in the 1990s when they consumed cheap TV dinners.

Kayleigh had always been popular with the boys, but it was only when she was fifteen—as Jilly held her hand in the waiting room before that first abortion—that Jilly found James had been setting her up with his friends. There seemed to have been a barter system—if you had a sister that James could have sex with, then he had a sister with a very pleasing figure who would reciprocate. Any boy who didn't treat her like a princess—albeit a tainted princess—had her big brother to answer to. As Kayleigh filled out, James's circle of friends grew, and the extended families of his friends were called to lay down their teenage women.

The first grandchild—Rafferty—came when she was 19. The father was still a matter of debate. She married before her second kid was born—but only due to an unfortunate miscarriage. That guy hung around long enough to father Jade and

Savannah, but he had left two months ago, leaving Kayleigh on her own with the three kids.

"They're running me ragged, babe," said Jilly to her daughter. "What time are you coming home?"

There was a ring at the door before Jilly could hear the answer. "Oh babe, really…" She pulled the crook of her right elbow more tightly around the baby and reached for the door with her right hand, levering it open while keeping the phone pressed against her ear with her left hand. "Babe. No. This is the third man in five days."

She paused, listening, observing the man standing outside her front door. "No babe, of course I love the kids, but they're your kids." He was dressed in a blue suit—a good suit that fit—and with a sensible haircut. He didn't look like the normal double-glazing/cavity-wall-insulation salesmen that often turned up at this time of day. "Babe, of course you're entitled to a life, but your kids need a mother." And he seemed quite happy to wait while she chatted. "That's too late, babe, what are you expecting to do—wake the kids up and take them home?"

She could hear Rafferty in the front room, or rather, she could hear his ball bouncing off the walls. Jade ran to see whether there was anything interesting at the door and stood, looking between her grandmother's legs, holding on tightly to her right leg. "Okay, babe. One drink, then get here as soon as you can."

She clicked the button to end the call and placed the receiver on a shelf under a mirror just inside the front door before turning to the man. "Hi."

"Hi—you must be Jilly? Gillian Crossley as was, now Gillian Walker."

She twitched, not knowing whether to acknowledge or deny.

Jade started rocking back and forth, knocking between her grandmother's legs with her head.

The man was relaxed, offering a door-to-door salesman's row of teeth, but something about his demeanor suggested he wasn't here to sell. "I'm glad I found the right place—Terry Meyerson gave me the address. I should introduce myself: My name's Boniface, and I've been asked to write a biography about the band Prickle. Obviously you will have known the band from your M-Stub8 days. More significantly, you will have known Dawn, who married Danny."

A football banged into the hall behind her. She ignored it, watching the man who called himself Boniface. "I was hoping you might have a bit of time when we could sit down and chat."

The football knocked the side of her head as it passed over her shoulder before leaving the house through the open door.

"Do I look like I've got time?"

Boniface stepped back, grimacing, and picked the football out of the flowerbed before rolling it past Jilly's feet to Rafferty. "Are you the next David Beckham?"

"Did you really need to do that?" Jilly's voice was a whisper. When Boniface returned a look of shock, she explained. "Now he's going to break my house even more before his mother arrives." She looked down at the baby. "Even you know that, don't you my angel?"

She talked to the baby for a moment or two, bouncing her as the infant gurgled, then looked up. "And why would I want to talk? You know the story—Dawn got away. I still see her every now and then on TV. She's done well—she lives in the country in a big house. I don't envy her the money, but it's shame she didn't reach back and help some of us she left behind. I guess she's got new friends now."

She didn't expect a response and went back to talking to the baby. When she looked up again, Boniface seemed to be waiting as if she had paused in the middle of a sentence. She elaborated. "What does Dawn tell her new friends? They're all lords and ladies in the country—hunting and fishing every weekend. Do they respect her? Or is she just tolerated, then groped by the husbands who are bored with their wives and fantasize about screwing her?"

Boniface seemed to be amused. Maybe he was humoring her. Perhaps he just didn't want to argue. "What about your time in the band?"

"There's not much to say that hasn't been said a million times. We were like sisters—it all ended the night Lorna died." She felt her bottom lip tremble. "But that's a load Dawn has to carry." Her voice trailed off. She inhaled sharply, her voice becoming steadier. "None of us knew how to deal with that pain, that guilt."

Boniface remained silent but tilted his head, raising his eyebrows expectantly.

Jilly shook her head, then blurted. "It was Dawn and Carmen—they were with Lorna. We were at a party and they went out for a smoke—I stayed back with some guy. They were playing on the bridge—Dawn wanted to dance on the balustrade and encouraged the other two to follow her. Dawn and Carmen got off, before Lorna…"

She wiped the tear from her eye.

"They called the police, the river police, everyone, but it was thirty hours before they pulled Lorna's body out of the Thames." She sniffed. "Dawn went inside herself—she couldn't talk. Carmen, she found other ways to keep blotting out the pain, and look at her now."

Jilly stared into the distance, jolting as Savannah screamed. "That's how it ended, and I haven't seen Dawn or Carmen for years. I don't think I can help you."

She shut the door on Boniface, sat at the foot of her stairs clutching Savannah, and sobbed while Jade watched.

twenty-two

There was a beaten-up Ford parked outside the black gates. Boniface wasn't sure which model it was, but it had that I-don't-earn-enough-to-care-how-I'm-judged vibe about it. The self-affixed sun visor and go-faster racing stripes running down the sides both pointed to a lover of all things 1980s.

Boniface pushed the wicket gate—the gate within the gate—and stepped onto the cobbles.

"What are you doing here, Boniface?"

The aggressive tone seemed familiar, but he didn't immediately recognize the small wiry man in front of him. Boniface looked down at the thinning hair—even in the dull lighting obviously dyed—and grinned. "Hello, Gray. I didn't recognize you with your clothes on."

"You got me in trouble—I've just been to the headmaster's office to have a word about my attitude problem. They don't give out detentions here—they tear your bollocks off." By the glass-paned door, the large black teenager lifted himself from the barrel he had been resting on.

Boniface stepped back to look at the other man—white dungarees spattered with paint over an equally paint-spattered dirty white T-shirt. "What are you doing, Gray?"

"I'm moving my gear—di'n't you see the car outside?"

The large black teen stared at the two men.

"You got me in the shit, Boniface, and now if you hang around here, you're going to cause problems for yourself." He cast a swift look behind him, then continued—his voice soft, his lower jaw fixed, his speech rapid. "Turn around and go, or they'll make you regret it."

"Mister Barrington," the black teen reached them, blocking out the light from the far end of the tunnel. "You must introduce your friend. Who is he?"

"He's no one, Jojo, no one." Gray cast a swift look back. "He came in the wrong door—he's just leaving now."

The black teenager let his gaze fall on Boniface, locking eyes. He waited.

"Gray used to be in a band," said Boniface. "I'm writing their biography—I was hoping we could chat."

The teen turned his gaze to Gray. "So he's a business associate of yours?"

"I am," said Boniface.

The teen slowly looked back to Boniface. "Then I must apologize for our earlier misunderstanding. Please do come in."

twenty-three

"I offered him a comfortable seat," said Jojo, continuing with some satisfaction, "in the room under the butcher's."

"That's good," said Ernie, resting on the side of his desk, tugging the collar of his shirt and then the lapel of his jacket. "Did he say what he wants?

Jojo shook his head. "Nah, man. He talked to that Gray guy."

Ernie sat up straighter. "He spoke to our little songbird?"

Jojo dropped his head once. "Gray said he didn't know him, but Boniface said he used to be in a band and he's writing a book about them."

Ernie stood and walked around his desk, dropping into his chair on the other side. "What do you think he wants, Irv?"

Iain Irvine sat in his customary corner, listening. "Two visits in one day—it's not an accident. He can't want nothing." Irvine turned to the black teenager. "He didn't give any hints."

"Nope. But you told me"—he turned to Ernie—"to hold him, so I put him in our best room." He paused. "He ain't wired. And he hadn't figured there's no phone reception down there."

"Am I the only one who doesn't like this?" said Ernie. "Think about it. Visit one—he asks for Billy. Visit two—Billy doesn't get a mention, but he sees Gray and says he's writing his biography. It's like he's two different people."

"Is he the guy that Gray told us knocked on his door?" asked Iain Irvine.

"Of course he is; who else would it be?" Ernie felt his voice catch in his throat. "Just Gray didn't tell us what a nuisance he is."

"What d'you want me to do, boss?" Jojo looked like a coiled spring who was coiling himself tighter.

"Is Wes around?"

Jojo nodded once.

"I'm going to have a pleasant chat with Mister Boniface. You boys can accompany me. I'll talk to him, but you need to communicate the message. We don't need to break anything, we don't need him to piss blood, but we need a bit of humiliation, we need a bit of pain so he remembers us tomorrow, and we need anyone he meets to notice his bruises."

"So the face," said Jojo. "I'll go and find Wes." There was a flash of brightness as Jojo opened the door onto the corridor outside, stooping under the doorframe as he left. As the door shut, the gloom he preferred returned.

"There's one thing, Irv, that no one seems to be mentioning."

Iain Irvine looked up.

"He calls himself a PR guy—he gives his PR card. But what's a PR guy doing looking for people or writing books? It doesn't add up to me." He exhaled. "I hate when people make me think this hard."

twenty-four

Veronica looked at the keypad, trying to remember what pointless logic Boniface had used for the security code. It didn't take long to remember that this time the choice had lacked any real sophistication. She hit the keys 2-4-6-8-3-5-7-9, waited for the click, and entered, turning into the first office on the left where the light was on.

"Hi Monty!"

"V-ron-ron!" Montbretia stood and hugged Boniface's former wife. "How are you?" Without waiting for a reply, she stood back and held her visitor at the shoulders. "And thank you for my tree."

Veronica laughed. "I wasn't quite sure what to get you."

"Well, you can be assured that yours was the only tree," said Montbretia, sitting back in her seat and gesturing to the only visitor chair in the room—the single-seat version of the sofa she knew was in Boniface's office. "It was lovely. Not what I expected, but then again, I'm not sure what I expected as a housewarming present...."

Veronica turned her back to the window crossing the far wall of the office and lowered herself into the chair. "I know you don't like flowers—and I wasn't quite sure what was appropriate, especially given..." she lowered her voice "...the circumstances."

Montbretia lowered her head. "It was very thoughtful." There was a pause, Veronica thought she could hear a sniff, then Montbretia looked up—her face a mask of joy, her eyes moist. "I wasn't expecting to become a house owner—and definitely not a house owner in London—but with Ellen..." Her face dropped, and the moisture because a small tear pooling in her left eye, slowly beginning its course down her cheek. "It's Ellen's anniversary in six weeks."

Veronica sat quietly, watching the younger woman as the memory of her late sister momentarily consumed her.

"Everything changed that day." She was cautious but firm. "I hadn't expected to stop traveling at that point, but after Ellen...I did. I didn't expect to be working, but when Boniface asked me to help out for a few days, it seemed like a good way to earn some cash. Days became weeks, and...here I am. And of course, there's the work I get from Chlodwig and Weissenfeld Shipping. We're about to deliver the second tranche of aid to Somalia, so if Boniface sucks I've got Chlodwig, and when Chlodwig gets too serious, there's Boniface. And I get to own a house and live in London—tired of London, tired of life, right?"

Veronica relaxed into the chair. "You're looking busy—what's he got you working on?"

"Work that earns the business money?" said Montbretia, the sarcasm bleeding through.

Veronica winced. "I thought he understood that he needs to keep earning money to keep the business afloat."

"So did I," said the younger woman. "So did I."

"I can hear the annoyance—let's change the subject." Veronica watched as Montbretia affirmed. "So what fool's errand has he got you spending you time on, safe in the knowledge that it will generate no income?"

"Amps," said Montbretia. "Guitar amplifiers, you know for…" she windmilled her arm as if a rockstar hitting a guitar on stage.

"I didn't know you knew anything about the subject."

"I don't," said Montbretia. "Or at least, I didn't until a few hours ago—but actually it seems simple." She shrugged. "Heads, cabs, stacks, and combos."

Veronica cocked her head, narrowing her eyes.

"A head is an amplifier. It's the box with the amplifier in it," said Montbretia. "A cab—or cabinet—is the speaker cabinet, and apparently the boys think twelve inches is perfect."

Veronica felt her eyes tightening.

Montbretia seemed to notice. "I'll spare you the fruit of my research into different tubes… Apparently this is all in pursuit of *the tone*. The tone, which no one can precisely describe, nor can they give a consistent recording of what exactly they mean—you go through YouTube, and everything is 'this microphone doesn't give the full sound' or 'this room is wrong.' It all sounds like a scam to me." She snorted. "And apparently feedback—you know, that horrible screech—can be good." She flopped back into her chair, which gently oscillated.

"So where do you fit in the world of *amps*?" asked Veronica.

"You will understand that because these things have valves, are constructed from marine ply, and are wired up by hand, they cost a lot of money."

"Suppose so."

"This means that the main market for these things is weekend warriors. Tubby accountants—boys that wear bad suits but have sensible haircuts—who want to, and I quote"—she made a sign of horns with each hand, holding down her middle and ring fingers with her thumbs while extending the outer fingers—"'rock out at the weekend,' provided they're in bed by 10:30. And the way to market to this audience is with slutty women wearing spandex and too much makeup."

"I think the way to market most things is slutty women," suggested Veronica.

"Opinion is split as to whether the sluttiness of the woman is in direct proportion or disproportion to how well an amp will deliver *the tone*. There's also some debate about whether blondes or brunettes have an effect, but all seem to agree that larger breasts are necessary." She shook her head, disbelieving. "Don't argue with me, I'm just the messenger. I'm only telling you what the internet told me."

"I think you have found the big dilemma for all marketers."

"But for guitars and amps, there is another way," said Montbretia, gaining fresh energy. "You can get a professional to endorse your stuff, and this is where I come in. Luca…he's the guitarist with this band, Prickle—I take it you've heard about them from Boniface…"

Veronica acknowledged wearily.

"Rather surprisingly, Luca is actually regarded as something of a guitar god. And from what I've heard in the last hour or so, he is actually quite good." Montbretia pushed her jaw forward, grimacing. "Again, I'm just telling you what the internet told me, but apparently in the world of the guitar, once you have got *the tone*, then you need to do *the solo*. To go with the solo, you need the face. I knew about the horns…" she held her hands up, making the sign of the horns again, "but I didn't realize about the face."

Veronica felt a slight nervous twitch cross her face.

"As I understand," continued Montbretia. "The song will be playing, the guitarist will be going strum, strum, strum, but when it's solo time, he needs to show that he is suffering; he needs to convey the emotion."

"He can't just do that through, you know, playing?" asked Veronica.

"Oh no. First, he needs to stand as if he's been shot and is clutching his wound. And then, the face." She frowned. "There's something about shredding. I'm not sure what it is—I think it just means playing very fast. Whatever it is, Luca seems to have a really good ear for melody, harmony, and just shutting up when he's not needed, where all the others just go on and on and on. And people seem to love Luca, but Luca needs new gear—Boniface had some bizarre story about his ex-wife selling off everything he owned...."

"I missed a trick in our divorce, didn't I?" said Veronica. "Then again, I'm not sure that Boniface had much worth selling. Ironically, he did have some Prickle CDs. He probably still does—I wasn't going to keep them."

"Seriously? He actually did like them?"

"Yeah. A lot. Went to see them live several times."

Montbretia looked uncertain. "Well, don't tell him I said this, but I've been listening to a lot of *rock*, trying to understand this whole amp thing, and Prickle really are better than most of them. They've got tunes, melodies you can actually hum." She blushed slightly. "I was in the bathroom with this tune going round in my head—it was only when I got back here that I realized it was one of Prickle's."

Veronica leaned forward and whispered. "Your secret is safe with me." She sat up straighter. "And talking of him, I haven't heard him stomping about, so I guess he's off chasing his youth."

Montbretia nodded. "I tried him on his mobile about five minutes ago. There was no reply; it went straight to voicemail. That's not unusual—it's not as if he's going to be in any physical danger. It's mostly his dignity that he's going to hurt...and the bank balance."

There was something strange in Montbretia's delivery. "You look worried," said Veronica.

"No," said Montbretia too swiftly, blushing as she seemingly realized her over-defensiveness. "I'm not worried about Boniface—I just think he might be...going in the wrong direction."

Veronica waited for the younger woman, letting the silence encourage her to talk.

"Boniface thinks this is about Prickle—he thinks it started with people saying things about Prickle on the internet." She sighed. "There's a level of that with every band, but nothing out of the ordinary for Prickle."

"So..." said Veronica slowly.

"It's not Prickle that are getting the hate, or even Danny—it's Dawn. She hasn't seriously been in the public eye, at least not more than a few TV shows here and there, for over twenty years, but the hate that's been coming at her from what looks like one or two people is just..." She seemed unable to form a word. "It's just horrid." She paused, seemingly having articulated her concern to her own satisfaction, and then slumped back into her chair. "So what brings you here, V-ron-ron?"

"I think you know why I'm here." The younger woman deflated. "What you're really asking is what fool's errand have I been obliged to perform this time?"

Montbretia affirmed.

"And the answer is, he asked me to check out someone for him. But if he's not here, I'll go and see if he's at home—and if he's not there, I'll let myself in and wait. It's getting dark, so he won't be that long."

twenty–five

Ernie Norton walked out of the glazed door, obscured with a dark curtain loosely held on the inside, and stepped into the cobbled courtyard, every surface a subtly different hue of darkening gray now that the sun, which only briefly reflected off the surrounding buildings, had disappeared many hours since.

Passing between the two barrels, he turned to his left and descended the staircase, disappearing under the rear of Abdul's butcher shop into a warren of exposed brickwork and aged concrete.

Wes and Jojo followed, both youths pumped with adrenalin, but both understood—Ernie had labored the point and threatened—that their sole role was to stand still and glare silently.

Stand still and glare until Ernie had left the room, after which he wouldn't really care enough what was going to happen.

He paused outside the door—the beige/gray tone contrasting with the dark blood dried across the foot of the kickplate. He waited. Jojo leaned forward, drew back the bolt, and pushed the door open, then stood back to allow Ernie to pass through.

"I don't believe we've had the pleasure, Mister Boniface."

The other man sat on an old wooden chair, his suit slightly rumpled, his shirt ripped, and—he knew from talking with Jojo—lacking buttons.

He was never sure when concern changed to fear. There was something in the anticipation—in not knowing what was going to happen. Once the first fist landed, once there was actual pain, then there was certainty—it became a matter of survival. Once you're in survival mode, you'll say anything, do anything to survive. When the man on the chair was in survival mode, then Ernie didn't need to be there—when someone will say anything to survive, then what they say is useless. All Ernie wanted to hear was the truth, and someone who was afraid, truly afraid, would be willing to bargain with the truth to avoid whatever future consequences their mind had conjured.

He heard Jojo and Wes shuffle in behind him. Jojo came second—he always stooped under the door, breaking his step. Ernie listened as the door slammed, holding back until the youthful feet stopped scraping, confident that one youth was now positioned on either side of the door.

Keeping his body still, he watched Boniface, noting the increase in the speed of his eyes—his pupils darting, down, to Ernie, back up, left, to the door, to Wes, up, right, to Ernie, to the lightbulb with its thin wire cage, to the top-left corner, to the bottom-right corner, to Wes, to Ernie, to Jojo, from the top-left corner down to the bottom-left corner, and back to Ernie, then dropping to his feet.

Boniface had been in the room for thirty minutes. For someone not used to incarceration, that was a long time to sit in a room with concrete-rendered walls and a concrete floor, only having an uncomfortable chair with one slightly short leg to sit on. It would be unpleasant to start with, but after thirty minutes—thirty minutes in a room where the only interior decoration had been the blood, piss, and shit of previous occupants—you would usually deduce two things. First, that there was no way out apart from the door. Second, that the only reasonable response to deduction number one was fear.

The only matter to be decided was how Mister Boniface was going to react to that fear.

"Why are you messing with my little songbird?"

From his reaction, this wasn't the question Boniface was expecting—or perhaps it was the question, but phrased in a way he wasn't expecting. In any event, the reaction was as he hoped and immediate—panic and confusion. Boniface was almost relieved when he started talking. "You mean Gray?"

Ernie noticed that this was the point where he paused.

This was the moment when Boniface was trying to determine how Ernie would react.

His voice was different when he continued—more confident, but far less authentic. Ernie looked at his eyes. In that pause, Boniface had relaxed and decided that his fears were unfounded. It was one thing not to respect Ernie, but it's stupid not to respect your fears.

"There's obviously been a big misunderstanding." Boniface was talking as if he was chatting to a cop—he was serious but believed they were on the same side. "I'm writing a biography about the band Prickle—I don't know if you've heard of them. Gray was the founder and the original lead singer, so he knows a lot that would be really good for the book. I was hoping he might have some old photos."

So this was how Boniface was going to react? With bullshit. Ernie wouldn't feel so bad about leaving him with Wes and Jojo if that was the other man's attitude. If he had started with the truth—or even made an acknowledgement that there was a truth to be told—then he might have reconsidered, but now...it didn't seem much point.

"A biography? And yet you haven't had the civility to talk to me?" He spun on his heel, slowly pacing around Boniface. "If there's money involved, then you should be paying it directly to me. I see no reason for middlemen who will want to take their cut or who might accidentally lose the money before it reaches me."

Boniface had the courtesy to introduce a tremble in his voice when he continued. "I'm sorry, I didn't know I needed to...Gray didn't..."

Ernie exhaled, continuing his pacing. "While I acknowledge that there was an apology—of sorts—wrapped up in your last few words, I'm still left wondering what else you haven't asked. What else should I know?"

Boniface seemed to change course. "It's been hard with the band's management problems...I didn't know I was...and I haven't—I mean there's no—at least not at the moment..."

"No what?"

"Money," said Boniface. "I'm not paying Gray for the biography."

"Let me get this straight," said Ernie. "You're not meeting our little songbird's debts and you're also trying to say there are management problems, which mean it's not your fault. But we're talking about my band and I find that a bit...confusing."

It was as if Boniface genuinely did not understand what he had just heard.

"For someone who says he's an author, you seem to be very persistent." Ernie stopped his circling, now standing face-on to Boniface. "But here's the interesting thing—you say you're an author, but the business card you left says you're a PR man. It doesn't stack up. And neither does it square with your first visit here."

Ernie stood back. "I don't issue threats and I definitely don't issue ultimatums—they just encourage people to do stupid things that they didn't really want to do in the first place—so I'll just say that I hope this is the last time we will meet in a business context." He turned to Wes and Jojo. "Will you two gentlemen be kind enough to escort Mister Boniface off the premises? Our business here is concluded."

Jojo opened the door and Ernie stepped out. The door slammed behind him as he followed the concrete and brick leading him to the stairs up to the courtyard.

twenty-six

The deadbolt turned.

The deadbolt turned the other way—of course he wouldn't have known that bolt was already unlocked. Unless he had called, and why would he?

Veronica leaned forward, picking up the bottle of whisky next to her handbag, and poured another measure. A large one.

The key tapped around the top lock and eventually found its home, zipping into the empty space before turning.

The door opened. Steps. The door closed. He knew she was there—either that or he thought very careless burglars had passed through—but he said nothing and didn't come into the room.

She heard the bathroom door open, and then there was nothing. There was no squeal of the door shutting. No sound to imply he was urinating.

Nothing.

She took a sip, replaced her tumbler on the table, and called: "Conventionally, when one has guests, one comes in and says good evening."

No response.

"Boniface?"

Veronica stood and walked through the lobby to the bathroom, cautiously rounding the final corner, letting Boniface come slowly into view. She gasped "what happened to you?" and ran forward, stroking Boniface's cheek with the back of her hand.

Boniface remained stationary, leaning on the sink and looking in the mirror. "Apparently I tripped over."

"And broke your fall with your face?" She almost sniggered, quickly lifting a hand to her mouth. "What happened? Did the big boys at the theater argue when you said you didn't like the color pink?"

"Ha, ha," said Boniface mirthlessly. "The unlicensed minicab driver who brought me back was scarier—the door had a broken catch and was held shut by one of those stretchy things with a hook at each end. Apparently he's getting it fixed tomorrow."

He raised a hand to his cheek, revealing a jacket seam under his arm that had been pulled apart, and then turned to face her, showing a ripped knee, his breast pocket pulled off the jacket, and grime stains scraped up his chest.

"You look like shit, Boniface. Perhaps it's time for you to start drinking again, darling." She stopped, not believing what she saw. "Where are your buttons?"

"Over a very wide area. But at least Jojo satisfied himself that I wasn't wearing a wire." He sighed heavily. "Not that Jojo would know what a recorder looks like—all he's seen are cop shows with a big clunky lump of wire taped to the cop's chest so that you know he's wired."

Looking at him straight on, the damage to his face looked worse than she had first suspected. His upper lip was cut and swollen. His left cheekbone was grazed, and his left eye would probably be black by tomorrow. "What happened to your cheek?" She heard the panic in her voice as she realized that the three-inch straight mark on his face was a gash.

"Wes—or rather, Wesley's knife. The knife was bigger than him." His hand moved to his left ear. "He started on my ear—trying to scare me. It worked. Then he was playing the big man—trying to scare me even by rubbing the blade on my cheek." His face loosened. "I think it scared him more than me when he cut the skin."

"Have you called the police?"

"No. And we're not going to, and we're not going to document...this." He indicated himself. "If we call the police, then I can't... And by the way, you're only seeing the edited highlights." He pointed around his face. "There's more below, but I don't think anything is broken."

Veronica ran forward, clinging to him, feeling the tears start to flow.

"Ow," whispered Boniface. "I hurt all over."

Veronica jumped back, tears flowing faster. "What hurts most?"

"Everything—but apparently I'm lucky. Ernie doesn't want me pissing blood tomorrow."

"Do you want a whisky?" asked Veronica.

"Thank you, but no. That's the thing about not drinking—you don't drink, even when you want one."

"Then you should have a bath—a long soak. When you get out, you can tell me all about it." She looked into the sink in front of the mirror. "Use the bathroom in your room—I'll clean up here."

twenty-seven

"I don't trust Boniface." Ernie ran a hand over his rough cheek. "Even after Jo and Wes have talked to him, I won't trust him. His story doesn't make sense—I can't even figure it from his perspective."

He inhaled deeply—a moist sound cultivated by fifty-five years of smoking.

"I don't trust Billy. Junkies are never reliable."

He paced the short distance from his desk to the door, turning and continuing to talk. "And I definitely don't trust Gray."

He reached his desk—a chunk of wood that was older than him and wider than he was tall—and rested on it. "As for those bastards at PAD Management...they're slippery. I've dealt with a lot of villains, but that bloke with the jewelry and his idea of truth..."

Iain Irvine remained motionless in the corner—his liver-spotted hide glistening in the few rays of light that Ernie hadn't scared out of the room. "Do you want me to handle this?"

"Yeah," said Ernie. He stood again and slowly began to pace around his desk. "But more than that, I want to know what their angle is. How does Boniface fit with Billy and Gray—is he onto us? And why did he seem to know about PAD?"

The muscles in his upper lip remained taut. Irvine spoke. "I'll apply some pressure—legal, of course. I am your lawyer, after all—in the right places. I'll go round first thing in the morning—I'll take Jojo or Wes to make sure that I articulate the message clearly."

"Make sure the message gets through," said Ernie. "But remember, this is about applying heat—not burning."

twenty-eight

About an hour after returning home, Boniface, wrapped in a white toweling robe with his damp hair combed back, shuffled into his front room and dropped onto the sofa diagonally opposite Veronica.

"For the record, I still hurt."

"Aren't you meant to make some joke about the other guy?"

"I believe that's the form—but they were both younger than me and clearly enjoyed their work. And I saw them walk away after they dropped me so delicately outside their boss's fine establishment, having doused me in cheap gin and left the bottle next to me so that anyone who passed would think I was drunk."

Veronica took a sip of her whisky, replacing the tumbler on the table in front of her. "So tell me what happened—start from when you left me."

Boniface exhaled, his mouth a tight circle. A tight, painful circle. "Kit. I saw Kit Flambeau. Nice chap, but he gave me nothing. Nothing. And for all the flamboyance—when you turn off the audience, he's a very quiet guy."

"So where next?"

"Fat Terry—he sends his regards, by the way. If ever you need his skills, just call." Veronica winced and Boniface continued. "He had the address for one of the girls who sung in the band with Dawn. Jilly Crossley, as was, now Gillian Walker."

"I don't remember the name," said Veronica. "I remember the band—or at least, I'm familiar with the story of the end. They were the lot where the girl fell in the Thames and drowned."

"Lorna," said Boniface. "The poor girl's name was Lorna Roscoe."

"If we could do today's forensic tests, then I'm guessing we would have found a lot of illegal substances in her system."

"That would be my guess, too," said Boniface. "And like you, I didn't know Jilly's name until Terry mentioned it, but then again, she didn't know who I was, so that made us even." He winced as his stomach muscles tightened. "When I got there she was having a bitch of an evening, and to be honest, my heart wasn't in it."

"That's not like you, Boniface."

"Quite the contrary," said Boniface, slowly maneuvering to face her more fully, "I give up quickly when there's no prospect of victory. When I got there she was having a row with her daughter on the phone and there were these three grandkids—a babe in arms, a clingy two- or maybe three-year-old, and this little bastard, Rafferty, who seemed to make everyone's life hell. I'm guessing she had been with the kids all day and the daughter had just dropped the kids on her for the rest of the night, so she was pretty cantankerous, and there was this image Terry left in my mind."

"I don't think I want to know about Terry's image."

"Do you know how hard it is to talk to somebody when all you can think about is their wonky headlights?" Boniface held his hands in front of him, raising one and lowering the other.

"That aside," said Veronica dismissively, closing her eyes.

"She seems to think Dawn was culpable—no, not culpable...but not without responsibility—for the death of Lorna."

"Did she elaborate?"

"Not really—but I didn't want to push. She seemed ready to snap with those kids, and I think I shocked her the way I sprung Lorna's death on her. From her reaction, I could believe that she sat down and wept after I left."

"So is there a link here—someone has an angle on Dawn about Lorna's death, Dawn gets windy and does a runner?"

"But why would Dawn suddenly run twenty, maybe thirty years later?" He relaxed back into the sofa, wincing as he released his weight into the padding. "And why would she react so badly when I chatted with her?"

"Call—see if Dawn's home—ask."

"Can't," said Boniface flatly. "If she's not home, all a call at this time of day will do is worry Danny even more."

Veronica started to disagree, then gave way. "You talked to Jilly—where next?"

"Jilly was in Leyton, so I jumped on the Central Line, got off at Bethnal Green, and walked up to Haggerston."

"Haggerston! Without an armed guard or police escort."

"It's not that bad."

"Allow me to get a mirror for you." She paused. "Why Haggerston?"

"Prickle's former lead singer Gray mentioned this club—he said this was where he had met the elusive Billy Watkins—the guy whose name scared Dawn. So I went to see if I could find Billy, and you know the rest. Well, apart from me scraping myself off the floor, crawling to the taxi office, cleaning myself in the dirtiest bathroom in London, and riding in the cab from hell over here."

"This is the Billy you wanted me to look into?"

"That's the one," said Boniface, feeling some enthusiasm for the first time since he met Ernie.

"Well, it's been a wasted beating you've taken: Billy's dead."

twenty-nine

Montbretia surveyed the wreckage.

Boniface called it his face. She called it what it was—wreckage. And apparently there was more damage under the suit, not to mention damage to yesterday's suit.

Yesterday's suit had been blue. Apparently that suit was no longer. It had sustained injury while undertaking duty on the front line and had later died from those injuries when Boniface got home. He and his former wife had paid tribute at the funeral.

Today's suit was charcoal gray, although it was unclear why Boniface felt the need to waste another suit, especially when what he should be wearing was cotton wool to protect himself from any new bumps. And if he was going out, surely he should be wearing jeans like her—clothes intended to sustain at least some physical stress.

She handed him a blister strip of paracetamol and a plastic bottle of ibuprofen. "You can take them together—they're different types of painkillers. The Tylenol"— Boniface frowned—"sorry, what you call paracetamol is probably better for pain, and the ibuprofen is an anti-inflammatory. Which you need."

He grunted.

"Have you eaten?"

Another grunt, but less committed. "I'm not letting you go anywhere until you have, but first..." She walked to the kitchen, filled a glass of water, and returned, placing it on his desk before leaning over to pick up the paracetamol and push out one tablet from the blister pack, dropping it on the desk in front of him. "Extra strength; you only need one." Then she picked up the plastic bottle, pressed on the top to open the childproof cap, and fished out a round tablet that she dropped next to the first. "Take. Now."

Boniface grunted, took a sip of water, then put both tablets in his mouth and swallowed before taking another sip and replacing the glass on his desk.

"You don't have to thank me," said Montbretia. "Just tell me what Veronica said about Billy Watkins."

"He's dead," mumbled Boniface.

"You said that. She didn't just say, 'He's dead, bye,' or even, 'He's dead; wow, it looks like you've got a shiner coming'—which, by the way, you have—'bye.'"

Boniface took another sip. "Veronica found a guy called Billy Watkins. He was a few years older than Dawn and was born a few streets away from Dawn."

"That's hardly conclusive."

Boniface shrugged, then closed his eyes, seemingly trying to block out the pain. "It's not, but it was New Addington."

"So? Where is it? What does that mean?"

"You've been in London for a year—there's a reason you've not heard of New Addington," said Boniface. "It was one of those areas they reinvigorated after the war. They used the greenbelt to circumscribe the urban sprawl, but they managed to fit this small island within the permitted zone. The idea was to build a vibrant community in the middle of what was effectively countryside, but which was actually in London."

"I'm already guessing..."

Boniface seemed to want to soften his face, but as he did he put his hand to his cheek. "They built the estate, but by the time they got round to building the transport they had run out of money, so it never happened—meaning no one in New Addington could travel to work, so no one got a job and crime rose, social security rates went up, gangs started to...you get the idea."

"But that still doesn't prove that Billy is Dawn's Billy—surely the guy could have got out of town. There must have been some roads."

"It doesn't prove—but this Billy stayed around New Addington. His criminal record tells us he didn't travel far from home, and Dawn told me she was there until she was 16, so it's not totally unreasonable to make an assumption."

"What happened to Billy?"

"Car crash in 1994. He died. The passenger—a woman—survived. That's all we know." He looked overwhelmed by the effort—as if his weakened body was having its energy sapped as he forced his brain to retrieve information and lay out a series of basic facts in a logical order.

"So you're going to leave it alone now?"

"Of course. If Dawn's back. If not..." He shrugged and seemed to regret the movement.

"Have you seen a doctor?" He moved his eyes—slowly, as if they hurt too—and focused on her, without the energy to keep his eyelids fully open. "Seriously, Boniface. You should."

"I'll be fine." He talked without moving a facial muscle—expelling oxygen without allowing his lungs to move his chest.

"And what did the police say?"

"Are you and Vron ganging up on me?" If he hadn't been so weak, Montbretia expected there would have been anger in his words. He tried to expel air through his nose, but seemed to find only discomfort, so he stopped. "We're not going to the police about any of this. Danny doesn't want the publicity or the embarrassment for Dawn. No one wants a potential nonissue—which this could turn out to be—becoming a matter of legal record."

"You reckon somebody beat the living..." She let the thought hang as she reformulated her words. "You think somebody did this to you over a nonissue?" She waited, not really expecting a response. "Do you even know what *this* is?"

"Do you?" His voice was quiet but accusing.

"What I know is this presented as a problem that Dawn and Danny had. They came in here—this room," she moved back from his desk into the middle of the room, "and, according to you, said that they—they, both of them together—had a problem."

Boniface's eyes made the slightest movement—this seemed to be an acknowledgement requiring the least physical pain.

"That's not what's being said on the internet," said Montbretia. "Dawn is the one getting the kicking...Danny and Prickle are secondary."

Boniface half-smiled. "But here's the thing—I go looking for the guy whose name scared Dawn, and everything I find relates to Prickle. Just before my pounding, Ernie said some crazy stuff—I don't quite remember what he said; I had other thoughts going through my head, and it wasn't really a matter of proper etiquette to ask if I could take notes." He leaned on his desk, wincing slightly. "There's a link—I don't know what it is, but there's a link." He moved his head to face Montbretia directly. "And I'll see what Danny thinks about it when I get down there."

"You're going there?" Montbretia could hear the concern in her voice as its pitch lifted.

"Yeah."

"Do you really have to? I really think you…"

"I have to." Boniface was moving slowly, but he seemed to be hiding any pain.

"Is Dawn back?"

"I'll find out when I get there." His tone indicated the conversation was at an end. "And when I get there, is there anything I can tell him about the amps for Luca?"

Montbretia brightened. "I found a company that love Luca and would like to talk about endorsement—they're called Zeimetz Tone Engines. I'll print out the details before you go."

She paused. "But once you've talked to Danny, please leave this alone. Walk away. And if you can't walk away, then call the cops."

thirty

Montbretia had insisted on going to fetch him a bacon sandwich. "With a face like that, you need food, Boniface. When did you last eat properly?"

He had complained, but not too loudly: It hurt, and if he was honest, once Montbretia had put the idea in his mind, he wanted a bacon sandwich but didn't want the hassle of going out and waiting in a line. Nor did he want people staring at his injuries while he stood in line.

She made him a cup of tea before she went out, which had reached drinking temperature when she returned with his sandwich. She didn't need to, but Boniface felt it was better to give way on some small things while digging his heels in for the things that mattered. His final sip of tea washed down two further painkillers, and before he left she wrapped two additional tablets in a tissue, slipping the wrap into his jacket pocket with instructions to take them at some point. "You're not going to overdose on six tablets," she said. "The injuries that those kids have inflicted on you will do you far more harm than a few over-the-counter pharmaceuticals."

And with those words, she had escorted him to the barge—the Mercedes permanently lent to him by his friend Gideon—which he then let drift him down to the Surrey Hills.

For this visit, he had two advantages that he hadn't had on his first trip. First, he at least had a clue about where he was going—he still clicked up the navigation thingy on his phone, but at least with this journey he recognized one or two familiar landmarks. Second, it was morning—before midday. With each minute, the sun got higher, and while this didn't add much to the ambient temperature of the early spring morning, it did bring an additional brightness as the sun's rays penetrated the dense canopies in the woods and copses, giving pools of light and pools of darkness to the narrow twisting road—a groove digging its way through the sandstone banks that he passed in the Surrey Hills.

In daylight it was much easier to see the cars coming in the opposite direction from some distance, but there was a new hazard: ramblers. Those that stood in the sun or moved were easy to spot. Those that saw a car and withdrew to the shadows became invisible specters waiting to jump out at him when his only hope of not killing them was to throw the steering wheel in the opposite direction. And as he threw the steering wheel—even with the power steering—he remembered the less than subtle message that Wes and Jojo had given him last night.

The Mercedes skidded on the imperfect surface of the road. The turnoff into Danny and Dawn's drive came upon him faster than he expected; she didn't say anything, but Boniface was sure that the woman giving him directions on his phone now thought a little less of him for not paying sufficient attention. He dropped the car into reverse, rolled it back twenty or thirty yards, and turned onto the stone driveway, pulling up in the small group of cars between the three buildings.

Luca was sitting just outside the kitchen door at a cast-iron table—white with patches of rust and enough space for four chairs, although there were only two. He had a cup of coffee in front of him and his phone in his hand. With the delicacy of movement that was only available to surgeons and musicians, Luca tapped out a message on his phone with his right hand while picking up his coffee with his left. The coffee returned to the table as the Italian continued to focus on his message—or more likely, messages.

Boniface eased himself out of the barge, slowly standing and wondering if this is what old age would feel like. At the studio door, he noticed Danny and raised his hand in greeting—the bassist returned the sign. Then Boniface pointed to Luca, tapped his wrist where most people wear a watch, and held up a splayed hand. Danny gave him two thumbs up and disappeared into the studio.

"Luca, hi. I'm Boniface."

Boniface held out his hand, ready to shake the Italian's. The guitarist continued typing with his thumb, then looked up and gently slapped his left hand across Boniface's outstretched palm as he started typing again. "Are you our new daddy? You seem to be around a lot.... Or should I call you uncle? Zio Boniface." Luca briefly lifted his eyes to scan Boniface as the Englishman pulled back the other chair. The Italian continued in his heavily accented voice. "Did you fight our last daddy—is that when you got hurt, Zio?" He seemed to want a reaction, but not a response.

Boniface cautiously lowered himself into the chair, feeling the hard iron patterning refusing to give any comfort to his back, arms, and legs. He sat as still as he could, and in modulated tones asked, "Have you heard of Zeimetz Tone Engines?"

"Of course. I'm not stupid, Zio. I use guitar amps for a living." The guitarist didn't look up from his phone.

"What do you think of their gear?"

The guitarist reached for his coffee, keeping his focus on his phone, gently rocking his head from left to right. "Some of the best."

"They want you to endorse them."

Luca looked up from his phone, his eyes widening, his long wavy hair settling after the sudden movement. "So you're not my uncle, but Santa Claus."

"I'm not the hero here," said Boniface. "It's you they want. I'm just passing the message."

"Now I know you're kidding."

The pain across his back and legs was too much—the concentration of his weight onto the narrow metal patterns of the chair was hurting and what he really wanted were feather pillows delicately supporting him. Circumspectly, Boniface willed his body to the vertical, walking behind the chair to use it as a support while he kept his gaze locked with the Italian's. "Seriously—they've got some nice shiny new gear, and they'd like to lend it to you. Permanently."

The Italian put his phone on the table and leaned back in his chair before taking a sip of coffee. "What do I have to do? You know I don't have sex with men."

"They're after a simple endorsement deal. You use the gear in public, and they have your picture in a few ads." The Italian showed no emotion as Boniface continued. "As a start, they'd like a video of you trying the gear for the first time—you know, plug in, turn some knobs, strum, and make warm noises about how good it sounds. You can shoot it in my office if you want—Montbretia will call and arrange a time." He pulled a card out of his breast pocket and dropped it on the table. "Here's the address." He released his other hand from the chair and stood straight. "And if you tweet about the stuff, I'm sure Zeimetz won't complain."

The guitarist dropped eye contact and picked up his phone.

thirty-one

"The other guy?" Danny raised his brows to widen his eyes. "Sit down." He sat on the edge of his desk and pointed to the sofa—the sofa where Boniface presumed Danny had slept on the night that Dawn disappeared.

The bassist's attire seemed to be his standard non-stage wear, but with a different shirt and no jacket. He had a sympathetic look as he seemed to study Boniface's visible injuries, and remaining quiet, he lifted his hand—pointing without accusation—identifying each individual wound.

"You might not use words, but your actions imply you don't see me as the street-fighting type."

The bassist laughed. "Tommy told me you were a good guy—he didn't tell me about your hobbies. What happened?"

"Long story," said Boniface. "I'll get to it."

The bassist shrugged. "Is Luca okay?"

"Very okay, I think," said Boniface, enjoying the softness of the sofa after the battering of the iron chair. "We've got him some amps—Zeimetz Tone Engines."

Danny rocked back on the desk, his lower jaw hanging. "How did you pull that off? Those amps have got quite a reputation. Hand-built in...I'm going to go out on a limb—Luxembourg, isn't it?"

Boniface tried to nod but felt talking might hurt less. "Zeimetz have got a new model that they were going to launch last week. They had another guitarist ready to endorse the gear, but he got arrested on kiddie-fiddling charges two days before. They needed to move quickly, we got lucky, and Montbretia sweet-talked them."

"That great!" said Danny. "Really great. Well done, Boniface." He paused. "What does Luca have to do?"

"A few photos. A hand-over video. Use the stuff live. Maybe a workshop." Boniface tried to shrug. "Maybe he'll tweet about it."

"He probably has already," said Danny. "And he's cool with all this?"

Boniface moved his head up and down, feeling the tension in his neck pull with each movement. He looked up, noticing that Danny's face seemed to have changed. The mood in the room was different.

Danny leaned behind him and flicked the door.

The dark-colored utilitarian lump of wood—which probably met the latest fire standards for offices—swung, thudding into the doorjamb, the latch clicking to confirm that the door would not open without human intervention in the area of the handle.

The sound in the alcove office slowly decayed, leaving a space unlike the oasis in the next room. Here, harsh white walls with hard, reflective surfaces were a contrast to the other room, with its soft fabric masking acoustic baffles and gentle lights to comfort.

"She's not back." Danny's voice was small. "I've checked—and checked again. She hasn't taken anything—no cash, no cards, no jewelry. She definitely didn't sneak in last night. I was waiting—I didn't sleep."

Looking at him, Danny didn't look too bad for his lack of slumber. Then again, he had probably spent most of his working life with unconventional sleep patterns.

"I sent out the roadies—Sven and Reuben—on horses to look. Trouble is, no one knows this area like Dawn—she's always out walking, riding, taking pictures, talking to people." He paused, exhaling heavily. "She loved the area from the first time we came here—someone recommended the Norman church at Albury for our wedding, so we drove down here one afternoon." He brightened slightly. "About 18 months after we released 'Tattoo Your Name on My Heart,' the royalties came through. I asked her: 'What are we going to do with the money?' She had one response—buy a house in the Surrey Hills. Somewhere where we can raise kids. Somewhere where we can grow old. Without Dawn, there would have been no 'Tattoo.' Without 'Tattoo,' there would be no income and Prickle would have died. I would have had to get a proper job and a boring wife. So it was my pleasure to buy this house with that money."

Danny was looking down, hiding his eyes.

"Of course, there were never kids. Some call it a sadness—and I'm sorry about it; Dawn would have been a great mother—but how can I complain about anything when I've got a wife I love and who loves me, and we live here?"

"I saw Kit." Boniface wasn't sure whether to change the subject, but he guessed that Danny didn't want to lose face and cry in front of him.

"What?" Danny replaced the maudlin introspection with incredulity.

"Because he was around and he might have a clue about something you don't think is relevant."

"She's my wife, Boniface. I think I would know whether someone is a good person to talk to—and Kit isn't. Lovely guy, but not relevant here."

Boniface could hear the simper in his voice—he knew he was only asking the question to hide his embarrassment. "Have you found a singer for the gig yet? What about Kit?"

Danny's voice was slight. "I'd love Kit to sing for us, but the set is too long—it'd put too much strain on his voice—and anyway, he's already working that night."

The room fell silent—the two men looking at each other.

Boniface broke the noiseless entente. "And you're sure you don't want to talk to the cops about Dawn, or go to the press, or whatever?"

There was a rip of anger in the bassist's voice. "Dawn would hate the intrusion—years later it would still be like a scar you need to put makeup over. She remembers things." His voice softened—a tone of disappointment. "I thought you understood this."

"I thought I did," said Boniface quietly. "But when I started asking questions, you can see the results..." He unbuttoned his shirt to reveal more bruising over his chest. He felt the accusation in his voice. "Are you sure there's nothing else?"

Danny trembled. It wasn't anger that Boniface could see. This was a man who'd been awake too long and had been worrying too long, who'd just had the PR man he'd asked to help instead suggest that the worst-case scenarios he'd been thinking about—all those still-awake nightmares that he dismissed as ridiculous, all those unfeasible possibilities that only happen to other people—well, perhaps they could be happening to him. He started slowly. "I trust my wife."

Boniface wondered if that was all Danny wanted to say. A simple incontrovertible statement that encapsulated a basic truth but also reflected the entire basis of his life.

"Does she have secrets? Perhaps—but they'll be..." The bassist waved a hand in the air as if mimicking a butterfly. "But I don't need to know everything—I trust her, she tells me what she wants to tell me. You've met her—she's a good person, right? What's the worst that she could tell me?"

He dropped his head, catching it with his right hand, and sobbed.

thirty-two

"I didn't know what else to do," said Montbretia, opening the door for Boniface. She seemed twitchy, on edge. "I'm sorry—I put her in your room. I couldn't think..."

Boniface moved slowly, cautious not to knock his injuries on the door as he awkwardly slipped past Montbretia and started walking toward his office. "It's not a problem—I'll..." he reached the door to his office, trying to give Montbretia a reassuring look as she disappeared even though he wasn't sure what the problem was.

"This is an unexpected pleasure." Boniface watched the baby giraffe move her legs, readying to lift herself to the vertical. "Please don't stand. These sofas are far too low to get out of, especially when you've got heels." Boniface offered his hand to shake, casting a glance at what was probably better classified as small tower blocks strapped to the feet of his guest before feeling the delicate skin of her small paw momentarily slipped into his.

Leaving his guest where she sat gave Boniface the opportunity to orbit and observe the lawyer, an opportunity not afforded to him when he had visited PAD Management's offices on Denmark Street twenty-four hours earlier. In the intervening period, Boniface hadn't felt the need to revise his observation that she was long and skinny—she would probably always be—although she did seem to settle her frame into the sofa with surprising grace. However, there was something about the face.

Most people have a nose attached to their face. Fiona Aldred, the A in PAD Management, seemed to have a face attached to her nose. A slightly asymmetrical face, which in combination gave the appearance of something that Picasso may have produced in an experimental phase when working with human beings.

It wasn't unattractive—quite the contrary, it was certainly interesting, and if he wasn't in so much pain, Boniface wondered whether that interest could actually reach alluring—but nonetheless it was an unusual face that gave him too many things to think about. It also looked like an angry face, or if not angry, then certainly stern.

Still, an angry lawyer was preferable to a weeping bass player and a missing former model.

"Mister Boniface."

He had forgotten the depth of pitch of the quiet voice.

"Please, just Boniface."

She seemed to acknowledge this but did not correct herself, instead continuing: "PAD Management is a professional firm." Her volume lowered as she articulated each word individually. "The practices that are presently being adopted are outside the expected norms of behavior."

Boniface felt his eyes narrow and his head cock instinctively.

"I feel we were far more frank with you yesterday than was necessary, or indeed may have been appropriate, but I hope we illustrated to you that there are some very real—although not insurmountable—problems in the relationship between PAD and Prickle. But even so, we are not looking to end the relationship."

Boniface was unsure why he was being told what he already knew and had clearly understood at the time.

"We believe that the talent and experience we bring to the relationship has led to results and will continue to lead to results beneficial to both parties."

Boniface felt an overwhelming urge to call her Fifi but resisted. "That was my understanding following our meeting, Fiona."

The lawyer stared at Boniface. "Your lawyer would seem to suggest otherwise. Those *gentlemen*," the word dripped contempt, "who accompanied him seemed to be of a similar opinion."

"What lawyer?" asked Boniface.

The lips on Picasso's experiment pursed. "Aaron Delcort was pushed. Very roughly." Her tone fired accusations. "That sort of behavior is simply not acceptable under any circumstances." She relaxed slightly. "As far as I can tell, I didn't get threatened because they thought I was just the secretary. It's not every day you find yourself the beneficiary of ignorant sexism."

Boniface waited a moment or two, attempting to communicate that he was considering, then continued with a softness he hoped would lead Fiona's attitude to a calmer place. "I don't have a lawyer. I haven't asked anyone to call on you or to..."

"You will forgive my skepticism." There was a newfound force in the lawyer's voice. "While I'm grateful for my own personal safety, I find this denial rather hollow given that it is quite clear you are working for Prickle."

Boniface felt the confusion returning, and a need for more painkillers.

"Beyond Mister Irvine," continued the lawyer, "what about this?" She held up her phone, pointing to the screen. "While we may have a dispute with Prickle, we still like to keep up to date with them, and Luca is very keen to document every moment of his day. Apparently Zio Boniface—*Uncle* Boniface—has kindly supplied him with some new amplifiers made by Zeimetz Tone Machines. That seems a very generous action for a man who claims only to be writing a biography."

"There's a..." started Boniface.

"Shh," said the lawyer, getting to her feet and looking down at him. "Let me be clear. We don't take well to threats—our next response will be to involve the police and to seek injunctions where necessary. As you will understand, that may have a reputational impact for your business."

She stepped back, seemingly judging the office. "As I've said, we believe we bring considerable talent to the relationship with Prickle. From what I've read about you, I'm not sure that you have the competence in this area or the resources to match what we offer. And if you do want to take the business of Prickle, you can be assured we will be looking for a considerable financial payment in settlement of our losses."

It only took her long legs two steps to reach the door, where she looked back. "One other thing." Boniface looked up. "Your lawyer. He isn't."

thirty-three

Boniface reached his office door in time to see Fiona Aldred step into the elevator.

"I really am sorry," said Montbretia as Boniface walked into her room and carefully lowered himself into the seat by the window. "She's..."

Boniface waited. When Montbretia offered nothing further, he threw out a few suggestions. "Tall?" Montbretia wrinkled her nose. "Skinny." Montbretia seemed to consider the description. "Odd." Apparently Montbretia couldn't dispute that characterization. "She might be odd, but I think she's competent, although perhaps a little misguided at the moment."

"Misguided?" asked Montbretia.

"I think there's some confusion," said Boniface. "I told Luca about the amps."

"I know," said Montbretia. Boniface frowned. "He tweeted about his amps and his new Uncle Boniface."

Boniface deflated. "Seems to be something of a theme here... Anyway, Luca is expecting a call from you when you're ready to make arrangements for the hand-over to be filmed, or whatever it is Zeimetz want." He leaned forward, feeling the pain. "Thank you for getting that sorted—in the world of Prickle, it is important."

"Talking about the world of Prickle, how was Danny?" asked Montbretia.

"Rough. Dawn's not back and he's not sleeping, which isn't that surprising."

"So that's the end of our dealings with them—apart from getting the amps to Luca?"

Boniface felt his head turning from left to right and back.

"So did he agree that you should go to the cops?"

"No."

"The press?"

"No."

"What did you agree on, Boniface?"

"Nothing. He wasn't in a state to agree to anything, and I didn't want to push him."

"You should have—you should have pushed him."

"He was in tears."

Montbretia let out an exasperated sigh. "And that is why you should have pushed him. If it matters enough to cry, then it matters enough to call the cops—especially because the evidence is only going to fade." She indicated the bruising and the cuts on his face.

"It's not important," muttered Boniface.

"He's been pushing you to help him—and it's in his best interest that everything is sorted—and when you get an opportunity to move things forward, you duck." She looked away, leaving the room quiet—the only sound coming from outside, where a delivery truck was reversing into the school grounds.

Boniface began softly. "I'm going to chat with Jilly again."

"The granny?" There was no approval in the question. "She's already told you to go away once. Do you think your war wounds will make you more appealing?"

"I want to see if she's a bit more amenable today. Hopefully I can get to her before the kids have worn her down."

"As an idea it's bonkers, but I'm not going to stop you." Her tone was resigned. "But please take some more painkillers before you leave."

thirty-four

"It's you again." She pulled the baby closer as she looked him up and down—her cynicism turning to concern. "You looked better yesterday." She squinted, as if looking at the detail of an oil painting. "A lot better."

"I felt better yesterday." The face of a granddaughter appeared between her grandmother's legs, her hands sturdily gripping a limb. "I came to apologize for yesterday—I got you at a really bad time and I intruded. And I was stupid to return the ball."

Her face softened. "Raff's at school, so it's calmer here. Us three girls together." She smiled at her two granddaughters, then pointed her head toward Boniface, questioning. "So what happened—who did you upset?"

Boniface looked down, feeling sheepish and not quite sure how to respond.

"Are you going to keep being a pain in the bum until I talk to you?" asked Jilly. He raised his eyes and twisted the side of his lip. "Do you want a cup of tea then?"

Jilly was already leading into the house before Boniface could respond. He followed her into the kitchen, where in one swing she flicked on the kettle and placed the baby in a high chair. "Savannah needs some lunch, so your tea will be a couple of minutes."

Boniface looked at the two-year-old still clinging to her grandmother's leg. "If you need another pair of hands..." Jilly turned to face him, a slight look of shock. "Let me wash my hands and I'll get straight on it."

She pointed to the sink and turned to the fridge. As Boniface dried his hands, she placed a small jar and a plastic teaspoon on the table next to the high chair where the baby sat. "Put this on." She handed him an apron from the back of the door. "Don't argue; that's a nice suit and Savannah will be wearing a bib, so you'll be even."

"This kitchen looks very new," said Boniface, sitting in front of the baby and unscrewing the cap of her food. "And it's all very clean and shiny. Do you have an army of people who come in to scrub and polish every night?"

"Ha!" Jilly threw back her head and laughed. "No—it is new. My ex is a plumber—I paid trade prices for the units, and he and two of his mates fitted it. They did the bathroom at the same time." She raised her eyes upward. "Turns out that in divorce he's not that unreasonable... Plus, he knew the grandkids would be spending a lot of time here, and he wants the best for them."

She looked over at her granddaughter swallowing another mouthful as Boniface cautiously removed the spoon. "You're good with kids."

"They see a kindred spirit—they recognize one of their own," said Boniface. "It's us kids against the world; no sense in fighting among ourselves."

"Any of your own?"

Boniface shook his head. "You've probably heard the story...my wife, now ex-wife, and I worked, I drank a lot, *a lot*, it was never the right time, I drank some more, I went to work for the government, I melted down, it all became ugly, the marriage ended. Good terms—but no kids."

"I'm sorry," she said quietly, watching Boniface feed her younger granddaughter.

"I've been talking to a lot of people over the past couple of days—one name came up which seems important." Boniface watched as Jilly's eyes brightened slightly. "Billy Watkins. Have you heard of him?"

"Heard of him. Met him," said Jilly softly. "He was the devil. At least as far as Dawn was concerned, he was all things that are evil rolled into one."

Boniface lifted another spoonful of puree and concentrated on the moving mouth in front of him.

"He turned up to an M-Stub8 gig one night. When I say gig, it was an appearance at a nightclub in somewhere like Stevenage, Letchworth, or Welwyn Garden City. One of those poxy commuter towns about thirty miles north of London. The Friday night crowd would be out on the prowl—those that pulled would go to their car and shag. Those that didn't would come and watch us lip sync while they leered and made the kinds of suggestions that only teenagers who have never had sex can make. The first we knew about Billy was when he took some kid out—the kid made a comment about Dawn, Billy fractured his cheekbone, and Dawn froze."

"Nice guy," said Boniface lightly. "The kind you'd want to invite round to meet your mother."

"He turned up quite a bit after that—it always upset Dawn. She'd known him from where she grew up and never wanted anything to do with him. He started chasing Carmen to make Dawn jealous; all that did was make Carmen unhappy and let Dawn get away." Her voice became reedy. "And then Lorna died and we fell apart. Carmen stayed with Billy—she didn't have anywhere else to go. We all clung to whatever driftwood was floating by—seems Dawn got lucky and grabbed a bit of solid oak."

She turned and faced out the window, her older granddaughter tugging at her leg. "So what's Billy done now?"

"He's dead," said Boniface.

"Dead?" She sounded almost relieved. "Does Dawn know? She'd be...well, it would be something she didn't have to worry about. She really was that upset whenever he turned up."

Boniface paused before he continued, his tone noncommital. "Do you know where Carmen is these days?"

"No." Jilly seemed apologetic. "I last saw her a few years ago—I don't think the years have been kind. I only got half the story—she was in a car crash, a bad one, left her in a coma. After she left hospital, she self-medicated and worked the streets to pay for her habit. She was in a squat for a while, and I think she did some porn—the really unpleasant stuff. When we spoke, she was in a hostel trying to pull her life together again."

She stood up straight, picked up a cloth, and came over to the baby, wiping her mouth. "Was that nice? Say thank you to Uncle Boniface." She turned to Boniface. "That sounds a bit odd, Uncle Boniface."

"Savannah wouldn't be the first person to call me that today," said Boniface.

Jilly picked up the baby, resting her over her shoulder and gently patting her back. "Don't get me wrong—I'd like to see you come round here and feed her every lunchtime...and perhaps you could take Rafferty to the park until he's about 35—but I don't know anything more. It was a long time ago, and lots of those memories still hurt today."

thirty–five

"Boniface!" Montbretia answered the phone. "Please tell me you're not in a hospital somewhere—I freaked when I saw your number come up. I thought someone might have lifted your phone off your dead body."

She dropped into her chair.

"So where are you?" She pushed the handset under her chin, clicked her mouse, and called up a map onto the screen. "Leyton—I thought you went to see Jilly." She paused, listening, watching as the map focused in on Leyton. "Oh. Jilly's in Leyton. Did she tell you to go away again?"

Montbretia clicked from the map view to the street view, dragging the cursor through the streets of Leyton in East London. The streets looked similar to the streets she had walked through in Bethnal Green when Boniface had dressed her up as a hooker from the 1980s and made her knock on Gray's front door. Perhaps these houses were more modern and maybe a bit larger. They certainly had front yards, so you couldn't bang on a door as you walked along the street.

"You fed her grandkids! I never had you as the Mister Mom domestic-tranquility type...you get too upset when your suit gets splashed in the rain." She continued listening, pulling the phone tighter under her chin, typing in internet searches as he spoke. "Sure, I can find—or at least look for—someone. Who are you interested in? Carmen Gallagher. Was in M-Stub8 with Dawn and Jilly."

She looked at the images appearing on her screen. Most were scanned from newspapers and magazines dating from the 1980s, but some were of a higher quality. There were pictures of her on her own—mostly, but not all, in a state of undress—and some pictures with the band, all clothed but dressed in a way that felt familiar given how Montbretia had dressed to visit Gray.

"Carmen Gallagher," she said to Boniface. "What am I looking for?" She clicked through more photos.

There was something striking about the woman—she stood out. Her skin was perhaps slightly darker than the other girls—with a name like Carmen, Montbretia wondered if one or both parents might have been Spanish—and her hair was darker: thick and rich with a curl that seemed natural. But what reached out from the screen and grabbed Montbretia was the woman's confidence.

Carmen was forward, Carmen was fearless, she lacked any form of self-consciousness, she roared, she had an animal-like sexuality, she was provocative, bold, assertive, vigorous, full-on, unabashed, unrepentant. Whether she was clothed, naked, or somewhere between, she was always smiling—not that fake model smile, but the smile that begins at the mouth, covers the whole face, and makes the eyes shine with complete joy. Smiling, shouting, cooing, and enjoying herself. Where so many models look as sexless as a three-year-old's plastic doll, Carmen—with or without clothes—always seemed to transmit the message that she *loved* sex.

"You want me to find her current location...might be a hostel in central London. Well, don't get too specific, Boniface. I'd hate to have an easy afternoon or to have any confidence that I can find an answer before you get back."

She scanned a few articles. Mostly old perverts with their own webpages reminiscing about the models from when they were teenagers—she decided not to look too closely in case Boniface's name was there. "Isn't this Lorna character important—might there be something in how she died? Yeah, I get that she's dead so she can't tell us anything, but what I'm saying is perhaps there's something related to her death and why Dawn disappeared."

The question seemed to make Boniface grumpy.

"Okay, okay. You can tell me why Carmen is important when you get back." She exhaled, pushing out her bottom lip. "So I'm looking on the internet and I'm not seeing any contact numbers—where do I start? Okay...I'll call Veronica for newspaper archives, but do we have a clue which hostel? Okay, I'll get on the phones."

thirty-six

Boniface decided to take the stairs. He was still in pain—and suspected he would be in some discomfort for a week or more—but he needed to stop behaving like an invalid, and it was only two flights of stairs. In any event, he hurt a lot less than he had this morning.

He stood outside the door and punched in the key code.

It was strange—usually the lights would be on. If not all the lights, then at least some. Switches were a thing of the past: All the lights in the office were on motion sensors coupled with timers. If you walked from one end to the other, the lights would come on, and then—according to some bizarre rules set by the electrician who did the fitting—the timers would progressively switch the lights off.

Theoretically, if you sat very still for a very long time, then all the lights would switch off, but the reality was that one or the other of them was always moving, so there would always be a light on somewhere.

Boniface opened the door and stepped into the main corridor, letting the door close behind him. The lights in the corridor clicked on, confirming there hadn't been a power cut. He stepped forward, and the sensor at the far end picked up the movement, firing more lights into action. When he passed the kitchen, there was a click and the light came on—he needed to call the electrician to fix that. There was no need to register someone passing. When he went into the kitchen to make tea, then he wanted light. When he passed, he wanted dark.

There seemed to be one thing missing: Montbretia.

He stepped into her room, lit only from the dull light outside, filtered through the tinted glass—a hangover from the 1970s. There was a buzz, and the light fired, revealing a floor covered with papers, scattered pens, and a broken mug, with what might be coffee splashed across the wall.

"Hello." A small voice came out from behind Montbretia's visitor's chair. "Has she gone?"

Boniface moved as quickly as he could to the chair and dropped to his knees, ignoring the pain as he maneuvered himself to look through the gap beside the chair, and into the space where Montbretia was sitting. "Hello," he said, looking at the figure sitting with her knees under her chin, her arms wrapped around her shins and pulling her legs toward her body. "Has who gone?"

"The woman who shouted."

"What woman who shouted?"

"The scary woman who shouted."

"I didn't see any woman—shouting or not."

"Go and look. Make sure she's gone." It wasn't a polite request. Montbretia had issued an order.

Boniface stood slowly. Maybe he should try not to kneel down on a hard surface for a day or two.

He walked into his room—the light flicked on—and checked behind his sofa and under his desk. No one, shouting or otherwise. There was no one in the meeting room—including under the long table. The two client rooms were similarly bereft of people, and both the kitchen and the reception area were empty.

He reached Montbretia's door before turning and checking the fire door, which was locked, and then checked the front door, which was properly closed.

"There's no one here," he said, looking down at Montbretia, who was still sheltering behind her chair. "Do you want a hand up?" He reached down. After a few moments Montbretia grabbed his hand and pulled herself to the vertical. She pushed the chair forward with her knees, slipping through the gap, and hugged Boniface. "She was scary and she shouted. Very loud. And she threw things."

"It's not like you not to fight back," said Boniface. "But please don't think I'm not grateful that I don't have to buy new carpets again."

"I don't like fighting on home soil. And I couldn't injure myself—one of us has to remain capable, and it's not you at the moment."

"I can feed babies. What further skill could I need?" asked Boniface mock-huffily. "Who was she?"

"I don't know. She was scary and shouted and threw things. Isn't that enough for you to identify her?"

"Probably," said Boniface.

"What did she look like?"

"Shorter than me. Slim. Angry. Long dark hair, straight. Asian, perhaps, Thai, maybe, but probably Filipino."

"Alone?"

"No—there was a big dumb lump, but he didn't say anything."

"Did she say what she wanted?"

"You mean in between throwing things?" Boniface nodded. "The gear—she said it was hers."

"What gear?"

"The gear—the gear for Luca." She stepped back and lifted her shoulders, then sighed deeply. "Has she really gone?"

"Mmm."

"She got really angry when I said the gear isn't here." Montbretia looked up, letting her hair fall over her face. "Who is she, Boniface?"

"I don't know, but my guess is you just met Bing-Bing, Missus Parzani, Luca's former wife."

There was a look of surprise on Montbretia's face. "Why did she...?"

Boniface raised his shoulders slightly. "My guess? Luca tweeted about the new amps, she saw the opportunity for him to make further reparations but didn't realize the gear hasn't arrived, and you got in her way."

"Really?"

"It's my best guess," said Boniface. "You still look shaken—let's get out of here and get some lunch."

"We can't leave," said Montbretia. "She'll be back. The last thing she said was, 'You'll be sorry.'"

"It was just an empty threat. Come on—let's get something to eat. If you're not here, she can't hurt you."

thirty-seven

Montbretia and Boniface left the first flight of stairs, turning onto the second flight leading up to their office. "That's a good place for lunch," said Boniface. "Good food. Not too heavy."

"I told you you'd like it," said Montbretia. "Now do you understand why I wanted to go there?"

"I do," said Boniface, reaching the landing and falling silent.

Montbretia walked around him, then noticed where he was staring. "Did you lock the door?"

"You say that as if locking the door would have stopped the glass getting kicked in." They looked through the lower half of the door to the glass—which had previously filled the pane, but which was now shattered and scattered over their carpet.

Part of the wooden frame that had held the pane had been twisted but not fully broken off, and was stopping the door from closing. "You wait here," said Boniface, gingerly pulling the door.

"No," said Montbretia, stepping into the passage and following Boniface as he pushed himself against the wall to avoid the broken nuggets of glass. "Did you set the alarm?"

"It was only a quick lunch," said Boniface, walking into Montbretia's office.

Her desk drawers had been removed, their contents tipped in a pile on the floor on top of the already scattered papers, and the empty drawers stacked roughly on the desk. He looked more closely: The faces of two drawers had been pulled from the rest of the drawer. The chair—her earlier buttress against invaders—had been tipped over.

"It's that bitch," said Montbretia. "She said she'd be back."

Boniface led into his room to see the sofa tipped over and the desk drawers open but not removed.

"So I tell you not to keep anything in your desk—I scan every document for you—and it's my desk that gets emptied."

Boniface quietly led into the conference room to see the table had been turned over. He poked his head into the two client rooms to see similar, and then looked in the kitchen, which seemed exactly as it had been when he'd last looked in.

"I'm telling you, Boniface. It's that bitch—she said she would come back. She said I'd be sorry." Boniface watched Montbretia. She stood straighter, uncurling her shoulders. She inhaled deeply. "I'm calling the cops."

"No." Boniface's voice was quiet, but the speed was reflexive. "Don't call them. Not yet."

"If not now, then when?" Montbretia's tone suggested her frustration at Bing-Bing was transferring into anger at Boniface.

"Apart from the door, there's no real damage. If, repeat *if*, it's Bing-Bing, then that will just be embarrassing for Danny and the band."

"What do you mean no damage? And who cares about embarrassment?"

"I mean this is a mess that will take us both..." he exaggerated the word *both*, pointing between them, "a while to clean up. But it will take far longer to talk to the police. And we all care about embarrassment—think how we'll feel if we call the cops and they can't prove it was Bing-Bing."

Boniface watched as Montbretia's face twitched.

"We need to get out of here," said Boniface. "It's not safe with all that glass, and I'm not leaving you here. Give Luca a call—don't tell him about this, but say we want five minutes to talk about the amps, away from Danny. While you do that, I'll call the carpenter."

thirty-eight

"May I just officially state for the record: The Surrey Hills are gorgeous. Why haven't you told me about them before?"

Boniface seemed to have decided that Montbretia's question was rhetorical.

"Is this place real? I mean, do people live here—it looks like a film set. You know, the kind of place where there's some busybody old woman who figures who committed the murder before the detectives. Then she just says 'hmm' when they ask and brings everyone together to confront the murderer...in the library."

"They do shoot a lot of stuff around here," said Boniface. "But these are real places. Real villages with real people. People actually live and work here."

"Wow," said Montbretia. "I'm coming down on my bike."

"The third best way to get around," said Boniface.

"Third?"

Boniface tilted his head forward as he steered along the narrow lane, flinching when the barge drifted close enough to sculpt the sandstone banks. "You need to understand the geography of the place."

"And you do?" Montbretia was not convinced.

"No," said Boniface. "But Dawn does, and she told me."

Montbretia accepted defeat and went back to looking out the window as Boniface continued. "There's the main road that goes through the bottom of the valley. And from this central road, there are spurs that jut off."

"Are we on a spur now?" she asked.

"Yeah," said Boniface. "And the difficulty with the spurs is that if you want to go from place A on one spur to place B on the adjacent spur, and you want to drive, then most of the time you have to go all the way out to the central spine and back again. And as you will have figured, that gives you a long journey along narrow, twisting roads."

"Narrow, but pretty—it's just so green out here, Boniface."

"It might be," he said, his tone unaltered. "However, if you're driving, your attention tends to focus on not wrecking your car on these sandstone banks."

"Okay," said Montbretia hesitantly. "But that still doesn't tell me why a bike is only the third best way to travel around here."

"You will have noticed the hills," said Boniface.

"I saw the sign," said Montbretia. "You pointed to it—it had the word *hill* on it. But they're not exactly massive hills, are they?"

"You mean, we're in the hills, not in the mountains," said Boniface. "And the thing with these hills is they're pretty irregular, so to answer your question, the best way to travel around here is on foot. The distances aren't huge, and you can go directly from one point to another without needing to come out to the central spine."

"You are aware that bikes can follow footpaths?" asked Montbretia.

"I am," said Boniface. "But they have wheels that can buckle and tires that puncture, which is why they're not as good as walking or the second best way to get around: horses."

The tree cover cleared, giving a view of the late afternoon sky but little sight of the surrounding land, which was separated by tall hedgerows on the sides. The road twisted again before inclining downward, passing through another tunnel formed by trees, giving way to a clear stretch of asphalt, lined below the height of the road by a row of red-brick houses with deep-pitched roofs.

Boniface slowed the barge and turned to the right into a large parking lot, its uneven surface covered by gravel.

"Where are we?" asked Montbretia.

"Exactly where you told Luca we would be."

"You said 'the pub in Peaslake.' I thought that was...code." She looked around. "Where are we?"

"Peaslake," said Boniface and pointed at a wide two-story building, rendered in white, with dark-brown roof tiles. "And that is the pub."

"But how will Luca know that this is the right pub?"

"Because it's the only pub," said Boniface. "I don't want to overstate the case, but with that row of houses," he indicated the row that they had just passed, "and those houses over there," he pointed to the houses on the slopes of a hill about 50 yards away—a mismatched collection of red brick and some mock-Tudor woodwork dotted between enough trees to suggest these building had just escaped from the woods, "that is the whole village. Come on, I'll take you to the heart of the metropolis."

Boniface led Montbretia out of the parking lot. "Where's the sidewalk?"

"There isn't one," said Boniface, leading Montbretia past the pub with a large red-brick chimney seemingly glued to the outside wall on top of the white render. The road forked as it reached a junction, forming a small grass triangle with a sign declaring that you were indeed in Peaslake. Boniface took two steps forward, indicating in turn the village stores, a small, squat building with a glass frontage divided into individual panes; the village war memorial, a simple stone cross; a red telephone booth; and a red letter box. "And here ends the official tour of Peaslake."

"That's it?"

"It's a village."

"It's...it's beautiful." There was a lightness to Montbretia's voice. "Tiny, but beautiful. I don't care what you say, Boniface. I am so coming back here on my bike. How did you find it?"

"I took the wrong road when I left Danny's." He turned back to the pub. "Let's go and sit down while we wait for Luca."

The two settled with a cup of tea and a mineral water, taking position on a not particularly comfortable sofa with a clear view of the door. "There he is," said Boniface as Luca came through the door, his long hair looking somehow out of place in an English village that seemed to have lost track of time somewhere around the mid-1930s.

Three people—two men and one woman—all in their sixties or seventies headed toward the door, blocking Luca's path. Their senses of style could not be more different. The rock god in jeans and a leather jacket, his flowing mane and the swagger. The pensioners' prevalent color of choice was beige; their style of dress—to be kind—could be described as elasticated easy wash.

Montbretia heard the end of the conversation. "Bella." The Italian was holding the older woman's hand to his lips—his gaze fixed on her face.

"Is he flirting with her?" she asked, keeping her lower jaw immobile.

"Don't be jealous," said Boniface. "Your turn will come."

Luca was beaming, holding the door for the three pensioners. As the woman passed, Luca's face dropped, and he released the door onto her two male companions before he turned toward the bar. Spying the barmaid his shoulders went back, his chest puffed out, and the edge of his grin returned.

"Are we going to have this with every woman in the bar?" asked Montbretia, her jaw becoming tighter. "I ask that because I think that dog over there is a bitch," she nodded toward a damp and muddy golden Labrador lying next to her master.

"I said your turn would come," said Boniface. "I'm just not sure whether you're in the queue before or after the Lab." The barmaid put a drink in front of Luca. He made a comment and she blushed, her cheeks getting redder as Luca continued talking. Finally, the guitarist picked up the glass, pointed to Boniface, winked at the barmaid, and continued chatting with her.

"According to Mel—Prickle's drummer—around this time of day he'll be looking to find a woman for the night using that fearsome combination of social media, his natural charisma, his complete lack of self-consciousness, and desperation."

"Desperation?" asked Montbretia.

"If he doesn't hook up with a woman who can provide recreation and a bed, then he has to spend the night in the hotel that Danny is paying for—and it's a pretty grim, tedious box out by the main road."

"Why doesn't Danny let him stay at his place?"

"Apparently—and I'm just repeating what Mel told me—Luca is very uninhibited and is very proud of his body. This combination meant there was far too much chance of *accidental* nudity—you could find that he'd come down for breakfast, get a coffee, sit outside and have a smoke, and the idea of putting on clothes wouldn't have crossed his mind."

"Oh."

"Danny could cope—he's been touring with the guy for years. But he didn't want to inflict that on Dawn."

"Zio Boniface." The guitarist was standing on the other side of the low table in front of Boniface and Montbretia's sofa. "You need to pay Chloe for the drink." He lifted his glass as if it explained fully, then turned toward the bar. "Chloe, bella." The barmaid blushed again.

Luca dropped into the chair opposite Montbretia, taking her hand and focusing his full wattage on her. "So, Uncle. Is this my next present that you're bringing me to win favor?" His gaze remained on Montbretia. "Are you trying to show me that you're a cool uncle?"

"This is Montbretia—who you should thank for sorting the Zeimetz Tone Engines deal."

"Ciao, Montbretia," said Luca without letting his gaze slip. "So she is my present. She is a very beautiful present, Uncle. Thank you. I will be sure to show her my full appreciation for all she has done to help me."

Montbretia pulled her hand away.

"Fiery," said Luca, a look of delight exploding over his face.

"We've got a slight problem," said Boniface. "Over here, Luca." He snapped his fingers, twice, and for the first time since he had sat down, Luca relaxed his gaze on Montbretia. "Bing-Bing came to try to take possession of your new amps."

"Which haven't arrived yet," added Montbretia.

A look of glee spread over Luca's face.

"She was pretty abusive. She got very aggressive."

A look of serenity crossed Luca's face. "She's a woman who knows her own mind."

"Then later," continued Boniface, "while we were both out, the office got trashed."

Luca shook his head—there was a slight rustling as his mane settled.

"You do see the link, Luca?"

"You're wrong, Zio. It wasn't her," said Luca. "Bing-Bing didn't trash your office."
He paused. "You clearly don't understand strong women, Zio Boniface."

"There's strong and borderline sociopath," muttered Montbretia, falling silent as
Boniface caught her eye.

The guitarist smiled at Boniface. "I like strong women. I like women with an
opinion. I like women who will stand up for themselves and tell me what they want."
He leaned forward, lowering his voice. "Take Chloe." He threw his eyes toward the
barmaid. "She is pretty, yes?"

"A bit young for me to be looking," said Boniface.

"Look at her, Boniface, she is pretty." Boniface shrugged as the guitarist continued. "But she's not interesting. She would just lie there and let me have sex with her."

He looked back at the barmaid.

"She *is* pretty, but where's the fun in that? I want to be surprised. I want to be
excited. I want to be thrilled. I don't want..." He spread his legs, tensed every muscle
in his body, and then relaxed. "Where's the fun in that? I'm sorry if that's what
your wife likes, but for me..." He shook his head. "No. Give me my equal. Give me
someone with spirit."

He stared up at Boniface, his eyes accusing. "Don't you like a woman with an
opinion, Boniface?"

"But Bing-Bing took everything you owned and sold it. She took all your guitars
and sold them. There were some beautiful handcarved pieces. Does that...?"

"Those are only objects, Uncle. She wanted my attention. She divorced me to get
my attention. That's all she's doing." He raised his eyebrows, delivering the words as
if he was stating elementary facts. "She wouldn't destroy your office—it wouldn't get
my attention."

thirty-nine

"You need to introduce that guy to Gideon—they could share stories."

"Share women more like." Boniface walked briskly around the side of the pub toward the parking lot. He could hear Montbretia following a step behind, seemingly surprised by his sudden decision to move.

"Why are we leaving? We haven't finished our drinks, and Luca's still on the prowl." She ran a step to draw level with Boniface. "I mean sure...I found him kinda creepy in a charming, oily sort of way, but you're moving as if you've left the gas on and if we don't get home in five minutes the house will burn down."

"Don't you see?" Boniface didn't wait for an answer. "We've got a problem."

Montbretia ran for another step, drawing level with Boniface as he turned into the parking lot.

"If it's not Bing-Bing—and I found Luca's rationalization totally plausible, even if I do want to wash some images off my brain with bleach—then that means it's someone else."

"So? It's someone else?" Montbretia reached the passenger door of the barge as Boniface dropped inside the car.

"I'm saying you were right," said Boniface, starting the car as Montbretia sat. He started moving backward before her door was closed.

"Right about...?" She yanked her door shut. Boniface put the car into gear and spun the wheels as the tires bit into the loose gravel surface.

"That whatever we're into is dangerous." He turned onto the road, heading in the direction from which they had come. "There's a USB thumb drive in that glove compartment—"

"So if you're agreeing it's dangerous, then are we going to the cops?"

"No." Boniface was accelerating—pushing the car faster than he felt comfortable pushing it in such narrow lanes. "We don't have time to explain the problem—the problem for which there is insufficient evidence—to flatfoots and wait for them to catch up. We need to do something now."

"Is this what you're after?" asked Montbretia, holding up an object.

Boniface flicked his eyes to the object Montbretia was holding—a silver plastic USB stick on a black lanyard—and immediately returned his view to the road, giving a single nod.

"What shall I do with it?"

"Put it round your neck."

"Done," said Montbretia. "Do you want to explain where we're going?"

"We're going to send out the bat signal. We're calling International Rescue." Boniface turned on the car's lights and accelerated.

"I don't understand, Boniface. Why are you driving like a loony and why don't you just use your phone?" She pulled out her phone and held it on the edge of his peripheral vision. "Use mine—just tell me who to call."

"I bought the drinks with a credit card," said Boniface.

"You know, that's legal. You don't go to jail for using a credit card or for buying three drinks in a public house in the English countryside."

"Yup, but there will be an electronic trace."

"There's a trace of your whole life somewhere."

"Precisely—but there mustn't be a trace for where we go next."

"Now you're talking in riddles. Where are we going?"

"Guildford is the closest town—it's close but far enough. And there's a university with lots of people, and we should be able to find an internet connection, which is when that gizmo round your neck will come into action."

"What? Wearing a necklace gives me superpowers? It makes me invisible?"

Boniface relaxed. "In a way it does. It anonymizes your connection on the internet, making you virtually untraceable—virtually, not completely, hence we're going somewhere that we've never been before and where we'll never go again."

Montbretia was breathing heavily through her nose, seemingly not able to decide which question to ask first out of the many that seemed to be bouncing around her brain.

"Why do we need this cloak-and-dagger stuff?"

"For Leathan's protection."

"Who's Leathan?" asked Montbretia.

"Leathan is...Leathan," said Boniface. "The point is, you don't know who he is. But more to the point, neither does anyone else know what Leathan looks like."

"So?" Her tone was more confused than accusatory.

Boniface sighed gently. "If it hasn't clicked already—if Bing-Bing didn't break our door, then Ernie did. Ernie who organized for my face to be rearranged last night. Ernie who doesn't know what Leathan looks like. And Leathan is good at dealing with this sort of challenge."

Montbretia paused before asking her next question. "I still don't see why we can't just call this Leathan or send him an email."

"Because those can be traced, and the reason that Leathan isn't living here is that he upset a few people. If we make him traceable, then he might end up dead, and dead is no use to us."

"So how do we contact him?"

"Facebook."

"But you're not on Facebook."

"I am. I'm a 14-year-old girl in Nebraska called Madison. I post about kittens, gummy bears, One Direction, and...well, all sorts of stuff I don't care about."

"It sounds a bit creepy," said Montbretia.

"It is. But with this identity, I post on my friend's page, and she is Leathan. I post that I've bought a new packet of gummy bears, and I'm about to eat them, and Leathan comes running. Or at least he picks up a phone that can't be traced, when it is safe for him, and if the Facebook logs are ever traced, no one knows who made the original posting or who read it."

Montbretia sat quietly as Boniface continued to thread the barge through the country lanes of the Surrey Hills. "I've been here for a year, and suddenly you tell me there's this guy called...what was his name?"

"Leathan. Lee...thn," said Boniface, emphasizing each syllable. "And you haven't heard about him because we haven't had a problem of this size before."

"Oh," mouthed Montbretia. "But isn't this all a bit ad hoc...Facebook postings and the like?"

"It is—that's why we're sending up a flare now. I'm relying on Leathan not being in trouble and checking the internet. Depending on what state he's in, he could call in five minutes, but he might not see the message for five weeks."

forty

"Are we going to every pub in the Surrey Hills?"

"This is only the second pub." Boniface let the barge wallow along the marginally less narrow lane, with a few less twists and permanent hedgerows replacing sandstone banks, until he reached a whitewashed brick house with Tudor beams.

He scanned the walls—the waves in every plane and the lack of any right angles told him that the building was old. There were three similarly constructed buildings—all clearly built at a time when tarmac roads were unheard of and the internal combustion engine would have been viewed as witchcraft worthy of the most serious consequences.

"Where are we?" asked Montbretia as Boniface let the barge drift around the lefthand bend, taking another left in front of the pub he had seen from the main road: another low-standing brick-built whitewashed building, but more modern than the wobbly houses they had just passed. This had some form and structure—this had a well-maintained slate roof. This had right angles.

"Sutton Abinger." He paused. "I can tell you're glad you asked."

The parking lot was maybe three times the length of the pub, but with only a handful of cars and a few motorbikes. The kind of motorbikes that were only run on weekends or when the owner could be sure there wouldn't be any rain. Certainly not the kind of bike that would appeal to a member of a motorcycle gang.

They had been sitting for less than five minutes when Mel Grant joined them. His tan leather jacket highlighted the rich, deep tone of his skin. "Hey Mel." Boniface stood to shake the drummer's hand. "I don't think you've met Montbretia."

"Haven't met—but I've heard good things about." He shook her hand. "Good to meet you, Montbretia. I hear you've sorted some amps for Luca. I should get you fixing my endorsements."

Montbretia flushed and mumbled something as the drummer sat.

"Why the secret squirrels, Boniface?"

Boniface winced. "Not secret…"

"You want me on my own—in a pub that's just that bit further away—and it's not secret?"

"Not secret," said Boniface. "Discreet. I don't want this conversation going beyond us—I don't want anyone to know we're having this chat."

"I'm not sure if that's better or worse," said the drummer, leaning back in his chair.

Although the pub was old, somehow the furniture and décor were the wrong sort of old. The tables and chairs were all the same theme that appeared in many pubs: thin stick furniture and varnished dark wood. Tables that were never quite level, meaning whenever they got knocked—which happens when you get a group of people around a table talking and drinking—the drinks got spilled. And spilled alcohol then flows off the edge of the table and onto the deep red carpet with blue diamonds outlined in yellow.

"I spoke to Danny this morning," said Boniface. "He seemed fragile. I don't want to add to his worries, which is why I'm asking you. All I want to know: Is there anything I should know?"

The big man's face relaxed. "I told you, Boniface. Danny's my brother." The drummer clenched his fist, beating his heart twice. "Genuinely I have nothing to tell you—not that I would blab if there was something."

Boniface let his head rock backward and forward, silently acknowledging the drummer's words but wondering whether silence would encourage the other man to elaborate.

"He's under a lot of stress. He feels it's his responsibility to find a singer, and without the management to help, that's a lot of work. And there's the cash—having the bank account frozen is a major worry. But I think the big problem is finding a singer. He's asked everyone—he asked David Coverdale, but he's got a throat problem. He asked Paul Rogers, but he's booked for another charity gig in New York that night. I'll tell you how extreme it's getting—he even thought about asking the guy who sold the gig on eBay."

Mel was repeating excuses. In Boniface's experience, when that happened, it was time to ask some more questions.

"But is there more—is there something I don't know?"

"Why should you know more?" Mel's attitude had changed. Suddenly the relaxed, easygoing guy was on the defensive. Questioning. Wondering. "What's your role here?"

"I'm trying to help find what the problem is Danny wants solved."

"What does that mean, Boniface?"

"Is there a problem with Dawn?"

The drummer fell back in his chair, which groaned with the momentum of the highly evolved body mass hitting it square on. Boniface was sure he could hear the wood starting to crack.

"I was the person he first played 'Tattoo Your Name on My Heart' to." A broad row of white teeth showed. "'Do you think she'll like it?' he asked."

Boniface leaned forward and went to rest on the table. Looking down, he saw the thin film of spilled drinks trickling like a stream running downhill and decided against leaning on the table.

"I thought it was a brilliant song—but more than that, there was this guy spilling out his emotions, trying to tell a girl that he loved her. We didn't realize it would be the song that would break us globally. We didn't realize that it would be the song that would make their relationship. We didn't realize that the song was the key."

Boniface sat up straighter as the drummer continued, his voice soft. "But it wasn't the song that won over Dawn. It's great song—she loved it and still loves it, and she was bowled over by the romantic gesture of this guy standing there emotionally naked, just for her. What got her—what won her—was the commitment."

Boniface felt his brow crinkle.

"Danny put everything into that song. He told her everything. But he also put everything into the band—into what the kids today would call *our career*. The day that Dawn first heard the song was the day that she realized Danny was totally serious about how he was going to make money to exist as a grownup. He proved he didn't want to behave like Luca. He wanted normal things that everyone wants—a house with the mortgage paid, a car without finance due, money for kids, holidays, pensions and savings. This wasn't a dream—this was a plan that Danny was putting into action. And that's all Dawn wanted: Mister Average, Mister Dependable. The honest, hardworking guy who loved a girl for herself, not because she was an appendage to his lifestyle, and not because of how she looked."

Boniface looked at Montbretia wearing the same white cotton blouse with brown buttons that she had been wearing all day—even when she hid behind the office chair, even after lunch when she managed not to splash herself. The cuff was now dirty where she had smudged her makeup as she mopped a tear listening to Mel's story.

"I was the best man at his wedding. I stood by him at the church—have you been to the church?"

Boniface shook his head.

"You should—stunning building, and it's only a few miles from here. Over a thousand years old. Ask Dawn; she'll give you all the history."

The drummer was looking down, seemingly lost in thought, then raised his head. "I was his best man—it was my privilege. It was my joy. Danny is my brother, and with that marriage I gained a sister, and I've been with them nearly every day since. I love them more than…" His voice trailed off, his eyes misting.

A few drinkers were talking at the bar, but Boniface was fixed on the big man.

As he began to speak again, his voice caught. He coughed and continued, his voice more steady. "They are two different personalities, but they work together and they communicate without words. He'll do anything for her. He won't treat her like a kid—but he will lay down his life. There's total trust."

"Have you seen her in the last couple of days?" asked Boniface.

"No, but that's not unusual. We play; she does her thing. She's got her own work—you've seen her pictures. You only get pictures that good by working hard."

"You're sure there's nothing there?"

The drummer leaned forward. His voice quiet, respectful. "You're coming from a good place, man, but I'm not comfortable with these questions. If you want to know something, you need to speak to Danny; you need to speak to Dawn. I won't tell Danny we had this meeting, but this is the end of the conversation."

forty-one

Boniface and Montbretia turned right out of the pub into the parking lot.

In the canopied lanes it would be dark. In the steeper-sided valleys—like the small valley with the pub where they met Luca, although *valley* was too strong a term for natural dip in the terrain—it would be getting dark. But out here with the comparatively flat, open space in front of them, without any woods or copses to bring shade, there was still sufficient light in the early evening.

Montbretia stared across the wooden fence and over the field that ran parallel to the parking lot and then farther.

When she had gone to the bathroom, she'd read a note about the pub where she and Boniface had just met Mel, the muscular drummer from Prickle. Apparently, parts of the building dated back to the sixteenth century. For such an old building it seemed incredibly well preserved—or maybe the main public areas were modern? Eighteenth century or something like that?

Boniface's pace was slower than normal—slower than it had been when they walked back from lunch. Something during the conversation with Mel had started niggling Boniface—he had never been able to walk at full speed and organize facts into a logical order. The slowed pace was one of the few signs she could recognize when something was troubling him.

But she wasn't sure what was making him think. Was it the love story? Had it tugged at something deep in his subconscious? Had it made him think about his marriage, which had ended but not quite ended? Was there some incongruence in Mel's story? Or was it the simple fact that Mel seemed unaware that Dawn was missing? Boniface only found out by accident when Danny thought she'd be back. Maybe Mel didn't know what was going on.

Boniface opened her door, then walked around and got in on the driver's side, firing up the engine before closing his door and putting on his seatbelt.

"Turn it off," said Montbretia.

Boniface looked toward her, a frown crossing his brow.

"The engine—turn it off. We need to talk."

The engine died.

"Please tell me that you're not going to screw this up."

"What?"

"Your conversation with Danny." She calibrated the tiny movements across his face—tightening micro-muscles, a slight loss of skin color in his cheeks. "You said he was fragile this morning. If Dawn's not back he's going to be even more fragile, and the last thing he needs is you accusing him or upsetting him, or wondering out loud if..." She became aware that her voice had been getting louder. She began again, softly. "What are you going to say to him?"

"I haven't even decided..."

"You have," she whispered. "You had decided before Mel left us." She lifted her voice. "I'm not disagreeing—it's probably the right thing to have a proper conversation with Danny—but before we go in, would you like to think about what you're going to say?"

"I'm going to ask him about Ernie."

"What in particular?"

"I'm going to ask him if he knows Ernie. If he does, I'm going to ask him what Ernie wants."

"And how are you going to react to what he tells you?" Boniface remained impassive. "Think about it—if there is a link, what's he going to tell you?"

Boniface pushed his jaw to the side.

"If he doesn't know Ernie, but there's still a link between our office being broken up and Ernie, then what can he tell us?" She paused. "I don't know what's going on—but I'm just saying, think what Danny might say if he doesn't know what's going on."

Boniface moved his mouth as if chewing air. Words didn't follow.

"And don't forget that pressure may be being applied directly to him. Heck—think what kind of pressure he's under with Dawn gone."

The mention of Dawn seemed to jab Boniface like a needle.

"So think hard: What are you going to say, how are you going to say it, and what do you really want to know? Remember, you're not being a journalist here. You want to encourage him to talk—not force him to defend himself."

He fired up the engine.

"And what about Carmen—don't you want to know about her?"

"In due course," said Boniface. "But for the moment, Danny is my priority."

forty-two

Boniface let the barge drift right and float over the stone driveway before coming to rest with the small group of cars that seemed to have made a tradition of congregating behind Danny and Dawn's house. This evening, there were only two cars—Boniface recognized neither.

"You'd better wait here," he said, then stopped himself. "I didn't mean stay here in this cage—I mean, I'd better go and see Danny alone."

"I already understood," said Montbretia.

"Do you want a coffee?" asked Boniface, casually. "The kitchen's just there." He pointed to the back door next to the table where Luca had sat that morning. "I'm sure they wouldn't mind if you helped yourself."

"I'm fine," said Montbretia. "Go and talk to Danny. And please don't mess it up."

Boniface closed the door and caught sight of someone he hadn't seen before.

Something screamed rock and roll.

Something also screamed not in the band. Or at least, not in this band.

Where Danny and Mel were on the less desirable side of 50, they were still in good shape—Mel more so than Danny, the more physically demanding role giving him a much better workout. However, this wasn't just about shape, this was long-term decisions, and the guys in the band seemed not to have made choices that they might be regretting now. This guy was different.

The tattoos covering each arm were as effective at covering his skin as a coat of gloss paint. Boniface couldn't quite be sure where the T-shirt ended and flesh began. He pondered—he hadn't seen Danny or Mel wearing a T-shirt. Maybe they had similar tattoos.

What they didn't have was a massive hole in their earlobe lined with some sort of dark material. The piercings on the man's face seemed minor to Boniface, but the stretched earlobe seemed...permanent, and not really something that could ever be covered. Boniface found himself staring as he neared. "Danny around?"

"In there," said the pierced, holed, and tattooed individual, in a hard-to-place Scandinavian accent. "My wife..."

Boniface looked back, not sure about the statement.

"My wife...I saw you looking." He held his arms, proudly displaying them. "My wife is a tattoo artist." Boniface tried to keep his face straight as the image of a body with no space between the tattoos took root in his brain. "Perhaps you would like one? Or your friend?" He tilted his head in the direction of Boniface's Mercedes.

"I'm fine, thanks," said Boniface, slightly distractedly. "But the ink is incredible. Such detail."

"I know," said the living artwork, continuing to walk toward the parking lot.

"How you holding up?" Danny was sitting on the sofa in the studio office as Boniface entered.

The bassist said nothing, communicating with a few indistinct hand gestures and facial twitches that could be interpreted as freely as an ink splodge. Boniface carefully maneuvered himself onto the desk, sitting where Danny had been sitting when the two chatted that morning.

"Ernie," said Boniface. "Ernie Norton."

Danny remained silent, his visual communication ending.

"Do you know him? Know the name?"

Danny pushed out his bottom lip.

"Any clue?"

A slow turn of the bass player's head.

"He seems to think he owns the band."

"He doesn't, and I don't know him." Danny's voice was controlled—a musician delivering the exact performance required. "How did you come across him?"

"Gray."

Danny exhaled, his exasperation visible, almost tangible. "I told you on day one that he's the root of the problems. This Ernie might be some bloke that Gray shot his mouth off to. Gray did that back in the day, and I'm sure it still happens."

The bassist returned to noncommunication mode, melting back into the sofa.

"But Ernie's more than some bloke Gray met in a pub—he's responsible for my face, and he broke up my office this afternoon." Danny stared as Boniface continued. "That's a lot of reaction for some bloke you don't know."

"What can I tell you, Boniface? However you want to phrase it, I don't know this bloke. That's not an endorsement of the man...that's not to suggest that I'm not concerned about your well-being, but it's not really the thing that has kept me awake." His voice fell. "I'm only concerned about one thing: Dawn."

"No news?" asked Boniface, his tone sympathetic.

"None."

"And you're sure there's no connection? You still reckon it's a coincidence—Gray mentions Billy; I mention Billy to Dawn and she disappears; I mention Billy to Ernie, who you don't know, and I get pummeled. You don't see any connections?"

"Why would I?" There was anger in Danny's voice.

"Because if I'm wrong, then Dawn has disappeared for another reason. A reason that is hidden from both of us—or at least, it's hidden from me." The annoyance on Danny's face didn't seem to be calming as Boniface continued. "People don't choose to disappear to get away from happy situations. You don't see it in the headlines: Happy housewife with a blissful marriage runs to get away from her happiness."

"Now you're being crazy, Boniface."

"But there's something here that I don't know," said Boniface.

"Whatever it is, I don't know either—and you seem to be implying I'm lying or it's my fault. You're meant to be helping, Boniface, not accusing me." He breathed heavily through his nose. "She's my wife. I love her, and I want her back."

A phone rang. Both men stared at each other. "That's mine," said Boniface, shaking himself free from the short staring competition and thrusting his hand into his pocket. He answered. "Hold on." He looked at Danny as he stood. "I need to take this. I'll be outside."

forty-three

He became aware, slowly.

His heart was beating faster. Not pounding, but a few extra beats per minute. Enough that he noticed.

As he held his phone, he could see a tremble in his hands. Maybe not unrelated to the increased tempo of his heart, but he still became aware and noticed it wasn't just his hand.

It was unlikely the temperature was any cooler than when he had entered the studio, but walking from inside to the outside, he could feel the drop. He pulled his jacket instinctively, then leaned against the wall just outside the door and spoke. "Leathan."

In his previous visits, he hadn't paid attention to the density of the woods or their proximity to the house. Danny and Dawn really did have a fairytale cottage—even if it was rather bigger than a cottage—in the middle of the woods. But maybe it wasn't a fairytale; perhaps it was the stuff of nightmares.

"It's urgent—I'm in deeper than I realized." He heard his own voice and turned away from Montbretia. He knew she was still sitting in the car, but somehow he didn't want to make a full confession about his lack of caution, even though she was out of earshot. "When does the train leave?"

He heard movement in the lobby of the studio.

"Okay...you need to get your passport." The steps inside became steps outside as Danny appeared. "I understand: *a* passport, not necessarily *your* passport." He felt himself starting to uncurl. "I'll be there when you get in.... Yeah, I know the procedure." Boniface slipped his phone back into his pocket and looked up at the bassist.

Danny looked sheepish but seemingly had no curiosity about Boniface's interruption. He held up his hands as if surrendering. "I'm sorry, man. It's tough, and I know you've got my best interests at heart." He looked more closely at Boniface's wounds. "And I know you've taken some blows for me. But I ain't lying: I love and trust my wife."

Boniface tried to find the words, but Danny continued. "Look, man. I thought he was a crank, but some kid turned up today."

"Kid?" asked Boniface. "Are we using Gray's idea of a kid or...how old was he?"

Danny's face softened. "Gray's idea of a kid—I guess he was early thirties, but I couldn't be certain. Hard-life twentysomething, maybe." He seemed to be lost in thought. "How he looked and how he appeared seemed at odds—I couldn't make it out."

Boniface tried to unscramble the description as he waited while Danny recalled each element one slice at a time.

"He dressed young, but young from the 1990s. Boots, old jeans, white T with a sleeveless denim jacket."

"That's hardly a look exclusive to an era."

"That was when this look was last common," said Danny. "We had lots of fans who dressed like that—at first I thought he was one. He seemed to know who I was."

"You spoke to him?"

"Yeah. I sent Sven to get rid of him—Sven can look quite aggressive with his tattoos and the holes in his ears—but this kid was quite insistent, so I went to speak to him." The tension seemed to dissipate slightly. "And up close, he wasn't pretty—I'd say there have been a lot of drugs over a long time. I'd say he ain't long for this planet with that level of usage. His skin had that look when all the energy has left it and his hair...it was dark, but was that sort of look you get when teenagers are experimenting and just mix everything together, and it just comes out the color of ick."

"So what did he say?"

"He wanted to see Dawn, but he wouldn't say why." Danny started hunching, pulling his fists tight. "He was...you know...tetchy...on edge...aggressive. Like he was wound up or needed his next fix. But there was more—it might have been fear, maybe nerves or anxiety. Whatever it was, it came out as aggression."

"What did you tell him when he asked to see Dawn?"

"I said she wasn't around."

"Which is true."

"But he thought I was talking bull, so I said she's gone to stay with her sister in Canada who's sick, and I don't know when she'll be back."

Boniface sucked air through his teeth. "If you're going to lie, don't elaborate. Don't get too specific—just give one detail."

"Thanks," said Danny sarcastically. "Why didn't you tell me that earlier?"

"He called you on it?"

"He said she doesn't have a sister. Then he was off. He took a couple of steps, turned, said 'I hate liars,' and was gone. I sent Sven to have a look—but he had gone."

forty-four

When Boniface got back in the car after talking with Danny, he went to say something to Montbretia, but then paused, as if trying to marshal his thoughts before he began his sentence.

He hadn't begun to speak as he nosed the car out of the drive and onto the narrow lanes of the Surrey Hills, drawing a smooth line along the middle of the road, equidistant between the high-sided embankments, and moving without the urgency he had shown earlier.

On the ground, as they threaded through the forest, it was night, but in the blinks of darkening blue sky that she saw as the trees occasionally yielded, it was clear that the day hadn't fully departed yet. It was dark enough to be dangerous. Dark enough to require Boniface's full concentration. But not yet dark enough that you could fully call it night.

Montbretia remained silent as Boniface navigated out of the Hills and back to a main road she soon recognized as the A3—the main artery into and out of southwest London: starting near the center of London just south of the river and soon becoming three lanes each way, finally ending at Portsmouth, the military and civilian shipping town on the south coast.

It was an easy route: All Boniface had to do was stay on the main road until they got to Tibbet's Corner, the junction—named after a highwayman who may or may not have existed, but who had now passed into lore as fact—on the A3 at the corner of Wimbledon Common. Here Boniface would take the road into Wimbledon and to the office.

It was an easy route and there was little traffic around, but Boniface had remained silent for the journey. Silent. He hadn't even cleared his throat.

Montbretia wasn't sure what was keeping Boniface quiet. It might have been his chat with Danny. It might have been the phone call—it was surprising that Boniface hadn't told her who called. Or it might have been that he was feeling rough so he was concentrating on his driving.

It might have been all three.

Whatever the cause, he was thinking. At several stages in the journey his breathing became heavier—almost as if he was inhaling, holding, then exhaling. He seemed to be holding his breath as they passed her turn—but this wasn't a problem; Montbretia was happy to go back to the office to pick up her bike. If she didn't, that meant public transport tomorrow—two buses.

He was still thinking as they approached Tibbet's Corner. The junction was an easy one—three lanes split. One lane turned off up to the intersection where they would join the road leading into Wimbledon. The other two continued, passing under the intersection and following the trail to London without interruption.

Montbretia waited for Boniface to think about the junction—he was in the middle lane, not the lane that filtered off. The car remained in the middle lane continuing into the underpass and avoiding the junction, exiting on the other side and continuing toward London. Montbretia waited to see if Boniface reacted. The car continued passing the Royal Hospital for Neuro-Disability, which apparently had once been called the Royal Hospital and Home for Incurables, only recently changing its name to its more hopeful current one.

"We're not going to the office, then?" Montbretia ended the quiescence. She knew Boniface needed time to think—time to process and play through every scenario, time to integrate whatever he had just been told with whatever he was thinking, with whatever hunch was buzzing around at the back of his head like a fly banging on a closed pane next to an open window…it knows there's a way out, but it doesn't have the brain capacity to know to move to the right and then fly.

But thinking had moved to acting, and clearly acting involved her.

"If it's not Bing-Bing, that leaves one person, and something Danny said is niggling."

Montbretia wondered whether it was time to suggest the police again, but waited. Boniface seemed ready to elaborate, at least a little.

"It's time to tell them we surrender. Time to tell them we're beaten." Montbretia felt her head jerk to look at Boniface, who was still focused on the road. "It'll give us some breathing space, which is what we need at the moment."

"What about this Leathan friend of yours?"

"Oh, he's coming," said Boniface. "But I want to roll out the red carpet for him."

forty-five

"Without wishing to be too crude about this, Boniface, where the hell are we?"

"Haggerston."

"To repeat. Where the hell are we, Boniface?"

"You can ask me as often as you want, but it won't cause us to miraculously move from..."

"Boniface." Her volume was quiet. Her tone stern. "Where—in the broadest sense—are we? Think politics, not geography."

He pointed down the street: on one side, terraced houses, the other and sweeping away from them, a housing estate—the projects, as Montbretia insisted on calling it—cheaply constructed low blocks of high-density housing run by a combination of the local authority and a social housing project. One side of the road had been called a slum and flattened; the other somehow survived. "You see at the end—a small row of shops."

"Just."

"Take it from me, there's a butcher and a pet shop that would like to believe it's a grooming parlor."

"You're taking me shopping?"

"It would be preferable, but no." He reached into his jacket pockets and pulled out his phone, his wallet, a small notebook, and a pencil. "Between those two is a black wooden gate—a fair size; it's big enough to get a van through."

"I'll believe you," said Montbretia, taking the contents of Boniface's pockets as he pushed them into her hands. "Wouldn't it be easier to park outside—then you could show me?"

Boniface twisted, trying to reach into his trouser pockets with his fingers. "You're staying out of sight." Slowly he disentangled his office keys from his pocket before twisting the other way to rummage in his opposite pocket.

"Why am I staying out of sight?" asked Montbretia. "And why are you giving me the contents of your pockets—I thought you said you were surrendering?"

"I didn't say we were surrendering," said Boniface, handing over the last few scraps he had pulled from his pockets. "I said we would tell them that we are surrendering."

"You mean lie," said Montbretia. "Lie to the people who did that to your face." She paused. "This is where we are?"

Boniface rocked his head forward.

"How can I express in words—words that you will understand and react to—that I think this is the stupidest thing you have done. Ever."

"I think you just did," said Boniface.

"No. I said understand and *react*. React as in decide not to do the really stupid thing." She paused as he continued to search through his pockets—now beginning a second check of each. "Stupid for you and stupid for me. You're leaving me here in what must be said is not the most salubrious location within this grand city."

"I wasn't sure how to raise that aspect of my plan, so thank you for that." Boniface smiled weakly. "If I'm not back in an hour, then call the cops. Tell them there's a knife fight, not guns—we want them to come in, not to put up a cordon and negotiate." He opened the car door. "The keys are in the ignition." He stepped out. "Get in the driver's seat. Lock the doors and stay safe. If it gets too hairy to stay here, then drive."

He gently shut the door before she could argue and began the short walk, arriving to find the small wicket gate within the larger gate ajar. He pushed the smaller gate fully open, pausing to survey the tunnel.

The painting equipment he had seen yesterday was gone, giving an unobstructed cobbled surface leading up to the door with its concealed glass. Lazily hunched on the barrel to the right of the door was an unwelcome vision: Wes.

Physically, Wes was unprepossessing—shorter than Boniface, he didn't look particularly muscular, but he had a sneer, worked on for years and which Boniface suspected would now be as hard to shift as a speech impediment.

The teenager said nothing, choosing instead to fix his unwavering gaze on Boniface.

"I need to see Ernie."

The teenager's stare remained.

"We had our fun yesterday, and now the grownups need to talk." Still no response. "Do you really want to tell Ernie that I came here to give him what he wants, and then you turned me away?"

The stare remained, but the confidence in the eyes momentarily flickered. "Waiting room." He flashed his gaze to the stairs leading under the butcher's shop.

Boniface let his head shake once.

"Ernie's office for this discussion."

The teenager remained impassive, keeping his vision fixed on Boniface.

"If I don't call home within an hour, then it's goodnight Saigon—they send in the napalm—if that's not something of a mangling of history." Wes looked at him with his best dead-eyed stare. "I'm not sure if you're trying to be scary or whether it's just a matter of you not having a clue about what I just said."

"Jacket," said the teen, snapping his fingers.

forty-six

Boniface looked around the room as the light disappeared. The harsh strip light in the corridor had been replaced by the yellow glow of a single lamp, which even at its brightest struggled to form a pool of light.

Boniface buttoned his cuffs, slipped on his jacket, and began to button his shirt. "I got the message."

He looked at the face—gray skin with old-man stubble, exaggerated with deep shadows—visible across the dust mote–filled half-light.

There was movement in the gray face. It might have been what passed for a smile—Boniface couldn't be sure.

"I would have preferred a carrier pigeon."

A small sound from the other man, a raspy chuckle.

"My preferences aside, I received the message loud and clear, and I don't want another message."

A tilt of the head seemed to be the extent of any form of reciprocation.

"Clearly we got off on the wrong foot," continued Boniface, looking for somewhere to sit but seeing nowhere. "I'm hoping we can rectify any misunderstandings." As his eyes became accustomed to the dark, he strained to see what was on the walls—it might have been framed boxing posters or it could have been movie posters. Then again, given the lack of light, it might have been crumbling plaster creating interesting patterns. "And in this spirit of understanding and cooperation, I have a simple question: What can I do for you, Ernie?"

The man behind the desk didn't hesitate. "Leave my band alone. Stop trying to make money off my act."

The door opened. Boniface's eyes spasmed with the light rushing like a burst water main. In the corner away from Ernie, he thought he could see someone sitting—thinning, slicked-back hair and a suit—and then the door was shut and whoever had entered rapidly crossed to Ernie.

A whisper. A grunt by Ernie. Then, as quickly as the person had entered—Boniface couldn't even be sure whether it was a man or woman—they had gone, with a brief burst of light confirming to Boniface that there were three people left in the room.

"When I was here yesterday—the first time—I saw a kid. Who is he?

Ernie grunted, the hint of self-satisfaction showing in the shadows around his mouth. "He's a junkie who thinks he can be helpful."

"Could I talk to him?"

"He's not here," said Ernie. "He's probably getting off his head on krokodil. Why the interest?"

"Someone thought they had seen him."

"I doubt it," said Ernie. "Now. Back to my band."

forty-seven

It was only when Montbretia released her hold on the steering wheel to feel for the key in the ignition that she realized she had been gripping the wheel—with her nails digging into her palms—since Boniface had disappeared from her view.

The car fired immediately and started to move without its driver taking her gaze off Boniface as he now walked toward her. Her eyes swiveled, taking in the mirrors, and she pulled into the center of the road, feeling the acceleration push her back against her seat. Boniface heard the car before he saw it—his head jerked until he locked onto the vehicle and moved swiftly, crossing the road as Montbretia pulled up.

There was a satisfying clunk as she released the central locking, and the passenger door opened at once, with Boniface slipping into the passenger seat. He was pale, but the tension around his eyes that had been present before he got out of the car had dissipated.

She hit the gas and the car started moving. Boniface finished closing his door, then pointed as if giving directions—the tremble in his right hand becoming more pronounced as he extended his arm.

"Mmm hmm."

"I've agreed to give him the band." As they came toward a junction, Boniface indicated the left turn.

"I say this with love, Boniface, but wasn't that immensely stupid?" Montbretia accelerated out of the junction, feeling calmer as they got farther away. "You've agreed to give him the band...but the band isn't yours to give."

"That's alright," said Boniface airily. "I've also agreed to procure anything that I don't already own."

Montbretia felt the need to look at Boniface and shout at him, but kept the barge moving steadily along the backstreets of northeast London, somehow feeling safer as each street seemed to lead to a slightly less minor street, which might eventually lead to a major road she might recognize. She fought the urge to turn but couldn't still her tongue. "And again, I say with love: That is even more stupid—Danny will never agree. Please tell me you know what you're doing."

She kept her concentration focused on the road, but somehow Montbretia knew Boniface was smirking. "And if you want me to top the stupidity table—catastrophic stupidity, you would probably call it—I made a deal but I don't understand what Ernie thinks he's doing." She shot him a look—he was smirking, but his face fell as they made eye contact. "He's trying to steal Prickle's back catalog. But that won't make him much money if he doesn't keep Prickle gigging, and he says he doesn't care if Danny, Mel, Luca, and Newton all die tomorrow. They're not in his plans."

"So let me get this right." Montbretia felt a calmness in her voice—if she understood what Boniface was saying he had just done, they were past the stage where panicking would achieve anything. "You've shaken things up, knowing that they will react, but you don't have any idea what you're going to do when they do react."

"I do," said Boniface as the car reached a junction.

"Home?" asked Montbretia.

"Saint Pancras—Eurostar terminal," said Boniface. "I didn't just go and see Ernie for the heck of it. What I've done will get him talking—there was another guy in with him, and we don't know how many other people there are in this venture. They're going to talk for a while, and hopefully they'll still be talking when Leathan gets in there."

"Leathan gets...in...there?"

"That's the idea," said Boniface, leaning forward and opening the glove compartment before starting to reload his pockets. "We know Ernie and his friends are our problem. Leathan will help us fix it."

"How?" Montbretia realized she was giving Boniface too much scope to be evasive. "I mean, what's this Leathan's history—why did you call him?"

Boniface groaned quietly. "When I was a journalist, it was acceptable to break the law a little. Do something cheeky, and that was fine."

"Really?" asked Montbretia.

"It was a different time—it was called showing initiative," said Boniface. "But there were things you couldn't be caught doing. It would be too embarrassing for the paper, not to mention perhaps beyond my skillset. But that didn't mean you couldn't outsource. I outsourced to Leathan. He was efficient, he didn't get caught, and he was productive. And for what I've got in mind, I need to do a bit of outsourcing."

"In short," said Montbretia, "you're telling me that he's a crook."

"Who amongst us has not broken the law?" asked Boniface. "There are good criminals and there are bad criminals. Leathan occasionally does bad things for a good reason." He patted his pockets, seemingly making sure everything had been returned to its rightful home. "I just hope Leathan's up for it."

forty-eight

"It might be something out of a horror movie, but I still like it," said Boniface, looking up at the dark-red brick Victorian gothic structure. "They used to call this the cathedral of the railways."

In front of them, four floors of red brick detailed with sandstone, all topped by a slate-covered mansard roof with gable-fronted dormer windows protruding. A square clock tower with a tall square spire and four small round spires on each corner stood at the far end of the building. "Turn by the clock, and I'll jump out round the corner."

Montbretia pulled up, avoiding three black cabs. Boniface's door was open before the car had drifted to a halt. "You're leaving me here? Alone? Again?" She winked. "Seriously, can't you just call him and tell him where to meet us?"

Boniface put his foot on the asphalt, grabbed the front pillar, and turned back to Montbretia. "His phone will have been switched off hours ago, before he got on the train." Montbretia's face didn't relax. "This is risky for him—being at a specific place at a predictable time. He needs to see me and be confident that I'm not being followed. He needs to be sure that no one is waiting for him. If I'm talking with someone—you, for instance—he'll freak."

"And when he sees you...is that when you have the big tearful reunion?"

"Once he has seen me—once he is sure it's safe—then he'll call."

"Call?"

"Yeah." Boniface relaxed. "You can put batteries back into phones." He stood on the road, leaning into the car. "We'll pick him up at a place where Leathan is sure he's not being followed—I'll call you."

"I'm beginning to feel like a chauffeur. I'm driving a Mercedes—all I need is a cap and a blue blazer, and I'm set." Boniface shut the door on Montbretia and headed for the station, stepping inside the Victorian architecture and finding a modern cream-painted steel-framed skeleton supporting the body's vital organs: commerce. A cathedral to transport had become an ecumenical meeting ground, inviting those who worship at the church of shopping to come join.

And to make them feel welcome, on the ground-floor level, between the cream-painted steel structure and the sandblasted red-brick skin, rows of glass units had been created. Home to faceless food and clothing chains as prevalent as cockroaches, plus those stores that you never quite know what they do but that seem to exist exclusively in public-transportation hubs. Apart from a few coffee shops, most of the units were closed for the night.

Boniface followed the signs to international arrivals, casually coming to rest about thirty yards away from the exit with his back against a cream-painted pillar. He scanned his fellow greeters—some individuals, some groups, some looking bored, others excited—everyone looked worthy of suspicion, and no one looked suspicious. All were gathered in a loose semicircle around the frosted-glass doors under the electronic display announcing that the next arrival was due in two minutes.

It looked so normal, apart from the upright piano.

Boniface had noticed this trend—leave a piano somewhere public. It seemed to be an idea taking hold; he had last seen one in Heathrow airport. A kid—eleven or twelve—resentful of having been dragged out of her house, resentful of not being trusted on her own, sat at the piano. Her parents—the mother plain, the father overweight—seemed not to notice or had long since stopped trying to communicate or take an interest in their daughter's passions.

She began playing an etude: the highly structured piece fully resolving with a simple melody as addictive as cocaine. The first time he heard it, Boniface thought it was sweet. The second time, he noticed a minor mistake. The third time the etude was repeated, he was bored with the tune. And by the fourth time, he wanted to find whoever thought leaving a piano was a good idea and suggest an alternate location for the instrument.

He tried to stare casually at the cathedral roof: glass supported by dark-gray steel spanning the entire width of the building, and the imposing clock—so big that he could see the minute hand move—at the far end. There was a sigh of air as the pneumatic struts pushed the doors open to allow a wave of people to flow from the customs hall that greeted newly arrived passengers.

At first a few drips—younger, self-important passengers. People with places to go and people to see, apparently, and practical footwear. But soon the drips became a wave of humanity, pleased to be released from their captivity in a steel tube traveling at 180 miles per hour for more than two hours.

Boniface looked through the passageway that was now spilling a flow of people. At each end, automatic doors gave the impression of a bad airlock, although he wasn't sure which side was infectious—or who was being protected from whom. Still, it was reassuring to know that only a single narrow retail unit had been sacrificed to allow passengers to get from their trains.

The passengers continued. Some dressed for comfort—their wardrobe a collection of elastic, soft fabric, and manmade colors. Some dressed to be seen—straight lines, very tight where they needed to be tight, and patterned to give a message. Whether they dressed for comfort or for show, there was one consistent factor: luggage. It may have only been a clutch purse with the heavy lifting delegated to someone else, but no one had empty hands.

Apart from one man.

Boniface caught the side of his face and averted his gaze.

One man—black leather jacket, jeans, black sneakers, and no luggage. Leathan swam in the middle of a shoal of people, his speed average and his movements slow, with his head rotating from left to right. The only fast movement was his eyes—fixing on a target, then jumping to the next and the next. He veered away from Boniface, the only acknowledgment a meeting of the eyes, which the train passenger held for a moment longer than a stranger would.

Boniface watched as Leathan passed about ten yards away to his left, then he took the righthand side of the expanse, soon finding his way back out. "North of where you dropped me—walking north." Montbretia answered on the first ring as Boniface started to pass the brushed steel and glass of the new part of the station, crudely bolted onto the gothic monument.

He checked behind—a quick jolt of his head over his shoulder, followed thirty seconds later by a stop to check his phone, giving him the chance to look in the reflection of the large pane and see whether he was being followed, not that he was good at this sort of thing.

The barge wafted up, and Montbretia reached across to open the door.

"Forward and left," said Boniface as he sat. "Under the tracks, then turn right."

Montbretia pulled out, carefully navigating the left turn. "Is he here?"

"Yeah, yeah. I went left; he went right. Right at the end."

Boniface's phone rang. He answered without speaking, listened, and hung up before pulling up a map. "Next left, then first right."

"Leathan?"

"Mmm."

"And?" said Montbretia as she pushed the car around the left bend, transitioning from a main road to a residential street with low blocks on either side—to the left, near-purple brickwork with concrete sills and lintels, to the right, near-orange brickwork with red tile sills. The wall and steel fence both said "we expect crime." Along the center was a strip of asphalt, marked with residential parking spaces on one side and a no-parking yellow line on the other. She slowed as the car approached a speed hump.

"And now we drive around this one block. Slowly—this sort of speed. Leathan will find us once he's sure we're not being tailed."

forty-nine

Leathan looked down at the plasticized cardboard container resting on the plastic table, its lid open to reveal what was to be dinner. He reached his fingers through the greaseproof paper and grabbed a chicken leg, taking a large bite with the side of his mouth while using apparently poor table manners as an excuse to scan the room.

It was a small restaurant—calling it a restaurant was probably an exaggeration. It was a chicken shop—nothing more—but as he bit, Leathan found that it was a surprisingly good chicken shop.

There was still a small crowd milling in front of the counter next to the glass and steel warming the food. Between the counter and the grills, there were two guys. He would call them men, but they were little more than boys—Indian perhaps, but unlikely. More chance they were Pakistani or Bangladeshi.

Both spoke atrocious English but were working incredibly hard and were very attentive to their customers. He hadn't quite understood when the offer was made, but slowly they overcame the language barrier, and Leathan understood that he was being offered chicken cooked to his tastes so he could specify just how spicy and which herbs he wanted.

He was too hungry to wait, but he liked the attitude. The immigrant spirit unlike the English, who just sat around and complained. One of these guys would be a millionaire, maybe both. The only question was how quickly. From their English, they had been here less than six weeks. However, Leathan was sure that within six months, they would both be speaking the language like a Londoner. Within eighteen months, at least one would be self-employed, and within five years, one would be millionaire. He could then afford to celebrate his twenty-fifth birthday in style.

Leathan watched as the man at the head of the line—well, huddle—took his food. A cardboard box carefully placed in a plastic bag. He had seen him come in: Most people were in groups, so someone on his own stood out. The man passed over some change and turned, leaving through the main door with his meal.

He continued his survey. What struck him most was how clean the place seemed. Clearly there was heavy foot traffic, but he couldn't see grease or the detritus that follows human beings who are not forced to clean up their own mess. The mirrors on either side reflected; there was an absence of fingerprints and accumulated dirt. Even the cards for local cab firms, a fixture in every other fast-food restaurant, seemed to have been cleaned away.

The tables were all clean. He looked at the diners—groups of two or three, and one of five—all clustered around their tables, engrossed in rowdy conversation. No one had that look people get when they don't want to lean on the table because they're not quite sure what the previous occupant left.

Three men at the table opposite, all in their early twenties and dressed in cheap hoodies, stood. The guy behind the counter who hadn't been serving was there before the last of the three stood up. The garbage was in a black plastic sack, the table was sprayed and wiped, and the plastic bench seats wiped. Seemingly pulled out of thin air, a mop appeared to wipe the floor. He was gone within thirty seconds, and the table was occupied by two women who didn't miss a word of their conversation as they sat and began eating.

"So why am I here, Boniface? What exactly do you want me to do?"

"Help." Boniface sat meekly on the other side of the table—he seemed to appreciate the warmth of the chicken shop as he crossed his arms, gripping the sleeves of his shirt.

Next to him sat Montbretia. "Call me Monty," she said as they got out of the car. She was shorter than he had guessed, but her hair was longer than he had expected as he looked at her from behind. She had been driving when Leathan got in. The car was on the second loop of the block and slowing as it approached a speed hump. Leathan opened the door without waiting for the car to stop—without even waiting to see whether they had noticed him.

Montbretia seemed unfazed by the new occupant and had then driven smoothly, making rapid progress and not drawing attention, while keeping the passengers comfortable. Having worked her way through a warren of back streets, she had found several places to eat—Leathan had chosen this one, and Montbretia had found a tight spot where she parallel-parked without incident.

Boniface, however, fussed and had insisted that she take his jacket. So now he looked cold, and she looked swamped by his gray suit jacket covering her white blouse.

Leathan grinned. "You bring me to this cheap chicken shop and ask me for help."

"It was your choice, Leath—I'll take you to the Ritz if that's where you want to go. But you wanted somewhere anonymous so you could feel safe, and apparently a noisy chicken shop is it."

"You got me there," said the new arrival, his eyes alternating between scanning the room, scanning anyone passing who was visible through the plate-glass window, and catching a glance of his food in an attempt not to smear it over his face. "Give me the problem again. Start with this Ernie—he sounds like a medium fish in a tiny pond."

"But he seems to want a different pond," said Boniface. "He wants—for lack of a better term—to own the band. As far as I can tell, he wants to take possession of Prickle's sources of income."

"Once a thief," offered Leathan.

"That's what I thought, but Ernie doesn't want the musicians. For a band like Prickle, that's an odd choice—no individual musician matters. But he needs a band that is out working—playing gigs, doing TV slots, being interviewed—in order to generate the publicity to sell the music that makes the money. Prickle are a working band—as soon as they stop, ninety-five percent of their income goes away overnight."

Boniface hesitated, seemingly considering something he hadn't thought about before. "He might have an angle, but from what I've been able to tell, he doesn't have the competence to make money from a band—he's way out of his league, and he doesn't have the contacts to help him."

"But you say he does have a musician."

Boniface exhaled. "Gray. Graham Barrington. He founded the band and was the lead singer, but he left nearly thirty years ago. It's not as if he brings an audience or has great connections."

"But there is a connection, right? Or rather, two."

"And that's where I'm really confused," said Boniface. "Gray mentioned this kid Billy Watkins who has hung around at Ernie's place—Ernie says there's a kid who's just a junkie. But when I mentioned the name Billy Watkins to Dawn, she disappeared."

"You say that as if you think she took herself out of the picture—you don't think there's a kidnap going on here?" asked Leathan.

"I think she ran," said Boniface. "And while it's tearing up Danny, I'm sure we'll find something made her run."

"And is there a connection between this Gray and Dawn?"

"Not that I've found."

Leathan took another mouthful and continued speaking before finishing chewing. "Gray has no money—although he does own property, so capital but no income—and yet he's managed to run up a gambling debt."

"It's not just that," said Boniface. "As far as I can see, he's still running it up, but he's paying in sweat. You get my point."

"I do," said Leathan.

"I don't," said Montbretia.

"You would expect someone with Ernie's finishing-school manners to deal with any debts in a practical manner," said Boniface.

"Isn't he doing that—you said Gray was probably doing some decorating."

"I think," said Leathan, "that what Boniface is suggesting is that we might expect Ernie to break Gray's legs to give him an incentive to repay the debt."

Montbretia's face registered shock.

"But instead," continued Boniface, "Gray is being encouraged to gamble more and so fall further into debt. In other words..."

"Ernie wants Gray in debt because he wants something from Gray. I get it," said Montbretia. "I still don't get how this relates to Dawn."

"Which is why Leathan is here."

"You're pretty hopeful that I'm going to agree with whatever you've got planned." Leathan finished his chicken and licked his fingers before wiping them on a paper napkin. "So what can I achieve now, tonight?"

"About an hour ago, I went to see Ernie to announce my surrender. I told him he could have whatever he wanted, I wouldn't stand in his way, and I'd help him get whatever I didn't have."

Leathan leaned back, dropping his napkin into the cardboard box and shutting the lid. "A strategy—and I use that term loosely—which is not without risk. If I may look at your actions in another light, we could even suggest that you've broken stuff in the hope that something happens."

"Yeah," said Boniface. "And I'm rather hoping you can get in there and find out what's happening."

fifty

Montbretia held the Mercedes steady, letting it find its own way along the back streets of northeast London. A subtle nudge here and there on the steering wheel, and the car maintained a perfect line down the street, low revs keeping the engine quiet in acknowledgement that it was midnight and they were passing through residential streets.

"Once past—slowly—and then park quarter of a mile up," said Boniface. "It'll be on the left in a moment, Leath."

Montbretia flicked her gaze. Both men seemed to sink down in their seats, pushing their faces up against the window.

"Pet shop, black gate, butcher," said Boniface. "That black gate is the entrance to Ernie's empire." The lights in the surrounding stores had been extinguished, with the exception of a few twinkles confirming that the refrigerated displays in the butcher's shop were still chilling. Around the black gate a lazy yellow light drifted, like fumes exhaled by a crowd of smokers. The wicket gate was not fully closed—its outline also etched in yellow light.

Montbretia flicked another glance. The two men's heads were moving slowly with perfect synchronization, seemingly each having their gaze locked on the gate. She let the car drift, neither accelerating nor decelerating—the engine tone remaining constant—as she watched the trip meter; the tenths of a mile turned over for a second time, and she looked for somewhere to pull over. Within 45 seconds of passing the gate, the car was stationary, the engine cut and its lights out.

Boniface turned and frowned. "It's a residential street, Boniface. A running engine is going to draw attention, and the lights illuminate the plates, so unless you want someone to notice us and to get a description..." She let the end of the explanation hang.

Boniface reached into his pocket and pulled out his wallet. "How much money have you got?" he asked Montbretia, grabbing all the paper money in his wallet and handing the bills to Leathan without counting and without breaking eye contact with Montbretia. "And your key to my place."

Montbretia wriggled her hand into a pocket, making three dives before all of her cash had been retrieved. She held out her hand to Leathan. "Count it first," said Boniface. "This is a loan, not charity."

"I, on the other hand..." said Leathan as Montbretia started counting, "don't really care about those fine differences. I just need cash."

"Twenty-seven pounds and thirty-two pence," said Montbretia holding out one hand to Leathan but looking straight at Boniface and fiddling in another pocket with her other hand.

"Thank you," mouthed Leathan.

Montbretia hooked her nail under the split ring and began to work Boniface's two door keys through the steel trap. The ring snapped shut as she liberated the two pieces of metal, holding them out for Boniface. "For him," said Boniface, throwing his eyes toward the passenger in the back seat. "He needs somewhere to go when he's finished here." He turned to face Leathan. "We'll find somewhere else for tomorrow night if you're still around."

Leathan took the keys silently, pushing them into a pocket.

"Anything more we can do for you?" asked Boniface, his gaze fixed on the man in the back seat, who was a lot less talkative than he had been in the chicken shop, preferring to communicate through body language alone.

Currently he seemed to be saying "I don't want to communicate" as he reached for the door handle.

"Take care," said Boniface.

"I have done this before." Leathan seemed to expend the minimum energy necessary to make the sounds.

"And look how well that turned out," said Boniface. "You're living in a different country constantly looking over your shoulder, sleeping in a different bed every night, and putting a new SIM card in your phone each morning." He paused; slowly Leathan's head lifted, his gaze toward Boniface. "Take care—you're no use to us dead."

In one continuous movement the door opened, he stood, the door closed silently, and Leathan started walking away from the car and away from Ernie's.

"He'll circle round," said Boniface as Leathan's figure came into view, his head down as he moved through the shadows.

"What's this about a different bed every night?" asked Montbretia. "You make him sound...I mean, can we trust him?"

"We can trust him."

"But leaving the country, a different bed?" She sucked her teeth. "I mean, he seems alright, but so do most crooks you meet."

"There are people you can trust—there are people you don't trust but have to work with. I trust Leathan. I told you, when I was a journalist and needed something that was just outside my reach, I called Leathan."

"I'm not questioning his skills," said Montbretia. "More his...I keep coming back to him sleeping in a different bed each night. Why did you bring it up?"

"Not to get this reaction," said Boniface, his voice was low but his mouth pulled tight. "I just wanted to remind him that he's not...invincible—things go wrong." He leaned back against the door. "We're mates. We were drinking buddies. Sometimes you need to use slightly stronger language to illustrate a point for a friend. It's not a criticism—I just made a point using shorthand."

"Drinking buddies," said Montbretia, not quite sure whether the term sat well with Boniface.

"What term do you want me to use?" asked Boniface, seemingly picking up on her hesitation. "Two heterosexual male friends who, in the past, frequently consumed too much alcohol together. What label should I apply?"

"So Veronica knows him?"

Boniface hesitated; there was a second of tension in his jaw, and then the softening of his face that usually preceded the admission of an error. "I think it would be fair to say that she's not a fan."

"Give me something positive about him, Boniface. Everything you tell me just digs a deeper hole."

"You're blowing this up," said Boniface. "Veronica doesn't get on with Leathan, and let's be fair here, Leathan ain't Vron's greatest fan." He leaned forward, resting on his elbow, his hand open, chopping the air for emphasis. "Veronica's problem with Leathan wasn't so much a problem with him—it was a problem with me. She didn't like what I did when I was with him. But what I did was my fault..." he brought his hand to slap his chest, emphasizing his guilt, "it wasn't Leathan leading me astray."

"Okay," said Montbretia cautiously. "Different bed each night..."

"I gave Leathan a lot of work. He even did a few bits after I started working for Gideon at the Department of the Environment."

Montbretia felt her eyes go wide and her head crane forward, wordlessly posing a question.

"You would be surprised what nonattributable information can help," said Boniface. "When I had my...incidents...and went to straighten myself out, I wasn't in a position to feed Leathan any more work, but he hooked up with an investigative reporter called Sam Cartwright." He paused, staring straight into Montbretia's eyes. "Sam is a good journalist. Hardworking. Honorable. Always wants the facts. Always after stories that matter."

"So why did he want Leathan?" asked Montbretia, trying to keep her tone light.

"Leathan is good. Leathan is dedicated. Leathan will do dangerous stuff. Leathan gives a monkey's about human beings."

Montbretia felt chastised. "Oh."

Boniface softened his voice. "Sam was doing a story about organized gangs in London—not small-time criminals like Ernie, but the new breed of international criminals that are coming to London. In particular, Sam was focusing on human trafficking—human trafficking for the sex trade. He had a story about a Bulgarian gang that was running brothels across London and all the major cities. It wasn't just that this gang trafficked in the girls—modern-day slaves by any other name—it was that they also stole other trafficked women. These women might have been brought into the country to work as domestic servants, but the Bulgarians got hold of them and made them work as whores." He exhaled. "Forget about Leathan, go and talk to Gideon; he'll tell you just how deep the problem is in this country and how horrific the conditions are for these people. I know you saw stuff in Turkey, but this is where the people you met end up."

"So how did Leathan get involved?"

"Sam wanted an inside man—someone who could give him better evidence."

Montbretia felt her face freeze.

"The Bulgarians are tightknit—the gangs don't let outsiders in, and as you've figured, Leathan isn't Bulgarian and wasn't on the inside. However, there's a lot of local knowledge that's needed, and that's where Leathan got in."

"He was working *with* the gang?"

"In order to get the story—which would then be followed with passing all the evidence to the police," said Boniface. "Leathan did some good work, but the trouble is that to get the evidence, Leathan had to see a lot, and that's where his problem came." Boniface snorted. "I call it a problem—Leathan did the decent thing, and the problem is now his."

"What happened?" Montbretia's voice was a whisper.

"Remember, I was in treatment at the time this happened, so I'm not clear on some of the details, but what I do know is that Leath got attached to a girl—I don't know who...I don't know how attached. It got to the point where he couldn't let her suffer, so he rescued her and blew open the part of the operation he knew about. There were police, arrests, and subsequently there have been convictions."

"So he did a good thing—what's the problem?"

"The problem is the Bulgarians. If they find him, he's dead. And we're not dealing with a small organization here—their tentacles stretch across Europe, and they've got a lot of people on their payroll. So Leathan's reaction was to skedaddle and drop off the grid, hence we communicate in odd ways—he doesn't leave an electronic footprint behind him, and he sleeps in a different bed each night."

"Oh," mouthed Montbretia.

"It puts a different gloss on your impression of him, doesn't it?" said Boniface. Montbretia nodded slowly.

"So do you see why I think he's got a pretty good idea about right and wrong?" Montbretia could feel her head still nodding.

"And at this point, I think we should leave Leathan to do what he does. He's got money and he's got the key to let himself in." Something changed in Boniface's tone. "Do you want to go home?"

"I'm not sure I'd sleep—I'm too wired...scared...anxious, so I..."

"I was hoping you'd say that," said Boniface. "If you're still twitchy, you can stay at mine—that way you'll be there when Leathan gets back. But before we go home, there's somewhere I want to go first."

fifty-one

"Isn't it a bit late?"

"You mean, isn't it a bit early," corrected Boniface. "Our problem isn't waking him up; our problem is whether he's back home yet. And anyway—it's not my problem, it's yours: You're knocking on the door. You're my lucky charm for getting in to see Gray."

Montbretia had pulled the car to the curb, diagonally across from Gray's house, before killing the engine and the lights. A few streetlights offered some illumination along the two brick rows with doors and windows punched into the walls.

"I'm not dressing like a hooker from the 1980s again," said Montbretia as they got out of the car.

"Some might say that wearing an oversized man's jacket has something of an eighties vibe," said Boniface. "Especially in the way you've turned back the cuffs. I think it'll be just Gray's thing."

Montbretia muttered under her breath. "The street's quiet."

"Yep." Boniface cast a glance along the brickwork rows—a few upstairs windows showed lights, and one downstairs window. "But we only care about one house, and I'm guessing from the glow that he's watching TV."

Montbretia pushed out her bottom lip.

"You know what to do," said Boniface quietly.

"Actually, Boniface, I don't."

"Make something up and get us in—we need to talk with Gray." He grinned. "And if you have trouble, just throw in the word threesome."

Montbretia raised her eyes and turned toward the door as Boniface flattened himself against the front wall.

She tapped the door lightly with her the tip of her index finger. Boniface heard a voice inside. "What?"

Montbretia pushed the flap in the mail slot, looked through, and then lifted her mouth to the opening. "Hey, Gray," she purred.

Boniface heard the TV go quiet. The glow of the front window faded, to be replaced by yellow light as an incandescent bulb lit. There were footsteps, and the door opened—a squeak as the expanded wood rubbed on the frame.

"Hi, babe," said Gray. His voice gravelly, his enthusiasm clear, his hopes clearer.

Montbretia lifted her foot over the threshold and turned to face Boniface, winking with her eye not in Gray's line of vision as she moved into the house. "Fancy a threesome, Gray?"

He was still stuttering as he turned to see Boniface standing in his door. "What happened to your face?"

"What happened to yours, Gray?"

"Jojo or Wes?" asked Gray. "Or did he bring in outside help?"

"Jojo and Wes," said Boniface.

"Ouch." The older man sounded sympathetic. "Must have hurt…must still hurt. But I did warn you, and you were determined to keep bullshitting."

Boniface stood in the middle of Gray's front room, which due to the location of his front door was also his entrance hall, and looked back at the former lead singer of Prickle. "Oh, do come in," said the singer, in a tone that was probably intended to be sarcastic, but that just sounded grumpy.

"Thank you," said Boniface, managing to get the sarcastic note Gray was looking for. "Is this where we're sitting?" he asked without looking at Gray. He caught Montbretia's gaze, then pointed with his eyes to the beaten-up sofa leaned up against the back wall of the room, indicating she should sit. He saw her hesitation.

First a bristle at the implied order, which soon changed to an understanding that Boniface wanted her sat for strategic reasons.

Then there was the look of horror in her eyes as she looked down at the beaten piece of furniture. The 1970s olive/tan stripe, fashioned out of a fabric that was probably over 90 percent nylon—the rest being grime. It was frayed, ragged, and torn and seemed to have been fixed by the last road crew who had passed through with pieces of silver duck tape. Boniface dropped onto the sofa, feeling it thump against the wall, and cast an irritated look at Montbretia, imploring her to sit. Tentatively, she moved to position herself—her body lowering as if it were being lowered into a bath of acid.

"Why don't you get yourself a chair," said Boniface as the singer turned into the room, having wrestled the front door shut, careful to avoid the stack of paint cans that had increased in size since Boniface's last visit.

"Make yourself comfortable," said Gray, again failing with the sarcasm as he walked diagonally across the room, exiting through the far doorway.

He returned a moment later with a dining chair, unsurprisingly of 1970s vintage with a winged oval wooden back and frayed leatherette-covered seat. He placed it in front of the television and sat. "Your face looks bad—you really did upset the boys, Boniface."

Montbretia was still looking around herself at the sofa: she had a look that said she was unsure whether it was damaging to her long-term health. Instinctively, she pulled Boniface's suit jacket tightly across her chest. Boniface looked down at the carpet—the color of indifference—and hoped Montbretia didn't follow his gaze.

"But I'm not pissing blood—apparently on Ernie's instruction—which I believe is a good thing."

Gray looked slightly self-satisfied as he sat back in his chair, straightening his dirty white T-shirt. "Why are you here?"

"Because we're your friends," said Boniface. "Friends call round. Friends drop in and say 'hi.' Friends just have a chat..."

"I get it," said Gray. "Now tell me why you're here and then get out of my world forever." The natural aggression in his voice was far better suited to these sorts of exchanges.

Boniface felt his face harden, his voice lose its lightness of tone. "Why does Ernie think he owns Prickle?"

"Because I do, and he reckons I'm going to sell Prickle to him."

"You own Prickle?"

"Stands to reason—I founded the band. I never gave away my rights, so I own them. And if Danny wants to fight me in court, then my lawyer assures me we will win."

"Your lawyer?"

"Yeah."

"You've got a lawyer, Gray?"

"Yes, Boniface. I have a lawyer."

Boniface paused taking in the room—it would have been regarded as being in need of some sprucing up thirty years ago. Now...now, Boniface couldn't even figure where to begin. He pointed to the large television behind the singer. "You're the last man in the country with a cathode-ray tube TV—everyone's gone flat screen—and yet you can afford a lawyer."

He let the observation hang.

Gray used a fingernail to loosen something caught between his teeth, continuing to talk and perform dentistry simultaneously. "He's a good guy—he knows his stuff, and he can be really aggressive."

"Who is he?" said Boniface calmly, his tone temperate, his attitude mollifying.

"Iain Irvine," said Gray.

"And he's been meeting people for you—talking about the situation?"

"Suppose so," said Gray, looking suddenly out of his depth.

"But he's a good lawyer?" asked Boniface with little conviction, more in the style of a cat toying with a mouse.

"Oh yeah," said Gray.

"Do you know where he gained his law degree?" asked Boniface.

"Why would I know that?" The aggressive tone was back.

"Just for my own interest," said Boniface, letting his face soften. "I'm always interested in where these people learn their trade."

Gray shrugged, pulling up his legs under his chin, his feet on the seat of his chair.

Boniface deepened his voice and tilted his head—his best empathic look. "You know Ernie's a criminal."

Gray shrugged again. "We're all dancing on the wrong side of a non-white line."

Boniface went to speak, then nodded his acknowledgement. "But it's a case of degrees. Ernie's more of a criminal—Ernie has people who make sure you trip up as you leave his fine establishment..." Boniface indicated his injuries.

"He ain't been criminal to me. And I find it hard to believe that your past is completely lilywhite...pure as the driven and all that."

"I've made a few mistakes," said Boniface quietly. "But what I've done isn't relevant. What is relevant is what you and Ernie are intending to do next."

fifty-two

"Shouldn't we go and see Danny? Tell him there's a lawyer."

Boniface shook his head and stirred his peppermint tea. Montbretia stood on the other side of the kitchen counter, staring intently. He looked at the clock on the microwave. "Have you seen the time? It'll be three before we can get there." He squeezed the teabag. "If we turn up, it'll freak him out—no one turns up at that time of day in person, except with bad news. And if Dawn's not back, then we've just increased his level of panic needlessly."

Montbretia's stare was fading and she glanced down at her rooibos, chasing the teabag around her mug. A South African—who had tried to start a chat in a coffee shop line and had asked for a date before the barista delivered her coffee—had told her she would like it. Montbretia had bought a box of rooibos teabags, but from her lack of enthusiasm, Boniface doubted the South African was right, and doubted the South African would be mentioned again.

"And what's the point in telling him? Danny's still got the same problems whatever we tell him." Boniface lifted his teabag out of his mug and dropped it into the food scraps recycling bin. "Anyway, that guy ain't a lawyer."

"What guy?"

"This Iain Irvine that Gray calls his lawyer. He's not a lawyer."

"You know him?" asked Montbretia.

"No." Boniface picked up his tea, walked around the counter into the lounge area of the room, and sat on the farther sofa, carefully placing his cup on a coaster. "But when I saw Ernie tonight, there was someone in that room with Ernie, and I'm guessing that was Irvine."

Montbretia, still wearing Boniface's jacket with the cuffs turned back, joined Boniface on the perpendicular sofa, placing her rooibos near to his peppermint. "Why did you ask where the lawyer gained his qualification?"

"Because this guy's behavior makes him sound like the *lawyer* who turned up to see PAD Management this morning—the one who took some heavies and started pushing them around. According to Fiona, the trainee giraffe with the deep voice, this guy ain't no lawyer. While I may not agree with everything Miss Aldred says, I think she's quite astute and would do the research and get that kind of detail right."

Montbretia took a sip of her tea and pulled a face. "It's too sour for me."

"Milk? Sugar? Honey?" offered Boniface, becoming increasingly unsure that his suggestions were helping.

"I'll suffer this—perhaps it's an acquired taste," said Montbretia. "So this guy who isn't a lawyer...I don't see what the significance is."

"The qualification, or lack of qualification, is a sideshow. What matters is this seems to be where the action is. Ernie's a crook—but he's got a so-called lawyer on his payroll, and as far as we can tell, that lawyer isn't a defense advocate. But more than that, Gray seems to think there's a legal claim, and PAD seem to think there's a legal issue..." Boniface stared into space, contemplating as he took a sip of his tea. "Ernie's a crook, so why is he acting as if he thinks he's got a legal case?"

Montbretia leaned forward. "But you can't fight a case without a proper lawyer, can you? This Iain Irvine can't stand up in court unless he's a proper lawyer—that would be..." she smiled, "fraud, or something—I need a lawyer to tell me the correct law that would be broken."

"It's not that simple. First, I'm guessing that Iain Irvine isn't a complete numpty—he's already been able to cause enough problems, even before fists flew. Second, and probably more importantly, there's the question of whether he might just be successful. Say Gray does have a legal claim—say there's something that Danny didn't pin down, or can't prove that he pinned down, all those years ago. And there's a third aspect here—say that Irvine ties Prickle up with litigation. That can last for years, which could destroy the band—Luca needs to earn, no singer's going to join if they're not getting paid... You get the idea."

"I thought this guy was just a low-life running a card school with the odd beating thrown in just for fun. That's quick money."

"And that's where I think we've underestimated him. Ernie just needs to wait. And if he gets bored of waiting, then he slaps a few people or makes a few threats. But he's not just threatening—he's like a pirate ship drawing up beside you. If they get one rope over—so what. Two ropes—okay. Three ropes holding you—there might be trouble. Four—start worrying. Every new rope—every pressure point is another advantage. The only question is what he's going to throw a rope over next."

"Well, if he's that smart, then shouldn't we be doing something?"

"I am doing something," said Boniface. "I'm sitting here waiting for Leathan." Montbretia frowned and Boniface continued. "There's no point in putting your trust in a guy and then not trusting him."

"But should we go and fetch him, something like that?" There was a hint of desperation in Montbretia's voice.

Boniface shook his head. "We could be seen—if Ernie makes the link between us and Leathan, that's bad for all of us."

"But we can't do nothing." Montbretia's voice had the hint of a whine.

"I'm not going to do nothing—I'm going to try to get some sleep, and so should you. The spare bed's made up. I'm not doing anything until I've heard from Leathan... or I've heard that Leathan's dead."

fifty-three

There was a noise.

Boniface wasn't quite sure what it was—he had been asleep, and the noise was in a different room. Perhaps something made of metal being knocked.

He rolled over, pulling the duvet tight, but dared to open one eye to look at the clock. It was still dark, and at best—best—he had been asleep for ninety minutes. He let his feet fall to the floor and his toes wriggle in search of slippers. It might not be much, but he wanted some protection for his feet.

He stood and walked around the bed, the only illumination coming from the streetlights pushing around the edges of his curtains and a faint yellow glow from his door. He leaned into his bathroom, put his hand around the door and grabbed a toweling robe, wrestled to find the sleeves as he walked into the passageway, and managed to tie the waist as he walked into the main room where he had sat drinking tea with Montbretia not long enough ago.

He became aware of the smell and looked at the items that had been spread over his kitchen counter. "I didn't have any bacon." He looked at the loaf of sliced bread standing vertically on the counter. "Nor bread."

"But Ernie did," said Leathan, turning to him, a smug grin firmly plastered. "And if you can't steal from a criminal with impunity, who can you steal from? I found all I needed for breakfast and figured it was time to get out of there." Leathan pointed at the pack of bacon and then looked up to Boniface, his eyebrows raised, questioning.

Boniface nodded. The other man pulled out the grill pan and carefully laid some more slices of bacon before returning the pan, noisily.

"There's a cab office just down from Ernie's..."

"I know."

"Thought you might. I got a cab, and the driver told me an interesting story when I said I wanted to go to Wimbledon. Apparently he drove someone well-spoken to Wimbledon yesterday. A guy in a suit but who looked like he'd been in a fight. Apparently the suit was ripped and the guy looked like he had received quite a beating..."

"Fancy that," said Boniface. "So you got in."

Leathan's grin was back. "The simple lines are the best. Imply you're a brother criminal doing work on their manor, and say you've come to pay your respects and to ask what taxes will be levied for safe passage."

"And it worked?" asked Boniface, although the bread and bacon already implied it had.

"It got me in." Leathan's tone was matter-of-fact. "And I've met Ernie."

"And stolen his bacon."

"Yeah." Leathan grimaced. "Ernie may seem like a bit of an anachronism—an essentially harmless, toothless tiger—but he's found a way to be relevant. He can administer pain, but he outsources the administration—and speaks very highly of his staff. Apparently these fine gentlemen from Brixton and Battersea..."

"I think I've met them," said Boniface.

"Well, then, you will know that they are very willing to take on work. Both sides seem to feel there's an advantage to using dark skins to do damage to light skins."

Boniface could feel his visage posing a question.

"It plays straight to the stereotype—a white person saying 'they were black' always sounds racist if you go to the cops, even if the cops are the biggest racists of the lot. But still you get into the 'how black' and 'what sort of black' conversations, and the cops don't know what to do because the pattern of crime doesn't fit their usual expectation of internecine gang wars."

Leathan pulled out the grill tray and started turning the bacon. "And Ernie's smart here—no one expects him to send in a bunch of black guys." He paused, finishing the turning, then placed the pan back under the grill. "The difficulty for us is that Ernie has these guys around for a reason."

The visitor walked to the end of the counter and leaned, resting on his hip and crossing his arms, watching Boniface. "Ernie has a problem—there's an influx of new criminals. Big gangs doing really unpleasant stuff."

"But that's not news for you, Leath—those gangs are why you left."

"Yeah—but Ernie probably doesn't have the advantages that I did…"

"You mean a French mother who taught you the language?"

"Helps," said Leathan. "But I was more thinking about my winning personality and the fact that I didn't have a business. Ernie can't just take his business to Paris, or Prague, or…wherever. So he's trying to adapt."

"Please tell me he hasn't been reading books."

"Nah…but he's being clever. He sees that certain areas are a no-go for him—the big ones are drugs and prostitution. These are the areas where you need the contacts and the logistics to get the merchandise into the country, and this is where the Albanian and Bulgarian gangs are dominating."

"Again, this isn't news to you," said Boniface.

"True. But at the moment, Ernie has an entente-lacking-cordiale with these guys. Basically, he's not stepping on their toes, and they're not breaking his toes. But he's worried about the gambling."

"How so?"

"At the moment, he makes his money through gambling. It's easy-ish money, and the new boys in town don't care about it. But it's a small step for these new boys to decide they want to get into gambling, and if they do—even with his army of South London thugs—Ernie won't be able to win that battle. And he knows it, so…he's expanding."

"Into music," said Boniface. "So Ernie thinks he's going to be an impresario. Thinks he's going to be like one of those folk-hero managers from the sixties: half silver fox, half thug hanging people out of the window by their ankles. He sees that as glamorous, does he?"

"Nah—Ernie's logic is quite good here. He reckons he can run a semi-legitimate business and make an income. But the clever part is that he reckons the earnings will never be so big that the Albanians, the Bulgarians, or whoever would want to get involved. Why would the gangs do something that makes them fifty thousand quid over a year, which has to be split ten ways, when they can do the same amount of work in a month and earn a million by trafficking in a bunch of girls?"

"I hate to admit it," said Boniface. "But there is some sensible logic there."

"Indeed," said Leathan. "And as part of this, he has recruited Gray."

"We know this."

Leathan nodded and continued. "He encouraged Gray to gamble and has rolled up huge debts."

"We know this, too."

"And he has offered Gray a way out."

"We had figured that."

"But have you figured what Ernie's going to do with Gray?" Leathan started looking around as if he had lost his keys or his phone. "Where do you keep your whisky?"

"There is none," said Boniface. "No whisky, no alcohol."

"None! Not even for guests."

"None," said Boniface. "Come on, Leathan. You of all people know how readily I would accept a drink. I'm sober now, and it's much easier to stay sober if there is never, ever any temptation."

Leathan shrugged dismissively.

"I can call Veronica if you like. She will have some whisky—and you know it will be very good whisky."

"There's only so much disappointed disapproval I can take in one lifetime. It would pain me—and it would pain your former wife—so let's not. I'll have a cup of coffee instead."

"The kettle's there," said Boniface, bobbing his head forward.

"How does Vron react to your new plaything?" He looked directly at Boniface— the glint in his eye that had always been there when he was trying to be provocative. "Very cute—I commend you on your selection."

"We're not in...there is no *us*," said Boniface.

"Really?" Leathan seemed half joking, half surprised. "So you won't mind if I have a swing."

"I mind if you upset, offend, or hurt her, but apart from that, Montbretia is her own woman. She's quite capable of telling you to get lost—she doesn't need my help for that." He sat back in the sofa. "Now, tell me about Gray and Ernie."

"Sorry," said Leathan, exaggerating the O in sorry. "I didn't realize it was a tetchy subject—case closed, end of discussion." Boniface stared and Leathan exhaled. "Ernie wants to put Gray in as lead singer of Prickle. He figures the only guy that matters in a band is the singer—everyone else can be replaced, so he wants the only living singer under contract, and then he'll fire the rest of the band and get some cheap session guys who have no rights. Once that's set up, he'll exploit the back catalog like crazy."

"That explains a lot," said Boniface. "Gray gets encouraged to run up the gambling debt, which can be paid off with assets in Prickle, and his legs don't get broken so he can perform with the band."

"Couple that with the lawyer he's got who's applying pressure to Danny and the management, and you could see this might work."

"Lawyer?" asked Boniface. "Iain Irvine?"

"You didn't think to mention him before I went in," said Leathan, an edge of exasperation grating his voice.

"New information—we paid a visit to Gray after we dropped you. What he said makes more sense now."

"I say lawyer," said Leathan. "But the way they're behaving, I think Ernie fancies Irvine as his consigliere."

"And Irvine?"

"My guess—Irvine sees himself as the heir apparent, not that he's that different in age."

There was a creak of floorboard in the entrance hall, and the door opened partially. Montbretia, her hair mussed, stepped in, knocking her shoulder on the door as she tied a toweling robe tight. "You're back," she said groggily to Leathan; her voice was tired, but the relief in her tone was clear.

She moved to the other sofa. As she turned her back to Leathan, he stared at Boniface, raising his eyebrows questioningly. He indicated the toweling robe and Boniface's robe, silently making an accusation based on their similarity.

"Your keys," he said, pointing to the end of the counter as Montbretia sat.

"Thanks."

"Although I see you managed to get in without them." He walked to the grill, pulling out the pan. "Will you join us for breakfast, Montbretia? Bacon sandwiches."

"That would be nice," she said. "I'll stay at this hotel more often if this is the service I get." She turned to Boniface. "I thought you didn't have any bacon—and I know you didn't have any bread."

"Leathan used his initiative."

Leathan placed three plates with bacon sandwiches on the low table, then dropped onto the sofa next to Montbretia. "I knew Boniface wouldn't take care of you."

"Thank you," said Boniface, reaching for the nearest plate. "So did you find anything else?"

"There's something that Ernie's not saying. He implied he has leverage, significant leverage, against Danny."

Boniface cursed as he chewed his sandwich. "Did he mention Dawn—even in passing?"

Leathan shook his head as he chewed.

"That's bad," said Boniface, putting his hand over his mouth. "That means problems for Danny through Dawn. We need to find her or find how Ernie and Irvine are using her as leverage." He looked over at Montbretia. "Eat up."

She frowned.

"We've only got one avenue that we haven't explored."

Her frown deepened.

"Carmen. I know it feels about a thousand years ago, but what did you find when you started calling hostels yesterday?"

Montbretia swallowed her mouthful. "I found nothing. A long list became a long list with about three hostels crossed off."

"Then we need to start knocking on doors."

"Am I okay to stay here and kip on the sofa?" said Leathan. "It's been a while since I slept, and you know I prefer not to go out in daylight."

"Take the spare bed," said Montbretia. "I'll change the sheets."

"No need—I'm fine," said Leathan. "I'll kip here. You two get going and find this woman."

fifty-four

"Oh, to be in Lambeth just after the night sky has cracked and is suggesting that somewhere—just somewhere—there might be a sun."

Montbretia sneered at Boniface, pulling her jacket tighter as she felt the bite of an early-morning breeze that had found its way from the North Sea and straight up the River Thames.

"Do I look sufficiently like a lawyer?"

Montbretia clapped her arms across her chest. "You'll do."

"And you don't think we've had enough trouble already with fake lawyers?"

"You're not really a fake lawyer—you're just..." Her voice trailed off.

"You didn't promise anything, did you?"

"I barely got a word in edgeways—as soon as they've found a way to say no, the calls ended."

"You didn't say there definitely *is* money?"

"I struggled to mention the subject with the speed the phones went down. It went 'I'm sorry, we can't disclose the identities of any residents past or present'—*click*."

"Okay, let's keep implying and let them extrapolate."

Montbretia looked at the façade of the office block—it had a certain facelessness. The brick frontage of orange-colored, wire-cut bricks produced cheaply in a factory for the minimum price seemed to have refused to weather in the forty years the building had been standing.

Two men came out of the entrance. Neither was a typical office worker. Their jeans were encrusted with filth, their footwear was indistinguishable—it was simply a dark color at the end of their legs. And their coats—such as they were—were tied with string for one and a length of plastic for the other. One man talked loudly, the other mumbled—neither seemed to be taking account of the other as they conversed.

Boniface had a look of sadness as he watched the two pass. "I guess we're in the right place. Does the address on your list say number forty?" He pointed to his eyes at the number forty on the tattered awning over the front door.

Montbretia pulled the list from her back pocket. "Forty it is."

Boniface pushed the brushed aluminum–framed glass door and stepped in, holding the door for Montbretia as they entered a reception area, which was only the reception area by virtue of the fact that it was the first place you reached in the building. To the side, a double door had been propped open, giving access to a corridor with offices on each side.

"Are you sure, Boniface? This looks like an office to me."

Boniface's voice was quiet, just above a whisper. "It probably was a few weeks ago, but while it's unoccupied and in need of complete refurbishment, landlords often let homeless charities use places like this."

Montbretia looked around and sniffed—a combination of institutional cooking and unwashed human filled her lungs. "Why would they?"

Boniface halfheartedly shrugged. "Buying their place in heaven. Also, if you've got people here, then they take care to a certain extent—it's cheaper than security guards. And as you will have noticed, the place needs to be completely gutted anyway, so it's not a huge deal."

A figure came out of the second door on the right, walking along the faceless corridor toward them. Montbretia guessed he was probably only around twenty, but he had that look when someone had been homeless—they could be anything between fifteen and fifty. She could see him taking in Boniface—the suit was conspicuous. "You couldn't spare us a tenner, could you?" he asked Boniface.

"Not unless you've seen Carmen Gallagher—and if you can take us to her now, there's fifty in it for you."

"Give me twenty and I'll ask around." He seemed better clothed than the two who Montbretia had seen leaving, but he didn't seem to have any respect for Boniface's personal space.

"I'll keep looking," said Boniface, stepping away and starting to move down the corridor.

"Is there an office here?" asked Montbretia.

"Up there," said the chancer over his shoulder, without breaking step.

Boniface was at the end of the corridor as Montbretia turned back. She ran the two steps to catch up as he tapped lightly on the door and confidently walked in. "Good morning," said Boniface. Montbretia followed him through the door. "Boniface," he held his hand to his chest, indicating himself, then indicated to Montbretia. "My colleague, Monty Armstrong."

"Lucy," said the woman behind the desk. Something about Lucy reminded Montbretia of herself. Lucy had shoulder-length brown hair—about the same length that Montbretia's had been when she arrived in the UK. She was slim—slimmer than Montbretia, slimmer to the point that Montbretia thought *issues with food*—and maybe two inches shorter. She also had that look of someone who was unaccustomed to exercise, or even, given her pallor, being outside.

Montbretia surveyed Lucy's office and hated it—peeling wallpaper, frayed and ripped carpet, and a strip light hanging by its wires that struggled to add to the gray light filtering through the filthy net curtain over the window. Then the realization came that this wasn't unpleasant because the homeless charity couldn't afford to undertake the maintenance—this was unpleasant because this is how the office was when the last paying tenants were here.

Boniface pulled out his phone. "I wonder if you can help us—we're looking for someone." He held his phone up for Lucy to see. "This is the most recent picture we have of her, but we also have pictures of her back in the eighties—she was a model then."

Lucy looked closely at the pictures as Boniface flicked through.

"Her name is Carmen Gallagher, and she's about forty-eight years old. We're looking for her in connection with a legacy."

Lucy paused, looking to Montbretia. "Did you call yesterday?"

Montbretia nodded.

Lucy sympathetically tilted her head—a look she was probably well practiced at delivering. "As I said, we don't disclose our residents—past or present."

"Does that mean she was here?" said Boniface.

"I didn't say that."

"True. But you said you won't disclose residents past or present. And since you won't disclose, that must mean she was here. If she wasn't, then you wouldn't be bound by a duty of confidentiality." Boniface seemed triumphant.

"We don't disclose details about anyone." Lucy gave a weak attempt to communicate an apology by scrunching her face. "In any case, our records are pretty sparse, and, newsflash, not everyone gives us a full name or their legal name. So if you want to take it that she's been here, go ahead—I'm saying nothing. If you want to take it that she hasn't been here, go ahead—I'm saying nothing." Lucy stood mute, but with the trace of a self-satisfied smile forming.

"I get that," said Boniface, continuing as if he hadn't really noticed that he had been rebuffed. "Look, as I said, I want to talk with Carmen about a legacy. We can meet somewhere public that suits her, she can bring a friend...you can be there...I just want to talk."

"It's still the same answer, I'm afraid," said Lucy.

Boniface jutted out his chin, admitting defeat. "If she does happen to get in touch, could you ask her to call me—here's my number." He reached into the breast-pocket of his jacket, then pulled his fingers out as if there was a trap. "I'm sorry—I don't have a card. I'll have to write it down for you," he said, pulling his notepad out of his inside pocket. "I just got the suit back from the cleaner."

Montbretia stared. He always had cards in his top pocket. Always.

Boniface finished scribbling his note and ripped out the page, placing it on the desk. "I just want to have a chat with Carmen." Lucy's face soured slightly as she stood, not touching the page. "Thanks, Lucy. It was good meeting you."

They followed the corridor toward the door. "You didn't tell me you had a recent photo," whispered Montbretia.

"I snapped it at Jilly's." He took out his phone and held the picture for Montbretia, who reached over to steady his hand as they walked. "It's good to see her with her clothes on."

"It's a photo of a photo, Boniface."

"I know. What was I meant to do? I didn't want to ask and have Jilly say I couldn't take the picture, so I snapped it while she wasn't looking."

His phone disappeared into a pocket as they walked out of the main entrance. "You were a bit harsh in there, weren't you?" said Montbretia.

"Yeah. But all lawyers are assholes, right?" said Boniface. "I had to be true to character. If I claimed to be a lawyer, she might have doubted, but if I behave like one, she'll believe I am."

"And what's the story about getting your suit back from cleaner?"

"It suddenly dawned on me that I can't give them my card: It says Boniface Communications. If she twigs I'm a PR guy scamming as a lawyer, then we'll never find Carmen."

Montbretia pushed out her bottom lip, weighing up the other option. "Suppose so. Where next?"

"First, I think we should get some cash—I feel we're going to want to pay for information before too long. Then we go to the next on the list. And then the next."

fifty–five

"How many hostels are there?" Boniface stirred his tea.

"Fifteen in Westminster. Well, fifteen that wouldn't admit she was a resident and wouldn't confirm that she wasn't." Montbretia spread butter over her toast. "That fifteen also excludes any hostels where Carmen didn't fit their entry requirements."

Boniface frowned as he took a sip of tea.

"Different hostels have different requirements—some only admit young homeless, some won't admit you if you have a reputation for violence or if you've got a criminal record. And not every hostel has a website or comes up when you Google, so I'm not sure I've found everything. But of those ones that I did find, the answer is fifteen in Westminster."

"And we've been to seven so far."

"In Westminster. More in Lambeth, of course."

"Of course." Boniface looked down at his silent phone lying on the Formica surface, then leaned back to survey the café. It was small—two tables, both arranged as booths. He occupied one with Montbretia; the other was empty.

Most of the custom seemed to be office workers getting a coffee or something to eat at lunch before scurrying off for a day's work. And from the stacks of various rolls and the amount of sandwich fillings being prepared by the four staff behind the counter, Boniface guessed lunchtime would be busy, too.

"And after Westminster," said Montbretia. "I mean...what happens if we don't find her in the remaining eight?"

"Then we go wider. Ever wider concentric circles." He twisted his face—he wasn't quite sure how to communicate *what other options do we have.* "We keep going, and hopefully we get lucky."

"And if we don't?"

Boniface smiled softly. "If we don't get lucky, then life is...suboptimal." He snorted. "Not that it's much better than that at the moment—I'm not sure I wanted to spend my day going round hostels." He looked up at Montbretia. "Not that you wanted to spend your day dragging around homeless shelters, either."

Montbretia bit into her toast with little enthusiasm. "I would say it's not what I had planned, but that would only be true because I didn't have anything planned."

"Why don't you go home? You sound more bored than I feel, and you look like you could do with a bit more than ninety minutes' sleep."

"It's tempting, but I left my keys at your place, so I'd have to go past there to pick them up."

"So?"

Montbretia's lips winced and twisted. "Leathan's there."

Boniface waited, forcing his face into the best expectant look he could given his lack of sleep and his lack of enthusiasm.

"He got...well...while you were getting changed...I'm not...but..."

"Leathan?"

"With you?"

"Mmm."

"And he said this?"

"Mmm hmm."

"To you?"

"To me."

"Right," said Boniface and paused. "What exactly did he say?"

"Well...it's this whole different bed each night thing." Boniface waited. "He sort of implied that maybe I could supply a bed—just for tonight. Not tomorrow, because...you know..."

"And I'm guessing he also suggested that a body to keep him warm might be nice."

"More implied...but that was my understanding." She sat up straighter. "I can handle Leathan—hell, I might even find him cute in certain circumstances. But I only met him yesterday, and it's too early in the morning. I need a cup of coffee before I have those kinds of conversations." She seemed to relax. "Do you want to split the rest of the list?"

Boniface pondered. "Nah...safety in numbers, and one of us is bound to be more inviting to her. The point is to get Carmen talking, not to scare her."

"And you're sure there's no other way of doing this, Boniface?"

"I'm all ears—if you've got an idea, then shoot." He waited a beat. "We've got cash and we're making noise—the best we can hope for is we get close and someone blabs." He exhaled deeply, the jet of air rippling his half full cup of tea. "If this is all about Dawn's past, then it must be related to Lorna's death—why else would she run? Carmen's the only person who I know was there and with whom I haven't spoken. The only other person who seems to know is Ernie."

Montbretia's face soured. "I'd prefer it if we didn't pay him a visit." She put the last lump of toast into her mouth, chewing as she talked. "I still think we should split up—we could cover four hostels each and be back here in an hour, maybe ninety minutes."

Boniface's phone rang. "I don't recognize the number."

fifty-six

She wasn't sure whether to trust this bloke.

Boniface sounded like a ponce's name. And to be frank, he sounded like a bit of a ponce on the phone, but if there was money, then it might be worth talking to him. Provided he didn't require pain and/or humiliation in exchange for the cash... Provided it didn't require her to commit another crime.

And the meeting place seemed safe enough. It wasn't a side street where she was looking for a parked car. It wasn't a hotel near Kings Cross where they charged by the hour and wouldn't care if a murder was committed as long as you paid in full, up front, in cash, and then left the room so that it could be rented to the next punter.

It was a café in Westminster. A café she knew by sight but had never been in. The sort of place where people who work in offices go to buy sandwiches or rolls made with Italian-sounding bread, thinking it made their lunch better or healthier. But at the end of the day, bread was bread, whatever you called it.

She walked past the window, slowly but not too slowly.

There was a man sitting in a booth with a woman sitting opposite him. He looked like he could be a Boniface—thirtysomething, confident—but she couldn't see his face well enough, she guessed around six foot but he was sitting, looked after his hair, and had a decent suit. The woman sitting opposite him twisted as she passed—Carmen sped up and only caught a glance of her, mostly seeing the chestnut hair that flicked as she turned.

She didn't look like she was being held against her will.

She didn't look like she was the muscle, there to bundle Carmen into a waiting van.

In fact, she looked like the woman that Matt at the shelter said had turned up with this Boniface bloke this morning.

Carmen kept walking, stopping when she was about thirty yards past the café, where she waited, watching the entrance as people passed. After about ninety seconds, a girl with curly blond hair loosely tied back walked in. Carmen walked back, slowing as she again approached the café, making sure the girl was standing at the counter.

The blond girl was—and as she stood, she blocked the passage between Boniface and the door. If Boniface made a lunge, then blondie was going to get hurt. Rules of the jungle, unfortunately, honey.

Carmen pulled the door and stood, her foot keeping the dark wood–framed glass door open. She took in the room, her eyes darting: three men behind the counter, blondie ordering, two tables—both probably fixed to the ground—one empty, the other with the man who was probably Boniface and the woman with the chestnut hair, a rear exit probably leading to the bathroom.

Boniface—assuming it was Boniface—made eye contact and started to slide out from his seat. The woman remained but turned her head and smiled.

"Hi. I'm Boniface." He leaned forward offering his hand, careful to avoid the blond. "You must be Carmen—it's so good to meet you."

She shook his hand once, withdrawing hers quickly, looking to see whether anyone else appeared.

"What do you want to eat?" Boniface had stepped back, leaving Carmen where she had been standing, and indicated to the menu boards.

"Umm...I'm not really sure," she said.

"Have you eaten yet today?" asked Boniface.

She shook her head.

"Full English?"

She nodded.

He turned to the guy closest to the grill. "Full English, please, for the lady."

"No black pudding," she said softly.

"No black pudding," relayed Boniface, then turned back to her. "Tea? Coffee?"

"Tea."

"It's builder's tea, but it's alright," said Boniface quietly, leaning forward. He talked like a wine snob, surprised at the quality of supermarket wine.

She nodded.

"And a cup of tea." He turned back and went to sit. "Please. Join us."

The woman slid across the bench seat to make room. "Hi. I'm Montbretia. Call me Monty," she said, offering her hand as Carmen cautiously moved closer. Carmen shook and carefully moved beside the woman who called herself Monty, sliding up the bench to sit squarely behind the table and diagonally opposite Boniface.

Matt at the shelter had said his face looked knocked about, and now, sitting across the table, Carmen could see that Matt was right: Boniface had a fat lip; several bruises displaying various shades of black, blue, purple, green, and yellow; roughed-up skin over one cheekbone; and on the other cheek a long, straight cut, the sort you get from a blade.

She pondered: If he was that smart, then why had Boniface got injured?

One of the guys behind the counter with a white shirt, black trousers, and white apron brought a mug of tea over, clunking it on the table and leaving.

"Quite a weapon, isn't it?" said Boniface, indicating the heavy white porcelain mug with the steaming brown liquid. "You could do quite some damage with that—scald someone, then clout them with it. They wouldn't fight back."

He didn't seem to realize he was describing her new emergency escape plan.

"Do you want to order something for later? A sandwich or something that you can take with you?" asked Boniface.

Carmen wasn't quite sure what to ask for.

"No hurry," said Boniface. "Think about it. Whatever you want—you can decide later."

The man in the apron returned with a large white plate, placing it in front of Carmen before pulling a knife and fork rolled in a napkin out of his top pocket. "Enjoy your meal," he said, turning away to leave Carmen looking at her filled plate, taking in each item: sausage, baked beans, bacon, two fried eggs, two fried tomatoes, fried bread, mushrooms, and hashbrowns.

Carmen unwrapped her cutlery and started to slice her bacon. "There, as I promised: breakfast," said Boniface.

"You said there was money," said Carmen, starting to chew her bacon, noticing that blondie had left.

"No, I said legacy," said Boniface. "And I may have allowed you to form the wrong impression—the legacy is M-Stub8's legacy." Carmen took another mouthful, her gaze fixed on Boniface. "But there is something for you." She opened her eyes wider, questioning. "I talked to Jilly Crossley—she thinks you're clean and you're pulling your life together. Is that right?"

"I'm clean," said Carmen, chewing. "Been clean for two years."

Boniface tilted his head as if he was listening intently.

"As for pulling my life together...that's harder. I don't have any real skills, and to try to get training at my age is hard."

"There are *no* offers?" asked Boniface.

"Who wants to take a chance on a former porn actress with a criminal record? I even thought about...you know...doing some more porn. But given what I've put my body through, there's not much—I'm at the extreme end of things." She cut into a hashbrown. "Do you know what the gangbang record is?"

"As in...?"

"As in the number of men one woman will have sex with in a single session."

Boniface shrugged. "It must be a big number, or else you wouldn't ask me."

"Mmm," said Carmen, biting into her hashbrown.

"Fifty," said Boniface.

"Do you want to guess?" she said to Montbretia.

"Seventy-five," said Montbretia tentatively.

"Just shy of one thousand the last time I looked." She looked between Boniface and Montbretia and saw disbelief. "I was asked if I wanted to have a go at breaking the record." She snorted. "They figured instead of just breaking the record—you know one-thousand-and-one, one-thousand-and-two—that we should smash it or set a whole new record for the largest number of double penetrations or triple penetrations."

"No." Montbretia's mouth was wide, the shock etched into her face.

"It's more appealing than the other offers."

"Worse than..." said Montbretia, her voice only just above a whisper.

"At least some of that stuff you might do for fun—the stuff I don't like is the pain...you don't want to know...and having guys crap in your mouth. Chocolate logs were never my thing...and never will be." She winced. "So do you get some sort of idea why porn isn't really an appealing option either?"

Boniface sat silently, then took out his wallet, opened it, and placed a £20 note on the table. He took a second and deliberately placed it on top of the first. Then a third, fourth, and fifth. Each note laid methodically and without hurry. He put his wallet away and looked up at Carmen. "Yours."

She reached forward, and he slapped his hand on the pile. "Yours for talking. And if we like what you say, we can help you—might even be able to find you a few bits of work. I'm not saying we can get you a change-your-life job—but a few days here and there so that you can tell people you've done some work. Maybe even help you get a reference."

"How do I..."

Boniface cut her off before she could ask the question. "How do you know you can trust me?"

She nodded.

"You don't." He paused—he seemed pleased with the answer he had given, even though it didn't help. "But what we do is this. I ask a question—just one. You answer. I give you the first twenty. Okay?"

She nodded again.

"We talk a bit more. When you think you've earned the balance of the cash, you say. Clear?"

"Clear," whispered Carmen.

"I'm not saying I'll pay you at this point—maybe I pay you nothing, maybe I pay you everything, maybe I'll pay you some—whatever I do, you'll get to see whether you can trust me, and from what you tell me, I'll see whether I can trust you. Fair?"

A single bob of the head.

"Ready?"

Another single bob.

"Billy Watkins," said Boniface. "Did you know him?"

Carmen felt her face flush and her stomach lurch. She dropped her head, unable to look at Boniface or the woman who called herself Monty.

She wasn't sure how long it was, but when she looked up, she could feel her eyes stinging. "I knew Billy." Her voice was hoarse.

Boniface lifted the top £20 and placed it on the table next to her. "You had a relationship with Billy?"

"Mmm hmmm." Carmen wiped her nose with the serviette. "He was the only man I've ever loved...the only man who loved me."

"Tell me about it—start from the beginning," said Boniface softly.

"I was in this band, M-Stub8—that's what you want to talk about?"

Boniface nodded, once. His head tilting as he leaned forward.

"There were four of us: me, Dawn, Jilly, and Lorna. We were all models...glamour models. They put us together in this band—we were awful, but it was a laugh."

Boniface remained still, watching. Listening.

"One night, we were doing this appearance, I can't remember where—some hole, Luton maybe—and Billy turned up. He was after Dawn—he knew her from way back...I don't want to say *love at first sight*, but you know when you see a guy and your heart just...you become aware.... You don't know why, but you know you've stopped breathing." Carmen looked at Monty. "You know that feeling."

Monty shrugged. "The last bloke I met recommended some South African tea. The only reason for my heart to stop was boredom."

Carmen laughed. "That's funny!" She leaned toward Monty. "Billy wasn't like that—he had a look about him...he was a guy that would fight. In fact, that night he did throw a fist. He was pure animal, and I was hooked. But as I said, he was after Dawn, and he didn't even speak to me." She turned back to Monty. "Seriously, he recommended tea—like..." She held up her mug.

Monty bit her bottom lip.

"Billy turned up a few other times, and we did get chatting—in fact, it was more than chatting—but he was only hitting on me to make Dawn jealous." She took a sip of her tea, and giggled "tea" under her breath before she continued, her voice becoming lower. "Dawn told me some things about Billy—they were quite...strong... serious accusations... But I didn't believe her—I thought she was just playing a game with Billy." Her voice took on a mournful tone. "I now know that everything she told me was true. Everything."

She reached under the table for Monty's hand and grabbed it, gripping it firmly. "We were like sisters, and it all ended the night Lorna died." She gripped more tightly, wiping a tear with her other hand. "None of us knew how to deal with that pain, that guilt. Jilly felt the loss—but you could see she blamed me and Dawn. It wasn't our fault..." She sniffed. "We weren't innocents—we encouraged Lorna to get up on the balustrade and dance with us—but we got down first and told her to get down, but she wouldn't. And then she slipped." She let out a sob. "We knew she was dead—we saw her hit head as she fell. It's the sound of her head hitting the balustrade that I hear when I wake up in the middle of the night. It was that sound that made me want to block out the world with a needle."

She wiped her tears with her fingers, breathing heavily. "Dawn went inside herself—she couldn't talk. Me, well, I found other ways to keep blotting out the pain. We all grabbed hold of what we could reach—I got Billy, and for once, he seemed to want me for me. He treated me well—I stopped having to show flesh, and life moved on. I lost contact with Dawn and Jilly, and life with Billy was good."

Carmen let go of Montbretia's hand, wiped her tears with her serviette, and brushed back her hair. "We were a family—me, Billy, and little Billy."

"Little Billy?" asked Boniface.

"Billy had a son: William. He was a nice lad—bit of a tear-away, but I liked him."

"How old was he?"

Carmen paused—running through dates. "I was there for his fifth birthday. I missed Lorna and the girls like crazy, but a kid's birthday gives you a different perspective. I would have been about twenty-two then, and you start thinking, you know..."

"Did it last?" asked Boniface. "You and Billy?"

"It was a bit on-and-off to start with. We'd be on; it was good. We'd be off; I'd have to work so I'd get my tits out. Billy would get angry—he didn't want his mates seeing me in the papers, so he'd come and have a go. One thing would lead to another, and we'd get back together. It would be good, then it'd be bad, then...you get the idea."

"I get the idea," said Boniface quietly.

"Then Billy's mum died. That hit him—that hit little Billy, who spent a lot of time with his nan. But it sort of brought me and Billy closer—we still rowed and were on-again-off-again, but we were more on than we were off." She looked across the table at the pile of cash. "I think it's time to pay."

Boniface picked up two £20 notes, showing each individually to Carmen, and placed them on top of the first note. "Part payment for part of the story. How did it end with Billy?"

"We were on and off, but mostly on. But we were out of it quite a bit—he was drinking a lot, I was doing a range of stuff, and that took up a lot of time."

"How long had you been together?" asked Monty.

Carmen paused, doing the sums in her head. "Little Billy—he was less little—he would have been about eleven or twelve, so what's that? Seven years?"

"Seven," said Montbretia quietly.

"I can't even remember where we were going, but Billy and I were going some-where. We were both under the influence, and he was driving fast. One minute he's driving, the next the car's wrapped around a bridge, and I'm unconscious.

Apparently it took forty-eight hours for Billy to die from his injuries. It took me a month to get out of hospital."

Montbretia gasped quietly. "And then?"

"What one of my counselors might have described as recreational drug use became self-medication, became addiction. Billy's family wanted nothing to do with me—not that they had ever wanted much—and I went back to work. I was seven years older—I was thirty, which in those days, in glamour-girl years, was more like 300, so I had to get involved in...you know...the dirtier stuff, so I took more to block out what I was doing...and you know how the story goes."

"What happened to the kid?" asked Boniface.

"Don't know," said Carmen. "His family—his father's family—took control. I never saw him again." She had the look of someone ready to leave the confessional. "I think that's the full hundred."

Boniface passed over the last two £20 notes. "Who was little Billy's mother?" he asked.

"Is there any more cash in your wallet?"

fifty-seven

"Do we trust her? Do we believe?" Montbretia was putting voice to the questions that were still swirling in Boniface's head as they walked through the doors into his apartment block, the light filtering through the glass panes in the doors soon losing its strength as they stepped across the marble-chip floors.

"I can't see any reason why she would lie." Boniface stood to allow Montbretia to ascend the stairs first, watching as she grabbed the brass handrail. "I'm not sure that I want to believe what she said, but would she really come up with that much of a story? You know, just keep talking with that level of detail?"

"By the sounds, she's done much worse for cash," said Montbretia, reaching the landing. "But that doesn't mean she was lying."

Boniface drew level and pulled out his keys. "Step quietly—we might as well leave Leathan if he's asleep." He slipped his key into the lock and held the black door open, following Montbretia into the apartment's lobby, which grew darker as he shut the door behind them, the only light pushing around the edge of the closed door to the main room.

Montbretia stood by the door, carefully placing her ear against it before turning the handle.

She stepped in and let out a small yelp.

Boniface followed swiftly and found the cause of her distress.

It took a moment to recognize the figure out of context, and another beat to recognize the danger. Boniface was more used to seeing Jojo Brooks standing outside Ernie's club, rather than leaning against the window in his front room. He was also conditioned to think of Jojo as one who used his fists, but the rusty pistol he was casually holding—as if it was the most natural thing that could be in his hand apart from his cock—suggested he might have other options.

"Sorry, Boniface," said Leathan. He was sitting on the sofa, his back to the door, facing Jojo, and didn't turn to apologize.

"Yeah, sorry, Boniface." Boniface turned to see the source of the second apology—the man standing behind the counter in the kitchen area. A figure Boniface half-recognized but had trouble placing out of context. Tall, gaunt, weathered skin with liver spots, and thinning hair combed back.

"I don't believe we've been formally introduced," said Boniface. "Mister Irvine, I presume?"

"The pleasure's all yours," said the other man.

"You were in Ernie's office yesterday."

Irvine ignored the comment. "Sit. Both of you." He indicated the spaces by Leathan. Montbretia sat next to Leathan, who was wearing jeans and white shirt with a buttoned-down collar, and Boniface took the perpendicular sofa.

"I'm sorry," mouthed Leathan with a look that was somewhere between apologetic, angry, and frustrated.

"Imagine our surprise when a driver from the cab company down the road came to tell us that he had just delivered someone to the same address as the guy who tripped on his way out. It didn't take us long to figure—two people, one address—and then there was the bacon. It's hard to say you came in good faith if you leave with my breakfast."

Leathan smirked.

"I'm a lawyer," said Irvine, apparently changing the subject. Leathan's smirk became a look of confusion, and he shot a glance at Boniface. "And as a lawyer, I think about contracts. There are four elements to a contract. Do you know what those four elements are, Mister Boniface?"

Boniface shook his head. Jojo looked bored and fiddled with the gun. Apparently he didn't care about contracts either.

"They're quite simple—it's probably what you would guess if you thought about it. The first part is the offer—like your offer to procure Prickle."

Irvine stood up straighter and walked out from behind the counter. "The second element of a contract is acceptance of the offer. You made an offer to Ernie, and Ernie accepted it."

He forced a look of pleasure across his face. "Now, most people think that's enough. But that's not a valid legal contract. Do you know what's missing?" He looked at Montbretia. "Do you?"

Montbretia shrugged. "It has to be written down?"

Irvine's mouth moved to become a rictal grin. "Good guess, but no. That's a very common misconception but it's not correct—a verbal contract is just as valid as a written one. No, there are two further elements—the first is that the contract must be legally enforceable. In other words, there must be consequences." He paused, letting his gaze linger on the three seated people. "And the fourth element—the one people always forget—consideration."

Irvine walked to the steel-framed window and stood toward the end away from Jojo before he continued. "Consideration. By which the law doesn't mean kindness—the law means payment." He looked at Leathan. "And with that bacon, we believe you have received suitable consideration to establish a valid contract. So let me now return to the third element of the contract and talk a bit about the legal consequences of not delivering on your contract, Mister Boniface."

"Bacon," said Boniface.

"Don't whimper—you offered the band. You're not going to tell me that you made an offer which you couldn't make, or that you were just bluffing." He stared at Boniface. "Good, so don't now start quibbling about the consideration."

"I..." Boniface stopped talking.

"You're going to deliver Prickle to us, Mister Boniface. And just to make sure you understand how serious we are, we're going to add a deadline. That way both sides"—he pointed to himself and then to Boniface, then back to himself—"can be clear about what's going on. So you have until midnight."

"Midnight," said Boniface.

"That's over twelve hours to do what you said you would do," said Irvine, checking his watch. "And if you don't meet our deadline, then Mister Featherstone—everybody's mate, Danny the bassist—will suffer. His wife may be missing—oh yeah, we know about that too, and we don't believe she's in Canada or wherever Danny told Billy she was—but we can still make her feel pain, unimaginable pain...pain that will destroy Danny from the inside."

He tilted his head at Jojo, who flicked the pistol in a move he had probably learned from a rap video, and walked in front of Irvine toward the door. Irvine remained still. "I presume you're that Leathan guy—the one our Bulgarian friends are hoping to meet." He shrugged as he started toward the door. "Maybe that makes things a little more urgent?"

fifty-eight

"Well, gentlemen. That was a rather disappointing interaction. What are we going to do now?" Leathan hadn't expected Montbretia to be the first to speak, but she had. And she seemed less downcast than him and Boniface.

Boniface, who sat back on the sofa, hopefully strategizing.

"You've gotta tell Danny," said Montbretia, who seemed to be far keener to act than the two men.

"Mmm," said Boniface. "But what am I going to tell him? What did Irvine *actually* threaten us with?"

"That he'd hurt Dawn," said Montbretia, talking over Leathan, who sat motionless apart from a small twist of his head as the conversation ping-ponged across him.

"And how is he going to do this?" asked Boniface. "I know that's what he said—what I'm trying to get at is what did he threaten to do? How is he actually intending to make good on his threat—especially as he doesn't seem to know where Dawn is either."

Montbretia stood up, removing the gray hoodie she had been wearing when she came in. Her voice was soft, encouraging. "What are the options? How could Irvine and Ernie hurt Dawn? How would that hurt Danny?"

Boniface mirrored Montbretia's calm tone. "Only one option I can think of—by going after her son. Hurt the kid, and Dawn feels pain that Danny can't fix."

"Excuse me." Leathan felt the need to break his silence. "When did we learn this little detail—that there is a son?"

"Carmen," said Montbretia.

"So you found her," said Leathan. Montbretia and Boniface nodded in unison. "Well done." He paused. "So who is the son?"

"I've seen him," said Boniface. "The first time I went to Ernie's place, he was hanging around there." Leathan felt his face register the confusion his brain felt. "It's worse than that, Leath. My blag to get in was that Billy had sent me—Billy Watkins, who was standing there. Billy Watkins, who I didn't recognize." He sighed, falling back into the sofa. "Which goes some way to explaining why I got beaten. They were on to me immediately."

"Hold on," said Leathan. "I thought Billy Watkins was dead."

"He is," said Boniface. "Billy Watkins Senior, his father, is dead—he died in a car crash with Carmen next to him. One name, two people."

"And you reckon Ernie's figured the Billy connection and he intends to use Billy Junior as leverage against Danny?"

"I don't know." Boniface leaned forward, resting his chin on his splayed hand. "I don't know, Leath. I really don't know."

"What's not to know?" Leathan stood up, moving toward the counter separating the kitchen from the main part of the room.

"Why did Dawn run?" asked Boniface. He looked up at Montbretia. "Any clue?"

"You mentioned Billy—she ran. Or at least, that's what I understood." She gave a slight shrug.

"Right. But if you're a mother, wouldn't you want to see your son?"

"I would," said Montbretia.

"So she must have thought Billy was Billy Senior, the father," said Boniface. "There was no reason for her to know he was dead, and that ignorance kind of makes sense if she cut herself off completely...which would be another reason to believe Carmen's story."

"But do you think Carmen's wrong? Do you have an alternative version?" asked Montbretia.

"Well, not an alternative version, but..." his voice trailed. "It doesn't fit with what Danny...implied."

Leathan started to fill the kettle. "I'll put the kettle on—you elaborate."

"The one thing we know to be true is that Danny and Dawn are the real thing—proper, true love."

"That's what everyone says," said Montbretia.

"Not even a hint to the contrary—wouldn't you agree?" said Boniface.

"Yeah."

"So, if it is true, why doesn't Danny know that Dawn has a son?" He looked between Leathan and Montbretia, neither responding. "But put that aside—Danny and Dawn don't have kids. Danny was pretty discreet, but he implied that they had been through all the medical procedures...and the problem seems—I say *seems*, because he's never going to say outright—to be with Dawn. So if she can't have kids, then the kid can't be hers—and if the kid's not hers, then that explains why she ran when she heard the name Billy Watkins, since there was only one Billy as far as she knew."

The room fell quiet—apart from the noise of the kettle starting to heat the water.

"You know what you've got to do." Leathan watched as Boniface looked up to meet his eye.

"I knew what I had to do the moment the words came tumbling out of Carmen's lips. But I don't know that it's the right thing to do." His voice became almost pleading. "I can't tell Danny he's got a stepson if I can't prove that it's true."

"But take the alternate view," said Montbretia, moving back to the sofa and sitting where Leathan had been sat. "Are you really saying you're going to do nothing?"

Boniface exhaled. "I've got to do something—I just haven't figured what that something is."

"Yet," said Leathan, leaning on the counter. "I guess the question is: How much do you believe this Carmen?"

Boniface snorted and ran his hands through his hair. He looked to Montbretia for agreement as he said, "She's more than plausible."

Montbretia nodded, seemingly not having anything else to offer.

"You've got to lay it out for him," said Leathan, resting against the end of the counter.

"But if it's true, Dawn didn't tell Danny for a reason. We can't prove Billy is her son without her DNA."

"Nor can Billy or Ernie or anyone else without Dawn's DNA," said Montbretia.

"But hold on," said Boniface. "We've got to assume that Billy is Dawn's son and make sure that no harm comes to the kid. You heard Irvine's threat."

"He's not our responsibility," said Leathan. "You need to look after Danny and Dawn."

"Think about it," said Boniface. "Whatever the situation, how does Danny get up in the morning if he is responsible, however indirectly, for harm coming to his wife's child—probably her only child? And how does he make a decision about giving away the band if he doesn't know for sure whether the kid is Dawn's."

"That's why they invented coins, Boniface," said Leathan, pulling a piece of silver out of his pocket and flicking it.

"Okay. You've convinced me. I don't know what I'm going to say, but whatever it is, I need to say it to Danny," said Boniface, standing. "Can I trust you two here together?"

He passed the kitchen counter as Leathan said, "Sure."

"You're not going to get yourselves held up at gunpoint." He reached the door and turned back, much as Irvine had done. "And Leathan—don't try to proposition Monty. You met her less than twenty-four hours ago, and I need you both on good terms when I get back."

fifty-nine

Boniface let the barge glide through the narrow country lanes of the Surrey Hills.

He didn't remember the route he had taken—he had navigated by muscle memory and electronics as he dedicated his conscious mind to the task of considering every permutation and each option. He knew he would have gone up Wimbledon Hill, through the village, and along the edge of the Common passing between the windmill and the Embassy of the Holy See before turning left at Tibbet's Corner onto the A3. Once on the A3, he would have followed the three lanes until he turned off and passed through the village of Ripley, shortly to turn south through West Clandon and climb to Newlands Corner, where he would have seen the panorama of the valley created by the Hills spread in front of him before descending and turning right into the narrow country lanes meandering through an occasional hamlet, until eventually he reached the house that was becoming familiar: Dawn and Danny's house.

Except without Dawn, it was hard to call it her home.

Danny saw him arrive from the kitchen and came out to greet him. Boniface was shocked at how rough he looked—the shock must have shown on his face. "I ain't slept," were the bassist's first words. "Not since she left."

"Have you eaten?" asked Boniface.

"Scraps. I can't keep it down—my gut's tied in knots."

"You could shave...have a bath..." Boniface surveyed the rocker's appearance. For a man who earned his living presenting an image, he seemed to be utterly unaware of how he looked from the outside.

"Thanks, Boniface. You've driven all this way to tell me to find a bar of soap." Danny indicated toward the kitchen. "You feel it's my personal hygiene that's keeping my wife away, do you?"

"I'm sorry," said Boniface, stepping through the kitchen door, pausing at Dawn's photograph of the Gothic tower that he had admired shortly before he mentioned the name Billy Watkins. "I'm just a bit distracted. Something on my mind that I'm trying to get straight."

"Sit down," said the bassist, clicking on the kettle.

"You'd better join me," said Boniface, pulling back the chair he had last sat in when he had dinner with the other man's wife on the night that Danny had met the prospective new singer. Boniface indicated the other side of the table. "Don't worry about the tea...other things are more important."

"Now you're worrying me, Boniface," said Danny, pulling back the bench on the other side of the table.

"You remember when we last spoke I asked you about Ernie Norton?"

"Gray's friend...comrade...business partner...whatever."

Boniface said, "You said you didn't know him."

"And I still don't know him."

"Maybe you should," said Boniface softly. "Maybe you will." He paused, looking for signs on Danny's face to suggest how he might react. "He's the root of your problems, and he's trying to unleash a whirlwind of torment for you."

"If he wants to do that, why doesn't he come here and face me?" asked Danny, his body stiffening as he sat up straight. "Face me, man-to-man."

"Because he's sent me instead," said Boniface. "He has figured—correctly—that I'm not going to refuse to pass on his message."

"You really are starting to scare me, Boniface. What is this message?" Boniface looked at the bassist, who was gripping the edge of the table, the color having drained from his face.

"He's proposing a deal. Not a nice deal, but a deal."

"Come on, Boniface. What is the deal?"

"He wants the band. He wants to own Prickle—every copyright, every contract, every source of income, and in return for that, he will be kind to Dawn."

The room fell silent apart from the sound of the kettle and Danny's breathing—a deep inhalation, silence as he held the breath, a long exhalation, and a pause before the cycle began again. Boniface fixed his focus, waiting until Danny finally broke the still. "You told him no?"

"I told him nothing." Boniface's tone was reassuring. "The decision isn't mine to make—either way."

Danny's left cheek twitched.

"But there's more."

"More?"

"He's threatening your wife, Dan, not you."

"If he lays a finger..." Boniface held up his hand to stop the bassist before he made a list of threats, only half of which he would intend to carry through on.

"You need to listen." Boniface's voice was just above a whisper. "And you need to stop thinking about revenge—if you're off dismembering people limb by limb, then you're not here protecting Dawn."

Danny stared at Boniface and exhaled deeply.

Boniface began slowly but deliberately, pausing after he had uttered each phrase. "I'm going to lay out the story as I have been told. I'm telling you so that you know what the threat is. I'm telling you so you know what people are saying. I'm not claiming this is the truth."

Danny remained still.

"Okay?" whispered Boniface.

"Okay," mouthed the bassist.

"The kid that turned up the other day asking for Dawn—the one that seemed like a strung-out junkie..." Danny nodded his head as Boniface continued. "There's a chance that he's Dawn's son."

The room was silent again.

Boniface watched Danny, checking the emotions playing across his face: anger, hurt, disbelief, understanding, rage, acceptance. Finally he whispered, "It's not true...he can't be."

"I spoke to Carmen—you remember Carmen Gallagher; she was in M-Stub8 with Dawn." Danny blinked his eyes as if to affirm. "She says that Dawn did have a son."

"Bullshit."

"She says that Dawn told her." Boniface watched, calibrating the reaction across Danny's face—perhaps hearing for the first time about his and Dawn's greatest desire: a child. Maybe realizing that his wife may have lied to him.

Boniface continued. "Carmen says that she had a relationship with the kid's father—a relationship over several years—and this guy said Dawn was the mother."

Danny's eyes glistened; his lower jaw trembled as it tightened. His lips opened and closed as if sipping small amounts of air. "It's…" He stood, turning away from Boniface, one hand clutched across his stomach, the other lifted to his face. When he spoke—still facing away from Boniface—his voice cracked. "I don't care if there's a kid—I just want my wife to be safe. I want my wife home." His voice trailed off, to be replaced by sobs.

Boniface stood and walked around the table to Danny, putting an arm around the other man's shoulder.

"I know, Dan, I know. We all want Dawn home—but we need to focus. We need to deal with this issue—I'm pretty certain that once we sort out Ernie, then all your other problems will disappear."

"What they're saying, Boniface. It's all lies." Danny's voice was a whimper.

Boniface took Danny's head between his hands, forcing the other man to look at him. "To do the best for Dawn we need to focus. We can't prove whether the story is true or not…"

"I don't care if it's true. I love my wife whatever, and she loves me." Danny's voice was pleading.

"Focus," said Boniface. "Ernie has given us an ultimatum and a deadline: midnight. He wants the band and all the rights and earnings that flow from the band. You, Mel, Newt, and Luca will be out, and Ernie will put Gray in as singer with a bunch of session guys. That's his plan."

"That's just stu…" Danny pulled away, visibly angry. "That's crazy—that'll never work."

Boniface clapped his hands. "Focus. That's what Ernie wants—the threat is that he'll hurt Dawn. To quote, *unspeakable pain* if you don't comply."

"It's a lie. This kid's a lie. There's nothing to hurt us with." Danny's face was reddening; his voice was reaching a crescendo. "Tell him no, Boniface. He can do what he wants. But there's no kid, and he's not having the band."

Boniface returned to the other side of the table and sat. He motioned to Danny to return to his seat. The bassist was breathing heavily, his shoulders pulled in as if taking the stance of a prizefighter.

Reluctantly Danny sat, and Boniface began softly. "I'm having trouble believing what I've been told, but let's just play through the options. Say this kid is Dawn's. Say she gave birth when she was fifteen—years before she met you."

Danny snorted.

"Just…pretend, for one moment, that this kid matters. Think of the options. Ernie could wheel out the kid and sell the story to the papers. Wife of a rich rock star ignores her child and keeps him secret for thirty years. Think how Dawn would feel if that story were plastered over the newspapers day after day after day. And as a secondary issue, think of the blowback for you and Prickle."

Danny's voice was quiet but firm. "The story ain't true, Boniface. My wife doesn't have a kid. We went through every test you can go through with some of the leading gynecologists around the world—I cannot say this any more clearly: Dawn cannot conceive."

"I hear you," Boniface's voice remained calm. "But just imagine that there's a possibility that there's a perfectly reasonable explanation for this, and the kid *is* Dawn's. If Ernie murders this kid, procures his death, or makes the kid suffer—permanently injures him, gives him some funny pills that make him blind or lose a limb, sends him to jail, whatever—think what that would do to Dawn if she is his mother." Boniface sucked his teeth. "Ernie's mean—he could make the kid suffer and also go to the press."

Boniface noticed that Danny didn't seem to be responding. Danny didn't seem to have heard.

When he started speaking, the warmth had drained from his voice. "If she doesn't have a kid, then there's no story. Right?"

He paused, his eyes boring into Boniface, challenging him not to respond to the rhetorical question.

"I love my wife. I trust my wife." He paused, breathing heavily. "These aren't just words, Boniface. This is the basis of our whole relationship. I'm not going to undermine everything we have together and say I don't believe her." He inhaled deeply. "You can tell this Ernie to go and play with himself. If the kid gets hurt, it's on him, not me."

His gaze remained fixed on Boniface.

"And just so we're clear. If Dawn did have a kid, I wouldn't care—I'd still love her completely. And as for the idea of using a kid to get at me...how much bad press could an illegitimate kid cause? I'd love her to have a kid! Seriously—if the kid were hers, then as far as I'm concerned he's my son, and I'd throw open our doors to him." He continued, his voice smaller. "And if my wife has lied, I don't care—she will have had her reasons."

Boniface sat up straighter, keeping Danny's gaze. "You're sure, Dan?"

"If it's a choice between who lives, me or Dawn, then I'll lay down my life like that." He slapped the table, hard, the echo bouncing around the hard surfaces in the kitchen. "But if you want me to be worried about some chancer when my wife's missing, I don't care. Let this Ernie guy do his worst."

sixty

"I know why Dawn ran, and I know where she is."

"Where?" Montbretia felt a combination of joy and enthusiasm, tempered with caution. She had been sitting on the sofa perpendicular to the sofa where Leathan sat, but was now on her feet as Boniface made his announcement. Leathan remained seated, but turned, his arm flipped over the back of the sofa as they both faced the new arrival.

Boniface stammered momentarily. "I don't know where she is *now*, but I know where she will be—and you're going to find her." He pointed at Montbretia.

Montbretia went to speak but stopped. It was as if her brain had been slow in processing what her ears had heard and was still trying to resolve how the two facts—Dawn's location and Montbretia finding Dawn—related to one another.

"What did Danny say?" asked Leathan before Montbretia could resolve her internal dilemma.

"Not good," said Boniface, holding his hand over the kitchen counter and dropping his car keys. "In some ways it was a complete waste of time going to see Danny—he's too distracted. All he can do is sit and wait for Dawn...he can't not be there if she comes back."

"Can't he go and look around the nearby area?" asked Montbretia.

Boniface dropped onto the sofa next to Leathan. "You don't find a moving target by moving—you find them by waiting at a point they may pass, and that is what Danny's doing."

Montbretia twisted her lip and flopped back on her sofa.

"But while I agree that he can't leave the house, I'm not sure that he's right about what we do about Billy," said Boniface.

"So you did ask him," said Montbretia.

"For all the good it did." Boniface sighed softly. "Danny is certain that this Billy isn't Dawn's son. Can't be Dawn's son. So Danny isn't going to take any action to stop Ernie hurting this kid—if that is Ernie's plan."

"Even if..."

Boniface cut across Montbretia. "There is no 'if' as far as Danny is concerned. For him, the matter is not open for debate—he will not bow to blackmail, since he believes the threat is fundamentally false. That's what trust in a relationship does for you."

Montbretia looked at Leathan—he seemed relaxed, leaning back on the sofa, as if unwilling to take a lead. Instead, he was waiting for Boniface.

When Boniface continued, his voice was soft. "I had quite a bit of time to think on the way home. We seem to have two options: Either we let the pieces fall and see where they land or..." he paused, a look of mischief crossing his face as he looked between Montbretia and Leathan. "Or we reject Ernie's offer."

"The sensible option must be to stay out of this, Boniface," said Montbretia. "Look in the mirror—you can see what Ernie does when he gets upset."

Leathan scrunched his nose but remained quiet.

"Unfortunately," said Boniface, "Ernie has threatened me directly, which, by the way, means he's threatened you, because he'll hurt you if that's the only way he can find to get at me."

"There's only one option, Boniface," said Leathan. "We need to hurt Ernie—take out Irvine or hurt someone who's close to him."

Boniface winced slightly. "If we were on one of those corporate team-building away-day things, in the spirit of always giving positive feedback, I'd say I love your creativity."

"But as we're not," said Leathan, "can I take it you think my idea is shit?"

"No, no...I like it," said Boniface. "I like the vindictiveness. It appeals. It's just... well...it's too criminal, we don't have the time, and we don't have the firepower."

"I was thinking about a kidnap," said Leathan.

Boniface shook his head, not disguising his disappointment. "The trouble is, we don't know who—or what—Ernie cares about, and we don't have time to do the research." He paused, seemingly thinking. "This needs all three of us. Are you..."

Montbretia and Leathan nodded slowly before Boniface finished his thought.

"There are three people who might get hurt," said Boniface. "Billy, Dawn, and Gray. We each find one, get them to safety, and then I'll go and see Ernie and throw the deal back in his face."

"Not Danny," asked Montbretia. "We don't need to tell him to move?"

"No. Ernie thinks he's got him by his hold over Dawn." He fixed his stare on Montbretia. "And on the subject of Dawn—can you go and find her and make sure she stays safe?"

"Sure," said Montbretia, pushing her jaw sideways. "Where is she?"

"Ah..." said Boniface, turning to Leathan without answering Montbretia. "Can you find Billy? Whether he's Dawn's son or not, he certainly seems to be the guy Ernie's using for leverage, so you might need to throw a fist or two to keep him safe."

"Would be my pleasure," said Leathan, smiling broadly. "I haven't been to the gym today."

"So you're going for Gray," said Montbretia.

"Half to protect him and half to stop him selling any other assets he doesn't actually own," said Boniface.

"You'd better explain what you want us to do," said Montbretia.

sixty-one

He checked the clock.

Three PM.

It probably was time to be awake, but he would have preferred to have made the decision himself, rather than have the obligation foisted on him by whoever was knocking at the front door.

And whoever was knocking seemed to be quite persistent.

Gray rolled over, leaving the sheets in a knotted twist, and stumbled for his robe. The robe he had liberated from a hotel in West Germany in 1979 on Prickle's first tour after Danny Featherstone had joined the band. The band had done a series of low-key gigs, mostly playing at American airbases—this hotel was their last stop before they went to France, and because of a late change in schedule, the hotel they were booked into was more expensive than they were used to.

He knew it was more expensive: Unlike their usual hotels, this offered complimentary robes, and so Gray decided to get a low-level refund, and the robe had found its way into his suitcase. He had contemplated taking more, but if he filled his suitcase that wouldn't leave space for essentials such as toothpaste and pornography.

He reached the small landing joining the two upstairs rooms and turned onto the staircase, which descended with a wall on either side, reaching the small passageway linking the front and back rooms of his house. He turned into the front room, turning off the television as he passed, and yanked the front door, which was stuck at the bottom.

As soon as he was earning—as soon as he was gigging again—Gray would replace the door and the frame. He would have some cash, and for once he would get someone else to fix his door—a proper chippy who knew what he was doing. And he'd get someone else to fix up the house, starting with the windows, which had been decaying for far too long and needed to be replaced.

Once the décor was updated, he'd get a new sofa and a decent TV—the current one was fifteen, maybe twenty years old and, to be frank, was pretty embarrassing in the way it filled up so much space for not a particularly large screen. And when the house was finished, then he'd have a holiday—or several. Perhaps he could persuade that Monty girl to go with him?

The frame released the door. "For fuck's sake, can't you leave me alone?" Boniface stood outside. He had a different look on his face. The really annoying, slightly smug PR man had been wiped away, and in his place there seemed to be concern. If not concern, his look was serious.

"Hi Gray." No smartass greeting—it must be serious. "Can I come in?" He leaned forward in expectation, but for once didn't push, and his foot stayed well away from the door. Gray stepped back and tilted his head toward the interior of the house.

By the time he had turned around, Boniface was sitting on the dining chair that Gray had brought in when Boniface and that Monty girl were there the other night. "We need to talk." Boniface's voice was low, but there was a rasp at the back of his throat—the sort of rasp that comes from stressing the voice.

As a singer, Gray knew this usually happened for two reasons: first, the voice getting overused, and second, nervous stress affecting the vocal cords. He suspected it was the latter with Boniface, and dropped onto the sofa. "Sure man, what's on your mind?"

As Boniface continued, the strain remained in his voice. "You need to get out of here for a few days." He reached into his jacket and pulled out his wallet, opening it and taking out some cash. He counted out six £50 notes, showing each to Gray before stacking them on the floor in front of him. "Does that give you an indication of how serious I am?" He paused. "Just in case it doesn't—I'm also going to pay your train fare. You must have friends somewhere—anywhere that's a long way away—that you can drop in on."

Gray reached for the pile of cash. Boniface bought his foot down on the notes, heavily. "You're not having that until you're ready to leave—get dressed, pack some hand luggage, and hurry up."

Boniface seemed dead serious. His usual faux friendliness—more like barely concealed tolerance of someone he clearly looked down on—was gone. Instead, it seemed to have been replaced by concern—what felt like genuine concern to Gray. "What's going on, Boniface?"

Boniface sat back in his chair, keeping his foot on the cash. "Ernie's grand scheme for getting into the music business is in the process of falling apart." For the first time since he had come in, a hint of a smile twitched at the side of Boniface's mouth. "I'm making it fall apart...with a little help."

"You fuc..." Boniface was on his feet before Gray could stand, and pushed him back onto the sofa. "That's my pension you're playing with, Boniface."

The younger man stood over Gray. "There is no pension."

Gray lay where Boniface had pushed him on the sofa, figuring how he could stand without Boniface stopping him. He tried to figure whether he could land a solid kick, but that would be difficult at this angle—and without shoes. And if Boniface had some strength, then he might be outclassed by the younger, taller man. "What d'you mean, there's no pension?"

"Ernie didn't recruit you to front a reinvigorated Prickle or whatever bull he told you—Ernie got you in debt so that you would sign over a bunch of spurious rights that you probably never owned in the first place and almost certainly don't own given how you and Prickle parted company."

"My lawyer," began Gray.

Boniface laughed, letting Gray see that he was laughing at him. Once Gray had noticed, Boniface sat down. His voice was calm, but there was still a hint of anxiety. "You don't have a lawyer, Gray. All you have is some bad advice from a bloke with no legal qualification—a man who owes his living to Ernie." He snorted. "They lied to you. They encouraged you to gamble knowing you would lose. They allowed you to keep playing, knowing you would lose more. Every loss was another debt—and that debt was leverage over you. And boy, have they levered you into position."

Gray felt the breath dragged out of him as his gut clenched.

"Ernie doesn't need you, whatever he told you. You're just as replaceable as any other member of the band—in fact, you don't need to be replaced...you've already been replaced by Kit and then Thad. Ernie just needs to find a new, young, good-looking frontman who can hold a tune, and he's set."

"But..." Gray began before being cut off again by Boniface.

"In fact, if you look at it from Ernie's perspective, once he's got your rights, then it might be easier if you're not around. Permanently. That way all income accrues to him directly, and you can never try to do to him what he's trying to do to Danny and Prickle."

Gray sat up, ready to ask a question.

Boniface kept talking, pulling out his phone and checking the screen. "I see what you're thinking."

"You don't even know..."

"I do. You reckon that all you have to do is nod your head and say 'yes, Boniface, I agree,' take the money, and then everything will be fine."

Gray felt the smirk twisting his mouth. "It's not a bad option."

"It's a dreadful idea. When Ernie thinks you're part of the scheme to break his dreams into a million little pieces, then he's going to come looking for you. Or rather, he's going to send some of his friends to look for you."

"But I'm not part of the plan to break Ernie's dream."

"You are," said Boniface, leaning forward, holding his phone with both hands. "Can we be honest?" His voice was just above a whisper.

Gray shrugged.

"Just between you and me...the rights relating to your time with Prickle...all this legal stuff against Danny, Prickle, and PAD Management...all this stuff instigated by Iain Irvine..."

"Yeah," said Gray.

"Just between you and me...it's bogus, isn't it? It's just your way to pay off your gambling debt, isn't it?"

Gray felt the smirk pushing again at his lips.

"Come on, Gray," said Boniface. "We're big boys—we can be honest, no one's listening. You agreed to claim these old rights just to settle your gambling debt, didn't you?"

"Yeah," said Gray, grinning. "You got me there. But you can't prove anything."

It was Boniface's turn to smirk. He held his phone between his thumb and forefinger and waggled it. "I can prove it—you've just given me the evidence."

Gray lunged forward, grabbing for the phone. Boniface twisted, moving the phone away from Gray and raising his elbow against the other man. Gray's windpipe made contact with Boniface's elbow and the older man slipped, his toweling robe billowing open as he fell to the ground.

sixty-two

Leathan crossed the road about fifty yards up from the black-painted wooden gates with the inset wicket gate. In daylight, from the other side of the road, the entrance under the archway looked quite benign, but still, he didn't see a need to take any risks, so he kept his pace swift and continued to let his gaze scan his surroundings.

The short parade of shops gave way to a row of faceless terraced houses. It seemed that the main way to distinguish between each residence was through a combination of the detritus left in the front yard and the state of the decay of the wood in the doors and windows. One house had a fridge-freezer in front of it, another a shopping cart from a supermarket, and a third a stack of car tires. The woodwork was almost exclusively white—or at least had been white once—and ranged from painted, badly, within the last five years, to not painted in the last twenty years, to the few where Leathan could see the wood rotting and crumbling even from the other side of the road.

He crossed the street quickly to check the front yards—none of them seemed to have anyone sitting in them. In the fifth house, an older woman was struggling to get herself and her shopping cart out of her front door. "Let me help you," said Leathan, starting up her path, watching as a look of fear froze the face of the resident.

Leathan stopped and took two steps back, looking at the gray-permed figure, wrapped tightly in an old raincoat, as she gripped the only shield at hand, her cart. "I'm sorry—I must have given you quite a fright bounding up your path like that." He indicated to cart, wedged in the front door to form a barrier between the woman and who or whatever predator she was avoiding today. "May I help you?"

"Now you've got me in this mess, you may as well," she said.

"I'm sorry," said Leathan, moving toward the door and lifting out the cart, placing it squarely on its four wheels, the handle toward its owner, who had locked her door and was squirreling her keys into the deepest recesses of her handbag, which she then placed inside the square bag held within the cart's cage.

He walked backward along the path, as if withdrawing from an audience with royalty, allowing the owner of the cart to step from her property onto the public path beside the road. As she went to turn, he began. "I wonder if you can help. I'm looking for my brother...younger brother. He's...not really an angel...the family is very worried. We think he might have found a bad lot...and maybe he's even been taking drugs. We want to get him help."

"Oh dear," said the cart-pusher. "We get a lot of that around here."

"Do you know where they congregate?"

Her face soured and with the slightest bow of her head she indicated the sprawl of housing across the road. "Not that one," she said, pointing to the collection of buildings to the right, "but that one," she indicated the estate to the left, her face souring further. "Won't go in there myself." A small shake of the head seemed to confirm that was all she could offer.

"Thank you," said Leathan, as she started pushing her cart in the direction of the parade of shops around Ernie's club. She was the only person in a street that was comparatively deserted apart the occasional car passing to note that humanity might pass through.

And in this neighborhood, there seemed to be two choices for cars: Either you had a beat-up wreck that was at least twenty years old and probably had a replaced panel or two, which would now be painted a different color from the rest of the car; or you chose a customized high-end German model with a booming bass sound system and tinted glass, so dark that no one could see in, and you probably couldn't see out. Apparently, there were no other options for cars—no family sedans were allowed.

Leathan crossed back to the side of the housing developments. The development directly opposite the cart-pusher's house—the one that drew the less sour face—was probably a 1980s construction, erected at a time when planners understood the mistakes made with the immediate post-war housing and were determined to make a whole new set of mistakes in the name of progress. The freshly painted railings denoted an intention to take ownership of the land, and the recently cut grass— grass, rather than mud—within the fencing and lack of litter suggested a certain level of care.

He carried on up the road, leaving the fenced-in development, delineating the border with its even more down-market neighbor. Where the first development had a certain cohesion, this second and older development didn't. The grass—or more accurately, mud—formed rolling undulations separating the street from the 1950s collection of four-story brown-brick and steel-window housing.

The noise of kids playing filtered through the development, but no kids were visible from the street apart from the occasional passing teenager seeking anonymity under a hoodie, pulled tight to hide his identity. From somewhere in the distance, passing a car standing on bricks rather than wheels, two uniformed officers on foot patrol approached cautiously. Leathan recognized the insignia: Police Community Support Officers. Civilians dressed in a uniform to suggest they were police, but without most of the powers of sworn officers. A political sop intended to reduce antisocial behavior and give people a feeling that there were police on the streets. In reality, they were probably just another authority figure for most of the residents to dislike.

She was tall, blond, and while pretty enough, could probably handle herself in a barroom fight or might just play rugby on weekends. He was short and Asian with a boyish grin—all of his physical attributes thrown into sharper contrast by his colleague.

Leathan stood straighter, and without increasing his speed he began to walk with greater purpose toward the two uniforms, doing everything he could to exude a casual confidence as the gap narrowed.

"Hi," he smiled at the blond. "Good afternoon," he acknowledged the shorter man.

The uniforms—in uniforms that simply didn't look like proper police with a dark shirt instead of white, and a blue band around a pointless hat—acknowledged in a somewhat socially awkward manner. Leathan wasn't sure whether this was them displaying a fear of violence or a fear of actually having to do something. They both made small noises that might have been greetings, but then again...

"This is a slightly awkward question..." Leathan paused, taking in the concerned look that flicked between the two. "I'm looking for where the junkies hang out." A look of shock passed between the officers. "Or maybe just the drinkers."

"Sir," began the Asian man, his accent clearly from London, his attitude one of minor royalty, which didn't seem to match with someone taking a low-qualification job that offered scope for violent attacks and yet didn't allow you to carry a gun, instead offering only a stab-resistant vest.

"I'm sorry. I should have made myself clearer," said Leathan. "I'm looking for my kid brother. We want to get him help. We want to get him off the streets and away from here so he's not a bother to you. I've heard he hangs out around here."

The two uniforms seemed to relax. The blond turned and pointed in the direction from which the two had walked. "To the end, turn left, two blocks over. There's a group of them—they get pretty lairy, so you'd better take care."

Leathan heard them before he saw them, and he soon recognized the distinctive uniform: cheap leisurewear—hoodies, sweatpants, football shirts—all displaying too much flesh for March. None looked healthy—several were overweight, most looked borderline malnourished, and none had the appearance of someone with a washroom in their hostel. Several of the group had already passed out, having probably been drinking since they got up—the rest were seated on a bench, a low wall, and a recently cut log that didn't have a corresponding stump anywhere in sight.

A collection of empty green beer bottles and cheap cider cans was scattered around the group like a ripple from a stone dropped into a pond. A few carrier bags, old but still holding something, suggested that the day's drinking was anything but finished.

In the group of eight that were still conscious, he recognized many of the accents—Eastern European of assorted varieties, although Leathan didn't have sufficient grasp of any of the languages to make a precise geographical location. Nor to engage in their mother tongue...

However, he could engage in the language they all understood and pulled out two £20 notes, rustling them between his fingers as he sized up the drinkers. Unlike the Police Community Support Officers, Leathan didn't feel intimidated—he was sober, fitter than each individual, and fitter than the group collectively. Plus, he was sure he could handle himself if one lunged for the cash, and certain he could run faster than all of them.

He rustled the cash with greater emphasis, increasing the volume as he tried to make eye contact with one of the group. The only one in the group with a jacket—an old, ripped fake leather jacket—stood, walked to Leathan, and held out his hand expectantly.

Leathan placed the first £20, keeping the second at eye level. "I'm looking for a guy called Billy. About thirty. Usually wears jeans, boots, T-shirt, and a sleeveless denim jacket, maybe a green sweater. Black hair." He tried to stare at the other man, but the man's eyes were focused on the remaining cash. "Have you seen him?"

The other man was silent—the remainder of the group carried on drinking. Clearly there was nothing out of the ordinary happening.

Leathan rustled the second £20. The man caught his gaze, held it, then returned to looking at the £20.

Leathan dropped it into the other man's hand without releasing his own hold. "Have you seen Billy?"

The other man momentarily closed his eyes as if affirming, and Leathan let go of the note.

"You've seen Billy?"

The man nodded—a single bow of his head.

Leathan pulled out another £20 and rustled it for the other man to see. "What's Billy's name?"

He shrugged, grabbing at the £20. "Billy Krokodil is what we call him." Leathan released the note.

"You know where I can find Billy Krokodil?" asked Leathan, sliding his hand into his pocket.

The other man tilted his head forward. "I know where he was going."

Leathan pulled out another two £20 notes. "These make one hundred. Where?"

"Home."

Leathan pulled his hand back, taking the note farther from the drinker.

"Prince William Estate," said the drinker. "In Tottenham." He grabbed the notes. "Gone to get more Krokodil, I expect."

sixty-three

When they had passed through in the barge, Montbretia had realized that the Surrey Hills would present a challenging cycling terrain.

When she came through with a bike—a loaded bike that she had taken cross-country—she realized that the terrain was far beyond tough. Indeed, some might start at the word *impossible* and work back from there.

Boniface had insisted that Montbretia take a change of clothes.

As soon as she had given way on that detail, Boniface's demands escalated. Not just a change of clothes, but warm clothes—and something warm if Dawn needed to change—a sleeping bag or two, cooking gear plus food, and lights—but don't switch them on until you've found Dawn. And even then, act with caution—you won't know who's around looking for Dawn, and if we've figured where she is, then someone else could have made the same deduction. It was enough that she had felt like a loaded mule on the point of collapse as she wobbled along the flat roads and pushed the bike up the hills and across the bridleways.

After she had hidden the gear near—but not in—the church, she had found cycling much easier. However, she had to admit—reluctantly, because she hated when he had been so pompous—as she looked at the mud spattered over the back of her legs, the mud she could see up her back as she twisted awkwardly and feel on the back of her head under her helmet, that Boniface had been right: A change of clothes would be necessary if she was going to spend any period of time roughing it—and roughing it without the chance of a shower. Apparently the Normans liked worshiping God but didn't feel the need to clean themselves before praising, and the rivers and streams she had seen as she followed the paths through the Hills looked quite chilly.

Finding a fallen tree, its diameter around four feet, Montbretia stopped, took out her map, laid the bike on its side, and jumped up onto the natural seat offering a view through the wooded hillside and over the valley.

She opened the edge of the map, cursed under her breath, and jumped down to retrieve her other map. That was something Boniface had also insisted on—two paper maps, since the area traversed where the maps met. She pulled out of her phone and found no signal—yet another correct call by Boniface.

Montbretia struggled to hold the maps together, trying to locate where she was and where she had been. Each map was somewhat over three feet wide and three feet deep; the paper had been folded in half and then concertina-folded to make the map a pocketable size. Assuming you had big pockets—big, long pockets.

Pocketable, but not readily open-up-able and spread-out-able, or look-at-next-to-another-map-able.

Montbretia gave up, jumped off the log, and instead opened up each map fully, spreading them across the fallen tree. She worked down the page until she found the railway line and then followed the line along until she found Gomshall, where she had alighted from the train with her heavily laden bike.

At Gomshall, Montbretia had worked out two routes to the church: the main road, a distance of 2.6 miles, or the backstreets and bridleways, a distance of

3.3 miles, plus as Montbretia had discovered, hills. It was obvious that if Dawn was hiding, she wouldn't hide on the main road, so the backstreets and bridleways seemed the obvious route.

And it was only 0.7 miles farther—nothing on a bike, even with a load.

It seemed far less obvious once she was spattered in mud, and as Montbretia traced the path she had followed from the station, she realized it would have been more sensible to take the straighter, flatter route and dump her load at the earliest opportunity.

But regret is part of the learning process, and lesson learned, she returned her focus to the map, trying to figure where Dawn would go and where she should go next to try to intercept Dawn. The main road—the road she should have followed along the valley floor—was the only road going east/west. Every other road—the minor roads coming from the valley floor—went broadly in a north/south direction. The only way to go east/west was to stay on the bridleways and footpaths, and since she was already muddy, that didn't seem to be much of a disadvantage now, although, as she had established, it was far from ideal cycling terrain.

With the map spread out, and now being able to compare the map to the terrain, Montbretia reflected on the task she was assigned: Find Dawn, keep Dawn safe. Don't do anything like try to take her home—find her, keep her safe.

And before Montbretia could keep Dawn safe, she had to find her. Boniface was bullish about where Dawn would spend her nights, but during daylight hours, his theory was that she would keep moving and make sure no one saw her. Montbretia stared at the paths—there were hundreds...and those were the officially recognized paths. If Dawn knew this area as well as Boniface said she did and had decided to disappear, then she would be untraceable. Forget Boniface's theory that you don't find a moving target by moving yourself...this was an exercise in logic, and Montbretia was determined to find Dawn.

And if she couldn't find Dawn, then she was determined to root out any signs of danger, even if she wasn't quite sure what danger looked like.

She looked back at the map, let her eyes follow the intended path, then got back on her bike and started pedaling.

sixty-four

By the time he had spent five minutes wandering around Prince William Estate, he knew what to expect: Leathan was starting to feel like something of an expert in North London low-cost social housing.

The look was familiar: six-story blocks, each intersecting to form something close to an S shape and perched on the top of a slope. In the foreground, the planners had aspired to give the residents some open green space. Clearly the residents had happily taken this space and used it as they saw fit to store old and unwanted furniture—two chests of drawers and one wrecked sofa—and unwanted electrical items, in particular, three unwanted flat-screen television sets.

Leathan scanned the red-brick blocks, the flat surfaces only differentiated from those you might find in Communist Russia by the meager balconies, detailed along their bottoms by concrete plinths that had once had their outside edges painted a uniform white.

A road snaked through the estate, but the footpaths were more akin to cow paths—tracks worn across the grass that had become the accepted route over time due to their usage, usually since they provided the swiftest means to travel from point A to point B. The cars were the mix Leathan was becoming used to: beaten-out wrecks that were twenty-plus years old and customized luxury German cars with very tinted windows and copious amounts of bling on the wheels and anywhere else additional trim could be added.

This combination of cars also had a third variety: those cars that had given their lives so that other cars might live. Leathan counted at least five cars, some on bricks, others just dropped on their bellies, which had given for others. All had given their wheels, some their doors and odd panels, some their glass, most components from their engines, and several their seats, so that the residents of the development could have somewhere to sit if they got too tired walking from one side to the other and the wrecked sofas weren't comfortable enough.

As Leathan surveyed the dead cars, he saw what he had hoped to find: a solitary male, sitting on a vinyl car seat, wearing old boots, jeans, and a blue T-shirt. His hair was a mess of darkish colors, and his skin had the clammy look of the soon-to-be dead.

Leathan approached and hefted another car seat next to the guy, who seemed unaware of the arrival of the other man.

"Hey," said Leathan.

The other man remained silent, his head bowed, his mouth open, the slightest rise and fall of his chest confirming there was life.

"How're you doing?" tried Leathan, dropping into the seat he had just hefted.

Still no response beyond the basic function performed by the autonomic nervous system.

"Billy," said Leathan, reaching over and pushing the other man's shoulder.

The man grunted and continued to assiduously ignore Leathan and the rest of the world as he sat on his car seat in the shadow of the red-brick block.

"Billy," said Leathan with greater force, giving the other man a determined shake.

The other man grunted louder and started to topple away from Leathan. Leathan grabbed his arm and pulled him back to the vertical. "Billy, listen to me."

"Yeah," grunted the other man as he started to flop forward.

Leathan stood and moved behind his seat to pull him straight. "So you are Billy?"

Another unqualified grunt, but this time sounding more positive.

Leathan knelt behind the seat—his head at the height of the other man—and tried to push his hands into the other man's pockets, looking for any form of identification. The other man seemed unaware and unconcerned as Leathan intruded first into this back pockets, where he found nothing, and then into his front pockets, where again he found nothing. Leathan pulled out his hand and looked at the fingers on his right hand, which had acquired a yellowy-brown stickiness. His sniffed his fingers and quickly regretted the action, choosing then to try to clean his hand on the other man's T-shirt.

"Billy." Leathan shook the other man as he returned to his seat, pulling out his phone.

The other man grunted. Again, a more positive grunt.

Leathan stayed on his seat, punching a number into his phone.

The call transferred to voicemail. "Boniface, it's Leathan. I've found Billy, but he's pretty spaced out at the moment. I'll stay with him until he's a bit more lucid, and then I'll get him somewhere else. Call if you need me."

He hung up and lay back in his seat, reaching down with his hands, grabbing for some way to change the angle of the seat.

sixty-five

In the gloom of Ernie's office, Boniface could see Wesley's eyes as the dull light from the brass banker's desk lamp with the green shade glinted off them. With each agitated blink of his eyes, the small teenager's dull mid-toned skin seemed to act as a complete camouflage, hiding him completely in the dark room. With his eyes hidden, the only confirmation that he was still present was his fidgety breathing and his sour breath.

"I hoped you'd come around." There was no joy in the voice—merely an attempt at menace.

"Figuratively or literally," replied Boniface to the would-be music mogul.

The pointed face with stubbly gray skin topped with thinning wiry hair seemed to ignore the question. "You've made the right decision, Boniface. It's so disappointing having to waste time waiting for an answer or expending energy persuading people. You've saved us all the bother by coming to tell me that you've sorted everything out."

"But that's the thing," said Boniface. "I haven't come round to your way of thinking." He sighed. "Quite the opposite, I've come to say thanks for the kind offer, but no thanks."

He tried to divine what Ernie was communicating as Ernie's gaze fixed slightly to Boniface's left with his eyebrows twitching.

Wes explained the finer points of the communication when his fist landed squarely in Boniface's gut.

Boniface remembered the force Wes could unleash. He was smaller than Jojo, but he seemed to be able to transmit a disproportionate amount of power through his right arm—so much power that Boniface instinctively hunched forward as the teenager's fist made contact, but he still fell backwards, unable to argue with the momentum of his body. Now Boniface was lying on the thin and dirty carpet, clutching his hands across his stomach with his legs pulled up in a fetal position. Winded and in pain.

Lying on the floor, Boniface felt that he had some sort of equality with Gray, who had ended up on the floor when he made a lunge for Boniface's phone—the phone on which Boniface had recorded Gray's confession that he knew his legal claim against Prickle was bogus. As Gray had lunged, his windpipe had made contact with Boniface's elbow, and the singer had ended up on the floor, whimpering.

Boniface wasn't sure whether he was whimpering about the pain, the fact that Boniface had tricked him, fear about Ernie's reaction, or distress about finding that the pension he had been expecting now would not be paid. Whatever the case, he was whimpering, and continued whimpering for what felt like an eternity to Boniface, who eventually decided to just ignore Gray and made his way to the singer's kitchen.

To call it a kitchen was probably hopeful. In reality it was more likely some sort of experimental laboratory where they were developing new antibiotics resistant to whatever forms of infection Gray had managed to grow through a lack of basic kitchen hygiene sustained over thirty years.

Boniface searched the kitchen, figuring that boiling water might kill off most bugs if he were to have a cup of tea. But he had been disappointed by the discovery of the milk—or to be more accurate, cheesy yogurt—and it was at that point when Gray decided to give up his whimpering and find out what Boniface was doing.

As Gray had decided to stop whimpering, Boniface had been able to encourage him to get dressed and ready to leave. When Gray had finally appeared, there had been no hint that he had spent any of the 45 minutes he had been out of Boniface's sight washing. He was dressed badly, and he had an overnight bag, although there would have been more dignity for him if he had thrown his possessions into a super-market bag.

With Gray dressed and packed, Boniface had called a cab and taken him to Euston train station, where he bought Gray a ticket—first class, plus a supplement for a single sleeper carriage, which seemed only fair for the other passengers—for Fort William, the second largest settlement in the Highlands of Scotland, best known for being next to Ben Nevis, the highest mountain in the UK.

Boniface hadn't argued when Gray told him he had a friend who lived near. Boniface hadn't argued because he didn't care. All he cared about was getting Gray on the train and making sure he left London.

Gray had waved sarcastically from the window as the train finally lumbered away from the platform, leaving Boniface relieved in the knowledge that the singer was on board a metal tube with locked doors that would not be stopping for at least ninety minutes. When it did stop, the train would be in Crewe, in the Midlands of the UK, where theoretically only boarding was possible, although Boniface didn't understand how boarding was allowed but disembarkation prevented. Even so, Gray was out of the way for at least three hours, hopefully more, and he had money in his pocket—a stack of cash that Boniface had given him—so even if he didn't make it all the way to Scotland, he should be hard to find for quite some time.

And if he did make it to Scotland, then Boniface had instructed him to call in twenty-four hours.

Having rid himself of the vexation that was Gray, Boniface checked his voice-mail. And now, as he lay on the carpet, having been floored by the thuggish teen, the indignity was mitigated by the reassurance that Leathan had found Billy, and while Billy sounded pretty spaced out, two out of the three were safe, and Boniface was confident that Montbretia would find Dawn, making three out of three.

It was only when he was confident that the extent of the damage Ernie could inflict on him was physical pain that Boniface had walked through the wicket gate inset into the black-painted wooden gate. He had been greeted by Wes, much as a hungry man would greet lunch.

However, the hungry man was disappointed—at least initially—when Ernie granted Boniface an audience, instead of asking Wes to communicate using his well-honed nonverbal talents in the lightless room under the butcher shop. From his perspective on the carpet, Boniface saw that the disappointment had been short-lived, and the frustration had built like a pressure cooker that had just exploded into his gut.

"Get him up," grunted Ernie. Boniface felt his suit jacket being grabbed as he was pulled to the vertical, his legs not feeling ready to hold his weight. He tried standing, but the pain on the side of his head from where his skull had made contact with the floor felt like the sole focus of his concentration.

"Do I need to make you stand up?" The sour breath accompanying the muttered threat was like smelling salts, reviving Boniface's drifting concentration.

"You disappoint me, Boniface. I knew you'd try to pull some stunt—I just hoped you might do something more imaginative than bullshit me," growled Ernie.

Boniface felt a spasm in his thigh and leaned on Ernie's desk, his wrists twisted as he gripped the edge of the flat surface. He kept his voice a whisper to hide any tremble. "Billy's safe. The game's over, Ernie."

The man behind the desk showed his nicotine-stained teeth, the blackened stumps grasping the receding gums. "As I said, I hoped for more than bull." A serenity fell over his bristly face. "I knew you'd want to save Dawn's kiddie—that's why I moved him away from here and got Jojo to babysit."

"Think again," said Boniface, trying to keep his feeling of superiority from showing on his face.

"Really?" asked Ernie. "You really want to try that line?"

"I don't need to try," said Boniface. "The truth speaks for itself."

Ernie moved a crumpled piece of paper into the pool of light under the green shade, flattening out the creases. Boniface strained to interpret the upside-down handwritten characters as Ernie ran his finger along what Boniface guessed was a phone number while he punched the digits on his desk phone with his other hand. "Still got our boy there?"

Boniface lowered himself to be closer to the paper as Ernie withdrew his finger, leaning back on his chair and glaring at Boniface.

"And he's behaving himself?"

It was an address and a phone number—written with the handwriting skills of someone who didn't know which end of a pen should be applied to the paper.

"Good. Good. And you've got that *very pure* heroin?"

Boniface picked up that the conversation was intended for him, not for whoever was at the end of the phone. He let his eyes make a final pass over the address before rising to see Ernie.

"You will be very careful with that heroin. Street junkies are terrible thieves, and his system wouldn't be used to something that pure. You know, if he stole it off you, it could have tragic consequences—he might overdose." Ernie had locked eyes with Boniface as he hung up the phone. "I think you were misinformed about Billy's whereabouts, Mister Boniface. But don't worry, he's safe with Jojo." The lightness in his eyes—the fun an evil child gets from tormenting an animal—disappeared. "What harm could happen?"

Boniface felt the urge to leave the room and call Leathan. "What about Gray?"

"Gray is weak. Your problem is Danny—he is pig-headedly in love, so I need to influence him in other ways."

"Are you sure about Gray?" asked Boniface. "I mean, really sure?"

The older man looked toward Wes and flicked his eyes toward Boniface. Boniface flinched. "Listen. It's time to stop playing the hero—it doesn't suit you, and to be frank, it's embarrassing to watch you go down on one punch." He stood up. "Go away and come back when you've got what I want and what you've said you will provide. I'm holding you personally responsible for anything that's not delivered." He turned to Wes. "Get him out of here. If he carries on like this, you're going to have a lot of fun at midnight."

sixty-six

Leathan liked to think that he could handle himself—even if that confidence was only that he could run faster than the other guy—and that he was prepared to go anywhere, but this place was sapping his soul.

He had crossed the main road from one housing development to another and had found himself transported to a different world. Prince William Estate had a series of joined six-story red-brick blocks and was comparatively compact. Across the road, King William Estate sprawled, seemingly with little logic in its layout.

Four tower blocks—Leathan counted sixteen or maybe seventeen floors on each—provided the only landmarks as he subsumed himself into 1960s concrete, erected with the sole purpose of warehousing the lowest echelons of society, the underclass that no one cared about, least of all any members of that social strata. It was somewhere that caged people with nothing to lose—the cage turned their anger inward, and having nothing to lose offered perhaps the ultimate freedom. And it was that unfettered freedom that scared Leathan: So often it led to the freedom to ignore even the most basic of human obligations and to have no conception about future consequences for present acts.

"You're sure he's not playing with us?" asked Leathan.

Boniface burned his ear off down the phone. He had the right to be angry: He was in pain—apparently Wes hit much harder than Jojo—and Leathan had messed up. Big time.

Leathan had been sitting with the guy on the car seat for about an hour when Boniface called. During that time, the best Leathan had got out of the guy was a grunt that seemed to be an affirmative answer to a question. After the call, Leathan shook the guy—vigorously, but not violently—and then squeezed the back of his neck with a vice-like pinch until he got a reaction: another grunt, but this time a grunt with his eyes open. Leathan asked, "What's your name?"

"What's your name?" said the newly awakened. "I'm Barack Obama."

Leathan increased the pressure. "Play nice."

"Vic."

Leathan released the pressure, taking in the mottled brown hair. Mottled brown, not self-dyed black. "Vic what?"

"Vic what has got a sore fucking neck." Leathan returned the pressure. "Vic Morton."

It was at that point that Leathan dropped Vic's neck, cursed his own stupidity, and started sprinting. He crossed the road and didn't stop running until he found himself disoriented in his quest for Chesterfield Terrace in the middle of the King William—King William, not Prince William—Estate.

The more he looked around, the more the development resembled a set for a TV show about inner-city deprivation. The four tower blocks—layers of beige concrete and white-framed windows with balconies set at each corner whose sole purpose seemed to be to provide a convenient location for satellite dishes—provided no differentiation sufficient to triangulate a location between the blocks.

The lower blocks—again, strata of beige concrete, but layered with open walkways punctuated by boarded-up properties—seemed to have been placed to fill up the gaps between the towers. Their exact location seemed to have been set according to a child's game, and Leathan expected that at any moment a child would pick up the estate and work a silver ball through the maze of gaps between the concrete.

Not that the ball would roll that well with the semi-regular piles of discarded furniture. Unlike the development across the road, these piles seemed to comprise ripped-up chairs, usually stacked in small heaps with bed frames, chests of drawers, all with added household rubbish seemingly sprinkled on top and left to marinate. Instead of being used by the occasional passing junkie, these seemed of interest only to the local rat population, which apparently had no fear of being seen in daylight, suggesting they probably carried knives for their own personal protection.

It took him another ten minutes of dodging through alleyways, avoiding thug-like eight-year-olds, and navigating small rubbish heaps to find Chesterfield Terrace, a sagging four-floor beige concrete-layered block where two out of every three residences seemed to be boarded up or so covered with graffiti that it was impossible to discern whether it was still inhabited.

Leathan took one flight of stairs, side-stepping the urine, feces, needles, vomit, and a dead squirrel as he ascended through the gray rectangle, which opened onto a broad walkway with properties on one side and on the other a low wall with a view over the only patch of open ground he had found on the estate.

He hesitated, stepping back down onto the penultimate step, craning his head to look down the walkway before slowly moving toward his target. Drawing level with the first front door, he checked the number—twice and then a third time, looking for any ambiguity.

Number thirty-six.

What was likely to be number thirty-seven was boarded up.

The next residence had a number eight loosely hanging by one screw. The ghost of the number three preceding the hanging figure suggested that Leathan had found number thirty-eight.

Thirty-nine and forty—if Leathan had understood the numbering system correctly—were both boarded, the heavier thickness of paint from the graffiti on number forty suggesting it had been vacant for longer.

And then he reached the end of the row. Number forty-one. Confirmed by the silver numbers screwed to the right of the mail slot midway up the door. On the walkway outside sat a baby stroller, rusted, probably dating from the 1960s, and two kitchen cabinets.

Gingerly, Leathan put his ear to the first window. Even at this distance, he could feel the vibration of the main road transmitted through the glass, but couldn't hear any sounds of humans in the residence. There was a sound—perhaps the firing of guns in a movie—but no voices, no doors banging, no one walking...nothing actively human.

He moved to the next window, surveying the frosted pane before leaning closer. Again, the only sound was like a movie where every character had more bullets than the whole of the US army, and weapons never jam. But he couldn't be sure whether this was a movie left playing or whether anyone was inside watching.

Leathan moved across the walkway to stand facing the door—two large panes of obscured glass in a wooden frame. One kick, and it would splinter and he would be in. One kick, and he could be dead—he had no idea how many people were inside. And if Jojo was there—or any of his friends—how armed they were.

He stared at the obscured glass, willing his eyes to see any signs of occupation—a lamp turned on, or the shift of light as someone moved across a room. He moved closer, hoping for a raised voice. All he could hear was shooting.

He straightened and looked away from the apartment. There was a group of feral ten-year-olds sharing a single cigarette on the other side of the open ground.

As he exited the stairwell, he started walking toward the young smokers. Initially they seemed indifferent to his approach, but as he got closer heads turned with greater frequency and their voices got louder. "You a cop?"

Leathan shook his head, his mouth reflexively lifting at the edges.

"Pedo?" The questioner seemed to be the alpha-male ten-year-old—the one who took a drag in between each pass of the cigarette.

"Nope," said Leathan reaching the group of five, all around the height of his waist, all with graying skin and a look of malnourishment. "Who wants to earn twenty quid?"

"See! You *are* a pedo," said the alpha, pointing his dirty face under a buzz cut at Leathan.

"If you don't want the cash, that's fine," said Leathan, turning away.

"Didn't say that." His retort was swift. "Just telling you what I won't do."

Leathan pulled a £20 out of his pocket and squatted in front of the group. "Chesterfield Terrace." He pointed to the block behind him.

"We ain't fucking stupid," muttered another in the group.

"One floor up, last door on the right, number forty-one." He waited for the group's eyes to follow. "See it?"

"Yeah." Alpha was back in control.

"Go and find if anyone's in."

"What?"

"Knock on the door—see if anyone's in," repeated Leathan.

"I'll save you ten," said the one currently holding the cigarette. "Give me ten, and you can knock on the door yourself."

"If you don't want..." Leathan started to rise.

"It's not enough," said the alpha, his strained voice reasserting his dominance as he retrieved the cigarette, taking a deep drag with his lips clamped tightly around the paper cylinder.

"Twenty," said Leathan. "And when you get back, I'll buy you a pack of cigarettes."

There was a spark in the eyes in front of him—a hint of excitement as they looked to one another.

"A pack each," said the alpha, seemingly less excited than his comrades.

"Tell you what," said Leathan. "Get whoever answers to come onto the balcony so I can see him from here—tell him there's a car on fire or something—and I'll buy you a carton. That's two-hundred cigarettes between you." He waited, fixing his stare on the alpha. "Deal?"

"Deal," said the alpha, grabbing the note in Leathan's hand. His eyes flicked to the tallest of the group, who wordlessly set off alone across the open space, disappearing into the stairwell shortly to appear one story up, only his head visible above the low wall as he moved toward number forty-one.

The top of his head was barely visible as he banged on the door—the fearless kind of knocking achieved only by kids and drunks. Leathan marshaled the remaining smokers in front of him until he felt sufficiently camouflaged.

The kid was clearly a dedicated smoker—from where he crouched, Leathan could hear when the kid banged for a second time. The head ducked, a sound of a kid shouting, and the head reappeared.

When it opened, the door opened slowly. The kid moved away—he was by the wall almost immediately, pointing at something in the distance insistently, looking back and calling whoever was inside to come out and look.

Leathan watched as Jojo filled the doorframe. Even at the distance, Leathan could see the large teen's vigilance—the way he observed, moved, stopped, observed, moved, stopped, and on. By the time he was fully out the front door, he seemed confident that there was no one waiting in the passageway. But from his body language, Jojo seemed unimpressed with the disturbance, and the kid's backward steps soon turned into a run.

"I believe I am in your debt," said Leathan, returning to his full height. "You'd better show me to the store." The alpha took the lead, walking swiftly away from Chesterfield Terrace, ducking into a narrow alley that wiggled between two blocks. He navigated two piles of furniture and refuse, finally bringing the small group—including the door knocker, who had caught up with them—onto one of the streets that carved its way through the estate.

He tilted his head across the road to a row of five stores: a launderette, a drop-in advice center, two boarded storefronts, and the last, Ali's Convenience, according to the sign in front of the heavy shutters covering both windows.

"Marlborough?" asked Leathan.

The alpha stared into space—a ten-year-old tobacco connoisseur—before wrinkling his nose and saying, "Yeah."

Leathan walked through the aluminum-framed door and straight to the counter. "Two-hundred Marlborough."

"In a carton," said the Asian man behind the counter, pulling out a carton before Leathan could respond.

"Could I also have two lighters and…" he scanned the shelves behind the store owner, "lighter fluid?"

The man Leathan presumed to be Ali placed the four items on the counter. "Anything else?"

Leathan shook his head once and watched as Ali rang up the price, expectantly standing without feeling the need to read the numbers displayed on his till. Leathan handed over two £50 notes and pocketed one of the lighters and the lighter fluid before picking up the change Ali had dropped on the counter without explanation. He pocketed the cash, then grabbed the cigarettes and a second lighter.

As he stepped out of the store, ten hands reached to him. "You earned a bonus," he said to the tall door-knocker and handed him the lighter. "There you…" he said, passing the box of 200 cancer sticks to the alpha. The five were running—moving as a pack, swiftly into the distance—before he could complete his sentence.

sixty-seven

"What do you mean *not there*?"

"What do you want me to say, Ernie? I can't say it any more clearly. I can't make him there when he's not."

Ernie looked up at Iain Irvine, his tanned skin showing a faint glow of perspiration. "I mean if he's not *there*, then where is he?" He felt his volume start to rise as his pitch dropped. "Or let me phrase it in a similar way to how you put the proposition to me... If our cash cow isn't in the field where we left it, then how can we take it to market?"

Irv seemed to get that surly defensive attitude that he took when he didn't want to admit he'd made a mistake. "What can I tell you—he was carrying a bag and left in a cab with some bloke in a suit."

"You mean he left with Boniface?"

"I don't know, Ernie." Irv seemed to be losing interest. "I'm sure there are other blokes that are about six foot and wear suits, but yeah, it sounds like he was with Boniface."

"And who told you this?"

"Next-door neighbor—some city type who thinks he owns the world." Irv sat on the edge of the desk. Ernie stared at him until he stood. Irv shrugged. "Only knows about the cab because the driver knocked at the wrong door—thinks he said he was going to Euston, but it could have been Kings Cross."

"This Boniface is being a right pain up my arse. First he puts Gray on a train, and then he comes round and tries to taunt me." Ernie slumped back in his chair. "Where has Gray gone, Iain?"

"We looked through his place. There was no sign that he planned this."

"Of course he didn't plan this—this is Boniface causing me trouble."

"I mean, he didn't even plan for thirty seconds before he left," said Irvine. "There are no notes; he didn't have an address book. The last number dialed was no use—he called for a pizza two days ago. He didn't leave a single breadcrumb."

"What about the cab?" Ernie wanted to punch someone to relieve his frustration.

"He didn't call them from the landline and whoever he called, it wasn't one of the local ones, but we're trying other firms."

"Try the chains," said Ernie. "It'll be a firm you can summon with a smartphone."

Irvine tilted his head, squinting. Wordlessly asking a question.

"Boniface," said Ernie. "Boniface will have ordered the cab, and he's the sort of git who will have used something flashy on his phone."

"I'll get on it," said Irvine.

"Yeah, and you won't get anywhere—he'll be using a big company used to dealing with celebrities. There won't be anyone we know who we can lean on...at least, not in time." He leaned forward in his chair. When he continued, his voice was quieter, but the emotion had drained. "This was your idea. The day Billy said his mother was famous—you made the link to Gray. You came up with the idea. Tie them up in litigation, cause them so much pain in so many places that either they give way and we win something, or they just offer us go-away money. It's easy."

Irv didn't respond. He just stood with that stupid sneer across his leathery face.

"And have you found the woman yet?"

Irv shook his head. "Not a clue where she went."

Ernie felt his anger burning. "How hard can it be to find a woman whose only talents are having big tits and neglecting her son?"

"It's not that easy—there are too many people around the house, including these two hefty roadies, and Wes and Jojo stick out. There are all these delicate little villages where they all eat cucumber sandwiches with the vicar and date their land back to Domesday. Our boys are the wrong color. They can't even look like tourists or school kids on a day trip."

"I'm not impressed, Irv. Do something fast."

sixty-eight

It seemed to take Leathan infinitely longer to retrace the route back to Chesterfield Terrace than it had taken to walk in the other direction with the ten-year-old smokers desperate for even one cigarette that didn't have to be shared with the others.

As he passed the second heap of discarded sofas, old paint cans, and bed frames, Leathan stopped.

Thinking.

It was a matter of basic logistics and practicality.

For the first journey, he carried three sofa cushions, an old mop, and a handle usually used to hold a point roller. For the second, he hefted a single bed frame. Two journeys each required less exertion than one unsuccessful journey trying to carry the whole load. Added to which he could be more discreet with smaller loads.

He dumped his load at the corner of Chesterfield Terrace, on the corner away from the open space. The heap didn't look out of place, and it was unlikely to be stolen as he completed a quick reconnaissance of the area. As far as he could see, Chesterfield Terrace was simply a lump of concrete, built on a concrete plinth, and was less than one-third occupied—assuming boarded up meant unoccupied.

The unoccupied property that was of particular interest was the one at ground level, at the end of the row. The property immediately below the one where he now knew Jojo Brooks was temporarily stationed, and where, by extrapolation, he suspected Billy Wilkins was also to be found.

The simple solution would have been to go through the front door of number forty-one, but since Jojo was holding a pistol last time he saw him, Leathan felt no urgency to bang on that door.

In any case, he had a much more straightforward solution.

He looked up at the boarding over the back of the ground-floor residence. Two rooms, two windows both covered with OSB—oriented strand board, cheap but effective engineered wood, constructed from glued flakes of wood giving a rough, tough, but cheap material used in construction sites across the globe.

The graffiti told him it had been up for a while. That the boarding was still attached to the window frame told him that the fitter and his nail gun had done a good job.

Leathan examined the bottom and the sides of the OSB. As he expected, nails had been uniformly shot, making a tight seal between frame and board. He guessed that the fitters probably had ladders and platforms—Leathan could only improvise and flipped over the bed frame, laying it vertically on its longest edge, balanced against the wall.

He stepped back and looked at the apartment above—number forty-one. He was sure he could still hear the sound of a movie with a lot of shooting. Stepping forward again, he looked left, looked right, and then climbed on the side of the bed frame, raising his eyes to the level of the top of the window.

There were fewer nails across the top, and the board had been cut short, allowing Leathan to see the top of the frame. Allowing Leathan an opportunity, as he took out the paint-roller handle—a sturdy piece of thin metal, essentially bent in a right angle with an exposed end and a plastic handle at the other. He tried to find a gap to wiggle the thin end into.

Leathan stabbed the point, looking for any gap between the board and the frame, but could find none, so he resorted to trying to hammer the point through a gap. His reward for a hand sore from banging the blunt end was the progress of the point behind the board. When the roller spindle was sufficiently behind the board, Leathan applied his weight to the handle, waiting until he finally heard a reassuring groan from a nail.

And then the board stopped. This nail would not release any further.

He scanned his surroundings again, then pulled himself up on the exposed roller handle to stand on the windowsill and placed his other foot to the side of the window as high as he could get it. Then he pulled and pulled.

The nails groaned, slipping slightly but refusing to release the OSB they were holding prisoner.

He dropped his foot back onto the sill and examined the gap he had created—it was wide enough to fit his thumb. He jumped down, grabbed the mop and climbed back again, inserted the wooden handle from his new tool into the gap, and leaned his weight onto his new lever.

The nails creaked and groaned, the OSB moved, but the nails still refused to give entry. He moved the mop farther down the board and applied his weight, bending his knees to give more purchase on his lever, rocking to give momentum to the application of his body weight.

A groan.

A creak.

A crack.

The nails gave way and released the board, which released the tension on the mop handle Leathan was pulling. He fell backward, managing to get a leg out as he hit the concrete plinth, but was not able to stop his momentum propelling him to the ground, to be followed by a window-sized piece of OSB landing on top of him.

He wasn't sure how long he waited before he moved, but when he did, it hurt.

A lot.

His leg, his ass, his elbow, his knee where the board hit, his head, which hit the deck and then got sandwiched between the ground and the board as it bounced—all hurt. Slowly he rolled out from under the board and got to his feet to admire his handiwork. The window was nothing special: a single-glazed casement window in three sections with an opening window on each side and a fan light at the top of the center section.

Leathan hunted for the roller handle, finding it under the OSB. He positioned the thin end on the glass just outside the handle and smacked the flat side with the butt of his hand; a spider's web of fracture spread across the window as he propelled the end of the roller handle through the pane. "I didn't want it broken," muttered Leathan as he manipulated the window's handle with the painting tool and opened the swinging pane.

With the window open, Leathan threw in the three sofa cushions, the paint-roller holder, and the mop, then jumped onto the bed frame before climbing through the window.

It was probably the smell of urine—stale urine, or at least what smelled like stale urine—that he noticed first. Impatient for his eyes to adjust to the lack of light, he stumbled forward, keen to explore the accommodation, only slowly becoming aware of the crescendo of shooting from above and the sound of stamping feet. He felt a smile cross his face. "I'll never understand computer games," he muttered.

Passing into a small hall he turned into the first room, his hand instinctively flicking the light switch inside the door as he entered. The light remained extinguished. Leathan pulled out his new lighter and flicked the flame into life. In the flickering orange glow, he could make out a kitchen—dirty dishes sat in a now-empty sink, and takeaway food wrappers littered the floor. He looked for an empty space on the worktop and ran his finger along the surface, rapidly pulling it away to inspect the accumulated grease.

He turned and crossed the passage, tugging the pull string inside the door. A click, but again no electric light. He lifted his flaming lighter, keeping his finger pressed, to view what he now knew to be a bathroom. A bathroom with a smell that stung more than the smell he had encountered so far.

Feeling the top of the lighter starting to get hot, he released the trigger and turned back into the passage, taking a left into the last remaining room, which was lit by the light that pushed its way past the OSB still fastened over the window. Two single beds were pushed into the far corners by the outside wall, and what looked like a stack of black trash bags covered the remaining floor.

Leathan returned to the room through which he had entered and scrabbled around, looking for his paint-roller holder. He found it and went back to the gloomy kitchen, pushing a space on the worktop, and climbed up to crouch under the ceiling. Gripping the roller handle as if he were gripping a pick, he waited—listening for shooting to start above—then jabbed at the ceiling, driving a small hole through the skimmed drywall panel. He pushed the horizontal length of the roller handle through the hole, leaving the other end to hang.

There was a burst of gunfire from the game in the apartment above.

Leathan jumped.

He launched himself toward the door, grabbing the handle with both hands, letting his weight and momentum transfer to the plaster ceiling panel.

As he swung, Leathan felt the panel give, releasing his hook as a chunk of the ceiling crashed to the floor, spitting dust in every direction.

As the crash quieted, Leathan listened to the continuing shooting above while he pulled out his lighter to illuminate his handiwork and found a hole, jagged but broadly circular about two feet across, exposing the rafters holding up the floorboards from the residence above. Holding the roller hook in both hands, he jumped, catching the long end in the newly exposed gap above the ceiling panel. He jumped two or three more times, yanking down more ceiling panel.

Having doubled the size of the hole, he moved to the bathroom. On the first leap most of the ceiling panel collapsed. It took three tugs in the bedroom to make a large enough hole and only two leaps in the room through which he had entered.

He bundled up the three sofa cushions and carried them to the bedroom, throwing them over the black trash bags before pulling out the lighter fluid, which he liberally sprayed over the cushions. Then he moved to the kitchen and doused some of the trash still left on the counter, emptying the rest of the fluid over two discarded sofas he found in the lounge.

Leathan walked to the window, pushing it fully open, then returned to the bedroom and ignited the lighter fluid–soaked cushions. The spreading flames momentarily hypnotized him, but the carcinogenic fumes of burning foam caught his throat, forcing him to remember his mission.

He darted into the kitchen and lit one pile of trash, leaving without waiting to see how it burned. As he moved through the hallway and into the living room, wisps of dark smoke trailed him. He lit the two sofas and took the short steps to the window, cautiously climbing out and resting on the bed frame, where he closed the window and looked back at his creeping flames.

He jumped down and manhandled the OSB he had worked so hard to remove from the window, leaning it back in position where it had come from in an effort to keep all of the smoke trapped within the residence and funneled through the ceiling he had just remodeled.

When he was satisfied that the OSB was sufficiently secure, he return to the front of the block and crossed the open space, squatting down where he had talked with the ten-year-old smokers, and watched the door of number forty-one.

sixty-nine

Montbretia had decided—temporarily—to admit that Boniface might be right. It might be a much more straightforward strategy to stay still and wait for a moving target to come to her.

It wasn't so much that she wanted to admit that he had a point; it was more a matter of practicality. She had been riding—energetically riding over rough, hilly terrain—for several hours, and the light was starting to fade. She hadn't found Dawn but instead was returning to the location where Boniface said she would find her. Hard as she thought about it, she couldn't find a way to finesse herself out of admitting that she was doing what Boniface had suggested.

She turned off the road and crossed the cattle grid as she entered the private grounds of Albury Park, passing the sign that confirmed that access was permitted to the land if visiting the Old Parish Church.

The church was less than five-hundred meters away, and although the obvious route was along the tarred strip intended for road vehicles—and probably to the disgust of whoever made the sign at the gate—Montbretia left the track, pulling up about one-hundred meters away from the church, where she dismounted and dropped her bike against a tree with a reptilian-scaled trunk too thick to wrap a bike lock around. If it got stolen—in what was essentially the middle of nowhere—Boniface could buy her a new one.

There were maybe ten or fifteen of the thick-trunked trees. Spaced, but the spread of the branches reached between each tree, which with the thick leaves gave her cover of near-darkness as she moved silently toward the church.

She reached the last tree in the group and stopped, letting her eyes drift across the view: a church more than a thousand years old, surrounded by a low ironstone rubble wall with a semi-horseshoe of trees behind offering some screening from two sides. Screening. Another way of saying "a place for the bad guys to hide if someone had the same idea as her."

Her eyes tracked across the panorama, looking for color, movement, or even smoke. Her ears tuned in for any sound, whether human or animal disturbed by human.

And then she broke cover, moving to the next group of trees, passing into the shadows as she worked her way toward the horseshoe behind the church. Pausing repeatedly to scan and listen, after about five minutes, Montbretia reached the baggage she had jettisoned several hours earlier. It was untouched—which she had hoped would be the result of hiding it eight feet up a tree. She pulled it down and began to quietly move the small heap to the outside of the ironstone wall.

She checked her phone. Boniface was right again. The Norman church truly did have the same phone coverage that the Normans had in 1066. With no way to know what was happening with Boniface and Leathan, the only option was to continue and get inside before the daylight was lost.

The top of the ironstone wall gripped her ass as she twisted her legs over before silently stepping toward the church, her head in constant motion, like a windshield wiper.

The tower of the church, constructed from yellowed ironstone and sandstone rubble with red-brick battlements, stood in the center. To the left a narrower and lower block had been added with a pitched red-tiled roof. To the right, another block stood—higher than that on the left—with a rendered wall, a steeper pitched roof, and a wood-frame porch topped by a gabled roof.

The handwritten note—*please be sure to shut the grill securely to keep birds out*—explained the function but didn't warn Montbretia of how high-pitched the hinges' squeak would be as it opened. The bird screen screeched again as Montbretia pulled it behind her, reaching for the iron handle, which, although large given the size of the wooden door, seemed insufficient. The spindle had worn loose in its hole through centuries of use, and it took her a moment or two to jiggle the latch up, with a substantial metal click that could be heard from the outside.

The heavy wooden door groaned, cartoon-like, on its hinges as it opened. Montbretia turned to pull the bird shield behind her, missed the step down, and stumbled backward into the church, finding herself drawn to look at her new surroundings. She closed the door with her gaze still being drawn up. The whitewashed walls were topped by a whitewashed roof supported by rafters that looked over a thousand years old.

The plaster on the walls was rough, but with occasional nooks with statues and detailing around pictures and memorials. She misstepped on the uneven flagstone floor, unable to draw her attention from looking up until she bumped into a substantial table with local guides and histories on display, together with a notice soliciting donations and giving details of how to make any payments tax-free.

From the airy square of the nave, she walked under the tower, staring up into the darkness of the inside of the unlit tower.

Boniface had mentioned part of the interior had been renovated by the owner of the estate during the Victorian era. As she looked down from the tower, her eyes fell upon what she presumed was the Victorian mausoleum. In the gloom, she couldn't make out much—a tomb, perhaps, a darkened window that was probably stained glass, a decorated wall and ceiling that just looked dull in the gloom—all separated from the rest of the church by a wooden screen to a height of about eight feet.

From the third open side under the tower, Montbretia found the altar. It was simple, little more than a table with a wooden cross, two candlesticks, and fresh flowers. In front of it, a pewter lectern stood—a bird of prey spreading its wings to hold a Bible.

Montbretia turned, returning toward the nave but stopping as she passed the screen separating the tomb, and moved up close to the screen, looking down behind it. A few neatly knotted empty candy wrappers were on the floor with three bottles of water in a straight line.

As she stood, she sighed. "You were right, Boniface."

Cautiously she opened the door and the bird screen, stepping from the chill of the church into the slightly less chilly, but still not warm, late afternoon before making three quick trips to retrieve the luggage that had been strapped to the back of her bicycle, dumping each load behind the door inside the church.

Montbretia picked up one of the backpacks and pulled out a blanket, dropping it on the ground in front of her. She dug deeper, pulling out some socks, clean sweatpants, and a fleece jacket.

She picked up a second backpack and took out a camping light, switching it on and placing it at the center of the nave. She returned to her unpacking and looked back at the light, wrinkled her nose, then returned to the light. "Better not," she muttered, flicking off the switch and placing the lamp next to her small pile.

She put on a jacket, then sat on the blanket, removing her shoes and replacing them with the socks before wriggling into the sweatpants.

"Okay, Dawn," she said under her breath. "I'm here, and I'm waiting for you. Where are you?"

seventy

"*This*? This is it?"

Boniface could hear himself shouting at the minicab driver.

"This?"

He pointed behind him at the housing development, the four beige-striped concrete towers blocking out anything that remained of the natural light of the day.

"This side? Not that side?"

"This side, sir," said the minicab driver, smiling broadly.

"King William Estate?" asked Boniface.

"Yes, sir," said the driver, his thick Bangladeshi accent coming through. His smile undimmed.

"How do you know?" barked Boniface, looking toward the towers and the low blocks. "Where does it say that?"

"That sign there," said the driver, pointing. His smile radiating from his eyes.

"And where's Chesterfield Terrace?" asked Boniface.

"I don't know, sir." The smile remained.

Boniface dropped a bill on the passenger seat before turning and jogging to the sign.

It probably did say King William Estate. There probably was a map of the estate, too. But all Boniface could see were the letters *Kin* toward the top-left corner and a few hints around the edge that the metal sign showed streets and walkways. For the most part, the sign was scratched, gouged, bent, burned, and covered in graffiti. Between the two posts holding it, Boniface stopped counting when he had seen fifteen needles.

The rush-hour traffic thundered down the road, penning Boniface into the beige concrete development. On one side, the smell of the internal combustion engine. On the other, the smell of something acrid starting to burn, fused with deep-fat frying, reached into his nostrils.

Boniface looked up at the low block in front of him. The sign, about ten or eleven feet off the ground, said "Burl..." The remainder had been graffitied over.

Not Chesterfield Terrace.

Boniface ducked to the right and followed the path passing Burl-whatever, which then twisted past some dark-brick two-story maisonettes, before curving away, becoming a narrower alley with a brick wall on one side. The alley passed a heap of abandoned sofas and beds, then turned, opening onto another block.

Croxton something.

The sign, as high as the one for Burl, had been snapped off and was dangling nearly vertically by one screw.

He saw a group of kids—probably no more than ten or eleven years old—smoking and throwing stones at the few cars that dared to pass. He avoided eye contact and turned in the opposite direction, becoming increasingly aware that the smell of burning he had noticed earlier wasn't dissipating. If anything, it was getting stronger.

Boniface looked up to the sky. Somewhere above the towers, there was a gentle breeze blowing, and it was drifting black smoke over his head. Black smoke that seemed to have its origin somewhere ahead.

It was as if a celestial force was leaving him a trail of breadcrumbs to Leathan.

Boniface picked up his pace, starting to jog as he followed another passageway, coming out near a row dilapidated shops. Across the road, he took another path—the smoke trail still in sight. He ducked around some more heaps of furniture and one with paint cans, finally coming out at an open space across from a long, low-slung block.

He recognized the back of the man watching the source of the smoke. "It's not a coincidence that you're here and there's a fire."

"See what happens when you leave me alone with matches."

"Shit, Leathan. You set fire to someone's home."

"Relax," said Leathan, although the look on his face didn't agree with the words falling out of his mouth. "The place was boarded up—it had been used by junkies as far as I could tell."

"But isn't it..." Boniface looked from Leathan's face to the smoke and back to Leathan. His brow was creased, his mouth tightening. "Isn't this a bit...I dunno...a bit dangerous?"

Leathan flinched and half-shrugged. "What did you want me to do? You weren't here, and I don't know who else is in there."

"Where?"

"First floor up—at the end. That's where Jojo is."

"And Billy?"

"Dunno. I only saw Jojo."

Boniface went to speak but stopped, catching Leathan's gaze, which swiftly moved to the funnels of black smoke coming out from behind the block. "I didn't know what weapons they had, so I thought it would be quicker to smoke them out—I knocked holes in the ceiling so the smoke would go through the floorboards." Leathan was speaking, but without commitment as he seemed to be focusing with increasing intent on the smoke. "At least, I hope it gets through the floorboards."

"A place like this will have huge slabs of particleboard on the floors—not stripped-back floorboards," said Boniface. "Then there will be carpets on top. How's the smoke meant to get through?"

The other man didn't reply.

"That's looking dangerous, Leathan."

Leathan winced, clearly not wanting to admit a problem, but seemingly having difficulty arguing with the assessment as he stared at the block.

"The plan was to save Billy, not to kill him in a different way before Ernie gets to him." Boniface moved his view from the side of Leathan's head to the block. "That smoke's getting thick. I'm going to have a look."

"Suit yourself," said Leathan, remaining still as Boniface started to walk toward the block.

Boniface had taken half a dozen paces when he heard footsteps behind him: Leathan jogging to catch up. "You need someone to supervise you," said Leathan, passing Boniface, who picked up his pace, then broke into a light jog.

By the time they reached the bottom of the stairwell, they were sprinting, jostling each other as they ran up the stairs, not noticing the smell in the stairwell—which had been masked by the acrid burning smell—and not paying attention to the vomit and dead squirrel.

They turned out of the stairs, slowing as they moved along the walkway toward number forty-one. "So how are we going to do this?" asked Boniface.

"I dunno," said Leathan. "I thought the smoke would force them out." The thick black smoke drifted around the end of the building. "I thought they'd just come running—look at it...it's much thicker than I expected."

"Are you're sure they're still alive?" said Boniface, feeling the tension in his throat. "We're not going to go in and find corpses?"

"What do you mean go in?"

"I mean you're kicking the door down."

"But we don't know who's in there or how many people are in there." Leathan was gabbling. "Or whether they're armed, or..." He stopped, turned to face Boniface, and continued, his voice simpering. "That's why I tried to smoke them out."

"And how's that working out?" said Boniface, continuing toward number forty-one. "You kick the door, then deal with Jojo and whoever else you find. I'll get Billy. In. Out. Finished."

"But..."

Boniface tried to get the annoyance out of his voice. "We're trying to keep Billy alive. Ernie's happy to waste him, so we don't have any option." He indicated the door. "Kick. Run."

Boniface leaned to the side of the door, leaving Leathan to stand in front of his target.

He breathed in once, shaking his shoulders loose as he exhaled. Inhaled again, more deeply, looking up at Boniface as he exhaled. Broke eye contact as he inhaled, and as he exhaled he lifted his foot, stamping onto the door where the cross-member halfway up met the side-member.

The cross-member flew in, and the left side of the door cracked. The lower pane of obscured glass shattered, with pieces scattering across the walkway and into the residence, and the top pane cracked as the muffled sound of music became clearer.

Boniface frowned, questioning the other man. "It was computer games earlier. He likes it loud—I think he's got trouble with his hearing," said Leathan, standing back and reloading his boot before he launched his foot at the cracked side of the door, which splintered, sending the door flying open. As it slammed into the back wall, the remaining glass in the top panel shattered.

"Go," said Boniface gently, tilting his head to indicate the entrance Leathan had cleared and softly slapping him on the back as he stepped up into the home. Leathan's footsteps crunched as Boniface turned, ready to follow the other man, who was ducking into the first room on the left before swiftly exiting and crossing the passage into the opposite room.

"There's no smoke, Leathan," hissed Boniface, becoming aware of the warm air that was pushing past him as he stepped up into the doorway, his feet grinding broken glass into the fitted carpet.

There was a noise—above the sound of music—coming from the room to the right at the far end of the corridor, and the door opened, rubbing along the carpet as it moved. As the door opened, the sound of a blaring TV—some rapper telling everyone how great he was, against a drumbeat that kicked Boniface in the gut and frizzled his ears at the same time.

Leathan exited the room on the right with a rolling pin in his hand, and the big black presence of Jojo filled the frame of the door at the far end.

"I've got a knife," shouted Leathan, moving toward the teen.

"Not as big as mine," said the oversized teen without a hint of fear. Leathan's bluff had been called.

Boniface caught sight of himself in the mirror just inside the door. His suit was clean and presentable this morning. Since then, he had been to see Ernie, where Wes had manhandled him, although thankfully not given him too much of a pounding. However, the cloth had taken a beating caused by Wes not understanding the subtle nuance between fear and respect. While the suit was probably beyond repair, it wasn't what he hoped to be wearing if he got into a fight in a tight passage.

He ducked into the kitchen and scanned the counter. Some beer—cheap, sharp, and over fizzy. Some peanuts, and that was all that was on display. Boniface opened the first eye-line cabinet and saw a row of squat tumblers. He grabbed the first one, feeling its heft. Then grabbed a second and exited back into the corridor.

Leathan was waving something at the big teen—bobbing and weaving as Jojo tracked his movements, seemingly more amused than frightened. Boniface took the first tumbler and pitched it, letting the weighty glass spin as it left his hand. The rotating object drifted right, clipping the wall and bouncing at a sharper angle than it hit, almost as if it picked up speed in its impact.

The big teen became aware of something fast-moving at head height and twisted to look at the incoming UFO, turning his head into the spinning tumbler as it made contact with his temple.

"Motherfucker!" shouted the teen, looking to the source of the projectile, which had fallen to the floor. Leathan ducked, grabbing for the first tumbler, and Boniface launched the second. The teen swayed out of its way, allowing it to hit the wall behind him and shatter, not realizing that he had moved in the direction of Leathan's wooden baton which made contact first with his cheekbone; Leathan's second blow landed on the side of the teen's head above his ear.

He bellowed as Leathan pushed forward, shoving the teen off balance and knocking him into the room from which he had come.

Boniface rushed forward. Where Leathan and Jojo went right, he went left, opening the door to what might be a bedroom with a figure sprawled on top of a duvet. Billy. Maybe unconscious. Maybe asleep.

seventy-one

A suppressed sound pushed its way through the thick church walls from outside: A latch rattled, followed by the groan and then slam of old wooden gate closing.

Montbretia waited, listening—her eyes scanning the nave of the church in the early evening gloom, which had rendered her surroundings in monochrome. She remained still—sitting on her blanket with her thick socks and warm jacket—pushed into the corner to shield herself from the line of sight of anyone entering the consecrated building.

Another latch clicked—the latch on the bird grill being lifted, and then the sound of the grill opening, the hinges squealing as the large metal mesh moved. Then the sound of the spindle in the wooden door, twisting to lever the latch out of its seat, ending with the latch hitting the stop as it was raised to its maximum level, leaving the sound echoing around the church.

The hinge beside Montbretia's ear moaned—a deep complaint about years of arthritic movement—and the door opened. A figure entered backward—ass first, the sound of the bird grill closing before the ass stepped backward.

A female ass.

An ass that Montbretia half recognized.

An ass that Boniface had admired.

Montbretia watched as the other woman swiftly looked around without looking behind and then crossed the nave, walking under the tower and to the altar, where she stood in silent contemplation for a moment.

Montbretia didn't interrupt the wordless invocation as she stood, moving forward, her socks not making any noise on the flagstones. "We've missed you."

Dawn let out a slight scream, reflexively bringing her hand over her mouth as the yelp echoed against the hard surfaces.

"It's alright—it's Montbretia. We met at Boniface's office."

Dawn dropped her hand but remained frozen, a look that Montbretia took to be fear spreading across her face. The other woman's face hardened, her lips thinning, her eyes narrowing, her head leaning forward. "Stay out of this."

Montbretia felt the aggression hitting her like a heat wave from a furnace. "I'm on your side, Dawn."

"You don't know what's going on, and I'm leaving." Dawn walked straight toward Montbretia, her shoulders pulled in as if readying for a fight. Her footsteps—which had been light when she entered—were now strides echoing around the thousand-year-old building.

Montbretia swiftly moved backward toward the door.

"Get out of my way." There was no softness in Dawn's voice.

Montbretia shook her head—the tiniest vibration. "I can't let you go," she whispered.

"Get out of my way," repeated Dawn, standing in front of Montbretia.

"No." Montbretia kept her voice low.

Dawn reached for the door, knocking Montbretia back against the ancient piece of wood. "Get out of my way." The older woman grabbed for the handle, and when she couldn't reach, she pushed Montbretia.

Montbretia bear-hugged Dawn, holding her arms tight against her body as the older woman struggled. "Let me go."

Montbretia gripped tighter. "We know about Billy."

Dawn's struggling became twisting.

"We know about both Billies."

Montbretia felt Dawn deflate and relaxed her grip while holding tight enough to realize that the other woman was trembling.

"I'm not worried about Billy." Montbretia stared at Dawn—the former model's anger seeming to turn into exasperation at Montbretia's incomprehension. Perhaps she was marveling at the younger woman's stupidity. "I'm worried about Danny."

"Huh?" said Montbretia, finally dropping her grip and stepping back from Dawn to look at her more clearly. "Danny loves you."

"Precisely," said Dawn. "Danny loves me unconditionally. He will do anything for me, so I had to be where Danny couldn't save me, because otherwise he'd give up *everything* for me." She shook her head, holding her bottom lip in her teeth—her eyes defocused and a smile forming on the side of her mouth not clamped in her teeth. "Everything. That man would give up anything and everything for me, and then we'd have nothing."

The older woman looked up, fixing Montbretia in her gaze, her voice soft, warm. "Danny would lay down his life for me—like that." She clicked her fingers. The snap echoed around the nave. "But I want a live husband—I don't want to bury the guy…I love him…and now you're just causing trouble."

Montbretia took two small steps backward, reaching the door and gripping the handle. "We need to talk and I want to eat." She softened her face. "Having looked at what you've been eating over the last few days, I reckon you could do with something sensible to eat, too."

seventy–two

Billy hadn't seen any urgency to get out.

Billy hadn't seen any urgency to even bother with opening his eyes.

When Boniface followed Leathan in, despite the fire downstairs, the residence had been smoke-free. With the front door open—permanently, thanks to Leathan's boot—there was now a through draft creating a vacuum, drawing smoke through the floor...or maybe the smoke was just coming in through the door. Thick, black, acrid smoke that was settling in Boniface's throat.

Boniface shook Billy as he lay on his back on the single bed. Billy grunted but refused to move. Even the racket from the rap video playing in the other room didn't seem to disturb him.

Boniface shook him again, more vigorously. Billy didn't even bother grunting.

"Billy. The place is on fire—it's time to get out," said Boniface.

The man on the bed gave no response. In the next room, there was the sound of skin-on-skin, punches being thrown, kicks delivered, and furniture taking a thrashing as human bodies came into contact. Another crash, and the music stopped.

"Come on, Billy," said Boniface. "Time to move, and if you're not going to do it yourself..." He rolled Billy onto his side, sliding his right arm behind the other man as he slumped onto his back. Slowly, he pushed his left hand behind Billy until it met his right hand.

He pulled his fingers together, tightening his grip on Billy's prone body and managing to grab his own wrists. He leaned back, holding his wrists tightly, and pulled Billy into a sitting position on the bed.

Not that Billy seemed to notice.

"You could make my life easier," said Boniface, releasing his grip, instead taking Billy's shoulder with one hand to keep him in a sitting position while he dragged his legs with the other, dropping his feet onto the floor. Billy half twisted into a sitting position, and Boniface returned his arms to under Billy's armpits, reaching his hands behind the other man's back and gripping his wrists before bending his knees and hefting the junkie to a semi-vertical position.

"I...ohhh." Billy groaned. Boniface felt his wrists slip and guided Billy back to the sitting position.

"Come on, Bill—you need to help me or burn," said Boniface, coughing as he looked at the thickening smoke. In the next room there was the sound of glass breaking—perhaps a window, maybe a mirror.

Boniface returned his arms around Billy, gripped him tightly, bent his knees, and raised him to something close to the vertical, pulling him so he was leaning forward. As the junkie started to topple, Boniface bent, getting his shoulder to the younger man's waist, gripping around the top of his legs and spreading his weight across his back as the other man flopped forward, before Boniface stood with the dead weight of the other man spread over his shoulder.

There was shouting from the other room as Boniface reached the bedroom door, then the now-familiar sound of one human coming into contact with another, followed by the noise of a sharp exhalation of breath. Boniface moved into the narrow corridor, feeling the weight of the man over his shoulder as he watched the smoke blowing out the door—the vacuum sucking more fumes from the floor below.

"Leathan—I've got Billy," shouted Boniface as he staggered through the front door, taking a few stumbling steps before roughly lowering Billy and leaving him sitting against the wall of the walkway facing the boarded front door of number thirty-nine.

Boniface stood outside the door of number forty-one, gulped a lungful of clean air, and reentered, turning into the room where Leathan had disappeared. "Help me, Boniface," said Leathan.

"Where's..."

Before Boniface could answer, Leathan leaned forward, brushing the smoke away to reveal Jojo lying on the floor. "Grab his arm." The two men took an arm each and started dragging the big teen toward the front door.

"There's a lot of glass," said Boniface.

"Better that he's cut than he dies of smoke," replied the other man, pushing through the door, followed by Boniface and the inert body.

They crunched over the glass, sweeping the shards with Jojo, then flopped the body down the front step, and dragged him just past where Billy sat.

"What happened to him?" asked Boniface, looking back at the smoke flowing out of the door from which they had just exited.

"I stopped him killing me," said Leathan.

"We'd better get these guys away from the smoke. Let's go with Billy first." He turned to the junkie. "Billy, meet Leathan. Leathan, meet the right guy this time."

"When you say it like that, I almost feel you don't appreciate me," said Leathan, grabbing Billy's arm as the sound of a siren began to fill the air. "Get his other arm." Boniface grabbed Billy's free wrist. "Ready?" Boniface nodded, and they pulled Billy to his feet, each holding an arm around their shoulders as they started to drag Billy along the corridor.

As they turned into the stairs, Billy changed from letting his toes drag along the ground to trying to get his feet flat. Something in the smell invigorated him, and by the time they reached the open space at the bottom, he was moving his legs, although not taking much weight on his feet.

The two got Billy across the open space and sat him on the open ground at the spot where Boniface had found Leathan. Billy sat, his legs pulled up with his arms wrapped around, his eyes now open and his head moving in slow motion. Boniface squatted next to him. "How're you feeling?"

Billy's skin lacked any tone—it was as if the color had dissolved and the muscle tone had departed. The only variation in shade was given by the bruises, rashes, and bristles. "I need..." he sniffed and continued his slow survey of his surroundings with his bloodshot eyes.

"Alright," said Boniface. "I'll be back soon; don't go anywhere."

Boniface stood up, stretching his back as he looked at Leathan. "Jojo hit you bad," said Boniface.

"I know—it hurt. That's why I had to put him down." He looked down, his voice trembling and only just audible against the sound of the fire engine, which was drawing near. "I think I might have done real damage, Boniface. He was too big for me, and I was more scared of him than he was of me, so I had to hurt him."

"Let's go get him," said Boniface, looking back at the block, flames starting to sneak out from the gaps around the shuttering on the ground level.

The two started jogging across the open space, Leathan then leading through the stairwell. "You can see he's a big lad," said Leathan, pointing his head at Jojo, who was laid out on the passageway, which was filling with smoke. "He was too big to fight in such a tight spot—I could move quicker. It was the only advantage I had."

They reached the big teen. He was still breathing, but it was labored. The bruising on his face was severe, and the cheekbones—previously symmetrical—were now misaligned.

"Let's get him out of the smoke," said Leathan, reaching for a wrist. Boniface grabbed the second, and they both leaned back to pull. Slowly, the friction holding the body—probably aided by blood and glass fragments—started to release its grip and the body began to move, dragging along the passageway.

"How are we going to do the stairs?" said Boniface, breathing heavily as they reached the top of the stairwell. "We don't want to permanently disable the guy by bouncing his spine on the concrete steps."

"One under each arm, and lift," said Leathan. "Let his feet bump." He exhaled. "You ready?" Boniface nodded and they lifted, both groaning as they walked backward into the stairwell.

"Which side was the vomit on?" asked Boniface.

"The opposite side to the piss and the squirrel," said Leathan. "And our friend's not paying attention, so he's likely to find it all."

Boniface stopped counting after the first ten steps, instead concentrating on holding the weight as he turned through 180 degrees on the half-landing.

The two pulled the near corpse-like body out of the stairwell and away from the building. They laid Jojo—dressed in black jeans, a drab olive jacket with breast pockets and hip pockets, and white sneakers, which were now mostly black—on the ground and stood, struggling for breath as they felt the damage the exertion had inflicted on their muscles.

Looking across the open space, Billy was on his feet—he didn't seem to be going anywhere, but at least he was standing—and the first fire engine had stopped, its blue light still flashing, but its siren extinguished.

"Shouldn't they come running?" said Leathan, pointing toward the first few fire crew who were opening up the equipment doors on the engine.

Boniface shook his head. "Risk assessment first." Leathan looked like he had been shocked by 1,000 volts. "They're here to sort things, not become part of the problem. There'll be someone with a clipboard. Let's go find them and tell them what we know."

They started walking toward the fire engine. "Listen," said Leathan, stopping. "Billy's safe, and the fire brigade are here..." He stopped talking but somehow seemed to fill the space with the anticipation of what he was going to say next. "Do you still need me here? I did start the fire and I hurt Jojo pretty bad—if you don't need me, it's a good time for me to be somewhere else."

"Go," said Boniface. "And thank you." He stopped, turned to Leathan, and embraced. They broke and he pulled out his wallet, taking out the cash he hadn't given to Gray or spent encouraging people to tell him about Carmen when he was searching for her that morning. He pulled out a couple of notes and gave the rest to Leathan. "That's all I've got, and I need to keep some back to get Billy out of here."

He looked over Leathan's shoulder as the other man took the cash. "And where is Billy?"

Leathan spun. "There. See? Staggering over to give Jojo a kick."

Boniface patted his heart. "He had me scared—there's no point in losing him now." He reached out and shook Leathan's hand. "Again, thank you."

"My pleasure."

"Eurostar and Paris?" asked Boniface.

"I'll get back to Paris in about a week—I'll take the long route home. Go and see a few friends along the way—take it slow in case Ernie really does have friends." He turned and started to jog in what Boniface thought was the direction of the main road.

Boniface checked on Billy—he had reached Jojo and was kneeling beside him. It was as if he were pilfering from a dead body.

"Did I see you up there?" Boniface spun to see a fire officer towering over him. He looked up to the white helmet, following down to the poorly fitting white vest denoting *Incident Commander* worn over his uniform. The officer cradled a clipboard in one arm and held a pen in his opposite hand.

"Yeah," said Boniface. "We got that guy down—he needs a paramedic."

"They're on the way," said the incident commander, making a note. "Where was he?"

"We got him out of number forty-one—that's one floor up, on the right." Boniface pointed loosely; the officer's gaze seemed to follow, and the notes continued. "I think the fire started immediately under." Boniface pointed to the ground-floor apartment where flames and smoke were now freely flowing. "Kids, I guess," said Boniface.

"Is there anyone else up there?" asked the officer.

"Not that we could see—we got the two out. That guy..." he pointed to Jojo, "and..."

Billy was gone. Boniface scanned the open space. A small crowd had congregated, including a group of kids Boniface had seen on the way into the development—all looked to be about ten years old and all were smoking.

"I need to go find him," Boniface said under his breath, turning away from the incident commander before he started sprinting toward Jojo.

seventy-three

"How did you find me?" Dawn looked at the other woman. Twenty-something, slim, good figure—she looked athletic, but perhaps that was more to do with how she was dressed in sweatpants, a fleece jacket, which seemed to be mandatory for every visitor who walked around the Surrey Hills, and with her hair in a plait.

When Dawn had seen her at Boniface's office, the young American woman had come across as very efficient but maybe standoffish, almost disapproving. Boniface raved about her—talking about her in terms of her being some sort of an organizing machine.

Dawn had formed an image in her mind of someone quite bookish, maybe rather withdrawn. But in reality, she was dealing with someone who was prepared to stand her ground—physically and emotionally, she'd already stood up to Dawn and stopped her leaving—and someone who had the gumption to sit alone in a thousand-year-old church when it was getting dark.

"I didn't find you," said Montbretia, the side of her lip lifting. "You came to the place where I was."

Dawn's eyes brightened, acknowledging the humorous rebuff. "Then why did you come here?"

"A guess...by Boniface. He figured it was the place you would feel safe." She pushed out her lower lip. "Sanctuary. The place that first drew you to the area. The place where you and Danny solemnized your vows." She lifted her shoulders. "It seemed pretty logical when he put it like that, but I hadn't thought about it that way until he said it."

She reached for a backpack and pulled out a blanket, spreading it on the ground, then produced two more, keeping them folded as she placed them on the first. "A bit of padding. Why don't you sit down, Dawn?" Montbretia then walked to the corner behind the door and picked up two more backpacks, brought them over, gently placed them on the floor, and then dropped onto a folded blanket, patting next to her to encourage Dawn to sit.

As she lowered herself, Dawn watched Montbretia unpack one of the backpacks. "Are you warm enough?" asked Montbretia. "Dry enough? I've got some sweatpants and a jacket if you want—you can sit on them or wear them." She wrested a lump of mixed fabrics from the backpack, dropped them between the two of them, and dived back into the backpack.

"Hungry?" Dawn watched as Montbretia took out an aluminum pot with an oversized lid held on with a narrow webbing strap. She dropped the strap, flipped off the lid, and pulled out what looked like three pots and a kettle stacked inside one another. From inside the kettle she took an orange polythene bag, which Montbretia revealed to be carrying a small brass pot.

Montbretia took the largest aluminum pot, which was perforated and had a large hole in the middle, and placed it upside down on the flagstones before picking up the brass pot, unscrewing its lid, and dropping it into the large hole in the center. A red bottle appeared from a backpack, and Montbretia squirted some liquid into the small brass pot.

"That's a rather interesting contraption," said Dawn. "It's like a Russian doll of cooking pots."

"That's exactly what it is," said Montbretia, striking a match and igniting the liquid in the brass container before taking the next cooking pot—which, when Montbretia lifted it, Dawn could see didn't have a base—and fitting it on top of the perforated pot, creating a cylinder.

"Cute, isn't it? It's a bunch of cooking pots," she grabbed the larger of the two remaining aluminum pots. "A frying pan," she pointed to the lid, "a kettle, a stand," she tapped the perforated base, "a windshield," she indicated the pot without a base set on top of the stand, "and a spirit burner." She looked at Dawn. "Home away from home. It's very quick, very efficient, lightweight, much safer than gas, and storm-proof. I've been able to make a cup of tea in the middle of a thunderstorm with no problem."

"Impressive," said Dawn.

"There is a downside," said Montbretia, exaggerating a grimace. "There's only one burner, so you're going to have to decide whether you want soup first or a cup of tea."

"Ooh dear," said Dawn, joining the younger woman in the humor.

"And before you make that decision, the soup is tomato—out of a tin, I'm afraid…I can't match your skills—and for tea you have a choice of English Breakfast, peppermint, and rooibos."

"Rooibos?"

"It's South African," said Montbretia, looking down and curling her lip. "Truth be told, I don't like it much—I'm trying to get rid of it."

"Shall we start with the soup?" said Dawn.

"I was hoping you'd say that," said the younger woman, pulling a can from the backpack and a paper bag, which she held up as she continued. "I've got some rolls as well—I'm sure they're not up to your home-baking standard, but they're quite good." She emptied the soup into one of the pots and balanced the pot over the flame inside the windshield before reaching into a sack and placing two yellow melamine mugs in front of her. "I must apologize for not bringing the finest porcelain."

The American woman reached into her bag again, pulling out something Dawn couldn't make out. She then turned over what she had thought was a lid but now knew to be a frying pan, and placed a tea light on the metal surface, lighting it and immediately returning the matches to the backpack. She turned to Dawn. "Enough for us to see, but not enough to highlight our presence through the dulled glass."

Clearly Dawn had been wrong in her initial assessment. Montbretia wasn't a quiet mouse of a librarian—she was practical, resourceful, and knew she was taking a risk, even if she hadn't expressed that risk directly.

She watched as Montbretia stirred the soup, resting the spoon in the second cooking pot before pulling out a roll of paper towels. "Just in case," said Montbretia.

"How's Danny?"

Montbretia's head swung to face Dawn as if her neck were spring-loaded. She paused, and when she started talking, her voice was soft, with no rancor in the tone. "He's in a bad way, Dawn. He's missing you." She paused. "I don't think he's slept since you left."

Dawn felt her eyes start to sting. "I should call him—can I borrow your phone?"

Montbretia shook her head and stirred the soup.

"I need to call Danny—I need to put him out of the pain I'm causing him."

"No." Montbretia's voice was just above a whisper. "Only Boniface and I know where you are. Another hour or two of worry isn't going to kill Danny, and as you said, if people can find you, then Danny's at risk."

"Please," said Dawn.

"There's no signal."

"I know—but if you cross the park and walk a hundred yards up the hill, there's a spot where you get a perfect signal."

Montbretia shook her head gently, looking back at the soup. "It's nearly ready..."

Dawn went to speak but was cut off by Montbretia. "I know you want to see him, but while people don't know where you are, then they can't force Danny to do anything." Her voice took a more businesslike tone. "We don't know how Danny will react if you call him—you know he'll do anything for you, and we don't want him to play the hero and make a stupid gesture." She picked up the pot of soup and began to pour it into the mugs. "Plus, your dinner's ready, and a church is probably safest place to be—people tend to be twitchy about killing people in a house of worship."

Montbretia placed the fuller mug in front of Dawn and opened the paper bag, offering her a roll. Dawn took a piece of bread and started to tear at it.

They dunked bread and sipped their soup. Dawn broke the silence. "You said you know about both Billies."

"Father and son."

Dawn felt her face flush. "Does Danny know?"

"About Billy...about your son?"

Dawn felt her throat tighten and the tears flow.

"He didn't believe it." Montbretia's voice was calm. "We saw Carmen—Carmen Gallagher—this morning. She seemed certain Billy's your son. Boniface spoke to Danny—Danny said Carmen was wrong."

"It's true," said Dawn, dropping her half-eaten roll as she put her head into her hands, starting to sob.

"Something else Carmen confirmed for us..." Dawn looked up, aware of her appearance and still feeling the tears. "Billy—by whom, I mean Billy Senior—is dead."

"No." Dawn became aware that she staring at the other woman and that her mouth was still open.

"Died in a car crash nineteen years ago."

"What about William?" Dawn fought to squeeze her voice out. "What happened...why didn't they tell me?"

"It's a conversation you need to have with Carmen...but from what I understand, Billy Senior's family took control." Montbretia's voice faded as she took another sip of soup.

Dawn looked down at her roll and the halo of crumbs, which she started to sweep up. When she spoke, she whispered. "How is William?"

"He's alive, but I haven't seen him," said Montbretia. "Boniface has gone to find him and get him somewhere safe. Once Billy's safe, then Boniface will come and find us."

"But he'll bring Billy?"

Montbretia winced. She seemed to be weighing up something. "Billy's not in a good way—there might be drugs, so Boniface might take him to get help." She paused again, still seeming uneasy, then blurted. "And you and Danny need to have a conversation before anything else happens. You need to have that conversation without any of us, including Billy, being around."

Dawn bowed her head, picking at her bread roll and taking an occasional sip of her soup. "Thank you for this," she said.

Montbretia smiled softly, sitting still, seemingly not ready to ask any questions.

"You must think I'm an awful mother," said Dawn.

"I know you've got a husband who loves you totally. Unconditionally." Her face brightened, a note of wonder creeping into her tone. "And he wrote a great song for you."

Dawn sobbed, bowing her head.

Gradually she looked up, wiping her tears with her fingers. Montbretia leaned forward and placed the kitchen roll beside her. "I haven't seen my boy since he was six weeks old. He's thirty-one now—that's older than you."

Dawn ripped off a sheet of paper towel and dabbed her eyes, then blew her nose.

Montbretia put a hand into a backpack and pulled out some black polythene, rustling it open to reveal a trash bag, into which she threw the soup can before placing the bag, open, near Dawn. "We've got all night—don't be shy about filling it."

Dawn blew her nose again and dropped the piece of kitchen roll in the black bag. "I suppose church is the place for confessing—and if there is a God, may he forgive me."

She finished her soup, then tore off a few sheets of paper towel, gripping them tightly in her hand. "I was raped when I was fourteen by Billy...William's dad. He lived near us, so I knew him, but he was quite a bit older than me." Her hand gripped the paper towels, trembling. "And when I say rape...he beat me, ripped my clothes... we're not talking about regret the morning afterward, we're talking about a four-teen-year-old kid being brutalized by a twenty-one-year-old man."

She looked up at the American, registering the shock and the questions on her face.

"Around where I came from, Billy was the scariest man alive. I wasn't alone—there were others, but he usually waited 'til the girls were older. But I had boobs, which made him think it was alright." She sniffed and dabbed her eyes. "That rape led to William." She felt a smile form and her face relax as she said his name. "For all these years, I've always thought of him as William... And he's really alive?"

Montbretia nodded reassuringly. "Yes."

"I'm not proud—I was fifteen when William was born, and only just fifteen. Billy knew William was his—more to the point, his mother and his family knew William was their family. I was a useless teenager without any family to support me, so they forced me to give them the baby." She felt the tears begin to rise. "At first, they said it was best for me—I could go back to school—and best for the baby that they looked after him, and that I could see him whenever I wanted. But that didn't last long. Within two weeks I was cut out of his life."

Montbretia sat silent, watching.

"I still saw Billy. He used to taunt me—'Be nice to me, and I'll let you see little Billy'... He knocked me around, lied to get me into bed, raped me several more times, and I got pregnant again. I was still fifteen." She felt herself go cold. "I didn't keep it—couldn't keep it. I went to a really dodgy place—they scared me so much that I never went for a checkup after, and I'm sure that's why I haven't been able to get pregnant since."

She picked up the jacket Montbretia had laid out earlier and threw it across her shoulders, pulling it like a shawl. "When I turned sixteen, I turned my boobs to my advantage and earned enough money modeling to get out. Billy tracked me down—he was after money; he said it was for William. Then he went after Carmen, thinking it made me jealous... How is Carmen?"

"She's had a rough time," said Montbretia. "But...I've only met her once—this morning—and she seemed like she was trying to sort herself out."

Dawn took in Montbretia's words. "Billy went after her. I warned her, but she liked a bad boy...and then Lorna..." She felt her voice go weak. "After Lorna, we all fell apart. I was lucky—Danny found me, and I never looked back. I put everything behind me and locked the door. I never told Danny about Billy and William—I was ashamed and Danny would have tried to fix that too, but I always hoped that William would find me, and now he has."

seventy-four

It wasn't unreasonable.

He had held Leathan at gunpoint this morning, and a few minutes ago he had come at Leathan with a knife when all Leathan had to defend himself was a rolling pin. That said, Leathan did say he had a knife.

Leathan had acted to ensure that Jojo would pose no further threat.

It wasn't unreasonable.

No threat to himself. No threat to Boniface. No threat to Billy.

But as Boniface looked down at Jojo, he recoiled.

The lump above his left eye was probably due to Boniface and a luckily pitched spinning glass tumbler. The gashes could not be attributed to Boniface, nor the broken tooth, nor the displaced nose, nor the cheekbones that now lacked the symmetrical appearance they held this morning. And Boniface was definitely not responsible for the blood, which was spread across Jojo's jacket and was drying across his face and in his hair.

Boniface knew what had happened—Leathan would have used Jojo's disadvantages against him. Jojo was big—in the tight space Leathan would have moved quickly, finding the gaps that the big guy couldn't reach. Leathan would have annoyed the teen. He would have taunted him—called him stupid, gay, ugly, bad with women, smelly—anything childish that would have made the teen disproportionately angry in the moment.

He would have said anything that would've distracted the teen. Anything that would have enraged the teen.

And once the teen was distracted and enraged, then Leathan would have struck. But most importantly, Leathan would have made sure if he got a chance to hit Jojo that it counted.

Looking down, Boniface understood just how much the blows had counted.

As Jojo struggled for breath, Boniface understood how Leathan had to be certain that there wouldn't be any retribution from Jojo while Billy was still in danger. Billy, who Boniface had last seen rifling through Jojo's pockets. Billy, who was now nowhere to be seen.

Boniface knelt down beside Jojo. In the early evening cold, the damp of the ground seeped into him through the knees of the second suit he had ruined that week. "Where's Billy?"

When it came through snatched breaths, Jojo's voice was little more than a strained whisper. "Fuck you and fuck that junkie."

Next to the fire engine, another siren had been switched off. Boniface looked up to see the blue light still flashing on top of the yellow/green ambulance, with a paramedic getting out of the passenger's side. Boniface raised his hand, making sure he caught the paramedic's gaze as she scanned the open space.

"I can still cause you pain," he said to Jojo. "Where's Billy?"

"Fuck you and fuck your psychotic friend," said the teen, without the strength to elaborate on his stream of abuse.

"You'd better take a look at him," said Boniface, standing as the green jumpsuit–clad paramedic approached. "He's not in a good way."

He didn't listen as she put down her bag and started talking to Jojo. Instead, he turned and headed for the stairs.

At the top of the first flight he looked left toward Billy's place. Thick smoke billowed along the walkway, hiding the legs of the white-helmeted incident commander with his clipboard, seemingly so keen to complete his risk assessment.

Boniface turned right and jogged along the walkway going away from the fire, his head in constant motion as he looked for any sign of Billy having passed or gone into one of the other residences. Toward the end of the passage, he turned into another stairwell and ascended to the next floor, completing a quick sweep before ascending to the next floor.

Having reached the top floor, he followed the stairwell down and exited from the back of the building, running for a short while before stopping, and muttering as he panted. "Where have you gone, Billy? Where have you hidden yourself?"

There was a woman pushing a stroller toward him. Bleach-blond hair stacked in a pile, wearing a black tracksuit with pink detailing, and with a cigarette clamped in the side of her mouth, which jiggled the burned end of its ash as she talked into the phone held to her opposite ear. She gesticulated wildly with her free hand when she wasn't using it to jerk the stroller forward, and when the free hand was being used to point at something for the benefit of whoever was on the other end of the phone, she knocked the stroller forward with her large belly.

Boniface leaned into her field of view, raising his eyebrows as if questioning. She kept talking, looking him up and down, her face sneering. "What?" she said, without giving any indication that the person on the other end of the line knew her focus had moved.

"I'm looking for a guy. Blue jeans, white T-shirt, denim sleeveless jacket, black hair, boots."

"I know, I know. Di'n't I tell ya." She seemed to have returned to her conversation.

"Have you seen him?" asked Boniface.

"Why would I?"

Boniface leaned into her field of vision again, pointed to himself and then to her phone.

"You, of course! Why would I see this bloke?"

"Because he..." Boniface inhaled. "Have you seen him in the last few minutes?"

"Nah. I was..." Boniface was jogging before the fourth word—following another rat run, searching in a rabbit warren. He followed an alley past several furniture and trash dumps—the last including two cathode-ray tube televisions—coming out to a block with a row of garages at ground level.

Each door—at least, each door that was still in place—had been graffitied. Most had been attacked in one way or another. Some were a bit bent, as if they had been kicked in the middle. A few had a bottom corner folded up, like a bizarre bookmark. Two had simply been removed from their tracks and were propped against the gaping hole behind them.

Boniface followed the row, opening each closed door—none was locked—and looking through the gaps left by bending, twisting, and mangling the other doors. Most seemed to be full of trash, furniture, old televisions. In one, he found a car, burned out and without wheels. Another was filled with empty metal shelves. Another was filled with car tires.

In none could he find Billy.

He took a path wheeling back in the general direction of Chesterfield Terrace. He passed several clumps of dark-brown brick maisonettes before coming out at the far end of Billy's block, facing the block's rear elevation. A group of firefighters were training a hose on the ground-floor dwelling at the far end, but thick black smoke was still billowing along the length of the building.

Boniface started shuffling in the direction of the fire, his head spinning as he passed boarded-up residences, what seemed to be a storeroom for dumpsters, and then across a back entrance to one of the stairwells. He stopped and jogged back to the dumpster store, pulling its wooden door fully open to reveal a tidy concrete-floored room with eight dumpsters, the two closest both with their lids open, and a third to the side with its lid open seemingly being fed by a large pipe coming in through the ceiling.

He smirked. The room seemed redundant. As far as he could tell, the residents had no need for formal waste-management arrangements—they dumped their trash wherever and whenever they wanted.

He had a quick look, saw something, and rolled out two of the dumpsters. "Billy!"

Boniface looked at the gaunt figure, comatose against the back wall, next to him a syringe, an old tablespoon that didn't seem sufficiently hygienic to go in a kitchen, and a lighter. He pushed his fingers into Billy's throat, just to the side of the windpipe, and felt a weak pulse. "For once in your life try and do the smart thing, Billy, and stay alive."

He turned and sprinted through the bottom of the stairwell and to the other side of the building, stopping as he reached a firefighter. "Where are the paramedics?"

seventy–five

"I know it's not your sort of thing." He listened to the response, feeling the tension in the back of his neck, but realizing that if he let his annoyance become anger he would achieve nothing. "I know. I know. But I'm asking a favor." His face relaxed. "Yeah, *another* favor. But I promise it's the last one today. In fact, I guarantee it's the last one I'll ask for... This week."

He laughed. "You got me. These are the last favors...zzz—not favor, *favors*—that I will ask for this week." He pushed his phone more closely against his ear. "Could you get the short version up on the website within thirty minutes and email me the link?" He winced, holding his tongue between his teeth to remind himself to shut up. "I know. I know. It's not a story that you want or that you would usually cover—but it is something *you* can trade for a favor. You must want someone else to be in your debt?"

Boniface sat on the concrete pathway behind Chesterfield Terrace, leaning forward with his knees pulled up, listening as his former wife, editor of the *European Daily Herald* newspaper, berated him for asking her to abuse her position and publish a story that 999 times out of 1,000 she would ignore.

About twenty yards in front of him, a paramedic securely closed the rear door of the ambulance before jumping into the passenger seat. Slowly, the large yellow and green van moved off, following along a pedestrian walkway unobstructed by traffic before dropping over the curb and onto the highway, and disappearing without flourish. No lights. No siren.

Boniface had been impressed by the paramedics. When he found them and led the first to where Billy lay, there had been no shock, no drama, no panic—just immediate attention and total focus on the person who mattered: Billy. Billy, who by then appeared to be in a deep coma. As the crowd formed and the second paramedic brought around the ambulance, the focus had remained total and the crowd that gathered had not distracted. The crowd that now seemed to lack any focus—the few who were left watched the lone policeman struggle to attach crime-scene tape around the dumpster store room before awkwardly standing guard.

"The sympathetic story needs to come first. There needs to be a focus on the tragedy of continuing estrangement because of the son's upbringing and the son's hard drug use." Boniface became aware that it was uncomfortable and cold sitting on concrete. "It's your turn to call in a favor. Find whoever can do the most sympathetic lifestyle story. This is gonna be all over the press in a few hours, and I can't stop it—but we can make sure that Dawn and Danny's perspective is understood... with your help."

The small congregation of people had started to disperse. Those who remained seemed to be there due to lack of anything else distracting them. Boniface stood up inelegantly—pushing with one hand while keeping his phone clamped on his ear—and looked down at his suit. Thick smoke, broken glass, running and searching, and his struggle to save Billy had all taken their toll: It was time to visit his tailor again.

"Within the next few hours I'll be able to get pictures to whoever you find to publish. The pictures will show that Billy was at Dawn and Danny's property within the last few days." He listened as his former wife noted the detail. "Yeah. Billy will show up on their security cameras. It will confirm the connection."

He watched as the next few people ended their conversation and left.

"Thank you," he said. "I'll leave it with you." He punched the screen of his phone and then returned it to his ear. "Danny. It's Boniface."

Boniface recognized the pile of blond hair before he saw the black tracksuit with pink detailing, and the fat belly being used to nudge the stroller as another small cluster dispersed.

"Danny, listen to me—it's time to bring Dawn home." He wasn't quite sure what Danny said, but he continued. "She's safe, she's with Montbretia—they're in the old church at Albury." He pulled his ruined jacket tight against the early evening chill. "Go now, Danny. But one thing—don't listen to the radio, don't check the internet, and leave your phone behind... Yeah, I know, but there's a lot you need to hear straight from me—not some media fabrication. Find Dawn and stay at the church—I'll be there as soon as I can. I've got somewhere I need to go first."

He dropped his phone into his pocket and muttered under his breath. "Montbretia, I hope you've got Dawn."

seventy–six

"This is how you PR men are dressing these days?" Ernie made a show of looking Boniface over, dishing out a sneer that Boniface guessed had been practiced over many years.

"From Paris to Milan," said Boniface. "If you left this gloomy place once in a while, you'd find that everyone is dressing like this."

"I like it here," said Ernie, his crumpled gray face lit by the banker's lamp on his desk, the only source of light for the room. "So you've got something to tell me, Mister Boniface. Our business is concluded, is it?"

"Our business is definitely concluded," said Boniface. "One or two Is to be dotted and Ts to be crossed...but that's just minor stuff."

"Good. Good," said Ernie in his gravelly way. "I knew you'd see sense in the end."

Boniface snorted. "I always saw sense. I just wasn't sure whether you would see sense."

Ernie went to speak, then stopped, as if his ears had been tardy in conveying the message to his brain. "What?" he barked. "What are you talking about, Boniface?"

"Where's Wes?" asked Boniface. "Jojo's not here. Wes isn't here. You've got a new kid on the door—what's going on?"

"Boniface!" There was a sharpness—a frustration—in Ernie's tone.

"Here's my guess," said Boniface, feeling a slight swagger in his delivery. "By now I'm guessing that you've tried to track down Gray—the lack of Wes and Irvine suggests they're out looking." He couldn't keep the glee from his face; he just hoped it wasn't too obvious in the gloom. "He's gone. Gray is beyond your reach. I'm sure you've broken down his front door by now and have checked his other haunts. Save yourself the trouble and call off your hounds."

"I own him," said Ernie, his teeth clamped together as he spoke, his lips carefully enunciating each syllable. "He has a debt that will be paid."

"No he doesn't," said Boniface, looking around for a chair. In the corner where Iain Irvine usually roosted was an upright 1930s dining chair. Boniface pulled it over and sat in front of Ernie, leaning forward to rest his elbows on his knees, lowering his eye line to match the older man's. "Gray has a debt because you made him gamble."

"I didn't force him..."

Boniface cut him off. "You didn't force him, but you made sure he kept gambling until he lost, and when he did—which I'm sure didn't take long, assuming he's as good at gambling as he is at living the rest of his life—then you lent him more money to gamble his way out of his losses, and then you lent him even more money to gamble out of his deeper debts."

Boniface noticed a slight look of self-satisfaction cross Ernie's face.

"You didn't try to collect because you wanted him to have a massive debt so that when you made your offer, he would only have one option."

"He's a grownup," said Ernie. "He knew what he was getting into, and he will repay his debt."

"Except he can't." Boniface let the statement hang as he pulled out his phone. "What you think he owns—the rights to Prickle—he doesn't, and he knows it. Always knew it. Take a listen."

Boniface tapped a button on his phone and heard his own disembodied voice come out of the small speaker: "the rights relating to your time with Prickle...all this legal stuff against Danny, Prickle, and PAD Management...all this stuff instigated by Iain Irvine..."

"Yeah." It was Gray speaking.

Boniface's voice returned. "Just between you and me...it's bogus, isn't it? It's just your way to pay off your gambling debt, isn't it? Come on, Gray. We're big boys—we can be honest, no one's listening. You agreed to claim these old rights just to settle your gambling debt, didn't you?"

"Yeah," said Gray's voice. "You got me there. But you can't prove anything."

Boniface pocketed his phone. "And before you ask, a copy of that audio file has already been sent to Fiona Aldred at PAD Management."

Boniface made a mental note to send the giraffe-in-training a copy of the file as soon as he got out, and hoped Ernie didn't make him pay for the omission and the lie.

"Let's be clear—what you thought you owned, you don't. Where you might have thought you could tangle Prickle in litigation for years in the hope of them cracking or agreeing to pay you off, they won't." He exhaled. "In short, you've got nothing."

Boniface watched the few dust mites swirling under the banker's lamp, with Ernie's face remaining stony in the background.

"You've got nothing, and that gambling debt you think Gray owes is cancelled."

Ernie slammed his hand on his desk, giving Boniface a look that had been practiced over many years, which probably worked if you were scared of the man.

"If you want to be angry with anyone, then it's Irvine you need to get angry at." Boniface saw a slight crinkle of confusion momentarily flit across Ernie's brow. "He lied to you. He's no more a lawyer than I am...or you. He's the one who has messed up your plans. Not me. Not Danny. Not Gray."

Something flickered in Ernie's eyes as he lifted his hand from his desk. Boniface wasn't sure what, but some of the certainty seemed to waver—maybe only for a moment, but it was still gone, even in the twilight of the poorly lit room.

His eyes narrowed—some would take this as shiftiness. Boniface knew better; this was Ernie feeling confident. This was Ernie about to play his ace.

"Aren't you forgetting something, Boniface? Or should I say, aren't you forgetting someone? Young William."

Boniface felt his gut twist and the energy drain out of him. He tried to inhale but had forgotten how to breathe—not that his body seemed to want or need oxygen at that moment.

When he spoke, it was a whisper. "Billy's dead. I don't know whether you killed him. I don't know whether he killed himself. I don't know what happened, but he's dead."

Ernie's face was fixed like a palsy sufferer.

"As for Jojo," said Boniface, his voice still subdued. "I don't know. He might be alive—he probably is—but he was in a bad way when I last saw him."

"But there's still the story," said Ernie. "Daniel wouldn't want to see dear Dawn in the press—the neglectful mother whose junkie bastard child died from a broken heart after self-medicating because his mother rejected him."

Boniface felt his face relax. "You're too late on that one, too—it's already in the press." He pulled out his phone and followed a link Veronica had emailed him. "There you are—*European Daily Herald*: Model's tragedy." He held his phone for Ernie to see. "The most sympathetic story you will ever see."

Ernie's face twitched.

Boniface stood. "And now, for once, I'm going to walk away from here without getting a pounding."

seventy-seven

Montbretia pulled the blanket tighter.

When Danny walked through the door of the old church, after the initial trepidation about who was arriving—Danny didn't have the lightest footsteps—Montbretia grabbed two blankets and a jacket, slipped her sneakers over her socks without tying the laces, and made herself scarce quickly.

She knew better than Danny that he and Dawn needed to talk. She knew better than Danny that he and Dawn needed privacy when they talked.

And in her rush to give Dawn and Danny their privacy—not that they even seemed to notice she was there—Montbretia hadn't considered what she was taking. She intended to return and get more, but as she looked back when she reached the old door, she realized that all she held was all she was taking. It was like looking back at a burning building—anything that was left was gone forever, although of course it wouldn't actually burn. It just meant she couldn't finish her cup of tea. If there was a God, then clearly he was sending a message that rooibos was not for her.

She initially intended to wait in the timber-framed porch with its pitched roof, but even with the wooden door fully closed, she could hear Danny sobbing, so instead she walked into the graveyard and chose a tomb. Respectful of what lay within, and with extreme care so as not to cause any damage, Montbretia slipped off her sneakers, lay her first blanket over the top of the waist-high platform, and then checked her clothes for anything sharp that might scratch or dig into the ancient memorial. Satisfied that she would not cause damage, she cautiously mounted the flat platform and wrapped the second blanket around her, soon wishing she had something softer to sit on and that she could light a fire in the graveyard for more warmth.

But whatever discomfort Montbretia was feeling, growing with each minute she sat, that was nothing to what Dawn was going through. The story she had told Montbretia—the story she was now telling Danny—was delivered in a manner that was harrowing, and yet in other ways matter-of-fact. It was a story of choices made, decision taken, and the consequences accepted, and now Dawn had to account to the man who loved her unconditionally for the lie at the heart of their marriage.

Somewhere in the distance—perhaps 500 meters away, near the entrance to the park—car headlights appeared. Two yellow streams hewing a path through the blackness. Two eyes staring into the distance, searching.

She watched the headlights bounce over the low speed humps and follow the road as it gently curved, listening as the familiar sound of the engine—the Teutonic marching song of a Mercedes—became louder, before drawing up where the road ended. The car jiggled backward and forward as it parked: an unnecessary exercise since it was the only car here and was effectively parking in the middle of a field, so there was hardly a need for it to be parked ready for a Le Mans start.

Montbretia sat still as the yellow eyes arced across the church, knowing that she would remain invisible in the shadows created by the artificial light unless the eyes hit her directly. And then the eyes died and the engine silenced. There was a weak light illuminating the inside of the car, which was swiftly extinguished with the sound of a familiar door clunk.

There were footsteps approaching, but Montbretia strained to see their owner with her night vision that had been assaulted by the headlights. There was a rhythm to the footsteps as they approached the gate in the ironstone rubble wall.

Then a foot kicked the wooden gate, and there was a mumbled curse.

Montbretia giggled and whispered: "Turn the handle, Boniface."

There was a rattling of the latch and a click as it lifted, followed by a slow creak as Boniface returned the gate to its closed position.

"What are you doing here?" he asked.

"I thought you wouldn't be that long, and I figured they had some talking to do, so I'm waiting here."

"How are they?" asked Boniface, hesitation catching in his voice.

"There were tears," said Montbretia. "Rivers of tears. Oceans of tears. A biblical flood of tears. I came out to collect wood and round up two of every animal. Then I ran down to the village and banged on the doors, telling everyone to head for the hills."

Boniface reached the tomb Montbretia sat upon.

"I think Dawn might have cried, too."

Boniface grinned. "And how are you?"

"Me?" said Montbretia. "My ass has gone to sleep, but apart from that I'm fine—I haven't cried. I'd like something warm to drink, and I could do with a pee...you know, in a proper bathroom, not behind a bush, but apart from that, I'm great." She looked up. "Pass me my sneakers—they're somewhere down there—and help me get off this thing. That would help."

"You're sure you're okay," said Boniface, bending down and patting the ground around the base of the tomb. "There you go." He stood, placing the sneakers on the flat surface.

"I've been away from you for a few hours, Boniface. I rode around. I had a chat with a nice lady and we had some soup. I've not really been exerting myself."

Boniface nodded. "You may not feel like you did much, but I am grateful. I'm grateful that you found and looked after Dawn." Montbretia looked at him quizzically. "It's been a shitty couple of hours, and I've done a lot that I said I wouldn't do." He shrugged and offered his hand to help her down. "Show me where they are—we need to talk."

Montbretia accepted Boniface's hand and cautiously lifted herself from the tomb before leading him through the graveyard, under the porch, and through the bird screen and heavy wooden door whose hinges announced their arrival. She stepped through the door first and closed it behind Boniface.

"Boniface," said Danny. By the time Montbretia had finished closing the door and turned into the nave, the bassist was embracing the other man like a long-lost brother, the snivel letting her know that tears were flowing again.

Montbretia remained by the door, watching. Dawn sat where she had sat earlier in the evening. The tea light burned low, casting dark shadows across her face, giving it creases Montbretia hadn't seen before. She looked worn, exhausted, emotionally drained, but managed to give Montbretia a nervous smile.

"Sit down, Dan." Boniface's voice had changed. Outside, he had been weary, frustrated, maybe angry. Now he sounded unsure, nervous, almost hesitant.

Danny sat on the blanket next to his wife, their bodies entwining, wordlessly melting to become a single figure. Boniface sat on the flagstones, the low-burning candle still balanced on the frying pan lid in the middle of the circle. Dawn leaned forward, her face drawn but expectation lighting her eyes.

Boniface was silent. Finally Dawn broke the still, "Where's Billy? Where's my baby?"

She heard Boniface sniff, saw him raise a hand to his face.

"Dawn, I'm sorry..."

"Where's Billy? Tell me he's alright."

Boniface sniffed. He voice a whisper. "Billy's dead."

Her roar of pain was animalistic. Prehistoric. The oldest sadness that any one human could endure. It seemed interminable as it echoed around the church. Husband and wife clung onto each other, inconsolable in their despair. Montbretia turned away, unable to watch as the two howled, neither able to be strong enough to comfort the other, but both clinging to the other.

She felt a hand on her shoulder and jumped. Boniface nodded at the door, holding his finger over his lips. She grasped the latch with both hands, lifting it silently, cracking the door sufficiently for Boniface to squeeze through. She winced as he squeaked the bird cage open, then followed him, shutting the door and the bird gate behind.

"What happened to Billy?" asked Montbretia.

"It may have been murder, it may have been misadventure," said Boniface. "My guess is we'll never be able to prove what happened." He shrugged. "But that's only half of it, isn't it?"

"What do you mean?"

"Look at them," said Boniface. "Dawn told a lie, Danny made a choice, and now Billy is dead. Danny is joyful his wife is back; Danny will forgive whatever Dawn said or didn't say—he just wants to support wife—but he met the kid, and he's always going to wonder whether he could have done something. Dawn abandoned the kid..."

"She had no choice," snapped Montbretia. "She got away from an abuser and buried the abuse so deep that she didn't even tell her husband."

"That won't make her feel better—that won't make either of them feel better." He sighed. "I'm not criticizing what she did when she was a teenager—I'm just asking how do you live with that going round in your head?"

seventy-eight

The vicar stood just inside the door, ready to perform the strange ritual of greeting his congregation as they departed.

"Thank you. It was a very moving service," said Boniface as he shook hands with the holy man before passing through the old door, under the timber-framed porch, and into the overgrown graveyard surrounding the church. The grass path between the church and the ironstone wall had been recently cut, carving a neat route to the wooden gate, which Boniface opened rather than walking into, as he had done a week before.

Gradually, the other members of the congregation passed through the gate, leaving the consecrated ground. Dawn and Danny clung to each other—their eyes the color red usually associated with tropical infection. They were followed closely by Carmen and Jilly, both looking far more relaxed than when Boniface had seen them a week ago, but still mopping their tears.

Gray was escorting Montbretia and appeared to be on his very best behavior and trying his hardest to be both charming and a bit of a bad boy—clearly someone had told him women like a bit of a bad boy. Sven and Reuben, the roadies, both wiped tears as they walked, as did the tattooed lady with them who Boniface guessed was Sven's wife. Kit Flambeau—or Christopher Edington, according to his passport—walked with Luca and Mel Grant while Newton Jubb, Prickle's keyboard player, brought up the rear.

Carmen laid a hand gently on Dawn's shoulder. The grieving mother turned and embraced her former bandmate, a new peal of sobs sounding across Albury Park. Danny left his wife and walked over to Boniface, offering his hand in greeting. "I don't think I've ever been to a—I don't know what you call it, a memorial, a celebration...who cares—I don't think I've ever been to a service in a consecrated church where the organ was a Hammond organ played by a keyboard wizard," said Boniface.

"Yeah, that was Newt's idea. He's spent the last few days with Sven and Reuben trying to figure how to get enough car batteries rigged together with a transformer to power a Hammond and the amps." He looked in Newton's direction. "It was a lovely idea of his—he reckoned there would be a lot of singers here, so why not make it more personal? Instead of getting in the local choir, he wanted people for whom the gathering would actually mean something, people who actually care about Dawn—people who love Dawn—and who understand that she has lost someone dear."

He wiped a tear and turned away, pulling a handkerchief out of a pocket.

"I didn't say thank you for handling the press and the fallout—that was a masterstroke you pulled that night. Whoever you persuaded to run that story as it was written, however you persuaded them, I'm impressed." Danny turned back to Boniface. "And now the legal stuff has gone away, PAD are back on side, and our finances will be released, so we can pay you." A mischievous smirk poked out from the sadness. "I'm not sure I should say, but I think tall Fiona quite likes you."

"How's Dawn?" said Boniface in an attempt to hide his embarrassment. "How are you?"

Danny deflated—his shoulders hunched as his head dropped. "It's hard to lose the stepson you never knew you had—it's even harder for Dawn to lose the son she knew she had, and then to find they were so close to reconciliation. Even if he was only after money, at least that would have been a start for communication, and we could have helped him."

He seemed unable to form the words of the next sentence—his mouth moved as if he was talking, and his hands moved as if he were explaining, but words didn't come quickly.

"It's hard to hear about your kid's fifth birthday when you weren't there but you should have been. But even though it's tough to hear, there's a joy in hearing what he was like as a kid. And from the people we've talked to who knew him more recently, obviously he was troubled, but he seems much more than just a plain junkie. He was as much a victim of his situation as Dawn. In fact he was more of a victim—Dawn escaped."

His gaze seemed draw to his wife, who was still being consoled by her former bandmates. He turned back to Boniface, mopping his eyes again.

"What happens next?"

The bassist sucked air through the side of his teeth. "Not much. We can't bury a body until the coroner has released it, and since there are murder charges being contemplated, that might take a while. As far as we know he didn't leave a will, so there's the question about who has rights—it should be Dawn as next of kin, but the family who never supported him sense there might be money, so I've asked Fiona to get a good lawyer for us." He shrugged. "So for now, we do the charity gig, which with all the publicity—it's a long time since I've been on the front pages of the nationals—has sold out."

Boniface winced. "Who's going to sing?"

"No one can replace Thad," said Danny. "No *one*. But many can pay tribute to a fallen comrade. So I'm going to take lead vocal for a couple of songs." He looked in the direction of his bandmates chatting with the musical theater singer. "Kit's going to join us for a few songs—don't forget 'Tattoo Your Name on My Heart' was written when he was singing with us, and the song was written with his range in mind."

The bassist's gaze seemed to wander, stopping when it found Montbretia, who was still humoring Gray.

"And Gray will sing a couple of songs."

"Gray?" Boniface could hear his pitch rising. "After he tried to destroy you."

"He's family, Boniface. The prodigal father has returned to our heart and will return to the stage with us. Kit is family, Gray is family, and it's one gig." He stopped, his eyes narrowing as if questioning. "Anyway, didn't you make his gambling debt miraculously disappear?"

"I felt bad—I lied to him, and I knew the debt was bogus." He stifled a naughty schoolboy smirk. "If I'm honest, I don't feel that bad that I lied to him, but I hope I didn't blow his last chance of earning money from music."

"You didn't," said Danny. "We need to act like a family and help him find some work. He's a good singer; he shouldn't be running a painting and decorating business."

Dawn looked across and smiled at Boniface, still keeping hold of her bandmates' hands. "See, Boniface," said Danny, following Boniface's gaze. "Family."

"Family still grieving over the one they lost when they were teenagers," said Boniface.

"You spoke to Carmen and Jilly, didn't you?" asked Danny.

"They both helped," said Boniface, looking at the three women. "And helping them will help Dawn."

Danny seemed unsure of what Boniface was suggesting.

"Jilly needs a friend. She needs someone she can talk to. Someone to help her when she feels overwhelmed with her grandkids. Let her come and stay and bring the kids with her." He remembered his first experience of the three. "They're a handful…. And it will hurt, seeing what Dawn will never have, but it will help."

"You think?" said Danny.

Boniface nodded slowly. "As for Carmen, she needs help to get on her feet and stay clean. It wouldn't be the first time you've come across someone in that situation. She needs a job—she needs to work to earn a living. She needs self-respect and a pension. She doesn't want charity—she wants a chance, and she'll prove herself fetching and carrying."

"Is there a suggestion in there, Boniface?" Danny seemed to have twigged where Boniface was pushing.

"You must have friends and contacts that hire people with unconventional backgrounds—perhaps PAD could take her on for a short while. You just need to make a few phone calls and call some favors."

The bassist pushed out his bottom lip.

"Think you can make that happen, Danny?"

Note from the Author

I hope you enjoyed this book. If you want to know more about me and my books, then join my readers' group.

When you join, I'll send you my introductory library and add you to my readers' group mailing list. Every month I'll send you my communiqué, Simon Says. This includes news about my books, special offers, and extracts, together with a few pieces I think you may find interesting.

Join my readers' group and get your free books here: simoncann.com/readers.

About the Author

Simon Cann is the author of the Boniface, Montbretia Armstrong, and Leathan Wilkey books.

In addition to his fiction, Simon has written a range of music-related and business-related books, including the *How to Make a Noise* series, the most widely ready series about synthesizer sound programming, and *Made it in China*, about entrepreneurs building businesses in China. He has also worked as a ghostwriter on a number of books.

Before turning full-time to writing, Simon worked as a management consultant, where his clients included aeronautical, pharmaceutical, defense, financial services, chemical, entertainment, and broadcasting companies.

He lives in London.

You can find more about Simon at his website: simoncann.com.

Printed in Great Britain
by Amazon

79479100R00385